PERFECT

Ariana Rivers

ISBN: 979-8-9998734-0-8 (Amazon KDP eBook)
ISBN: 979-8-9998734-1-5 (Amazon KDP Edition Paperback)
ISBN: 979-8-9998734-2-2 (IngramSpark Edition Paperback)
ISBN: 979-8-9998734-3-9 (B&N Press Edition Paperback)

First edition 2025

DEDICATION

For the person who reminded me that one must still have chaos in oneself to give birth to a dancing star.

For the person who sees that chaos in me and chooses to love it every day.

RESOURCES

Perfect deals with heavy topics such as domestic violence, sexual assault, substance abuse, mental health issues, and eating disorders. Help is available.

National Domestic Violence Helpline
1-800-799-7233
Text BEGIN to 88788

Suicide and Crisis Lifeline
Text 988

National Sexual Assault Helpline
1-800-656-4673
Text HOPE to 64673

Substance Abuse and Mental Health Services Helpline
1-800-662-4357

National Eating Disorders Association
1-800-931-2237
Text NEDA to 741741

CONTENT WARNING

Reader discretion is advised.

Perfect contains mature themes and content that may be distressing to some readers.

This book contains sexually explicit content, depictions of abuse (verbal, physical, emotional, and sexual), domestic violence, sexual assault, mental health issues, substance use and addiction, graphic violence, eating disorders, and references to child abuse, among other things.

Complex relationship dynamics are at the heart of this book, including elements of psychological distress, complex trauma, and sexual situations involving power imbalance and non-traditional consent.

You can review the full list of content warnings at the end of this book or on my website, www.arianarivers.com.

CONTENTS

1

ALEX

SATURDAY, MARCH 18

When I was twelve, my mother painted me with a blue ribbon in my hair, holding a panicked-looking white rabbit. Now, the painting hangs in Danny's office and watches as I open the safe, pulling out all ten thousand dollars of emergency cash we keep on hand and slipping the stack of bills into my belt bag.

The rabbit's red, beady eyes watch as I pull out my cell phone and call a taxi, whispering the address twice and begging them to hurry. Time seems to stretch out into years as I wait, and I lock eyes with my painted self. We stare at each other, both of us silent and unmoving as we listen intently to the sounds in the house.

It's so quiet that I can hear the kitchen clock ticking downstairs, but I'm focused on catching the slightest sound from our bedroom. I'm freezing, but I can't risk waking Danny by going into the bedroom for different clothes, so I'll have to pick up something warm on the way.

Something with less blood on it, preferably.

Eventually, the taxi's headlights sweep across the house, illuminating the painting briefly. *Down, Down, Down* was one of my mother's more celebrated paintings, but I never liked it. The girl trapped in the painting always seemed frozen and unsure, and it felt like my mother took something of mine, something raw, and gave it to the world without asking.

People have been taking from me my whole life, and I'm tired of it.

I share one final glance with the girl in the painting before I leave, both of us thinking the same thing:

"Would you tell me, please, which way I ought to go from here?"

***

I tell the cab driver I'll pay him an extra hundred dollars if he won't tell anyone about the ride. He takes in my split lip and my bloody shirt and the bruise starting to form around my eye, and he agrees quickly. He asks me if I need help, but his voice sounds far away as I sink deeper inside of myself.

I can't afford to get numb like this, not right now, not when I need to focus on running, but I can't help it. I'm too deep inside myself to respond, so we spend the rest of the ride in silence, the news filtering softly through the radio. I try to get my breathing under control and get back into my body, which barely works.

I stand shivering in the cold as I wait for the two-fifteen bus to New York, crossing my arms over my chest when I notice that my face and the dried blood on my thin white t-shirt are drawing attention from the other people milling around the station. Someone here will be able to tell the police they remember seeing me, and the thought makes me panic as I climb onto the bus.

I need to find a way to hide myself.

I get into New York around six in the morning and check the times for departing buses before I leave the station, reentering ten minutes later in an oversized hoodie and large sunglasses, keeping the hood up and my head down. Half an hour later, I'm headed to Seattle, flipping through my transfer tickets and trying to figure out what I'm supposed to do now.

I've got my ID, a ton of cash, and nothing else. Well, almost nothing. I stare at my left hand before pulling the three-carat round-cut diamond ring off my finger and slipping it into my belt bag.

I never liked that fucking ring anyway.

***

I have an hour-long layover in Minneapolis, and the station attendant writes down the directions to a Target a few blocks away. I run there, quickly grabbing a prepaid debit card and a pay-as-you-go smartphone, but I freeze when I go to grab a change of clothes. The hoodie I'm wearing was bought out of necessity, but these are the first clothes I'm buying for myself outside Danny's control.

I can choose whatever I want.

What the fuck do I want?

I stand there frozen with indecision for a long moment before I grab an oversized cream sweater and a pair of soft, wide-leg black pants. I don't know what I want, but I know I *don't* want anything tight or revealing, so that's a start. I duck into the bathroom and change quickly, shoving all my old clothes into the trash can before I hurry back to the bus station, fighting off a panic attack.

So far, I've been working on instinct alone, but I'm starting to realize just how fucked I am. I can't use my identity at all. I have money, but that's all I have for the foreseeable future. Ten thousand dollars will barely last me a year if I'm careful, and I don't know how to be careful with money.

I start to feel numb as the panic starts rising again, so I force myself to focus and make a list of what I need to do when I get to Seattle. I stay awake until I transfer buses in Billings, then finally fall into a fitful sleep on the bus to Spokane, jolting awake every so often, my heart pounding in my chest.

I spend the final leg of the trip to Seattle figuring out how I'm even supposed to find an under-the-table job and an apartment I can pay for in cash, much less a fake ID. I make a new email address and post a Craigslist ad before responding to help wanted ads in Washington and Oregon, and even a few in Alaska.

By the time the bus pulls into Seattle, I'm slightly less panicked but extremely exhausted, so I find the cheapest hotel near the bus station that I think I'll be safe at, and I sleep on and off for two days.

***

I can't stay in Seattle just in case Danny somehow finds out what bus I took, but I need to be harder to identify before I leave. I go to a cheap chain salon and have my waist-length hair cut to just above my collarbones and dyed from my natural honey blonde to a rich brown before I head to the train station. I take the train down to Portland, finding a crappy hotel near the college and paying for a month in advance before I wander around the city, keeping my head down and nervously glancing at any man who bears a passing resemblance to Danny.

Portland is different from Boston, but it's nice. I spend most of my time walking around the city trying not to get wet in the near-constant drizzle and avoid people screaming on the sidewalks. I visit parks and explore the neighborhoods, eating at food carts and window shopping at vintage stores, finally starting to feel safe in my anonymity.

It takes two weeks before I find a woman who makes fake IDs. I barely sleep the night before I meet her, convinced that it could be a setup by the police or a sex trafficker. Even if it isn't, she could rob me or kill me, but I'm desperate enough to risk it.

I don't have much to lose at this point.

I'm numb as I press the buzzer on the old warehouse door and answer the garbled question coming from the speaker box. Someone buzzes me into a dingy stairwell, and I force myself to climb the stairs to the third floor. A thin, tattooed woman with gold facial piercings opens the door into what looks like an industrial print shop. I don't miss how she takes in the fading bruises on my face before she leads me to a small back room, where she passes me a form and asks me who I want to be.

I stare at her for a long moment before looking at the paperwork she hands me.

Who *do* I want to be?

I flush and stammer out an apology, asking her for a few minutes to figure it out. She offers to make up a name for me, but I tell her I'd prefer to choose it.

I get to make my own choices now.

I choose something that sounds close enough to my name that I'll respond to it if I'm not paying attention, then write down a long, feminine version of the name. I keep my birthday and middle name, and I use the last name of my favorite summer camp counselor from childhood. I pass the woman the paperwork and my Massachusetts driver's license before I cake on makeup to hide the last of the fading bruises on my face.

Five minutes later, when I hold the new, fake license up to my old license, I heave a sigh of relief.

Alice Murphy doesn't exist anymore.

I'm Alexandria Shearer now.

I pass over the money and give the woman the first real smile I've given anyone in a long time.

***

LOOKING FOR WORK & HOUSING

26 year old woman escaping DV situation looking for employment and housing.

I'm a quick learner, exceptionally reliable, extremely personable, and I am willing to do almost anything.

I can cook and clean, I have basic computer skills, and I have experience organizing charity fundraisers.

Will move anywhere.

No children, no pets.

No access to a car.

***

I wasn't smart about how I worded my desperate Craigslist post, so I've been getting hundreds of solicitations for sex or worse every single day for the last two weeks. I'm tucked away in the corner of a large coffee shop scrolling through bullshit responses when one catches my eye:

SREED61, APRIL 17, 2023, 3:53 PM:

> Hello, I have a receptionist position available for a small law firm in Astoria, Oregon. Our office is currently staffed by women only. Please let me know if you're interested.

I respond, and the person must be at their computer because they message back a moment later. After a few messages, we arrange to meet later in the week for an interview, and I spend the rest of the week anxiously anticipating it. I've never had a job or interviewed for anything, but I know I need to look professional, so I buy a black dress and a pair of sensible heels.

On the day of the interview, I do my hair and makeup and show up at the restaurant fifteen minutes early, making sure not to show how nervous I am as I wait.

I'm good at hiding my feelings, good at lying, good at pretending everything is fine, because I've been doing it for years.

I stand up when a woman in her sixties with short red hair, thin eyebrows, and warm brown eyes approaches the table and introduces herself as Suzie Reed. I *need* to make a good impression, so I try to keep my nerves under control and force myself to be the charming, perfect version of myself I've practiced over the years.

It's like a second skin I can pull on, familiar but slightly too tight.

Suzie orders us wine for the table, and I force myself not to drink as much as I want to as we make small talk. After we order our food, Suzie peers at me over the rim of her wine glass appraisingly.

"So, Alexandria, how much work experience do you have?"

I give her a bright smile. "Please, call me Alex. And I've been incredibly involved in charity fundraisers over the years, at least two a year. I'm exceptionally organized, to the point that I'm a little obsessive about color coding my calendar," I say jokingly, even though it's not a joke. I like the feeling of control it gives me.

Suzie smiles at me. "Well, I'm fairly unorganized, so you'll have to show me your system sometime. Did you go to college?" I blink quickly and freeze the smile on my face, trying to seem nonchalant. I didn't even graduate high school, but I'm not telling her that.

"No," I say, keeping my voice even, "but I was in all AP classes in high school, I've done a tremendous amount of reading over the years, and I've taken various online classes in my spare time. I'm not stupid." I sound defensive even to myself, so I smile and try to play it off. Suzie raises her eyebrows and sips her wine.

"No, you're not."

I take a small sip of my wine before asking her questions about where she went to law school. When the waiter brings us our food, I act charming, thanking her and complimenting her earrings to show Suzie I'm personable.

I look down at my plate and try not to groan. I ordered the cheapest thing on the menu in case I had to pay, and the salad looks delicious, but it's meager portions. Suzie looks at my plate and at her pasta dish and stops the waiter before she leaves.

"Excuse me, but we asked for plates to share. Would you mind bringing those over?" Suzie gives me a small, conspiratorial smile as she pours me more wine. I want to cry, but instead, I smile back at her and ask her the right questions about the job. She tells me the job won't be hard, mostly just filing, organizing, and scheduling.

"That sounds like something I'd be good at, and I'd love the opportunity to work in the legal field." God, I hope I don't sound as pathetically desperate as I feel.

"Well, Alex, I think you'd be a good fit. I have no idea why the *temp agency*," she says slowly, making air quotes with her fingers, "we're hiring you from asks us to pay you in cash every week, but you've come so highly recommended that no one will ask any questions. No one will even know about it." I stare at her for a second, realizing that not only is she offering me the job, but she's saving me from saying that I need to be paid under the table.

I give Suzie a genuine smile, trying extremely hard not to cry.

"I promise I won't let you down."

She smiles at me warmly. "I don't think you will."

Suzie orders us dessert and coffee, and I finally start to relax as we chat about the town I'm moving to. On our way out of the restaurant, we exchange phone numbers, and she tells me she has a client who might have an apartment available, and that he'd most likely take cash.

I look at her, overwhelmed and confused by her kindness. I don't ever accept help, and I don't understand why she's so willing to offer it.

"Can I ask why you're helping me?" I blurt out, wincing slightly at how vulnerable I'm being. Suzie levels me with a serious, knowing look.

"Good help is hard to find sometimes, isn't it?"

***

The next morning, I'm going through the small stack of bills in my bag and panicking.

Between transit tickets, the hotels, the ID, and everything else, I've managed to go through almost three thousand dollars in the last month. Suzie said I had the job, but that's not a guarantee. She might have changed her mind about me.

I'm about to start going through the other responses to my Craigslist post when my phone chimes.

Suzie, 10:30 AM:

> Good morning, Alex. The apartment I mentioned yesterday is available.

> It's not a great part of town or a great apartment, but it is inexpensive.

> Please let me know if you're still interested.

Alex, 10:31 AM:

Absolutely. When could I move in?

Roger can drop the keys at our office today.

When would you be able to start work? I assume you'll need time to relocate.

I can be there tomorrow, and I can start work on Monday.

With the knowledge that the job is actually happening and I'm not completely screwed anymore, I spend the day buying clothes that I think will be good for an office job. I still have no idea what I like to wear and figuring it out is overwhelming. I drift from store to store, getting used to only thinking about myself when I pick things out.

That night, when I lay out all the clothes I bought on my hotel bed, I realize with a pang of grief that everything I bought reminds me of the clothes my mother liked to wear.

***

The next morning, I pack my few belongings into my new suitcase, check out of the hotel, and take the bus to Astoria to pick up the keys from Suzie's office.

Cairn & Reed is a small, converted house a few blocks from the quaint downtown. Suzie introduces me to her partner, Catherine, a woman in her early fifties with salt and pepper hair piled on top of her head artfully, and their paralegal, Bailey, a woman in her late thirties with a mass of curly black hair and bright red nails.

They're kind and welcoming, and I wonder how much Suzie has told them about me. Not much, most likely, because I avoided talking about myself as much as possible, but it's entirely possible they know about my situation.

I hope not.

Suzie leads me out to her car, her blue and gold license plate proclaiming Oregon as a "PACIFIC WONDERLAND," and she drives me to a small, crumbling Victorian on the south side of town. She lets herself in and I trail behind her up the narrow stairs, grimacing at the peeling wallpaper and faint smell of dampness as we approach a small landing on the third floor.

She opens the door to the apartment, making a quiet, displeased noise as she shows me inside the converted attic. It's old and drafty, with sloping ceilings and paper-thin walls covered in cracking plaster. The shallow, stained laminate breakfast bar juts out of the tiny kitchen into the small living space, and the hardwood floors are scratched and unpolished. The cramped bedroom won't fit a queen-sized bed easily, and the ensuite bathroom has a tiny, stained porcelain tub.

Suzie looks at me, seeming embarrassed, and I keep my face neutral as I survey the absolute shithole I'm about to live in.

"I'm so sorry about this, Alex. I promise that Roger *did* say it was nicer than this." I shake my head at her, smiling a little too widely.

"It's great. I don't need much, Suzie, just something that's mine." She gives me a tight, understanding smile and lets out a long sigh.

"Well, the rent's $750 a month, although that seems extremely steep to me now. It's due on the first of the month, and you can leave your rent in the mail slot of the first-floor apartment. Roger lives there, but he's a long-haul driver, so he's not home that often. The second floor is a vacation rental, so you might have strangers in and out, but based on your apartment, I'm going to hazard a guess that it's not the nicest rental around, so I'm not sure how often you'll have people there. I think Roger said the laundry is in the basement." Tears prick at my eyes, and I look away briefly as I blink them away.

"Suzie, I really can't thank you enough. I don't know what I'd do without this."

"I'm happy to help. Lord knows I could have used it, once." I raise my eyebrows at her, and she gives me a tight smile. "I'll see you on

Monday." With that, she leaves me alone in my empty, shitty apartment with two sets of keys.

I look around the place I've ended up in, as a different person than I was, and I curl up on the floor and I cry until I feel empty.

For the first time in my life, the emptiness feels like an opportunity.

2

ALEX

MONDAY, MAY 1

"You stupid fucking bitch!" The empty wine bottle flies towards my head, and I duck out of the way just in time. I lose my balance and fall to my knees as it smashes into the wall behind me, and I can feel glass shards hitting my shoulders and back.

I wish I could take one of them and drive it into his thick fucking neck.

"I don't know how I ended up with such a pathetic fuck up of a wife!" I look up at Danny's face, at the hideous shade of red he turns when he's angry, and I laugh at him. I know it's the wrong thing to do, that it's dangerous to provoke him, but I'm too drunk and furious to care anymore.

"You *don't?*" My drunken, bitter laughter sounds manic. "Well, *Daniel*, let me fucking tell you -" I pause as I push up off the floor, steadying myself against the wall, and then I start to yell at him. I've never yelled at him before, but I'm so angry I can't control myself. I don't stop yelling when he tells me to shut up, or when he starts screaming back, or even when he charges at me and shoves me into the wall so hard my head spins. I stop briefly when he punches me in the stomach, but the rage and adrenaline coursing through my body dulls the pain, and I start yelling at him the second I can breathe again.

I only stop when I'm staring down the barrel of his loaded gun.

"If you *ever* speak to me like that again, you worthless fucking cunt, I'll put you in the *ground*." He grabs a fistful of my hair and shoves me down to my knees, the gun pointed at my forehead. "Apologize, Alice. *Now*." I feel the cold metal of the gun touch me between the eyes, and I start to sob.

"*NO!*" I shout as I sit up in bed, panting heavily, my heart pounding out of my chest as I look around the room, confused. I'm not in the kitchen, I'm in bed. I look beside me, but I'm alone in the small bed in the tiny room with the cracking plaster walls, and I heave a sigh of relief.

It was just a dream.

I'm in Astoria, Danny isn't here, and I'm still safe - for now, anyway. I flop back onto my mattress and run my hands over my face, trying to force the panic back down and ignore it.

It's just shy of five in the morning, but I know I'm not getting back to sleep, so I slip out of bed and change into sweats and my one pair of sneakers. I search for the nearest high school and make my way to the track, where a few older women and a handful of high school students are using the track before school starts. I warm up and run some quick drills before I sprint as hard as I can, not stopping until the constant churn of anxiety in the back of my head goes quiet.

Once I'm calm, I go home and get ready for my first day of work.

***

"So, you only *really* need to know two things to do this job: first, there always needs to be coffee, because some of us have horrifying caffeine addictions." Bailey points to herself with a wink. "Secondly, you'll see Mrs. Hart often. She's got a ton of money, no kids, and nine nieces and nephews. She usually comes in a week after every holiday to make changes to her will." I raise my eyebrows, and Bailey gives me a playful smile and nods. "She usually writes them all back in after Christmas, although her nephew Jeremy has been out in the cold for years. No idea what he did." Bailey shrugs, walking me from the kitchen to the desk in the comfortable reception area, and she spends the morning training me.

Bailey is chatty and warm and a little overly familiar in a way that feels endearing instead of irritating, and I get along with her at once. Suzie and Catherine both come in later in the day, and I spend all day trying to make a good impression on the three of them.

From what I can tell, I think they all like me.

I have to go into the bathroom several times during the day to breathe, and I have to pinch myself a few times so I don't cry. I have a new name, a job, an apartment I spent all weekend furnishing with things from the thrift store, and Danny isn't here.

It feels surreal and overwhelming, but this is my life now.

***

After work, I go home and pull a microwave meal out of the freezer. I don't love eating things like this, but after years of being expected to cook three meals a day, food for parties, and elaborate holiday meals, I'm not cooking another day in my life if I can help it. I take my microwaved food into the living room and turn on the TV, putting on a cooking show in the background while I eat.

I might not want to cook ever again, but I still find the process soothing and familiar.

I try not to think about how long it took me to learn to cook the way Danny liked, or what happened if I didn't do it right. I force myself not to think about the nightmare from this morning, and I do my best to ignore everything that happened to me before I moved here.

It didn't happen to me, it happened to Alice Murphy, and I'm not her anymore. There's a defined before and after, and I can choose to shut it all out, so I do.

***

For so many years, I barely got to make any choices for myself. Even if I got to make decisions about something, I had to consider Danny's preferences. I have to make so many choices now, about *everything*, and I'm the only one who has to be considered. I get to wear whatever I want, eat whatever I want, go wherever I want, speak to whoever I want, everything. I'm in complete control of my life.

It's overwhelming.

It's terrifying.

It's fucking *amazing*.

I furnish and decorate my shitty little apartment with things I find at the thrift store, trying to make the space as comfortable as I can. I make up a past for myself. I make lists of things I need to do, things I want to do, and things I've never done. There are things that I can't do, like get a car or health insurance or tell people about my life, but I control whatever I can. I begrudgingly budget, split up the remaining emergency cash, and hide it all over the apartment. I also hide the ring and my ID, just in case I need them.

I get to know Suzie, Catherine, and Bailey better while trying to keep them from getting to know anything about me beyond the surface level.

I buy a paper planner and start organizing my new life like I used to in high school, using different colored pens to block out my days, and I organize the calendar on my phone and my work computer the same way. Seeing the structure of my life taking place feels grounding, and it reassures me every time I look at the planner that I'm in control. I buy myself nice running shoes and start running regularly for the first time since I left Boston. The recreation center is a ten-minute walk from work and has fitness classes available during my lunch hour, so I start taking whatever they offer during the week.

Between the control, the constant physical activity, and the fact that Danny *still* hasn't found me, I start relaxing enough that I can sleep long hours regularly, and the nightmares get less frequent. The lack of stress makes my appetite return fully in a way I haven't experienced in years, and I start gaining weight. It terrifies me initially, but Danny's not around to throw a fit over it, so I let it happen. It's my fucking body.

I take the bus into Portland on Saturdays and recreate the way I spent the first few weeks of my new life, walking around doing whatever I want to, trying hard and often failing not to spend money.

I explore Astoria after work and during my lunch breaks, getting to know my new home. It's charming, small enough that you start to recognize the same strangers, but large enough that it's not boring. The slow, constant trickle of tourists adds some interest to the working-class families and rich retirees. The town is set back slightly from the coast, but getting to live near the ocean excites me.

The coast here is so different from the coast back home, but it's stunning. The dense wall of evergreens abruptly changes into dunes coated in pale beach grass, which give way to a long, flat stretch of dark grey sand that disappears into the frigid blue-grey waves. Large trucks drive slowly on the beach, and it's cold and slightly foggy every time I go.

I walk past an art supply store one Sunday and realize that I want to make something for the first time in years. I spent my entire childhood attempting to be as talented of an artist as my mother, but I gave up making art entirely after she died. Walking into the store makes me feel like I'm coming home, in a way, and I abandon my budget. I fill my basket with sketchbooks and canvases and pencils and paints and inks, and I leave the store feeling a little more like myself.

I start spending every Sunday at the beach with the decaying iron skeleton of a ship's hull buried in the sand, sketching and painting it in different mediums and styles. I see a small herd of elk in the park surrounding the beach, and I do my best to sketch them from a distance. I sit out on the pier and paint the ships drifting up and down the mouth of the river, and I draw the old, intricate Victorian houses that are peppered throughout the town. I start hanging up the pieces in my bedroom, surrounding myself with reminders that I can express myself again.

As the weeks start to pass, I realize that even with all the lying and pretending, I'm more myself than I've ever been.

I found it hard to be Alice Silva.

I hated being Alice Murphy.

I fucking *love* being Alexandria Shearer.

3

ALEX

FOUR MONTHS EARLIER

My phone pings as I park in the driveway, but I ignore it as I grab my gym bag and water bottle and head straight for the kitchen. Going to Pilates was a mistake. The bruises on my arms are finally gone, but I almost passed out doing oblique crunches.

My ribs still aren't healed, apparently.

I drop my stuff in the kitchen and grab a half-empty bottle of vodka from the freezer, eyeballing what will make me feel less anxious and in pain as I pour it into a glass. I'd prefer wine, but vodka will make the discomfort go away quicker.

I lean against the counter stiffly and pull my phone from my leggings, sipping my drink quickly as I open my texts to find a text from my Pilates instructor with a link to an Instagram video.

Gabi, 1:39 PM:

So great to see you today! Feel better!

BTW I'm volunteering with this great non-profit and just did a video for them - can you watch it so I can get more views?

Alice, 1:46 PM:

missed you too! can do :) see you next week, hopefully!

I open the video she sent, letting it play in the background as I pour another drink. It's an affirmation video, and I let Gabrielle's calm, cheerful voice wash over me as I sip my vodka, cringing a little at the stupidity of the affirmations. I finally look down at the screen as the video plays to see Gabrielle dressed in purple, moving through heart-opening yoga poses in a room decorated in shades of cream and purple. I look at the name of the account, @purpleribbonyoga, and click on the page.

It's a non-profit for domestic violence.

I tense up immediately, thinking back to anything I've ever said or done that could get back to Danny. I know Gabrielle does stuff for charities all the time, so I'm sure that's all this is. I aimlessly scroll through the videos on the page, drinking quickly to combat the cold dread creeping up my spine as I listen to what's being said on the videos. I pause on an aesthetically pleasing infographic about the cycle of abuse and stare at it for a second.

The glass in my hand starts to shake as I read it.

It's my life, reduced to a fucking chart.

I put my phone down and drain my drink before emptying the rest of the bottle into my glass.

It's not like I don't know what my marriage is, what my *life* is. It's not like no one has ever tried to help before, I just didn't want to hear them.

I don't know what's different now, but I hear every message from every video and post. They hit like bullets, lodging themselves in my drunk brain and breaking apart the carefully constructed compartments I sort my life into.

I stare at the empty vodka bottle, trying to remember how full it was half an hour ago. My brain is fuzzier than it should be, but instead of feeling numb, I'm feeling all the emotions I keep locked away. I head to the fridge and grab a bottle of wine, seething.

Things have been good for over a month, but Danny's been spending more time at home lately. This morning, he snapped at me over a shirt not being properly folded, even though it *was*, and I know without a doubt that he'll be looking for reasons to make me apologize soon, and then he'll freak out about *something* and fly off the handle.

It used to take so much longer before he'd freak out again.

I keep scrolling, unable to stop myself, and before I realize it, I've spent all afternoon scrolling through Instagram, jumping between hashtags and accounts and posts, crying on and off, drinking through the whole bottle of wine.

I'm so tired of my life.

I hear the garage door open, and I scream, dropping my phone. My eyes fly to the clock on the wall. *Fuck, fuck, fuck,* I lost track of time. Panic slices through me and I grab my phone, quickly deleting the texts from Gabrielle and my Instagram search history before running around the kitchen and frantically putting together dinner.

Maybe he won't be mad.

He slams the garage door, his heavy footsteps heading for the kitchen, and I work hard to keep my cool and act sober. I look up from the salad I'm preparing and force a smile that feels too tight, but I take one look at his face, and I know I'm fucked.

He's already mad.

"Hi, pumpkin," I coo, pitching my voice a little higher to hide how shaky it is. He doesn't say anything as I look back down at the avocado I'm halving, trying to push down the anxiety and ignore my churning thoughts. He walks towards me, looming over me and looking down at the salad I'm throwing together.

"How many times do I have to tell you I don't like avocados, Alice?" Danny's voice is low and menacing. I stare down into the salad, realizing that in my panic, I started making something I usually only make for myself.

"Oh, god, Danny, I'm so sorry," I say quietly, and I set the knife down and start picking the chunks of avocado out of the salad greens with trembling hands. He's either going to explode now or save it for later, and I'm not sure which is worse. He scoffs and walks towards the fridge, pulling out a beer.

"Jesus, Bunny, you're so stupid," he mutters, heading out of the kitchen and leaving me standing there, my hands shaking with anger and fear. My eyes lift from my hands to the recently repaired drywall in the kitchen from when Danny threw me into the wall almost two months ago.

Looking at it now, you'd never even know it had been damaged.

Something inside me that was already broken beyond repair finally shatters, and all I feel is bitter, horrible resentment. I grab another bottle of wine from the fridge and drink directly from it, fury and contempt roiling in my stomach.

Fuck this.

Fuck him.

I dump all the avocado chunks back into the salad, hastily cutting open another, roughly slicing it, and dumping it in before I grab another, draining the bottle of wine as I go. I'm furious and shitfaced by the time Danny comes in for another beer, asking me where the fuck dinner is.

FRIDAY, JUNE 2

I lay on the yoga mat in savasana, breathing deeply and trying to clear my mind. I don't want to let the memory bother me, but it won't stop replaying in my mind. I dream about that night all the time, how he threw the salad and the wine bottle at me, how I got too drunk and made the mistake of telling him everything I thought about him and our relationship and all the things he'd done to me, how I had to run in the middle of the night with no plan, no preparation, and no fucking idea what I was doing.

It's working out okay so far, though.

I get changed after yoga in the rec center locker room and hurry back to the office, pressing my lips into a thin line as I focus on drafting billing emails for Catherine and Suzie. Despite my best efforts to keep the past in the past, it's not working that well. Between waking up from another nightmare about Danny, seeing a large blond man at the coffee shop this morning, and fighting off that memory in yoga, I've been a bundle of nerves all day.

I do my best to hide it, to smile and act normal, but I think the women at work are starting to be able to tell when I'm having a hard day.

I hate it.

I walk home quickly after work and open a bottle of wine, setting up paints and a canvas on my coffee table. I search online until I find the video Gabrielle sent me back in March, and I play it on repeat in the background while I paint a peony on a small square canvas, focusing on detailing it with a fine brush. Like exercising, painting helps me manage the constant, nagging fear that I'll lose control of my life again.

I breathe deeply as I paint, practicing the affirmations Gabrielle asks me to repeat, letting her familiar voice comfort me.

I love myself.
I love who I am becoming.
I am doing the best I can.
I am stronger than I think.
I am grateful for my freedom.
I am worthy of love and respect.
I deserve to feel good about myself.
I deserve to be happy.

I repeat the affirmations to myself over and over until I'm grounded in the truths and almost believe the lies.

***

I go to Portland the next morning and focus on burying my feelings under an avalanche of brunch and shopping. I walk away from the restaurant, drunk off mimosas, following my phone's map and peering into the large glass windows as I walk past the shops. I pause when I come to a shop with frosted windows and discrete signage, slipping my phone into my bag as I step inside. I'm immediately overwhelmed by the brightly lit, well-organized shelves full of things I'm unfamiliar with.

I've never been in a sex shop before.

"Can I help you?" I glance at the tall, androgynous person behind the counter and shake my head quickly.

"Just looking," I say, ducking my face to hide the blush creeping across my cheeks. It's definitely the mimosas making me blush and not the fact that I'm an adult woman who's never owned a sex toy, much less masturbated until about a week ago.

"Cool, let me know if you need help. I'm Sienna." I nod, flipping through an explicit, illustrated book on display and putting it down quickly. I head to the back of the store, picking up a long flesh-colored dildo that I can't fully wrap my hand around. It's *very* different from what I'm used to. Could that even *fit* inside of me? What would that even feel like? I set it back down, glancing around at the other items laid out nearby. There's a leather harness with a hole in the front, a string of silicone balls, cylindrical pumps, handcuffs, ropes, clamps and pinwheels and things that look like they might hurt, and an enema kit.

Oh my god, I'm in way over my head here.

I just want to buy a vibrator.

I turn towards the front of the store and balk at the wall and small display tables full of vibrators. I had *no* idea there were so many kinds to choose from. I pick one up and turn it on, and I accidentally drop it in surprise when it starts gyrating. I can feel my face turn bright red as I hurry to grab it from the floor, desperately trying to figure out how to turn it off. Sienna comes back from around the counter and points to the bottom, and I turn it off and set it down.

"I need help," I blurt out, staring at my feet. God, I fucking hate asking for help.

Sienna leans casually against a display table. "For sure. How can I help you?"

"I don't know. I haven't really ever...I don't think I need all of *this*," I say, feeling my face start to turn red again as I gesture vaguely around the store, "but I need...something?" I look up and see Sienna smiling at me warmly.

"We have *so* many somethings. Do you have an idea of what you might like?" I shake my head slowly. "No worries. Let's do a quick run through of what we have and go from there." I trail Sienna as they walk me through the store, calmly explaining what most of the things in the shop are.

I leave half an hour later with a much more in-depth understanding of exactly how little I know about what I like, a slim purple vibrator, a smutty book, lube, a handwritten list of porn sites, apps, some book recommendations from Sienna, and the distinct, triumphant feeling that I've just taken back control of another massive part of my life.

***

I wander through Powell's a few hours later, killing time before the bus leaves for Astoria by aimlessly browsing titles, drifting through the literature section into the poetry section. Of all the things I'd left in Boston, I wish I'd been able to take the books. My parents had turned one of the spare bedrooms into a library before I was born. It was the only room in the house I could keep Danny from changing because he thought it looked impressive.

I trail my fingers absently along the shelf, and my heart stutters when I see a battered collection of Neruda poems that looks almost familiar. I pull it off the shelf and flip it open, searching until I find Sonnet XVII. Underlined twice in a heavy hand is my father's favorite line, the start of the stanza he wrote into his wedding vows.

I love you without knowing how, or when, or from where.

A pang of grief echoes through me as I think about the copy of this book I left back in Boston, the one my dad bought for my mom on their first date. The spine was broken open to this sonnet, and my mother underlined the entire last stanza in red pen at some point a decade before they got married.

> *I love you without knowing how, or when, or from where.*
> *I love you directly without problems or pride:*
> *I love you like this because I don't know any other way to*
> *love,*
> *except in this form in which I am not nor are you,*
> *so close that your hand upon my chest is mine,*
> *so close that your eyes close with my dreams.*

I close the book gently, clinging to it as I navigate towards the checkout counter, wondering what it would feel like to be loved like that.

Now that I'm free of Danny, maybe I'll be able to find out.

***

When I get home from Portland, I stand in the entryway on the ground floor of the crumbling house for a minute, inhaling deeply. Aside from running into him once or twice in the basement when I was doing laundry, I rarely see Roger, and I only know he's home if the ground floor smells like cigarette smoke. Apparently, he's out of town right now.

I listen closely as I walk past the second floor, but the rental is only occupied a few times a month, so I'm certain it's just me in the house right now, which means the water and the radiator will get hot. I let myself into my tiny apartment and sigh, setting down my tote bag and jacket.

The apartment has felt homier since I started decorating with thrift store pieces and hanging my canvases on the walls. It's still a dingy little apartment in severe disrepair, but the fact that it's all mine makes up for that.

There are other things that are all mine now, too.

I rifle through the tote bag at my feet and pull out the lube and the vibrator, heading for my bedroom.

***

I don't think I've spent more than fifteen minutes in bed before I feel loose and hazy, every nerve ending in my body tingling from multiple orgasms. I lay on the small bed, staring up at the ceiling, sexually satisfied for the first time in my life, and I start laughing deliriously.

I'm glad no one else was in the house because I was *not* quiet.

The number of orgasms I had during my marriage barely surpasses single digits, and *none* of them got close to what I just experienced. Danny was so vehemently against me masturbating or owning any kind of sex toy because he was convinced I didn't need anything but him, which was fucking *bullshit*. Somehow, of all the things Danny kept from me or took away from me, this one pisses me off the most.

I'm not letting anyone take anything away from me ever again.

4

THEO

MONDAY, AUGUST 7

My grandparents' estate attorney, Catherine, volunteers to pick me up from prison. She brings coffee, and after a painfully awkward attempt at small talk, she pivots to explaining the inheritance again. She visited me after Nana died, and we've gone over this before, but it's a safe topic and it takes long enough to go through that we'll be close to Astoria by the time she's done speaking. I barely listen to her as I watch the low, flat sprawl of Salem give way to the agricultural fields of the Willamette Valley.

Was this drive always so pretty?

I hum in response to whatever Catherine's saying about the trusts as we navigate away from the wide interstate cutting through the suburban mess outside of Portland to the highway that heads towards the coast. The low, densely wooded hills slowly transform into dense copses of trees as the road narrows to two lanes, and I stop listening to Catherine entirely once we start driving through the Tillamook Forest. I never realized how much I missed how the light filters through the tall evergreens and illuminates the ferns and mossy tree boughs. Even the fresh clearcuts we pass seem scenic to me, the mismanaged undergrowth fully visible around the tree stumps and through the mess of tree limbs scattered across the forest floor.

I start to get anxious once we pass through the coastal mountain range and start driving through the drab seaside towns with their squat, weather-beaten buildings. When I see Astoria rising out of the Columbia River, my body tenses and my knee bounces quickly.

I have no idea what the fuck I'm supposed to do with myself now.

Catherine drives us to her firm on the edge of downtown, and I follow her into the converted house and upstairs to her office. I focus on breathing as I take my time pretending to reread the paperwork before signing it. I've read it thoroughly before, but I want to delay facing my new reality for as long as possible. Catherine hands over a large keyring with keys to the Anderson House, the house in Yachats, the safety deposit boxes, Boss's old Chevy, Nana's Prius, and my beater Subaru from college. My head is buzzing looking at all the keys, and I excuse myself to the bathroom just to get some space.

As I walk down the stairs into the main level, a young woman gives me a warm smile as she heads into the reception area, and I catch the faint scent of her floral perfume as she walks by. I stop short on the last step and stare at her, but she doesn't notice.

She's fucking *stunning*. She's short, with dark hair that falls at her shoulders and big brown eyes. She's wearing a loose, emerald green dress with a neckline that shows off her long neck and sloping collarbones, and I'm immediately, painfully aware that she's the first attractive woman I've seen in person in nine years. I lock myself in the bathroom, splash my face with cold water, and take a minute to calm down. I take a few calming breaths, trying to compartmentalize.

I need to get the fuck out of here. I need to get to the house and be alone.

I need to not think about that woman.

As I head back upstairs to wrap up with Catherine, I can't help but peer into the reception room. The woman is completely unaware of me, mindlessly running her full bottom lip between her teeth as she focuses on the computer in front of her. She's not wearing makeup, and I can see she has a small spray of freckles across her nose and cheeks.

God, she's so cute.

I shake my head and head back upstairs, vaguely listening to Catherine as she passes me a portfolio of paperwork and all the keys.

"Our receptionist will send you the final statement later this month. The statement is just for your records—Dottie put the money for the probate services in trust before she passed." I nod and try to smile, thanking Catherine and taking the keys and the paperwork.

When I leave, the receptionist is chatting quietly with a tall woman with red hair, so I don't have an excuse to talk to her.

That's probably for the best.

***

"Good afternoon, Theodore. I'm Dr. Mills." I shake her hand before sitting in the chair across from her, giving her a polite smile.

"Nice to meet you." It's not. This is bullshit.

"Is there a name you prefer to go by? Please feel free to call me Melissa." I feel my mouth thin out. I have no fucking interest in being familiar with her.

"Theodore is fine, Dr. Mills."

"Okay. You're scheduled to meet with me every other Thursday as part of your parole. Does that work for you?"

"That's fine."

"Salem's a long drive from Astoria. I can do virtual, if you prefer?"

"I can come to Salem for our appointments." It'll give me something to do, at least.

"Will that pose an issue once you get a job?"

I smile politely again. "I won't be needing a job. Money isn't much of an issue for me."

She nods and scribbles another note. "Well, financial stability is important, but jobs can also bring a lot of social fulfillment, and social connections are important for successful reintegration. Are you religious at all? Involved with churches, or any secular organizations?"

"No."

"Do you have any friends you're still in contact with?"

"No."

"Did you have friends inside?"

"Friends of convenience, so, no."

"Any family?" I try hard not to roll my eyes.

"My grandparents are both dead, and if you read my file, you'd know my father is dead." Dr. Mills purses her lips in concern.

"What about your mother?" I can feel my jaw tense, so I force myself to relax.

"With one exception, we haven't spoken in almost two decades." She frowns at me.

"Theodore, reintegration can be extremely hard for people with robust support systems, much less people who don't have one. There are lots of programs that can help fulfill the need for community."

"I'll be fine. I don't have many social needs, honestly."

"Well, what *are* your social needs?" I look out the window and shrug, thinking briefly of Catherine's pretty receptionist.

"I'd like to meet someone." Dr. Mills's face is smooth as she considers what I've said.

"Given your history, I think you should deprioritize romantic attachment for the time being. I think it's a good idea to focus on yourself first." That is *such* bullshit.

I clear my throat and force another smile. "I've participated in therapy for almost a decade, and I've come to terms with the issues that landed me in trouble in the first place. I've done all the work I needed to do."

Dr. Mills crosses her legs and gives me a patient, neutral look. "That's wonderful, but there's always more work to be done. Will you still be taking your medications?"

"No."

"Why not?" My patience finally runs out, and I roll my eyes at her and her asinine questions.

"Because I've spent nine years feeling like a fucking zombie with no sex drive," I snap. I take a deep breath, exhaling slowly. "*Sorry.* I don't like the medication, and I don't agree that I need it. I'm fine without it."

Dr. Mills nods slowly. "Side effects can be difficult, but you might just be on the wrong medications. It usually takes some trial and error to find an effective combination. I think you should at least schedule an appointment with another psychiatrist and see what they have to say."

"I'm fine, thank you."

"Well, let's keep it in mind as an option. Have you looked through the resources I've emailed you?"

"No."

She exhales slowly, looking down at her notes. "Theodore, I'm going to encourage you to engage more deeply with this process. Reintegration is jarring and difficult. I'm here to support you and help you navigate it."

"I'll be fine."

"Be that as it may, I think we should create a support plan for you." I glance at the clock. I haven't even been here that long. I sigh and look back at her, trying to be polite.

"Fine."

***

After nine years of a routine with very little autonomy, the most challenging part of being home is choosing what to do with my days. I actually listen to one thing my therapist says and give myself structure right out of the gate. Wake up, make breakfast, work out, find something to do, make lunch, find more things to do, make dinner, find another fucking thing to do, go to bed. There's so much time in the day to fill that I make a long list of projects and throw myself into them as hard as possible.

I clean out the house, box up everything I can't handle looking at but don't want to get rid of and donate things I don't want or need anymore. I get rid of the ornate wood pieces my grandfather cherished and replace most of them with pieces that remind me of the mid-century furniture my grandmother loved. I donate everything in my closet and buy all new clothing, I set up a gym in the basement, I buy a nicer computer than I need and set it up in Boss's old office, and I work on all three cars and get them running properly again.

I meet with Officer Dent, report on all I'm doing, take my drug test, smile, nod, and shake hands. I work with Catherine to take care of all the bullshit paperwork I need to, like getting everything put in my name, getting insurance, whatever. It's not really her job, but she helps anyway because my grandmother paid her to. I make a point not to talk to the receptionist, whose name is Alexandria, mostly because I don't remember how to talk to women I'm attracted to and she's *so* fucking gorgeous.

After a few days off my medication, my sex drive comes back with a vengeance, and I finally find something interesting to do with my time. I do not listen to Dr. Mills at all, because she's a fucking idiot. I barely used dating apps when I was in college, and I find the profiles daunting to set up, so while I figure them out and start talking to women online, I also start driving down the coast, spending every night at different bars, relearning how to speak to and flirt with women.

I lie about what I do, since "just released from prison" isn't usually a turn-on.

I lie about pretty much everything, and no one seems to notice.

The first few encounters are awkward. I'm too forward, too honest, or too obviously bored by what they say. I'm attractive enough that the women are often forgiving, but it takes me a few tries to remember how to be charming. It's harder than I remember it being, mostly because I'm genuinely not interested in any of the women I talk to.

Nothing's *wrong* with them, they're just not *right*.

I ask questions, I listen, I engage, and I make lists in my head of everything that I find interesting or attractive about them. Then, whether or not I like them, I focus on getting them into bed.

The first time I get a woman in bed, it's been so long that it's overwhelming, and I come embarrassingly quickly. I spend half an hour going down on her in apology, fuck her properly, then leave.

Between online dating and going to bars, I start fucking as many women as I can, as often as I can. I pay attention to what they respond to, what they like, and I try to see if I like them more after I fuck them.

I don't, usually.

One woman holds my attention long enough to see her a second time, but not a third.

She's not right, either.

The first time I see Alexandria in town, she's out jogging the river-walk on a Sunday in a hoodie and a pair of baggy sweats. The first time

I think of her during sex, I dismiss it as me having seen her that day in town and finding her prettier than the woman I'm fucking.

The second time I see her, she's sketching in Shively Park. The second time I think about her during sex, I think it's because the woman I'm fucking has similar hair.

The third time I see her is at the cafe near her office right before her workday starts. Without realizing it, I've started to think about her a lot, and even started trying to figure out where I can see her.

Once I understand what I'm doing, I force myself to stop and spend time on the stupid dating apps until I set up a date with someone.

The third time I think about her during sex, I force myself to be present with the woman I'm fucking, and it almost works.

I don't tell Dr. Mills any of this at our next session. I'm not interested in her opinion about the fact that my sex drive has started running my life in the two weeks since I've seen her. I have no interest in her opinion about *anything*, especially anything that has to do with women, or a specific woman I'm not thinking about. I talk about my daily routine and the self-help book I'm forcing myself to read, and I tell her which of her resources I've skimmed. I'm sure we both know I'm bullshitting her, but I lie anyway because it's a parole requirement for me to sit in this room with her for the next year and get her to approve of me.

I don't need her help with anything. I spent years working on my issues in prison, and I'm fine now.

After therapy, I head back to Astoria and stay in the house all weekend, trying to figure out what to do about how I'm feeling. It's been a decade since I've felt interested in someone, and this is so different from last time.

I decide to avoid Alexandria for a bit and ignore my desire to get to know her. I'm running out of projects around the house, but I keep looking for things to do to occupy my time. I work out. I meditate. I replace all the lightbulbs in the house. I masturbate. I cook. I clean the house. I listen to an audiobook. I tighten all the screws in the house. I watch TV.

I do anything not to think or feel, and it almost works.

I need to go grocery shopping by Monday. After years and years of prison food, it's nice to have control over what I do or don't eat, and I enjoy being picky about it. I loved cooking before I went to prison, and it's the only thing that really makes me feel calm lately, so I take a lot of time planning meals, picking ingredients, and focusing on the process of cooking.

I'm looking at wine when a short, plump woman on her phone bumps into me as she reaches for some chardonnay. I glance over at her quickly as I step back, and she looks up from her phone for a second and gives me a guilty smile.

"Sorry, excuse me!" She pushes the phone between her ear and shoulder and grabs two bottles of wine. "Hi, Alex. Are you still at the office?" I glance back at her as she turns away. Doesn't she work with Catherine? My mind empties out at the possibility. "Can you check if I turned off the heater under my desk? *Shit.* You're a lifesaver, thank you!" The woman hangs up as she walks away, and I stare at the wine in my hand.

I could be totally wrong. That woman might not work with Catherine. Lots of people work in offices, and Alex is a common name for both men and women. She probably wasn't talking to Alexandria. It's probably someone else. Even if it was her, I've decided to avoid her, and that's what I'm going to do. I'm done shopping, though, so I check out quickly and head home. Only once I'm driving do I realize I'm on a road that will take me past the law office. I see Alexandria – does she go by Alex? – several blocks ahead, walking quickly up the hill into the residential area of town.

I drive slowly, watching her. Does she live alone? With her parents? Roommates? Boyfriend? Girlfriend? Those last two thoughts irritate me, which is ridiculous.

I pass her and park my car at the top of the hill that runs through town, slouching down to watch her through the mirror as she crests the hill behind me. She has on large, over-ear headphones and seems to not be paying attention to her surroundings as she walks.

What does she like to listen to?

She walks past my car without noticing me and keeps walking downhill towards the south side of town. I let her get several blocks ahead before starting the car again and following her at a good distance.

Eventually, she turns down a street of run-down houses, and I watch her enter a decrepit-looking old house with peeling paint and an overgrown yard. She lives *here*? I'm almost positive this house was a hovel when I was a kid, and it's even worse now.

A minute later, the lights on the top floor go on. She lives in the attic, so I assume she lives alone. Is she single? She's certainly not married, because she doesn't wear a ring. Is she on any of the dating apps I'm on?

I realize what I'm doing and drop my head on the steering wheel in frustration. I followed her, which is the opposite of avoiding her. Goddammit.

I turn the car around and head home, bringing the groceries into the kitchen and starting to make dinner, berating myself. I did so much fucking work on my impulse control issues in prison, but apparently not enough. I start pulling out groceries and try to lose myself in cooking.

This is just me readjusting to being in the world again. It's temporary. I'm fine, I just need to get back in control.

I grab my phone and check my email while the curry simmers. I've been checking my email a lot, but I'm not sure why until the email I didn't realize I've been waiting for pops up.

AShearer@cairnreed.com, August 28, 2023, 4:45 PM:

Good afternoon, Mr. Anderson,

Please see attached the final billing statement from Dorothy Anderson's estate and probate matter.

Please let me know if you have any questions.

Best,
Alexandria Shearer
Cairn & Reed LLP

I turn off my phone instantly. It means nothing that she emailed me right before I followed her, and I'm not thinking about her anyway. I finish dinner, eating slowly and thinking, trying to taste each individual spice in the curry. I take my time cleaning the dishes and head upstairs to my office. I'm just going to look her up, which is a thing people do.

That technically doesn't count as giving in to an impulse.

Alexandria Shearer has no online footprint, no photos of herself anywhere, and no social media - not even an old AIM, MySpace, or Facebook from when she was younger. She doesn't have a phone number registered, and her personal and work email addresses are new. That's interesting, but it doesn't matter, because I'm avoiding her.

I'm going to go down the coast or into Portland tonight and see if I can pick someone up to fuck this out of my system. It's not technically a *healthy* way to deal with my feelings, but I need to focus on anything other than how I'm starting to feel when I think about Alexandria.

I'm in control of myself, my feelings, and my impulses.

I'm fine.

5

ALEX

TUESDAY, AUGUST 29

"What are you up to tonight?" Bailey fills her coffee mug with her fourth cup of coffee as I pull my boxed salad out of the fridge.

"Um, I was thinking about checking out this trivia thing I saw a flyer for."

"That's cool! Are you going with someone?"

"No, I still barely know anyone here. I thought I could make some friends," I say, trying not to sound as pathetic as I feel. I haven't had friends in so long, and I want to be more social now that my life feels established. I was always friends with Danny's coworkers' wives, but I couldn't be myself with them, so I don't think that counts.

Bailey is the closest thing I've had to a real friend in almost ten years.

"Friends, *right*," she says, rolling her eyes. "I had those before Dylan knocked me up and moved me out here to be close to his sister. He just wanted me all to himself." She laughs, pulling her curly black hair into a bun, and I force a smile. I know she's exaggerating - Bailey is close with her sister-in-law, has a standing monthly girls' night with her college friends back in Portland, and has a best friend in Seattle whose life is so chaotic that everyone in the office occasionally gets long-winded updates about her over coffee - but even the idea of being kept isolated like that makes me anxious.

"Well, at least Miles is good company?" She laughs, making a face.

"He's okay. If you ever want the company of my spoiled toddler, let me know. We pay top dollar for good babysitting."

I smile, spearing a tomato. "Sure. I used to babysit all the time, actually. I make killer mac and cheese, I'm a nut about flossing, and I don't pay attention to bedtimes on weekends."

Bailey laughs and shoots me an interested look. "You got lots of nieces and nephews or something?" Danny did, but I shouldn't tell her that. I shouldn't be telling anyone anything too personal, which might make having friends hard, now that I think about it.

"Oh, uh, friends with kids. Back home. In Maine."

Bailey shrugs. "Well, if you're serious, I'd *love* a date night."

***

I didn't look into trivia at all before heading there after work, which might have been a mistake. I didn't realize there were teams, or that you couldn't play without a team of at least two, or that there was a two-drink minimum.

I take a deep breath and push down the anxiety. I'm determined to try something new, so I tap the shoulder of a tall blonde girl around my age and ask her who runs the trivia, explaining that I'm here alone and hoping to find a team. I want to die of embarrassment, but she's sweet and tells me I can join her team.

She introduces herself as Anna, and I sit with her and a few of her coworkers, who are all around my age and work at one of the local parks as rangers or something like that. She tries to loop me into their conversations, but they all know each other so well that it's easy for them to slip into talking about work drama or people I don't know.

Still, it's nice.

It's new, at least.

Someone buys a pitcher of beer for the table, and I have a drink to calm down. Once the game starts, I have a reason to be part of the conversations, and interacting is easier. I find trivia boring, but I'm surprisingly good at it, and I'm having a nice time with Anna and her coworkers. I try to pay Anna back for the beer when trivia is over, but she waves me off with a sweet smile.

"Don't even worry about it." She leans in close with a conspiratorial smile. "Will's parents are real estate developers in Bend, so he can afford to buy us a round once in a while," she says, laughing a little. "Did you have a good time?"

I smile at her, nodding. "Yeah, it was fun. You and your coworkers are great."

"The guys are cool, but you *need* to meet Jessica. She's awesome, and she's definitely coming next week, so you should join us again if you want to. No pressure," she says, smiling a little shyly.

I beam at her. "Absolutely. I'd love that." I sound too eager, but Anna doesn't seem to notice as she pulls out her phone to swap numbers with me.

I think I just made a friend, and she's going to help me make *another* friend.

I leave the bar feeling giddy.

***

When I get home, I change out of my work dress into baggy sweats and an oversized green knit sweater that I found at the thrift store last week, which has quickly become my favorite. It has a few yellow and white stripes bracketing the word OREGON, and it's the perfect amount of worn in without being worn out. It must have just been donated when I bought it, because the thrift store smell hadn't gotten to it yet. I sniff the sweater again, a little disappointed that the clean, warm, faintly spicy smell is fading so quickly.

When I'm done getting ready for bed, I crawl under the thick duvet and grab my vibrator. I lay back in bed, turning on audio porn on my phone, and let the man's deep voice start guiding me through masturbating.

My reference for porn before going to that sex shop a few months ago was whatever Danny liked. He'd make me watch it with him to show me what he wanted and to tell me how I should be acting, and I thought all porn was horrible. Apparently, some porn is kind of amazing - I just didn't like what Danny liked.

It took me every night of June and July to figure out the basics of what *I* like.

June and July were *the best*.

I used to think I hated sex. I'd only ever had sex with Danny, but from the very first time it happened, I hated it. I'd occasionally want it and even enjoy it, but those occasions were few and far between.

Now, I think I only hated sex with Danny.

You're supposed to want to have sex before it happens. On top of that, your partner is supposed to care if you like what they're doing.

All of this was news to me.

Now that I'm on my own and I know I like sex, I can masturbate whenever I want, as much as I want, and I do it every day.

Every. Single. Fucking. Day.

Right as I'm starting to come, I have this overwhelming fear that Danny's about to walk in, and the tension in my core starts to falter. I try to ignore it and keep going, but it ruins it for me, and I lose my orgasm. I huff out an angry breath and stare up at the ceiling, pissed.

He's still trying to take things from me, even though he's not here.

I'm not going to let him.

I take a few calming breaths and navigate to a video I love and start over. I have so many questions about what I like and why I like it, but I'm not asking them. It's not like I'm having sex with anyone, so I don't need to worry about having to explain wanting to try something that would be embarrassing to talk about. It's just me, so I save whatever makes me come to a bookmarked folder on my web browser, even the videos I'm sure would make me cry if they happened in real life, which are most of them.

I don't know how I'd feel about being tied up, but it seems scary.

Maybe someday I'll get to figure out if it's not.

6

THEO

THURSDAY, SEPTEMBER 7

I think about Alex a lot.

It's not that I can't stop myself, I just don't want to.

I keep seeing her around town. Her office is near my house, and we're regulars at the same coffee shop in the mornings. We also run a similar route on Sundays, but at slightly different times. Seeing her is the best part of my day, but I don't think she's noticed me once. Not that she would, because she seems somewhat unobservant.

It's fine. I'm not trying to get her attention.

Not yet, anyway.

***

"You seem distracted today, Theodore."

"Uh, yeah. Sorry."

"What's going on?" I stare at Dr. Mills for a minute. I can't tell her that I've been out of prison for a month and I'm already having a hard time controlling my impulses. She probably wouldn't give me a chance to deal with it by myself. She'd probably think I'm a recidivism risk and recommend that the parole board revoke my parole, and I'm *never* going back to prison. I do have to talk to her, though, so I need to figure out how to talk about this casually.

"I might have met someone." The tiniest crease forms between her eyebrows.

"Have you been trying to meet people?"

"Yes."

"Why?" I raise my eyebrows at her, but she waits me out, staring patiently back at me. I can't believe she's going to make me say it.

"Because," I say slowly, "it's been a *while*."

"Ah," she says, looking down at her notes quickly. "Were you intimate with anyone in prison?"

"No."

"Have you been intimate with anyone since you've been released?"

"I'm thirty-one and I just told you I didn't have sex for nine years, so I'm *pretty* sure you can figure that one out for yourself." She doesn't seem fazed by how condescending I'm being.

"May I ask how many people you've been intimate with since your release?"

I grimace at her. "Do you *need* to know that?"

She shrugs. "I'd like to know, if you don't mind telling me. Sex and romantic attachment have been some of the biggest areas you've struggled in, so it feels relevant to me. I think it's important to be honest about these things." I stare at her and feel my knee bouncing quickly, which she clocks immediately.

"Three women." She blinks and purses her lips at me slightly, which I've noticed that she does whenever she doubts that I'm being honest.

She does it a lot, which is fair. I'm usually lying about something.

I'm *definitely* lying about this.

"Were all of the encounters casual?"

I shrug. "Pretty much."

"So, this person you're telling me about...?"

"Alex."

"How did you meet them?"

"At my lawyer's office."

"So it wasn't on purpose?"

"No."

"What makes them different?" I frown, looking out the window and thinking about it for a minute. How have I not thought about this?

"I don't know. I just have a feeling about her."

"What kind of feeling? Is it a good feeling? A bad feeling? Something different?" I force myself not to roll my eyes at her. I don't know how I got saddled with the stupidest therapist the state has.

"Obviously it's a good feeling, or I wouldn't be interested in her." Dr. Mills nods, keeping her face neutral and humming in a cliched, patronizing way.

"Have you felt the same way about anyone before?" It feels like she just dumped a bucket of ice water on me. Is she making this about Ashley? Oh, of fucking *course* she is. I take a second to compose myself before I shake my head slowly.

"It's very different from anything I've felt before." It's much stronger, for one thing.

"Different how?" I narrow my eyes at her slightly.

"Like I said, I don't know." Dr. Mills considers me for a second, her lips pursed slightly.

"Do you think you're ready to get involved with someone right now?"

"We're not *involved*," I insist. "We just met. I want to get to know her better, that's all."

"I'd like you to consider not pursuing it any farther than that for now." I stare at her blankly, trying to hide my irritation. "I understand that it might be difficult, especially if you have a good feeling about Alex, but I think it would be wise to hold off on building a relationship with someone until you're more settled. What do you think about that?"

I think it's fucking stupid.

"I'll take it into consideration." She blinks and purses her lips at me again.

***

I think about the conversation with Dr. Mills all the way back to Astoria. Something about Alex calls out to me in a way I've never felt before, but I don't know what it is. The feelings I have when I see or think about her are so different from the ones I had about Ashley.

When I met Ashley, I felt like something between us harmonized, like we complemented each other, but it was softer, subtler, less consuming. I made some impulsive, shitty choices with her, but I was able to control most of the impulses I had until she broke up with me.

I'm having a much harder time doing that with Alex.

I need to be careful and do things differently this time. With Ashley, I jumped in and started pursuing her immediately, and I overlooked all the warning signs I should have noticed. I was wrong about her.

I don't want to be wrong about Alex.

I need to take my time and get to know her first. I need to make sure the feelings I have about her are right before I invest in starting a relationship with her. I'm not going to be impulsive about this.

The question is how to get to know her.

I know the way I *should* do it.

I know the way I *want* to do it.

In the back of my mind, I know the way I *have* to do it.

I don't know exactly what I'm going to do or when I'll do it, but it'll probably be soon.

7

ALEX

SATURDAY, SEPTEMBER 9

I come home to my wi-fi being out. I text Roger, but get no reply.

Shit, I wanted to watch the Red Sox game.

I don't care for sports in general, but my parents and I never missed a game, and it was one of the few things I got to keep when Danny came into my life. I know there's a divey sports bar a few minutes away, so I walk there and feel relieved that they have the game on.

It's dingy but warm inside, and I sit at the bar and order the first beer I recognize, grateful that the bartender doesn't even ask for my ID. I sip my beer slowly, looking over the scores at the bottom of the fourth. I relax into watching the game and enjoying the hum of conversation and the tinny sound of the electronic slot machines in the corner.

I've never been to a sports bar alone before, and even after months of being on my own, I still get a rush whenever I do something new.

About ten minutes into the fifth inning, a tall man in a red flannel shirt slips into the seat next to me. I stiffen slightly, shooting a quick glance his way.

"Is this seat taken?" His voice is low and friendly, and my cheeks heat the longer I look at him. There are plenty of other seats open along the bar, but he's cute, so I shake my head. I turn away, taking a quick sip of my beer and trying hard to focus back on the game.

Interacting with men I find attractive hasn't gotten easier yet. I'm still expecting to get yelled at if I look at them for too long or seem too interested in what they're talking about, so I usually avoid them.

The guy orders a shot and a beer, and we sit silently, watching the game. I watch his long fingers curl loosely around the half-empty shot glass, spinning it absently, and I can't help but sneak a few glances up at him. He's got a sharp jaw and dark, wavy hair that falls over his forehead and curls around his ears, and his eyes crinkle at the corners a little as he flashes me a quick smile when he catches me looking at him.

Fuck, he's *really* cute.

I look back at the TV, and he turns his head towards me just a bit, his eyes still glued to the game.

"You an Orioles fan?"

I snort. "No, I actually *like* baseball."

He laughs. "Wow, harsh. You from Boston?"

I sip my beer, trying to keep calm. I don't think my accent is strong enough to peg me, but it's undeniably present. Hopefully, he's from here and won't know better.

"Maine, actually, but I like to think I have good taste," I say, smiling, glancing at him but trying not to make eye contact. He smiles back at me and taps his beer can against my bottle of Coors Lite.

"Not if you're drinking that, you don't," he says, his tone warm and amused. Are we flirting? There's no reason we couldn't be. I blush and look at the tall can in his hand with a large red R on it.

"That's better?"

"Depends on who you ask."

"I'm asking you." I'm pretty sure we're flirting.

"Mmm, I think it's better, but they're both fucking *terrible*," he says, rolling his eyes and chuckling.

"Then why are you drinking it?"

He shrugs. "I'm thirsty, and I think it legally counts as water." I laugh and look away as the game comes back on. When I finish my beer, I order a vodka soda, and he orders another shot and a beer, and we chat a little bit, mainly about the game. I try not to make eye contact or look at him too directly out of habit, but I want to.

When the game is over, I throw cash down on the bar and walk away to use the bathroom before I head home. The flirting was exciting, but that's enough for me tonight. I probably don't need to think about men right now, anyway. The guy leaves at the same time I do, holding the door open for me when he notices I'm right behind him.

"I'm Theo," he says, sticking his hand out as we leave the bar. His hand is large and callused and warm around mine.

"Alex," I say. I start walking up the street and he keeps step with me.

"So, what part of Maine are you from?"

"Bangor."

"Is Stephen King required reading in schools there?"

"Oh, *totally*. I did my fourth-grade book report on *The Girl Who Loved Tom Gordon*." That's not even a lie.

He whistles softly. "Deep cut. You do a lot of hiking since fourth grade?" I giggle, glancing up at him.

"I haven't hiked alone since." He laughs, shooting me an amused look in return.

"Makes sense, if that's your frame of reference. How long have you been out here?" How many questions he's asking me is making me nervous, so I focus on turning them back on him.

"Oh, um, I moved here for a job a few months ago. Are you from here?"

He nods. "Mostly, yeah. Do you like it out here so far?"

I hum in agreement, shielding my eyes against the headlights of an oncoming car by looking up at him. "It's great, actually. So, what do you do?"

He shrugs. "Nothing interesting. You?"

"I'm a receptionist, so I mostly just drink coffee and do crosswords."

"That sounds like a perfect day, although I'd prefer to do those things in bed."

"Even the billing emails?"

"Oh, especially those," he says, shooting me a sly smile. I blush, looking away from him quickly. I have no idea what to say to that, so I just hum a little and nod. We're approaching the street I need to turn down, and my heart starts racing as he slows down when we approach the intersection. Is he following me home? We're probably just walking in the same direction. Bailey loves true crime and keeps telling me horror stories because she's worried about the fact that I live alone, and it's making me anxious. Theo slows to a halt, jerking his chin up the street.

"I turn here. Do you want me to walk you home? It's pretty late."

"Oh, um, no thanks. I'm right there." I give him a tight smile as I hook my thumb over my shoulder, indicating the big apartment complex a few blocks down. I'm being paranoid, but it's better to be safe than sorry. His face is blank for a moment before he smiles.

"Cool. Get home safe, okay?"

"Yeah, you too." He looks me up and down with interest, and my stomach flips at the slight smirk he gives me before he turns away.

"See you around," he calls, waving as he walks up the street. I turn and keep walking towards the apartments in the distance, sighing in relief when I look back and he's nowhere to be seen. I shake my head at myself and turn up the next street, doubling back towards my apartment. I was *absolutely* being paranoid. He was just being friendly, and possibly trying to get laid based on the look he gave me.

I sit on the couch and put on a movie at random, but I barely pay attention to it.

I'm too distracted thinking about what would have happened if I'd invited that guy home.

I've only ever slept with Danny, and I've *never* had casual sex, so I don't even know what that would be like. Thinking about being vulnerable like that with a stranger makes me nervous, but it's also exciting. It feels more and more like there's a real possibility that I could start dating someone at some point when I'm ready. Having someone be so openly interested in me and flirting without making a total fool out of myself felt nice, so maybe casual dating would be nice.

Maybe casual sex would be nice, too.

When I crawl into bed that night, I grab my vibrator and think about the guy from the bar.

God, I hope I see him again.

8

THEO

I lean against the tree at the end of Alex's block, keeping in the shadows as I watch her walk up towards the house from the opposite end of the street, her face lit up with a pretty smile.

I'm absolutely fucked.

I can tell my feelings about her are right.

I need to be methodical about getting to know her, and this was the first step. It went *so* fucking well. I try to calm down on the walk home, but I feel like I've been struck by lightning, and every part of me is thrumming with energy. I head down to the basement the second I'm inside to work off some of the excitement, but it doesn't help.

All I can do is think about her.

I can't let myself get carried away here, so I go upstairs, pour myself a drink, and set a timer. There have to be limits, even if they're arbitrary, so I'm giving myself *one* hour to think about her as much as I want to, and that's it.

Everything about her is so perfect. She's got a beautiful smile and a cute laugh, and she blushes *so* easily. She's a little reserved, but very friendly. She's also a shitty liar. I would've noticed that at some point, but knowing she was lying about her apartment showed me that she briefly skates her teeth over the innermost part of her bottom lip when she lies.

It's adorable.

She's adorable.

I imagine what would have happened if she'd invited me back to her place, and after coming to the thought of her on her knees blushing up at me, I pour myself another drink and go to my office to make several impulsive purchases.

I *need* to control myself, so once the timer goes off, I do my best not to think about her. It's impossible, and I last all of five minutes before I give in and spend the rest of the night drinking and thinking about her, getting progressively more drunk and thinking about getting to know her the way I want to, the way I *have* to. I spend time looking at everything I would need to do that, and then I lose complete control of myself and start buying things.

The drunker I get, the more ill-advised and impulsive the purchases get.

***

I wake up late the next morning in fucking agony. I haven't been drunk in a decade, but I don't remember hangovers being this excruciating. I spend the entire day nursing my hangover and going through every impulse management skill I've learned in the last ten years to keep from thinking about Alex.

None of it helps, and I dream about her when I sleep.

I'm eating breakfast the next day when a pile of packages gets delivered to my house. I stare down at them with trepidation, glancing at the shipping labels. Did I seriously pay for expedited overnight shipping? Oh, for fuck's sake. I don't need the things in these packages, and I'm going to return them. They were stupid, impulsive purchases I made because I was drunk, and I need to calm down.

Alex is a normal, ordinary woman. She's just a normal, charming, gorgeous woman with huge, light brown eyes that I could get lost in and, the more I look into her, possibly a fake identity. She's just a normal, intriguing, magnetic woman that I can't stop thinking about, no matter how hard I try.

I need to try *much* harder.

I know I should return all the packages, that I shouldn't even touch them, but I bring them inside and set them on the kitchen counter, my mind spinning as I stare at them. I should return them and keep running into her in person, like last night, and get to know her that way. It'll take a long time to do that, but it's what I should do.

It's not what I want to do, though.

I leave the packages on the counter and go for a run, forcing myself not to pass by her office. I come home and make lunch, my eyes darting to the pile of packages every few minutes. I spend an hour cleaning the house, debating whether or not to pick someone up tonight. I haven't answered any dating app messages or thought about fucking anyone lately because I'm no longer interested in the idea of anyone but Alex, but that's a problem.

I should be interested in other women, interested in trying to get to know someone else in any way at all, even if it's just sex. I take all the packages and put them in the attic with all the boxes of things I have no interest in seeing or thinking about, resolving to go out tonight and talk to someone, *anyone*, just to prove to myself that I can think about women other than Alex.

I drive into Portland, rent a hotel room, and start at sleek cocktail bars during happy hour, talking to busy, polished women just off their corporate jobs, but none of them smile like her. I move on to hip, used-to-be dive bars, talking to beautiful women with tattoos and stylish clothes, but none of them blush like her. I wind up at an annoyingly loud, trendy bar and end up speaking with a recently divorced woman named Maya, who's being openly flirtatious. She's tall and pretty, with long legs, generous curves, and short black hair, and I'm more interested in her than any of the other women I've spoken to.

When she speaks, her vowels and how she drops her r's sound almost exactly like Alex's faint accent. I ask her where she's from, and she says Boston, which almost certainly confirms that Alex isn't from Maine.

I realize I'm thinking about Alex and try to stop myself and focus on *Maya*, who is a naturopath in town for a conference for the next two nights. *Maya* was married to her college boyfriend for fifteen years, and their divorce was finalized last week. *Maya's* asking if I want to get out of here. I'm trying to stay present with *Maya*, enjoy kissing *Maya* in the hotel elevator, and focus on the sex that *Maya's* initiating. I keep my eyes on *Maya* as she sucks my cock, and I'm only thinking about *Maya* when I eat her out. It's *Maya* moaning and calling me Daddy as I fuck her, which I don't like, but she seems so into it that I don't say anything. *Maya* is great in bed, and I'm able to focus on fucking *Maya* until I flip her over and can't see her face anymore.

Then I can't help myself.

I call out Alex's name when I come and feel an immediate wash of guilt and shame because I'm *such* a fucking asshole. I apologize immediately, making up some story about a recent breakup I'm not over, telling her she was amazing and apologizing again for being such a dick. Maya ignores me, gets dressed quickly in angry silence, and leaves. I fall back on the bed and run my hands over my face, groaning in frustration.

Everyone else is off the table.

That's probably not good.

***

I don't sleep. I delete the dating app before I check out of the hotel and drive home, heading straight for the attic and bringing the packages down to the dining room table. I open most of them and lay out the contents in a neat row. I worked hard to make sure that I wouldn't give in to my impulses, and I'm not, technically, because most of this is fine.

I eye the unopened packages, which make me slightly uncomfortable. The impulses I have about Alex are different than I'm used to, and I bought those things when I was very drunk and not even trying to control myself, so I put them back in the attic.

I should return them, but I won't.

I spend the day trying to talk myself out of how I'm feeling. I work out. I cook. I go for a run. I go down to a brewery and have a beer. I watch a movie. I masturbate. I meditate. I read. I do anything I can to distract myself, to redirect the feelings, but in the back of my head is constant chatter that's populated entirely by thoughts of Alex.

It's getting almost impossible to fight it, so I don't.

***

Early Wednesday morning, I put on my running shoes and go for a jog, finding myself near Alex's place and making a few loops around her neighborhood until I see her lights flip on. I turn back and run towards her office and sit at the cafe down the street, pretending to scroll through the news on my phone, occasionally sipping my coffee.

I start planning as I wait, growing excited the more I think about it.

It's not exactly a foolproof plan, but it should be fine.

Just before eight, I see Alex walk into the cafe in a long, loose grey dress with her hair twisted up, showing off her graceful neck. She looks so pretty as she stares off into space while waiting for her coffee and bagel, focusing on whatever she's listening to.

I wonder if she's thought about me at all.

Once she's been in her office for half an hour, I head back to my place and change into jeans, a plain t-shirt, and a nondescript work jacket, packing my backpack quickly. I'm buzzing with energy as I walk to her place.

I'm vaguely aware that I'm not doing the best at controlling myself at this point, but it's fine. I need to be careful and methodical, and this is part of that. My impulses aren't acceptable, but I don't think they're wrong, and I'm *barely* giving in to them, anyway. This will help me get to know her, see what she's like, and make sure I'm right about my feelings. It's basically like bypassing the part of dating where we lie to each other and find out later that we're different people.

It's safer this way.

The locks on the front door are so pitiful that it barely counts as breaking in. I walk upstairs, hearing a couple on the second floor having sex as I pass. I wonder who else lives here.

I should look into that.

Her apartment door takes a little more effort to pick, but not much, and the door swings open to reveal her tiny apartment. The living space is so small it barely holds the battered loveseat and coffee table, which are placed in front of a half-full bookshelf with a small TV perched on top. Her furniture is mismatched but somehow works together, giving the space an eclectic vibe.

There's a random assortment of unframed, abstract paintings on the wall, and the warm, muted colors are soothing. I don't like abstract art, but these are nice and done with some skill. Leaned against the wall next to the bookshelf are an easel, a bunch of blank canvases, and painting supplies.

Wait, did she paint these?

I *love* them.

I crouch down to look at her bookshelf and assortment of battered second-hand books. *Jane Eyre. Song of Achilles. Persuasion. Alice's Adventures in Wonderland. North and South. Norwegian Wood. Atonement. Anna Karenina.* There's a copy of Peter Stark's *Astoria* and a few other nonfiction books, as well as poetry collections by cummings, Plath, Neruda, Whitman, Keats, and Dickinson. We don't have the same taste, but I like some of these a lot.

I pull out the collection of Neruda poems, flipping through until I find my favorite poem. Alex has underlined *"I love you without knowing how, or when, or from where,"* twice, the pen pushed down on the page so hard that it left divots. I stare at the pen marks momentarily before closing the book and slipping it back onto the shelf.

I can feel a soft humming starting in the back of my head, but I try to ignore it. It's a famous line from a famous poem and it's a second-hand book, so maybe *she* didn't underline it.

It probably doesn't mean anything.

I move into her minuscule kitchen that barely has enough counter space to cook. Her fridge is full of take-out containers, her freezer is full of premade foods, and her cabinets are mostly filled with snacks and things that don't require cooking. She has no pots, pans, or cooking utensils at *all*, just cutlery and one large kitchen knife. Does she not know how to cook? I could teach her how to cook, or I could just cook for her. I would *love* to do that.

I drift into her bedroom, where the walls are covered in expressive sketches, watercolors, and pen and ink drawings of the coast. Many of them are of the wreck of the *Iredale*, and the humming in my head gets a little louder. I went out there constantly in high school when things were too hard to deal with, but it's a popular beach with a cool attraction. Her spending time there probably doesn't mean anything, either.

I examine each drawing, finally removing a small pen and ink drawing I like and slipping it into my backpack. There are also a few tiny canvases scattered on the walls here and there, and I take one of a small, detailed peony. Nana grew peonies in the front yard, and I love how they smell.

Alex's small bedroom is crammed with a full-sized bed, a narrow nightstand, and a slim, low set of drawers. I frown down at the bed. I'm tall enough that it's going to be a pain in the ass to sleep here if we *do* start dating, but putting anything bigger in here would eat up what little floor space she has.

Her closet is small and full of new clothes, with a hamper of dirty clothes on the floor. I rifle through her drawers, pausing when I reach her underwear drawer. Apparently, she wears thin mesh bras and tiny thongs under all her loosely cut clothing. God, I really wonder what she looks like naked. Without thinking, I grab a soft, lacy black thong and slip it into my pocket before I close the drawer.

Alex keeps a planner and a little cup full of colored pens on top of her dresser, and her planner details everything she does in a day in color-coded, bubbly handwriting. I flip through her planner, happy to find that we both like structure and wondering how she decides on her color coding.

She works from eight to five Monday through Friday, written in blue. On Tuesday nights, she does trivia with someone called Anna, noted in orange. She spends half her Saturdays in Portland, which is written in purple. She tracks her periods and monthly breast exams and IUD string checks in pink, and I'm grateful to know she's on birth control. She takes various rec center fitness classes during her lunch break, sprints on Fridays after work, and goes for a long run on Sundays, all written in green. If staying active helps her manage her feelings, we're alike in that regard, too. I take photos of the past entries and of her upcoming month to review later.

I wonder what color I'd be in her planner as I move to her cramped bathroom, which isn't decorated at all. Next to the small clawfoot tub is a tiny metal rack that's packed with skincare and haircare and a massive bag of Epsom salts. I go through her medicine cabinet, finding very little of interest. There's her toothbrush, some floss, a small first aid kit, a box of hair dye, and some normal, over-the-counter medications. She has some makeup, even though she barely wears it, and there's a small, half-empty glass bottle of an expensive-smelling peony perfume. I spray a little on my wrist and inhale deeply. It's fresh and floral and warm, and I'm almost positive she was wearing it the first time I saw her.

I wonder how it smells on her skin.

I put the perfume away and go back into her bedroom to rifle through her cluttered nightstand. There's a glass water bottle, a romance novel next to the bulky lamp, and a little dish with a phone charger, some lip balm, and a spare set of keys. I slip the keys into my pocket and check my phone, noting the time.

How have I been here for almost half an hour? According to her planner, she's got Pilates at the rec center today, so she probably won't come home for lunch, but I should leave soon just to be safe. I glance back at her nightstand, my eyes landing on the romance novel.

I think I can stay here a *little* longer.

I flip through the book, noticing she's dog-eared an explicit sex scene. I sit on her bed and feel something under the covers, pulling back the duvet to reveal a slim purple vibrator. I can feel myself getting hard just looking at it. Did she masturbate this morning? How often does she masturbate? How compatible would we be in bed?

I lay back on her bed and start to read the sex scene, undoing my pants slowly. The sex scene is tame, all things considered, but it's still hot enough that I'm getting harder. I pull her underwear from my pocket and rub the soft lace up and down my length, gripping myself hard in one hand and the book in the other. I imagine it's us that I'm reading about, and I try hard to imagine what she'll feel like wrapped around me. When I come, I clean myself off with her panties, doing my jeans back up and shoving the wet fabric into my back pocket, swallowing my irritation with myself.

It's going to take time before we have sex, and thinking about it is going to distract me from getting to *know* her. This was a problem with Ashley – I was so distracted by the sex that I didn't notice anything was wrong for a long time.

Looking back, I think she used that against me.

I can't let myself get distracted by the sex this time. I need to get to *know* Alex. That's why I'm here.

I look over at the pile of clothes by the foot of her bed and freeze when I see a familiar worn, dark green knit sweater tucked under a pair of sweatpants. I pull it out and hold it up, the humming in my head starting again as I look at it. It's a knit University of Oregon sweater that looks exactly like the one Nana bought me when I started college.

There's no fucking way.

Lots of people went to that school and had this sweater in this size, so there's genuinely no fucking way this is mine. I grab the neck and see *TRA* written in my grandmother's handwriting on the tag in faded Sharpie, and I'm so shocked that I drop the sweater on the bed. I stand there, staring at it as the noise in the back of my head takes over everything.

I donated that sweater less than a month ago, and *she* bought it.

The feelings I have about her *are* right.

Alex and I are *connected.*

I don't know how long I stand there, stunned, but I try to clear my head as I step back into the living room. I was right to follow the impulse to come here. I'm starting to feel like we're meant to be together, but that's just a feeling, and I need evidence. I think it's entirely justified if I put a few cameras up. I brought them in case I thought getting to know her better was worth it, and now I'm positive that it is. I'll watch her routines, get to know her tastes, see how she is when she's alone, and once I'm fucking *sure* that my feelings are right, I'll figure out the best way to pursue her.

I look around her living room, scoping, scrutinizing. She's got some house plants and decorative tchotchkes, but her place is still small enough that I need to be careful. Thank god these cameras are so small.

I pull out my laptop and set it on her couch, linking it to my phone's hotspot before I pull out a handful of cameras. I pair them to the software and then start placing them, tucking one behind the leg of her TV, one on top of her fridge near a plant, one on top of her undusted medicine cabinet, one in her closet, one in the base of her nightstand lamp, and one on the low dresser underneath the lip of a metal dish that has a random assortment of hair clips.

I check the camera feeds for the angles of the cameras, adjusting as needed, placing a few more for good measure until I've got a view of her apartment from every angle. The cameras are small and out of the way enough not to be noticed, and she doesn't seem to be super observant of her surroundings, anyway.

I'll have to come back regularly to charge them, but that's not a problem. I want to be here more often. The longer I'm in her apartment, the calmer I feel. It feels like a home in a way that my place doesn't.

I pull out her cheap laptop and open it up, the home screen popping up at once. I shake my head in disbelief at her lack of password, jamming in a USB drive and installing a rootkit. Now that I have her keys and eyes on her and the ability to see what she looks at on the internet, I'll be able to get to know her on a deeper level.

I try to ignore my excitement about having this kind of access to her.

I check my watch, realizing it's almost noon, so I reluctantly leave, locking the door behind me with her spare keys. I'll get these copied and return them soon, so she won't even know they were gone.

I'm glad I don't have to see my stupid therapist tomorrow, because I need to calm down. Some of this counts as giving into my impulses, and I should take some space. It doesn't matter if Alex and I are connected, which we *are*, I shouldn't watch the cameras yet.

I shouldn't even be near her right now, just in case.

When I get home, I drop my backpack and phone inside and get back in my car, heading down the coast for the house in Yachats before I can stop myself. I breathe deeply and try to get my shit together on the drive, but every time I inhale, I smell her perfume.

I'm somewhat aware that I'm not in control anymore, but I don't think I need to be. I need to be smart about this and take my time, but I don't need to fight my impulses anymore.

They led me to *her*.
Now I need them to lead her to me.

9

ALEX

FRIDAY, SEPTEMBER 15

"Still on to watch Miles tonight?" Bailey's voice is excited, and she comes bearing a coffee and a croissant, which she dramatically presents to me, making me laugh.

"Yes, but you didn't have to get me anything. You're already paying me."

"A spoiled babysitter is a babysitter who might consider showing up again. It's nice to have some time to remember why I like my husband so much," she says, winking at me, and I laugh at her as she heads upstairs.

I'm looking forward to babysitting. I liked spending time with Danny's nieces and nephews because kids are easy. They don't say one thing and mean another, and you always know where you stand with them. Plus, they can be silly and fun in a way adults aren't.

When I return from lunch, there's someone sitting in the reception area, a cup of coffee in his hand, his knee bouncing quickly. He's dressed in light grey pants and a thin, dark blue sweater, and his hair is pushed back from his face, and it takes me a second to realize it's the guy from the sports bar. It's a small town, so I shouldn't be surprised to see him, but I am. He looks up from his phone, cocking his head a little as he recognizes me.

"Hi, Alex." My stomach flips as he smiles at me, and I notice that one side of his mouth picks up more than the other. God, he's way cuter than I remember. My cheeks heat and I smile back at him as I walk over to my desk and lean against the edge of it, realizing with horror that I've forgotten his name.

"Hey," I say in a sweet tone, trying to hide the fact that I'm panicking. *Fuck*, what was his name again? "Um, it's Leo, maybe?" I ask slowly. His smile fades and my heart sinks. God, I'm so stupid.

"It's *Theo*," he says, frowning slightly. "Occasionally it's *Theodore* if I'm in trouble with my grandmother," he says with a tight smile and a quick roll of his eyes.

I flash him a quick, guilty smile. "I'm so sorry. I'm bad with names, but I *really* like yours," I say, hoping I'm being flirty. I think I nail it, and relief floods through me as his face softens back into that cute smile. "Uh, did you get in trouble with your grandma often, *Theodore*?"

He laughs a little and rolls his eyes. "You have no idea."

"What'd you do, steal all the hard candy from her purse?"

"Cigarettes, actually. They taste much worse than butterscotch, though." I wrinkle my nose at him in disgust. I hope he's not a smoker. Danny smoked, and I *hated* it.

"You know smoking's bad for you, right?" Theo looks confused and a little concerned, and I kick myself for criticizing him.

"Alex, what are you talking about? Smoking is one of the healthiest things you can do."

I gape at him. "*Please* tell me you're joking."

"I'm extremely serious," he deadpans before flashing me a quick grin. "So, what's *The Girl Who Loved Tom Gordon* doing here?" I'm thrown off for a second. How did he remember that?

"Uh, I work here. This is the job I moved here for."

"Nice. Catherine's cool. Did you do this sort of thing in Maine?"

"No, I...uh," I falter, trying to remember what I tell people I used to do. Something about how much eye contact we're making is overwhelming. "I, uh, I temped, I think."

I think? I'm so fucking stupid. I need to get away from him for a second, so I force a smile.

"Can I get you something while you wait for Catherine? Water? Coffee? I think we have muffins. Do you want a coffee?" He looks amused and shakes his head slowly, taking a sip of the coffee he has in his hand. "Right, you *have* a coffee. Um, okay, uh, please excuse me," I say quickly, heading towards the kitchen.

What is *wrong* with me? I'm so good at being polite and polished and social with strangers, but *one* cute guy smiles at me and I become an awkward teenage girl again. I pour myself a cup of coffee, taking a deep breath before heading back into the reception area, keeping my head down. I'll just make an idiot out of myself if I keep talking to him, so I avoid looking at Theo as I sit at my desk. I pull up a blank email, and type out the word *stupid* repeatedly, looking intently at the screen.

When I glance over at him, he's smiling down at something on his phone.

I stare at him for a second, noticing his thin knit sweater is tight enough to show off his broad shoulders and the fact that he definitely works out. He catches me looking at him, and I pointedly stare back at my computer. After a few minutes, he stands up and approaches me, resting his hands on the edge of my desk and leaning over my computer to get my attention, and I look up at him immediately. Up close, I can see that his eyes are the most startling hazel I've ever seen, pale green at the edges and a dark gold in the center, the transition nearly seamless.

"Do you know how long Catherine's going to be?" It takes me a second to realize he's asked me a question, and I blink quickly and jerk my gaze away from his to look at my computer.

"Oh, um, Catherine's in the middle of a meeting right now," I say, frowning. Was he even on the schedule before I went to lunch? Maybe she changed it at the last minute. "What's your last name?"

"Anderson."

"Mr. Anderson? Welcome back," I say slowly as I flip through the calendar, realizing halfway through saying it that I'm saying it out loud. I'm hoping he doesn't catch it, but he laughs, his expression bemused.

"Are you making a fucking *Matrix* reference?" I avoid looking at him, feeling my cheeks heat up in embarrassment.

"I'm so sorry. I rewatched it a week ago, and that just came out of my mouth," I say, cringing slightly. "Please ignore me, that was *so* stupid." I bite my lip, focusing hard on my computer but not seeing anything in front of me.

"No, it was *cute,*" he says, his voice low and amused, "and I have *no* interest in ignoring you, Alex." Butterflies explode upwards from my stomach into my throat as I look up at him, his warm, crooked smile making me blush. I look away quickly, unused to this level of attention. I suck in a sharp breath and refocus on the calendar on the computer screen again, and frown.

"Um, you're not here. What time is your appointment?"

"I don't have one." I raise my eyebrows at him.

"Most people make appointments to see their lawyer, unless they're in trouble." He shrugs, smirking a little.

"I'm definitely in trouble." I frown at him, concerned, but he looks relaxed.

"You know Catherine doesn't do criminal law, right?" He laughs.

"Oh, I'm aware, but I'm not in that kind of trouble. I'm in *Catherine has a pretty receptionist* trouble." He flashes that cute smile again, and I can feel my face burning as I look down at my keyboard. I don't even know how to respond to that, so I don't. He's flirting with me, and I'm making an idiot out of myself. I shouldn't even be flirting with him since I'm at work, so I put on my chipper receptionist voice and try not to look directly into his eyes.

"Um, Catherine will be done soon," I say, my gaze landing on his mouth. His lips look soft. "Can I get you anything while you wait? We have muffins." He laughs a little, and I realize I didn't notice his faint dimples before. Those are so fucking cute.

I wonder what kissing him would feel like.

Okay, I can't look at his mouth. I glance at his nose instead, flustered.

"You're *really* pushing these muffins, huh? I'll try one, but only if you made them." I frown at him, meeting his eyes again.

"Why would that matter?" Theo frowns back at me, looking a little confused.

"Am I doing this wrong or something?" He asks with an almost nervous laugh.

"Doing what wrong?" I take a sip of coffee, and he looks at me incredulously.

"I'm hitting on you, Alex. You *know* that, right?" I choke on my coffee and look away from him as I struggle to catch my breath. He slips the coffee cup out of my hand, my nerves lighting up from where his fingers graze against mine. "Shit, you okay?"

"Wrong pipe," I choke out, refusing to look at him. "Um, I have a lot of work to do. Excuse me," I say, flashing a tight smile somewhere in his direction and grabbing a stack of paper off my desk, hurrying into the other room to pretend to file them.

After a few minutes of hiding in the other room, berating myself for being such a fucking idiot, I hear Catherine and her clients walk downstairs and listen as she starts speaking quietly with Theo. I fix my face into a neutral expression and walk back to my desk, trying to ignore the amused smile he's giving me. I slump down in my chair once they're upstairs, covering my face with my hands.

Fuck, that was embarrassing. I'm twenty-six and I've been married for almost a decade, so I haven't been hit on much and I have *no* idea how to deal with that sort of attention. I've barely flirted with anyone, but I'm positive that's *not* how you do it.

God, I'm *so* stupid.

When Catherine's door opens half an hour later, I hurry to the kitchen to avoid having to see Theo again. I hear the two of them chatting quietly in the front hallway and only head back into the reception area when I think he's about to leave, but they're waiting for me. Theo's standing behind Catherine with his arms crossed loosely, giving me that same amused, slightly crooked smile. Catherine turns towards me, holding up a sheaf of paper and smiling.

"Hi, Alex. Are you a notary?" I force a smile back at her, hoping I'm not blushing.

"No, sorry. Bailey's here, though, so I'll go get her." I set my coffee down and hurry up the stairs, popping my head into her office and bringing her back down. Bailey's chatty with Catherine and Theo as she notarizes the documents, and I do my best to ignore them all and look busy.

Every time I glance up, Theo's looking at me out of the corner of his eye.

When Bailey heads back upstairs, she catches my eye and points at Theo and back at me, her eyebrows jumping a few times. I shake my head quickly and look into my coffee as Theo tucks the papers into a large envelope.

"Thanks for squeezing me in, Catherine. I appreciate it." I watch out of the corner of my eye as he turns towards me. "It was *really* nice to see you again, Alex." I look up at him and feel myself blushing the second I meet his eyes.

"Uh, yeah, you too. Um, I'll see you later?" I say, smiling a little. That's probably wishful thinking on my part. His smile broadens, his dimples more visible.

"Looking forward to it." I look down at my hands to hide that I'm blushing, and Catherine gives me a brief, appraising look after he walks out of the office.

"Do you know him? You two seemed friendly."

"No, we just met at a bar the other night." She frowns.

"Got it. Did he ask you out?" Her tone is a little odd. She probably thinks I shouldn't be dating clients.

"No, he didn't. I'm not dating right now, anyway." I shouldn't be, at least. I don't know how I'd let someone in after Danny. That's a sobering thought, and one that bothers me for most of the afternoon.

It's good that Theo didn't ask me out.

I would have said yes.

***

"No inviting boys over," Bailey says with a wink as she slips on her coat, and I groan.

"It's nothing. Please drop it."

"Drop what?" Dylan walks downstairs with Miles, who is carrying a well-loved stuffed orange cat that looks identical to their cat, Biscuit.

"One of Catherine's clients was seriously eyeing Alex today. He was cute, too," she says in a teasing tone.

"Jesus, Bails, leave the poor girl alone." Dylan shoots me an apologetic look. "Ignore her." Bailey rolls her eyes and opens the door, shooing Dylan out.

"Alex, you have our numbers, and my sister-in-law's contact info is on the fridge. We'll be back around eleven. Miles, give Mommy a kiss and be good for Alex, okay?" She kisses Miles and hustles out the door, leaving Miles and I looking at each other. He's cute, with big blue eyes like Dylan and wild, curly black hair like Bailey, dressed in green dinosaur pajamas.

I crouch down to get on his eye level. "What do you want to do?"

He breaks into a shy smile. "Wanna play dinosaurs?"

I grin back at him. "I *love* dinosaurs." His smile broadens, and he pulls me into the living room, chatting excitedly.

***

"I am Allie! Allie Saurus! Queen of Dinosaur Island!" I make a roaring sound and jump off the couch towards Miles, who screams in delight and runs for the kitchen, flapping his arms and jumping as he runs, making pterodactyl sounds while Biscuit looks on in annoyance from the windowsill.

We play until he gets hungry, and I make him dinosaur mac and cheese, which is just boxed mac and cheese with a bag of microwave-steamed broccoli mixed in, the way Danny's youngest nephew liked.

It's the most cooking I've done since moving here, but I don't mind doing it for Miles.

I like Miles.

***

When Bailey and Dylan get home, I'm sitting on the couch with Miles' head in my lap as he sleeps, Biscuit curled up at his feet, and a nature documentary playing on mute in the background. Dylan takes Miles up to bed, and Bailey pulls out some cash.

"Thanks so much for doing this, Alex. We haven't had a real date since our old babysitter went to college," she says, pulling an exasperated face.

"Yeah, anytime. Miles is great."

She beams. "We like him. Let me drive you home, okay?" I shake my head quickly. I don't want to walk home this late, but I do *not* want Bailey to see where I live. I suspect that the women at work pity me a little, and I have no interest in fostering that.

"It's fine, I can walk." She shoots me a shocked look.

"Alex, it's eleven-thirty at night."

I shrug. "I live close, don't worry." I don't, but I'm not telling her that.

Bailey presses me for a while, talking about a true crime book she's reading to scare me, but she finally relents when I promise to call her in ten minutes when I get home. I hug her goodbye and leave, putting my headphones on and starting my audiobook of *Anna Karenina*.

It's dark out, with the moon barely a sliver and the streetlights in this part of town few and far between. I walk quickly, a little bothered by what Bailey was saying about the book she's reading. I don't know how she stands reading that stuff.

Real life is hard enough without focusing on the things that make it bad.

10

THEO

FRIDAY, SEPTEMBER 15

"Um, I'll see you later?" Alex says, smiling up at me hopefully. She seems as excited as I am by that prospect, and I grin.

"Looking forward to it," I say, forcing myself to turn away and walk out the door, nodding at Catherine briefly, ignoring her raised eyebrows.

I pull my phone out of my back pocket, slip in my headphones, and log into the camera software. As well as the rootkit on her work computer, I placed a few cameras in her office while she was on lunch. One shows the reception area, another is tucked in the corner bookshelf behind her desk, and another shows the kitchen area.

I'm absolutely going to save the video of her pulling up a blank email and typing a string of words to look busy while sneaking looks at me. I watched her do it while I was sitting there, and it was hard not to laugh.

She's so fucking cute.

I watch her brief conversation with Catherine, which is slightly concerning. Catherine knows who I am and knows why I was in prison, but she didn't say anything about it to Alex. I know Alex knows my name now, but I'll do what I can to ensure her computer crashes if she searches for me.

I'm sure she'll understand why I was in prison when I tell her.

"I'm not really dating right now, anyway," Alex says to Catherine, sounding dejected. I smile and slip my phone into my back pocket as I approach my house.

That'll change soon enough.

***

I drop the paperwork from Catherine at home and grab a backpack, shoving in a few more cameras and a swimsuit before I head to the rec center. I sign up for a day pass and take the facilities tour, surreptitiously checking all the rooms for any surveillance system, grateful that there's none. The group fitness classes are held in a room off the main hall, and I head back to the room after the tour. The next class isn't for another hour, and the rec center is relatively empty anyway, so I can quickly place a camera without being seen. I swim a few laps to kill time and make it look like I came to use the rec center, and then I leave and drive over to Alex's place.

She's not off work for a few more hours, so I have time. I need to charge the cameras, but mostly I want to be close to her, to smell her perfume lingering on her clothes and her pillow, to lay in her small bed and look at the art on her walls, to flip through the books she's reading and see if she's underlined anything else.

I turn on her TV and scroll through her recently watched movies and shows, smiling. Alex is *such* a romantic. She's a big Nora Ephron fan and seems to like romantic comedies in general, as well as dating shows. This is precisely the kind of thing I need to know about her. I want to pursue her in a way that feels good to her and makes her feel adored and desired, and my next move is so simple now.

I'll start running into her more, not so much that she's suspicious but enough that I'm on her mind. I don't need more help from Catherine right now, so I'll start running into her at the coffee shop, or join trivia, or take one of her exercise classes. However I do it, I'll become a fixture in her life and take every opportunity to make her feel wanted. I'll ask her out as soon as possible, I'll let her get to know me better, let her see for herself how great we are together, and then she'll feel our connection for herself.

I think I'm the only one who can feel it right now. I felt fire race through me the second our fingers touched, but she didn't seem to register it.

I need to be okay with the fact that pursuing her like this might take a while. I *can* be patient, even if I hate it, but I don't think this will take that long.

Based on how seeing her today went, I'm positive I could have just asked her out right then. I would have, but she pretended like she forgot my name, and I'm not going to reinforce bullshit games like that.

She's so adorably awful at flirting that I'm surprised she even tried to pull that move, but she made up for it by obviously being interested in me. My showing open interest in her seems to make her shy and a little uncomfortable, and while I don't understand how someone that gorgeous isn't used to that kind of attention, I like how easily flustered she is by it. She blushes *so* much when she's flustered, like when I caught the way she was staring at my mouth.

I check the time on my phone and sink back into her small couch, leisurely masturbating to the thought of bending her across her desk and making her scream my name.

***

I go home and make dinner before changing into black clothes and driving to her coworker Bailey's house, parking down the block in a poorly lit spot. I watch in my mirror as Bailey and her tall, thin husband drive off before I pull my hood over my face and walk towards their house, finding an inconspicuous place in the bushes along the side of the house to watch through the window at how Alex interacts with their son, Miles.

She's sweet with him, animated and goofy in a way I didn't know she could be as they play whatever games he wants. The windowpanes are old and thin, so I can hear them making silly sounds as they play, and I watch the two of them for hours.

At one point, when it's late and they're piled on the couch, Alex seems more relaxed than I've seen her before. She looks down at Miles with this wistful, content look, and I start to wonder if she wants a family.

I could give her that.

I begrudgingly walk back towards my car a few minutes before Bailey and her husband get home and watch in my mirrors as Alex starts to walk home.

Did they seriously not offer her a ride home? Fuck these people.

I stay in my car for a minute before following her on foot, keeping about two blocks behind her. I don't want to scare her, but she doesn't notice me. She doesn't look around at all, she just walks quickly with her head down and her headphones on.

She's so fucking vulnerable.

I walk a little faster, trying to make a lot of noise. I'm a block behind her now, and she still hasn't heard me. Oh my *god,* I feel like I'm going to crawl out of my skin.

Why is she putting herself in so much danger?

After about ten minutes of this bullshit, she pulls her phone out, her voice drifting back to me.

"Hey, Bailey. Yeah, no, just walking up to my door now. Yeah, we had a great time! I'd be happy to watch him again. I'll see you on Monday."

What the *fuck?*

I follow her all the way home and she doesn't notice me *once,* which is terrifying. Alex lives alone, seems to have no close friends or family, and is either so naive or stubborn that she's taking stupid risks with her safety. Is she entirely ignorant of what could happen to her? I had an insufferable serial rapist as a cellmate for a few years, and I'm aware of just how much danger Alex is unwittingly putting herself in.

Fuck, I need to make sure she stays safe. I think of one of the un-opened packages in the attic, full of microchip GPS trackers, and I knew there was a reason I didn't return them.

I'll start tracking her soon, just for her safety.

Once she's inside her apartment, I turn around and log into her camera feeds as I walk back to my car. I love having this kind of access to her, but I need to remember that it's *only* to help me get to know her better. I just want to make sure she gets inside safely – I can't watch her all the time or anything like that.

She lets herself in, takes off her headphones and coat, and drops her bag on one of her breakfast bar stools before heading straight to the kitchen. She pours herself a glass of wine as she starts playing French jazz from her phone, and I feel the frisson of connection again.

How many hundreds of times did Nana play that Django Reinhardt record when I was a kid?

Alex sips her wine and throws some olives, pickles, and crackers on a plate before sitting on her counter. I walk back to my car, watching her eat something that isn't technically a meal and pour herself another drink. That's a lot of wine in a short amount of time, but it's Friday, I guess.

I'm down the street from my car when she gets up and starts pulling her shoes and socks off, and as she heads into her bedroom, I realize she's about to get undressed. I run the rest of the way to my car, torn between the overwhelming impulse to watch her and the knowledge that the first time I see her naked should be in person, when I'm the one undressing her. The cameras are for getting to know her, her tastes, her likes and dislikes, her routines, not *this*.

I should stop watching.

I sit in my car as she starts to strip, trying to convince myself to close out of the camera feeds, but all thoughts of what I should do evaporate from my head as she pulls her dress off.

Alex wears looser clothes with chic, boxy silhouettes, things that don't give a real indication of what her body looks like, which is fucking *criminal*. She's got a fit, athletic build, but with a softness to the curves of her body that makes me hard immediately. I'm aching to get my hands on her. I want to wrap her long, sculpted legs around my hips and dig my fingers into her round ass while I watch her full, perky tits bounce in my face as I fuck her.

My erection is bordering on painful, so I jam the car seat back and undo my jeans quickly, grateful that it's late and that I'm parked on a dark part of the street. My fist is so tight around my cock it hurts, but all I can do is work myself furiously to the sight of her walking around her bedroom, slipping off her bralette and taking her hair down. She slips her thong off and keeps her legs straight as she bends down to pick up her clothes off the floor, and on the tiny, dimly lit phone screen, I can see the shape of her cunt between her legs.

I come instantly, unable to tear my eyes away from the phone until she walks into her bathroom. I absently wipe my hand on my jeans as I sit my seat back up, and I throw my phone in the back seat before I drive home, praying no one saw me.

That's it. That's all I get. This is about getting to know her, not getting to fuck her. I know the sex will be amazing and will help her feel how connected we are, but I can't get focused on that yet. It'll be too distracting.

I snatch my phone from the backseat and check the cameras the moment I park in my driveway. In the time it took me to get home, Alex finished her second glass of wine and started taking a bath. The bathtub is so small that she can't put her legs all the way down, and her knees and chest protrude out of the bubbly water. I shouldn't watch her like this, but I can't help it – she's so breathtakingly beautiful.

I watch as she gets out of the bath, puts on my sweater, and pulls her hair into a messy topknot. Okay, *that's* it. I should log out of the cameras now. I don't, but I go inside and head to the kitchen to grab something from the fridge, pretending to ignore my phone until she lies on her bed, reaching for the book on her nightstand.

Oh, *fuck.*

I lock my phone, head down to the basement, and jump rope quickly, trying to distract myself and work off some of the energy I have pent up in my body. I hold out for about two minutes before I can't help myself and sprint up to my office, filling my three monitors with the different camera feeds from her room to see her in better detail. I turn the sound up as I watch Alex lying there reading, dragging her hand slowly up her thighs and stomach and back down. She turns a page and drags her fingers over her bottom lip as she reads, slipping her fingers into her mouth, and I'm hard again in a second. I undo my pants, touching myself slowly, matching her glacial pace.

Her back arches as she slips two fingers between her legs, and her soft little whimper is the sexiest thing I've ever heard. I watch her rub herself in slow circles before she finally starts fucking herself with her fingers, pausing to awkwardly flip the page once or twice. Her thumb starts to thrum against her clit, and she lets out a long, breathy exhale as she writhes under her own hand. I'm paying more attention to her than to myself, trying to memorize what she reacts to. She pulls her fingers out of herself and licks one finger as she tosses the book to the side, and I want to die because she's so fucking hot.

She pulls her laptop out from under her bed and starts searching, pulling up a bookmarked page. She bookmarks her porn? She's making this so easy for me, like she knows exactly what I need to get to know her better.

She sits back against her headboard, pulling her vibrator out from under her pillow and turning it on as she plays the video. One of the cameras I've placed in her room gives me an unobstructed view of her laptop screen, and my eyebrows raise at the porn she's chosen. There's a woman tied down spread eagle on a table, and the man in the video edges the woman mercilessly.

We have similar tastes.

I fight a smile as I try to gauge what exactly about this video Alex is into, watching her reactions closely. The man switches from edging the woman to forcing her to orgasm over and over, praising her in a deep voice, and Alex seems to respond to *that*. Her moans move from breathy and low to higher pitched, bordering on a slight whine that makes my cock throb in my hand as I jerk off to her enjoying herself. I watch as her right leg tenses up, the muscles in her calf and thighs beginning to twitch right before she moans loudly, her back arching up and her body shaking as she comes.

I'm coming before I'm even aware of it, too focused on her to notice anything else.

I sit there after we come together, dazed, watching as Alex closes her laptop and turns off her vibrator, lying back on her bed and slowly dragging her fingers up and down her body, humming to herself quietly with a soft smile on her lips. She's the most beautiful, erotic thing I've ever seen.

As she lies there in post-orgasmic bliss, wearing my sweater, all thoughts of going slowly with her flicker out of existence for just a moment.

While she gets ready for bed, I pull up her computer in another window and poke around until I find the bookmarked folder full of porn. We're going to have sex at some point soon, so I should study what else she likes.

After two hours of going through every porn video and audio she has bookmarked, I can't focus on anything besides the video feed of Alex curled up in a ball as she sleeps.

I don't know why I'm so surprised by how perfect we are for each other, but I am.

Alex and I don't have similar tastes.

We have the *same* tastes.

***

I don't sleep. I try, but it doesn't work. All I can do is think about Alex.

It's Saturday, and her schedule says she's going to Portland, but not *why* she's going. I make breakfast as I watch her wake up and get ready. It's fine, honestly, because this is all part of getting to know her.

She wears one of her nicer dresses, does her makeup, grabs a tote bag instead of her everyday purse, and leaves her apartment. I get in my car and drive towards her place, catching her walking downtown, tailing her in my car as surreptitiously as possible. Eventually, she gets to the bus station, and I follow the bus into Portland, parking near the train station and following her a block or two behind on foot once she's off the bus. I don't have a way to find her if I lose her, but I can fix that soon.

I assume I'll need to be careful because Alex is slightly more observant of her surroundings here, but she doesn't notice me at all.

God, that makes me fucking nervous.

We spend the day together, sort of. She spends the day indulging herself and I spend the day watching her, impatient to be part of her life.

She starts with brunch and then takes herself shopping. I can't follow her into all the shops, but I do my best to follow her and notice what she likes. After shopping, she gets lunch and takes herself to an indie movie at the art house theater, and I sit in the back of the theatre and watch her watch the movie. I don't love it, but I like it, and I desperately want to know how she feels about it. I wish we could talk about it together. After the movie, Alex goes downtown to shop more, wandering around Powell's for an hour before heading back to the bus.

I make sure she gets to the bus safely before doubling back towards the shops she went to. Alex craves creature comforts in a way that makes me think she's used to them. Besides her clothes, everything in her apartment is either secondhand or cheap, but her tastes certainly aren't. She shopped at trendy boutiques and ate at nice restaurants, and while she probably doesn't make much money, she seems to spend a *lot* of it without thinking.

I don't think she's ever been broke before.

Before I leave Portland, I buy everything she looked at but didn't buy for herself, anything I saw her like even a little bit. It's overkill, but I want her to have everything she wants. I speed a little to catch up with the bus she's on and follow her home in my car, making sure she gets home safely before I go home and watch her. Her night is spent drinking wine, painting, and listening to an audiobook. When the book turns out to have an explicit sex scene, painting becomes her masturbating on the couch. She gets close but doesn't come, which is odd.

Only when she gets into the shower do I realize that I haven't eaten anything all day. I cook myself some dinner, watching her sleep on the camera feed on my phone, irritated at the battery warning on the cameras. They should last longer, but I'm constantly watching her now, so I'll have to charge them on Monday while she's at work.

On Sunday, I pass her on the tail end of her run down along the riverwalk. She's adorably sweaty and exhausted, and when I wave at her in passing, I watch her face turn red when she sees me. I wasn't planning on being noticed, but I couldn't help it. I wanted to see her, but I also wanted her to see me.

Later in the day, she takes the bus to the beach, spending her time sitting on a dune and drawing. I'm happy to just watch her as I walk along the beach, keeping her in my sight the whole time.

She doesn't notice me once.

***

I adjust the structure of my life to Alex's. I watch her wake up and get ready for work. I go to the coffee shop and watch her when she comes in. I go home and watch her work. I watch her work out at the rec center. I follow her when she walks home from work. I watch her eat takeout or her ridiculous excuses for meals, paint, read, watch TV, masturbate, take long baths, and go to sleep. I follow her to the high school and watch her sprint from a distance. I follow her around town the next Saturday as she runs errands, and I cross her path again during her Sunday run. She waves and smiles at me, and I wave and smile back at her, watching her cheeks flush a soft pink. I still want a little more time to get to know her, but I'll ask her out next week.

I can barely wait any longer.

***

I already know we're connected, but the more I get to know Alex, the more I realize she truly is the perfect woman for me.

She's friendly and sociable, which I need in a partner. I can be charming, but I generally find people boring and don't see the point in interacting with them. Alex, on the other hand, is friendly with *everyone*. She's a bit shy sometimes, but she smiles easily and seems interested in other people, and she gets people to open up to her even though she artfully avoids talking about herself beyond surface things.

I'm not the most open, either, but I want us to be open with each other.

Besides her casual friendliness with some regulars in her workout classes and her closeness with her coworker Bailey, she regularly sees friends on Tuesdays for trivia. There's a small rotating group of people, mostly men, but Alex seems most comfortable talking to a tall blonde woman with large glasses and a short androgynous woman with her coiled hair styled in long twists. I've noticed that she seems more comfortable with women in general. One of the men who joins them frequently looks at her appreciatively, buying her drinks and making a point to sit next to her. Thankfully, she doesn't seem to pay him any extra attention beyond the basic friendliness she shows to everyone.

She certainly doesn't look at him the way she looks at me.

Seeing Alex at home is seeing another facet of her entirely. She loves comfort. Her clothes are all loose and soft, her blankets and towels are all thick and plush, and her baths are all hot and long. She drinks wine and dances around her apartment to music that was popular a decade ago, songs she knows all the words to, rarely anything new. She watches an eclectic variety of movies and shows, including some of my Nana's favorite old films, but she seems to watch her favorites over and over. She spends a lot of time making warm, inviting paintings, or curling up on her couch and reading for long stretches of time.

I want to be with her when she does all of it.

I want to make her happy.

She might be perfect for me, but there are some concerning things about her. She never cooks, she eats like shit, and she drinks a *lot*. Sometimes she'll sit curled up on her couch or bed and stare into space for a long time, and she cries often, seemingly out of nowhere. She sleeps in a tight ball buried under her duvet and has horrible nightmares occasionally. Strangely enough, she has a tough time with sexual pleasure.

She masturbates most nights, but the first time I watched her was one of her more successful endeavors. She tries so hard, and seems to get close, right on the precipice, but is unable to get there. The handful of times I've seen her come, it's exceptional, but other than that, she's *so* frustrated. I watch her every night, and if she doesn't come, I don't let myself come. I want to feel her frustration, and it's awful. It's been less than a week, and I don't know how she stands it.

She won't have to stand it much longer.

***

"So, are you still seeing Alex?" Dr. Mills cocks her head slightly, smiling openly at me. I glance up at the clock. Fifteen minutes and I'm free.

"Mmhmmm."

"How's it going?" I shrug, looking out the window.

"Good."

"Have you two been intimate yet?" I look back at her in surprise.

"No."

"I think that's wise. Is that your choice or hers?"

"I'm still getting to know her, so it hasn't happened yet."

Dr. Mills smiles a little. "How do you feel about that?"

"I'm trying to be patient," I say slowly, working hard to keep the condescension out of my voice.

"Tell me about that."

I cross my arms over my chest, frowning at her. "*Why*?"

"Well, sex and romantic relationships are big for you, so I think being open about them will help us address any potential issues early." I look out the window, running my hand through my hair and resenting how nosy she is, which she seems to pick up on. "You can be as detailed or vague as you feel comfortable being," she says softly.

I sigh. "Fine. I care about Alex, and I want to wait until it's the right time, but it's hard to be patient." Especially because I watch her constantly and I haven't let myself come in days because she hasn't, but Dr. Mills does *not* need to know that. She gives me a searching look.

"Would you consider answering a very personal question for me?" I raise my eyebrows at her. "How many sexual partners have you had?"

I snort and look away from her. "Um, a *lot*."

"Were these girlfriends or casual encounters or something in between?"

"Aside from Ashley, it was usually just sex."

"Why is that?" I shrug, glancing back up at the clock.

"I lose interest quickly."

She hums thoughtfully. "Why do you think that is?" I shrug again. These questions are making me uncomfortable.

"I've never felt connected to anyone besides Ashley."

"So, you feel connected to Alex?" I struggle to keep my face neutral.

"I guess so." From the look that flits across her face, she knows I'm downplaying.

"What was your sex life with Ashley like?"

I narrow my eyes at her suspiciously. "We had a lot of sex, which is normal considering that we were in college and I was in love with her."

"What did Ashley think about your sex life?"

Oh, fuck her. She's *absolutely* read Ashley's victim impact statement if she's asking this. I take a deep breath, tamping down my anger as I look up at the ceiling.

"I think she called me a sex addict who'd rather fuck her than talk to her or something like that. What's your point?"

"Do you agree with her opinion at all, in retrospect?" I work hard not to roll my eyes at her.

"I acknowledge that it's how she felt, but I disagree. We'd always been on different pages about our relationship, apparently, and I think she was unnecessarily harsh because she was angry about what happened." Dr. Mills hums in acknowledgement and looks down at her notes briefly.

"Do you think your relationship with sexual desire is healthy?"

"It's fine," I say quickly.

"It feels like it takes up a lot of space for you," she ventures, looking at me appraisingly.

"What's your fucking point?" Her eyebrows raise slightly at my tone.

"Theodore, I think you might use sex as a sort of shortcut to the deeper emotional connection you want in a relationship, and I'm concerned you're going to repeat that pattern with Alex." A chill sweeps through my body, but I ignore it. "I understand that new relationships are exciting, and sexual connection is a healthy part of that, but if you're pursuing a real relationship instead of a casual one, I'd like you to consider that the most important part of any connection you're building needs to take place outside of the bedroom."

"I'm aware of that." She blinks and purses her lips a little, but I'm not lying. Maybe I'm misreading her expression.

***

After considering the conversation on the drive home, I resentfully acknowledge that Dr. Mills *might* have a point.

I know Alex and I are connected, and I think she can sense it, but she still needs to see it for herself. Any plans I made definitely got sidetracked after I watched her masturbate, which I should have known was going to be a problem.

I take a deep breath and think of the things I like about Alex that have nothing to do with sex. She's sweet. She's friendly. She's creative. She's sensitive. She's smart. She's perfect for me, and our relationship will be perfect.

Fuck it, I'll run into her tomorrow and ask her to dinner. I know she'll say yes, and she might even let me make her dinner, which would be ideal. Either way, it'll be nice to make her eat a proper meal, because how she eats is bothering the shit out of me. She had a jar of kalamata olives and two pears for dinner last night, which is ludicrous. She should have a nice meal every night, just like she should get to come every night. I can give her that, but I need to be patient for a bit longer.

I'll just suffer in the meantime, watching her eat random ingredients and unsuccessfully masturbate and sleep alone every night.

I pull up my driveway and head for the basement rather than my office or bedroom, working out for an hour and trying to refocus myself. I *need* to be patient, and I *can* be patient for her. We'll be together soon, I just need to keep my shit together and follow my fucking plan. I don't really want it to take that long, but *she* might need it to take that long.

I want things to be based on her wants and needs, not mine.

I manage to avoid watching the cameras as I make dinner and take a shower, but I head to my office the second I'm out of the bathroom. I just want to check on her and see what she's doing. It's early, barely eight, so she's probably reading or painting or watching a movie.

Maybe I'll watch the same movie and casually bring it up when I see her tomorrow.

I pull up the camera feeds and all thoughts eddy out of my head. She's on her bed, watching porn, writhing in skimpy red lingerie and fucking herself. I barely notice that I'm jerking off, because it's agony to watch her.

I want those to be my fingers inside of her.

She switches to her vibrator, and I can tell she's exceptionally frustrated from her needy little whimpering sounds. She alternates between thrusting the vibrator inside of herself and focusing on her clit, turning it all the way up as she gets closer. She gasps as her leg tenses up, and I start coming just as her whole body jerks violently. Her eyes snap open, and she huffs angrily before throwing her vibrator against the bed.

Oh, my god.

She didn't come.

My plans and my tenuous patience disintegrate immediately as I watch her cover her face with a pillow and groan in frustration. All of my impulses about Alex have been right, and my overwhelming impulse right now is to go over there and take care of her.

I quickly clean myself up, throw clothes on, dump some things I bought for us into my backpack and into my pockets, and I'm in my car before I know it.

The conversation with Dr. Mills today seems so irrelevant now. Her bullshit doesn't apply to this situation because Alex and I are *connected*, and I know what she needs. We're basically together at this point, anyway, and everything will fall into place after we have sex. I think she probably connects best through sex the same way that I do, and I'm positive she'll feel our connection the second we touch. I've been trying to make sure everything goes perfectly, but I don't think that's going to work with Alex. I think I need to be more intuitive with her, like right now.

I know I'm right when I hear Alex crying softly through her front door.

She doesn't need me to be patient.

She needs us to be together.

11

ALEX

THURSDAY, SEPTEMBER 21

The video is played out, but heat is pooled in my spine and I'm so fucking close I can taste it. I tilt the vibrator exactly right, and my mind drifts towards the object of my stupid, childish crush, and then I'm almost there -

"Jesus, Alice, can't you do anything right?" My eyes snap open as Danny's voice blasts through my head, and I lose it entirely. I fling the vibrator away from me and press a pillow over my face, screaming in frustration. I don't know why this has been happening so much lately, but all I want to do is make myself come uninterrupted by some intrusive memory of that fucking bastard.

I storm into the kitchen and pour myself a full glass of wine, drinking quickly and pouring another. I'm so angry that I start to cry, and then I feel self-conscious once I realize that I'm crying into my wine while wearing lingerie, which has to be some sort of lonely girl cliché.

I've just finished my second glass of wine when I hear my dead-bolt flip.

Panic rushes through me, and my eyes snap towards the door, my tears stopping instantly as I watch in horror as the door opens. I scream, dropping my wine glass in shock. It shatters on the floor, bathing my feet in glass shards as a tall man in black jeans and a pale green sweater walks in.

I can't move or I'm going to cut up my feet, but I should at least grab a knife. Instead, the panic makes me freeze as the man looks at me with concern.

Oh, my god.

It's *Theo*.

"Sweetheart, what's wrong?" A chill rolls down my spine as Theo looks me up and down, and his eyes widen when he notices the glass on the floor.

"Shit, don't move, okay?" My body goes rigid with terror as he drops the backpack slung over his shoulder and walks towards me quickly. I whimper and slam my eyes shut, waiting for the blow. Instead, his strong, warm hands grip my waist as he lifts me easily and sits me on the kitchen counter. I look up at him in shock and he smiles a little, brushing a tear off my cheek.

I work to get my breathing under control and force myself to say something, *anything*.

"Th-Theo?" It comes out as a whisper, and his smile widens.

"Hey," he says in a low, warm voice as he gently takes my face in his hands. "Come here," he whispers as he pulls my face towards his, leaning down to kiss me. A thrill goes through me when his lips touch mine, and my frozen body unlocks. I pull away from him, but he leans further into me, trapping me against the cabinets. I reach up and grip his wrists, trying to yank his hands away from my face, but his arms tense and his hands don't move at all, except to tilt my head back slightly as he deepens the kiss.

I gasp when he gently bites my lower lip, and his tongue sweeps into my mouth, heat and fear shooting through me as I move my hands to his chest, pushing weakly. He doesn't move at all, but he finally breaks the kiss, his bright eyes wide and surprised when he pulls away from me, his gaze glued to my lips.

"Holy fucking shit," he says under his breath with a laugh, dropping his hands from my face and slipping them down my body, resting them around my waist. I freeze again at the feeling of his hands on me, and he grins and laughs a little, looking excited before he kisses me again quickly. He backs up, running his hands through his hair, looking down in surprise at the crackling sounds coming from under his shoes as he steps on a few large shards of glass.

"Oh, shit, *right*. I'll clean this up, okay? Let me get you some more wine." He reaches into my cabinet, takes out another glass and hands it to me, pouring in a small amount of wine before grabbing my broom and mop from the small space behind my fridge. My hands are shaking so badly that the wine sloshes around inside the glass as I watch him clean.

How did he know where everything was?

Once he seems satisfied there's no more glass on the floor, he tucks the broom and mop back behind my fridge and leans against the opposite kitchen counter casually. He crosses his long legs in front of him and gives me that same crooked, amused smile from the other day.

"That's the first glass of wine I've ever seen you ignore," he teases, and I stare at him in shock and confusion, my voice trapped in my throat and my mind spinning in wild circles.

What the fuck is *happening*?

Theo steps forward and tilts my chin up gently as he pulls the wine from my hands, bringing it to my parted lips. He tips the glass up, filling my mouth with wine.

"Swallow." I do, ignoring my body's reaction to the commanding tone of his voice or the smirk that plays across his face. I gulp down air, forcing myself to breathe. There's a man in my house forcing me to drink wine, I have no idea how he got in, and I'm in fucking lingerie.

Oh, my god, he's going to kill me.

I can't die like this.

"What...the...*fuck*?" I'm barely whispering, but once I choke out the first few words, the rest start coming quickly. "What are you doing here? How did you get in? What do you want? Get the fuck out!" My voice gets louder and more frantic until I'm yelling at him. He steps back and cocks his head slightly to the side, looking confused.

"Alex, calm down." Anger blooms suddenly in my chest, and I throw the wine glass at him. He flinches to the side and swears loudly as the glass explodes against the cabinet behind his head. I jump off the counter, praying there's no glass on the floor as I run for the door, but his strong arm grabs me around the waist, pulling me up off the ground and back into him as he hauls me into the living room and throws me on the couch. I land with my legs over the arm of the loveseat and my head flat on the seat, and then he's in my face, gripping my jaw and forcing me to look at him.

He looks *furious.*

"Do not throw things at me, Alexandria," he bites out, his voice low and harsh. He grabs my wrists in his hands, and I realize how absolutely fucked I am as he pulls out a pair of handcuffs from his back pocket. I start screaming for help as he quickly fastens my hands in front of me, and one of his large, warm hands slips over my mouth.

"Stop it," he snaps. "Roger's not home and there aren't any renters this week, so no one will hear us. Just sit there for a minute while I clean, *again.*" He stands up, watching me as he slowly lifts his hand to make sure I don't start screaming again, but I stay quiet. I see a muscle twitching along his tense jaw as he sighs heavily and heads back to the kitchen.

When I hear him start cleaning, I try desperately to push through the fear and think. I barely know this man, and he's acting like it's no big deal that he's somehow in my house and has me handcuffed. How does he know we're alone? Did he make sure that happened? What was that *kiss*?

Fuck, I need to get out of here.

He's preoccupied with cleaning my kitchen, so if I'm careful, maybe I can make my way to the door. It's worth a shot, at least. I slowly pull my knees towards my face, wedging my feet against the arm of the couch and pushing myself into a sitting position as silently as I can.

"Alexandria Marie Shearer, *don't move.*" I freeze at the sound of Theo's irritated voice, trying not to panic.

There's no way out.

I scramble into a sitting position, curling up in a ball on the couch once I see him finish up in the kitchen and walk towards me. He sits down next to me, running a hand through his hair before looking at me, his face torn between frustration and concern.

"Give me your feet." I curl up tighter, shaking my head. He rolls his eyes as he grabs one of my ankles, and I whimper as he pulls my foot close to his face and makes an exasperated sound. "I fucking knew it.

You've got glass in your foot. *Don't move.*" He gets up and heads to the bathroom, immediately returning with tweezers and my first aid kit.

"How do you know where everything is?" I blurt out, but he ignores me as he bends down, gently pulling my foot towards him again and working a small shard of glass out of my big toe. He cleans the area with an alcohol wipe and applies ointment with a cotton swab, bandaging it before holding out his hand for my other foot. I tentatively stretch it forward and, after inspection, he pulls a fairly large shard of glass out of my heel and repeats the process in silence. He drops the bloody glass and the tweezers on the table and gives me a tight, forced smile.

"Let's try this again, okay? Do you want some more wine? You can't have another glass, though. I really don't want to sweep again," he says, smiling a little as he gently rubs the arch of my foot.

Is he *joking*?

I stare at him, my eyes wide, and his smile fades as I yank my foot out of his grip and curl up tighter into myself. I take a few deep breaths, trying and failing to wrap my head around what's happening.

"What the *fuck* are you doing here?" He winces slightly at the shrill pitch of my voice.

"I came over because you needed me," he says, his voice slow and patient, like he's explaining something to a child.

I scoff in disbelief. "I *need* you?" He nods, his pupils dilating as he looks me up and down, and my blood turns to ice.

Oh, *no.*

He stands up and grabs the backpack he left near the front door, slipping off his shoes and coming back towards me. Panic starts to numb my body as I watch him, and I sit there paralyzed with fear, trying hard to force air in and out of my lungs.

Not this.

"You can walk into the bedroom, or I can carry you. It's up to you," he says, flashing me a quick grin. I stare at him blankly and he smirks, bending down quickly and picking me up, carrying me bridal style into my bedroom. My body is rigid in his arms, my hands tight against my chest as he lays me down gently on the bed. I clench my legs together, pushing myself back towards the headboard and curling up as small as possible as he opens the backpack and pulls out some lengths of rope.

"*Please*," I choke out. He looks up at me with a wicked smile as he grabs one of my ankles and pulls me back to the center of the bed, making quick work binding my ankle to the corner of my bed frame. I try to keep my legs locked together, but he snags my other ankle and makes quick work of tying that leg down. I fight back tears as I realize I can't close my legs at all. He walks towards me with more rope, and I force myself to push through the overwhelming panic and not shut down.

"*Please, do-*" He presses his thumb against my lips, dragging it across my bottom lip slowly.

"You're so impatient. I *love* that," Theo says as he starts to loop rope through the handcuffs, pulling my wrists over my head and tying them to the headboard. He spends a long moment staring at me, his lips parting faintly as his eyes move slowly over my body. "*Fuck*, you're gorgeous."

I have no idea what to do. I'm helpless like this, spread out with little ability to move and no one to hear me scream, and I'm starting to get numb.

"Theo," I force out, failing to keep my voice from shaking, "*Please* st-" He covers my mouth with his finger again, smirking at me.

"You're *so* needy," he teases as he bends down, cupping my face in his hands and kissing me again. A sharp thrill passes through me, but I don't kiss him back. He tilts my head back anyway, making a low, content sound as his tongue glides against mine, and I start to cry. He pulls back slightly, his eyes wide.

"You feel it, don't you?" I just stare at him, and he smiles, his face almost relieved as he pushes my hair behind my ear. "Don't worry, Alex. I've got you now," he says, and I feel his fingers trailing up my leg. I shut my eyes, crying harder as his hand moves closer to my core. "Look at me, sweetheart." I reluctantly open my eyes, and he gives me a soft, sweet smile. "Hey, I'm here now. Everything's going to be okay." My body tenses up as he touches me gently, slipping my thong to the side, his finger gliding against me effortlessly from how wet I am.

I'm only this wet because I masturbated earlier, but his eyebrows shoot up and he grins at me.

I open my mouth to tell him to stop, but nothing but a soft exhale comes out. Fuck, I'm so confused and overwhelmed that I can't even speak. Theo's eyes flit between my face and my cunt, his breathing increasing slightly, his eyes dark. He starts rubbing my clit softly, watching my face intently, and I'm frozen in fear as I stare back at him. His brows furrow slightly, and he presses harder against my clit, and my hips jump involuntarily. He smirks, continuing that pressure as his other hand reaches for my face, softly stroking my bottom lip with his thumb.

My core burns, and my eyes widen when I realize my body is so pent-up and frustrated that I'm starting to react to his touch. I try not to visibly react to him, but he seems to be able to tell that I'm holding back. He pulls his hand away from my cunt and delivers a quick, soft slap against my clit. I gasp at the sensation, and he grins.

"There we go," he says, almost to himself, as he pushes his thumb into my mouth, letting it rest heavily on my tongue before he slips one of his fingers into me, and I can't help moaning. Theo pushes his thumb deeper into my mouth, and he makes a satisfied sound when I whine involuntarily. He bends his head down, biting my nipple through the lace cup of my bra and withdrawing his finger to gently pinch my clit. I arch up hard, my breath stuttering at the joint sensations, my leg tensing involuntarily as scorching heat races down my spine.

He grins up at me, slipping two fingers inside of me and crooking hard, making me gasp.

"Do you want to come, sweetheart?" I try to say something in protest, try to scream at him, try to tell him to fuck off, but I can't. When I try to shake my head, my chin bobs slightly instead, and he gives me a satisfied smile.

"Let's make it good, okay?" He withdraws his fingers, moving to the end of the bed and bending down to grab something from the backpack. I hear a soft buzzing, and my head feels too heavy as I look down at the large wand vibrator in his hand. He keeps it on low as he kneels between my legs, starting to drag it against my inner thighs, close but not close enough, avoiding anywhere I want him to touch me with it. I shut my eyes and let my head flop back onto the pillow, willing myself to detach from my body.

I can usually do that so easily, but not right now.

Theo leans down and kisses me deeply, his tongue thrusting into my mouth as he presses the vibrator hard into my clit. It only takes a few seconds before I feel the orgasm building in my core, my body starting to tense up, a long keening sound escaping me as I get close. He moans into my mouth and kisses me harder, biting and sucking my bottom lip while his other hand grips my throat, squeezing gently on the sides. I let out a series of soft little whines that make his grip tighten on my throat further, sending a wave of heat down my spine.

"*Come.*" I'm confused for just a second at how my body reacts to him saying that, and then I scream as the tension in my core snaps. My entire body feels hot, my vision goes white behind my eyelids, and my brain shuts off as I'm completely overwhelmed by the pleasure running rampant through my body.

I lie there, panting hard as I come down, my body humming with pleasure and twitching with aftershocks. I couldn't form words if I tried, and my mind feels hazy, soft and slurring, gliding over everything. I open my eyes and stare at the ceiling, completely confused.

My body doesn't seem to want to register that he's going to fucking *kill* me, because that was the most intense orgasm I've ever had.

"*Fuck*, you're so pretty when you come for me," Theo says, his hand tightening against my throat before releasing me, and I close my eyes again as he slowly pulls the vibrator away. I feel him repositioning his body and kissing his way up my right leg, dragging his tongue slowly up my inner thigh, nipping at the soft skin there. I moan as his velvety tongue drags gradually up the length of my cunt, and I start panting hard as the tip of his tongue flicks against my clit. I raise my head and lock eyes with him, surprised.

I had no idea that head could feel this good.

His hands grip the tops of my thighs, and he makes a long, low moan as his tongue pushes inside me. He looks up at me as he draws his tongue up the length of me with torturous slowness before he finally drags his tongue against my clit. A soft, strangled sound escapes me when I feel him kiss and lick and suck me there again and again, and an orgasm builds in my core rapidly.

My right leg begins to tense up and twitch, and my breath starts getting shallower and coming more rapidly. Theo makes low, encouraging sounds as I start coming, my body shaking and my vision flickering at the edges, moans pouring out of me as the orgasm tears away the last of my thoughts.

He's going to kill me, but at least I'll have finally gotten some good head before I die.

"You taste fucking amazing," he says, hovering over me and leaning down to kiss me, dragging his tongue across mine, every part of his mouth tasting of me. When he pulls away, I whine in protest, and he laughs quietly as he stands up and undoes his pants.

"I can't wait any more, either," he says as the rest of his clothes drop to the floor. I turn my head and stare at his cock for a long moment, my eyes widening before I look up at him and shake my head quickly.

His expression turns smug instantly. "Oh, you can take it," he purrs, stroking himself slowly as he kneels between my legs, notching the blunt head of his cock against my entrance. One of his hands buries itself in my hair and he holds my head in place, staring into my eyes with an intense expression. I can't look away from him and I can feel him pressing into me, feel the weight of his body on top of me, and I start hyperventilating.

He pushes inside of me in one smooth thrust, bottoming out with a shout, and I scream, arching up into him as much as I can, the stretch burning and the pressure aching as my body tries to adjust to the feeling of him inside of me.

He's too much, and I can't relax around him.

Theo lets out a long, low moan and doesn't move for a minute, his body tense and heavy on mine as he takes deep, shaky breaths. We stay there for a minute, tense and still and quiet before Theo presses soft kisses along my neck, groaning in pleasure.

"You feel so much better than I imagined," he says quietly against my skin, and I start sobbing hard, barely able to take a breath. Theo lifts his head, looking down at me with wide, shocked eyes, and he smiles a little.

"I know, sweetheart," he whispers, "I feel it, too." He kisses me sweetly as he pulls out slowly. "It's like you were made for me," he says quietly against my lips as he starts fucking me with long, slow strokes. I slam my eyes shut to get away from him, but he's all I can feel and hear and smell and taste.

I can't process what's happening anymore, because my terrified mind is trapped somewhere deep inside my body, and my body only wants to feel good. I can't move, so all I can do is take him, gasping over and over at the sharp pain followed by a dull ache as he starts to slam into me too deeply.

"That's it, take it just like that," he pants, thrusting impossibly deeper. He kisses my neck, biting gently as his pace picks up, his breathing getting shallower. The sensation of him moving inside of me is agonizing, too much in every possible way, and my sobs turn into whimpers when the friction and the feeling of him becomes mind-numbingly exquisite. My leg starts twitching against the restraints, against *him*, and Theo's answering moan is laced with approval.

"Come - for - me - right - fucking - *now*," he grits out through his teeth, punctuating every word with a harsh thrust, and the low, commanding tone of his voice pushes me over the edge.

I scream, feeling like I'm on fire as wave after wave of orgasm rolls through my body, burning away anything that isn't pleasure. Theo swears, keeping up his bruising pace for a moment, then makes a low, startled sound as his body tenses and his hips jerk several times before stilling.

As I come down from my orgasm, I can't feel anything except him, his cock still hard and insistent inside of me, his large body heavy on mine, his breath hot on my neck.

"Oh, *Alex*," he says in a soft voice, his thumbs wiping tears from my cheeks as he cradles my head, kissing my forehead gently. "You're such a good girl, coming for me like that." When he pulls out of me, I gasp at how empty I feel.

All I can feel now is emptiness.

"You're so fucking perfect for me," I hear him say from somewhere far away, and my body begins to go numb as he gets up and undoes the ties at my ankles and wrists. My arms drop to the bed as he grabs the handcuff keys from his pants pocket and unlocks my wrists before he pulls me into him, whispering into my hair as he rubs his hands up and down my limp body.

It's all too much.

I'm boneless in his arms, my eyes open but not seeing, not fully processing anything he's saying or doing. I don't know what will happen to me now that he's done, but I know it won't be good.

I've let so many terrible things happen to me, but at least this one *felt* good.

"Don't worry, sweetheart, I've got you. I'm going to take care of you," he murmurs as he leans down to place a soft kiss on the top of my head. I don't totally understand what he's saying, so I just nod, and he makes a smooth, happy hum as he reaches down and pulls the duvet around us.

Am I cold?

I'm shaking, so I must be.

This kind of numbness is different than I'm used to.

I don't feel cold or hollow the way I usually feel after sex. Instead, I'm warm and weightless, my body too relaxed and overwhelmed for my mind to take part in what's happening.

Theo pulls me tight, petting my hair and kissing my face and praising me in a soft voice, telling me how good I was for him, how well I took it, how amazing I feel, how gorgeous I am when I come. I'm still shaking and wrung out and confused, but I let him hold me close, let him touch me and talk to me and kiss me.

It feels good, even though it shouldn't.

Nothing about this should feel good.

***

He says something in my ear, but his words skim across my mind, not landing anywhere before his lips press against my skin, kissing slowly down my body before he parts my legs. I'm not really aware of what's happening, just aware of the warm, slick feeling of his tongue, the tip of it flicking against my clit, the way it dips inside of me, the soft kisses he presses into my skin, the way his moans sound, the way his cock feels as he pushes in, the way his tongue glides against mine as we kiss, the way his heated skin and soft hair feel under my fingers.

I stay outside of my body, my mind somewhere far away, my body beyond feeling anything but pleasure, enjoying the last time I'll feel good before I die. I let myself welcome him in and take what he's giving me, let the way he sounds when he says my name make me feel warm, let him kiss me deeply and fuck me slowly until we come, let him keep my mind in a place where nothing makes sense and everything has a soft glow to it, and let the affection he's giving comfort me until I drift away.

***

I'm so *warm*.

I crack my eyes open, and everything is dimly lit, bathed in a soft, dreamy wash of pink light. I can feel a man's large body curled around me, arms embracing me and hands lazily stroking my skin. I close my eyes again, and the man presses tender kisses onto my shoulders and neck. I snuggle back into him, humming contentedly.

This is *such* a nice dream.

I can feel his cock hard between my thighs, gliding against me easily because I'm already slick with wanting. His arms grip me tighter as I rub myself against him, and he mutters something approving as I tilt my hips back, lining us up. He nudges into me, kissing the back of my neck as he takes his time pushing inside me, and the feeling of him is unbearable and exquisite at the same time.

I'm *definitely* not dreaming of Danny, that's for sure.

He wraps an arm around my shoulders and almost chokes me as he pulls me back against his chest, and I moan at the feeling of him thrusting gently into my aching cunt. His other hand drags slowly down my body and slips between my legs, his fingers circling my clit with just the right pressure. I gasp at how good it feels, how close I am to coming so soon after being touched.

This feels *so* much more intense than my other sex dreams.

"*Please,*" I beg as I arch back into him, keeping my eyes closed and focusing on the feeling of him. My head kicks back, resting on his shoulder as I reach my hand back to run my fingers through his soft, thick hair. He hums in pleasure and kisses my neck, dragging his teeth gently across my skin, making me shiver.

God, this feels so real.

He pushes me higher and higher until I break, my body starting to shake as I come apart in his arms. My orgasm is long and languorous, and he moans as he fucks me through it. Soft, affectionate words of praise tumble out of his mouth when a second orgasm follows almost instantly, and he buries his face in my neck as he comes, groaning before tracing my skin with gentle kisses.

This is the best dream I've ever had.

I feel a rush of wet warmth against my inner thighs when he pulls out of me. He starts stroking my body from my shoulder to my hip in a soothing way, kissing my temple before rolling me onto my back. I finally open my eyes, looking up at the dream smiling down at me adoringly.

Oh, I'm dreaming about *Theo* again.

The last sex dream I had about him was barely detailed, a jumble of blurry images and a strong sense of desire, but this is intense and lucid in a way my dreams usually aren't. I smile up at him, grazing my fingers over his high cheekbone and trailing them down his sharp jaw, watching his face soften and light up as he leans into my touch.

It would be so nice to wake up to him like this.

"Hey, you," I whisper, pulling him down towards me. He flashes me that cute, crooked smile, his dimples showing.

"Good morning," he whispers before kissing me sweetly. I twine my arms around his neck and deepen the kiss, sucking on his soft bottom lip and running the tip of my tongue against it, eliciting a moan from him, his arms wrapping me in a tighter embrace. I'm hazy and spent as I curl up against him, tangling my legs with his and tucking my face into the crook of his neck.

In my dream, he smells the way my favorite sweater used to.

Theo's fingers draw slow patterns against my skin, and his lips move against my hair as he whispers something I can't quite make out. I hum contentedly, loving the warm, safe feeling of being enveloped in his arms. Being held by Danny felt so claustrophobic, but this must be what my brain thinks it should feel like to be held.

As I drift off again, a troubling thought glides across my mind, catching my attention for a fraction of a second.

How can I go back to sleep if I'm already dreaming?

***

When I wake up, I'm alone in my bed, my room painted in bright, mid-morning light. I close my eyes again, trying to process the series of dreams I had. Those were the weirdest fucking dreams of my life. God, where did that stuff even *come* from? I don't know if I could ever look Theo in the eye after dreaming about him like that.

I'm lying there, embarrassed, when I hear a noise from my kitchen. Is someone in my house? I sit up quickly, confused as I register a sharp pain between my legs.

That's not good.

I get out of bed slowly, realizing that my whole body is exhausted and I can barely put my legs together. I grab a sweater and sweats off the floor, pulling them on slowly as I make my way to the bathroom, and I gasp softly at how painful it is to pee, at how fucking *sore* I am.

Oh, *no*.

I wash my hands slowly and splash cold water on my face, my anxiety building the more I wake up.

Last night *happened*.

This morning wasn't a dream, that *happened*.

Theo's *here*, in my kitchen.

Oh, god. He's probably going to keep me alive for a while before he kills me.

I steel myself before I open my bedroom door slowly, peeking out into the living room. I have the distinct feeling that I'm looking into an alternate universe. There's a huge bouquet of pink peonies on my coffee table, a row of gift bags lined up neatly on the breakfast bar, and I can smell something sweet and cinnamony from the kitchen. I walk slowly through the living room, peering into the kitchen, where I see Theo standing at the stove in a pair of joggers and a t-shirt, his posture relaxed and his hair a little messy. He looks up and sees me, his faint dimples appearing as his mouth picks up into a crooked, affectionate smile.

"Hey, sweetheart," he says, his voice warm and slightly raspy from sleep. "I'm making French toast. You want coffee?" I blink slowly, confused. My brain isn't working right, because I can't understand anything that's happening. His smile falters when I don't respond, and he comes into the living room, reaching out for me.

My body floods with fear and a familiar helplessness, and I flinch away from him. His face becomes confused and hurt as I back away from him quickly, my shoulder hitting the door frame of my bedroom.

"Alex, are you okay?" My brain comes back online fast as he reaches for me again.

I didn't leave Boston to die like *this*.

"Don't touch me, you fucking *psycho*!" I shriek, shoving past him and running into the kitchen, grabbing the big kitchen knife from the drawer and spinning to face him. I see him walking towards me slowly, his hands up in a placating manner, and I thrust the knife out in front of me.

"Don't move!" He frowns but doesn't come any closer.

"Alex, put the knife down," he says slowly, his voice low and soothing.

"*No!*"

"Um, okay," he says, frowning and glancing to my right. "Can you please turn off the stove and move the pan off the heat? The toast is burning." I'd think he was trying to distract me if I didn't smell the burning from next to me, but I keep my eyes on him as I reach out blindly, finding the correct knob and turning it off.

I reach for the handle of the pan but grab the hot rim instead, shoving it backward as I cry out in pain. I clutch my burnt hand to my chest, keeping the knife raised towards Theo as he stares at my hand in horror.

"Sweetheart, I can tell you're upset, but *please* let me look at your hand. That pan was really hot." I hesitate before I raise my hand, my palm facing him, and he grimaces. "*Fuck*. Okay, um, shit. How about you keep the knife, but you let me bandage you up?" He walks backward slowly, watching me as he heads towards the first aid kit he left on the coffee table.

My eyes dart towards the door.

"*Stay right there,*" he says, noticing me glance at the door. "Run your hand under some cold water." He keeps his eyes on me, only briefly glancing away to rifle through the first aid kit, so I don't think I can make a run for it. I move quickly, setting down the knife to turn on the faucet. The cold water stings my hand, and I hiss in pain as Theo walks slowly back into the kitchen with gauze and a small roll of tape, looking concerned. I snatch up the knife and point it toward him, trying and failing to keep my hand from shaking.

We stand there, staring at each other and the quivering knife between us.

Theo takes a deep breath and tries to smile.

"Alex, I'm not going to hurt you, I *promise*, so will you please let me look at your hand?" I bite the inside of my cheek to keep from crying. This man broke into my house, raped me, and now he's going to kill me. I know I shouldn't let him touch me, but my hand really hurts.

I need some kind of control over this situation.

"If you make one wrong move, I'll fucking kill you," I say, trying to sound tough even though I can hear my voice wavering. Theo nods and moves very slowly, turning off the water and looking at my palm closely, seeming more upset about my hand than the knife I've got a few inches away from his body. He starts to dry my hand carefully with a paper towel.

"It doesn't look too bad, probably just a first-degree burn," he says quietly. "Let me wrap you up." He's so gentle as he places gauze across my palm, and I get distracted for a second by how nice it is to be cared for. I lose focus, watching the way he carefully presses down the tape on my hand, obviously trying not to hurt me.

Losing focus is a fucking mistake.

One of his hands shoots out and grabs my wrist, twisting hard and fast, and the knife drops out of my hand, skittering across the floor and under the fridge. Theo's face becomes tense and frustrated, and I scream as he backs me into the wall. He pins me with his hips, one hand still on my wrist, the other coming up and gripping my jaw, lifting my gaze to meet his.

"If you're upset with me, fucking *talk* to me. Don't *ever* threaten me with violence again. That's not how we're going to handle conflict, understood?" I stare at him blankly.

What the *fuck*?

I'm so scared and confused that I'm completely unresisting as he pulls me away from the wall, leading me out of the kitchen and pushing me gently down onto the couch. He goes back into the kitchen and returns with two cups of coffee, sitting next to me and handing me one, but my hand is shaking so badly that the coffee spills over the rim. He runs his hand through his hair, exhaling harshly.

"Okay, why don't you tell me why you're upset? That came out of fucking nowhere." Is he joking? I set the coffee down on the table slowly, my mind racing.

"Why are you doing this?"

"Doing what?"

"Breaking in? Being here? Doing..." I gesture to the bedroom, "...*that*." The panic and fear break to the surface, and I start to cry. "What is *happening*?" Theo looks confused and worried as he sets his coffee down and reaches for me, but I flinch away from him. He winces and touches me anyway, his hands rubbing my shoulders soothingly.

"Alex, calm down, okay? I think you're just overwhelmed. This isn't *exactly* how I thought things would go, but you needed me so badly last night that I knew it was the right time." I stare at him and cry, not understanding what he's talking about. He takes in my face and frowns. "Come here, sweetheart. Everything's okay." He pulls me close, and I try to get away from him, but his arms tighten and he won't let me go. "This is all going to work out, I promise."

"What are you *talking* about?" Theo pulls back and gently brushes the tears from my cheeks, giving me a reassuring look.

"I'm talking about our relationship, Alex."

I freeze up, my body going cold and my heart starting to race.

No way.

No fucking way.

"We're finally together now," he says with a soft smile.

Suddenly, I'm seventeen again, numb and devastated and confused in the backseat of a car, the scent of stale cigarette smoke surrounding me.

"This means we're together, Alice."

I can feel more tears streaming down my face as I start hyperventilating, and Theo frowns at me.

"Hey, everything's okay. I've got you." His words start mixing with Danny's in an inescapable cacophony.

"I'll take care of you now."

"Can you take a deep breath for me? You don't have to cry."

"Can you stop fucking crying?"

"I know it's a lot, sweetheart."

"Don't act like you didn't want this."

My vision starts tunneling, so I close my eyes, shutting out Theo's scared face. I can hear him talking, but I'm too deep inside myself to make out his words. I can feel him moving my body, but I'm not there anymore. I dive deeper into the small, secret place inside myself where I can't feel anything, and I hide.

***

I don't know how long I'm gone for, but I slowly become aware of soft pressure on my chest and stomach, and I can feel Theo's hard body pressed into my back. He pulls in a deep breath, and I pull in a shuddering breath a moment later. He exhales slowly, and I follow, exhaling shakily. I start to feel more sensation return as my breathing slows down and deepens, and we stay like that, breathing together until I can feel my hands again.

I open my eyes and look down at how we're sitting, our legs across my small couch, Theo's bent at the knees and bracketing mine. He's placed his hands on my chest and stomach to help me to breathe with him. I pull away from him and stand up, but I can't totally control my body yet, and he helps me to my feet when I stumble.

"What do you need?" His voice is soft in my ear, his hands gentle on my shoulders. I don't respond as I walk to the bathroom slowly, staring down at the bathtub for a long moment before I can make my hands turn on the tap. Theo disappears for a second as I wait for the water to get hot, returning with an array of gift bags. I ignore him, keeping my unbandaged hand in the stream of water.

Nothing exists for me outside of the slowly rising temperature.

Once the water is finally warm, I plug the tub and strip, sitting in the filling bathtub and pulling my knees to my chest. I rest my arms across my knees and curl in on myself, laying my chin on my arms as I watch Theo. His face is blank, and he seems calm as he pulls things out of the bags, uncorking a glass vial of salt and rose petals and dumping it into the bath. He grabs a small wooden tray and fits it over the tub's rim, creating a shelf in front of me that he starts putting things on. Salt scrub. Body oil. More vials of bath salt. He gets my coffee and a glass of water and sets them on the tray, turning off the water once the bathtub is full. He sits on the rim of the bathtub, looking at me with that same blank face.

"Does that happen to you often?" I roll my head back, looking at the ceiling. I debate lying, but I'm so exhausted that I just answer him.

"Not since I left."

"Left where?"

"Home."

"Do you know what triggered it?"

"You." His brows knit together, and he cocks his head slightly, frowning deeply. I close my eyes, blocking him out. "You're taking everything away. Why are men always taking things from me?" He's quiet for a long time before he responds.

"I'm not taking anything from you, Alex. We're together now, so we're *adding* to each other's lives. I know it's a lot, and I was overwhelmed at first, too, but I promise everything will be okay. You'll see." I shake my head and close my eyes.

I'm too tired to cry, so I don't.

He's broken into my house, he's raped me, *and* he's fucking insane.

He's probably going to kill me soon.

That would be a relief.

Once the water is cold, Theo pulls the plug and helps me out of the tub, offering me a plush bathrobe. It's always easier if I don't fight it, so I don't. He wraps me up, drying my legs with a towel and squeezing the water out of my hair. He won't stop touching me as he leads me to the bed, and I feel an overwhelming sense of helplessness as I drop the bathrobe and lie down, closing my eyes and opening my legs.

I just want it to be over already.

When Theo pulls the duvet over me, I open my eyes and look at him in confusion. His jaw is tight and his eyes are wide, and he seems concerned, for some reason.

"You should rest, okay? We can talk later." He kisses my forehead and slips out of my bedroom, closing the door behind him.

When he doesn't return, I curl up into a tight ball and fall asleep.

12

THEO

Once I'm sure Alex is asleep, I start to panic.

I'm glad I sent Catherine a text from Alex's phone saying that she felt ill, but that was supposed to be so I could make her breakfast, shower her with gifts and affection, fuck her until neither of us could walk, and finally get to *be* with her. Instead, she thinks I'm ruining her life.

I *might* have fucked this up a little bit.

I run my hands through my hair, pacing back and forth. I need to go home. I need to give her some space. I need to regroup.

Fuck, fuck, *fuck*.

I quietly slip out of her house and ignore my car, focusing on my breathing as I run back to my place. I don't understand how this happened. Everything felt perfect this morning when we woke up together, and then it was like a fucking switch flipped.

I *might* have let my impulses get the better of me here.

I know I'm not wrong about us, but I think I fucked this up by being too impulsive. I need to get myself under control again. I had a plan.

I was going to get to know her, make sure it would work between us, and find out how to make her happy. I *did* that, and it was easy because Alex and I are supposed to be together.

I was going to let her get to know me, pursue her in a way I knew she'd like, and let her see our connection for herself. I did *not* do that, but I thought it was the right time because all my impulses about Alex have been right so far.

I *might* have been wrong about the timing.

I can't believe this is going so badly, but I can fix it. This is still going to work. I can still pursue her in a way she'll like.

I thought Alex and I were the same and that sex would help us communicate, but I might have been wrong about that. I felt like my entire body was on fire the moment I kissed her, and all I could feel was our connection, but maybe she didn't feel it.

I need to be more mindful that no matter how similar we are, we're still different people. She seems a lot more sensitive than I thought she was, and I need to find a different way to show her that we're connected.

She might be having a hard time accepting it right now, but we're perfect for each other.

I just have to figure out how to get her to see that.

I get to my house, leaning on the porch railing and trying to catch my breath, massaging a stitch in my side and shaking my head in frustration. Stupid fucking Dr. Mills might have been right, and I can't let amazing sex get in the way of a perfect relationship.

Oh, my god, the fucking *sex*.

I didn't know sex could feel like *that*. It was like the feeling I got when I kissed her, but so much stronger. Feeling that kind of connection with her the second I was inside of her and *not* coming immediately is probably the most significant achievement of my life. Fuck, she was so ready for me, too. I've always had to take my time and let women adjust to me, but she just welcomed me in like she was made for me.

We fit together.

She's so perfect for me. She's so sensual, so responsive, and *so* easily overwhelmed. *That* was amazing to find out because I fucking *love* that. I've never been with anyone who needs that much aftercare, and kissing and praising her and hearing her small, happy sounds as she trembled in my arms made me feel euphoric and accomplished in a way I've never felt before. I want that forever, and I want to give her that forever. Fuck, I want to make her come forever. She's such a vision when she comes, and

I got to see it again and again. She needed me, just like I knew she would, and she fucking *loves* the sex as much as I do, just like I knew she would. God, the way she was with me this morning, so needy and passionate and sweet, with her soft little whimpered *please* -

I'm coming hard before I even realize that I'm leaning against my porch railing and masturbating in broad daylight. When the fuck did I even start jerking off? I groan as I wipe my hand clean against my pants and head inside. Thank *god* my house isn't that visible from the street. What the fuck is my problem? I am going to keep fucking this up if I can't get my shit together.

I check Alex's cameras to see that she's still asleep, curled up in a tight ball under her duvet, her hair fanned out around her head like a halo. I watch her for a few minutes, longing coursing through me.

She's an absolute angel, and I'm a dumb fuck who needs to fix this.

I take a shower, thinking about how *scared* Alex was this morning. She's obviously never been in a fight or held a knife against someone before, but she felt like she needed to. She doesn't need to be afraid of me, so *maybe* it wasn't about me. Her panic attack was scary, and I think she almost passed out. I did my best to help her regulate her breathing the way I was taught to, but it took her the better part of an hour to finally calm down.

She said it hasn't happened since she left, but left where? Why did she leave? What did she say - *Why are men always taking things from me?* What does that mean?

I groan and drop my face into my soapy hands. I'm such a fucking *idiot.* I've been so overcome by our connection and so distracted by my desire to fuck her that I've entirely glossed over the fact that she's probably living under a fake identity. How did I overlook something so important?

When she goes back to work on Monday, I'm going to figure out who the fuck she was.

I get out of the shower and check the cameras, but Alex is still asleep. I don't want her to be alone when she wakes up, so I'll head back soon to take care of her. This weekend will be about calming her down, winning her over, and helping her see what we have. I'll make her dinner, take her out and spoil her, show her how connected we are *outside* of the bedroom, and we'll get to know each other better and adjust to our relationship.

I can fix this.

***

She's still asleep when I get back to her place, so I go grocery shopping for her to kill time. I picked up what I needed for breakfast this morning, but she still barely has any food in her place. I focus on buying her things that are quick and easy to prepare since she has an aversion to cooking, but then I go overboard and buy her everything I think she should be eating.

It's fine, I'll just cook for her.

I eye the bouquets of flowers on my way out, grabbing one I think she'll like. When I get back to her place, she's *still* asleep, so I put everything away quietly, organizing her fridge and cabinets so everything faces label out. I slip into her room to put the flowers on her dresser, and she stirs a little but doesn't wake up. I clean up the attempted French toast and coffee from this morning before cleaning the kitchen top to bottom. I clean up her living room, even though it's tidy. I dust, making sure the cameras are still hidden. I look at the small still lifes she's been working on lately.

She stays asleep through all of it, and I get nervous enough to check on her, but she's just sleeping.

I open a bottle of wine and pour myself a glass, grabbing her copy of *Persuasion* from the bookshelf. I'm so distracted and nervous that I keep reading the same sentences repeatedly, and it takes me an hour to get through the first chapter. When Alex finally emerges from her room, her hair is messy and she's wearing my college sweater and her sweats.

She stops when she sees me, her face blank.

"You're still here?" she asks flatly.

I take a deep breath and try to smile at her. "Of course. I thought maybe we could talk?" She ignores me and grabs the bottle of wine, sitting on the small couch as far away from me as she can and curling into a tight ball. She turns on the TV and puts on the BBC *Pride and Prejudice*, which I've seen her watch at least twice.

"I'm more of a *Persuasion* person," I joke, lifting the book in my hand, but she still ignores me. She watches the show for a few minutes, slowly sipping the wine from the bottle. At one point, her entire body tenses and she sniffs at the wine.

"Is this drugged?" I laugh at her, but she seems serious.

"No, it's a Malbec. I picked up some wine and groceries while you were sleeping."

"More apologies?" Her voice is bitter.

"What?" Without looking at me, she gestures to the unopened gift bags on the breakfast bar.

"Um, that's not...*no*, those are just gifts that I knew you'd like." She looks at me, her face blank but her eyes sharp.

"How do you know that I'd like them?" I stare at her appraising-ly. Based on her reaction, she may not be ready to hear about that. She'll understand once we're better adjusted.

"Um, I know you pretty well," I say, aiming for nonchalance.

"*How?*" I shrug. I can see her thinking, her face hardening the longer she considers me. "I didn't just happen to meet you at that bar, did I?" I try to keep my face neutral, but her eyes widen. "My office?" I say nothing, and she looks away quickly, drinking more wine and curling into a tighter ball. I want to comfort her, but I know I need to follow her lead right now, especially since she's so upset, so I don't reach for her.

She puts the bottle of wine down slowly. "I'm calling the fucking cops," she says, her breathing unsteady. I grimace and look up at the ceiling.

She's *really* going to hate this.

"Sweetheart, we both know that's not an option for you," I say, keeping my voice soft. Her mouth drops open in shock. "Plus, I have your phone," I mutter, and she blanches, looking around frantically. "I'll give it back to you on Sunday, okay? I think we should take this weekend to get to know each other better." She freezes, her face horrified as she stares down at her hands, her voice a hoarse whisper.

"You're going to kill me, aren't you?" I feel a surge of indignation, trying to remember that she doesn't know me or fully understand what we have yet.

"Alex, look at me." Fuck, she looks so scared, and I just want to hold her. I grip my knees tightly to keep from reaching for her. "I am *never* going to hurt you, okay? I promise. I just want us to spend the weekend getting...adjusted."

"Adjusted to *what?*"

"To our relationship. We should take some time to get to know each other better. Together. As a *couple.*" The more I talk, the wider her eyes get, and she's so pale she looks ill.

I didn't expect this to go perfectly, but this isn't even going *well.*

I feel a spike of anxiety and start babbling, trying to explain it to her, hoping she'll understand. "What we have is really special, Alex. We work well together. We're complementary, but we're also similar in a lot of ways that will make building a life together easy." She starts to hyperventilate, but I can fix this if I can just make her understand. "Woah, hey, calm down, *no* pressure. I don't expect us to get married and have kids tomorrow, you know?" I try to smile at her, but the look on her face kills it immediately.

I should probably stop talking now, but I can't.

"*Do* you want kids? You're so good with Miles that -" Alex starts to cry, and I can't stop fucking talking. "Okay, wrong time. I'm just saying this is *new* - take some deep breaths, okay? - and we need time to *adjust* before - oh, no, please don't -" I finally stop talking because Alex is having another panic attack.

I'm such a fucking asshole.

I move very slowly, gently taking her face in my hands as I talk her through counting her breaths. Her eyes are round and watery and locked on mine the entire time, and we finally get her breath into a slow, deep rhythm. I grab the blanket from the back of the couch and pull her close, wrapping my arms around her and covering us with the blanket.

She doesn't pull away from me, but she's completely nonresponsive.

We sit like that through several episodes of *Pride and Prejudice*. She starts shaking in my arms at one point, and when I realize she's crying, my knee starts bouncing quickly. I focus on the fact that this is kind of like the normal nights we'll have together soon, minus the fact that she can't stop crying and I'm so anxious I want to vomit.

It's still a step in the right direction.

I finally relax a little when she falls asleep in my arms, and then I start to freak out. I drop my head against the back of the couch, staring at the ceiling and trying to meditate, to compartmentalize, to manage my feelings, to figure out how to get back in control of the situation.

I totally fucked this up, but it's going to get better.

It's an adjustment for *both* of us.

13

ALEX

I'm the sad little girl in the painting, and the rabbit and I climb out of the frame and into the Alice in Wonderland mural my mother painted in my childhood bedroom. We fall down the rabbit hole and land in the kitchen where my parents are laughing and dancing, and Danny is standing in the corner, screaming silently. The kitchen lights become the bright summer sunlight of Cape Cod, and the rabbit becomes my grandmother, yelling at me for swimming out farther than I'm supposed to.

I keep swimming out, the water beneath me getting deeper and deeper, when something grabs my leg and pulls me under, dragging me down quickly. I kick it off and swim towards the light rippling across the surface of the water, but no matter how hard I swim, I can't seem to get any closer. My lungs are burning with the need to breathe, and I gasp for air. Water rushes into my nose and mouth, pouring down my throat and into my lungs, and I start choking as the edges of my vision fade.

I drift farther away from the light, and the last thing I feel is the thing beneath the surface grab me again.

I wake up gasping, my heart racing as I struggle against the arm wrapped tightly around my waist. I take deep, shaky breaths, trying to get my heart rate down, aware of the oppressive heat of Theo curled around me, still asleep, one arm underneath my pillow and the other locked around my waist.

I've woken from one nightmare to find myself in another.

My new life has become an alternate version of my old life, and I have no idea what to do. I'm not in control of anything anymore.

I need to get back in control.

Theo stirs behind me, and I can feel him hard against me. I try to ignore how my body reacts to him and move to get out of bed, but he pulls me back into him. His lips graze my neck just below my ear, and his warm hand pushes down my stomach and into my sweatpants. I feel a surge of warmth between my legs as his hand slides lower, and he makes a content, barely-awake sound.

It's going to happen either way, but I can choose to let it happen.

His hips press forward as his fingers find my clit, and I bite my bottom lip hard, holding my breath, focusing on how nice it is to be touched. If I can't control anything else, I can control myself, and I'm choosing to enjoy this.

Theo's half-awake now, kissing my neck with slow, lazy kisses, and I arch back into him, my head resting against his shoulder. His fingers slide easily against me and he groans, moving his fingers in soft circles. I jam my hand down my sweats, covering his hand with mine and softly moaning as I use him to get myself off.

I'm in control.

"I need to taste you," he murmurs into my hair, and I keep my eyes closed and nod. He pulls me to the edge of my small bed, pulling my sweats off and pressing his face between my legs, his pace languid as he drags his tongue along my center. I whimper at the sensation of the slow, deliberate strokes of his tongue and try to lose myself to the feeling of his mouth against me, of his hands pushing up my body to cup my breasts, of my nipples rolling between his fingers.

Nothing exists for me outside of those sensations.

My orgasm builds low in my spine, and Theo moans in encouragement as my leg tenses up. He slips two fingers inside of me, fingering me gently as he lavishes attention on my clit, and his other arm moves quickly against my leg as he jerks himself off. I reach down and pull his face closer as I start to come, let him take me through the orgasm, and then push him away when I'm done.

He's good at this, at least. Danny only ever did it once a year on my birthday for a few minutes before he fucked me, and it was always somehow worse than nothing.

Theo stands up quickly, and I feel his cum spill across my cunt as he lets out a soft moan, but I keep my eyes closed. I let him do that because I'm in control. I wasn't in control with Danny for a long time, and I learned that lesson the hard way.

Theo seems intent on making me come, at least, so I'll use him the way I use my vibrator.

Until he kills me, at least.

My eyes snap open as his tongue starts dragging up my cunt again, and I look down at him in surprise. He's staring at me, his hazel eyes darker than usual as he licks my cunt clean. For just a second, I forget about being in control and focus on what he's doing.

He crawls up my body and kisses me hard, shoving his tongue inside my mouth and coating it with his salty, rich taste mixed with my own sweet, musky flavor, and I can't help moaning. I kiss him back, sucking on his tongue gently, getting lost in the moment. He pulls away and looks down at me, breathing hard, staring at my lips with a small smile.

Goddammit, I lost control.

"Good morning," he says, his voice soft. He leans down to kiss me again, and I flinch away. I force a smile and sit up, pushing away from him quickly, ignoring the confused, hurt look on his face.

"I'm going to take a bath." I hurry into the bathroom without looking at him again.

***

I scrub my body until I'm red, thinking hard. I need to figure out how I'm going to get out of this. I don't know much about Theo, but he seems like Danny, possessive and sex obsessed. I can work with that. He's been stalking me to some extent, and he's talking about us being in a relationship now, so I guess that's just how men are with me.

He seems really invested in this relationship idea, almost like it's been going on in his head for a while, so maybe he's fucking delusional. I don't know what to do about that. Is it safer to play into it? He seems to have a bit of a temper, so I don't want to push him.

No matter what he says, I know he's going to hurt me, so I need to be careful.

He said we're spending the weekend together, so I'll just get through the next two days. I can do that. I'll run on Sunday, maybe Monday if he spends the night. I've been saving a little bit here and there, so on top of what's left of the money I took from Boston, I'm set. Maybe I'll go somewhere in the middle of the country, like Michigan or Kansas or Texas. I'll find another job, another shithole apartment, and I'll start over again. I'll be even more careful next time. I'll avoid all men, especially ones that I'm attracted to, even if they seem normal when they hit on me.

I can't believe I thought that I could have a guy pay that kind of attention to me and have him not turn out to be a total psycho.

I'm so fucking stupid.

I look in the mirror as I apply moisturizer. I'll have to cut and color my hair again. I think I can find a red that goes with my complexion, and a pixie cut would suit my face. I steel myself for the day as I dry myself off and dress in jeans and my favorite sweater. I need to be smart about this and figure out how to deal with him. I won't play into his bullshit, I'll try not to piss him off, and I'll figure out what he wants from me. I just have to stay sharp and stay focused.

I can't get worn down or numb, and I *need* to stay present.

I'm not usually great at that.

Theo's sitting in the living room on his phone, wearing a tight, cream-colored sweater and dark blue pants, and he looks up at me and smiles.

"You look so gorgeous." I shrug, trying to smile back at him as I stand there awkwardly, unsure of what to do. He stands up and pockets his phone before he grabs the car keys off the table.

"You ready?" He seems tense and slightly nervous, which is probably bad for me.

I work hard to keep my voice even so he can't tell how terrified I am. "Where are we going?"

"I have a fun day planned for us," he says, his voice tight.

"What's your idea of a fun day?"

He smiles at me. "Normally, I'd want to stay in bed, but your planner says you were going to go to Portland today, so we're doing that. I looked at the list of restaurants you want to try and chose a few, and we'll go to the bookstore, and there's that showing of *You've Got Mail* that you were looking up times for, and then maybe some shopping?" I nod absently, struggling to keep my face neutral as I feel the numbness creeping in.

He really *has* been stalking me.

"That sounds great," I say, hoping he can't hear how forced my voice is. He smiles at me, relieved, and reaches his hand out for mine, gripping hard.

"Let's go."

***

Theo's old Subaru doesn't have an aux port, so we listen to the radio. He lets me tune it to public radio so I can listen to a news quiz show, and he grins and tells me it's his favorite. Listening to it keeps us from talking for most of the car ride, and I focus on my breathing.

I just have to get through today and tomorrow.

We go to a little brunch place Bailey recommended, and I order something light, mostly just drinking coffee. It's awkward. Theo watches my every movement, my every reaction. Danny was unobservant if he was in a good mood, which made my life easier, but I have to be on guard with Theo no matter what. I don't want to talk to him, but I need to know what I'm dealing with.

"Um, did you grow up in Astoria?" He looks out the window.

"Kind of. I lived in Yakima until I was twelve, and then I moved in with my grandparents."

"Why?"

"Just worked out like that," he says with a shrug before turning back to me. "Where did you grow up? I know it wasn't Maine, by the way," he teases, and I grit my teeth and scramble for another answer.

"North Carolina." He narrows his eyes at me, smiling a little.

"Nope." I shrug, flagging the server for a refill of my coffee.

The day has barely started, and I'm already having difficulty staying focused by the time we stop at the huge bookstore downtown. Theo stays close to me, mostly watching what I pick up, occasionally grabbing something and flipping through it.

"What do you like to read?" I ask, watching him out of the corner of my eye. He shrugs, grabbing a battered copy of *The House of the Dead* and flipping through it.

"I liked this one," he says as he passes it over. I skim the back, feeling frozen in horror as I read the words *murdering his wife*, but Theo doesn't seem to notice my reaction and keeps talking. "I'm used to reading whatever's available, so I'm not picky. I like your taste, though. You're a bit of a romantic, you know that?" He rubs my back and I flinch, turning away from him.

He asks me questions and talks to me about books, but I can't really respond after that. He buys me whatever books are on the list I keep on my phone and others that he thinks I'll like, and I focus on my breathing.

The movie is two hours of respite. As long as I ignore that he looks over at me frequently, I don't have to perform for him, and I'm able to calm down enough to focus again. We talk about movies over lunch, and it's an easier conversation, but he notices I'm not eating much and asks if I'm feeling okay. I have no interest in telling him that stress kills my appetite, so I pretend I don't like what I ordered.

He looks confused. "You have pad see ew once a week for lunch, and this place is *way* better than the place by your office. Is it too spicy?" I look down at the food to hide my shock at how much he knows about me.

How long has he been stalking me?

"Yeah, I guess." I drink my beer slowly, trying to steer the conversation back to an easier topic.

I'm completely overwhelmed from constantly being on guard by the time he takes me shopping. It's awful. Theo *really* wants to buy me things, *nice* things, *expensive* things. I think of all the unopened gifts at my apartment and try to find ways to dissuade him.

When I mention something's too expensive, he just shrugs, says it's not a problem, and buys it. When I say I don't need something, he gives me a weird look, says I should have anything I want, and buys it. When I tell him I won't use something, he tells me I should have it just in case, and buys it.

He's about to buy me a pair of heels I'll never wear, and I pull him to the back of the store, keeping my voice low.

"Please stop buying me things."

"Why?"

"I don't like it." He frowns.

"Alex, you like everything I bought you." He seems so sure of himself, and my patience finally runs out.

"Stop trying to *buy me off*," I snap, and his face twists.

"Jesus, is *that* what you think I'm doing?" He pushes my hair behind my ear and strokes my neck. "Sweetheart, I like giving gifts. If you don't like these, I won't buy them, and I'll return something if you actually don't want it, but it's just a way I express affection, I promise." He leans down to kiss me, and I flinch a little, not kissing him back.

I'm not accepting *anything* from him.

He sighs and runs his hand through his hair. "Are you tired? We've done a lot today, and it's getting late. Do you want to go home?" He's so overwhelming, and I'm worn out, so I nod.

He buys me the fucking heels anyway.

We don't talk on the drive home much. He asks what I'd like for dinner, and I tell him I'm not hungry. He turns the radio to the classical station, and I rest my head against the window, closing my eyes. I can feel my brain starting to shut down and my perception becoming fuzzy. By the time we get back to my apartment, I just want to go to sleep.

I go straight to my bedroom, stripping and getting underneath the duvet. Theo apparently misunderstands because he starts kissing me, running his hot hands over my body as he slips his tongue into my mouth. I can feel him getting hard against my thigh, and something inside me crumples.

I can't do this. He can do what he wants, but I don't have to be here. I can choose to do that. I'm *good* at that, so I tune out of what's happening.

Unlike Danny, Theo notices instantly that I'm not reacting to him, and he stops.

"Are you okay?" His voice is concerned. I don't say anything, I just withdraw further inside myself. He pulls me to the edge of the bed, sitting me up and kneeling in front of me, his hands rubbing up and down my arms.

"Sweetheart, look at me." His face is anxious and concerned, his mouth tight. "Alex, *please* talk to me. What's wrong? What can I do? Let me take care of you." His hands cup my cheeks, and his thumbs stroke against my temples. I close my eyes, shaking my head a little.

I don't want to feel anything anymore.

I stand, pushing him out of the way as I walk to the kitchen, grab two bottles of wine, open them both, and head back to the bathroom. Theo's standing in the doorway to my bedroom, looking concerned as I push past him, starting in on the first bottle of wine.

"What are you doing?" I ignore him as I turn on the faucet and drink fast, waiting for the water to heat up. Theo slips in behind me and starts going through my medicine cabinet, surreptitiously pulling out my razor and pocketing it. He doesn't need to do that, but maybe he'll be nicer to me if he thinks he does, so I don't say anything. I drink and wait for the water to get hot, plugging the tub and sitting in it as it fills slowly. I finish the first bottle of wine, setting it down on the floor and grabbing the second. Theo grabs my wrist, trying to get me to look at him.

"Sweetie, that's *not* water," he says, his voice tense, but I ignore him, pulling my hand and the wine bottle free. "Alex, you really shouldn't drink like this. You're worrying me."

"Fuck off," I mutter into the second bottle before I start drinking.

The bathwater is hot on my skin and I'm drinking fast on a mostly empty stomach, but I'm not escaping how I need to. This has always worked before, so it'll work now. It has to. I turn the faucet off and set the half-empty bottle of wine on the little tray before I grab the vials of bath salt. I pour all of them in, coating the bottom of the tub in hard crystals that dig into my skin. Theo's leaning against the door frame, his body tense and his face alarmed, his arms crossed tight over his chest as he watches me closely. I drain the bottle of wine and lean back, letting my head hang off the back of the tub as my head starts to swim.

I close my eyes, frustrated that I can still feel my body, feel how upset my stomach is and how my skin is starting to itch from the salt. The scent of roses is overpowering, my head is swimming, and I start to feel nauseous.

Goddammit. Usually, I start to feel numb.

I glance over at Theo and let out a bitter, angry laugh. "Do you know what it feels like when you don't have control over a single fucking thing in your life?"

"Yeah," he says quietly.

"How does it feel to you?"

"Like I'm trapped, I guess."

"Do you like feeling like that?"

He snorts. "No, I fucking hate it."

"Then why are you doing it to *me*?" I hear my voice crack on the last word as I start to cry. He steps into the bathroom, leaning over the tub and cupping my face.

"I'm not," he says as he brushes my tears away with his thumbs, his voice soft and pleading. "Please don't think that. This relationship isn't like that, okay?"

I pull away from him and curl up, crying harder. He sits on the rim of the tub and stares at me, opening his mouth and closing it like he's searching for something to say. I'm so drunk all of a sudden, and I drop my head onto my knees, moaning.

How am I still not numb?

"I never would have left if I'd known I was going to end up back here," I slur out.

"What are you talking about?"

"I don't want to do this again," I sob, letting my tears drip into the bathwater.

"Do what?"

"I'm going to have to start over." I really shouldn't be saying this to him.

"Oh, sweetheart, we can try again tomorrow. Today went better than yesterday, right? Tomorrow will be better, too. You're just adjusting. *We're* adjusting." I sob harder. *Adjusting.* I adjusted to Danny, but I refuse to adjust to this. A familiar wash of despair rises inside me, and I let it take me back to an old place.

"I should have been in that fucking car."

"What car?" I shake my head, my vision tunneling a little and my mouth watering. I gag and lean over the side of the tub, vomiting up wine and bile. Theo pulls my hair back with one hand and reaches away from me with the other to pull the plug and turn on the cold tap. Once my stomach is empty, Theo gets me a glass of water and I take small sips, lying back in the cooling bathwater, my head spinning.

I can see my mother's painting behind my eyes, the rabbit's beady red eyes judging me, young me staring at me with disappointment, and I pass out thinking about that fucking rabbit, trapped in my arms, desperate to be free.

14

THEO

SUNDAY, SEPTEMBER 24

Alex passes out and I push down my panic as I get her cleaned up and dried off and tucked into bed. I ignore the pit in my stomach as I clean the bathroom. I swallow the creeping nausea as I methodically comb through her house, checking for loose baseboards and tiles, looking under every piece of furniture, and going through all her clothes and bags.

It takes me an hour to find everything.

Small piles of cash are hidden throughout the house in obvious places, amounting to just over seven thousand dollars. A platinum diamond ring is tucked away in an empty bottle of aspirin, and my first thought is that it doesn't look like something Alex would wear, even though she doesn't wear any jewelry besides small gold hoop earrings. Her driver's license takes me the longest to find, because she taped it underneath the bottom of the bookshelf.

I put it all in a neat pile on the table and stare at it, panic overtaking me.

I never would have left.
I don't want to do this again.
I'm going to have to start over.
Oh, fuck, she's going to run from me.
I know what I have to do to stop her, I just don't like it.

It's the middle of the night and Alex is passed out drunk, so I have hours. I grab everything and head to my house, taking everything into my office. I pull up the camera feeds of Alex's room on one monitor and pull up search engines on the other two, grabbing her license and looking up her real name.

The first thing that pops up is a homemade missing persons poster from March. The photo looks like it was taken at a holiday party, and I barely recognize her. She's thinner, with waist-long honey-colored hair styled in a wavy, layered blowout, and she's wearing heavy makeup.

Her smile is wide, but it looks wrong to me somehow.

She's got on a tight, short dress and leans against the arm of a tall, muscular man in a dark blue suit, a thick platinum band on his left hand. He's maybe my height or a little taller, built much broader than I am, with sandy hair, blue eyes, a ruddy complexion, and a very square jaw.

He's not unattractive, he just looks like a fucking asshole.

I look at the information on the missing poster, nausea churning in my gut.

MISSING PERSON:
ALICE MARIE MURPHY, nee SILVA
DOB: 2/26/1998
HEIGHT: 5' 2"
WEIGHT: 100 LBS
HAIR: BLONDE
EYES: BROWN
LAST SEEN: 3/9/2023, JAMAICA PLAIN, BOSTON
CONTACT DANIEL MURPHY WITH TIPS

There's an official missing poster put out by the Suffolk County Police Department with her ID photo on it and an article about her going missing from March, full of photos of her. There's one of Alex in a pink bikini top at the beach, her hair in a coiffed twist, and one of her wearing a Red Sox jersey sitting in box seats with her husband, and another of her holding a mimosa with an untouched plate of picture-perfect food in front of her.

She's always smiling, always poised, always a little tense around the eyes.

I find her Facebook and her Instagram next. Her Instagram is sparse, with a few nicely framed photos of flowers, museum exhibits, and food, all with vague, positive captions. The several most recent posts are all missing person posts, obviously made by her husband.

Her Facebook is less sparse. Her husband has posted and tagged her in tons of missing person posts, at least once a week since she disappeared. I scroll back to the year she made the account and start going through it. There's standard teenage girl stuff, innocuous posts about her life and things going on at school. There are photos of a happy teenage Alex with lots of friends at summer camp, school dances, birthday parties, track meets, and lots of selfies with silly filters.

It takes me a minute to realize that I've never seen Alex smile like she does in these photos, unguarded and giddy and sweet. The smiles I've seen from her are polite and friendly and warm, but not *real*.

Oh, fuck. I've never seen Alex actually smile.

I keep going through the photos on her page, and there are lots of old photos with her parents. She's with them at Red Sox games, in matching pajamas on Christmas, sightseeing in San Francisco, at art openings with her mom or running a 5K with her dad, and my heart hurts looking at them.

They all look so happy together.

I search her parents' names and feel a wave of nausea as I read an article from a local paper about a college professor and his artist wife who died in a car accident. It was raining hard, and they got rear-ended by a drunk driver at an angle, spinning their car out into the next lane, where they were hit by a semi.

I should have been in that fucking car.

Oh, my god.

William and Andi Silva look like they were nice people. Her father was a tenured engineering professor at MIT, and her mother was a fine artist, a painter who was well-known on the East Coast art scene. Her father had no social media, but her mother did, and Alex features in most of her mother's posts. There's one where her mother calls her their "miracle baby," the attached photo of a beaming Andi and William in a hospital, maybe in their late thirties or early forties, holding a swaddled newborn Alex.

I scroll through more posts, seeing a happy woman with a happy marriage and a happy family, pausing on a photo of Andi and an adolescent Alex standing next to a massive painting of Alex holding a white rabbit. The rabbit's gaze is nervous and trapped, and the painted version of Alex looks lost and scared, in stark contrast to the content, happy version of her standing with her arm around her mother's waist.

From what I can tell, Alex was a happy kid who was wanted and loved, probably spoiled, and most likely very sheltered.

I flip back to Alex's page, dread creeping up the back of my neck when I see that Alex's social media gets sparse and concerning after her parents died. She made one long post memorializing her parents the week they died, then posted nothing until her status changed to *Married* five months later, a few days after her eighteenth birthday. She posted infrequently after that, maybe once every three or four months, and every post going forward references her husband.

There's no posts or photos of her alone or with friends, nothing indicating any hobbies, nothing without him.

The first two years of their marriage, based solely on pictures, changed Alex immensely. She lost a *lot* of weight, her body going from athletic to delicate looking. She grew her hair from her shoulders to her waist, got it highlighted and cut in soft layers rather than the blunt cut she'd worn before, the way she wears her hair now. Her skin got tanner and her whole wardrobe switched from normal but stylish clothes to extremely feminine things, tight and short and usually in pale colors. She's beautiful, but based on how she looked before she got married and how she looks now, I don't know that any of it was entirely her choice.

Alex looks perfectly put together in every photo with her husband, her smile poised and radiant and never reaching her eyes. She looks fragile next to him, and I feel uneasy when I notice how she seems like she's always curling in on herself slightly.

I click onto her husband's page and swear quietly, finally realizing why Alex has gone to such extensive measures to hide.

Detective Daniel Paul Murphy has been employed with the Boston Police Department since the year after he graduated high school.

He's also eleven years older than Alex, and since they got married right around her eighteenth birthday, he's a fucking piece of shit on top of being a bastard.

I scroll through their pages simultaneously. Daniel was promoted to Detective four years ago, and around the time he got promoted, Alex started going longer without posting anything. By the time the first missing poster pops up on his page, she hasn't posted in over eight months.

Daniel, however, posts about her. He calls her "Bunny" and seems to like showing her off. There are photos of her in the kitchen making Thanksgiving dinner, her smile strained as she holds up a perfectly roasted turkey, photos of her surrounded by his nephews and nieces in a pool, photos of her in a tight white dress posed perfectly in front of a ten-foot Christmas tree in their giant, charming house that I doubt he afforded on a cop's salary.

There's a series of glossy Christmas photos with his family from over the years, and Alex always looks perfectly happy, unless you line the images up against the ones of Christmas with her parents.

Then, she looks downright miserable.

I sit back, reeling, watching Alex sleep. No wonder she's not adjusting well. She probably has huge fucking trust issues and isn't ready for such a serious relationship yet. If I had known about her marriage, I would have known I *needed* to follow my plan and take it slow. I knew she probably had a fake identity, and I should have looked into it before. I was in her apartment, I had access to all of this, and I overlooked it.

God, I'm a fucking idiot.

I don't know everything that happened, but I've got enough missing pieces to start making assumptions, and none of them are good. She can fill in the details later, but right now I need to recalibrate and figure out how to get her to trust me. Getting her to see our connection is going to take a *lot* longer than I thought.

I push my hands back through my hair, sighing harshly. I can't keep being a fuckup. She deserves better, and I can *be* better. We'll start this over. I can fix this.

I just need her to not fucking run away from me first.

I look down at the money, the ID, and the ring, and I start thinking. I can just keep everything, which is what I *want* to do, but it's not a great option because she'll get upset and never want to trust me. I *should* put everything back and find another way to prove that she doesn't need to run, but I have to know I can find her if I do that.

We're definitely connected, because I prepared for this before I knew it would be a problem.

I grab the unopened packages from the attic and set them next to Alex's things on my desk. I was going to put a few trackers in her things anyway to help me keep her safe, I just have to go a little bit farther now. I don't want to do something this drastic, but I know enough about her past now that I don't trust her not to run. This way, if she tries, I'll know where she is and if she's safe.

I can't believe I've fucked this up so badly.

It's fine, I can fix it. We'll take this slower. I'll scrap my plans of having dinner with her every night. I'm still going to *make* her dinner, though, but I'll let her have a few nights to herself. I'll stop giving her the gifts I buy for her until she's better adjusted and we've had a long talk about love languages. I have no idea what hers are, but I'm sure her rejecting the gifts is just her adjusting poorly.

I have *no* idea what to do about the sex.

That was supposed to be the easy part, but even that's complicated. This morning was amazing, but the way she lay underneath me after she initiated tonight, her face blank and her body non-responsive, makes me viscerally uneasy. That whole situation was really fucking concerning, and I don't know what I'm supposed to do.

Everything about this relationship is going so differently than I thought it would, but I know this works.

It has to.

I grab the packages and Alex's stuff, trying to calm down as I head down to my car.

I can fix this. I just need to try harder.

***

I start by slipping small GPS microtracking chips into things she owns. Seams of coats and jeans, her purse and backpack and wallet, her suitcase, her shoes, a few scrunchies. I pop the back off her phone and slip one in there just in case she finds and disables any or all of the location tracking programs I've downloaded onto her phone.

I pull up the tracking app and label each tracker with the item I put it in, and after two hours, the app shows about fifty little flags in Alex's apartment.

It's a little over the top, maybe, but couples share locations.

I'd give her mine if she asked.

I stare at her, longing roiling inside of me. We'll be so happy together once we get this figured out, and I'll spend the rest of our lives making up this one little thing to her, whether she ever finds out about it or not. She's going to have an easy, happy life with me. She'll go back to being spoiled, sheltered, and adored the way she deserves. If she wants, we can have a family. I just need to make sure she can't run before she sees how good we are together.

Alex is dead asleep while I set up, and a tiny lick of guilt curls in my stomach. Ideally, she'd know about this. She'd *want* this, maybe even ask for it. I tell myself it's just temporary. I won't tell her about it, and I'll take it out when things are better.

I roll her onto her stomach and swab the skin between her shoulder blades before I prep the syringe and inject a local anesthetic. She's so passed out that she doesn't even flinch, but she still doesn't deserve to feel any pain. After a few minutes, I take the larger implantation needle, pinch a fold of skin and slowly push the needle in, injecting the small tracker. I pull the needle out and rub her back with an alcohol swab, holding a piece of gauze to the injection site for a few minutes. It's injected shallowly enough that you can feel it if you push hard, so I'll be able to find it when I need to take it out, but it's very small and placed in the area of her back that's a little hard for her to reach, so she probably won't find it accidentally.

I clean up, throwing everything back into the box and tucking it into my backpack to throw away at home before I turn off the lights and strip down to my boxers, sliding into bed next to her. I lay on my back and gently pull her into my arms, tucking her head into my neck and pulling her arm across my chest.

This isn't even that bad, really. It's just an extension of us location sharing, and I'll take it out once she's adjusted. It's fine.

I lay awake for another hour holding her. All relationships take work, and ours just might take a lot more work than I initially expected. That's fine. She stirs briefly, her arm moving up around my neck and her thigh slipping over mine, her small, soft body pressing flush against me. I relax into her, letting her even breathing lull me to sleep.

It's all going to be *fine*.

***

When I wake up, Alex is gone. I shoot out of bed, panicking, until I remember to check my phone. She and her running shoes and wallet are moving slowly across town. It's Sunday, her long run. I'm surprised she can run with how hungover she must be, but I'll take care of her later.

I make the bed and take a bath, checking my phone occasionally to see where she is. She takes the bus out to Warrenton, running through Fort Stevens to the beach. I change into fresh clothes and spend time putting all the cash back, replacing the ring and the ID before driving out to the beach and looking for her.

I find her on top of a dune, surrounded by swaying beach grass. Her eyes are closed, and her pale, sweaty face is turned up to the weak sun filtering through the clouds, a half-empty plastic water bottle in her hand.

Part of me doesn't want to approach her, doesn't want to see how her face will change when she sees me, but I walk up to her anyway. I sit beside her, leaning back on my hands and watching her, longing pooling in my stomach as she refuses to acknowledge me. I want her to look at me, to smile at me, to be happy to see me.

It'll happen, I just need to be patient.

She's still adjusting.

"How'd you find me?" she asks as she finally opens her eyes and looks at me. I can't discern her expression, but it's certainly not happiness or affection.

I lift the back of my hand to her clammy forehead, ignoring her flinch. "How are you feeling?"

Her lips turn down into a tiny pout. "I vomited twice."

"Maybe you should take it easy today. Let me take care of you."

"What do you mean by *that?*"

I shrug. "Parking you on the couch, putting on a show you like, making sure you drink water and eat something, maybe keeping you away from wine?"

She scoffs. "Then you'll give me back my phone and go home, right? It's Sunday, and I need to get ready for work tomorrow." She's trying to seem normal, but her eyes are sharp, and I know she's going to run. I sigh, knowing I need to let her. "I'll see you soon, I'm sure," she says, her voice placating.

She's going to see me a lot sooner than she thinks.

"Yeah, sweetie. Whatever you want." I can see her relax a tiny bit, giving me a small, forced smile, but there's no warmth on her face, nothing but apprehension and determination.

This is going to *suck*.

***

I try to take care of her, but she's despondent. She lays in bed, facing away from me, barely acknowledging me. I leave her house at four, heading home and pulling up the camera feeds. She waits about twenty minutes after I leave before moving quickly, changing all her clothes and leaving everything but the cash, the ring, and the ID.

She wears my sweater, which makes me feel a little better about having to do this. It's a thread of connection she can't see yet, but it lets me know we're still on the right path.

I debate whether to head her off at the bus station or let her get her to Portland before I stop her. Letting her leave Astoria will make her feel like she tried, but stopping her in Portland will dissuade her from trying again.

I feel like such an asshole for thinking about it like this, because I'm *not* this guy.

I drive to Portland, anxiety churning in my stomach as I park a block away from the train station, thinking about how wrong this could go. I slip inside the station, staying out of sight while waiting for the bus to arrive. I hate that she thinks she needs to do this, and I hate that she's going to be so upset with me when I stop her.

Alex doesn't see me as she gets off the bus, even though she's glancing around quickly, more observant than I've ever seen her. I duck back so she doesn't see me as she enters the train station and heads for the ticket counter, walking as quickly as she can without running. I catch up to her, and she jumps and whirls around when I gently grab her arm, looking devastated when she sees me.

This is not going well.

"Hey, don't worry. It's just me," I say softly. She lets out a short, sharp exhale and closes her eyes, her face contorting as she starts to cry quietly. I pull her into a tight hug and kiss the top of her head, trying hard to keep my shit together as I turn her away from the ticket counter and lead her out of the station.

She doesn't say anything, doesn't scream or fight me the way I was worried about. Instead, she lets me lead her back to the car, crying quietly the whole time. I try to stay calm enough for both of us as I start driving, but it's hard when I see tears running down her cheeks as she stares blankly ahead.

I need to fix this.

"Sweetheart, I'm sorry you felt like you had to do this," I say quietly, but she doesn't respond. "I know you're upset and overwhelmed right now, but I also know this isn't just about me." She jerks, staring over at me with wide eyes. "I don't know what happened to you before you came here, but I want you to know that you don't need to run from me. I can make everything better if you just talk to me, I promise."

She doesn't talk to me.

I take her home and get her upstairs, where she sits on the bed staring blankly at the wall while I unpack her small bag, putting everything back where I know it goes. I feel like such a fuck up as I sit next to her and pull her close, ignoring her flinch when I kiss her temple.

"Sweetheart, everything is going to work out, okay?"

"Okay." Her voice is quiet and soft, and a wave of relief washes through me. I don't know what changed, and I'm not going to ask. I hold her tight, ignoring the fact that she keeps flinching whenever I touch her.

We don't really talk after that. She gets up and starts getting ready for bed like nothing's wrong, and I make her dinner while she takes a long time in the bathroom. When I look at the cameras, she's lying in the bathtub, staring at the ceiling with wide eyes. She eventually comes into the kitchen wearing my college sweater and soft leggings, looking a little lost and ignoring me entirely. She eats very little of her dinner as she watches an episode of some soapy teen drama she's rewatching, and I stay in the kitchen, cleaning slowly, giving her as much space as possible in the small apartment.

When she turns off the TV and finally looks at me, my heart jumps into my throat.

"Are you staying?" she asks in a small voice, and I grip the kitchen counter until my knuckles turn white. I know I should go, even though I don't want to. She's had such a tough weekend, and I think she probably wants to be alone, so I'm going to do what I should for once in my fucking life.

I shake my head. "I was going to go home, if that's okay with you. I think we need to take this a little slower." Her eyebrows raise in surprise. "How about I make you dinner on Wednesday?"

"Okay." She bites her lip, taking a few quick breaths. "Are you going to have sex with me?" I tamp down the flare of desire I feel at the idea as I stare at her, trying hard to read her.

She didn't ask if *we* were going to have sex, so I'm going to play it safe.

"Um, you seem tired, so...no?" She visibly relaxes, and we stare at each other for a minute before I grab my keys off the counter. I step towards her slowly, leaning down to kiss her, and she flinches a little.

I fucking *hate* that.

"I'll see you soon, okay?"

15

ALEX

MONDAY, SEPTEMBER 25

I curl up on my couch and stare out the living room window, drifting between numbness and panic as I try to wrap my mind around the situation I've found myself in.

The guy I have a crush on broke into my house, tied me down, raped me, *and* he thinks we're dating. I need to figure out how to escape him, but I can't run from him like I did from Danny.

I have no idea what to do.

My phone chimes, startling me, and I see a new contact name pop up.

Theo, 1:49 AM:

> Sweetheart, go to bed. It's late.

How would he know I'm awake? It's not like he can see me or -

I stare at the phone, horror piercing through the confusion.

Oh my god, he's got cameras in my house. How long has he been watching me? Where are the cameras? I look around quickly, but I can't see anything obvious. What should I even be looking for? I pull out my laptop to search for surveillance equipment, but my search engine glitches and shuts down. I try it twice more, but it does the same thing each time.

Is he in my *laptop?* I need a fucking drink.

I open my fridge, finding it packed with more food than I can reasonably eat. It looks like a health food store exploded in my fridge. There are glass containers with sticky notes on them, and neat, blocky handwriting listing what's inside, the date it was made, and reheating instructions. I pull one of the containers out and stare at the salmon, vegetables, and rice suspiciously. I do some rough math, and indignation flares through me.

This asshole is fucking *dieting* me.

I worked so hard to get my life under my control, and he's taking it all away from me. I can't go to the cops or get a rape kit, because if my real name goes into the system, Danny will find me. I can't run, because Theo's tracking me somehow besides my phone. I'd look up ways to track people, but my laptop is no longer a resource. I reach for my phone and then pause, considering. He had it all weekend. Can you even hack a phone? Probably.

Fuck. I'm trapped.

I breathe deeply and think of the affirmations I've been repeating for months, but I can't seem to remember them.

Theo, 2:02 AM:

You should get some sleep.

I don't sleep, but I lay in bed and pretend so that he stops texting me. I replay the weekend in my mind, getting stuck on the sex. Rape? Sex? I don't even know what I think that *was*, and I can't handle how it made me feel, so I try to ignore it. This has to be about more than sex if he thinks we're dating, but I don't know. He's going to kill me either way, but if I play along, maybe he won't hurt me until then.

How did I end up in this situation? Maybe this is just what happens with me and men. Maybe this is my fault, somehow, the same way Danny was.

I close my eyes and exhale harshly, pinching myself.

I can't think about it like that anymore – there's no fucking way that was my fault, and this isn't, either.

I lay there until my alarm goes off then get up and start getting ready quickly, staying as clothed as possible. When I walk out into the living room, I groan when I notice all the gift bags. I can't accept anything from him, but I can't piss him off by throwing them out, so I put them all under my bed.

My phone chimes repeatedly, but I ignore it. I need to play along with him, but I can't lean into his delusion, so I'll just try to ignore him for the most part.

Theo, 7:00 AM:

Good morning. How are you feeling?

You haven't had insomnia before.

Theo, 7:14 AM:

You forgot your lunch.

I get to work early, skipping the cafe just in case he knows I go there, and I sit at my desk and stare into space trying to figure out how to handle this.

Theo, 7:53 AM:

Why didn't you come to the coffee shop?

Of course he's been stalking me there. God, how did I not notice *any* of this?

Theo, 8:32 AM:

Why aren't you eating breakfast?

Oh my god, he's got cameras in my office, too. Is *that* why he was here last week? How long has he been following me?

I pull up the web browser on my work computer and start looking for surveillance equipment to see what I should be looking for, but my web browser crashes. I pull up the browser again, searching for "THEODORE ANDERSON OREGON" and the browser crashes. I search for what to do if you're being stalked, and the browser crashes *again*.

I'm on the verge of tears when I hear my phone chime.

Theo, 9:17 AM:

> Please don't be upset.

> This is just while we adjust.

Theo, 10:09 AM:

> You look gorgeous today.

Theo, 10:20 AM:

> You don't usually have this much coffee.

Theo, 11:41 AM:

> Are you going to respond at any point?

At lunch, I run down to the rec center, leaving my phone at the office to get some reprieve. I try to lose myself in the yoga class, but I'm so scattered that I fall out of a pose, and I spend the rest of the class in child's pose, just trying to keep myself from crying.

Theo, 12:22 PM:

> Are you okay?

> That fall looked painful.

Theo, 12:49 PM:

> You forgot your gym bag at the rec center.

Okay, so I'm constantly under surveillance. Fuck, he's taking *everything* away from me.

Theo, 1:15 PM:

> Alex, you need to eat something.

I pretend everything is fine, but I think Suzie can tell something is wrong. She keeps giving me this concerned look and asking if I'm okay when she comes down for coffee, which she's doing far more than usual. I just force a smile and tell her I have insomnia, and I think she can tell I'm lying, but she grabs her purse and slips me an Ambien anyway, telling me to get some sleep.

Theo, 2:39 PM:

> Please don't take medication that's not yours.

Theo, 3:18 PM:

> You shouldn't have caffeine this late.

I sigh in agitation, shoving my phone in my desk drawer. He's going to kill me, but apparently he's going to mother me first.

Theo, 4:45 PM:

> Do you need a ride home?

I leave work a few minutes early and walk home quickly, looking for him everywhere, but he's nowhere to be seen. When I get home, I look around my apartment for anything suspicious, but nothing seems to have changed, except that my planner now has "DINNER" on Wednesday written in red ink. I close the planner and slip it into a drawer.

I guess that's not mine anymore, either.

Theo, 5:55 PM:

> Are you seriously not eating at all?

Theo, 6:02 PM:

> How about dinner tonight?

> Alex, please answer me. You're being rude.

> Fine. I'm coming over.

Panic flares through me and I scramble to leave my apartment. Ignoring him isn't going to work, and I need to get out of here. Roger is still gone, and there's no one in the rental right now, but maybe someone else can hear me scream if I'm not in my apartment.

I walk up the hill towards the center of town, silencing my phone to ignore the chiming. I'm jumpier than usual, constantly looking over my shoulder for any sign Theo, taking streets I'm not familiar with.

I end up in an older neighborhood that looks out over the river, full of nicely kept Victorian houses on big plots. I panic when I realize I've walked down a short, dead-end street. There's only one large house at the end, partially obscured by trees, and there aren't a ton of streetlights.

I need to get to someplace better lit, with a lot more people. I pull out my phone to help me navigate downtown and another text pops up.

Theo, 7:03 PM:

> Can you please fucking answer me?

"Crazy asshole," I mutter as I read the message.

"What is your problem today?"

I scream and spin around, finding Theo right behind me, looking down at me with a cold, polite smile and his arms crossed over his chest.

Fuck, he's quiet.

"Um, I didn't sleep well, and I'm not feeling like myself. I didn't mean to upset you. I'm sorry," I say, trying to keep my voice sweet and placating as I take a small step back from him. I can make this work, but I need him to not be angry with me. He sighs and cocks his head to the side a little, scrutinizing my face. Whatever he sees makes his expression soften into something concerned but still irritated.

"Well, I don't like being ignored *or* insulted, okay?"

"Okay," I say quietly, taking one more tiny step away from him.

"Let's get you inside."

"What are you talking about?" He frowns and hooks a thumb over his shoulder silently, and I look behind him at the large house visible through the trees.

There's no fucking way.

"Is that *your* house?"

He looks at me, puzzled. "Yeah, I sent you my address when you started walking. Did you seriously not read *any* of my texts?"

"My phone was on silent."

"Wait, so you weren't even *trying* to get here, and you still ended up here?" He looks extremely excited for some reason, which is probably bad.

"I guess so." Theo's whole demeanor softens, and he steps close to me, rubbing his hands over my shoulders and gripping me hard the second I try to pull away from him.

"Wow," he says softly, smiling at me. "Listen, let me pick you up next time, okay? I don't want you walking alone in the dark." He loops a tight arm around my shoulders and guides me towards the steep, tree-lined driveway at the end of the road towards a massive, well-kept Victorian. All the lights are on, giving the house an inviting air that feels wrong given the circumstances. The property looks out over the town and river, and the lights from the houses and ships and the bridge twinkle softly beneath us.

It's beautiful, and for just a minute, surprise washes away all of my fear.

"Dinner's going to take a while," he says apologetically as he leads me up the steps of the large wraparound porch before opening a front door with an ornate, leaded glass pane making up most of the center. The door opens into a narrow entryway with a living room on one side and a large staircase on the other, and Theo ushers me into the house, where I can hear soft French jazz drifting into the entryway from a brightly lit room down the hall.

Theo's house has dark wood walls with cream wallpaper, leaded glass panes in all the doors and windows, and mid-century-style furniture that looks brand new and completely out of place with the house's ornate wood paneling and picture rails and old-fashioned sconces. There are a few pieces of art, but they're impersonal, as though they're placeholders.

His house is spotless, but there are so few signs of life that it feels like it's been staged.

He closes the door and locks it behind him, looking down at me with direct and overwhelming eye contact, and all my panic returns in an instant.

I'm in his house.

It's just us here.

He's going to kill me.

"Shoes off, please," he says, slipping off his sneakers and placing them on a shoe rack by the door that I didn't notice. I follow his instructions, placing my tennis shoes next to his, and he takes my hand and pulls me into the large kitchen at the end of the hall. It's the most updated room in the house, with new appliances and a large island. It's as clean as the rest of the house, but between the cookbooks and the phone charger, it looks more lived-in.

Theo pulls out a stool at the island, and I sit as he starts rummaging in the fridge.

"Do you like coq a vin?" I stare at him blankly. "Alex?"

"Uh, I don't know." He frowns down at the bowl of marinated chicken in his hands.

"Well, it's got wine in it, so I figured it might go over well," he says. I can tell he's trying to joke, but it's sharp and forced. He walks close to me and pulls a bottle of red wine from a full wine rack and uncorks a bottle, pouring it slowly into a decanter sitting on the counter.

Who the fuck owns a *decanter*?

He catches me looking at it and flashes me a small smile. "I know you like wine, so I've been getting into it, too. I've got some pinot gris before dinner, if you want?" I nod. I probably shouldn't drink around him, but I'm pretty sure I'm going to die, so I don't see the harm.

He grabs a bottle from the fridge and pours me a glass, but when I don't take it right away, he shrugs and takes a long sip, refilling the glass and setting it before me. I watch him cook for a minute and then drink the whole glass at once, not tasting it at all. It doesn't help my nerves, so I pour another one to the brim and start drinking quickly.

We're quiet as he focuses on cooking, Theo humming to the music as the kitchen starts to smell of bacon and butter and chicken. He smiles at me tightly as he catches my eye.

"How was your day, sweetheart?"

"Um, long. I'm tired."

He frowns a little. "Do you get insomnia often?"

"Uh, no, not really."

"Okay, well, *please* don't take that Ambien that Suzie gave you, okay? You shouldn't take it if you drink." He looks between the bottle and the wine glass in my hand, surprised. "Especially with how *much* you drink," he mutters. I nod slowly, ignoring his passive-aggressive comment as I work through the second glass of wine and empty the bottle into the glass. I can *finally* feel the wine hitting me, and I realize I've had almost a whole bottle of wine on an empty stomach in less than half an hour.

Whatever. If I'm going to die, I'd like to experience it as little as possible.

"Why couldn't you sleep?"

I snort, and I can't filter myself in time. "Some crazy asshole broke into my house and raped me," I snap. His head jerks up towards me, his eyes wide.

"Alexandria, what the *fuck* are you talking about?" I choke out a laugh. Is he seriously this delusional?

"It was *you*," I say, drawing the words out. Theo's face goes from horrified to angry.

"That is fucking *bullshit*," he snaps as he walks towards the island, leaning close to me. "First, I have keys, so I didn't break in. Second, you *loved* the sex." My cheeks burn, and his face slowly turns from angry to somewhat relieved. "Third, please stop insulting me. I don't fucking like it." He grabs my wine and starts drinking it as he retreats to the stove, removing the chicken from the large pan with an incredulous, frustrated look. "I don't understand why you would fucking say that," he mutters, shaking his head.

"Because that's what happened." I know I shouldn't push, but if I'm going to die, I'd rather die being honest for once. He looks over at me, shocked and concerned as he stares at me intently.

"Say that again. Right now."

"That's what *happened*," I say slowly, and Theo's eyebrows quirk together a little. He blinks, his face becoming intensely focused.

"What's your full name?"

I frown at him, confused. "What does that have to do with anything?"

"Answer the question."

I roll my eyes. "Alexandria Marie Shearer." He blinks quickly, his head tilting to the side just a little.

"Where are you from?"

"Bangor, Maine."

"Did you like the sex?" Heat creeps into my face.

"*No.*" He smirks a little, leaning against the counter and crossing his arms, suddenly more relaxed.

"Oh, so you *didn't* like getting tied up and forced to come? That's not something you're into?" he teases, and I go cold immediately.

"No."

Theo looks amused. "Uh-*huh*." His smile fades, and his brows knit together as he considers me momentarily. "Alex, do you honestly think I raped you?"

"You fucking *did*," I snap. His eyes narrow at me before the tension bleeds out from his shoulders.

"Jesus, Alex, come on," he says, rolling his eyes before looking back at me with interest. "Would you have liked it if I had? Is that why you're pushing this?"

"*What*? No, you fucking *freak*." He watches me closely when I speak and his eyes widen, his lips quirking at the corners in amusement.

"Okay, *got it*. I don't think I'm into that, but I'm happy to accommodate you," he says as he turns back towards the stove.

What the fuck is he talking about?

We're silent as he finishes cooking and washes his hands, leaning against the sink and staring at me contemplatively as he dries his hands.

"Dinner's going to take a while. Why don't we go hang out in the living room?" The wine swims through my head, and the first thing I think pops out of my mouth.

"Oh, are you going to rape me *there*?"

He looks surprised. "Sweetie, do you want to do this *right now*? We can watch TV or something." I cross my arms and glare at him, feeling the full force of the bottle of wine washing over me.

"It's not like *I* get to choose, *right*?" Theo grimaces slightly before shrugging.

"Whatever you want, Alex." He's across the kitchen in a few long strides, grabbing my arm hard and pulling me down the hall to the living room. Panic starts to cut through my drunken haze, and I try to pull away from him, but he's much stronger than I am. He yanks me close, looming over me and pulling my arms behind my back, both my wrists gripped in one of his hands. I struggle to get my breathing under control as he undoes his belt with one hand and pulls it off quickly. I flinch when it makes a snapping sound, panic making my body lock up and I slam my eyes shut.

Did I seriously fucking push him to do this?

"Stop," I plead, but he doesn't listen to me as he grabs me, spinning me around and shoving me forward across the arm of the couch. He ties my wrists with the belt, cinching it so tightly that the leather bites into my skin. I whimper in pain as he fists my hair in his hand and pulls my head back, my back arching towards him.

"Theo, please." He shoves the skirt of my dress up and pushes my thong to the side, and he laughs a little as he slips two fingers inside of me easily. My face flushes. I don't understand why I'm so wet. His fingers slide out of me, and I shake my head as I hear him undoing his pants.

"Please stop," I beg, and he releases my hair, his arm slipping across my throat and pulling me back into him as he shoves inside of me, bottoming out in one rough thrust. I scream, trying to struggle but unable to move as he starts thrusting, choking me slightly with the crook of his elbow as he grips my ass with his other hand.

"Doesn't feel like you want me to stop," he growls into my ear as he thrusts into me mercilessly. I gasp as a rush of heat floods down my spine, and I bite back a moan as his hand slips up my body to cup my breast.

What is happening? I don't understand why this feels so good. Do I *like* this? Why the fuck would I like this? What is wrong with me? I start to cry, confused and terrified and unwillingly turned on.

"You look so pretty when you cry for me," he whispers. I shut my eyes against his voice and the feel of him. I can't be into this. I can't like feeling overpowered like this. I can't like the way my body feels. I can't enjoy the sounds he's making. This is so fucked up.

I panic as my leg starts to tense up and the heat in my spine builds.

"See? You fucking want it, you little liar." There's no way this is happening. There's no way I like this. I'm not about to let myself come from getting raped.

"Stop! *Stop*! Please stop, *please*," I sob, and Theo freezes. His hand comes to my jaw, tilting my face up and back towards him. I whimper in discomfort. My shoulders hurt from my arms being tied behind me and being pulled backward off the couch by Theo, and looking up at him makes my back bow farther and my shoulders hurt worse. His grip is gentle on my jaw, and his face is concerned as he looks at me.

"Do you *actually* want to stop? I can't tell," he says, his voice a low whisper. I'm so shocked that I stop crying, blinking up at him in confusion.

I don't understand what's happening.

"Yes," I whisper. Theo looks at me for a second, his eyes dropping to my lips, and then he grins.

"*Right*," he says, drawing out the vowel and rolling his eyes a little before the arm around my throat tightens and the hand on my jaw covers my mouth as he thrusts into me hard. I scream, hearing his soft laugh in my hair. "Shut the fuck up and take it," he says, his voice low and harsh as he drives into me. My eyes roll back from the sensation and the lack of air as his arm tightens around my throat further, and traitorous heat pools in my core again.

I feel so helpless and overwhelmed that I start to cry again. I don't want to come for him, don't want my body to like this, and I start shaking my head as much as I can.

"No, no, *no*," I mumble under his hand as the pressure builds in my body until I can't take it anymore.

"You're going to come for me," he whispers, moving his hand off my mouth to start circling my clit hard, "whether you want to or not." My eyes go wide, and I start unraveling beneath him, the tension in my spine snapping quickly and pleasure flooding my body, whimpers and moans slipping from my mouth.

"*Fuck yes*," he says under his breath, his hips snapping into me hard. He swears as he comes, the arm around my throat slipping down across my shoulders, his hand gripping my arm hard. My body slumps forward as he finally drops his arm, and I groan from the pain in my upper back and the feeling of emptiness as he pulls out of me.

My orgasm washes away my ability to fully understand what's happening, and everything seems hazy as I lie across the arm of the couch. At some point, my wrists are unbound, and my arms fall to my sides. My body feels limp and my brain feels like mush as Theo gently pulls me off the arm of the couch and into his arms, pushing my skirt down around my legs. He grabs a blanket off the back of the sofa and wraps it around me, kissing my hair as he holds me against him. I stare into the empty fire grate, warmth and tingling numbness coursing across my skin. Theo holds me close, his fingers trailing along my skin and his lips buried in my hair, praising me for being so good for him, for taking it so well, for doing such a good job.

I hate to admit it, but it feels nice.

The other part felt nice, too, but I don't understand why.

I *never* liked it when Danny did it.

I barely even felt it when Danny did it, I just pretended it wasn't happening. I didn't want to pretend it wasn't happening with Theo, but I don't know why not.

I don't understand why Theo seemed concerned about me at one point. Danny never fucking noticed me.

I sit there, staring into space, too confused to be scared. I feel Theo's knee start bouncing against my leg, and I see out of the corner of my eye that he keeps looking down at me with a concerned expression, but he keeps stroking my skin and saying sweet things, which makes me feel less numb.

I settle back into my body just as a phone alarm goes off in his back pocket.

"Sweetheart, I need to go check on dinner. Are you okay?" I look up at him, and his face is momentarily concerned, but whatever he sees on my face makes him smirk. "Oh, you're *definitely* okay." He kisses my forehead and stands up, settling me back on the couch. I sit there dazed and not fully present while he does something in the kitchen. I struggle to think as I hear him moving around the kitchen and dining room, but every thought is like water in my hands.

He's gentle with me when he comes back into the room to lead me into the dining room, where the table is set with plates of fragrant food and glasses of water and wine. He pulls my chair out and kisses my temple as I sit. I look up at him smiling softly at me, and then back down at the food. The chicken smells divine, but I don't touch it.

"Is this drugged?" He looks taken aback and lets out a startled laugh.

"Jesus, of course not." I watch him start to eat and then cut off a small piece of chicken and spear a mushroom and place it tentatively into my mouth, surprised at how good it is. The food grounds me a little, and I have some of the meager amount of red wine in the glass in front of me, which grounds me more. I wait for a minute or two, pushing food around on my plate, and when I don't feel drugged, I eat another bite.

The more I'm grounded back in my body, the more stressed I am, and the less of an appetite I have. I put the utensils down, catching Theo staring at me with this weird, focused look.

"Don't you like it?" I blink at him for a second before the first thing I think spills out of my mouth.

"It's a good last meal, I guess." Theo looks startled before his face breaks into a grin.

"I didn't know you had such a dark sense of humor." I shrug and don't eat any more, which he frowns at. "Are you *seriously* not hungry? You haven't eaten all day." I cut another small piece of chicken and eat it to appease him. I'm *not* hungry, but he seems weird about food.

We eat in silence for a while as I attempt to figure out what I'm supposed to do here. He's going to kill me, but my mind is blurry from the wine and the sex, and I'm too tired to play along or even care that much.

"Why are you doing this?"

Theo shrugs. "I know we were supposed to do this Wednesday, but you didn't eat anything today, and I thought making you dinner would be nice." I frown at the earnest look on his face.

Does he seriously think I'm talking about dinner?

"Why are you *stalking* me, Theo?" His mouth tightens and his jaw clenches as his expression closes off.

"Alexandria, I know this weekend was tough and it didn't really go how I thought it would, but we're together now, so please stop being rude to me. Also, you came here tonight, okay?"

Oh my god, he's insane.

"Why did you rape me?" Theo grimaces and looks away from me as he sips his wine.

"Can we please keep that one in the bedroom? It makes me uncomfortable." I stare at him, my eyes wide, and a small lash of anger cuts through the haze in my mind.

"Oh, does being called a rapist hurt your feelings or something?" He looks at me with confusion before his eyes widen in horror.

"We're on the same page, right?" he asks slowly, his voice strained.

"What *page*?" His eye twitches slightly, and he takes a long, deep breath as he gets out of his chair and crosses over to mine, getting in my space and pushing me back against the high back of the chair, his expression serious and his voice quiet.

"You're starting to worry me, so I need you to stop lying and playing games. Tell me if you wanted it. *Now.*" He's watching me intently, and I look away from him, embarrassed.

"I *didn't* want that." He exhales harshly and turns away from me.

"Jesus fucking Christ, Alexandria," he hisses, leveling me with a stern look as he sits back in his chair. "Don't scare me like that. That's fucked up, honestly." I blink at him, stunned.

"What is *wrong* with you?"

"Well, my girlfriend sucks at boundaries, for one thing," he says under his breath as he grabs his wine glass. Anger floods through me and I have to keep from throwing something at him.

"I'm not your fucking *girlfriend*!"

Theo raises his eyebrows in surprise. "Okay," he says slowly. "It's new. We can wait on labels, I guess."

"You're fucking insane!"

"Don't talk to me like that," he snaps.

"Why not? You're just going to kill me!" His face flashes with shock.

"Are you fucking *serious*? I would *never* hurt you. You don't need to be afraid of me, Alex." He seems so earnest and hurt that I laugh at him.

"You're a great liar."

"Oh, *Jesus fucking Christ*," he hisses, snatching up the abandoned plates and leaving the room.

I stay in the dining room while Theo tidies the kitchen, drinking more wine and staring at the wall, trying hard to think. If he's serious about this boyfriend delusion, maybe he's not going to kill me tonight. Maybe I can get out of here and regroup.

When he returns to the dining room, the decanter is empty and I'm pretty drunk. Theo leans against the doorway, eyeing me critically and frowning when he sees all the wine is gone.

"Let's get you to bed. It's been a long day, and you've had a *lot* to drink, which explains your fucking behavior," he mutters. I try to keep my face neutral and not roll my eyes at him for being so fucking passive-aggressive. He's still acting like a pissed-off boyfriend, not a murderer, so I think I have a chance.

"Um, thanks for dinner, but I'm going to go. I have work tomorrow, and all my stuff is at home." Theo sighs and comes towards me, grabbing my hand and pulling me out of the chair.

"You have stuff here, and we can swing by your place for your bag tomorrow." He pulls me up the narrow staircase and down a long hallway to a large bedroom with a king-sized bed and a small fireplace. I notice there are no personal effects, no photos, nothing indicating someone lives here. Just like downstairs, it's so neat it seems staged, and that takes up all the limited space in my drunk, overwhelmed brain.

"Did you just move in?" His mouth twitches into a quick frown.

"Kinda. I grew up here, but I just moved back two months ago."

"Why aren't there any photos?"

He shrugs. "They're in storage, I think. I haven't finished unpacking." His smile is tight as he leads me to a bathroom down the hall. "Why don't you get ready for bed? I'll lay out some clothes for tomorrow." He closes me into a large bathroom with a clawfoot tub, and I focus on my breathing.

The medicine cabinet is small but tidy, everything facing label out. There's a small shelf filled with unopened skincare products from a brand I used religiously when I lived in Boston, a large glass bottle of a perfume I love, two expensive electric toothbrushes, toothpaste, a heavy silver safety razor, a small bottle of shaving cream, and not much else. I ignore the skincare and perfume and brush my teeth for a long time, not looking at myself in the mirror.

How long has this been going on for him?

As I walk back into the empty bedroom, I keep my eyes down, noticing a small pile of clothes on the dresser and a short, silky nightgown lying across the bed. I don't want to accept things from him, but I *really* don't want to sleep naked with him. I put on the nightgown and crawl into bed, sitting up against the headboard and wrapping my arms around my knees, waiting. Theo comes in a few minutes later with a glass of water and two pills, offering them to me. I look at the pills and shake my head quickly, and he rolls his eyes.

"It's fucking ibuprofen," he mutters, popping one in his mouth and taking a sip of water. I watch him for a minute before taking the other from him and draining the glass of water. Theo leaves the room, and I can hear him brushing his teeth. I lie on my back and close my eyes, fighting off tears.

I thought getting away from Danny would be enough to keep me safe, but I was wrong. I know what's coming next, so I'll choose to let it happen. I was right to drink that much, because being drunk makes everything easier. It always has.

The lights go off, and the mattress dips as Theo gets in bed next to me, leaning over me and cupping my face in his hand before kissing me gently. I flinch and don't kiss him back, but I will my body to stay relaxed.

Theo will probably kill me during sex, so it's going to be easier if I'm relaxed.

He pulls away with a displeased sound. "Can we talk about the flinching?" I keep my eyes closed but scoff at him a little. "Alex, look at me," he begs, his voice pleading. I open my eyes to see him hovering over me, his face concerned. "Sweetheart, please talk to me." I'm so exhausted and don't have the energy to play along, so I roll my eyes at him.

"Just do it," I say, my voice flat.

I watch as his face moves from concern to confusion. "*What*?"

"Just kill me already." A horrified expression creeps across his face.

"What the *fuck*?" He stops touching me immediately and rolls onto his back, sighing hard, his hands scrubbing over his face and back through his hair. I don't say anything as I look up at the ceiling, focusing on a long, thin crack in the plaster. We lie there in silence, listening to a ship's horn blare in the distance. After a long moment, one of his hands finds mine under the blanket, and I flinch as he twines our fingers together.

"Alex, I'm never going to hurt you, I *promise*. We're adjusting, and part of that is learning to trust each other. It'll be so much easier once you trust me," he says softly. I slip my hand out of his and turn away from him, curling into a ball and shoving my emotions down so I can think.

He's delusional, but he wants to think he won't hurt me, which means I can push until I figure out the boundaries of his delusion and then find a way out. I'm smart, and I can make this work if I'm careful. I can get through this, whatever the fuck *this* is, the way I used to – minute by minute, hour by hour, day by day.

And then, when I can, I'll fucking run.

16

THEO

WEDNESDAY, SEPTEMBER 27

I lay in bed reeling, listening to Alex's breathing even out and focusing on a long, thin crack in the plaster on the ceiling.

I'll add that to the endless list of things I need to fix.

I have no idea why this isn't going the way it should. She keeps misinterpreting everything I do and acting like she can't feel how connected we are. Maybe she *can't* feel it, or maybe she can, and she's just lying to herself. She seems to be *really* good at that.

This is so different than I thought it was going to be.

I turn to my side and pull her into my arms slowly, slipping an arm under her pillow and curling my body around hers. She relaxes out of the tight ball she sleeps in and pushes back into me, and I breathe a sigh of relief into her hair. She can't lie to herself when she's asleep, at least. I kiss her shoulder softly and hold her a little tighter, syncing my breath to hers to help calm myself down.

I might have overestimated how well I got to know her, because she's *so* different than I thought she was. She's guarded and seemingly incapable of opening up, and sensitive in a way I didn't expect. She's kind of an alcoholic. She's got such insane trust issues that she thinks I'm going to *kill* her. She barely seems to understand affection, and keeps flinching any time I touch her, unless we're having sex. I know it's not about me, but it's hurtful, not to mention concerning.

I definitely underestimated what a liar she is.

I know Alex was lying through her fucking teeth about the rape thing, but she seemed insistent about it, almost like she needed to believe that's what happened. I get that she's into that, but I didn't like it. I'm still slightly worried we're not on the same page, so that shit's off the table until she can communicate better.

I think *sex* is entirely off the table for the time being. I know she loves the sex, but that doesn't matter anymore. I think I underestimated how bad her marriage was, so I think we shouldn't have any sex *she* doesn't initiate. Her motivations for initiating might be complicated to figure out, so probably not until she's begging for it. That's going to suck, but I want her to know that this is a good relationship and that she can trust me.

Alex rolls over in my arms, and I roll to my back, pulling her close. She slings one of her arms across my chest and makes a low, content sound, and I feel the hum of our connection radiating through me.

I know I'm right about us. I didn't expect I'd have to work so hard to get *her* to see it, but that's fine. This is an adjustment period.

I have to adjust, too.

***

I give Alex a day to herself. She acts fine when other people are around, but the second she's alone, she seems scattered, and she's so exhausted that she leaves her fitness class early. No matter how much I text her, she won't even look at her phone.

She goes to trivia with her friends, and I watch her from the bar across the street as she drinks too much on an empty stomach. I follow her home, horrified that she's walking home alone at night while fucking drunk.

Does she have a death wish?

Wednesday starts the same, and I can't stand it. I catch her on her walk home from work, falling in step with her after a few blocks. Her face falls the second she sees me, and my heart sinks.

"Hey, sweetheart," I say, keeping my tone light and pretending like nothing's wrong as I steer her in the direction of my house. "How was your day?"

"It *was* going well."

"Uh, how was Pilates?" I know she didn't go, and she knows that I know that.

She shrugs. "It was fine."

"Sure. What do you want for dinner?"

"Does it matter?" she snaps. "*You're* dieting me, so *you* fucking choose." I stop short and stare at her incredulously, but she keeps walking.

"Hang on," I call out, catching up to her quickly. "What the fuck are you talking about?"

She barks out a sharp, bitter laugh as we walk up my driveway. "I'm not stupid, Theo. I looked at the food you made me. You obviously did the math on what I roughly burn in a day, and if I eat all the food you're making in the portions you're serving, the calories are pretty close to maintenance. I assume you'll start lowering them slowly until I'm in enough of a deficit to start losing weight." She shrugs, and I stare at her, appalled. I did *not* think she'd notice that I did the math, but I only did it to make sure she's eating enough. She hasn't eaten almost anything in the last week, and I'm worried about her.

One of us has to be.

"I'm concerned about your eating, maybe, but I'm not fucking *dieting* you." She snorts as I usher her into the house, shooting me a dirty look.

"Thanks for the concern, *mom*, but I'm going to eat whatever I want to."

"That would mean you'd need to *eat*, Alex. Coffee is not a meal."

"If you're not dieting me, then why do you keep cooking for me? Is it a weird sex thing?" I shrug, keeping my face neutral to hide my shock. Did her husband seriously never cook her dinner?

"I like to cook. That's it." She eyes me suspiciously as I herd her into the kitchen.

"So, you don't care what I eat?"

I grimace. "Not really, but I'd prefer you eat a home-cooked meal with actual nutrients in it."

She gives me a skeptical look. "So, you just want to cook for me all the time because you like cooking?"

"Yeah."

She crosses her arms, leaning against the counter. "And you expect me to believe that?"

"It's the truth," I say, trying to smile at her. We stare at each other for a long second, her eyes narrowing at me slightly.

"Fine. I want cheesecake for dinner."

"That's a dessert." She raises her eyebrows, and it takes me a second to realize this is a test. I shrug and open the fridge, looking through what I have. She's being so combative. I know she's adjusting poorly, but does she have a temper in general? I can't imagine her having a temper, but I'm realizing that there's a lot I don't know about her. I close the fridge and start herding her towards the entryway.

"We're leaving."

"Why?"

"I don't have cream cheese." She gives me a weird look, like she wasn't expecting me to do what she wanted.

***

I take her to the co-op and grab graham crackers, cream cheese, raspberries, and whatever else I need, but I get sidetracked by lamb shanks.

"Sweetheart, do you like osso buco?" She shrugs, so I buy the ingredients anyway. I try to keep from asking the next question, but I can't help it. "Why would you think I'm dieting you?" I ask in a quiet voice.

"You think we're in a relationship, right?" I stare at her, confused.

"We *are* in a relationship, but so what?" She blinks back at me, also seemingly confused.

"*So,* you think that means you get to tell me what I should weigh and how I should look." I stare at her, reeling. "I'm not doing that again, so you might as well just kill me now." A woman passing down the aisle eyes Alex with concern.

"I'm *not* going to kill you. You do realize that's not normal, right?"

"What?"

"What you're saying. That's *insane,* not to mention fucking abusive." She raises her eyebrows at me in surprise. "That's not what's happening here."

"Uh-huh." Her tone is still skeptical.

"I mean it when I say I just like to cook, and I don't care what you look like. I mean, you're fucking gorgeous, but I think you'd be gorgeous no matter what."

She scoffs. "Yeah, *right.*"

I wince slightly. What the *fuck* was her marriage like?

***

Alex frowns while she watches me cook, seeming shocked when I make the cheesecake she asked for. She eats half a slice of it slowly, looking at me like I'm insane when I ask her what she likes to eat so I can start meal planning for us. She gives noncommittal answers and makes another shitty comment about me dieting her, but that's fine. I'll figure it out. I can adjust the food I make and how I portion it, so she doesn't feel like she's being scrutinized or dieted.

I refuse to adjust to the fact that Alex does not seem to like me or trust me at *all,* because I know this fucking works.

It will, anyway, once she stops fighting it.

She seems confused when I make us tea and put on *Sleepless in Seattle.* I know she likes it, so I thought it would make her comfortable to see that I like it. I don't, actually, but I act like I do. Alex relaxes enough to start joking about the movie, and she tells me halfway through that it's her least favorite Nora Ephron film, and that she sort of hates it.

I relax a little. She's opening up to me, and we're more similar than I thought. This is working.

She's *very* confused when I don't initiate sex. I can't help that it's obvious how much I want her, but I ignore it and hold her in my arms, focusing on syncing my breath to hers. It takes her a long time to relax, but once she falls asleep, she melts into me the way she only does when she's sleeping.

The next morning, I greet her with a kiss, ignoring that goddamn fucking flinch of hers. She keeps giving me these wary looks over breakfast, but she eats most of the omelette I make her. When I drop her off at work, I'm sweet to her and pretend everything is fine before I go home and do everything in my power to keep my shit together.

I just need to focus on the small list of things that are working rather than the laundry list of things I have to fix.

My phone chimes, and I almost drop it when I see the texts from Alex.

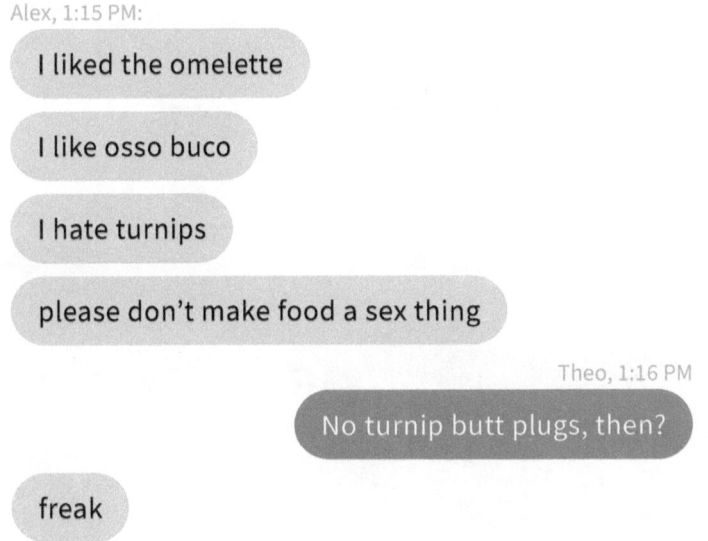

Alex, 1:15 PM:

I liked the omelette

I like osso buco

I hate turnips

please don't make food a sex thing

Theo, 1:16 PM

No turnip butt plugs, then?

freak

I grin down at my phone, feeling lighter. We're joking around. This is finally going in the right direction, and I just need to keep working for it.

I didn't realize it would be so much goddamn work, but I know the extent of her trust issues now, and I know I need to work a lot harder to earn her trust. I'll do whatever it takes, because Alex is worth it.

She's mine whether she likes it or not, but I want her to like it.

17

ALEX

SATURDAY, OCTOBER 7

Theo and I have reached a weird detente where he pretends we're dating, and I pretend that I'm not afraid of him. I'm still sure he's going to kill me, but I can't keep living in fear every moment of my life, so I do my best to ignore my feelings and pretend nothing is wrong.

I spend my days at work trying to think about how to get out of the trap he's set, but it seems impossible. Bailey and Catherine don't seem to notice that anything's wrong, but I think Suzie can tell. She's asked me out to lunch more than once in the last two weeks, but I keep finding reasons to put it off. I don't want to ask her for more help until I figure out what type of help I need, or if Theo's a danger to anyone else.

He's a danger to me, even if he seems to buy his own lie that he won't hurt me. I know it's bullshit, but his insistence means I can push him hard enough to figure out the boundaries of his delusion.

So far, I've found that anything that challenges his delusion is either ignored or twisted to suit it.

He does *not* like being called a stalker. He hates that I flinch when he touches me. He likes it if I'm nice to him or if I act domestic with him in any way. He seems to be able to tell when I'm lying and doesn't like it. Any time he notices anything about us that seems similar or complementary, he seems really excited.

Those moments are concerning because they seem to drive him deeper into the delusion, and they happen *often*.

Since he thinks we're dating, I mostly see him before and after work. He texts me during the day, but I've found that acknowledging a few texts throughout the day makes him likely to text less. There's no point in trying to avoid him. I don't tell him where I'm going, but I'm no longer surprised when he shows up.

He *always* shows up.

My biggest concern is that he's stopped having sex with me. He touches me, he kisses me, he holds me in bed, but he doesn't fuck me. I can tell he wants to, but he doesn't, and it makes me nervous. I don't want to initiate sex and play into his delusion that we're together, but I'm concerned that if we don't start having sex soon, he's going to change his mind about hurting me.

I won't initiate sex, but if I did, it would just be to make sure he didn't hurt me.

No other reason.

***

Theo's up early, making me breakfast and rifling through my things. I try to ignore him and go back to sleep, but the smell of coffee and bacon makes it hard. Once I give up and get out of bed, I see he's in a good mood, smiling at me and buzzing around the kitchen, telling me he has plans for us this weekend.

He might kill me.

He might fuck me.

He's definitely going to cook for me.

I doubt it'll be anything else.

We spend the day driving down the coast, listening to the classical station on the radio. I haven't been down the coast that much since I don't have a car, and it's beautiful. It's different from Cape Cod, with large cliffs visible down the shoreline and craggy rocks jutting up through the water off the coast. It's cold and overcast, a soft drizzle turning the beaches a dark grey.

The first beach we go to is particularly windy, and Theo pulls a slim red puffer jacket out of the trunk of his car for me. He says it's an ex-girlfriend's and that I can borrow it, but it's new and it's my size. I let him lie and I take it, grateful to have it.

The beach looks familiar, even though I've never been here before. Theo tells me it's where they filmed The Goonies, and I laugh, telling him my dad loved that movie. I get quiet for a moment, a sharp pang of grief piercing through me, and Theo seems to register that I've used the past tense.

I wonder, not for the first time, how much he knows about my life in Boston.

He walks close to me but doesn't touch me, waiting for a while before he starts in on his normal bullshit of asking me questions about myself. I give him short, vague answers, and when he asks something I don't want to talk about, I redirect the question to him instead. He gives me a knowing look when I do it, but he plays along anyway.

I don't like showing interest in him, but I need to get to know him better to deal with him. I've been trying to ask him about himself more lately, but for all his expecting me to be open, he's cagey in his own answers. Most of them are so vague that I'm sure he's lying about pretty much everything. By the time we get back to the car, the only new thing I've learned about him is that his dad also died when he was a kid.

We keep driving down the coast, and I watch the scenery pass by in silence. Theo seems relaxed, which is new. When I met him at the bar and again at my office, he seemed laid-back, but in reality, he's very high-strung. He seems calmer today, more like before, which makes me feel less nervous around him.

I know it's a mistake to get comfortable with him, but I can't help it.

After a couple of hours, we pull into a small town and park along the two-lane highway, which serves as the main street through town. Theo grabs two pairs of binoculars from the trunk, and we walk down to a lookout point with a squat, concrete building. He hands me the binoculars, standing behind me and pointing out seals on rocks, and birds, and boats in the distance.

It's beautiful.

Theo swears excitedly at one point and turns my head slightly, directing my sight farther out into the water. I'm amazed as I see the slick back of a whale push up slightly from the water, another following a second later. I see the very tips of their tails break the surface, and I'm awestruck for a moment.

"Oh my *god*," I whisper as I lean forward. I try to follow them, but they don't surface again. I pull the binoculars down and look over at Theo, finding myself blushing at how he's looking at me with open affection.

"Have you ever seen whales before?" I shake my head, and he grins. "This time of year can be iffy, so I'm glad they were here." I smile at him for just a second, then look away quickly when I realize what I'm doing, training my binoculars back out on the water. We stay there for a while, waiting to see if any other whales appear, and I berate myself silently for letting my guard down for a second.

Theo puts the binoculars back in the car before leading me down a little path by the whale-watching building to a cluster of tide pools. I'm able to forget the situation entirely for a moment as I peer down into the pool, and nothing exists to me outside of the slow march of a sea star across the rocks until I hear a camera shutter. I look up in horror at Theo, phone in hand.

"Delete that, *now*," I snap. Theo seems taken aback.

"It's just a photo." I debate with myself for a second, figuring out if I want to push it, but my anxiety wins out.

"Theo, *please*. I don't want any photos of me taken, *ever*," I beg. He considers me, frowning for a moment before he unlocks his phone and hands it over. He's got one photo in his camera roll, and it's me crouched down on the rocks, looking into the tidepool. I almost feel bad when I delete it, but I can't risk it.

"No photos, I promise," he says quietly as he slips the phone out of my hands, being careful not to touch me. When I look up at him, he seems earnest, and I nod at him, feeling a little too vulnerable.

PERFECT

We stay there for a while, Theo mostly watching me, occasionally pointing out something that he thinks I'll want to see, and trying to keep me from slipping on the rocks in my sneakers. Things feel less awkward eventually, and he seems excited by how much I'm enjoying myself.

"I thought you might like this, but I didn't know you'd be so into it." I shrug, squatting down to watch a cluster of anemones sway gently.

I shrug. "I loved tidepooling as a kid." He crouches down next to me close enough that our shoulders brush together, and I can see out of the corner of my eye that he's looking at me.

"Me, too," he says softly.

"Thanks for bringing me," I say, trying hard not to look at him.

"Yeah, of course. There's a million places on the coast, and we can go whenever you want."

I want to do that, just not with him.

When it starts to get dark, he helps me back up the steep path and leads us back to the car. When I try the handle, the door is still locked, and I look up at Theo, suddenly nervous.

"Can we go back now?" He shakes his head, and my stomach sinks.

"Uh, we're not going back to Astoria," he says slowly, and panic shoots through me.

He fucking *kidnapped* me, of course he did. Maybe he's going to murder me here.

"I thought it'd be nice for us to have a weekend away, so I rented us a house down here. I booked a whale-watching tour for tomorrow, too." His voice is quiet, and he seems almost shy when he looks at me.

I think this still technically counts as kidnapping, but I don't think most kidnappers do things like this. I don't know whether to be anxious or touched, but I'm kind of both.

"Um, okay. That sounds...good?" He smiles, one side of his mouth picking up a little more than the other, and he seems relieved.

***

159

The house Theo rented is tiny, with wood-paneled walls and rooms decorated with tacky beach-themed items, but the back deck and the master bedroom overlook the beach, and we can hear the ocean in every room. We drop our things off and walk down the path to the beach, not talking much, but the silence is somewhat comfortable.

For a moment, it feels like I'm on a weekend trip with someone I'm dating, but I push the feeling away.

That's probably what he thinks this is.

Dinner is nice, mostly. The clam chowder we have is good, but not as good as what I'm used to, which Theo finds hard to believe. I remind him that New England clam chowder is best in New England, and he shakes his head at me and tells me that for someone who's supposed to be from Maine or North Carolina, I seem to have spent a *lot* of time in Cape Cod. I shrug and tell him my grandmother lived in Hyannis, which is true.

When he asks me more about my grandparents, I say very little and ask him about his, and he says very little back. We deflect each other's questions for the rest of dinner, and it almost becomes a game of who can reveal nothing while saying something.

I think he's slightly better at it than I am.

After dinner, we go back to the house and we sit out on the porch wrapped up in thick blankets, drinking wine and listening to the waves. He's back to asking me things, inane things, things that are too personal, seemingly anything that comes to mind. I've had enough wine that I give him slightly longer answers and deflect slightly less than earlier. I even ask him more questions about himself, and he seems to give me more honest answers.

I learn we have similar tastes in movies. When I mention an old Cary Grant movie my mom loved, he gets excited and tells me it was one of his grandma's favorites, and we find we both watched it a lot growing up. When it gets too cold and rainy to stay on the porch, we head inside, and he finds the movie on a streaming platform.

We sit on the couch, close but not touching, drinking hot tea and watching it together.

It's comfortable.

When we go to bed, I'm *positive* he's going to fuck me, but he doesn't. He lies on his side, his head propped in one hand while his other hand trails slowly up and down my waist under the covers, and we just talk. I try not to make eye contact with him, but I can't help it. He's kind of magnetic.

He's being chatty and sweet, pushing my hair behind my ear and telling me I'm beautiful, smiling wide enough that his faint dimples show, and as we lay there, it's kind of hard to remember he's my stalker who's going to kill me.

Sometimes, for a few minutes at a time, it seems like he's just the cute guy I met at that bar.

The bar he stalked me to.

Right.

Stalker.

When we finally go to sleep, he pulls my back flush against his chest, and I lie there with his arms around me, listening to the ocean. I try to ignore how nice it is to be held, but it's hard. He feels so warm pressed against me, and he smells good, like soap and laundry detergent and something warm and familiar, somehow. I get tired quickly, and without thinking about it, I push back into him a little. He makes a content sound and kisses my shoulder as his arms tighten around me.

It feels too intimate.

When the alarm goes off early the next morning, I lean across him, fumbling for his phone. Once I get the alarm shut off, he wraps an arm around my waist and rolls me to my back, cupping my face with one hand and kissing me gently. I almost don't flinch, and I almost kiss him back.

This is kind of nice, honestly.

"Good morning, sweetheart," he says, his voice thick with sleep. "You want coffee?" I nod, fighting my urge to smile at him.

What is *wrong* with me?

***

161

We drink coffee down at the dock while we wait to board the boat. Theo's not asking me endless questions today, he's just quiet and relaxed, his posture loose. We don't talk much, mostly listening to the guide tell us about the wildlife and local history, and pointing our binoculars out into the water.

Theo occasionally points something out to me, but that's as much as we interact until a whale surfaces for a second, its large tail appearing and rising high out of the water. He swears softly at the same time I do, and I can't help laughing and smiling up at him after the whale disappears. He looks thrilled as he smiles back at me, and I look away from him quickly, hiding the blush I can feel heating my cheeks beneath my binoculars. I keep staring out into the water, enjoying the moment, and it takes me until he laces his fingers through mine as we're getting off the boat to realize that he got me to let my guard down.

Not only am I playing into his delusion, but he got me to join him in it for a minute.

Theo's a different kind of manipulative than I'm used to, and he's *really* good at it.

***

Once we're in the car, I lean my head against the window and close my eyes, tired from the early morning and the beers I had after the boat tour and everything that's happened since Theo broke into my house. It's only been two weeks, but it feels like it's been years.

The humming of the tires on the road is soothing, and the classical concerto coming from the radio is calming, so I start to drift. I flinch slightly when I feel Theo's hand rest gently on my knee, but I let it stay there, enjoying the warmth and the feel of his thumb gliding back and forth across my skin.

He gently shakes my knee a second later.

"Sweetheart? We're home." I open my eyes and look around, confused. We're at his house, so I must have slept the whole way here. His hand stays on my knee as he leans into me, and I can tell he wants to kiss me from the way he looks at my lips. I almost let him before I realize what's happening, and then I get out of the car quickly, hurrying towards the porch. He joins me, unlocking the door and holding it open for me.

"I think there's a Red Sox game on if you want to watch it while I make dinner. I was thinking of something light since lunch was pretty heavy. Do you want a glass of wine?" His voice is low and affectionate, and he seems so different to me right now, calm and at ease in a way that's new. I hum in agreement and walk into the living room, and he comes in with a glass of wine a minute later, our fingers brushing when he hands it to me. He smiles and kisses my forehead before he heads back to the kitchen to make us dinner.

I turn on the TV, raising the volume to cover the sound of my rapid breathing as I curl in on myself, starting to panic. I can't believe I'm this fucking stupid. I let my guard down with him this weekend, and I didn't even realize it until it was too late. This was the problem with Danny, too. Things would go well for a while, and I'd get complacent. Theo's trying to make this all seem normal to me, and he's doing an excellent job. The trap he's set for me is domestic and comfortable, but it's still a fucking trap.

Why am I even buying into his bullshit a little bit? Because I'm lonely? Because he's nice to me? Because I want to fuck him? God, I'm such an idiot. He's a terrifying, violent stalker who hijacked my entire life, and I can't get complacent and let my guard down with him again.

I can't risk letting him in.

18

THEO

SUNDAY, OCTOBER 8

I look over at Alex asleep in the passenger seat, relieved that this is *finally* going well. I think she's adjusting. I was right that not having sex is what she needed to open up to me, because Alex has been so warm towards me this weekend. The way she smiled at me this morning was *real*. It only lasted a second, but it happened.

I can't believe how badly I fucked this up from the start. If I'd just followed my goddamn plan, maybe this would have been a perfect weekend. Maybe she would have answered my questions instead of dancing around them. Maybe she would have curled up in my arms while we watched the movie. Maybe she would have smiled at me for longer than a second. Maybe she'd kiss me back. Maybe *this* would have been the right time for us to have sex.

I should have known better than to give in to my stupid impulses.

This is so different from the last time I felt connected to someone. Ashley and I worked *immediately*, and controlling my impulses with her was easy, at least until she left me. I can barely fucking control myself when it comes to Alex. My impulses are so different with her - they're stronger, and more possessive, and much harder to ignore.

I loved Ashley so much that I wound up in prison, and I didn't have nearly this level of connection with her.

That's a little scary to think about.

***

Alex is tired when I leave her in the living room, but she's still the same person I've had all weekend, the person I want her to be with me. When she walks into the kitchen for more wine, though, that person is gone. Her face is neutral, but she avoids making direct eye contact with me as she pours herself another glass of wine.

Goddammit, she's withdrawing from me.

"Dodgers are up," she says absently before heading back to the living room. I follow her, abandoning dinner.

"Sweetheart? Are you feeling okay?"

"Yeah, just tired." I watch her mouth when she speaks. She's not lying - she *is* tired, but I can tell that's not the whole truth. Does she know that I can tell when she's lying? That would make this harder.

"Um, okay. It's pretty early, but maybe you should go to bed."

"I'll just go home, actually," she says softly, not looking at me.

"Sure, we can go to your place after dinner." She raises her eyebrows at her wine glass and takes a long sip, gearing up to withdraw from me further.

"It would be nice to be alone tonight." I smile at her, trying to hide my displeasure. That's not going to fucking happen, but I don't want to tell her that.

I've learned that the more alone time she has, the more she withdraws from me, and letting her withdraw when things are going well is a bad idea. I want her to want what we were sharing this weekend.

The longer it takes me to answer, the more resigned her face gets.

"Never mind," she says quietly. "Let's go after dinner."

"Sounds good, sweetie," I say, heading back to the kitchen. I know I'm being an asshole, but I don't understand why she's pushing me away like this. She was *finally* opening up.

She keeps pushing me away all night. She barely talks to me and barely eats, but I don't say anything because she's sensitive about food.

She drinks, though, and the more she drinks, the more irritated she seems. When we get back to her place, she seems pissed that I'm there and snaps at me when I ask if she's okay, slamming the bedroom door in my face.

I'm working hard to keep my temper under control, but she's being a fucking brat.

Oh. *Oh?*

I turn the TV on, turn the volume up, and pull up the camera feeds. I watch as she undresses quickly, storming around her room and drawing herself a bath.

She knows I watch her and has been spending as little time naked as possible, but not today. Today, she's walking around her bedroom in nothing, even though her apartment is frigid. I force myself to stay on the couch, but my knee starts bouncing.

Not fucking Alex has been what she's needed to open up to me, but it's only been manageable because she hasn't seemed to want sex at all. When I watch her grab her vibrator and head into the bathroom, I know I have to leave immediately. I need to wait until she asks for it, but knowing she wants it and isn't asking is going to make it harder for me to control myself.

That's what got us into this fucking mess in the first place.

I walk into her bedroom and knock on the bathroom door gently, watching on the camera as she hears me but doesn't stop. I can hear the low buzz of the vibrator in the water through the door.

I think she *wants* to get caught.

I need to leave *now*.

"Sweetie, I'm going to head home, okay?" I watch on my phone as she drops her head back over the rim of the tub, closing her eyes. I can't keep watching this.

"I thought you were going to stay the night?" She sounds *so* hopeful. I slip my phone into my pocket and back away from the bathroom door. I need to get away from her.

"Um, no. *Please* text me if you need help coming, okay?" I call out over my shoulder as I force myself to leave her apartment.

"You have a camera in *here?* You fucking pervert!" I hear her shouting through the paper-thin walls as I hurry down the stairs and rush out of her building. By the time I'm home, she's in bed and trying again, and finally seems to be getting somewhere.

She *knows* I'm watching. Is *this* her asking?

Theo, 10:15 PM:

Do you need help?

Please say yes. I watch her flinch when she hears the text, and it seems to ruin it for her.

It's definitely not her asking.

She grabs the phone, puts it on silent, and starts again. She gets close, but after a few more minutes, both of us realize it's not going to happen for her.

She hasn't masturbated since we started dating, and I know she wants to have sex with me, but she's fucking stubborn. I don't want to have sex with her until she asks, which means my life is about to get a whole lot harder.

I *need* her to know that she can trust me.

As I watch her, I realize that I need her to trust me sooner rather than later. She's lying in bed under the covers, curled into a ball and shaking a little bit, crying so quietly that I can barely hear her. She's trying to hide it from me, and I'm starting to get concerned about her.

I wish she'd just let me in.

19

ALEX

TUESDAY, OCTOBER 10

Theo's taking everything away from me.

I can't come from masturbating anymore. Danny's voice isn't popping up, but every time I get close, I start thinking about Theo, and I refuse to come while thinking of him.

I have no desire to paint. I want to cry whenever I look at the paintings hung on my walls because I miss expressing myself. Theo's asked me why I stopped, but I can't tell him. It feels too personal.

Exercising is no longer a release since he's started joining me on my long runs and showing up at the track whenever I sprint. The only reason he doesn't take the fitness classes at the rec center with me is because he doesn't like them, but I know he's *watching* me.

He cooks every meal for me. He puts things away in my apartment where he thinks they should go. My planner, which I've started using again, is covered in red ink. I'm only alone if he wants me to be, and he really doesn't want me to be.

The only things I have left to myself are work and my friends, and it's only a matter of time before he ruins those, too.

***

I can't keep ducking Suzie forever, so I let her take me out to lunch. Since she hired me, I've been friendly but distant, and I'd like to keep it that way.

Suzie and I walk down to a brewery nearby that has good pizza, and when we order food, she orders a beer and winks at me, so I order one, too.

"The best part of being a lawyer in the eighties was the three martini lunches," she jokes. I force a smile. I used to have six martinis for lunch sometimes, but I don't think she needs to know that about me.

"How'd you get anything done?" Suzie taps the side of her nose, and I laugh.

"You're joking, right? This sounds like a bad stereotype." She shrugs, sipping her beer.

"Stereotypes occasionally have a basis in reality. I moved away from that a long time ago, though, so I'm not really sure what they do now." Suzie smiles and shrugs. "So, how are you settling in, Alex? We haven't had a chance to catch up lately." I fix a smile on my face. I can tell she's worried about me, but I can't tell her about Theo.

"I'm good. The apartment is working out, I have a routine, and I'm making friends. I love the job," I say, smiling warmly. That's not a lie. "I love Astoria, too. It's so different from B...where I'm from." Suzie blinks but otherwise doesn't seem to register that I almost revealed something personal. I smile again, and she smiles back, but hers is subdued.

"How are you doing? You've seemed a little on edge the last few weeks." I try to keep my face neutral, but over her shoulder, I watch Theo walk into the brewery.

"Uh, I'm good, honestly," I say, taking a sip of my beer to hide my expression. "I mean, not everything is perfect, you know? I'm still pretty nervous about being here sometimes. I don't want to be found." Her eyes widen the slightest bit, and I realize that Theo threw me off enough that I revealed something *very* personal about myself to Suzie, who now looks concerned.

I look briefly over her shoulder at where Theo is sitting at the bar, watching me with a somewhat blank expression. He's probably here to make sure I don't ask her for help.

Fuck him.

"Is it likely that you'll be found?" Suzie keeps her voice quiet, and I get time to collect myself before answering because our food arrives. I take a deep breath and try to act as normal as possible.

"Uh, maybe. I'm fine for the time being, but there's a lot of things I can't do." Why am I being so honest with her?

"You know that Catherine and I will do whatever we can to help, right? Bailey as well, I'm sure." I blink hard, looking away from her but nowhere near Theo.

"Thank you, Suzie. You've been so kind to me, really. I wouldn't have anything without your help." She waves a hand dismissively.

"Bullshit. You have you, and that's more than enough." I stare at her, taken aback, and she levels me with a serious look. "You can do anything you want to, Alex. You're free to live your own life now."

"Yeah," I say, feeling hollow. "Yeah, I guess you're right." She clinks her beer glass to mine, and we drink. I excuse myself to the bathroom quickly, holding back my tears until I'm locked in a stall, and then I cover my mouth to dampen the sounds of my quiet sobbing.

I can't afford for Suzie or Theo to see me this vulnerable, so I force myself to calm down and dry my face. I do my best to make it look like I haven't been crying, but it's obvious.

I'm not surprised to find Theo leaning against the wall outside the bathrooms. He cocks his head to the side and frowns when he sees me.

"Sweetheart, are you okay?" I stare at him, getting so frustrated I start tearing up again, and his face becomes concerned. "Alex, what's wrong? You can talk to me." He reaches out for me, and I shake my head and walk back to my table.

I apologize to Suzie, telling her that I just get a little emotional sometimes. She nods, looking concerned, but doesn't mention it.

When we leave, I lock eyes with Theo, who looks frustrated.

***

I'm at trivia that night with my friends, and Theo is at the bar, sipping a beer and watching me. First lunch with Suzie, and now this? I'm fucking livid.

I'm trying to pay attention to Jessica's story about her cousin that's studying in Italy, who got drunk in Venice and fell into a canal, but Theo's staring at me with this intense, watchful look, and it's hard not to be aware of him.

I need to drink a lot more to deal with him.

"I'm going to get another drink. Does anyone want anything?" I take a few orders, and Ben offers to help me carry them back, but I need to be alone to talk to Theo, so I politely decline.

At the bar, I stand just close enough to talk to Theo without looking like I know him.

"Hi, sweetheart. Are you having fun?"

"Why are you here?"

He shrugs. "I thought I'd make you dinner after trivia. Do you like salmon?" I'm dealing with a lunatic.

"I'm not hungry. Please leave."

"Why? I'd like to get to know your friends." I shoot him a dirty look, and he seems surprised.

"Absolutely *not*. *Don't* come here. *Don't* do this." He doesn't get to trap me and take everything away from me.

I'm not letting that happen again.

I take a deep breath, trying to calm down enough to try a different tactic. "I am *begging* you, Theo, just let me have friends."

"I'm not keeping you from having friends, Alex," he says, his voice insulted. "I'm not a fucking *asshole*." I laugh bitterly as the bartender passes over the drinks.

"Prove it. Don't come here again. I don't want you to know my friends." He sighs, exasperated and obviously hurt.

"Great, I fucking *love* it when you shut me out. Do you want help carrying those?"

"No." I turn away quickly, spilling the drinks a little because I probably did need help carrying them to the table.

Theo doesn't leave.

I'm tense through trivia, drinking much more than I usually do, leaving quickly when I'd normally stay and chat, ducking Theo and starting to walk home by myself. He catches up to me within a few blocks, and I flinch as he grabs my arm gently and pulls me to a stop.

"Sweetie, you're drunk and you just walked off without me. You have to be careful, okay?"

He links his fingers through mine as we walk. I leave my hand open, not gripping back, which seems to frustrate him, and I refuse to talk to him on the walk back, which makes him more frustrated.

I try to keep ignoring him, but Theo tries harder to get me to engage once we're back at my place. I sit at the breakfast bar as he starts getting things prepared to make dinner, asking me about my friends, what I like about them, why I like doing trivia – anything to get me to talk to him.

Every question he asks makes me feel more irritated.

I open a bottle of wine and start drinking fast, giving him a tight smile and one-word answers, getting progressively more drunk. I can tell I'm wearing on his patience, but I need to have control over something.

If all I can control is pushing him until he kills me, I'll fucking do that.

After I pour my third glass of wine, he snatches it off the counter, grabbing the empty bottle as well.

"Jesus, Alex. You have a drinking problem, you know that?"

I give him a sharp smile. "Give me back my fucking wine, *Theodore*. It helps me get through things that are unpleasant, like spending time with *you*." Theo's jaw tenses, and he gives me a cold, condescending smile as he slowly dumps the wine into the sink.

I snap, grabbing the first thing in my reach, which ends up being my keys, and I hurl them at his face. He ducks out of the way, and then he's immediately in my space, somehow still towering over me even though he's leaning over the breakfast bar.

"Don't fucking *throw things* at me! We are *not* doing that, *ever!*" His voice is raised and stern, and he's not quite yelling at me, but he's so intense it's scary. My anger dissipates quickly, shame and anxiety creeping up on me.

Why the fuck did I just do that? This is a dangerous situation, and I can't push him like this. Plus, I hated it when Danny got mad and threw things at me.

I look down at my hands, shaking my head. What is wrong with me?

Theo sighs hard, and I flinch when his hand comes to grip my jaw lightly, tilting my face up so I have to look at him.

"We *talk* in this relationship. I am *never* going to hit you, or throw things at you, or hurt you, so don't fucking do it to me." I nod. "Good. I *never* want to have this conversation again, understand?" I nod again. He lets go of my face and turns into the kitchen, picking up my keys and pocketing them, shaking his head. "*Jesus fucking Christ,*" he mutters under his breath. I don't say anything, feeling ashamed.

I need to calm down and get through this, one day at a time. I'm not going to keep pushing him to his limits because I'm tired of dealing with him, and I'm *not* going to be like Danny.

No one deserves that, not even this fucking asshole.

Theo finishes making dinner in tense silence, passing me a plate and eating his in the kitchen. We don't talk for a long time. Finally, he sucks in a breath and blows it out fast.

"Have you ever been hit, or had something thrown at you before?" I shrug, not looking at him. I don't want him to know me. "Well, I have, and I fucking hate it, okay? So just talk to me, *please.* Why are you so mad at me?" I shake my head. He's got to be fucking kidding.

"I'm not *mad.*" I stab a Brussels Sprout. "I'm *frustrated.*" I shove the sprout into my mouth to keep from telling him how I really feel, and Theo gives me a disbelieving look.

"You are *such* a shitty liar," he laughs out. "You know, you can just ask me to fuck you if you're so frustrated."

I shoot him a dirty look. "That's *not* what I meant."

"Maybe not, but you're much nicer to me after you've come. I seem to be the only one of us who can make that happen for you." His lips twitch into a small smile, and I flush with embarrassment and anger. I take some quick, deep breaths to keep from throwing something else at him.

This is *bullshit.*

"You know what? *Fine*. Fuck me. Maybe *that* will make spending time with you tolerable." He considers me, his mouth tight.

I realize, belatedly, that I'm pushing him again, and I'm pretty drunk if I'm asking my stalker to fuck me.

"I'm good," he says, his voice casual but his hands gripping the counter until his knuckles turn white.

"So, what you're saying to me," I grit out, plastering a smile on my face and talking slowly, "is that you broke into my house because you wanted to fuck me so badly, and now you're not even going to do that?"

"You're adjusting to our relationship poorly, and the last time we had sex was concerning, so it's off the table until things between us get better." He looks at his plate, making a face. "Believe me, I wish this was going better," he mutters.

"No, you just wish you were getting laid."

"You're drunk and you're being an asshole, Alex. I'm not going to fuck you just because I want to."

"Oh, *that's* new." He shoots me a warning look.

"*Don't.*"

"You could always just *rape* me again," I say, flashing my teeth at him.

"Knock it the fuck off. We have *talked* about this, and I'm not playing that game with you again until you learn the difference between fantasy and reality."

"You're the one who doesn't want to face reality! We're not together!"

"Alexandria, you're being delusional."

I gape at him, horrified. "*I'm* being delusional? *Fuck you.*"

"You have quite the temper, you know that? I didn't expect that, and I don't love it."

"*I do not have a temper,*" I shout. Theo just looks at me, raising his eyebrows slightly, and I flush in embarrassment.

I put my head in my hands and take deep breaths. Why am I reacting so much? I used to be able to keep this under wraps, even when I was drunk, at least up until the end. Today has just been so hard.

"It's fine to be angry, sweetie, but you have *terrible* anger management skills. You should look into that." His tone is so condescending that I want to punch him.

"Oh, and you're the pinnacle of anger management?" His face gets somber, and he looks away from me quickly.

"Not historically, no."

"Great! I'm sure that means you killed the last girl you stalked when you got tired of her, so when are you going to kill *me*? I'd rather be dead than have my life taken over by my stalker that keeps *making me fucking dinner*." His head snaps towards me, and I can tell he's pissed.

"First, I'm not going to kill you, so knock it off. Second, I *hate* how you view our relationship. Third, you're still barely eating anything, and it's fucking concerning!" He gestures at my barely touched plate.

"If I eat, will you leave?"

"No. I'm spending the night." Of fucking course he is.

"But *not* fucking me?" He laughs and shakes his head.

"Definitely not. You're being a dick." He takes my plate and pulls out a glass container from under my counter, starting to put the leftovers away.

"*You're* being a dick," I snap back. Theo snorts, shaking his head.

"Very mature response, Alex." I slip off the stool and storm into my room, slamming the door behind me and stripping my clothes off. I know he watches me, but I'm drunk enough that I don't care. I want any kind of fucking release, and I'm so tired of crying all the time. I want to feel good for once.

Fuck it, I'm going to push.

When I come back into the living room, I'm wearing the skimpiest bra and panties I have, and I give him a tight, forced smile. I can see him tense up and watch his knee start bouncing quickly as he folds his arms over his chest tightly. He swallows hard, clearing his throat.

"Sweetie, you look *so* gorgeous, but I'm still not going to fuck you." His voice is strained.

"*Fine*," I say sweetly. "I'll do it myself." I head back to my bedroom and pull out my vibrator, and I hear him swearing to himself. When I turn around, Theo's leaning in the doorway of my room, his body rigid, his arms crossed as he watches me with a frustrated look on his face.

"Can you please talk to me for once instead of acting like this?" I laugh at him.

"You can stop pretending that you give a shit about me."

"I wouldn't be putting up with your behavior if I didn't give a shit about you," he snaps.

"Putting up with my behavior? Oh, I'm *so* sorry. Am I not the girlfriend you thought I was going to be when you stalked me?" His face goes blank, and he doesn't respond at all. I laugh and shake my head at him, throwing my vibrator back into my nightstand so hard I think I break it.

I walk over and stand in front of him, watching him get more tense as he looks me up and down. "You seem to be fine taking what you want from me, so go ahead."

He rolls his eyes. "See, *this* is why I'm not fucking you. You have such a distorted perception of our relationship."

"That's bullshit. We're not in a relationship, so stop acting like you care!"

"Yes, we *are*, and I *do* fucking care! I want you to participate in this relationship, Alex."

"Not gonna happen, so just fuck me already, okay?"

He shakes his head, smirking. "No," he says slowly, "I think I want you to *beg* for it."

"I'm not begging you for *shit*."

He raises his eyebrows, looking me up and down slowly. "You're standing in front of me, in *lingerie*, trying to goad me into fucking you. You want to rethink that?" I get frustrated with his self-satisfied tone and grab his hands, placing them on my waist. He grips me instantly, pulling me closer, although it seems almost involuntary.

"You want me? Just fucking take me." I see his pupils dilate as he stares down at me, his face so openly hungry that he looks almost predatorial.

What am I *doing*?

I can feel his hands shaking, feel his fingers digging into my waist, and I realize I've been playing a dangerous game. I shrink back as he starts leaning down towards me, and he seems to stop himself, exhaling hard and pushing me away.

"*No,*" he chokes out, rushing into the bathroom and slamming the door. The tiny window in my bathroom means there's no fan, and I hear him spit and start breathing hard.

Oh.

I sit on my bed with my back up against the headboard and stare at the bathroom door as I listen to him masturbate, feeling heat between my legs as I listen to his breathing get harsher.

Why am I so disappointed that he didn't fuck me?

Is he serious about wanting me to ask for it? I've never asked for sex in my life - it just happens when someone else wants it. I don't know why he wants me to participate in his delusion so badly.

His breathing picks up, and I hear him swear softly, the sink running a few seconds later. He comes back into the bedroom, his face tense and frustrated as he walks towards the bed. He plants his hands on either side of my head, gripping the headboard as he leans down and kisses me hard. The second I sigh and lean into the kiss, he pulls away and gives me a mean smile.

"You're going to have to fucking beg for it, Alexandria, and I know you will." I stare up at him, furious and horrified.

He's right, and I hate him for it.

He's cautious not to touch me in bed that night. I lay there, staring at the cracking plaster wall across from me, realizing I've lost a crucial battle.

He's taken everything away from me, and now he's made me want something from him.

I wait until I'm sure he's asleep before I slip into the living room and curl up on the couch, pushing a small throw pillow against my face to absorb the sound of my sobs.

It takes a long time for me to calm down.

When I'm finally done crying, I look up and see Theo in the doorway of my bedroom, looking confused and upset. I head back into the bedroom, pushing past him and crawling into bed. I'm sure he's going to start badgering me to talk to him, but he doesn't. Instead, he pulls me close and holds me, trying to comfort me with soft, murmured reassurances, which only makes it worse.

He makes *everything* worse.

20

THEO

FRIDAY, OCTOBER 13

I am in hell, and I have no one to blame but myself.

Well, maybe Alex, a little bit.

She's stubborn as fuck and has such horrific trust issues that she won't let me in, even for a second, and she has a hell of a temper.

I don't know how I didn't see that before.

Her voice has a clipped quality to it, her movements are quick, and her body is always slightly tense, even when she's stretching or sleeping. I thought she had anxiety, and maybe she does, but mostly she seems angry - *especially* with me. It seems like everything I'm doing pisses her off, but I think the fact that I'm not fucking her is pissing her off the most.

The only time she's not angry with me is when she's asleep. I haven't been holding her when we go to sleep, but I wake up with her in my arms anyway, her body flush against mine. I've watched the cameras back, relieved to see that she's the one who gravitates towards me in the middle of the night.

It's reassuring to know that, on some level, she feels how connected we are, especially since she doesn't want to speak to me, doesn't want to share her feelings with me, and does her best to ignore me if she's not trying to get me to fuck her.

Instead of asking for sex, she's keeping up her bullshit attempts to get me to lose control with her. I've almost lost control with her so many times. Her apartment is freezing, but she keeps walking around in lingerie, standing closer to me than usual, laying her legs across my lap on the couch when we watch TV, anything other than *asking* me. Every time I ignore her attempts, she gets furious and sulks.

I have to wait her out, but it's so fucking hard.

I'm not any better at controlling myself or my impulses – I just have a much stronger motivation *not* to fuck her. I need her to know that she can trust me, and I know the payoff of her finally opening up to me is going to be worth it. I'm getting tired of her being angry with me all the time, and of her lying to me, and of her acting like I don't actually care about her. Most of all, I'm *so* fucking tired of catching her crying quietly in the middle of the night. She shuts down any time she realizes I've caught her, and she won't talk to me or let me comfort her at all, no matter how hard I try.

I know she's got a lot of baggage, but it's not like I don't have any fucking baggage, and it sucks to be the only one who's trying to make this relationship work. I hate how long it's taking her to adjust, and I hate that she's actively fighting against it, but I know that it will get easier soon.

It needs to, for both of our sakes, because I'm starting to lose my fucking patience with her.

21

ALEX

SATURDAY, OCTOBER 14

I'm having another sex dream about Theo.

I can feel him behind me, one hand splayed across my ribs and the other gripping my stomach, his lips moving slowly up my neck. I lean into his touch, and his hard cock twitches between my thighs as I push my hips back into his.

I wish he'd just fuck me already. These dreams are excruciating.

I whine a little, moving against him, so wet that he slides against me easily. I tilt my hips back until the head of his cock notches into my entrance. His arms tighten around me and his hips jerk forward, and I cry out as he shoves inside of me fully.

I realize I'm not dreaming roughly at the same time that he fully wakes up.

We both freeze, and Theo's body shakes as he tries to restrain himself. I push my hips back into him, trying to get him to break, and he makes a strangled sound as he pulls out of me.

"*God fucking dammit,*" he chokes out as he shoves away from me and rolls out of bed, walking quickly into the bathroom. I curl up against the headboard and listen to him masturbate, furious and frustrated and embarrassed.

I hate that I want him this badly.

When he comes back out of the bathroom, he pulls on his sweats, which I swear he was wearing when we went to sleep, and I can't help but notice how good they look slung low on his hips.

"For the last time, you need to fucking *ask* for it," he snaps, crossing his arms, and I look back up at his face. His jaw is set, and he looks *pissed*. "I'm getting really fucking tired of you pushing me like this."

"You were the one who *pushed,* actually," I snap back.

He rolls his eyes up to the ceiling, shaking his head. "Yeah, well, I wasn't totally awake." He looks at me for a second and runs his hands over his face, pushing his hands back into his hair. "Also, for future reference, I *love* waking up like that," he mutters.

"I don't know why you didn't keep going, then." He exhales hard and shoots me an irritated look.

"I can't believe I have to explain to you that you need to fucking participate in our relationship. Judging from this morning, I can tell you *want* to participate," he teases, although his voice has a frustrated edge to it.

"Not really."

"You're not even *trying* to lie, sweetie," he teases.

I cross my arms and change the subject. "What bullshit do you have planned for today?"

"That depends. What do *you* want to do today?" he asks, flashing me a crooked grin. I huff angrily and get out of bed, trying hard to avoid him in the small space of my bedroom.

"I have plans today."

He frowns. "We haven't made plans yet."

"*I* have plans, *alone.*"

"No, you don't. There's nothing in your planner, or your phone, or your work calendar." Fucking stalker.

"I had plans to spend the day by myself."

"That's *nice,*" he says, and I can tell from his passive-aggressive tone that it's not going to happen. I storm past him into the bathroom and shut the door, pouring myself a bath. I groan when I see the little tray laid across the bathtub, full of bath salts and body oil and scrubs.

This is ridiculous.

Recently, Theo has been pulling the gifts out from under my bed and trying to put them away. No matter how many times I put them back under the bed, they reappear. I look down at the body oil again, feeling a mix of emotions. Theo has bought me everything Jo Malone makes in my favorite scent, which is obscenely over the top. As much as I hate to admit it, Theo's really good at giving gifts.

I don't trust gifts.

Danny gave me a *lot* of gifts, usually as apologies for losing his temper or hurting me, but the gifts Danny gave me were things *he* liked. Tight, short dresses. Big, showy diamond jewelry. Bags with large designer labels visible. Cute, fruity perfumes. Frilly, silky lingerie in pale colors. He liked me to look sexy and show off our money - *my* money, my *parents'* money, money he spent freely because it was *our* money in his mind - and he expected that I would love everything, fawn over him for it, show gratitude, act like it fixed everything.

Gifts meant something bad had happened.

Theo's bought me things I've shown a genuine interest in, at least, but he only found out what I like from *stalking me*. It feels too familiar, like an apology for the stalking.

I stare at the body oil in my hand, conflicted. I want it, but I can't accept anything from him. If I do, it's like I'm accepting the apology and buying into his delusion. I set the body oil back on the tray and steel myself for the day.

Things between us have been tense, and they're not getting any easier.

When I walk into the bedroom, the bed is made, and there's a cup of hot coffee on my dresser. I ignore it, turning to my closet and getting dressed quickly before walking into the living room. Theo's dressed in jeans and a hunter green button-down, looking at something on his phone, sipping coffee.

I hate myself for wanting to crawl into his lap.

"Is there *any* way to get you to leave me alone?"

He gives me an exasperated look. "We can do whatever you want, but we need to spend more time together. We're still adjusting to each other. Last weekend was nice, right?" He flashes me a small, hopeful smile, and I cross my arms and look down at my feet.

Last weekend was horrible. I let my guard down for one fucking second, and he doubled down on his delusion.

"Fine. I want to go to Portland, but I want it to go differently than last time."

"Whatever you want, sweetheart," he says, his voice affectionate. It pisses me off for some reason, and I look up at him, my temper settling into defiance.

"I want to choose the restaurants."

"Of course."

"I *don't* want you to buy me gifts. I don't like them."

He frowns. "You don't like the gifts I got you, or you don't like receiving gifts?"

"I don't like getting gifts."

He nods, looking disappointed. "Can I ask why?"

"No." He's obviously irritated but gives me a polite smile.

"Okay," he says slowly, drawing out the vowel. "Anything else?"

"I *don't* want you to pay for me."

He cringes slightly, shaking his head. "I was raised kind of old school, so that one's off the table. It's nothing against you, but I'm pretty sure my grandfather would come back from the dead and shoot me on sight if he saw me letting a woman pay for herself."

I scoff at him. "That's *so* sexist."

He shrugs. "Oh, absolutely, but it's not a concession I'm going to make. What else do you want?" I blink at him for a second, figuring out what else to ask for.

"Um, I want to choose the movie. There's a new superhero thing I want to see."

His face falls immediately. "There's that special showing of *Singin' in the Rain* you were looking up times for? It's a classic, and I know we both like it," he says, sounding hopeful. I do want to see that instead, but he *really* doesn't seem to want to see the multiverse thing, so I shake my head, smiling at him spitefully, and he sighs. "*Fine.*" He's being so acquiescent, and I'm angry enough that I start pushing.

"I don't want you to touch me." He frowns, looking slightly concerned. "I don't want you to stand close to me." He rolls his eyes at me, catching on. "I don't want you to talk to me." He sighs heavily and pushes off the couch, grabbing his keys and opening the front door. "I don't want you to come with me," I snap, trailing after him.

He laughs, shaking his head. "Oh, I'm *aware*. Can we go? All I want is to have a nice day with you." He seems to mean it, and I stare at him for a second before walking through the door, getting close to him and jamming my finger into his chest.

"*You* are not going to have the day *you* want." He raises his eyebrows, seemingly amused.

***

I do everything I can to ruin Theo's day.

I tune the car radio to a conservative talk radio station, and when he changes the station quickly, I change it back, telling him I want to listen to it. He shoots me a disgusted look, and I spend the car ride reveling in his increasing irritation and muttered rebuttals to what's being said on the show.

Once we get into Portland, I choose a greasy spoon diner that I know he'll hate, order the worst-sounding thing on the menu, and then sweetly ask him to switch plates with me. He gives my food a horrified look before he takes it, reluctantly handing over his omelette. He doesn't eat much, he just drinks coffee and tries to talk to me, and I give him vague, mostly one-word answers, which I know he hates.

I drag him around stores and ignore him, chatting animatedly with any halfway attractive male employees. Theo has a tight, polite smile plastered on his face as he watches, but I can tell I'm pissing him off.

At lunch, I choose a burger restaurant, order the greasiest thing on the menu, and make him switch food with me again. His jaw clenches as he swaps our plates.

"Are you having a good day, sweetie?" he asks, his tone tense and condescending. I give him my most saccharine smile, enjoying how miserable he seems.

"Oh, *absolutely*. Aren't you?" I ask, mimicking his tone. He leans across the table with a small smirk.

"No," he says quietly, "but I *am* enjoying how hard you're trying to turn me on." My nipples harden and I look away from him, and he lets out a low, mean laugh.

He shouldn't get to make me feel like this.

I sneak my card to the server when I go to the bathroom, and when he realizes I've paid for lunch, he seems to lose his patience. As we leave the restaurant, he slings an arm around my waist and pulls me tight, not letting me go when I push away from him.

"You need to stop being a fucking *brat*, Alex," he whispers into my ear. The harsh tone of his voice sends an anticipatory shiver down my spine that I can't ignore. I cross my arms, my anger flaring as I look up at him.

"You think we're together? Fine, but *this* is what you're going to get from me. I hope you fucking like it, asshole." He pulls me to a stop and looks down at me, leveling me with a warning look.

"I don't think *you'll* like what you get if you keep acting like this," he says, his voice sharp, and he gives me a cold smile. "Consider that a warning. Also, I'm done with your bullshit rules for today."

He hurries me into an expensive lingerie shop and doesn't leave my side, his hands constantly on my waist or my lower back. He starts talking to me under his breath as he picks things out for me, telling me how sad it is that I can't come anymore and that he'd love to help if I would just open my pretty mouth and ask. I keep my arms crossed and try to ignore him, which is extremely difficult.

I hate that what he's doing is turning me on so much.

When we get into the car to drive to the movie theater, he pulls my face towards him and kisses me hard. I don't kiss him back, but he seems amused rather than frustrated as he kisses his way down my neck. I have to bite my lip to keep from moaning and clench my fists to keep from touching him, and he can tell. He plays with my hair as he drives, dragging his fingers down my scalp and trailing them down my neck in a way that makes me shiver. He's overly affectionate in line at the theatre, so I make him sit behind a group of loud teenagers that I hope will be annoying. He looks displeased, and his leg starts bouncing the second we sit down.

Half an hour into the movie, I'm bored and wish we'd gone and seen the movie both of us actually like, and Theo looks zoned out. He's not entirely focused on the screen, but he's also not focused on me for the first time all day. The teenagers in front of us are being irritating, and I eye Theo's bouncing leg.

Fuck it, I'm going to push him.

His leg stills when I gently drag my fingers up it, slowly caressing his inner thigh. He has to readjust himself almost immediately, pulling himself up against his stomach and trapping himself with his waistband. His jaw is clenched when I look over at him, and I graze my hand higher. He shoots me a charged look, shaking his head in warning. I ignore him and do it again, rubbing the very edge of my hand against his erection until he's shifting in his seat uncomfortably. He leans close to me, his lips pressing against my ear.

"You need to ask or fucking *stop*," he says, his voice strained. I scoff and keep going until he grabs my wrist with a shaking hand and jerks my hand away. The look he shoots me is pure frustration, and I give him a mean smile as I sit back in my seat, crossing my legs to ease the ache in between them.

After the movie, he tries to drag me back to the car, but I flag down a canvasser and let him trap me in a prolonged conversation about whatever he's raising money for. I flirt with him and ignore Theo entirely until I look up at him sweetly, leaning into him and calling him *baby* as I ask him to make a recurring contribution for *us*. Theo raises his eyebrows and stares at me for a long moment, his body rigid against mine. I can tell he's pissed, but he gives the canvasser a fixed, polite smile as he fills out his information.

His arm winds around my waist as we walk away, and he leans down, keeping his voice low.

"This is your final warning, Alexandria. I'm not fucking with you."

"Yeah," I say, pushing him off, "I'm *aware*."

When we sit down to dinner, he leans across the small table and keeps his voice low.

"I wouldn't recommend whatever bullshit you're thinking of pulling," he says, and I give him a sweet smile.

"I don't know what you're talking about." He leans back in his chair and crosses his arms, unimpressed.

I make him switch plates with me again, but it's a mistake. Apparently, Theo can eat much spicier food than I can, and he looks incredibly smug as I eat almost nothing while he enjoys the sushi I'd rather be eating. I spend the rest of dinner flirting with the waiter, who has no interest in me, but I know it bothers Theo either way. I can tell he's holding onto his patience by a thread by the time we head home. I wait until he seems somewhat calmer, and then I reach for the radio.

His hand shoots out and grabs my wrist hard.

"Alexandria, do *not* keep pushing me," he says in a stern voice. I stare at him defiantly as I jerk my hand away and punch the radio on, turning it up. His knuckles turn white on the steering wheel, and I watch him take deep breaths, trying hard to keep his cool. I smile wickedly at him, enjoying making him so miserable.

"Did you have *fun* today, *Theodore*? Is it *fun* to be in this *relationship* with me? Aren't you glad you've taken over my entire fucking life?" He pulls the car to a stop at a red light and turns the radio off, staring straight ahead, his hands shaking.

"I'm trying so hard to control myself, but you're making it *impossible*. If you want to play your shitty little games when I'm trying to be nice, you're going to fucking pay for it," Theo grits out through his teeth, his voice low and terse.

He's either going to kill me or he's not, and I'm so angry and frustrated that I don't care what happens to me right now, so I push.

"What are you going to do? You keep telling me that you're not going to hurt me, right? Then how, exactly, am I supposed to *fucking pay for it?*" He barks out a sharp laugh and gives me a look that makes me nervous.

"*Great* question, sweetie." Theo makes a sharp right on red, driving us down towards a mostly empty moorage on the river. He throws the car into park, undoes his seatbelt quickly, and then he's on me. He kisses me, biting my lips until they part, his tongue thrusting into my mouth as his hands cup my breasts and grip my thighs. My body responds to him immediately and I moan, gripping his shoulders as I finally kiss him back.

Right now, I don't care that he's stalking me or that I'm trapped in this situation. I'm so fucking horny, and I can't make myself come, but *he* can. Theo bites my bottom lip, dragging it through his teeth slowly, making me whimper as he breaks the kiss.

"Beg for it." I keep my eyes closed and nod faintly.

"Please," I whisper. His laugh is sharp and frustrated.

"You need to beg better than that, and you better fucking look at me when you do." I open my eyes and see how frustrated his face is, how wanting and angry he is, and I hate myself as I cave, but I can't help it.

"Please fuck me, Theo," I whisper, and he instantly looks smug. "I want it," I whine, reaching out to touch him, hating myself a little more with every word. "*Please*."

He undoes his pants quickly, pulling out his hard cock and grabbing the back of my head, pushing me down too quickly for me to resist.

"You want it? There you fucking go." I open my mouth and drag my tongue across his blunt head, and he swears loudly and pushes up into my mouth, shoving my head down. I feel a spike of panic and try to pull back, but his hand traps me. I close my eyes and breathe, waiting for him to make it rough, but he doesn't.

"Take as long as you fucking want, sweetie, but you don't come until I come." I let out a soft sigh of relief before closing my lips around his cock and sucking hard. "Oh, *fuck*," he hisses out, and I start bobbing my head slowly, sucking him in a little further each time, learning the feel of him in my mouth.

"That feels amazing." His voice is affectionate again, and his grip on my hair loosens, leaving him running his fingers through my hair, tightening his hand occasionally when I do something he likes. I hate giving head, but the sound of his heavy breaths and the muttered *good*s and *fuck*s and *perfect*s slip out of his mouth and straight down my spine, and heat pools in my core.

The feel of him in my mouth and the taste of his skin starts to turn me on.

I suck him in as far as I can go comfortably, humming around him, grabbing the base of his cock and jerking hard, hollowing my cheeks out as I suck him off. His hand tightens in my hair, and he tenses as he makes a deep, satisfied groan as his cock pulses on my tongue and his cum floods into my mouth. A low moan escapes me at the taste of him, and I'm surprised as the sound comes out of me.

I didn't realize giving head didn't have to be awful.

"Good girl," he pants out as I swallow him down, pulling off his cock with a wet pop and licking up all the cum that spilled out of my lips. When I look up at him, his eyes are wide and dark, and he's looking at me with unbridled need as he pushes me back into my seat, kissing me hard and slipping his hand up my skirt.

He slips my thong to the side, and I'm so wet that he pushes two fingers inside me easily. I dig my fingers into his hair and gasp at how good it feels, keeping my eyes locked on his. I can't seem to break eye contact with him, and I'm touching any part of him I can reach as heat pools in my core quickly. His face splits into a smug grin as he wrings another moan out of me.

"If you want to come, you need to beg for that, too," he says in a teasing voice. I force my eyes shut so I don't have to look at him.

"Please, Theo," I beg softly, sounding pathetic. "Please make me come. I'm so close, *please*," I whine as my leg starts to tense and my core clenches around his fingers. Just as I'm on the edge of release, he pulls out of me and throws the car in reverse, quickly heading back to the road. My eyes snap open and I stare at him in shock, my body aching with unreleased tension.

"*What the fuck*?" My voice is shrill with frustration. He laughs, shaking his head.

"I told you not to push me. You want to be a brat and play games? Here's a game: you're not coming until I fucking let you, no matter how much you beg for it." I sit back in my seat, crossing my legs to get some friction, indignant and frustrated.

"You're a fucking asshole!"

He snorts. "You started this game, Alex. I'm just going to finish it."

"I didn't start anything, you delusional *freak*." He shoots me a harsh look.

"First of all, don't insult me, I'm fucking tired of it. Second of all, you're a goddamn liar, and now you're not going to come at all tonight."

"Fuck you." He smirks at me.

"Open your legs." I spread them so fast that Theo laughs as he pulls my skirt up and slips one hand between my legs, playing with me, stroking me softly, never hard enough to do anything but make me want more. I reach down to move his hand, to touch myself, but he stops touching me the second I try to take control. We drive along in tense silence until we hit a long stretch of straight, empty road, and Theo pushes his fingers back inside me, keeping his hand still.

"*Beg.*"

"Please," I moan, slouching down in the seat and grinding into his hand. "Theo, please. I need it." He makes a satisfied-sounding hum and starts fucking me slowly with his fingers, but the second I get close, he stops. I scream in frustration as he laughs harshly and pulls his hand away, slipping his fingers into his mouth. I sit back in my seat, frustrated and furious and aching to be touched.

"You're so fucked when we get home, sweetie. You have no idea." I glare at him, and he glares back, seemingly just as angry as I am. The last twenty minutes of the car ride are silent and tense. I can tell he's getting more and more worked up, and as we pull into Astoria and start heading up towards his house, my arousal starts fading, being replaced by real fear.

What the fuck am I *doing?*

"What do you mean when you say I'm fucked?" I ask, my voice shaky. He laughs and parks the car, getting out quickly and dragging me out and up toward the house, his hand tight on my arm. He pulls me inside, slamming the door behind him, not bothering to turn on any lights as he hauls me upstairs. He's walking so fast that I trip and almost fall, but he smoothly grabs me around the waist and lifts me up, carrying me down the hall into his bedroom, shoving me towards the bed. I bump into the edge of the mattress and turn around as he flips on a dim nightstand lamp and faces me, his body blocking the door, his face angry and amused and frustrated and very, very hungry.

I'm frozen with fear as he walks over to me slowly, getting into my space.

"You need to learn that actions have consequences, Alexandria. I'm not going to hurt you, but I don't think you'll like this," he says, his voice soft and menacing. He fists a hand in the back of my hair, pulling my head back gently, leaning over me as he brings his face down close to mine, his expression intense and ravenous. I try to pull away from him, but his grip on my hair keeps me in place.

"Wh-what are you d-doing?" My voice wavers, and he shakes his head slowly as he stares at me.

"I'm going to show you what happens when you push me too far," he says, his voice quiet and tense. I can feel him shaking against me, and I realize that he's absolutely furious.

Oh, fuck.

He releases my hair and caresses my cheek. "Get undressed. *Slowly.*" I can't tell if I'm terrified or turned on by the way Theo looks down at me, watching every move I make until I'm bare in front of him.

"Turn around. Hands behind your back." I look at him in alarm and shake my head, panic coursing through me.

"Theo, please do-"

"Right fucking *now*," he snaps, his voice going from soft to sharp in a moment. I flinch and turn around slowly as he opens his nightstand. A moment later, he binds my wrists behind my back tightly before he reaches up and he grabs my jaw.

"Open wide," he whispers in a poisonously sweet voice in my ear. I shake my head, and he bites my neck, laughing softly. "You want to make it worse? Keep resisting." I reluctantly open for him, and he slips a small ball gag into my mouth carefully, fastening it behind my head. He turns me around and pushes me back until I'm sitting on the bed, smiling down at me sweetly.

"You look so pretty right now," he says, his voice soft again as he leans down over me. He slips a hand between my legs, and I close my eyes, embarrassed at the whine I let out as he rubs his fingers up and down my slick, aching cunt. I try to shift my hips to get him to touch me where I want, but he doesn't.

"Do you want me to fuck you, Alex?" I nod slightly. "Is that why you've been acting out? Because I haven't been fucking you?" I nod again. "Look at me, sweetheart." His voice is soft but commanding, and when I open my eyes, he gently cups my face in his shaking hands.

His jaw is set, his mouth is tight, and I can tell he's *pissed*.

"You should have opened your pretty mouth and asked nicely. Instead, you've been pushing me to my fucking limits so you can lie to yourself and pretend you don't want it. I'm fucking *tired* of it, and now I'm going to make you regret it." I yell at him through the gag, but the silicone ball muffles everything I'm trying to say. He strokes my cheek with his thumb.

"Here's what's going to happen, sweetie. I'm going to push *you* to the edge, over and over, and we're going to see how you like it. We're going to do it again and again, and I'm not going to stop until I make you *cry*. And once you cry? I'm going to keep fucking going." I shake my head hard, and his eyes widen as he gives me a terrifying smile, nodding slightly.

"Oh, *yeah*. You need to understand how this relationship *can* go. I want to be sweet to you, Alex, I do, but I don't *have* to be. You need to be punished for how you've been acting, and I'm so goddamn fucking frustrated with your behavior lately that this is going to be *really* fun for me." I glare at him, trying to communicate how much I hate him. He leans forward and kisses my forehead softly. "It's not going to be fun for *you*, though."

He kneels between my legs and dips his head down to suck one of my nipples into his mouth, biting softly just as his fingers lightly graze over my clit, barely touching me, and the sensations combined are fucking torture. I moan softly, trying to beg through the gag. He takes his time, undoing his jeans with his other hand and stroking himself as he barely touches me. I get fed up with him and jerk my hips forward, rubbing my clit hard into his hand. He yanks his hand away and fists it in my hair, pulling my head back, his voice stern.

"Absolutely the fuck *not*." He stands up and pulls my face towards his cock, jerking himself off quickly. "Look at me." I look up at him, furious and frustrated, and his gaze softens for just a second before he smirks and comes on my face. I close my eyes as his cum hits the bridge of my nose and my eyelashes, swearing at him through the gag as he laughs and smears his cum across my face with the head of his cock.

"You look *so* beautiful like this," he says, sounding less angry and more affectionate. He yanks me up and turns me around, bending me over the edge of the bed and shoving my face down into the mattress. He delivers a sharp slap to my ass, stinging hard enough that I flinch but not hard enough that it feels like he's trying to hurt me. He waits a second, resting his warm hand on the skin he just hit, then pulls back and slaps it again in the same spot, and I whimper.

I don't like being hit, but this kind of feels good.

He spanks me again, and again, and again, palming my ass in between sharp slaps. My ass is aching and my cunt is throbbing and I'm in agony as he drags his fingers between my legs and starts rubbing my clit slowly, taking his time working me up until I'm on the edge of pleasure. I can feel my body tense up, heat pooling in my spine, and I moan and push my hips back towards his hand. He pulls his hand away instantly and slaps my other cheek hard enough to make me yelp, palming my ass and waiting a second before slapping me again. By the second or third spanking, I start thrashing and screaming at him, which elicits a soft laugh out of him.

"I know, sweetie, I know," he says right before he spanks me again.

My body is full of weeks of pent-up energy, and my skin is tingling all over by the time his hand goes back to my cunt. He strokes my slit with long, soft touches, entirely avoiding my clit, and I think I'm going to die. I make pleading sounds through the gag, whining and whimpering, anything that I can do to beg, and he grips my hair and pulls my head back, kissing my temple softly.

"What's that?" I whine. "You said you love this, and you want more?" His voice is amused and condescending, and I hate this passive-aggressive prick with every fiber of my being. I shake my head hard and scream at him, and he laughs as he slaps my ass again, making me whimper. "I think you need more, too. I think you need to learn your fucking lesson."

He picks me up and repositions me face down in the middle of the bed, moving away from me and coming back a moment later to grab my ankles and spread my legs. Rope wraps around one of my ankles as he ties it to the bed, and I try to pull my other leg out of his grip, but he slaps my ass where it's sore and I go limp.

Theo pushes the very tip of his finger inside of me, and I whine in desperation. He withdraws it, slaps my ass hard, and then pushes his finger just barely inside me again. Every sensation is too much to handle but not enough to get a release, and the tension in my body keeps ratcheting up to the point that I feel like I'm going to snap.

My entire body feels like it's on fire, my nerves pained and excited all at once, and it's so overwhelming that I can't help the tears that start streaming down my face. Theo makes a satisfied sound behind me and pushes one long finger inside me, fucking me slowly.

"*There* we go. That's it, sweetie, cry for me *just* like that." He slips in a second finger and curls them down, pressing hard against my g-spot. My leg starts to shake, and I'm moaning, begging for it, but he takes it all away just as I need it most. I scream at the top of my lungs through the gag, bending my knees and dragging myself backward, pushing my hips in the air. He laughs at me, gripping my hips and kissing my cunt slowly until I'm writhing. I whine when he stops, and a moment later, he moans just as his hot cum spills across my cunt. I cry harder as he presses his thumb against my clit, gently circling it in an irregular rhythm that does nothing but frustrate me more. I scream and cry and writhe, and he keeps making soft, low, amused sounds.

I *hate* him, I hate that I want him, I hate that he's doing this, and I hate that there's a small part of me that likes that he's doing this. Mostly, I hate myself for being stupid enough to push him this far but not stupid enough to push him farther.

He slaps my ass again where it's sore, and I go limp, dropping my hips on the bed and sobbing uncontrollably. Only once I'm able to catch my breath does Theo grab my face, turning my head gently and wiping away the cum and tears. I open my eyes to find Theo's smug, satisfied face in front of me.

"Are you having a good time, sweetie?" I shake my head slowly, sniffling. "No, I didn't think so. Are you going to be nicer to me from now on?" I nod reluctantly and he grins. "Yeah, you are. Are you going to fucking participate in this relationship now?" I nod again, hating myself for it. His smile becomes softer, and he kisses my forehead. "That's my good girl," he says, his voice tender. "Remember, *this* is what's going to happen if you act like a brat." I whine pathetically and he wipes a tear from my cheek, licking it off his thumb.

"Do you think you've learned your lesson yet?" I nod frantically, and he starts stroking my body slowly. I hum at how good it feels to be touched. "Me, too. You've been so good for me, and I want to keep you tied up just like this and make you come until you cry for me again. Do you want that?" I nod desperately, making needy little whimpers, and he grins at me. "Do you want me to fuck you, Alex?" I moan in agreement, begging him with my eyes. "You want to come on my cock and have me fill you up like the little cumslut you are?" I'm moaning and nodding frantically now, begging, but his eyes narrow at me as he laughs harshly.

"Well, you lost that privilege today because you're a fucking liar. Now, *neither* of us are going to get what we want." My eyes go wide, and he smirks at me. "You need to learn this lesson the hard way, apparently, so we're going to keep going." I start swearing at him through the gag, and his smile is so fucking smug I want to punch him. "You're doing *so* good, by the way. You should see how perfect you are like this. It's *so* hard for me not to fuck you, so I'm going to go get a drink and let us both calm down a little. When I come back, if you're *very* good for me, we'll only go for a *little* bit longer." I shake my head frantically and try to talk through the gag, trying to beg him to stop, trying to tell him I'll do anything, and his expression becomes more and more amused.

"Well, since you asked so nicely, I *will* push you until you break. I don't know how long that's going to take, but we're going to find out." My eyes get wide, and I start screaming at him again.

His answering grin is evil.

I fucking *hate* him.

***

When Theo finally stops, I'm sweaty and wrung out and limp on the bed, drooling around the gag, his cum drying on my skin. My shoulders are aching, my jaw is screaming, my cunt is throbbing, and I'm fucking miserable. My body is exhausted from almost coming over and over, and my mind is entirely unrelated to my body, everything taking on a hazy and confusing quality. I'm not even angry anymore – I'm just needy. I'd tell Theo I loved him right now if I thought he would let me come, and I'm so fucking sensitive that I think I'd come if he touched me anywhere.

He starts to unbuckle the gag, and I almost sob in relief because my jaw hurts so badly from biting down on it for so long. He wipes some of the drool off my chin and kisses my lips softly, and my nerves are so overstimulated that the slight touch feels electric.

"I think you owe me an apology," he teases. Panic cuts through the haze, clearing my mind a little bit, and I shake my head slowly, hoping that he'll take pity on me. My jaw is so sore I can barely open it, and my voice is soft and slurring through my teeth.

"I can't."

He smirks down at me. "Sounds like you can talk to me." I look up at him, pleading with him silently.

"I can't do the other part," I whisper, tears burning behind my eyes. Theo's brows knit together, and he cocks his head to the side, looking confused.

"What other part?" His tone is no longer teasing. I shake my head and start to cry, and he strokes my hair softly. "Alex, what are you talking about?" he asks, his voice slightly panicked.

"Please don't make me," I beg. "It'll hurt."

"What the *fuck*?" He unties my wrists a moment later, and my arms flop to my sides, my shoulders screaming as Theo unties my ankles before he's on the bed, pulling me into his arms. My back rests against his chest and his legs bracket mine as he pulls a thick duvet over us and tilts my face up to him, his eyes wide and worried. He massages my jaw gently, and I start crying harder because it feels so good.

We stay like that for a while until I start feeling calmer and less afraid, but I'm still exhausted and pent up and painfully sensitive. My body feels wrong, and I'm so confused by everything right now except that being held feels nice.

"Sweetheart," Theo says, his voice slightly shaky, "I'm going to take care of you, okay? You were *so* good for me." I don't totally register what he's saying or doing until I feel his hand between my legs, and I start whimpering immediately, pressing back into him as he touches me softly.

My body is so pent up, and his touch is so overwhelming that I start crying again. I *never* cried this much during sex with Danny. He didn't allow it, but Theo just makes soothing noises and strokes my skin with his other hand as he touches me.

"It's okay, sweetheart, I've got you. You're going to feel good in a minute, I promise," he says as he slowly pushes his fingers inside of me, and I moan as I start to feel my orgasm building rapidly. He goes back to circling my clit with his fingers, and I can feel my leg tense as my hips move against his hand, my body flooding with heat quickly. I break apart in his arms, coming so hard my vision goes black for a second. I'm shaking and crying, and his body is tense around me, but he's gentle when he touches me, kissing my hair and stroking my skin. I'm so oversensitive that every graze of his fingers feels like heaven, and nothing makes sense anymore except that he didn't hurt me, and he made me feel good.

I feel a rush of gratitude and drag my hand along one of his arms.

"I'm sorry," I slur as he starts massaging my jaw again.

"Fuck, no, *I'm* sorry, I'm *so* sorry. Come here," he says, rolling me gently until I'm lying on my side. He curls around me and holds me tightly, kissing my hair and shoulders, telling me how perfect I am.

I can't tell which one of us is shaking, but he's so warm and I'm so exhausted that I fall asleep almost instantly.

***

When I wake up a few hours later, the clock on the bedside table tells me it's close to four in the morning, and Theo is nowhere to be found. Everything is still hazy, and my body feels heavy, so I take my time getting out of bed, grabbing a soft crewneck sweater and a pair of grey sweats from his dresser.

When I use the bathroom, the mirror shows me I look as miserable as I feel.

I walk down the hall towards a door that's slightly ajar and spilling light out into the hallway, opening it to find Theo behind a large desk. He's looking between the three monitors in front of him, his brow furrowed and his hand across his mouth. The walls of his office are hung with large, framed sepia photos of trees and piles of logs, but aside from that, the room seems just as staged as the rest of his house.

He looks up and sees me in the doorway and stands up quickly, running his hand through his hair.

"Hi," he says, his voice tight as he crosses the room immediately. He pushes my hair back from my face and kisses my forehead, rubbing my arms and looking into my eyes with an intense, concerned look. "How are you feeling?"

"Why are you up?"

"Uh, I couldn't sleep. Are you okay? Can I get you anything?" He's speaking rapidly, obviously stressed about something, and when I pull back to look up at him, he looks even more upset than a second ago. My brain feels sluggish. *Do* I need anything?

"Food." He nods and escorts me out of the office and down the stairs, turning on lights as he goes. I sit at the island as he starts moving around the kitchen quickly, occasionally running his hands through his hair in agitation.

"Do you want breakfast or dinner?" I shrug. "Okay, um, breakfast. Eggs? Bacon? Yogurt? Quiche? Oatmeal? What do you like?"

"Oatmeal?" He nods, rifling through his pantry with sharp, jerky movements. He's so high-strung right now, but I'm too tired to care.

He's probably just upset he didn't get to fuck me before I fell asleep.

Once he puts a pot on the stove to boil, he leans over the kitchen island towards me, staring at me with a concerned look.

"Can I ask you some questions?" I shrug faintly. "How did he make you apologize?" A hazy recollection of how freaked out Theo was by the apology thing swims through my mind, and I look away from him. I don't want to talk about this, but I'm so worn down that I answer.

"Um, he'd use my mouth, but he was...rough." Understatement. Theo's hand very lightly touches my jaw and lifts my chin until I'm looking up at his bright, concerned eyes.

"That's not how we're doing apologies, okay?" I don't believe him, but I'm too tired to argue with him about anything. He looks at me, frowning when I don't respond. "How long were you married?"

"Nine years." Did I tell him I was married?

"How old were you when you met?"

"Seventeen."

"How old was he?"

"Twenty-eight."

"How'd you meet?" I raise my eyebrows and sigh, looking down at my hands. I'm too tired to lie to him right now.

"He was one of the cops that came to tell me my parents died." Theo makes a choking sound, and when I look up at him, he looks furious. I smile a little at his reaction. "I know, right?" I say softly. "I haven't told anyone that, *ever*."

Theo runs his hands through his hair quickly as he paces back to the stove to check on the pot of water, staring at it for a long moment before he walks back towards me. He leans against the island next to me and strokes a hand over my shoulder.

"Sweetheart, did he ever hurt you?" His voice is quiet, and I nod slowly, not looking at him. "How often?" I shrug. "What made you leave?" I place my head in my hands, pressing the heels of my hands against my eyes gently.

I don't like to think about any of this, and I'm done talking about it.

"*Stop.*"

"Okay. One more question, and it's not about that, I *promise*." I groan, looking up at him. He pushes my hair behind my ear, giving me a tight smile. "What do you like in your oatmeal? I've never seen you eat it." I blink, taken aback.

"Honey. Lots of honey."

"You got it." He moves back to the stove and the boiling water, and I stare after him, trying to figure out why him asking me what I like in my oatmeal seems sweet.

It's probably just because I'm thinking about Danny.

22

THEO

Since that first weekend with Alex, since I found out who she was, I assumed things were bad before she ran away. I knew she had some trust issues, but I assumed that she would let her guard down and feel how connected we are once we got past them. It wasn't supposed to be this hard or take this long, but now I know why she's a fucking minefield of issues that I have to navigate.

Daniel Murphy is the biggest fucking piece of shit, and I'm going to kill him.

After Alex fell asleep on Saturday and I had a panic attack in the basement, I went into my office and started digging, trying to figure out what the fuck happened in her life to make her so tricky to deal with. I'd found out enough by the time she woke up to know it was a lot worse than I'd initially thought.

Then she told me how they met, and I had to work ridiculously hard not to freak the fuck out in front of her.

She shared it with me, though. That's something.

I've spent almost every second I've been away from her looking into her past. Between my own limited hacking skills, buying more complicated hacking programs off the dark web, and the information available on Daniel and Alex's social media, I've put together a basic timeline and have a rough understanding of what happened, and everything I've found makes me want to kill him even more.

Alex's cell phone number was noted down in the police report. The phone records aren't available anymore, but I'd bet money that Daniel started reaching out to her immediately. She was placed in foster care for a very brief period, and from what I can find, her foster mom is close to one of Daniel's aunts. Alex seems to have spent a lot of time around the Murphys right after her parents died, and there are a few photos from that time on his aunt's Facebook. Alex looks like she's not there, and Daniel's extremely close to her in all the photos, which is *very* upsetting.

I got into her Facebook and Instagram accounts, and she had a small army of people who had reached out at the time - her friends, her teachers, friends of her parents, people who cared about her and tried to be there for her. She wasn't exceptionally responsive, understandably, but she started ignoring *all* of them about three weeks after her parents died.

Alex's high school guidance counselor saw her twice a week following her parents' death and listed concerns that Alex was dissociative and potentially suicidal, but she started refusing all help offered to her with no explanation three weeks after her parents died.

I don't want to know what happened three weeks after her parents died, but I *know*.

Alex petitioned the court for legal emancipation a few weeks later. Because she was a straight-A student who was a few months away from being eighteen and had considerable resources and community support, it was granted. The "community support" listed on Alex's emancipation petition seems to have been compromised entirely of her foster parents, the Murphy family, and their church, even though she didn't seem to know any of these people or go to that church before her parents died.

She moved back into her house after her emancipation was granted, and Daniel moved into Alex's house, her *parents'* house, a week later. Shortly after that, Alex, a straight-A honors student who co-captained her track and field team, was involved in extracurriculars, and was *actively* working on college applications, dropped out of high school.

Alex's parents had money. Not Anderson Timber money, maybe, but both of her parents came from well-off families, did well for themselves, and were smart about managing their assets. Setting aside their million-dollar house in a nice neighborhood, Alex inherited roughly four and a half million dollars.

Five months after her parents died, Alex got married on her eighteenth birthday with no prenup, and Daniel's quality of living improved *significantly*.

Alex's medical charts have notes about domestic violence concerns for *years*. She always said everything was fine and turned down any help offered, even when her arm was broken about two years into their marriage.

I don't understand how this fucking bastard manipulated Alex into any of this, or why it went on so long, but I can make some assumptions. Alex drinks, dissociates, lies to herself and everyone else, and tries her best to pretend like everything is fine. If I had to guess, she probably spent her entire marriage trying to avoid conflict that way.

She certainly doesn't do that with me. We're *always* in fucking conflict, and she pushes me hard on everything. On some level, that means she knows she can trust me. Even if she doesn't acknowledge it, I know it's because she can feel we're connected. I know that she wants to be with me, but she's probably afraid to be happy. Maybe she doesn't know how.

I'm going to need to work *much* harder to get her past her trust issues.

I have fucked this up so badly, but I really want to fix it. I can't stop thinking of her face as she sat in my kitchen. She looked so genuinely miserable, and I hated it, hated that she wasn't happy, hated the idea that maybe I was a small part of why she felt that way. This is *not* what I thought this relationship would be like, but she's mine and I want to take care of her.

I just don't know *how* to do that yet.

***

"Theodore, this is *very* concerning to me. Do you know why?"

"Because her ex is a *fuck* and now she's got all these issues that she shouldn't have to deal with?" I don't want to talk to Dr. Mills about this, but I need a *little* bit of advice on how to take better care of Alex, and she'll have to do.

"Yes," she says patiently, "but I'm mostly concerned that you've found yourself in a relationship with a very recent survivor of domestic abuse. I think you, specifically, might trigger a lot of her trauma by accident." I shoot her a dirty look and cross my arms.

"What are you *talking* about? I don't hit women." Dr. Mills gives me a serious, considering look.

"Maybe not, but stalking is a form of domestic violence."

"I'm not *stalking* her, I'm dating her." I'm doing both, technically, but it's different with Alex. She's mine, so it's okay.

"You've stalked women in the past."

I roll my eyes at her. "*One* woman." Technically. "I've taken accountability for that, I've apologized, and I've worked on myself a lot since then. I'm fine now." Dr. Mills blinks and purses her lips as she scrutinizes me.

"Theodore, please consider this seriously: you've spent nine years completing whatever therapy you've been required to participate in, but you've had very little ability to test your skills in the real world and *no* ability to test them in regards to romantic relationships before this point.

"You've discontinued your medication, you've barely reintegrated into society, you have no family relationships, no friends to speak of, and no involvement in any sort of community. You have, essentially, isolated yourself and fixated on finding a partner. That's concerning enough to me for *your* sake. On top of that, you've now found yourself in a relationship with a vulnerable, traumatized young woman who has only just left an abusive situation and has not, it sounds like, begun to seriously process or move past her trauma.

"What's concerning to me, for *Alex's* sake, is that you've found boundaries specifically challenging in the past. I'd guess that she might find being pushed on any of her boundaries, spoken or unspoken, exceedingly difficult to handle. Do you see why I'm concerned for both of you?" Her words skip over my brain, making shallow waves that ripple out.

I'm sure that would be concerning if that's what was happening here, but she's way off base. This woman barely knows me, she doesn't know Alex at all, and she's missing a *lot* of context, like the fact that Alex and I are connected.

That context is critical.

"I can understand where you're coming from." She gives me a sharp look.

"Okay, let me ask you this: do you think that sounds like a good situation for Alex?" Anger flares in my chest, and I force myself to keep my face neutral. I'm making it a good situation for Alex. I might have gotten this wrong at the start, but I'm recalibrating. I'm taking her past into account now and adjusting everything to suit her better. I can make her happy. I can make this work for her. We *work*. We *fit*.

"I think Alex can decide if it's a good situation. I trust her judgment." I will, anyway. She's very confused right now, but I trust that she'll see that this is good for her soon.

"I'm concerned that she may not be in a place right now to judge what's best for her." My knee starts bouncing, and I give Dr. Mills a tight smile. I really fucking dislike her.

"Your concern is misplaced." She blinks and purses her lips.

***

All I want to do after therapy is spend time with Alex and reassure myself that Dr. Mills is wrong, but my stomach sinks as I watch Alex open the door and sigh in defeat when she sees me. She drops her bag and coat on the floor and beelines for the cabinet where she keeps her wine, pouring herself a glass almost to the brim. I force a smile as she comes into the living room, sipping her wine quickly and not looking at me as she curls up on the couch as far away from me as she can get.

This is off to such a bad start.

She's been subdued and kind of depressed since Saturday, and I know it's because I fucked up and lost my temper and went a *little* too far. I could tell she enjoyed it, though. I think it was fine until the

PERFECT

misunderstanding about the apology thing. I think that's where it all went wrong.

"What are you cooking and how are you fucking me?" Her voice is flat and she's drinking quickly, still not looking at me, and my knee starts bouncing quickly. I need her to see I'm a normal boyfriend, not an abusive fuck like her ex, but she's so guarded that even that seems like a huge hurdle.

"I thought we could order in and watch the Red Sox game?" Her face flickers with interest, and relief washes through me as she finally looks at me. *This* was the right move. She nods, turning on her TV and pulling the game up.

"What do you want to order, sweetheart?"

"Whatever *you* want." In general, I hate eating out because I can't control how the food is made, but I can't tell her that. She has her own hang-ups about food, and she still barely fucking eats as is. She's definitely lost some weight since we started dating, which is concerning because it's only been a month.

"Honey, what do *you* want?"

"Burgers. Fries. Milkshakes. Some fucking *alone time*." I nod, pulling out my phone. At least she chose something. Something I don't want to eat, maybe, but something. I hand over my phone and let her scroll through the brewery menu, looking through the menu after her and choosing the least disgusting-looking thing I can find.

I do *not* eat burgers or hot dogs on anything remotely resembling prison food anymore on fucking principle.

"Um, how was your day?"

"Fine." She's almost done with her wine, and she's been home for ten minutes.

That's a nice Viognier, I wish she'd take the time to taste it. I also wish she'd address her drinking problem.

We eat dinner in silence, mostly. I try to engage with her, but outside of occasional comments about the game, she's completely shutting me out. Today's conversation with Dr. Mills rolls around in the back of my mind, seeming like an idea that's almost real, but not quite.

Maybe I should go home and look up how to be a better boyfriend to Alex. I don't want to keep triggering her by accident like I did on

Saturday, so I clean up the dishes once the game is over, determined to go home. She wants alone time, which I hate, but I want her to see that I can give her what she wants.

"Okay, I'll see you tomorrow. Think about what you want to do on Saturday?"

She looks confused. "You're leaving?"

"You said you wanted alone time, right?" I think it's too much to hope that she'll ask me to stay.

"Yeah?"

"So, I'm going." I give her a tight smile and kiss her forehead, ignoring how much it hurts that she still flinches. I know it's not about me, and I'm focusing on the fact that it keeps getting smaller and less pronounced every time I touch her.

We're getting there, slowly but surely.

She grabs my wrist when I reach for my car keys, and I stop, looking down at her in question. She lets out a long sigh and doesn't meet my eye as her face flushes a bright pink.

"Come on." She walks into the bedroom, stripping quickly as she goes. I trail after her apprehensively, leaning in the doorway and considering her. She's naked, sitting in the center of her small bed, curled in on herself and not looking at me.

I haven't initiated sex since Saturday, and this is the second time this week Alex has initiated. She seemed embarrassed last time and didn't want to look at me, or talk to me, or kiss me, insisting on being taken from behind and refusing to be held afterward.

It felt informal and transactional, and I did *not* like it.

"Alex, why do you want to have sex?" She looks embarrassed, flushing a deeper shade of pink and looking away from me. I instantly know the answer, and I fucking *hate* it.

"Can you shut up and just fuck me?" I feel a sinking sensation in my stomach, followed by a curl of irritation.

"No. I'm your boyfriend, not your fucking vibrator." She gets angry immediately, grabbing a pillow to throw at me. She stops herself, making a frustrated sound and throwing it into the wall before she jumps off the bed and gets in my face, shoving her finger in my chest.

"You're not my *boyfriend!* You just show up constantly and feed me and fuck me and bother the shit out of me!" I grin down at her.

"*Definitely* your boyfriend," I tease. She's not having it, and my smile slides off my face as angry tears well up in her eyes.

"What *is* this? You won't leave me alone, you won't kill me, and now you won't fuck me again?" She's getting worked up, pacing the floor, waving her arms around. "What am I to you? A pet? A doll? A fucking object? I'm not property, goddammit, I'm a fucking *person!* At least, I *was* until you showed up." I don't even know what to say. Is this seriously how she thinks about our relationship? It's like she doesn't know me at all, like she's misinterpreting everything I do on purpose.

"Honey -"

"What is the fucking *point* of this?"

"We're together, Alex," I say, trying to keep the hurt out of my voice.

"No, we're fucking *not!*" she shrieks. It's getting difficult to deal with her when she acts like this. I understand this is just about her ex, but it feels sort of personal. "Can't you just fucking kill me already? I'm so *tired* of this."

I'm ignoring that one entirely.

"I'm not having this fight with you. I know you're adjusting -" Alex barks out a laugh.

"Yeah, adjusting to being someone else's fucktoy! I had nine years of that already, so what's the difference, right?" She looks at me as though she expects an answer, but I can't think of anything to say, and she lets out a bitter laugh. "The *only* difference between you and Danny is that *you* can actually make me come, so can you please fuck me already?" Anger courses through me.

She seriously thinks I'm anything like her husband?

"You want me to fuck you, Alex? *Fine,*" I snap, grabbing her by the waist and hauling her against me. She seems instantly nervous, and when I cup her face in my hands and kiss her softly, she makes a confused noise and doesn't kiss back. I pull back and look down at her, taking a deep breath to try to calm down.

I'm so frustrated with her trust issues, but I can't get mad at her like this.

"Sweetheart, if you don't kiss me, I'm not going to fuck you. I'm your boyfriend, so act like it for once, *please*." She looks angry but nods as she sinks to her knees. "Oh, *Jesus fucking Christ,* that's not what I meant," I mutter as I bend down and pull her to her feet, drawing her back into a soft, slow kiss. She seems frozen, barely reacting as I cup her face again and kiss her, tilting her head back slightly to deepen the kiss. She starts to undo my pants frantically, and I reach down and push her hands away gently to make her stop.

"Alex, slow *down*." She flushes and makes a frustrated noise.

"What do you fucking want from me?" Is she serious? From the angry look on her face, I think she is.

"I want you to be *here* with me, sweetheart," I tell her, keeping my voice soft. "I want you to be present and enjoy what's happening, to connect with me and feel how much I care about you." Her eyes are wide and confused as I tuck her hair behind her ear and brush my thumb over her cheek. "You know, boyfriend stuff," I say, rolling my eyes a little and smiling at her.

She shakes her head slightly. "I don't know how to do that," she says in a small voice, and I struggle to keep my face from showing how angry I am.

I am *absolutely* going to kill the piece of shit that came into her life when she was young and naive and treated her like a piece of meat. She's so damaged, and it's his fault that making this work with her is so hard.

I try to stay calm, taking a deep breath and kissing her forehead.

"Just try for me, okay?" I lean down slowly to kiss her again, and she kisses me back tentatively. I let her set the excruciatingly slow pace, focusing on keeping my touch slow and gentle as I slide my hands up and down her waist. Eventually, her hands come up my chest, sliding slowly up the back of my neck and burying themselves in my hair. I sigh in relief as she pulls me forward into her, pressing up onto her toes and wrapping her arms around my neck as she leans into me, deepening the kiss.

There she is.

I bend down and pick her up, letting her legs come around my hips before I climb onto her bed and lay her down. I lean over her, undoing my shirt as I kiss her, tossing it to the floor and pulling away to yank off my t-shirt quickly. She's laid out beneath me, soft and warm and naked and looking so nervous.

For the briefest second, I think this is what her first time should have been like, with someone who gave a shit about her, who wanted to take care of her and make her feel good.

I know that's not what happened.

I undo my pants slowly, standing up and pushing them off before taking my time kissing up her body. She makes faint, wanting sounds in the back of her throat as I trail my lips up the soft expanse of her skin. Alex doesn't seem to know what to do with her hands, running them up and down my chest and sides and arms until they land tentatively on my shoulders. I lift my head to kiss the back of her hand, and she exhales softly, looking surprised.

She needs *tenderness*, and I can give her that.

"Can I take care of you?" She nods, her face still nervous. I smile at her reassuringly and start kissing my way back down her body, kneeling in between her legs, dragging my tongue up the soft skin of her inner thighs until I'm pressing light, barely there kisses against her cunt. She whimpers as I kiss her clit, and her chest arches off the bed briefly. I moan as I dip my tongue into her, tasting her, and then again when she cards her fingers through my hair, her nails dragging along my scalp.

I kiss my way up her cunt, sucking on her clit and making her yelp, her breath becoming heavy. I don't touch myself, even though I'm aching, because right now is about connecting with her and showing her the difference between what she had before and what she has now. I flick my tongue against her clit as I run my fingers against her, touching her softly but not pushing inside her. Her grip tightens in my hair, and she moans quietly as I kiss my way back up her body, slipping one finger inside her as I run my tongue over her nipple. I add in a second finger once I hear her breath catch in her throat, and I press my lips against her throat as I start to finger her slowly, feeling her pulse skyrocket beneath my lips.

I kiss her to keep from talking to her, from encouraging her, from being commanding. I focus on her, on her body, on her feelings, and she tilts her hips to lean into my touch, panting a little as my thumb circles her clit. Her hands slip over my chest and shoulders again as I kiss her, and I get dizzy when she sucks on my bottom lip before she runs her tongue against mine, tasting herself. Her hands grip my shoulders, and I pull back to watch her as I bring her to the edge.

When I feel her telltale leg muscles twitch, I rub her clit a little harder, finger her a little faster, just enough that she makes a shuddering gasp and starts to come, her body shaking softly. Her eyes close, and her face and chest flush as her mouth opens in a little O, and a soft moan escapes her. The flood of her arousal coats my fingers, and she opens her eyes halfway, looking at me with something close to affection. Warmth spreads through my body as I look down at her.

This is what she needs from me, and she's finally trusting me to give it to her.

She's so much more responsive now, her kisses no longer tentative. She makes a soft moan when she slides her tongue against mine, her hands trailing down my chest and stomach until she lightly wraps her hands around my hard cock. Her touch feels like fire, and I moan into her mouth, trying hard to keep myself from rutting into her hand and failing miserably. She lets out a soft, amused sound, stroking me slowly. She tightens her grip and makes my eyes roll back in my head before she releases me, moving her hands to my lower back and pulling me closer.

"Can we...?" I nod down at her, repositioning myself between her legs and kissing her for a moment before I push into her slowly, exhaling hard against her lips as she parts around me. Her eyes go wide and roll back in her head, and she moans loudly, her hands gripping my hips as her head kicks back. She's so fucking ready for me, and I know she can take it all at once, but I give her time to adjust to me, kissing the soft column of her throat as I work myself inside of her, loving the tiny whimpers and whines that going slowly elicits from her. I swear quietly as I bottom out, and Alex huffs a laugh and looks up at me almost fondly. I kiss her again, pressing my body flush against hers, letting her feel the weight of me on top of her. Her hands roam up my back as I start to move in her slowly, and she kisses my shoulders and neck, her fingertips and lips leaving fire in their wake.

"You feel so amazing, Theo," she whispers sweetly, and my stomach flips. Something about her saying my name hits me hard, and I have to focus on not coming instantly. It's difficult, especially with the way she's smiling up at me.

She pulls me down into a passionate kiss, moaning and nipping at my bottom lip. I thrust hard once, and she laughs, nipping at my lip again and earning another hard stroke. Fuck, I love it when she laughs. I look down into her eyes, wide and warm and not nervous anymore, filled with desire and what might actually be affection.

This is what I want from her.

"You're so beautiful, sweetheart." She blushes and smiles shyly, and I can't help but laugh a little. I'm balls deep inside of her and she blushes over me telling her she's beautiful.

"You're okay to look at, I guess," she says as she winds her arms around my neck, her tone teasing and a slight smirk playing across her face. I thrust hard twice, and warmth spreads through my chest as another laugh bubbles up out of her.

Oh, my god, this is amazing. We're having *fun*.

She tilts her hips, pulling me deeper inside of her. "I need more."

I nod, picking her legs up and bringing them around my waist before I plant my forearms on either side of her head. She locks her ankles together as I build up my pace slowly. She closes her eyes and her head kicks back as she lets out a low, throaty sound that makes me groan in response, and we move together, our moans mingling as we kiss.

The closer she gets, the more aggressive she gets, drawing her nails down my back hard, biting my lip and panting into my mouth, and that's going to make me come if I'm not careful. Her leg twitches against me, and I slip my hand between us, rubbing her clit. She pulls back and looks into my eyes, nodding quickly as she gets closer, burying her hands in my hair and making a high-pitched whining noise.

"*Please*...more...oh my god...right there...that's...*Theo* -" My name trails off into a long moan, and I'm on fire as I look down at her, trying to memorize the sound of her moaning my name like that. Her eyes close and she arches into me and starts shaking, and the second she clenches tightly around me, I'm done for, holding her close and moaning her name into her hair as I come with her.

This is so different.

I fucking love it.

We lay there panting, wrapped up in each other's arms and staring at each other. Alex smiles at me in such an unguarded way that it fully reaches her eyes, and joy and hope flood through me as our connection hums through me stronger than I've felt before. She can feel it too, I'm fucking sure of it, because she's *here* with me. We're finally, totally, completely connected for the first time.

I didn't understand what that meant until right now.

Alex isn't just *mine*. I'm *hers*.

Oh, *shit*.

I look down at her gorgeous, happy, flushed face and open my mouth, snapping it shut again when I realize that I'm about to say something catastrophically stupid. I kiss her instead, not trusting myself to speak until I can push the impulse down.

The last thing I need is to scare her off just as she's finally adjusting.

"How was that?" I ask, and she laughs as I pull out of her and lay down next to her. I run my hand across her chest to cup her breast, feeling her heart pounding beneath her ribs, and she looks at the ceiling, trying to catch her breath, her fingertips grazing against my hand.

"Is *that* how boyfriends are supposed to fuck?" I chuckle, kissing her shoulder.

"Good ones, yeah." She rolls her eyes, looking over at me with a warm expression before cupping my jaw and pressing her body into mine as she kisses me. I lose myself in her easy affection, in the content sounds she makes and the feeling of her smiling against my lips, at how she laughs at the petulant whine that escapes me when she moves to get up, at the way she kisses me once more before she walks to the bathroom on wobbly legs.

I lay back, shocked and exhilarated. I was right initially – we *do* connect emotionally in bed, and we *can* build on that. I absolutely fucked up the timing and made this so much harder than it should have been, and it's taken us time to get back on track, but this is finally *working*.

We're finally adjusting.

Alex comes back to bed, grabbing my college sweater from her dresser and slipping it on, and a rush of hope and affection floods me. *This* is what I want - I want to connect with my gorgeous, perfect girlfriend and then have her wear my clothes and curl up in my arms as she finally recognizes what we have together. I want her to finally open up to me and let me in and start loving me back.

It's what I want.

What I get is Alex lying close but not touching me, her expression already closing off. The smile she gives me is small and polite but not very affectionate, and her demeanor is less warm and less open, and panic shoots through me when I see how quickly she's withdrawing. I don't want to lose what we shared this quickly – I want her to stay with me in the moment. I glance down at the sweater and rub my hand down her arm, hoping this is the thing that keeps her in the moment with me.

"I didn't know you went to U of O," I say, working hard to keep my tone light.

She looks confused. "What?"

"The sweater? It's a University of Oregon sweater." She frowns down at it and shrugs.

"Oh, I didn't know that. I didn't go to college. I didn't even graduate high school, but I wanted to go to NYU. My mom and I did a campus tour once, and I loved it." Alex *never* volunteers information about herself like this. She might be withdrawing, but she's being more open than usual, which means this is still working.

"Where'd you get this?" She looks down at the sweater and smiles.

"I found it at the thrift store. It's not anything I'd normally wear, but I loved it when I saw it. It even smelled good. It felt like it was already mine, which sounds stupid." I grin, feeling the hum of connection between us again.

"It's not stupid at all. It *was* already yours, because it was mine." She gives me a confused look. "I donated all of my old clothes a few months ago. Nana bought this for me when I started college, and I wore this thing constantly for years. If you check the tag, my initials are there." Her face is incredulous for a second before she yanks the sweater off and checks the tag. She stares at the tag, dumbfounded, before she closes her eyes and laughs.

My hopeful smile fades at the bitter tone of her laughter.

"I don't even get to have a favorite sweater anymore without you ruining it for me," she mutters as she stands up and throws it to the ground. She pulls another sweater out of her dresser drawer as she heads to the kitchen, where I can hear her opening a bottle of wine.

I stare after her, frozen, a pit opening up in my stomach and sucking away all of the happiness I felt a moment ago. For the first time in years, I have to fight off the overwhelming urge to cry.

I don't talk to her as we get ready for bed. I can barely look at her, and she seems equally happy to ignore me as well, which makes my chest ache. I turn away from her in the small bed, barely sleeping at all.

When I wake up early the next morning, she's curled up in my arms, her face pillowed on my chest, and I pull away from her so immediately that she jerks awake. I don't make her breakfast, I don't talk to her, and I don't look at her, but I catch her looking at me all morning out of the corner of my eye.

"Um, I'll see you tonight?" she asks as I park in front of her office. I shake my head a little, still not looking at her.

"I have some stuff that I need to take care of at home. You can have that alone time you want."

"Or I can come over after work." I finally look at her, confused. Why the fuck is she volunteering to spend time with me after last night?

I shrug. "Fine." She gives me a small smile and waits, her hand resting on the door handle. Does she want me to kiss her? I can't handle her flinching away from me right now. When I lean over to kiss her, she doesn't flinch at all and barely kisses me back, but she *does*.

That's new.

I watch her with confusion as she gets out of the car and walks up the stairs into her office, waving back at me slightly. What the fuck is happening here? Why the fuck would she push me away like that, only to change her mind immediately?

Oh. *Oh.*

My chest fills with warmth as I realize she *did* feel our connection, she just got *scared*.

23

ALEX

SATURDAY, OCTOBER 21

I thought this whole boyfriend delusion of Theo's was just about sex and control, or a weird justification for breaking into my house to fuck me.

It might be those things, but that's not *all* it is. He's definitely sex obsessed, but what he really seems to want from me is *affection*. I don't know why I didn't see it sooner, especially because he's so insistent about it.

He *actually* wants me to be his girlfriend.

I can use that to my advantage.

I've been pushing Theo so much because I thought the only way out of this situation was him killing me, but I think I found another way out. He let his guard down with me when I was sweet to him, and I was able to hurt him by rejecting him, so I'm positive that I can use affection to get him to do what I want.

If I can get him comfortable enough that he slips up, I can get away from him. I'll have to engage with him emotionally and toe the edges of his delusion to get him to let his guard down, and if I can do that without letting *my* guard down, I can finally get the upper hand here.

That might be hard.

I accidentally let my guard down the other night. Theo was so different and so *sweet*, it took me completely by surprise. The sex was different, too. It felt like it wasn't about having sex. It felt like being cared for, in a way.

It was the best sex I've ever had.

That's a problem.

***

"Honey, *this* is what you want to do with your day? We've been in line for almost an hour," Theo says, checking the time on his phone again. I pull my jacket a little tighter and roll my eyes at him.

"You're free to leave, but you're not going to, so shut up." He laughs, shaking his head at me. "The brunch is worth the wait, I promise. They split their hollandaise the last time I was here, though, so maybe avoid the eggs benedict." Theo gives me an incredulous look.

"*You're* being picky about food? Alex, you ate a can of baked beans for dinner on Monday when I went to Salem. *I* left you fresh spinach tortellini, but *you* chose to eat beans, *cold* beans, *out of the fucking can* like a cartoon hobo." How indignant he is makes me genuinely laugh, which in turn makes him smile at me in a soft, unguarded way.

"I didn't want to cook. And yes," I say, catching his disbelieving face, "boiling water for pasta and heating up beans counts as cooking."

He rolls his eyes. "That's *insane*. You're so lucky I like to cook, especially for you."

"I guess so," I say, smiling up at him. His smile becomes more vulnerable as he snakes an arm around my waist and pulls me close, leaning down to kiss me. I don't fully lean into him, but I rest my hands against the hard plane of his stomach and kiss him back. I don't usually return affection outside of sex, and he notices instantly, grinning at me like he's won something.

I've been working all morning to see how hard it is to get his guard down if I'm sweet to him, and he's shockingly easy for me to manipulate.

This is *perfect*.

"Holy shit, Ted? Ted Anderson?"

Theo's demeanor changes so fast it's scary. One second, he's slouched against the wall of the restaurant, relaxed and leaning in to kiss me again, and the next he's tense, standing to his full height, his face stony. I turn around and see a short, thick man with stringy blonde hair walking towards us, waving at Theo. Theo steps between me and the man, his arm passing across my body and his hand snaking back and resting on the outside of my hip as he shoves me behind him.

He's so obviously upset that I want to rub his back in reassurance, but I quash the urge.

That's too much affection.

"Adam." Theo's voice is lower and completely flat, and something about this is making me nervous.

"Damn, man, I thought that was you! It's been forever, how are you?" Adam reaches out as if he'll hug Theo, who doesn't move at all. Adam puts his arms down awkwardly and sees me looking out from behind Theo and smiles. "Hey, is this your girl? It's Ashley, right?" He shoves his hand out towards me. "I'm Adam."

I reach out to shake his hand, but Theo holds me back slightly. I lean forward and shake Adam's hand anyway, looking up at Theo as he grips my hip and levels me with a scary, warning expression.

Who's Ashley? I've *never* heard Theo talk about an ex.

Did he stalk her?

Did he *kill* her?

I look back at Adam and force a smile as I catch his eyes flitting down my body in a way that makes me uneasy.

"Um, hi. I'm Alex." Adam's face goes from confusion to embarrassment.

"Oh, sorry about that."

"It's fine," I say, keeping my voice friendly. "How do you two know each other?"

"Theo and I *roomed* together for a while," he says pointedly.

"In college?" I shoot Theo another look and see his jaw tense, a muscle in his neck twitching as he glares at Adam. I look between them, confused, and something in Adam's expression changes as he glances back at Theo.

"New girlfriend?"

"Oh, I'm n-" Theo's hand grips me tightly, his thumb pressing into my hip bone so hard I think I might bruise, so I nod, digging my nails into Theo's wrist. "His girlfriend," I finish, and Theo's grip on me relaxes, his thumb stroking over my skin in quiet approval.

"It's *new*," Theo says with a weird, tense emphasis on the word. Adam's mouth twitches up at the corners.

"So, she doesn't -"

"*No*," Theo says in a low, harsh tone of voice before clearing his throat. "Excuse us," he says, his voice cold and forcibly polite. "Sweetheart, let's go." Theo wraps a tense arm around my shoulders and starts pushing me away from the restaurant, keeping his body between me and Adam. I let him steer me up the street as I look back at Adam, who looks at me with narrowed eyes, his flat expression making my skin crawl. When I look up at Theo, he looks furious.

"Who's he?"

"Stop asking questions for ten fucking seconds and *walk*," he hisses. I don't like this situation or the way he's speaking to me, so I stop dead. He almost pushes me over from how hard he's trying to make me move, and he's so tense he's shaking.

I need to get him to calm down.

"Theo, what's happening? You're scaring me," I say, keeping my voice soft as I gently pull his arm off me. He stops, his whole body rigid as he looks up at the sky and exhales harshly through his teeth. He turns towards me slowly, angrier than I've ever seen him as he grabs my shoulders and bends down to get his face closer to my eye level.

"Alexandria, *sweetie*, I need you to get in the fucking car, okay?" His eyes are wide and he's speaking slowly through clenched teeth, and I can tell he's trying to manage his anger, but it actually makes him scarier. I want to be anywhere other than near him right now, but he doesn't wait for me to respond before he places his arm around my shoulders again and drags me up the street.

Once we're in the car, Theo runs his hands through his hair and swears under his breath as he drives away quickly. The tension inside the car is so thick it makes my shoulders start to curl in on themselves, and I sink down in my seat, leaning against the door and staying quiet as we navigate onto the freeway, immediately winding up in bumper-to-bumper traffic. Theo swears under his breath and leans over to open the glove compartment, pulling something out quickly.

"Honey, can you look at me for a second?"

It's a mistake.

The second I look at him, he grabs the wrist closest to him and snaps a handcuff around it, quickly placing the other one on his wrist, and I scream, starting to panic.

"What the *fuck*, Theo?" I jerk my wrist away, but he grabs my hand, forcing his fingers through mine and pulling our entwined, locked hands towards him.

"I need to talk to you."

"You can't do it without fucking *handcuffs*?"

He grimaces. "I don't know. Can you calm down for a second?"

"*No!* You flipped your shit and handcuffed me after I met your friend!" Theo barks out a harsh laugh.

"We're *not* friends," he spits. "I fucking *hate* that guy. He's a real piece of shit, you have no idea. I had to deal with him for two years, and they were the longest two years of my life. He *never* shut the fuck up, and I wanted to beat the shit out of him constantly." He makes a disgusted sound in the back of his throat before he takes a deep breath. "We were cellmates," he says quickly.

I freeze, looking over at him with wide eyes.

"Like in *jail*?" He shoots me a worried look out of the corner of his eye as he squeezes my hand.

"Um, more like *prison*," he says quietly, "because I was in prison for nine years." I stare at him, panic welling up inside of me.

"Why?" I ask quietly, leaning away from him.

"*Sweetheart*, listen to me, okay? In college, I had this girlfriend, Ashley. We were together for almost a year before she broke up with me," he says quickly, squeezing my hand so hard it hurts.

Oh my god, he *did* kill his ex.

"When she broke up with me, she said it was so she could focus on getting into med school. I assumed she was just overwhelmed with classes and her internship, and I thought we'd get back together once she saw that she didn't have to give up our relationship to get into med school. I tried to show her that, but she started avoiding me, and then she filed this *bullshit* restraining order. When I went to talk to her about it, I found out that we were on *very* different pages about our relationship," he says, his voice slowing and getting terse.

Hasn't he told me *we're* on different pages?

Oh, *fuck.*

"Apparently, she filed the restraining order because she'd been fucking my asshole roommate for *six months*, and she knew I wasn't going to take it well." He takes a deep breath in and blows it out quickly. "I *didn't* take it well. I couldn't really control my reaction – I was young, you know? – and I absolutely *lost* it." He grimaces. "I wanted to take my time telling you, maybe wait until you and I were in a better place and you were more adjusted." He raises our hands to his mouth and presses a gentle kiss to the back of my hand. "It seemed like that was *happening*," he says under his breath, his tone sad and a little resigned.

He looks over at me, but I'm looking out the window, staring at the car ahead of us as I struggle to get my breathing under control. He killed her, and now he's going to kill me.

Now that I'm not pushing him to do it, it's so much scarier.

I can't believe I've been stupid enough to think I can handle this.

I start hyperventilating as Theo takes the exit to get us on the highway towards the coast. He's going to kill me when we get back, I'm sure of it.

"Woah, hey, deep breaths, okay?" He squeezes my hand again. "I know this is a lot to take in, but it's not as bad as it sounds, I promise. Why don't we -"

"Please don't kill me," I beg, and he shoots me a wounded look.

"Alex, come *on*. That's fucked up."

I gape at him in horror. "I just found out you killed your fucking girlfriend!"

"Wait, *what*? I didn't kill Ashley! I didn't fucking *touch* her. Jesus, Alex, you know me better than that," he says, his voice indignant and hurt. He squeezes my hand again, frowning at me. "I tried to kill *Kevin*, sweetie. I got really close, too, before Ashley knocked me out with a baseball bat, but I still beat the ever-loving shit out of him and put him in a coma. I mean, technically, his *doctors* put him in a coma, I just gave him the brain damage that made it necessary." He snorts and shakes his head slightly. "Ashley was a softball player in high school, so Kevin wasn't the only one with brain damage," he says, rolling his eyes at me. He seems to realize that joking is the wrong move once he sees my face, and he looks away quickly. "*Anyway*, he's awake now and lives with his mom, I think. He kind of *has* to," he mutters the last part under his breath, but I catch it.

I stare at him, horrified.

"*That's* supposed to make me feel better?"

"Um, yeah?"

"You have got to be *fucking kidding me!*" My voice is so shrill that Theo flinches.

"It's not *that* bad, honey. I'm not going to tell you what Adam did, but I'm a fucking saint compared to him, I promise." I give him a questioning look, and he shakes his head a little bit, staring ahead at the road. I think about how he was trying to keep me away from Adam, and I shudder.

I don't think I want to know.

"What happened to Ashley?"

Theo shrugs. "Last I checked, she was about to finish her residency, but that was a few years ago."

"Why are you bothering me if you were so fucking in love with her?" I ask, and he winces.

"Um, after she gave her victim impact statement, I found out that we'd never had the relationship I thought we did. She didn't even love me, she loved *Kevin* - just not enough to stay with him after all that brain damage," he says, sounding both disdainful and smug. He shrugs and then looks at me, a little bemused.

"Wait, Alex, are you *jealous*?" I blanch at the suggestion, and he laughs. "Seriously, sweetheart, don't be," he says, kissing the back of my hand. "That was *so* different from what we have. Honestly, I basically didn't even give a shit about her compared to how I feel about you." He smiles at me sweetly and I burst into tears, jerking my hand out of his to cover my face as I sob.

"*Fuck*," he mutters, letting me take back my hand and smoothing his hand over my hair as I sob. "Sweetheart, *please* don't cry. Everything's fine." He keeps trying to comfort me, his voice getting increasingly panicky, but everything he says makes it worse. Eventually he stops talking, taking my hand in his and running his thumb over the back of my hand in small circles in an attempt to be soothing.

I don't stop crying until we get back to his house.

I got lulled into this false sense of security, convinced myself that I could handle this because he's affectionate and hasn't hit me and he's good in bed, but he's still going to *kill me*.

He parks and turns toward me, pulling my face towards him with his free hand, looking at me with concern.

"Let's get you inside, okay? I'm so sorry you found out like this. I wish I'd been able to tell you on my terms, but we're going to get past this. It's all going to be fine." He pulls handcuff keys out of the center console and uncuffs me, and I let him lead me inside and guide me to the couch. I'm starting to get numb, so I just stare at him as he kneels between my legs, cupping my face and giving me a nervous smile.

"I know the prison thing is freaking you out, honey, but I promise that I'm in a better place now. I did a lot of work on myself while I was in prison, and I see a therapist now." I school my face into an expression I hope looks neutral and not horrified.

I don't want to know what he was like when he was younger if this is him *better*.

"You don't need to be afraid of me, Alex. I made bad choices, but I'm not a bad person." I take a shuddering breath and try to stay calm.

"Theo," I say, my voice shaky, "can you understand why I'm scared?" He looks at me, frowning. "It's just that I don't really have a choice of whether or not to be here, and I don't actually *know* you at all, and I've been letting you *fuck* me, and I *can't* go to the cops, and you're a *stalker*, and almost a *murderer*, and you're probably going to *kill* me, and -" Theo covers my mouth with his hand, which is for the best.

"Alexandria, you need to stop spiraling. You've got a skewed perception of our relationship right now because you're upset, but you're being mean. You *do* know me, okay? You just didn't know this *about* me." I'm glad his hand is still over my mouth because I want to laugh at how insane he sounds. "Also, you haven't been *letting* me fuck you. You've got this idea that our sex life and relationship are one-sided, and it's hurtful because they *aren't*. You're a very active participant in both."

He finally drops his hand from my mouth, but I have nothing to say. He sighs in frustration and looks away from me, rubbing the back of his neck.

"Listen, I'm sorry today sucks, okay? I felt like things were going well this morning. Why don't we try to reset? We were going to get brunch, so let me make you brunch. *I* won't split the hollandaise." He gives me a small smile, and I stare at him, dumbfounded. His smile falters, and he nods. "Okay. I'm going to be in the kitchen."

I pull out my phone the second he's out of the room and search "THEODORE ANDERSON OREGON" but my search engine shuts down immediately. It was worth a shot. I look around and see his phone and keys on the coffee table, and I grab his phone as quietly as I can. I look at the lock screen and type in my name, and it opens. Of course.

I search his name and click on the first item.

LOCAL STUDENT ARRESTED ON ASSAULT CHARGES
February 3, 2014

SALEM, Ore. - A University of Oregon senior is being held on a $150,000 bond after he was arrested on charges of assault in the first degree, stalking, and harassment.

Police say Theodore Robert Anderson, 21, was arrested after assaulting his roommate, Kevin Eric Jackson, 21, in the apartment of Ashley May Chen, 21. Chen has an active restraining order against Anderson dated January 17, 2014, and she alleges that Anderson began harassing her and stalking her following their breakup on December 27, 2013.

Anderson was allegedly hiding inside Chen's house when he discovered Chen and Jackson romantically involved. Anderson brutally attacked Jackson, only stopping when Chen hit Anderson over the head with a baseball bat and was able to contact law enforcement.

Jackson is currently in an induced coma as he recovers from the traumatic brain injury caused by Anderson. Chen's lawyers have requested her whereabouts be kept confidential.

Theo comes back into the room with a cup of coffee, grimacing when he sees me looking at the phone. He walks over and pulls it from my hand, scrolling through it briefly before sighing and setting it down on the coffee table.

"Alex, don't freak out, okay?" I can feel the edges of my perception starting to get blurry, but I can't afford to get numb right now. I need to focus.

"You were in her house?" He grimaces as he sits next to me and grabs my hands, gripping them tightly.

"Uh, yeah. I needed to talk to her, and she was avoiding me."

"Can you blame her? Being stalked is terrifying." He winces slightly, but I don't think the jab lands fully.

"I've tried to apologize." He makes a face. "She has *not* accepted."

"Would you have killed Kevin?" Theo looks up at the ceiling, his jaw tense.

"Probably. I was *very* upset at the time."

"How are you even *out*?" He shrugs.

"I had good lawyers, I took a plea deal, and I got out on parole for good behavior." He seems so nonchalant about it, and I narrow my eyes at him.

"Have you ever killed anyone?" His face goes blank instantly, and I lean away from him. He looks over my shoulder, and his mouth becomes a thin line.

"Um, *yeah*," he says quietly, "I killed my dad when I was twelve." My eyes widen uncomfortably, and I lean farther away from him, feeling his hands grip mine tighter.

"You killed your *dad?*" Theo's face hardens, and his eyebrows jump up as he looks at me.

"It was self-defense, and he deserved it, *believe* me. That fucking meth-head piece of shit knocked up my mom when she was sixteen and used to beat the shit out of both of us. I don't think anyone was that upset about it, honestly."

I highly doubt *that*.

"What about your mom?" Theo scoffs and rolls his eyes.

"Oh, Melissa *hates* me. She fucked off to Florida while I was being held in juvie and didn't speak to me again until last year, and she only talked to me because Nana left me everything. The first thing she said to me in almost two decades was that it was unfair of me to steal her kids' futures by keeping all the money for myself." He rolls his eyes again. "She conveniently forgot I'm *also* her kid, I guess. And before you think I'm a total asshole, I offered to have Catherine set up a trust for her other kids. She *freaked* out, calling me a monster and a financial abuser and all this shit just because I wouldn't just give *her* the money. Mother of the year, right?" His tone is almost joking, but I can tell from the tight, clipped edge of his voice that it bothers him a lot. My brain seems to skip over the broader context of the conversation and focuses on that.

"I can't imagine parents like that. It sounds awful." He looks a little shocked at my response but rubs his thumbs across the back of my hands.

"Um, yeah, but Nana and Boss were basically my parents after that. They adopted me, actually. Melissa signed over her parental rights for, like, five grand or something." He tries to smile, but his mouth is too tight. "I was definitely a handful, but they were great. I know they would have *loved* you, especially Nana." I have no idea what to say to any of this, so I just nod. He looks at me, his face softening, his smile small and a little crooked.

"God, you're so sweet. I'm so fucking sorry about today. Again, this is *not* how I wanted you to find out about any of this." He shakes his head. "If I ever see Adam again, I'll fucking kill him." My mouth drops open in horror, and he holds up his hands. "I'm kidding! Bad joke, sorry."

I don't think he's joking.

He runs a hand through his hair and stands up, pulling me with him. "Right, okay. *Brunch.*"

We don't talk while he starts to make food. I sit at the kitchen island and watch him, my mind reeling. My stalker is a murderer who has a bad relationship with his mother, and the last woman he stalked meant *less* to him than I do. Bailey tells me about all the true crime shows she watches, and this sounds like one of those.

This is bad. This is very fucking bad.

The one thing I keep coming back to is that he didn't hurt Ashley. It's the only thing keeping me from spiraling into a full-blown panic attack.

"Alex?" Theo looks at me expectantly.

"Huh?"

"I asked if you like orange or grapefruit mimosas?"

"Whatever you're having."

"What do *you* like?"

"Uh, grapefruit." He smiles at me.

"You got it." I stare at him, thinking hard. I need some answers or I'm going to completely freak out.

"Um, Theo, can I ask you some questions?" He sets the drink down in front of me, looking a little nervous.

"Yeah, anything."

"Did you and your mom ever get along?" He freezes and swallows hard, nodding once and turning away from me, walking back towards the food on the stove.

"Yeah. She, uh...we were best friends when I was little. Jason went from logging to driving a long-haul truck, so it would be these long stretches of just me and Melissa, but then he'd come home, and it was a fucking nightmare." I feel a pang of sadness for him and try to quash it. He's going to kill me, so I don't need to feel sorry for him.

I sort of do, though.

"Was it ever good?"

He shrugs. "Sure, maybe sometimes, but in general, having a meth head for a dad fucking *sucked*." I frown. That sounds like an understatement.

"Why'd you kill him?" He shrugs again, his shoulders tense.

"He got *really* high and threatened to kill Melissa, and I fucking *lost it*. He was waving his gun around in her face, so I got it off him and shot him in the head." My eyes widen, and I stare at him in shock. He did that at *twelve?*

"And she just left you?" Theo raises his eyebrows, shaking his head and sucking in a deep breath.

"*Yeah*. Never came to visit or answered any of my calls, and then Nana and Boss showed up and told me they'd be adopting me and that I'd be living with them."

"Fuck." He crosses his arms and nods his head at the pan in front of him, his eyes wide.

"Mmhmmm." Something about the rigid set of his shoulders tells me I need to drop this line of questioning, so I pivot.

"Why'd you go for Kevin and not Ashley?" He looks up at me with a serious, pained expression.

"Come *on*, Alex. I *never* would have hurt her." I can't tell if I believe him or not.

He seems to believe himself, but I'm pretty sure I don't.

"Do you feel bad about almost killing Kevin?" He looks away from me again.

"It's...complicated," he says, laughing humorlessly. "Honey, can we talk about something else now? I try not to think about this stuff."

"I think I get to ask you these questions," I say, trying to keep my voice even.

He lets out a harsh sigh. "You *do*, but I'm only talking about this shit because you feel like you don't know me. I hate thinking about it, and I'm *begging* you to change the subject," he says, the last words brittle.

"Don't you have to talk to your therapist about this stuff?"

"Fuck, no. I talked about it in the past, and I'm fine now," Theo says, his voice clipped and tense.

"You know that talking to a therapist doesn't mean that you're actually dealing with anything, right?" My tone is sharp, but the laugh that he lets out is sharper.

"How the fuck would *you* know? You don't talk to anyone about anything, especially not your fucking feelings," he snaps, and my anger flares in my chest.

"I don't need to talk about my feelings. They're *my* feelings, and I'm the only one who needs to know about them," I say, and he shoots me a dirty look.

"That's so fucking unhealthy," he scoffs. "It's also a shitty attitude to have in a relationship." Anger and stress coil tightly in my chest and I snap.

"This isn't a fucking *relationship*!" Theo closes his eyes and takes a deep breath, looking up at the ceiling and shaking his head.

"I know you're upset with me right now, sweetie, but this *is* a relationship," he grits out through clenched teeth. He lets out an aggravated sound and stirs something in the pan in front of him. "Whether you like it or not," he mutters under his breath.

"I don't!" I scream at him, jumping off my stool and stepping towards him. "If you ever fucking listened to me, you'd know that!" He rounds on me, his face frustrated and his jaw clenched.

"That's bullshit!" Theo's not quite yelling, but his voice is louder than usual. "I'd listen to you, but you're constantly fucking lying to me, *and to yourself*, about your feelings."

The implication that *I'm* the one in this situation who's lying to myself makes something in me break. I'm angry in a way I've never felt before, angrier than I was with Danny the night I ran. Waves of heat and years of pent-up aggression course through my body, and I move without thinking, swinging my hand up to slap him.

Theo catches my wrist, and both of us stand still for a minute, shocked. His face goes blank, and his hand shakes slightly as his grip on my wrist gets so tight that it hurts.

He's going to kill me now.

Maybe he should, if I'm the sort of person who would hit someone out of anger. My eyes start watering, and his face slowly changes into a look of deep hurt. He shoves my wrist out of his hand, and I step back from him, scared and ashamed.

He looks away from me, and his voice is quiet and ice-cold when he speaks.

"Get the *fuck* out."

***

I don't notice the walk home. I only notice that, at some point, I'm in the bath with a bottle of wine, sobbing.

I don't know if I'm more upset about the fact that Theo might have been angry enough to kill me, or that I almost did something I didn't think I would ever do to another person.

I should be more upset by one of them, but I don't know which one.

24

THEO

I give Alex space after Saturday, mostly because she's freaked out about the prison thing but also because *I'm* freaking the fuck out about our fight. She tried to *hit* me, and then I kicked her out like a fucking asshole instead of talking to her and resolving the issue. I know she's dealing with a lot because of her ex. I know that's probably all this is, but it felt personal, like she really wanted to hit me.

Maybe she did.

For the first time, I wish I could actually talk to Dr. Mills about my feelings.

It felt like right before Adam walked up, things were finally easy between us. Alex stood closer to me, she was affectionate with me, she gave me a genuine smile when we were joking around – she was *adjusting*.

Now I have to start over.

Fuck, why is this so hard? We work so well together, but she just won't let it happen. I've been more open with her than I've been with anyone in a long time, but she just won't let me in. She went home on Saturday and cried for hours, and she hasn't eaten much in the last two days, but she still won't call me.

She watched a video on YouTube about managing her anger, though, so she's trying.

Alex, 4:39 PM:

can i come over after trivia

we should talk

Holy shit, she's reaching out to fix it. She's *really* trying.

Theo, 4:41 PM:

I'll make dinner.

I do my best to stay calm. I clean, I meditate, I masturbate, I work out, I repeat. I'm something approaching calm by the time Alex's trivia thing starts, so I go down and watch her from the bar across the street. She seems subdued, not as chatty with her girlfriends as usual. Two of their other friends are there, people I've seen before, but I fixate on the blonde guy sitting next to Alex.

Does she realize he kind of looks like Danny? Similar hair color, similar jaw shape, shorter but with a similar build. He's so obviously interested in her, so how the fuck does she not see it? Does she see it, and she just likes the attention? Is she going to run into this guy's arms anytime we have a fight?

That won't end well for him.

I'm getting worked up, so I focus on my breathing and think about it logically. I've seen Alex flirt, and she's terrible at it in a cute way, but it's very obvious when she's doing it. She's not flirting with him, as far as I can tell. I think about how she is with me in public - somewhat standoffish, but very aware of me and generally accepting of my affection. I think about the few videos of her and Danny on his social media, how she seemed to stay close and slightly behind him, as if she were hiding from him.

For someone so unobservant, she's extremely aware of the person she's with.

I watch closely at how she interacts with this guy, and she seems to be genuinely unaware of his attention towards her. The way he sits near her and reaches up to tuck the tag into the back of her sweater makes me want to fucking punch him, but the fact that Alex barely registers it makes me feel marginally better.

He finally gets her undivided attention, and I fucking *hate* that Alex seems even somewhat interested in what he's talking about, so I pull out my phone to text her.

Theo, 8:49 PM:

What do you want for dinner?

Alex grabs her phone in the middle of him saying something to read my text, and he looks irritated as she starts responding immediately.

Alex, 8:49 PM:

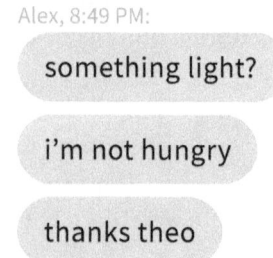

something light?

i'm not hungry

thanks theo

I let out a long breath, tension bleeding out of my shoulders as she looks back up at the guy, seeming to apologize as she puts her phone back on the table, screen up. I think she'd grab it again if I texted her right now, so I need to calm down.

Couples fight, but that doesn't mean she's going to fucking cheat on me.

I don't think she's like that.

I stay at the bar, watching Alex and trying to stay calm. Our relationship is so different than I thought it would be, and every time I think things are going well, something happens to fuck it up. I know our conversation tonight is going to suck, but it might also be an opportunity to fix things between us.

It'll work out.

It has to.

Once trivia is almost over, I pay out and cross the street, waiting outside the bar for her. She walks out with her friends a few minutes later, not noticing me at all, and I watch closely at how they interact.

"...don't know who chose the theme this week, but it sucked," the blonde guy says, and Alex laughs in a way I can tell is slightly insincere and placating.

"I liked it, but I like classic literature," she says, shrugging. "My mom read a ton of it to me as a kid, although reading a six-year-old *Anna Karenina* is a weird move, in retrospect." Her friends laugh, and a pang of jealousy rings through me.

Why isn't she telling *me* things like that?

"Yeah, I guess it was cool," he says in response. "Do you need a ride home tonight, Alex?"

I'm absolutely going to punch this fucking guy.

"No, thanks. I'm meeting a friend soon."

Are we friends? Are you supposed to be friends with people you date? I walk up to her group, approaching Alex from behind.

"What *kind* of friend?" her shorter girlfriend asks in a teasing tone.

"A good one, hopefully," I say, stepping close into Alex's space. She startles, turning around into me and taking a quick step backwards. She doesn't meet my eyes as a blush spills across her cheeks, and she turns back to her friends, leaning slightly back towards me, obviously flustered.

I shove my hands in my pockets to keep myself from reaching for her.

"Oh, um, guys, this is Theo," she says quickly, gesturing at me. "Theo, these are my friends Anna, Will, Jessica, and Ben." Greetings are exchanged, and Alex gets a curious look from her friend Anna, while Jessica looks me up and down before smirking at Alex. I nod at Will, who seems polite but disinterested, and I meet Ben's eyes briefly, smiling at him when he looks vaguely irritated.

I want to claim Alex in some way, but I know she'd be pissed if I touched her right now. We're still fighting, and she seems extremely protective of her friends, but I can't fucking help it – I need to tell them she's mine somehow. I lean down slightly into her space, keeping my voice quiet, but loud enough to be heard by all of them.

"Are you ready to go? I've got dinner waiting at home." Alex shoots me a cold look over her shoulder.

"*Sure*," she says tightly, and I can tell she's not pleased with me. "I'll see you guys next week," she says to her friends before she turns away and lets me lead her back towards my place. I don't touch her, but I walk close to her, hearing her phone ping a few times as we walk in tense silence for a block.

"Did your mom actually read you *Anna Karenina* as a kid?" Her demeanor softens, and she smiles a little wistfully and nods.

"Yeah, she did. Went right over my head, but I dreamed of wheat fields for a while." I look down at her and smile, wondering what she was like as a little kid. "She also read me kids' books, like a normal mom. My favorite was *Alice's Adventures in Wonderland*. I made her read it to me a hundred times, easily. It was her favorite as a kid, too. It's why she na-" Alex fakes a cough, and I try to hide my smile.

She basically just told me why her mom named her Alice.

"She painted a ton of the art from the books on my bedroom walls when I was born," Alex continues, and a sharp thrill shoots through me as I realize this is her trying to be more open. "It stayed like that until Danny -" She forcibly coughs again. "Anyway, it got painted over at one point," she says, getting somber.

"I'm so sorry."

"Yeah. I cried about it for a year," she says with a humorless little laugh. I'm going to kill him.

"Why don't you tell me stuff like this more often?"

She shrugs. "It's personal."

"I'd like to hear more of your personal stuff."

Alex scoffs and crosses her arms. "You don't tell *me* anything," she mutters.

I run my hands back through my hair, sighing. "Sweetheart, I said I was sorry."

She levels me with a skeptical glare and snorts out a laugh. "Yeah, *right*. I don't believe you would have told me in the first place."

"I was going to, I just...I wanted it to be on my terms."

"*Everything* is on your terms," she snaps. "You get to control my life and come over whenever you want and fuck me and play house, and I just have to take it." God, I hate how she views our relationship.

"Alex -"

"I don't know why I thought I could actually talk to you," she interrupts. "You know what? We'll just fuck. That's all you care about anyway." She storms off ahead of me, turning down the dead-end street leading to my house, and I stare after her, frustrated and confused.

How did that go so poorly so quickly?

I scrub my hands over my face and let out a long sigh. She *wants* to talk to me. She's mad that I *didn't* talk to her. She wants more from me, just like I want more from her. That's a good sign. I can do that. I follow her slowly, letting her burn off some of her anger, and find her waiting impatiently on the porch.

"I was going to apologize, so should I blow you here or wait until we get inside?" I grit my teeth and ignore her snide comment, bracing myself to be open the way she wants from me.

"Um, Melissa didn't read to me that much, but someone gave her the first *Harry Potter* book one year when I was little, and that was really nice for about two weeks." I unlock the door and open it, glancing back at Alex. Her anger deflates instantly, and she gives me a pitying look that I fucking *hate*.

Ashley used to give me that look, which is why I never talked to her about anything.

"I thought you said she was a good mom?" Alex's voice is gentle in a way that puts me on edge.

"I said she was my best friend, *not* a good mom. Are you coming inside or not?" She nods and walks in, glancing up at me as she slips her shoes off.

"What about your grandma? Was she a good mom?" I nod, staring at my feet as I unlace my boots.

"I mean, yeah, definitely. She was sweet and tough and sharp as hell. I was a handful, and she was super fucking strict, but she loved me a lot."

"How were you a handful?" I give her a sly look as I kick off my boots.

"I was emotional and had impulse control issues as a kid, so I did a *lot* of stupid shit. I got into fights, I set fire to an abandoned barn, I ditched school to get drunk at the beach, I crashed my first car into a tree, shit like that. Oh, and I got caught fucking Carrie Osman in the bathroom my freshman year during third period. Twice."

She lets out a soft laugh. "*That* one sounds like you," she says, her voice almost teasing. I can't tell if she's making fun of me, but her mood seems better, and I decide to use it as an opening.

"What were you like as a kid?" She looks at her feet and shrugs.

"Uh, normal? My parents were great, but they expected a *lot* out of me. They were both ambitious, so *I* had to be ambitious. They succeeded, so *I* was supposed to succeed." I frown slightly at her bitter tone.

Was her childhood not as happy as I thought it was?

"I did everything my parents wanted. I took all AP classes, I got straight As, I co-captained my track team, I was president of the art club, I was on yearbook, all of it. I barely partied or dated or had a life. I mean, I drank, but only at home and only alone," she says in a reassuring tone, as though that's not extremely fucking concerning. "*My* big high school rebellion was that I ditched school once during my sophomore year and got stoned with Tim Klosterman. I let him finger me in his hot tub when his parents were at work." She glances up at me, blushing a little. "It was the first time I ever came, but I ended up getting a yeast infection because of the chlorine," she says, rolling her eyes. I smile a little, fighting the urge to touch her.

"Was he your high school boyfriend?" She gives me a sheepish look and shakes her head.

"He was someone's." I raise my eyebrows at her in surprise.

"Wait, seriously?" She nods, looking a little smug, and I laugh. That doesn't fit with my idea of her, but I love that she's sharing all this with me.

She looks almost different to me now, but I don't know why.

We stand there in the entryway looking at each other, and it feels like the tension between us has finally evaporated. I realize that this is my opening to try to fix things with her, so I step closer to her.

"I'm really sorry, sweetheart. I don't just want to fuck you and play house, I want *this*. I want us to be open with each other." Her face shutters, and she looks at her feet.

"I don't," she says quietly. "It makes this harder."

"How?" She levels me with a look I don't totally understand before she shakes her head and sucks in a deep breath.

"It doesn't matter. Listen, Theo, I am *so* sorry about the other day. I didn't mean to almost hit you, I really didn't. I'm not like that, I swear." I nod, glancing away from her quickly, discomfort flooding my body.

"I know. I'm sorry I kicked you out. I just...I don't like getting hit," I say quietly, looking back at her after a moment.

She wraps her arms around her waist, her eyes tearing up. "Me, either." My heart breaks a little as she looks at her feet to hide that she's crying. "I'm so sorry. I really don't know what happened. I was so scared and upset, and I got *so* angry, and I felt like my body moved without me being able to control it." I reach for her, resting my hands gently on her shoulders and pulling her closer.

"Honey, I know what it feels like to be that angry, *believe* me." Maybe being more open with her is how I help fix her trust issues, so I push myself. "I got in so many fights as a kid because I only knew how to express anger through hitting people. That's what Jason did, so that's what I did, you know?" Alex looks up at me, her face sad and vulnerable.

"No, I don't know. Anytime I got angry, bad things happened, so I didn't *get* to be angry. Right before I left, I got *so* drunk and *so* angry that I screamed at Danny. It was the first time I'd ever really yelled at him, but I couldn't stop myself because I was so fucking mad."

"What did you yell at him about?"

She shrugs. "My feelings about our marriage."

I have to work hard to keep my tone even. "What did he do to you?"

She huffs out a sharp exhale and looks down at her feet. "He, um...uh, he beat the shit out of me and pulled his gun on me. He told me he'd kill me if I ever spoke to him like that again, and I knew he'd do it, so I waited until he fell asleep and then I ran." I step closer to her and gently tilt her chin up so she's looking at me.

"Alex, you can get angry with me, okay? I'll never hurt you, I promise." She gives me a skeptical look. "I mean it. You're *allowed* to be angry, okay? You just need to start letting yourself feel it and deal with it in healthier ways so that it doesn't take over your life or keep being an issue in our relationship."

She snorts and rolls her eyes. "You sound like a fucking therapist."

I shrug. "I'm basically quoting a therapist. Anger management is *huge* in prison, for some reason." I grin at her, and she laughs. I rub my hands up and down her arms, and something inside me unwinds a little as she leans into me slightly.

Holy shit, I think I fixed it.

"You want dinner? I'll make whatever you want."

She lets out an exasperated sound. "Should I just start texting you a list of what I want to eat every day?"

I laugh a little, kissing her forehead. "You could do that, you know. I wouldn't mind."

"You're *insane*," she says, but it's teasing and almost affectionate.

***

Alex, wine glass in hand, sits close to me on the couch after dinner. She puts on some horrible reality TV show, but I ignore it. I'm too busy paying attention to the fact that she keeps shifting closer to me until her arm is looped through mine and her head is resting on my shoulder.

Then she starts asking me detailed questions about the show because she can tell that I hate it and she's trying to force me to watch it with her. She's being a dick, but she's having fun with me, so I play along.

She falls asleep in my arms on the couch, and when I take her up to bed, she barely wakes up enough to brush her teeth. She strips and climbs into bed immediately afterward, humming contentedly as I pull her into my arms. I lie there as she relaxes against me, and my breath catches in my throat as her hand slips under the pillow, her fingers threading through mine before she falls asleep.

It feels more intimate than sex, somehow.

25

ALEX

SUNDAY, OCTOBER 29

Despite what he says, Theo just wants to fuck and play house, and I'm fairly sure that he won't kill me if we keep doing that. It's nice, sometimes, and if I keep him at arm's length, I can keep control of the situation. If we stop getting to know each other, everything will be fine. If I can ignore how I'm starting to feel about him, I can keep this going until I figure out how to get away from him.

***

Alex, 11:45 AM:

hey, i'm inside. i'll get popcorn?

Jessica, 11:46 AM:

i'm out. food poisoning. do NOT get the teriyaki burger at Mikes.

oh no! i'm sorry

Will, 11:48 AM:

too hungover

feel better!!

I sigh, disappointment and irritation rising. I'm trying to make plans with my friends, but so far, everyone seems a little flaky. I'll take what I can get, though, because I still get to have friends. Theo's weirdly respectful of that, even though he seems to have no friends whatsoever.

"Hey, Alex." I look up to see Ben walking towards me from the ticket counter. "Zach couldn't make it. Guess it's just us?"

I force a smile. "Oh, um, I haven't heard from Anna yet, so maybe not?"

Anna, 11:51 AM:

I got called on shift last minute! You guys enjoy the movie.

Rain check???

I stifle a groan. Anna chose the movie, and I don't want to spend three hours watching another franchise action movie. I only watch them to annoy Theo, who hates them just as much as I do.

Alex, 11:52 AM:

shoot!!! definitely rain check :)

"Anna's out?" I look up at Ben and nod.

"Yeah. What do you want to do?" I ask, hopeful he won't want to see this movie either, but he smiles, pointing towards the concession stand.

"I'll get the drinks if you get popcorn?"

I force a tight smile. "Sure."

***

Ben and I go to lunch at a brewery after the movie, which was the plan I'd made with the group, but it's a little awkward with just the two of us. Ben's nice, but he's boring, and we don't have much in common. He seems eager to talk to me, so I mostly ask him about himself and act interested, which he seems to buy.

I don't think about how it looks that we're having lunch together until I see Theo sitting at the bar, watching us. His face is locked in a tight, cold smile when he catches my eye, and I can tell that he's furious.

Why is he even here?

Right.

Stalker.

I'm looking over Ben's shoulder at Theo when I realize Ben is still talking to me.

"...a ride?" I glance back at Ben, trying to figure out what he just asked me.

"Huh? Oh, no, I, um, I have one today. I should get going, actually. Thanks for coming to the movie," I say, grabbing my purse and standing up quickly. Out of the corner of my eye, I see Theo stand up, throwing cash on the bar.

"Yeah, it was fun," Ben says enthusiastically. "We should do this again sometime."

"Sure, okay," I say, tracking Theo's slow approach.

"Awesome. I'll see you Tuesday?" Ben goes to give me a hug, and I let him, barely returning it as I watch Theo's face flash in anger. He tries to school it back into a neutral expression but fails miserably.

"Uh-huh, see you then," I say, not looking at Ben or Theo as I hurry towards the exit and start walking away from the brewery, trying not to panic.

Danny was a jealous prick, but as long as I didn't look other men in the eye when I spoke to them and didn't seem too interested, he usually didn't freak out. I have *no* idea what Theo's going to be like, but since his ex cheated on him, I assume he's going to be a fucking nightmare.

He probably won't hit me, at least.

Theo grips my arm halfway down the pier, and I look up at him, opening my mouth to explain. He shakes his head tightly and starts guiding me back to his car, and I spend the walk figuring out how to get him to calm down.

He's quiet when we get in the car, but the air around him is crackling with anger.

"Theo, it's not wha-"

"*Don't,*" he snaps at me.

"Theo, I need you to listen to me," I say sweetly, resting my hand on his forearm, which is so tense it's shaking slightly. "Everyone else canceled at the last minute, but Ben showed up before I could leave." I pull up the texts and hand him my phone, and I see his eyes flick down and read the texts when we hit a red light. "Ben wanted to get food afterward because that was the plan the group made originally, and I was really hungry." Theo's jaw tenses and I start to get angry, but I keep my voice even. "You said you weren't going to keep me from having friends, right?" Theo drags in a long, deep breath and exhales it slowly, shoving my phone back in my hands.

"I'm not keeping you from having *friends*," he grits out, "but I'm not fucking stupid. That was a *date.*" I can't help rolling my eyes and groaning.

"I wasn't on a *date*, Theo. I'm not stupid, either – you'd proba-bly kill me." He shoots me an angry, insulted look, and I gesture at his rigid posture and white knuckles. "Look at how you're acting right now! You're being a jealous fucking maniac over me having lunch with a friend." He turns up his driveway and parks the car, looking out towards the house, forcing himself to take deep breaths.

"That wasn't *lunch*," he says, his voice menacing. I groan in aggravation, my patience completely gone as I wrench the car door open.

"You're so fucking *paranoid*," I snap, slamming the door and hur-rying up the porch. Theo gets out of the car, following me up to the porch with slow, deliberate movements. Everything about him still seems strung tight and furious, and his jaw is clenched hard as he leans down, crowding me back into the door and looming over me.

"You can't be this fucking naive, Alexandria," he says through gritted teeth. "*He* thought that was a date." My temper flares, but he's not listening to me at all, so I need to try a different tactic.

"Baby, you're being crazy," I coo sweetly, and his eyes widen as his head tilts to the side slightly. I put my hands on his chest and lean up against him, and he slowly straightens up.

There we go.

I wrap my arms around his waist and look up at him with wide eyes, resting my chin on his sternum and rubbing his back, feeling some of the tension ease out of him.

"Theo, I get that you're jealous, but you need to listen to me. Ben's just a friend, and not even one I like that much. I would *never* date him, so calm down, okay?" Theo's rigid body relaxes a little more, and I take the keys from his hand, opening the front door and pulling him inside. "For the record, he's *not* my type," I say quietly.

I don't think I have a type, but Ben looks a little bit like Danny, and that's definitely *not* my type.

Hearing this seems to calm Theo down further, and he seems less worked up than a minute ago, but he's still tense and quiet, watching me intently as I turn around to kick off my shoes and set down my bag.

"Honestly, Theo, you're bei-" I scream in surprise as he grips me around the waist and picks me up, quickly heading up the stairs. "Put me down, you fucking lunatic!"

He barks out a humorless laugh but puts me down on the second-floor landing, shoving me back up against the wall, kissing me furiously. I gasp and his tongue sweeps into my mouth as he bends down, his hands gripping my ass hard enough to bruise as he picks me up, shoving his hips in between my legs. His teeth are sharp against my bottom lip and my jaw and my neck as he bites his way down, slamming me back into the wall with his hips, the friction of his jeans against my thin underwear making me writhe.

He carries me back towards his bedroom and throws me down on the bed, pulling my clothes off so aggressively something rips. Theo's got all of my clothes off within moments and he seems nearly feral, grabbing me roughly and making low, angry sounds as he kisses me brutally, his hands roaming my body, his fingers digging into my waist and thighs and ass.

He's intense in a way I'm unfamiliar with, and it's genuinely scary, but heat pools between my legs all the same. I grab onto his shirt and pull him closer, but he pulls away and starts undressing quickly.

"If you *actually* think, for one *fucking* second," he says, ripping off his shoes and socks and throwing them across the room.

"That fucking *asshole* is your *friend*," he snarls as he reaches behind his head and yanks his sweater and t-shirt off in one movement.

"You're the one who's a fucking *lunatic*." He rips his belt out of his pants with one hand, and I flinch hard, but he's looking down and doesn't notice my reaction. I relax when he throws the belt to the ground without a second thought before he shoves his pants off and stands in between my spread legs. He grabs my throat and shoves me flat on my back, his grip firm but not painful, and leans down over me, his pupils blown wide as he stares at me.

"You're *mine*, Alexandria," he snarls, and I stare at him, speechless. It's not surprising he feels that way, but I'm still shocked at the hard, possessive edge to his voice.

What's more shocking is how my body reacts to his words.

He tightens the hand around my throat as he grabs my jaw with his other hand, hooking two fingers against my bottom teeth to hold my mouth open. I make a shocked noise when he spits into my mouth and pushes his spit down my tongue with two rough fingers, finally breaking eye contact to watch his fingers slide deeper into my mouth. He makes a low, satisfied sound when I gag on his fingers.

Suddenly, it feels like a part of my brain shuts off, and I'm beyond thinking, beyond feeling anything other than what's happening in my body. He keeps his eyes on my lips, his face focused and intense as he raises his eyebrows expectantly. I suck on his fingers, and he nods in silent approval before he pulls them out of my mouth and slips them between my legs.

"*This*," he says, pressing his fingers against the slick entrance of my cunt, "is *mine*." He punctuates the word by shoving his fingers inside me, making me whimper. Uncomfortable heat courses through me as he starts to fuck me with his fingers rougher than I usually like, but something about it feels so good that I react instantly, writhing underneath him and panting softly, his hand around my throat keeping me in place.

He watches me, his eyes intense and serious as he squeezes the sides of my throat, cutting off enough air that my head starts to swim. His expression is pure hunger, and I can't look away from him, even when he crooks his fingers and pulses hard against my g-spot, his thumb circling against my clit a moment later. My leg starts twitching as more scorching heat pools in my spine, and I start clawing at the hand around my throat, at his arm, at his chest, nodding and moaning and trying to force out the word *please*.

He watches me closely as he brings me to the edge.

"*Come.*" His voice is rough and commanding in a way that causes the tension inside me to snap and my nerves to catch fire. He releases my throat, and my head feels light as I suck in air, making everything so much more intense. I reach for him desperately as my back bows and my hips start shaking, and I hold onto him for dear life as the orgasm rips through me. I collapse back onto the bed, panting heavily as I open my eyes to see him looking down at me, his jaw clenched.

"*That's* mine. You *only* come for me, do you fucking understand?" I nod absently, running my hands up his chest and across his shoulders, dragging my nails down his arms as all thoughts slip out of my grasp. I'm used to how Theo can be during sex, but this is new.

I don't know what about this is different, but how overwhelming he is right now feels so good.

That's probably bad.

He straightens, pulling me up to sit on the edge of the bed and standing in front of me, his cock flushed and angry and dripping precum. He looks down at me, dragging his thumb across my bottom lip.

"This is mine, too," he says as he slips his thumb into my mouth, and I freeze as I feel his other hand fist tightly in my hair. Anxiety cuts through the haze of pleasure, and I slam my eyes shut as I start to panic. He releases my hair a moment before his thumb drags out of my mouth, and both of his hands come to cup my face forcefully.

"Look at me," he orders in a harsh voice, but when I look up at him, he doesn't look angry at all. His gaze is intense and almost concerned as he looks down at me, and he shakes his head faintly, his eyes locked on mine. "Just fucking *trust me*, Alex." He still sounds angry, but it's not a question and I don't know what else to do, so I swallow hard and nod faintly. The corner of his mouth lifts slightly.

"Open for me," he demands quietly, his voice sending a thrill down my spine and making my cunt clench with need as I slowly open my mouth and stick out my tongue. He grips my face tighter and pushes his thick cock into my mouth slowly, watching me carefully.

"*There* we go, that's it," he says as I wrap my lips around him and suck gently, letting my eyes drift closed. "You need to look at me, sweetheart." I open my eyes and look up at him, feeling extremely vulnerable and trying to get my breathing under control as he starts to slowly, shallowly fuck my mouth.

"You're doing *such* a good job, Alex," he says, steadily thrusting deeper, but keeping his pace unhurried. My fear and hesitation start to dissipate, and I'm able to calm down enough to focus on my breathing.

I hate this, I have *always* hated this, but I don't hate it right now. Theo's not making me apologize for anything, he's not berating me, and he's not trying to hurt me, which means this isn't a punishment.

This is something *different*, but I don't know what.

"You look so pretty with my cock in your mouth." My eyes widen and my cheeks heat, and my head starts to empty from how much I like hearing that. I stare up at him and focus on the way he's fucking my mouth, starting to enjoy what he's doing. I like the feel of him in my mouth, the taste of his skin as his cock slides against my tongue, and the gentle way he strokes my cheeks as he starts thrusting deeper.

Theo keeps his eyes on mine, watching me carefully, gripping my head firmly but not painfully, his face approving and pleased as I start matching his movements in a way that makes him swear loudly. I whimper and try to relax as he pushes his cock down my throat slowly, choking on him before he pulls back to let me breathe.

"You're taking it so well for me," he moans as he grazes his thumbs across my cheeks again. He stares down at me possessively as he thrusts deeper, picking up his rhythm and making harsh, low sounds every time he hits the back of my throat. I love the way he sounds, and I'm starting to relax enough to enjoy the way his cock feels when it pushes against the back of my throat.

This is *so* different.

I raise my hands and run them up and down his body, and he moans in approval. He starts to get rougher with me, an uncontrolled edge to his movements, but he seems to inherently know what I can handle and what I can't. I breathe through my nose frantically, gagging on him and drooling a little, looking up at his intense, hungry face as I drag my fingernails down his body, which makes him moan and thrust a little deeper. I feel a surge of warmth between my thighs as he makes me choke on him again, and his eyes roll back in his head as he swears harshly. A moment later his cock pulses in my mouth and I taste his cum flooding the back of my tongue. I moan and swallow twice in quick succession before he pulls his cock out of my mouth, stroking my hair as he drops to his knees before me.

Theo's expression is still intense, but there's a softness in his eyes that wasn't there before, and it makes me more nervous than his anger did.

"I'm so proud of you," he whispers, and my eyes widen as I stare at him. Unwanted tears prick at the corners of my eyes as my throat closes up, and I suddenly feel much more naked than before.

He starts kissing me again, pushing me back towards the center of the bed, but his movements are less angry, his kisses less savage. He holds me down as he kisses me, grabbing my wrists and pinning them over my head with one hand. I can feel him getting hard again, and I writhe beneath him, whining, trying to get friction. He pulls away, his other hand gripping my throat again as he stares down at me with open need.

"You belong to me, Alex. Do you understand that?" Before I can think better of it, I nod the smallest amount, barely moving my head at all, but he catches it.

His face transforms from hunger into something else, something satisfied and triumphant.

He pushes into me and I hear him exhale roughly, and then he's covering my body with his own, bracing himself on his forearms and bracketing me in, his hands tangled in my hair as he stares down at me with an intense expression I don't want to understand. I close my eyes and let him fuck me with long, deep strokes that leave me breathless, letting the feeling of being so completely overwhelmed by him work its way up my spine, ratcheting the tension closer and closer to breaking.

"You need to tell me you're mine," he says quietly as he thrusts harder, and I keep my eyes shut, shaking my head slightly as I start tearing up again. He kisses my neck just below my ear and up my jaw, making me whimper. I'm so close to coming I can almost taste it, and he pushes me closer and closer to the edge.

Just as my leg starts to tense up, he pulls out of me and flips me over quickly, his hips shoving mine down and pinning me to the mattress, his body heavy on top of me. I let out a low, needy sound as one of his arms wraps around my neck, choking me slightly and pulling me back against him as he pushes so deep inside of me that it makes my vision swim. He stops moving, and I start sobbing nonsense, begging for more, my choked-out words and his harsh breaths getting tangled up. He grabs one of my hands, twining his fingers with mine and pinning my hand down.

"If you want to come, you need to say it," he whispers into my ear, tightening his hold around my neck slightly. "*Now,* Alex." The aggressive command in his voice has me opening my mouth before I can stop myself.

"I'm yours," I breathe out, trying to ignore how I feel as it slips out of my mouth.

"That's my perfect girl," he says, his voice softer but still aggressive, and a thrill passes down my spine. Theo tightens his grip on me and keeps me immobile while he fucks me, and I start crying as my orgasm finally rips through my body a second later, the heat dancing along my spine obliterating all awareness that I've just fucked up somehow.

He presses his lips against the back of my head as his pace picks up, and his low voice is so quiet that I can barely make out what he's saying, but the words *good* and *perfect* and *mine* break through again and again, and something about how possessive he sounds and the arm he's got around my neck and the intimacy of our hands interlocked puts me over the edge. Another orgasm rolls through me, and I sob harder as the heat in my core radiates fire into my exhausted body.

Theo barely fucks me through it before he starts coming, his loud moans and the way his arm tightens around my neck and the feeling of him pulsing inside me as he comes sends another wave of heat coursing through my body. I scream, shaking in his arms so hard that he loses his balance and collapses on top of me, his warm body flush with mine. I gasp for air and my tears start to subside, all complicated thoughts and feelings eddying out of my head as I come down from the orgasms. I'm drained and spent, and I feel light and airy, thoughtless, hovering just outside of my body, and everything is edged in a slight glow.

All I can feel is Theo's body pressing me down, feel how his heart is pounding through his chest and into my back, feel the sensation of his breath hot on me as he presses a hard kiss against the nape of my neck, his teeth scraping against my skin. He groans as he pulls out of me, falling to the bed next to me and running his hands through his hair as he stares up at the ceiling, panting.

How could feeling this good possibly be a bad thing?

I smile at Theo as a rush of affection for him courses through me, and he looks over at me with an unadulterated obsession that makes my stomach flip, and I lay there breathing hard, melting under his piercing gaze. He looks at me for a long moment, the angry tension slowly returning to his face and body before he leans over me and grips my chin, turning my face up towards him.

"I never want to see you with anyone else again, understand?" I look up at him, feeling amused and wrung out and loopy.

"That's stupid," I mutter, laughing softly as I trail my hand up his clenched jaw. Why would I want to be with anyone else? He makes me feel so good.

An alarm bell goes off in a distant corner of my mind, but I can't figure out why, and Theo's expression hardens, and he shifts his body until he looms over me, his stern face inches from mine.

"I'm fucking *serious*, Alexandria. Promise me it won't happen again." I laugh a little at how intense he is, at how aggressive he's being, and at how he relaxes the second I graze his cheek with my fingers and smile lazily up at him.

He's so easy.

"Okay, baby," I whisper, "I promise." He softens a little more, and I push my hand through his hair again. He hums as I drag my nails down the back of his neck and closes his eyes for a moment, and when he looks down at me again, he's calm and adoring. I wrap my arms around his neck and pull him into me, a content sound slipping out of me involuntarily as our lips meet.

"That's my girl," he whispers, his lips grazing against mine before he deepens the kiss, and I lose myself in how hearing those words makes me feel. He embraces me tightly and starts murmuring praise in between the soft kisses he presses against my cheeks and eyelids and neck, and I lie back and relish in his affection.

Somewhere in the back of my mind, I'm aware that I've lost another battle, ceding some unknown territory to him, but I ignore it.

I know I'm not in control of this situation at all right now, but I feel so good that I don't care.

***

I sit at the kitchen island, sipping my wine as Theo puts together dinner. He seems different, and I take my time watching him closely, trying to figure out what's changed.

There's always something slightly tense about Theo, but not right now. I don't think I've ever seen him so completely at ease before. His posture is unusually loose and he's smiling, humming along to quiet indie music as he prepares a salad, shooting me amused looks as I sneak cucumber slices from the bowl he's dumped them into. I wish he was like this more often.

Dread pools in my stomach as it slowly dawns on me what's different about him.

He's *happy*.

I'm not handling this situation as well as I thought. I've mostly learned how to manage Theo at this point, but it requires keeping him at a distance. I have to let him in just enough to get him to drop his defenses, but not enough that I drop mine. I don't know exactly what happened, but something about the sex this afternoon made me let him in, *again*.

I can't believe I'm so fucking stupid.

Theo heads for the fridge, kissing the top of my head on the way, the action seemingly involuntary. I watch him closely, and he looks up from grabbing things out of the fridge and smiles at me with that same possessive, adoring look he gave me in bed. Something other than dread churns in my stomach, and I force a smile and look away quickly, drowning the feeling with more wine.

I think it'd be easier if he just killed me, because I can't ignore how much I'm starting to want him.

Not just the sex.

Him.

26

THEO

THURSDAY, NOVEMBER 5

"How are you, Theodore?"

"Fine." Dr. Mills looks me over quickly, frowning.

"Is everything alright?"

I shrug and slouch back into the chair. "I didn't sleep very much last night." I haven't slept in about 36 hours because I've been going through Danny's social media with a fine-tooth comb to learn what phishing emails would work best on him. Something involving Joe Rogan, creatine supplements, or some Blue Lives Matter bullshit, probably.

Idiot.

On top of that, I had to check on Alex about fifteen times last night because she kept coughing so much that she could barely sleep. I think she's getting sick, and I want to be at home taking care of her.

"Theodore, how much do you sleep on average?" I'm not so tired that I don't know where this is going, and I narrow my eyes at her.

"I sleep a normal amount, Dr. Mills."

"Have you made an appointment with a psychiatrist since you've been home?"

"No."

"I'd like you to consider it. I think maybe finding medication that works for you would be a good next step in terms of your reintegration." I take a slow, deep breath and give her a small smile.

"I'm fine, thank you. We've discussed this before, and my feelings haven't changed. The medication wouldn't benefit me at all." I know what she's about to do before she does it, so I blink and purse my lips at the same time she does, but she doesn't seem to catch it.

"Alright. How are things with Alex?"

I smile a little. "They're going really well."

"I'd like to hear more about that. What do you think makes you two good together?"

"We just fit. I think Alex needs someone she can trust, someone who makes her feel safe and cared for, and I do that." Dr. Mills' mouth twitches slightly.

"What makes her a good partner to you?"

"Everything, honestly. She's smart and creative and kind of funny, and she's so fucking sweet. She's wonderful." Dr. Mills smiles.

"Sounds like it. You've mentioned something you provide for Alex, so what does she provide for you?" I blink once, carefully keeping my face neutral as Dr. Mills' gaze becomes slightly scrutinizing.

"Connection, definitely." She smiles and raises her eyebrows like she wants me to keep talking. "Um, she makes me feel accepted, I guess." Dr. Mills blinks and purses her lips, and I try not to wince.

It's not a lie, it's just not the truth *yet*.

***

When I get to Alex's place, she's curled up on the couch, coughing.

"Unless you want this cold, go away," she snaps, coughing again. I don't get sick easily, so I go out and get things to make her chicken soup, loading it up with turmeric, garlic, and ginger. She barely eats it, she barely drinks any water, and she gets angry when she realizes that I've used her phone to text Catherine and Suzie that she'll be out of work the next day.

"Stop fucking mothering me," she mumbles, sinking down into the couch and refusing the tea I hand her. She's coughing and blowing her nose constantly, but insists she's fine.

She's kind of an asshole when she's sick, apparently.

She's worse on Friday, but she refuses to take anything, continuing to insist she'll be fine. I go to the store and get her bullshit homeopathic cold remedies as well as normal cold medicine, but she refuses *all* of it. She has *no* idea how to take care of herself, and she refuses to accept any help from me, and I start to lose my patience with her as I kneel in front of her with a mug of tea.

"Drink this." She shakes her head and burrows further into the blankets. "Sweetie, you need to let me take care of you."

"*I'm fine,*" she mumbles in a petulant voice.

"Alexandria Marie Shearer, drink this *right now*," I snap. She pouts, but she drinks half of it. She gets woozy when she stands because she's barely eaten since Wednesday, so I scoop her up and tuck her into bed, trying to keep my temper in check.

She develops a low-grade fever later that night, and she refuses to do anything to help herself, even take a cold bath. She says she just needs to sweat it out, and she refuses *everything* I try to do for her, snapping at me any time I try to help her. She mostly lays in bed and sleeps, her head in my lap with the soft drone of a nature documentary series playing on her laptop. I coax her into drinking fluids anytime she wakes up, even though she keeps telling me she's fine.

I understand she's stubborn, but this is ridiculous.

When she wakes up on Saturday, her fever hasn't broken, and I start to get pissed with her. I force her to eat, and she's too tired to fight me, but I can tell she hates it. She's too exhausted to be mad at me when I put her in a cold bath and make her drink water, but she saves all of her energy to fight me about not taking any type of medicine or fever reducer, insisting she'll be fine and she'll hate me forever if I force her to do anything else. Her fever doesn't break and even starts to climb, and I don't sleep at all, checking on her every hour.

Sometime early Sunday morning, I decide I'm done with her bullshit. She can hate me if she wants to, but I'm not letting her die of the flu just because she's stubborn. She whines a little when I pick her up out of bed, but she wraps her arms around my neck and seems reluctant to let me go when I put her in the car.

"Honey, come on." Her eyes open, and she shakes her head when she sees the sign for urgent care, mumbling something about *no doctors*. I pull her face towards me until her glassy eyes are focused on mine, stroking her hair softly.

"Alex, listen to me. No one will know you were here, okay? I'm going to take care of you." She looks like she might cry, but she nods softly and lets me take her inside. I fill out her name and as much of her health information as they need and use my address and information for everything else. Alex looks too pale and shivers even though she's wearing warm clothes, so I wrap my arms around her while we wait, and she starts to fall asleep against me.

I carry her into the room the nurse leads us to and do most of the talking because she's barely awake, frustrated as I explain to the doctor that she's refused everything I've tried. The doctor looks Alex over and says it's just a bad flu. She hooks her up to an IV, hands me a prescription for antivirals, and tells us she'll be back in half an hour.

I sit in the room with Alex, who gives me a tiny smile and barely squeezes my hand.

"Thanks, Theo," she murmurs, "I never get sick." All my anger melts away, and I smile back at her and push her slightly damp hair back from her face.

"I've got you, sweetheart. You need to let me take care of you from now on, okay?" She nods and squeezes my hand gently, and I relax entirely. When we get home, she does everything I tell her to, and she curls up with me and lets me hold her as she sleeps, snoring a little because she's so stuffed up.

By Monday afternoon, her fever is gone. When I return from the store, she's curled up in bed, her laptop playing some old sitcom I know she's seen before, and she looks up at me and smiles, pausing her show.

"How're you feeling?" She whines and burrows further under the blanket, pouting a little.

"Terrible."

"Terrible, but better?" She nods, and I feel her forehead just in case before I crack the lid on the bright blue sports drink she asked for and hand it over.

"I have no idea why you want this. It's all sugar." She laughs softly.

"Didn't you do any sports as a kid?"

I shake my head. "I hated team things."

"Makes sense," she says, smiling. "I'm sure it would have made your grandparents' lives easier." I laugh.

"Yeah, probably. I picked up running when I was fourteen because Nana told me I was driving her fucking nuts and that I needed to do something to deal with my energy other than get in fights or jerk off all day." Alex snorts out a laugh.

"You must've been a nightmare."

I frown down at her, crossing my arms. "Like you were perfect."

She shrugs. "*I* never fucked anyone in a school bathroom at ten in the morning." I roll my eyes, fighting off a smile.

"You're definitely feeling better if you're being a dick." She reaches out for my hand, trailing her fingers against my palm.

"I get to be a dick. I feel *awful*," she pouts, twining her fingers through mine. "Come to bed."

My stomach flips and I take off my pants and sweater and climb into bed with her, feeling a thrill run down my spine at how her head immediately goes into my lap as she plays the sitcom again.

"Thanks for taking care of me," she murmurs as she drapes an arm across my legs. I look down at her, surprised.

"Yeah, of course, sweetheart," I say softly. I start stroking her hair, and she reaches for my other hand, threading her fingers through mine as she cuddles into me.

I like this version of Alex.

On Tuesday, Alex seems to enjoy being taken care of for the first time, and it's only then that I realize that she probably hasn't been taken care of like this since she was a little kid. I double down on doting on her, and she becomes affectionate in a way I've never seen.

It seems like the more I do to take care of her, the more she relaxes into the relationship and opens up to me.

***

On Saturday, I let her sleep in and then drive her into Portland because she wants to see an exhibit at the art museum. She's openly affectionate as we walk around the museum, holding hands with me, leaning into my touch when I hold her as she stares at paintings, and smiling at me anytime I catch her eye.

Alex is chatty and knowledgeable and more than a little pretentious about art, but I love listening to her. She tells me that her mother was a fine artist, that she spent every summer at a creative arts camp in Maine, and that she ran her school's art club. I know all of this, but I'm thrilled that she's finally sharing it with me.

When I ask her why she's stopped painting recently, she closes off and says she hasn't felt like it, but she misses it.

She shuts down a little after that, spending a long time sitting on a bench and contemplating a black and white photo of a man's hand holding a lock in front of a chained door. She seems tired and slightly sad, and I want to do something nice for her, so I slip out of the gallery hall and book her a massage a few blocks away.

She's exasperated when I tell her about it as we leave the museum, but I'm insistent that it doesn't count as a gift. I tell her that it's for her *health*, that it's good for her circulation after being sick, and she looks at me with amusement and rolls her eyes but acquiesces.

I wait for her outside of the art museum, scrolling through a hotel rental. Alex seems to be adjusting so much better since she was sick, and I want to reinforce the positive direction things are going in any way I can, and I think sex is how we connect best emotionally.

When I notice her walking towards me, I keep my face pointed down at my phone but look up at her for a second. She doesn't notice immediately, and I'm stunned when I see the emotions on her face.

Desire. Affection. Adoration. *Happiness.*

I raise my head, and she schools her expression quickly, but it's all still there.

27

ALEX

I'm happy and relaxed as I walk back to the art museum to meet Theo, who is sitting on a bench, doing something on his phone and sipping coffee. I slow down and take a second to study him as I walk towards him.

He seems different to me now.

Based on the way he took care of me when I was sick, I don't think he's trying to manipulate me anymore. He's still my delusional stalker, but he cares about me in his own weird, intense way, and what he feels for me is real to him. He's sweet and thoughtful, and the sex is fantastic, and he *loves* taking care of me.

A soft ache pulses through me as I realize that if things were different, he'd be a *really* good boyfriend, exactly the kind of boyfriend I would want.

Exactly the kind of boyfriend I *do* want.

That realization rings around like a bell in my head as he looks up at me and smiles warmly.

"Hi, sweetheart." He stands up and slips his phone into his back pocket as he leans down to kiss me, handing me a warm coffee cup as he does. "I got you ginger tea. I know you feel better, but I still thought it would be nice. How was the massage?" I lean into him a little, and his free arm wraps around my waist reflexively.

"It was great, thank you."

"I'm glad. Let's go."

"Where are we going?" He looks down at me with a warm, hungry expression.

"There's a nice hotel a few blocks away with a huge bathtub and good room service." He shoots me a quick grin. "I thought it might be nice to connect a little." I roll my eyes at him but don't say anything, because it sounds amazing.

It feels incredible to be cared for like this.

That's a problem.

***

As we check into the hotel, he wraps his arm around my shoulder and kisses my temple absently, as if being affectionate towards me is natural for him, like he's been doing it for years. It's impossible to ignore how much I want him, even though I shouldn't. It's so new to feel cared for like this, and I like it so much that I'm willing to overlook the fact that I'm trapped, just for a little bit.

For the first time, I let myself sink into the fantasy he's so invested in.

It's overwhelming how easy it feels.

We're barely in the elevator before I push him back into the wall, pressing onto my toes and kissing him deeply. He seems shocked for a moment before he grips my hips and pulls me in tightly, making a low, content sound in the back of his throat as he kisses me back.

It's nice to pretend this is normal. It's nice to completely ignore the fact that he's stalking me, to flirt and kiss and undress, to let him softly kiss my cunt while I order us a bottle of champagne and room service, to drink and joke and make out in the bath, to act like he's actually my boyfriend.

I let myself pretend all of it is normal as he sits back against the headboard and I crawl into his lap, gripping his shoulders as I lower myself onto him slowly, taking my time and teasing him. His hands tighten on my ass, his moan low and appreciative, his eyes bouncing from my lips to my tits to where we're joined and back again.

I have to lower myself the last inch or two carefully, tilting my hips forward and back until I find the most comfortable angle, moaning when he's finally all the way in. His hazel eyes are wide as I start to ride him, his face torn between adoration and lust and something I don't really recognize.

If I didn't know any better, I'd say it was hope.

I twine my arms around his neck, leaning into him, grinding slowly as his hands roam over my back and come forward to cup my breasts, his thumbs running over the peaks of my nipples. His touch feels intoxicating, and an electric current hums through my body when he kisses me. I close my eyes and melt into the feeling.

It's never felt like this before.

"What hasn't?" I look at him, slowing myself until I'm barely moving. Fuck, did I say that out loud? All of a sudden, I feel too naked, and the sex feels too intimate.

"Uhm, this. It feels...different." His eyes widen, his pupils large in the low light, and he looks surprised as he searches my face and wraps his arms around me tightly. "Theo," I say slowly, "why are you looking at me like that?"

"You feel it, don't you?" Theo's voice is an excited, low whisper, and his body is tense beneath me. I try to pull away from him, but his arms are like a vice around me, and he won't let me move. "Oh, my god, you *do*. Alex, you're *here* with me."

"What are you talking about?"

He smiles at me tenderly, pulling me closer. "You're finally letting me in."

Oh, god, he can tell.

What the fuck am I *doing*? Why am I giving into this bullshit delusion of his? I'm so fucking stupid if I think I actually want him, that he's not just manipulating me successfully. I can't be desperate enough to have someone be nice to me that I'm willing to overlook the fact that he's a violent fucking asshole who broke into my life and took it away.

That's pathetic.

"No, I'm not," I blurt out. "I don't want to be here. I don't like this. I don't like *you*." His expression shifts into deep hurt, and his eyes flick down to my lips as he grips me tighter.

"I *know* you don't mean that." Intense anger surges through me, and I need to get out of here. I need to get away from his feelings, from *my* feelings. I start pushing away from him, but his arms are locked around me. "Sweetheart, please don't push me away," he says, his voice pained. "I know you're scared of being happy with me, but you don't have to be."

Oh, *fuck him,* and fuck me for letting my guard down like this. I need an out, *any* kind of out. He shouldn't get to make me feel like this.

Fuck it. I'm going to push.

"You really think that? The only thing I'm scared of is *you*," I spit. "You're an insane, manipulative *stalker*, and you're going to kill me." I watch anger and hurt flash across his face, and I push again. "You think I want *this*? You think I want *you*? No one would want you! You're fucking *unlovable*."

I know immediately that I've pushed hard enough when Theo freezes, his face going instantly blank. There's a tense moment of silence as the word hangs between us, and then I'm on my back before I even realize he's moved. He's already off the bed, grabbing his clothes and throwing them on as he faces away from me. I can hear his breathing, loud and shallow and fast, and I curl up into a ball and start to go numb.

I'd rather die than want him like this.

He starts pacing at the end of the bed, every muscle in his body so tense that he's shaking.

"This is such fucking *bullshit,* Alexandria. You're lying to yourself if you think you don't want this, which isn't surprising because all you fucking do is *lie*. You can be *such* a shitty girlfriend sometimes, you know that? I have to beg you to talk to me, you barely tell me anything when you *do*, and you've got all these big fucking issues that you just bottle up and take out on me whenever I get too close. I fucking let you, because I want to take care of you, but you treat me like shit and shut down any time you let me in! I have to work so fucking hard to get so fucking little from you, and it *sucks*." He stops pacing and looks up at the ceiling, making a loud, frustrated sound, shaking his head and scrubbing a hand over his eyes.

"I didn't think this relationship would be so difficult, I really didn't. I've been doing everything I can to make this work, and you've been fighting me at every turn. I don't understand why you're working so hard to try to push me away, but I'm fucking tired of it." He grabs his keys off the dresser and finally looks at me, frustrated and hurt and on the edge of crying.

"Why can't you make this easy for *once* and just let yourself be happy with me?" He sighs and drops his keys, rubbing his hands up his face again and pushing them back through his hair. "Fuck this," he mutters as he moves towards me quickly, reaching out for me. I flinch away from him and curl tighter into myself, and he freezes. His face is shocked, then incredulous, then pained.

"Are you fucking *kidding* me, Alex? You think I'm going to *hurt* you?" He turns on his heel, grabbing his keys and his jacket. "I'm the only one getting hurt here," he snaps out as he wrenches open the door and storms out.

I sit on the bed, frozen and confused and unsure of how to feel. I stay glued to the same spot for an hour, but he doesn't come back. I have no idea what to make of what just happened, so I don't think about it. I order more wine, pour myself a hot bath, and drink to numb myself.

I don't sleep at all, but he never comes back. He's not at the bus station in Portland the next morning, or at the bus station in Astoria, or at his house, or at my apartment.

I know he'll show up. He constantly shows up, whether or not I want him to.

I don't know if I want him to or not.

28

THEO

The beach is barely above freezing when the sun finally starts rising, and the delicate, frigid mist from the fog rolling in off the water has dampened my clothes enough that my skin is chilled. I don't remember how I got here, or how long I've been here, or where *here* even is.

All I can think about is how scared Alex looked when I tried to kiss her.

I bury my face in my hands, looking down at the craggy rocks and the shadowy tide pools below me. I think Alex would love it here, wherever it is. She should be here with me, or I should be back at that hotel with her. We shouldn't be fighting like this. I don't understand why this relationship is still so fucking hard, because it shouldn't be.

We're supposed to be together – we're fucking *connected*.

I had no idea what that meant until I met Alex. I told Dr. Mills I felt connected to Ashley, but it barely even counts in retrospect. I knew something was different about her from the moment I met her, but it took me a while to figure out that we were connected, and it wasn't nearly as strong as the connection I have with Alex.

Ashley, as much as I loved her, was never *mine* the way Alex is.

I wasn't lying when I told Alex that I hardly cared about Ashley compared to how I feel about her. Things with Ashley were so easy, and I never would have tried this hard to make things work with her. I wouldn't have let her go easily, maybe, but I would have let her go, eventually – I *did* let her go.

That's never going to happen with Alex.

I think that's why Ashley and I had different perspectives on our relationship – we didn't *belong* to each other. It makes so much sense now. She doesn't lie to herself like Alex does, but she has a different outlook on things than I do. How she talked about me in her victim impact statement felt wrong, like she was misinterpreting everything I did on purpose. I thought she was just angry about what happened, and it took me years to accept that it was actually how she felt. According to her, I was too much to handle, had *always* been too much to handle, and I only got worse after I told her I loved her. She said she was afraid of hurting me, not because she loved me back, but because she was worried about how I'd react.

Kevin wasn't too much to handle, though.

Kevin was a funny, charming, easygoing piece of shit who was fucking my girlfriend behind my back for months and lying to my face about it. Things were going well between me and Ashley before he took her away from me, but I was too young and stupid and in love to notice when that happened. He knew how I felt about her and told her that I was going to propose, and said she'd never be able to get away from me if I did.

He wasn't *wrong*, but I didn't want her to see it that way.

He manipulated her into feeling like she was in danger, which she wasn't, but I think me giving into my impulses and stalking her only helped prove his point. Ashley said the stalking was so bad that she considered dropping out and moving back to California just to get away from me, but she didn't think it would have stopped me.

To be fair, it probably wouldn't have.

She talked about the lengths she and Kevin went to hide their relationship from me, how they didn't text or email at all, how they only met off campus when they knew I'd be occupied, how they were both afraid that I'd freak out if I found out about them.

They were right, of course.

They just didn't know how *badly* I'd freak out.

I remember how Ashley looked at me when she saw me step out of her closet, when she realized that I'd watched Kevin fuck her and heard her tell him that she loved him.

Alex might think she's afraid of me, but she's never been *that* afraid of me.

We both know that being happy is the thing she's actually afraid of, and she's only pushing me away because she *knows* I can make her happy. She just got scared because I acknowledged that she was finally starting to let me in, and she lashed out.

That's *all* this is.

Dr. Mills says she thinks I'm sensitive to rejection and while she's generally wrong about me, she *might* have a point there. I'm used to being rejected by people I love, but I know that Alex doesn't mean to reject me. She didn't even mean what she said to me, but it keeps playing in my head on an endless loop anyway, cutting deeper and deeper each time.

I *know* Alex doesn't mean to hurt me. She only pushes me away so I can show her that I'm not going anywhere and that she can trust me, but it sucks nonetheless. She's been fighting me and rejecting me every fucking step of the way, and all I get with her are these brief, shining moments when she finally lets her guard down and connects with me.

I *know* I'm right about us and our connection, but it's starting to feel like her trust issues are too big to get past. Sometimes, it even feels like she's trying to sabotage this relationship on purpose.

I'm at a loss on how to fix things with her. I know I *can* fix them, I just don't know *how*.

My phone chimes in my pocket, and I pull it out, shocked to see how late in the morning it is. I open up the security system app and stare at my phone, a deep ache coursing through me as I watch Alex walk up my driveway, stopping short when she realizes my car isn't there. She stands there for a minute before she shakes her head and walks away.

The relief I feel is so intense it's almost painful.

It starts raining, but I stay on the beach and watch her location as she walks home, my fingertips losing feeling by the time she gets into her apartment. I open the camera feeds to see her curl up on her couch under a blanket, turning on the TV and staring blankly at it. She's not watching anything, letting the carousel of advertised movies and shows on the home screen play through, because she's too busy checking her phone every other minute.

I can tell she's upset, and I know she wouldn't be this upset if she didn't care. She certainly wouldn't have stopped by my house if she didn't care, and I think she needs time to realize that. I know she wants me to reach out, but it's time for her to stop fucking lying to herself and invest in this relationship.

I don't know what I'll do if she doesn't.

29

ALEX

Theo hasn't shown up.

I keep checking my phone, but he hasn't called or texted me. I keep expecting to wake up to him in my apartment, or in my bed, or in *me*, and I'm weirdly disappointed that it hasn't happened.

I don't know why it's bothering me, but it is.

He's my delusional fucking stalker, and I shouldn't be upset that he's finally leaving me alone. I shouldn't want him, either, because that means I'm being successfully manipulated by him, which is what he wants. I can't give him what he wants, and he's going to snap eventually and kill me because of it.

That's what I keep trying to tell myself, anyway. I know it's true, but it's not how I feel. I push him constantly, and this time I pushed him so hard he *almost* snapped, but he didn't. He didn't scream at me or insult me or hit me. He just seemed hurt.

I can't stop thinking about how hurt he looked.

What seemed to hurt him the most was me flinching away from him like I thought *he* would hurt *me*. At this point, I'm not entirely sure that he would have. If I'm honest with myself, I'm positive he was going to kiss me. I know I would have caved if he had, and that might have been worse than him hurting me.

"Babe, are you okay?" I startle slightly, looking up into Bailey's warm, deep brown eyes. I didn't even notice her come into the room, much less set a cup of tea in front of me.

"Uhm, no," I say quietly, and Bailey leans a hip on the edge of my desk. "I'm, uh, kind of seeing someone. We got into a fight and now he's not talking to me." Bailey makes a soft sound of understanding.

"I've been there. He probably just needs some space. How upset was he?"

"*Very* upset. I was...harsh, and then he got close, and I freaked out and flinched, and he was really upset by that." Bailey's face becomes deeply concerned, bordering on anger.

"Alex, has he ever hurt you?"

I shake my head slowly. "No, I just reacted badly because we were fighting."

"Does he know about -" Bailey cuts herself off with a grimace, realizing I've never told her I'm hiding here. Suzie definitely said *something* when she hired me, and I should be mad, but I'm too preoccupied with this situation to care.

"Sort of. I don't like talking about it." She nods thoughtfully.

"Did you mean what you said to him?"

I look out the window, thinking for a minute. "I didn't mean *some* of it," I say quietly, aware Theo's possibly watching. He's definitely an insane, manipulative stalker, that's for sure.

"Do you think you'll break up because of it?"

I fake a cough to keep from laughing. "No, he's not going anywhere. He cares about me a lot, he's just *really* emotional."

"Do you care about him?" I look up at Bailey and nod slightly, keeping my movements small.

God, I hope Theo's not watching.

She smiles at me, tucking her hair back. "You know, before Dylan and I started dating, I'd been with this guy for years who made me believe all of his insecurities were my fault. He told me constantly that I was never good enough, he acted like I was stupid, he treated me like I was an embarrassment, *all* that shit. I believed him, and it *totally* wrecked my self-esteem.

"When Dylan and I got together, it was a hard adjustment to be with someone who cared, to be in something good, you know? *Really* hard. It took a long time to learn how to be in a healthy relationship, but if you find the right person and you both work on it, you can build something good. Whether or not it's this guy, you deserve to be loved for who you are. You don't deserve anything less than the best, babe."

I'm tearing up as I nod at Bailey. She's so wildly off base, but I can tell she actually cares about me, and it's nice to be cared for.

"You should focus on yourself and do things that make you happy, so just put this fight into a box and open it later. Get back to a good place with yourself before you try to get back into a good place with him. Call me if you need anything, okay? And let me know if I need to fight him for your honor or something," she says with a wink, and I laugh a little, smiling at her. She leans down to hug me tightly, and I realize that I haven't been hugged by another woman like this in years.

"Thanks, Bailey," I say, my voice watery as I work hard to keep from breaking down in her arms. I head into the bathroom the second she heads back to her office, and I can't hold it in any longer. I let myself sob, covering my mouth with my hand to keep silent. Once I'm able to calm down, I dry my face and brush my hair forward to cover how red my eyes are, keeping my head down as I return to my desk, grateful no clients are coming in for another hour.

On my lunch, I go downtown to a little boutique and go shopping, seeing a short, tight black dress with a low scoop neck that I can't afford. Bailey's right – I *should* get to do things for myself, even if I'm constantly being watched, and what I want to do is dress up and have fun with my friends tonight. I stare at the dress with longing before ignoring the price tag and buying it.

After work, I go home and blare pop music from my phone as I drink a glass of wine, dancing around my apartment as I get ready. I should still get to feel joy, even if I'm trapped. I curl my hair and do more makeup than I've done since I left Boston and put on the dress. Dressing up for myself feels good, and even with Theo taking over my life, trivia with my friends is still mine.

When I walk into the bar, it's just Anna and Jessica at our usual table, and Jessica's mouth drops open when she sees me.

"Excuse me, did we miss the memo? I'm in *overalls*," she whines.

"You look hot in overalls," I say as I hug her, and she laughs.

"Yeah, but not like *that*," she says, waving her hand at my dress.

"How'd you get your hair like that?" Anna asks as I give her a hug. "My hair won't hold a curl no matter what I do." I beam at them as we talk about hair and clothes as we get our drinks, just because it's *so* nice to have girlfriends. I'm thrilled that we're getting to have a girls' night, at least until Ben shows up fifteen minutes later. The three of us exchange a look, and I know they feel a little disappointed, too.

"Maybe the three of us should get brunch sometime," I venture quietly as Ben approaches the table with a pitcher of beer, and the enthusiasm that Anna and Jessica respond with fills me with warmth.

During the intermission, Ben gets us another round of drinks, and the three of us shift back into girls' night mode as Anna tells us about a date she went on over the weekend.

"He didn't ask me a *single* question! He just talked about himself the whole time. I had to listen to him talk about his *CrossFit* regiment." I scoff, and Jessica lets out a groan. "*And* he said he forgot his wallet, so I paid for both of us, and he *still* hasn't paid me back. It was awful."

Jessica rubs her hand over Anna's shoulder soothingly. "You still fucked him, didn't you?" Anna drops her head in her hands and Jessica cackles, and I almost spit out my drink as I laugh.

"He was really hot, okay?" Anna says, looking up at us. "Like I said, *CrossFit*."

"Please tell me the sex was good enough to make up for such a bad date," I tease, and Anna flashes me a sly grin. Jessica and I laugh, and she eyes my dress as she sips her drink.

"Are *you* going on a date after this?" I shake my head, finishing my beer quickly as Ben returns to the table with more drinks.

"No, I just felt like dressing up to come out. I'm not even seeing anyone." I almost cringe as I say it because it feels like a lie. Jessica exchanges a shocked look with Anna.

"Wait, what about that guy we met? I thought you said you two were sort of a thing," Anna says, and I shrug as I grab the drink Ben puts in front of me and take a long sip.

"I have *no* idea what's going on there." It's not a lie, but it's not the truth.

"So, it's a situationship?" Jessica asks.

"You have *no* idea," I say, rolling my eyes.

"Does the sex make up for it, at least?" Anna asks in a teasing tone, and I almost spit out my drink, blushing deeply. I'm not answering that question in front of Ben, but she and Jessica see the answer written on my face. "Well, *that's* good, at least," she says, and I try not to laugh.

"God, men fucking suck. Oh, sorry, Ben," Jessica says when she sees Ben scowl. "Listen, Alex, he's an idiot to fumble you. You should let the guy who's been staring at you all night buy you a drink." I cock my head slightly, confused.

"What guy?"

Anna laughs in shock. "Alex, *come on*. The guy who hit on you at the bar?"

I shrug. "Oh, he wasn't hitting on me. He was just being friendly."

Ben looks over at me incredulously. "Can you not tell he likes you?"

I shrug, and Jessica laughs. "Girl, you are *blind*. Listen, I'm setting you up with one of our coworkers while your situationship gets his shit together." She winks as she pulls out her phone and starts scrolling through contacts. "Let's see...Will's gay, Louis is shit in bed, Nathan's got a girlfriend, Rob's hot, but he's, like, *forty*. Are you into older guys?" I shake my head quickly. "Gotcha. Maybe you'd get along with Zach? What do you two think? You both know him better than I do." Ben looks at Jessica for a long moment before shrugging at me.

"He's cool, I guess, but he's not our only single coworker."

"Yeah, but he's much better than the other guys we work with," Anna says quickly. "The rest aren't worth your time, *believe me*." Her face tenses as her eyes dart to Ben quickly, and I can see Ben scowling again. I don't think he likes being part of our unofficial girl's night conversation very much. "Plus, Zach's *definitely* worth getting to know," she says teasingly, and Jessica snickers. I raise my eyebrows at Anna, and she nods a little.

"*Oh.* Um, I'll think about it, okay?" I think Theo would go fucking ballistic if he even heard me having this conversation.

"You should," Anna says with a wink, and I force a smile and finish my beer quickly as the trivia starts back up. Thinking about what might happen if Theo caught me on a date with someone is sobering, and I have no intention of thinking about that, or *him*, or being sober.

Anna, Jessica, and I are bad at the trivia theme for the week, and we start a drinking game where we drink every time we get an answer wrong, which is almost every time. I also drink whenever I think about Theo, so I'm pretty drunk when trivia is over. The girls and I make plans for brunch while Ben closes out, and I use the restroom when they go outside to catch their ride.

I sit in the stall, checking my phone, but there's still nothing from Theo. I want to go over and apologize tonight, but I'm not sure if he's back from wherever he went yet. Even if he is, knowing him, he'll get pissy about me being so drunk.

He's such a fucking *mom* sometimes.

When I leave the bar, it's pouring rain, and I groan, pulling my light denim jacket tight around me. I can't believe I forgot to check the weather. My rain jacket is at Theo's, anyway, and I'll be freezing and soaked by the time I get home. I pull out my phone and pull up his number, my thumb hovering over it. I don't think I'm ready to talk to him yet, and I don't want to ask him for anything before apologizing, but I know he'll come get me. At least, I think he will.

Maybe he doesn't want anything to do with me now.

That shouldn't bother me as much as it does.

Fuck it, I'm going to call him.

"Hey, Alex. Need a ride?" I look back and see Ben leaving the bar, holding up his keys, and I smile back at him. I can call Theo once I'm home, and I *really* don't want to walk home in the rain, so I slip my phone into my pocket.

"Yeah, I do. Thanks." The ride to my place is quick, and we mainly talk about whatever Ben brings up, although I can't track the conversation entirely because I'm drunker than I thought I was. He parks across from my house, watching me as I unbuckle the seatbelt with some difficulty.

"Hey, can I use your bathroom?"

"Sure."

I lead him upstairs and show him to the bathroom as I hang up my jacket and head into the kitchen to make dinner. I'm not hungry, but I haven't eaten much in the last few days, and I know I should. At the very least, it will soak up some of the alcohol in my stomach. I feel a slight pang as I look at the lone glass container with a sticky note on it sitting in my fridge. I grab it and look at the neat, blocky writing on the note.

11/10
BRAISED LAMB + ROOT VEG PUREE
ADD 2 TBSP WATER
MICROWAVE 2 MIN
LID PARTIALLY ON

Fuck, I need to apologize to Theo. Maybe I'll ask him out to dinner or do something nice to make up for how awful I was. That's probably a bad idea, but I feel terrible enough about what happened to do it.

"So, you and that guy aren't together?" I look up at Ben as he enters the kitchen, then back at the sticky note. This is the last day I can eat this unless I freeze it, and it's possibly the last thing Theo's making for me for a while.

"Oh, um, I don't know," I say, feeling guilty as I slip the glass container into the freezer.

"He's an idiot if he's not into you." I laugh, almost losing my balance as I bend over to grab a bottle of wine from the bottom cabinet. *That's* definitely not the problem, but I'm not talking about this with anyone, except maybe Bailey. "You look so beautiful tonight, Alex," he says quietly. Something about Ben's voice sets me on edge. I look up at him, realizing that I'm bent over and that he's close behind me, looking at my body appreciatively. I stand up quickly, my head spinning a little.

I'm not sure I should drink more right now.

"Oh, um, thanks, I guess," I say quickly, wrapping my arms around myself. Ben steps closer to me, backing me into the kitchen counter, and I get nervous. Why didn't I ever notice how big he is? He's shorter than Theo, maybe, but he's kind of got Danny's thick build and he's *much* bigger than me.

Didn't Theo make me promise I wouldn't be alone with Ben?

I'm not so sure he was just being jealous anymore.

"You know that I'm into you, right? Maybe you just thought I was being friendly." I tense up, leaning away from him as he stares down at me, his eyes glued to my lips.

"Ben, we're just friends."

He steps even closer. "We could be more than that," he says with a soft smile.

I squirm slightly as he leans down over me, his arms bracketing me in. "Uhm, I should go to bed."

Ben laughs a little, his eyes drifting down the open neck of my dress. "We can do that." It takes me a minute to realize what he's saying, and I shake my head, feeling slightly dizzy as I do. Theo's going to freak out when he sees this on the cameras, but maybe he'll come over here and make Ben leave.

"That's not what I meant," I say quietly, but I can barely get the words out.

"Right. The kitchen works, too, I guess," he says with a smirk as one of his hands drags up my body and cups my breast. My breath starts coming faster as he leans closer, and I pull back as far as possible, but I can't go much farther.

"I don't think this is a good idea." My voice sounds high-pitched and panicky.

"I know you like me, Alex." Ben pushes his hips against mine, and I freeze as I feel him hard against me. Why isn't Theo blowing up my phone? Is he not watching me? Did I actually get rid of him right when I needed him?

Oh, fuck, I wish he was here right now.

"No," I whisper out, but Ben must not hear me. I'm frozen as his other hand drifts up my thigh and grips my ass hard as he leans down to kiss me. I work hard to move my arms, putting my hands on his chest and pushing, but he doesn't move. "*Don't*," I say a little louder, forcing the word out.

Ben's brow furrows as he leans over me, staring down the open neck of my dress. "Jesus, Alex, you're such a fucking tease," he says, his voice surprisingly angry. Ben's leg pushes in between mine, his thigh pushing up until he's rubbing his against me roughly. I whimper in protest at how harsh it feels as he leans down and kisses me aggressively, and I feel the familiar cold, numb sensation of disconnecting from my body.

I don't want this, but it's going to happen anyway, so at least I don't have to experience it.

Suddenly, Ben pulls away from me and a second later slams into the wall with a yelp, and in his place is a furious-looking Theo.

"*What the fuck is this?*" I startle at Theo's harsh voice, and all the sensation and panic rush back into my body as I stare up at him, tears starting to form on my lash line. I open my mouth to say something, but nothing comes out. His face goes blank, and he looks over at Ben, who looks between the two of us with genuine fear.

30

THEO

TUESDAY, NOVEMBER 14

By Tuesday, I'm crawling out of my skin and nothing is distracting me. Alex isn't sleeping or eating much, and she's checking her phone constantly. When I watched her leave for work this morning, she seemed distracted and frazzled, leaving without her phone and reappearing two minutes later.

I can't keep waiting for her to come to me.

I watch her talk to Bailey, grateful that Alex has someone who cares about her like that. I don't watch the cameras or check her trackers after I hear her talk to Bailey. If Alex feels like she needs time to herself, I can give her that. I know Alex told Bailey she didn't mean some of what she said, but I know she didn't mean any of it. She got scared and lashed out, and we just need to talk about it. We'd finally started to talk more before this happened, and we're going to keep doing that, because that's what couples do.

I need to fix this as soon as possible, so I'll go over after trivia and make her dinner. I'll show her that she can trust me, that she can let herself be happy with me, that I can make her happy if she lets me, and then she *will*.

I need to get the fuck away from my computer and phone if I'm going to give Alex privacy, so I leave everything but my wallet at home when I go on a run, purposefully running in the opposite direction of her office before heading to get groceries. I take a long time buying groceries, thinking about what she might like for dinner, taking my time debating which wine to buy her and which flowers she'd like most.

When I get home, I spend a long time making a salad and lobster ravioli, trying to lose myself in the process. Once I'm done and realize I still have a few hours, I do what I can to work off some of my anxiety. I clean the house. I work out. I jerk off to a video of us fucking that I have saved to my computer. I make a key lime pie. None of it helps that much, but it eats up the time I need it to. Trivia's usually over by nine, and it takes her half an hour to walk home, so I pack the food, wine, and flowers in a tote bag and get to her place fifteen minutes before she gets home.

She'll walk in the door, and I'll be there making dinner with a chilled glass of wine ready for her, and then we'll talk. She'll love the flowers and the food, and we'll spend the whole night making up. It'll be fine. I know she has trust issues because of her ex, I know she didn't mean any of what she said, and I know she's just scared of her feelings.

It's all going to be fine.

When I get up to Alex's floor, I can hear her talking with someone through the thin walls, which sets me on edge. She shouldn't be home yet, and she's so embarrassed about her apartment that she never has anyone over except me. Her door is already unlocked, and I start to freak out as I open it slowly.

"...a fucking tease," a man says bitterly, and I see Alex backed into the kitchen counter, Ben looming over her, one of his legs jammed in between hers and his hands all over her body. She's looking at him with wide eyes and her hands flat against his chest, and my body floods with hot rage when I watch him passionately kiss her.

There's no fucking way this is happening.

I'm across the room in an instant, ripping him off her and shoving him into the wall.

"*What the fuck is this?*" Alex startles at my voice, looking up at me with wide, teary eyes. She opens her mouth to say something, but nothing but a quiet huff of air comes out. God, she looks gorgeous. Is that a new dress? Why is she so dressed up?

Every thought fades when I look at her face.

Alex looks *scared*.

I look over at Ben, taking in his frustrated, terrified face, and my stomach twists in anger.

Were they on a date?

She should be afraid *for* him if that's the case.

I set the tote bag on the ground and try hard to stay calm as I step in between them, the small kitchen crowded with the three of us.

"What the fuck is your problem, dude?" Ben says, his voice panicked and angry. My fists clench and my arms tense up because I want to punch him so fucking badly, but I stop myself. The last thing I want to do is scare Alex off anymore, so I need to work a *lot* harder to stay calm.

"Get the fuck away from my girlfriend," I say, trying to keep my voice even.

"She said she was single, I swear!" I whip my head around and stare down at Alex, but she's glaring at Ben.

"*Alexandria*?" We're going to have a long fucking talk if she said she was single.

"I didn't...it wasn't...Ben was just leaving," she says, her voice shaky, and he looks at her incredulously.

"What are you talking about?" I'm holding on to my composure by a fucking thread, and I don't know who to trust until I hear Alex scoff. I look down at her, and she looks back at me with wide eyes, her jaw set and her face flushed.

She's not just scared.

She's *furious*.

Oh.

"Sweetheart, did you *want* him to touch you?" My voice is slow and quiet, but it sounds wrong, as if it doesn't belong to me. Her eyes widen, and she and I stare at each other for what feels like an eternity before she shakes her head the tiniest bit.

"No," she whispers, and a loud, angry buzzing starts in the back of my head as the edges of my vision swim with red.

He's fucking *dead*.

"Wait, *what*?" Ben's voice is panicky, and Alex must see how I feel, because she pales and reaches a hand out towards me.

"Theo, calm down," she says, her voice soft and placating. "It's just a misunderstanding, okay?" I laugh at her as I look over at Ben, who seems to realize how much shit he's in.

I don't even try to stop myself.

I grab his head with both hands and slam his face into the kitchen counter twice in quick succession, his nose making a loud crunching noise. He yells in pain, and Alex screams my name as I pull him up and finally punch him in the face. He's trying to hit me back, but he's obviously never been in a fight before because he's just flailing his arms towards me. I hit him in the stomach, and he doubles over, and I throw him to the floor and follow him down, jamming my arm across his throat and pressing my weight into it.

I punch him again with my other hand as he starts turning purple. He's hitting me in the ribs and pulling at my arm frantically, but I'm too angry to feel any pain. Alex is yelling at me, her voice terrified and pleading, but I can't tell what she's saying. It doesn't matter, anyway.

The only thing that matters is that this motherfucker pays for what he was going to do to her.

I pull my arm back to hit him again, but Alex grabs my elbow, yanking back hard. The moment I register the feel of her hands on me, my mind clears just enough to hear what she's saying.

"*Baby, stop,*" she begs in a low, terrified voice, and I freeze. Ben takes the momentary interruption as an opportunity to punch me in the face. Alex screams at him and lets go of my elbow instantly, and I press more of my weight into the arm across his neck, making him choke harder as I hit him in the face once more before I shove off him. Alex grabs me around the waist the second I stand up, but it doesn't stop me from lifting my foot and driving my heel into Ben's side. He screams as one of his ribs snaps, and Alex starts yelling at me angrily.

"*Theodore, stop it right now!*" She tries to pull me away from him, and I let her, angling us towards the front door and keeping myself between her and Ben. I slide a hand behind me to grab her hip, focusing on the grounding feel of her arms tight around me and her body pressed into my back.

She's okay.

Ben scrambles off the floor and backs into the living room, looking furious and scared once he realizes he's blocked from leaving. His face is dark red, his lip is split, his nose is bleeding freely, and he's bent over, clutching at his side. It's so fucking satisfying to see him in pain that I can't help smiling at him, and his eyes widen until there's a rim of white completely circling his irises.

"You're a fucking psycho, man! I'm calling the cops!" The smile drops off my face immediately. Shit, I didn't even think about that. Alex lets go of me and walks towards him, her hands out in front of her like she's trying to calm a skittish horse. I keep close behind her, one hand hovering over her waist, and he backs away towards the wall quickly.

"Ben, this is all just a misunderstanding, okay?" Her voice is shaky, but she's trying to be calm and placating. "I'm so sorry. You misread the situation, and Theo's a little...protective. We don't need to call the cops, right? We can deal with this ourselves. I can give you money for the medical bills, and Theo can apologize." I bark out a harsh laugh, and Ben flinches. "Um, just hang on for a second. Please don't call the cops, okay?" She rounds on me and mouths *apologize* before she hurries out of the room, and I wait until I hear her rifling through her closet before I step closer to him, keeping my voice quiet.

"You touch her again, and I'll fucking kill you," I hiss as I lean towards him, and the blood drains from his face as he shrinks away from me. From the look on his face, he knows it's not an empty threat. "I wouldn't recommend calling the cops, either." Ben shrinks against the wall and nods once.

"Theo?" I back away from him the second I hear Alex's shaky voice. I see her walk back into the living room with a small stack of cash that's easily a thousand dollars, looking nervously between me and Ben. I cross my arms and glare at him, working hard to keep myself from hitting him again.

"Get the fuck out," I snap. He takes the money from Alex and bolts, slamming the door behind him. I'm still so fucking angry that I'm breathing hard, clenching and unclenching my hands, anything to calm down as I turn back towards Alex. She wraps her arms around herself, her mouth a thin line as she looks at me. She just watched me beat the shit out of someone for her and she doesn't seem afraid of me, which is a good sign. I take a few deep breaths, trying to keep my voice calm.

"Did he hurt you?" She stares at me but says nothing, and my temper spikes again. "*Did he fucking hurt you?*" She flinches a little at how loud my voice is but shakes her head. "Why the fuck was he here?"

She looks at her feet and shrugs, turning away from me. "It was raining, and he offered me a ride," she says, slurring slightly as she heads into the kitchen. She wobbles a little as she reaches for a bottle of wine, and I exhale loudly when I finally realize she's drunk.

Oh, goddammit, of course.

I follow her into the kitchen, staying close to her as she unscrews the wine and takes a long sip directly from the bottle. I shake my head, gripping the counter behind me to keep myself from grabbing the bottle and pouring it down the sink.

"You promised not to be alone with him, so why the *fuck* was he in your apartment?" She won't look at me, but her face contorts with anger.

"He said he needed to use the bathroom," she says in a quiet, bitter voice.

"Because he was trying to get you *alone*," I snap at her, snatching the bottle of wine out of her hands as she goes to drink more. "You're not stupid, sweetie, and you would have realized what he was doing if you weren't so fucking *drunk*." Her face hardens into something cold and resentful.

"Oh, *fuck you*." My blood boils and I slam the bottle of wine down on the counter.

"Goddammit, Alexandria! He was going to fuck *you*, whether or not you wanted him to!" She starts crying the second it comes out of my mouth, and guilt overtakes me.

"You think I didn't *know* that? You think I didn't...you think I *wanted*...He thought...I couldn't...I just..." She drops her head in her hands and sobs, and shame courses through me.

I want to hold her, but I don't know if it's the right thing to do. I need to give her a minute to calm down, and I need a minute to calm down, so I stare at the ceiling and force myself to take deep breaths as she cries. I fucking hate myself right now. It's not her fault, and I shouldn't have said that to her. When she finally calms down a little, I can't help but reach out and touch her lightly, running my hands up and down her arms in a way I know she finds soothing.

"You don't get to be mad at me about this," she whispers.

"I'm not mad at you, sweetheart, I promise. I'm upset because that piece of shit could have hurt you, but it's not your fault at all." Her shoulders relax a little under my hands. "You should be mad at me right now because I'm such an asshole. I'm so sorry I yelled at you. Are you okay?"

She shrugs, her movements sharp. "Nothing happened." She sniffles a little, wiping her cheeks and looking up at me, her face twisting into an expression I don't understand. She sighs and pulls away from me, grabbing a dish towel from the counter and wetting it in the sink before stepping toward me again.

"Your nose is bleeding," she says as she gently wipes blood from my chin and lip before pressing the towel against my nose, putting her other hand on my jaw and gently tipping my head back. Warmth rushes through me the second her fingers touch my skin, and I feel a soft humming in my body as I realize she's looking at me with *concern*. I stare at her out of the corner of my eye, but she won't make eye contact.

This is the first time she's ever tried to take care of me.

I don't want to scare her off, and it takes everything in me not to wrap my arms around her. She hands me the towel and lets go of my face, and I keep the towel pressed against my nose, staring at her with wide eyes as she turns away, opening the freezer.

"You should have called me if you needed a ride, sweetheart," I say quietly.

"I didn't want to bother you." She grabs an ice pack from the freezer and hands it to me.

"You're never bothering me, even if we're fighting, okay?" I press the ice pack over my face, wincing as she reaches for the wine on the counter.

"Well, I'm fine, so you can go back to ignoring me now," she says bitterly, and a small part of me is delighted at how angry she sounds.

"I wasn't ignoring you, honey, I was trying to give you *space*." She glances up at me, surprised. "I hated it, and I missed you, and I thought we should talk. I didn't even think you'd be home yet, so I was going to surprise you. I made you dinner. And a pie. And I got you flowers." I gesture at the abandoned tote bag with my foot, and Alex looks at it with wide eyes before she stares down at her hands.

"Why are you being nice to me right now?"

"Because I lo-" I bite my tongue hard enough that I taste blood. I don't think she caught my slip up, thank god. I slump against the counter and look up at the ceiling, putting the towel and ice pack down as all the remaining anger and frustration drains out of me, leaving nothing but exhaustion.

"I'm fucking *trying*, Alex, but I don't know what to do here. I'm having a hard time figuring out how to make this relationship work because you won't work on it with me. Any time you let me in, you push me away immediately, and you keep telling me that you don't want me, and it hurts. I don't buy it because you're *constantly* lying, but it still fucking hurts." She's staring at the counter and fidgeting with a potholder nervously, assiduously avoiding meeting my eye.

"I promise you that I'm not going anywhere, but it sucks that you're constantly telling me to fuck off in one way or another. I fucking *adore* you, and I want you to be happy, so *please* let me in." I can hear how pleading my voice gets at the end, halfway to begging, but I don't care.

Alex shakes her head faintly. "I don't want that." Her voice is small, and she's looking at her feet again.

"You don't want *what*?"

She runs her hands over her face and shrugs. "I don't know."

"Well, what the fuck *do* you want, Alex?"

She looks up at the ceiling and shakes her head. "*I don't know*! I want you to stop being fucking crazy, and I want my goddamn life back, but I...I don't know, I feel so...*goddammit*, this is so confusing!" She exhales loudly, pressing her hands over her eyes as her shoulders drop, and she leans against the wall a little too heavily. "I don't want you to fuck off, okay? I do, but I don't," she says, her voice almost inaudible, and something inside me unwinds instantly.

I was *right*. Of course I was right, because I fucking *know* her.

She wants this as badly as I do, she's just *scared*.

She makes a groaning sound and wraps her arms around her waist again, but she still won't look at me. I watch her closely, focusing on her mouth as I hold my breath.

"I didn't...when I flinched, I just reacted. I didn't think you were going to hurt me." I fucking *knew* it. "I was going to call you tonight to pick me up, but I didn't want to ask you for something without apologizing." My hand jerks from how badly I want to reach out for her as she rubs at her eyes, smearing her makeup a little. "When Ben...he thought that I...I *didn't*, I swear, but he was going to...I just fucking froze, and I wanted you here, and then you were here. You're, like, really fucking scary when you're angry, by the way," she says softly, and I wince at the nervous edge of her voice. She finally looks up at me and shrugs, the corner of her lips picking up into a shade of a smile, her expression open and vulnerable. "I'm so happy to see you, Theo, and I'm *so* sorry about the other night."

Relief floods through me, and I stand there staring at her gorgeous, upset face for a long moment before I'm across the kitchen in one stride, pulling her into my arms until her toes barely touch the ground. Her arms grip tight around my neck, and I don't even know what to say, so I just breathe her in. Her breathing adjusts to mine, or mine to hers, and we stand in the kitchen holding each other, breathing slowly, calming each other down, finally connecting in a way that feels unguarded.

She pulls away to kiss me and makes a displeased sound when she realizes my nose is still bleeding. She makes me sit down on the couch, standing between my legs and fussing over me, looking at me with soft eyes as she examines my face carefully, telling me I'm going to have a hell of a black eye and chiding me for beating up Ben so badly. Her touch is gentle, and she keeps giving me a small, fragile smile whenever she meets my eye. I run my hands over her hips and waist slowly, in awe of how good it feels to have her take care of me.

I'm stunned when she climbs into my lap and kisses me, pressing her body flush against mine and sighing as she grinds down into me. I hold her close, and she makes needy, frantic sounds as she deepens the kiss, nipping at my lip and tongue as she undoes my belt. She pulls back and looks into my eyes, her face anxious as she quickly reaches down to undo my jeans.

"Can you not..." She strokes me roughly as she pulls my cock out, and I groan, my eyes rolling back. "Let me...just...I need to do it, okay?" I nod, kissing her neck as she hikes up her dress and slides her thong to the side, ignoring my hiss of discomfort as she plunges herself down onto me. She's too tight, wet but not quite ready, but she forces it over and over until I'm fully inside of her. I open my mouth to say something, but she slams a hand over my mouth and tells me in a harsh voice to shut the fuck up, so I do.

Alex is rough with me in a way she usually isn't. She's demanding, snapping out orders and telling me how and where to touch her. She bites my lip hard when we kiss, bites my neck and shoulders as she rides me aggressively, pulls my hair, digs her nails into me until it hurts and drags them down my skin, leaving long red scratches. It's so fucking hot, but I can tell it's mostly about control, so I do whatever she asks and take whatever she gives me.

I want her to know that I can give her what she needs, no matter what that looks like.

She starts picking up speed but losing her rhythm, and she makes that fucking whining noise that drives me crazy, and I can't help gripping her hips and thrusting up into her hard. She gasps, moaning out something unintelligible as she rides me faster. Her leg starts tensing against me, and she's getting closer, her eyes fixed on mine and her head nodding, her moans low and harsh. My eyes stay locked on her flushed face and the way she's looking at me with desire and something else, something new, something deeper and more vulnerable than I've ever seen from her. We stare at each other, and I can feel an electric current of connection running between us.

From the slightly scared look that flits across her face, I know she can feel it, too.

"*Theo*," she whispers, but it's more of a question than anything else. I pull her closer, gripping her tightly.

"I've got you." Her eyes widen, and she whimpers my name again and starts shaking in my arms. The second her muscles flutter around my cock, I come with her, spilling up into her without breaking eye contact.

She's panting hard as she comes down, her hands carding through my hair, and I pull her so close that there's no space left between us.

"I didn't mean it," she whispers as she strokes her hands down my neck. I watch her mouth closely, and when she doesn't bite her lip, I feel like I can finally breathe again. I give her a reassuring smile as her eyes start tearing up.

"I know you didn't."

"I'm so sorry." I push her hair behind her ears, shaking my head slightly.

"It's okay."

"I didn't - with Ben, I didn't -"

"I know, honey."

"Thank you for showing up." I gently cup her face in my hands, looking deep into her eyes.

"Alex, I'm always going to show up, I fucking *promise*. You're mine, and I'm never going anywhere, okay? I'm never going to let anything bad happen to you." Her bottom lip quivers for a second before she starts sobbing and collapses in my arms. She buries her face in my neck, and I hold her close until she calms down, trying to help her slow her breathing.

We barely talk for the rest of the night, but something feels settled between us. We're totally unguarded with each other, and things feel right in a way they haven't before. I make her dinner, and she stays in the kitchen, sitting on the counter and watching me, smiling whenever I look at her. We curl up on the couch after dinner, drinking tea and watching something I ignore because I'm focused on how Alex is leaning into me and shaking slightly, even though I don't think she's cold. I pull her into my lap and wrap a blanket around us, which seems to help her relax. I keep her locked tight in my arms and press my lips against her skin, telling her over and over that she's okay. When we go to bed, she curls into a much tighter ball than usual, and she digs her fingers into my skin when I wrap an arm around her waist.

"I've got you, sweetheart," I whisper into her hair as I hold her tighter. I revel in how she unfurls in my arms instantly, turning over and burying her face in my chest, her hands gripping my shirt tightly. She starts shaking a little, and I can tell she's crying, so I just hold her and try to soothe her.

She's finally trusting me.

I knew we'd be able to work past her trust issues. I knew she wanted this, wanted *me*. I know she understands that we're connected somehow.

I know she *can* love me back, that she's *going* to love me back. I'm not stupid enough to think she won't still be guarded and scared, or that she won't still push me away, but this is massive progress.

I hate that it happened this way, but I think what she needed to start truly accepting our relationship was to see how much I love her.

I think I needed to see it, too.

I can't believe she was able to stop me from killing Ben.

No one's ever been able to get me to calm down when I get that angry. Melissa couldn't do it with all her screaming and crying, and Ashley only stopped me because she cracked open my fucking head. All Alex had to do was ask.

I don't think she realizes what would have happened if she hadn't stopped me.

That's probably for the best.

***

"You expect me to believe you got that black eye from running into a door?"

"That's what I said."

Dr. Mills looks unimpressed. "You realize you're not even trying to lie, right?" Her tone almost sounds amused, and I can't help but smile as I shrug at her. "Okay, I'll bite. What happened to *the door*?" The smile slides off my face as I think about walking in on Alex and Ben.

"Oh, *the door* is fine, unfortunately. Broken nose, maybe a rib, but nothing serious."

Her eyebrows shoot up. "Don't you think that's serious?"

"No, I think he deserved worse since he tried to fucking *rape* my girlfriend," I spit, my tone venomous. Dr. Mills' eyes widen in horror, and she lifts her hand to cover her mouth, and it's the most unfiltered emotion I've ever seen out of her. She takes a moment to compose herself, letting out a sharp breath.

"How's Alex?" She seems genuinely concerned, and I feel instantly warmer towards her.

"She's fine." It's not this woman's business that Alex is stressed and wants to be held constantly. She's bordering on clingy lately, but I don't mind that. "I got there in time, so nothing happened." Dr. Mills stares out the window, her face tight.

"Theodore, I don't condone violence, and with your history, it's extremely concerning," she says, looking back at me, "but I can't criticize your motivation in this instance. I'm glad nothing happened to Alex." I blink, slightly shocked. I think this is the first time I've ever liked Dr. Mills. "Your heart was in the right place, but I still don't think you should have started a fight." I scoff and roll my eyes.

"He started it when he fucking touched her. She didn't even let me finish it," I mutter, but I know it's a mistake the second it slips out of my mouth.

"What does that mean?" Shit, fuck, goddammit.

"Nothing." She blinks and purses her lips, humming slightly.

"Given the circumstances, I won't speak to Officer Dent about this." I look at her in surprise. "However, we should revisit some basic anger management skills today."

"I don't think that's necessary." She pointedly stares at my black eye and raises her eyebrows impatiently, and I roll my eyes. "Oh, for fuck's sake, fine."

Never mind. I still don't like her.

***

"This is a one-time thing," Alex hisses as we walk into the bar and towards her friends, her hand interlaced in mine. "Guys, this is my boyfriend, Theo. You met the other week, I think?"

My mind empties out for a second, but I can't help the smug grin on my face as I greet her friends. The other guy at the table, Zach, is quiet and very stoned, Jessica is chatty and fun, and Anna is sweet like Alex, but much more open.

Ben doesn't show up.

Once trivia starts, I realize I hate it and have no interest in participating. I can't tell if Alex actually likes it, but she seems to have a knack for remembering obscure bits of information, probably because she was a total overachiever as a kid. She's also highly competitive, constantly checking her team's scores against the other teams, which is adorable.

She leans over in between rounds, her hand drifting up my thigh. "I shouldn't have brought you," she whispers. "You're atrocious at this." She grins at me, squeezing my leg gently.

"I'm very good at other, less trivial things," I say quietly, smirking down at her. Alex blushes a deep pink and turns away, leaving her hand where it is, and she seems happier than she has all week.

During the short intermission, she goes to the bathroom while her other two friends go to the bar for another round of drinks, leaving Anna and I alone. We make an awkward attempt at small talk that neither of us seem interested in, and she gives my still-bruised eye a curious look.

"Do you know Ben?"

I shrug, taking a sip of my beer. "We've met."

Anna's eyebrows jump, looking back at my eye. "Did you know he got mugged last week?"

I snort. "Must have happened after he drove Alex home." Anna's face drops, and she frowns at her beer. I don't know her, but I can tell the tightness around her mouth and eyes probably isn't normal for her.

"He was really messed up," she says quietly.

"He was asking for it," I say, looking at her pointedly. Her mouth thins out until her lips are barely visible.

"Is she okay?" My eyes flick over to Alex joining her friends at the bar, her posture extremely straight and her shoulders slightly higher than normal. A week later, she's still more anxious than usual, but only if you know how to see it. "Sorry, you don't have to tell me anything," Anna says quickly. "I just care about her."

I give Anna a warm smile. "She's fine. Nothing happened," I say, and her face relaxes. "If Ben knows what's good for him, though, he'll listen to me and stay the fuck away from her."

"He's not big on listening to people," Anna says quietly. I glance at her, immediately concerned, but she's smiling at everyone as they return to the table, the tenseness from her face completely gone.

Alex sits closer to me than before, and I place my arm around the back of her chair, loving how she leans into me and the feeling of her hand gently pushing down on my knee to keep it from bouncing.

As much as I like finally getting access to this part of her life, I'm glad this is a one-time thing. Her friends are boring, trivia is boring, and I don't understand why they do this every week. Still, I sit through it and participate and engage with her friends, and when it's over, I drive her home and fuck her in the car because I can't wait the two minutes it would take to get her inside.

She *finally* called me her fucking *boyfriend*.

31

ALEX

WEDNESDAY, NOVEMBER 22

"What are you doing tomorrow?" I paste a smile on my face even though I'm so anxious I want to cry.

"Nothing," I say, smiling tightly. I fucking hate Thanksgiving, but I don't want to be mean to Bailey. She loves Thanksgiving, and her entire November revolves around planning a themed Thanksgiving dinner for her friends every year. "It's too much fuss for me, but the guy I'm seeing might want to cook."

Theo will *absolutely* want to cook, and I need to find a way to avoid him.

"Well, if you don't have plans and want to stuff yourself to death on Ethiopian food, you're invited to my place. Suzie and Catherine are stopping by, and you can bring your mystery boyfriend. Dylan and I will play good cop, bad cop about his intentions with you," she says with barely contained glee, and I force a laugh.

"I'll let you know," I say, my smile straining my cheeks. I'd much rather go to Bailey's than deal with whatever Theo's planning. He's not one for restraint and he loves the holidays, which is about to be my own personal nightmare.

I don't go to the rec center during my lunch. Instead, I go to a bar and have two vodka sodas, grateful not to receive a mothering text from

Theo about drinking during the day. On the way back to the office, I pick up two tall cans of alcoholic seltzer. I usually wouldn't drink at work, but it's a slow day and Theo's about to be so fucking overbearing and overwhelming that I know I'm going to have a tough time dealing with him.

I take a large coffee mug and the seltzer into the bathroom, pouring it into the mug and tucking the empty can in my purse. Theo doesn't text me, and I spend the last few hours of work buzzed, preparing myself.

I walk to his house after work, dread coiling in my stomach, and I freeze when I enter the kitchen. I was *right* – he has gone insane. He looks like he's preparing to feed roughly twelve people, even though it's just us.

He looks up and smiles at me broadly enough that his dimples are noticeable.

"Hi, sweetheart." He's buzzing with energy as he pulls me into a deep kiss. I break away from him and look around the packed kitchen, my heart rate skyrocketing.

"This is...a lot," I say, trying to keep the panic out of my voice. He gives me a sheepish look as he pours me a glass of wine, and I look at it in surprise.

He must not have been watching me at all today.

"I know, but I *love* Thanksgiving. Boss was big on it, so Nana and I would cook for two days straight. Boss would invite around some employees that didn't have families, so there were always different people to talk to, and we'd watch the parade and the game and eat an illegal amount of food. I don't know what you did as a kid, but maybe we could do something new? Like, we could cook dinner together?" His voice is eager. "For our first Thanksgiving? It'll be perfect."

Cold panic seeps through my body. He wants us to cook a perfect Thanksgiving together. I blink at the bread he's breaking apart to toast for stuffing, the brussels sprouts, the green beans, the massive turkey defrosting on the counter, the brine solution in the sink, and I start going numb.

Danny wanted the perfect Norman Rockwell Thanksgiving every year, and I was expected to cook and host it at our house, *my* house, for *his* family. Every year, I had to make a perfect turkey, which is *hard*, and I had to make perfect side dishes and desserts on top of that.

If I didn't get everything right, Danny got really fucking angry.

That first Thanksgiving was the worst.

I sip the wine quickly, and Theo seems to sense my apprehension but pushes on, his voice tighter. "I *know* you don't cook, but I thought it could be fun. I'll do almost everything, but I thought maybe you'd break your no cooking rule this one time? For me?" he pleads. I look at him blankly, drink the rest of the glass in one go, and pour myself another glass, drinking quickly. His smile falters.

"Okay, so you don't have to do *anything*, but maybe you hang out in the kitchen with me all day?" I look over at the turkey, and I drink. "Maybe you slow down and taste your wine? We've talked about this, sweetie." Theo slips the glass from my fingers, setting it out of reach. I look at him, panic rising in my body.

"I *hate* Thanksgiving," I whisper. He looks instantly dejected, but a thought seems to cross his mind, and he stares at me appraisingly for a second.

"*Why* do you hate it?"

"Please don't make me explain." He purses his lips.

"You don't want to do this at all? You don't even want me to make dinner?" My eyes go wide at the thought that he won't make me go through with this.

"*Please*, no." He frowns, drawing in a deep breath.

"You got it." Theo hands me my wine glass and starts chopping celery angrily. "Why don't you get comfortable and go watch TV, okay? I'll finish this and take all the food to the soup kitchen, and I'll order dinner when I'm back." He points to the bottle of wine with his knife, giving me a stern look. "That's a nice burgundy, Alex. Go slow and *taste* it, for fuck's sake."

I sip it slowly, barely holding back tears.

"Are you mad at me?" It comes out as a whisper. Theo drops the knife and looks at me with concern, wiping his hands on a towel before gripping my shoulders and kissing my forehead.

"Fuck, no. I'm not mad at you at all. Please don't think that. If you don't want to do it, we're not doing it, and you don't have to talk about it at all, either. I just want you to relax while I deal with this, okay?" I look up at him. His jaw is tight, but he's smiling at me, trying to be comforting and not angry. I wrap my arms around him and bury my face in his chest, breathing in his warm scent.

He seems to know *something* about why I'm reacting like this, and I don't like that, but he's not asking and he's immediately accommodating it. He rubs my back, and I start to feel calmer.

"Thank you." He holds me tightly for a second, breathing deeply.

"Yeah, of course." He kisses my forehead lightly. "Go relax. That god-awful dating show you've been making me watch has a new season, and there's some really comfortable stuff in your closet." I pull back and blink up at him in confusion.

"My *closet*? I have a drawer." He winces.

"Uh, yeah, you also have an entire closet in the big guest room. You don't like getting gifts, so I don't *give* them to you, but that doesn't mean I don't buy them for you. Maybe you could pretend they're not gifts? There's a cashmere lounge set in there that I know you'll love." I gape at him, appalled, trying to calculate how much money he's spent on the Thanksgiving food, or food in general, or the number of expensive gifts he's bought me, which I've apparently seen very few of.

How have I never thought about this?

"Theo, what do you do?" He blinks, confused.

"Uh, I don't know. I spend a lot of time thinking about you, that's for sure. Outside of that, I mostly cook and clean and work out. There's usually an audiobook involved. Right now it's *IQ84*. Have you read it? I think you'd like it." I look at him incredulously.

He needs a fucking life.

"What do you do for *work*, Theo? You spend *so* much money."

He looks a little surprised. "Wait, are you serious? Alex, I'm an *Anderson*. Why do you think I live in the Anderson House?" he says, gesturing vaguely around the room as I stare at him blankly.

"The *what*?"

"The Anderson House? Anderson Timber?" I raise my eyebrows at him, confused. "Right, you're from...not *here*. Okay, so my family's company was one of the first big timber companies in the state. The biggest, for a long time, actually. We had sole control of the company from 1885 until about a decade ago, and everyone along the line was smart about business and good at investing. Nana had a great sense for that part - she forced Boss into buying Microsoft and Apple shares super early, even though he thought it was bullshit." He laughs a little. "She was sharp."

I blink at him. "Is *that* what you do? Run a business?"

He scoffs. "*God*, no. Boss sold our majority in the business after I went to prison. I still own forty-nine percent of the company, but I let other people run it for me and I live off a trust fund."

"So," I ask slowly, surprised at how casual he's being about this, "you're saying that you're the heir to a timber fortune?"

"*Heir* and *fortune* are exaggerations," he says, looking a little uncomfortable.

"Are they?" He shrugs, turning me around and pushing me out of the kitchen.

"No more questions. Go get changed." I walk upstairs, wine glass in hand, peeking into the office and looking at all the old, framed photos of timber yards, which make sense now. I ignore the guest room entirely, and Theo doesn't seem bothered when I come back down in his clothes instead of something he bought me.

I wrap myself in a blanket on the couch and sip my wine slowly, watching the dating show. At some point, Theo leaves with all of the food, and I consider how sweet he's being.

Alex, 7:45 PM:

> we might drop by tomorrow

Bailey, 7:45 PM:

> YES! Miles will be so happy.

I'm not particularly excited about any sort of Thanksgiving, but I kind of want to make it up to Theo that I've ruined his holiday.

When Theo gets back, he seems tired as he orders food in and pours himself a full glass of whiskey before settling in to watch a show he says he hates but seems to like. His arm goes around me the moment I curl up against him, and I keep my eyes on the TV but put it on mute.

"We kept it small, as a kid, just us. My dad cooked, I helped, and my mom drank champagne and called it *managing*." He looks at me, shocked, but I don't look at him. "There were two or three side dishes, different every year, and my mom hated turkey, so it was always duck or Cornish game hen or something. I also hate turkey, by the way."

"Got it."

"My mom would go to bed right after dinner, and then my dad and I would do the wishbone wishes, even with the tiny bird bones. I wished for the same thing every year, but I never got it." Theo hums, kissing my hair, and I lean into him. "We're invited to Bailey's tomorrow. The only reason I'm going is because there's going to be no Thanksgiving food. Would you like to go?"

"Yes, please."

"She's going to ask you a million questions to see if you're a good boyfriend or not, so watch out for that." Theo doesn't comment about me calling him my boyfriend again, or push me to talk about my parents, or ask why I hate Thanksgiving, or ask what my yearly wish was. He just kisses me and holds me and criticizes the takeout for being too oily and the men on the dating show for being shitty.

I agree, because they are shitty.

So is Theo, but he's also kind of the best.

32

THEO

"ALLIE!!!" Miles collides with Alex's shins and beams up at her.

"Hi, buddy!" He pulls her into the house, chattering at her. She looks back over her shoulder and smiles at me, but it's not a real smile. She's been pissy all day, and me hiding all the alcohol in the house didn't help.

I'm such a fucking idiot. I should have remembered those photos of her, perfectly made up, obviously unhappy, holding a perfect-looking, gigantic turkey. She was probably expected to do that and hated it, but I don't think that's enough to make her react the way she did yesterday.

She looked genuinely panicked when she saw the food in the kitchen.

I trail in after Alex and Miles into Bailey's frenetic, cramped dining room. Dylan, Catherine, Suzie, a small blonde woman in a bright pink pantsuit, a couple dressed vaguely the same, and a tall woman who looks like the female version of Dylan are all crammed around the table loaded with Ethiopian food. Catherine watches Alex and I enter together with a surprised expression, and I start to feel antsy at the idea of socializing with all of these people.

Fuck, I *really* wanted it to be just Alex and I for our first Thanksgiving. I wanted to cook together, fuck in the kitchen, eat a ton of food, and fall asleep on the couch. That would have been perfect.

This will be fine.

A slightly drunken Bailey flags me down immediately and sits me next to her, asking me questions that get progressively more invasive. Catherine and Suzie watch from nearby with amused interest, but neither intervene. Alex sits across from me next to Miles, ripping off pieces of the sour flatbread and eating tiny bites of the food with her hands. She either doesn't like it or is too anxious to be hungry, and after tasting it, I decide it's the latter. She drinks a *lot* of wine and avoids looking at me anytime she pours another glass.

Bailey is boisterous, funny, and fairly engaging, but I have difficulty focusing on her because I keep looking over at Alex and Miles. It's hard not to get distracted by how focused she is on him, how sweet she is to him, and how *silly* she can be with him. I've watched them together before, but seeing them interact in person is different. Seeing it up close, I can so easily picture what a family with her would look like, and I realize that I fucking *yearn* to have that with her.

"You better wipe that look off your face before she sees you," Bailey whispers, and I jerk slightly, realizing that she's been watching me watch Alex and Miles. I run my hands through my hair and smile at her sheepishly.

"Thanks. I don't think that would go over well," I say, forcing a laugh.

Bailey snorts. "Not *yet*, maybe. Give it time," she whispers, winking at me.

I've never liked anyone as much as I like Bailey at that moment, so I smile at her broadly, trying hard to focus on her.

"Bailey, this food is delicious. Did you put together the berbere mix yourself?" Her face lights up at the question and she gasps, nodding emphatically.

"I did, actually! You're the only person who noticed."

"It's extremely well balanced. This is honestly the best Doro Wat I've ever had."

Her grin is loose and tipsy and approving. "Oh, I like *you*. Alex, I *like* him," Bailey says loudly enough to get Alex's attention. She looks up from Miles and smiles, but it doesn't reach her eyes.

***

Alex, for the most part, continues to ignore everyone but Miles. I leave her alone because it's the first time she's seemed relaxed since yesterday, and I want her to have a good day, but I wish she'd talk to me. I end up talking to Catherine instead, who gives me a somewhat scrutinizing look.

"So, *you're* the mystery boyfriend. I should have guessed." I smile at her, shrugging. "How long have you two been dating?"

"It's new, and we're taking it slowly." Catherine looks over at Alex thoughtfully.

"That's probably for the best. And she knows...?" Catherine's always been kind to me, and I love that she cares about Alex, so I try not to get defensive when I hear the suspicious tone in her voice.

"Yeah, she does. All of it." Most of it, anyway. Catherine's eyebrows raise slightly.

"Well, good. I'm surprised she's so understanding, to be honest, because of -" Catherine cuts herself off with a grimace, apparently realizing I might not know much about Alex's past.

"She doesn't like to talk about it," I say quietly, "but I think it's justified that she's hiding. I assume you know about it to some extent." She shakes her head.

"We don't know anything besides the fact that she's hiding. The three of us worry about her, Suzie especially. Alex is reserved and always says she's fine, but she still seems fragile."

I look over at Alex and consider what Catherine's saying. Alex is sensitive, she's got a lot of fucking issues, she cries at pretty much everything, and she's been emotionally all over the place since we met, but I've never thought of her as *fragile*.

"She's not, Catherine. She's really not." Catherine looks at Alex, contemplating her as she and Miles sit on the couch, coloring.

"I hope you're right." She looks back over at me, her mouth tightening. "So, what *are* your intentions with her, exactly?" I grin down at Catherine before glancing back at Alex and Miles.

"I just want to make her happy," I say, looking away once Alex notices me staring.

***

Once Miles goes to bed, I assume I'll finally get to spend time with Alex, but she still avoids me. She ends up in a long conversation with the blonde woman in the pantsuit, turning her back to me. I realize it's because she's drinking a *lot* and she knows that I'll cut her off, so I keep an eye on how much she's drinking from across the room.

I end up talking to Dylan, his sister, and the couple, who are Bailey's friends from college. They're all friendly and welcoming, and I get to avoid talking because Dylan's an insatiable gossip. He tells us in hushed tones that Catherine and Suzie have opened up their relationship recently and invited their girlfriend, gesturing surreptitiously at the woman Alex is speaking to. I try to stay engaged, but I keep looking at Alex, who is now on her fifth glass of wine and a third small piece of baklava.

She's eating something, at least.

When she finally walks over to me, she leans into me a little too hard and I realize she's *very* drunk. I think maybe I miscounted the glasses of wine, until I remember that she wouldn't eat yesterday, or today before dinner, and didn't even eat much dinner.

God, her drinking is so fucking concerning, and she just ignores me about it. I really need to sit her down and try and talk to her about it. Maybe if I –

"Baby, can we go home?" she slurs sweetly, and every other thought evaporates from my head. I want to keep my face neutral, but it's hard not to grin at her.

"Yeah, sweetheart. Let's go *home*." She smiles up at me, drunk enough that she doesn't even notice the emphasis I place on the word.

***

I hold back Alex's hair as she vomits into the bushes outside my house, then get her inside and give her a glass of water while heating up some of the mashed potatoes I made for myself. She eats them slowly, glaring at them with animosity.

"I *hate* Thanksgiving," she slurs, and I cringe as she salts the potatoes for a third time.

"Is that why you got shitfaced?" She groans, shaking her head.

"Theo, don't. Not today," she says, frowning down at the mashed potatoes.

"Fine, but we're talking about this soon, Alexandria."

"*We're talking about this soon, Alexandria,*" she parrots back in a snide voice. "Your kids are going to *hate* you." I bite my tongue hard as I watch her lean against the kitchen island, drunk and miserable and beautiful. I try not to say anything, but I can't help it.

"They're going to *love* you." I whisper it quietly enough that I don't think she'll hear me, but she freezes for a second, her eyes widening before she goes back to eating. I know she heard me, but it doesn't matter. She's drunk enough that she won't remember it in the morning.

That's fine - we're not there yet. Alex has *barely* adjusted to our relationship, she's kind of an alcoholic, and she's still married to someone else.

I need to fix one massive issue at a time.

We'll get there, eventually.

33

ALEX

SATURDAY, DECEMBER 2

Theo looks down at my feet and frowns. "Sweetheart, we're going *hiking*. Don't you have hiking boots?" I look down at my sneakers and shake my head.

"No. I didn't really have a way to go hiking before we started..." I pause as I realize I'm about to say *dating*, and I stutter out a hurried "...hiking together." He doesn't notice my fumble and frowns at my feet again as he opens the car door for me. We drive across the river on a long, narrow bridge and drive up the coast, his hand high up on my thigh, and I laugh when I see the signs for the state park we turn into.

"Cape *Disappointment*? Is that what I'm in for today?" Theo huffs out a laugh and starts telling me the history behind the name, and it feels normal. *This* feels normal now, whatever this is. He's still stalking me, but fighting it seems futile, so I don't.

That's a problem.

He's fully entrenched in his delusion, and he's starting to pull me down the rabbit hole with him. We spend so much of our time together that we have a weekly routine. Theo's got enough stuff at my house that he has a whole drawer, and enough of my things are at his house that certain rooms are starting to look lived in.

That's another problem.

When I babysat Miles the Saturday after Thanksgiving, Bailey and Dylan invited Theo to babysit with me. Miles made him play dinosaurs, which Theo kind of sucked at, almost like he didn't remember how he used to play as a kid. He and Miles seemed awkward with each other until Theo made him brownies, and then Theo was his favorite of the two of us.

How I felt watching them interact was a huge problem.

Bailey started teasing me at work on Monday about how Theo's "audition" went, and he immediately texted me asking if I would ever want kids, like he's really my boyfriend and those are conversations we should be having. Sometimes, it actually feels like he's my boyfriend, and I almost responded to him about the kids thing.

It's all a big fucking problem.

***

When I wake up on Sunday, I have the overwhelming urge to paint something. I shove Theo's arms off me and jump out of bed, ignoring his questions as I pile my sketchbook, watercolors, and brushes into a tote bag before running out my front door. It's six in the morning, the sun is barely up, I have brunch plans later, I'm in pajamas and it's freezing, but I don't fucking care.

I want to *paint*.

It's clear outside, thankfully, so I run to Shively Park and up the steps, camping on the wet grass and setting up quickly. I start sketching the ionic portico of an old hotel that's been placed in the park, flanked by bushes and trees that render the path behind it totally dark in the early morning. I don't focus on anything other than the desire to make something, and I'm blissful as I lose myself in the flow of drawing for the first time in months.

Theo shows up with my winter coat, two coffees, and a book. He's unusually calm and doesn't bother me at all, sitting close by and reading quietly. It's only when he gently tells me I need to get ready for brunch that I realize we've been there for hours.

I look down at the almost finished painting in my hands and smile slowly. My fingers are tired, my back aches, I'm cold, but I get to have *this* again. Theo doesn't ask any questions, he just looks at the watercolor and smiles tenderly, telling me it's lovely. When we get back to my apartment, he hangs it up on my bedroom wall while I get ready.

I startle when I see it on the wall, dread coiling in my gut. I leave it up because Theo will notice if I take it down, but I refuse to look at it again.

What I've painted is a beautiful, enticing doorway leading down a dark path.

***

"Wait, *that's* why he beat the shit out of Ben?"

I nod at Jessica, sipping my Bloody Mary. She looks horrified, her fork full of eggs hovering halfway to her mouth. Anna looks on the verge of tears, and I catch her eye, giving her a questioning look.

"Anna, what's wrong?"

"I'm so sorry, Alex," she sniffles. "I should have said something, but I didn't know...I didn't think..." Jessica's head swivels around so quickly her twists flip over her shoulder, and my stomach sinks.

"What do you mean?"

"Ben and I went on a date once," Anna mumbles, pushing around food on her plate. "We had...different experiences of how it ended." A wave of sympathy rushes through me, and Jessica reaches for Anna's hand and squeezes.

"Are you okay?" she asks, keeping her voice quiet.

Anna shrugs and sips her mimosa. "Um, I guess? It was a long time ago, and I was pretty drunk, and he doesn't think *that's* what happened, so...I don't know." I down my Bloody Mary quickly, fighting off my body's desire to freeze up because I want to be here for Anna.

"That fucking piece of shit," Jessica spits. "Can we get him fired for that? Arrested? Anything?"

"*Is* there anything we can do?" I ask, even though I doubt it.

Anna looks at me and shakes her head. "No. I mostly just try to ignore him. We work together and he's part of my friend group, so I can't *not* talk to him, which sucks." She stabs a potato viciously. "*He* sucks."

"Maybe if everyone else knew what kind of person he was, they wouldn't want to be friends with him," Jessica says as she slams her coffee cup on the table.

Anna shakes her head hard. "Please don't."

I reach across the table and grab Anna's hand, squeezing tightly. "We won't," I say quickly, and Jessica's anger deflates as she reaches for Anna's other hand.

"Sorry. We definitely won't. I just want to kick his ass now."

Anna smiles at her. "At least I'm not alone in that anymore."

"No, you're not," I say, locking eyes with her and smiling at her. "I think I know someone who would love to kick his ass for you, if you want," I offer quietly. "I'd probably help, honestly," I mutter. Jessica looks shocked and lets out a low whistle, and Anna raises her eyebrows in surprise.

"That's okay, but I *really* appreciate the thought," she says, unable to fight off a small smile.

"You're kind of a savage, aren't you?" Jessica asks.

"I don't know about *that*," I say, pulling an olive off the skewer and popping it into my mouth.

"Oh, I think you might be," Anna teases. "You're just so sweet no one notices." I laugh at her and shrug as I flag down the waiter for another round of drinks.

No one needs to know how good it felt to watch Theo beating the shit out of Ben, least of all Theo, who walked in ten minutes ago and sat at the bar. I'm not surprised he's here, but I'm ignoring him entirely because I'm here with my friends.

Our conversation drifts to less serious topics, but the feeling of warmth in my chest keeps spreading. For the first time in years, I have real friends, women who I can be open with and get closer to.

It's only dampened by the fact that I can't be open about everything, and that I'm not here with just them.

ARIANA RIVERS

***

Sometimes, I think about how thrilled I would have been if Theo had asked me out when we met, when he was just a guy at a bar. I'm glad he didn't, because he'd still be who he is and I'd still be trapped, but it would have taken me a long time to realize it.

I was able to get away from Danny, but I don't think I'd ever be able to get away from Theo. I think the only way I *can* get away from Theo is if I push him too far.

I still think about doing that sometimes, but less and less often as time goes by.

***

Theo's reading on the couch and I'm painting him when we hear the couple in the rental below my apartment start having loud, passionate sex. Theo glances up at me with a wicked smirk as he puts his book down, scooping me up and moving us into the bedroom where we can hear the couple better.

Both of us stay quiet as we undress and lay on the bed next to each other, kissing quietly as we listen to the man's low grunting and the woman's loud, squeaky moans. Theo slips his hand between my legs and raises his eyebrows at me in surprise when he finds me already wet. He grins at the blush staining my face, and I shrug slightly, not meeting his eyes.

The woman downstairs lets out an exaggerated sound of pleasure, and Theo huffs a laugh as he slips his fingers inside me, making me gasp.

"She's faking it," he whispers in my ear.

"*Definitely*," I whisper back, wrapping my hand around his cock and stroking lazily. He lets out a satisfied exhale and kisses his way down my chest, biting one of my nipples softly.

"I don't know how he can't tell," Theo says quietly as he drags his lips across my skin.

"Theo, *most* men probably can't tell." He freezes before looking up at me with a mischievous smile.

"Maybe he should hear what it sounds like when someone *isn't* faking it." I raise my eyebrows at him in surprise as he starts fingering me harder, and I stifle a moan as I look at him, horrified.

"Absolutely *not*," I hiss.

"I heard *absolutely*." He grins and crooks his fingers at just the right spot, circling my clit with his thumb, and I stifle another moan and slap his shoulder.

"You're an asshole." He laughs softly, leaning down and kissing me quickly.

"You just figured that out?" He slips his fingers out of me and pinches my clit, making me squeal. "Don't hold back, sweetheart," he says, tracing my neck with soft, open-mouth kisses. "You make the prettiest sounds for me." I shake my head, trying not to laugh.

"I'm not playing this game with you," I whisper as Theo covers my body with his, lining us up.

"I'm not giving you a choice," he says before he sinks into me deeply. I scream, clinging to him, and he shoots me a wicked grin when we hear the couple downstairs go quiet. "*That's* my girl," Theo whispers as he starts fucking me harder than usual. I can't help the sounds I make as he thrusts into me deeply enough that the pressure is painful.

"*Theo*," I whisper, and he shakes his head.

"Louder for me, honey." Theo grips my throat tightly as he fucks me, which he knows drives me crazy, laughing as we hear the couple downstairs start up again. I can hear them, but I'm more focused on the mischievous smile on Theo's face, his dimples deepening every time he elicits a loud response from me.

His face lights up at one point, and he pulls out and flips me over quickly, yanking me onto all fours before he grips my hips and slams into me so hard it makes me scream again. Theo's low, appreciative moan is obscured by the man downstairs swearing and coming with a shout.

Theo starts laughing hard, and I bury my face in the pillows, my face heating up in embarrassment.

"You did *such* a good job," he says, smug and amused, and I whip my head over my shoulder to glare at him.

"You've made your point," I hiss. Theo bends down over me, wrapping an arm around my neck and slipping his other hand between my legs, kissing my temple.

"Not yet, I haven't," he whispers in my ear as his fingers circle me gently, "but I'm about to."

Theo takes his time making his point because he's an asshole, and he makes his point more than once to show off to the people in the apartment beneath us. We lay there afterward, listening to the decidedly tense murmurs of the voices below us, and Theo looks at me with a satisfied, crooked smile.

"You're really fun, you know that?" He tucks a bit of my hair behind my ear, and I shake my head at him, genuinely amused.

"You're okay, I guess." He laughs and gives me a soft, affectionate look.

"I mean outside of bed, too. I have a lot of fun with you." I roll to my back and stare at the ceiling, unable to look at him. He's been more vulnerable lately, and it's a problem.

"Yeah." His fingers twine through mine, and he squeezes my hand. I barely squeeze back, but he notices it. He notices everything.

"Have you ever faked it?" I laugh out loud and look over at him, grateful to see the vulnerability wiped off his face.

"I pretty much always faked it."

"For *nine years?*" I nod, and Theo looks horrified. "Oh, honey, you should have told me that sooner," he says, reaching into my nightstand and grabbing a vibrator and rope. "Get the fuck over here."

Theo would have made a very fun boyfriend, and when we're having a good moment like right now, I let myself pretend he is.

It's a huge problem.

***

"Alex, you can't be fucking serious." Theo looks at me incredulously as I chew my dinner. "You've lived here for *months,* and you haven't been to the Gorge?"

I shrug, sipping my wine. "I don't have a car, Theo."

He waves a hand dismissively towards his driveway. "I can give you a car. I have an extra that I've been meaning to sell, anyway." I look at him, surprised by the offer, and for just a second, I think that having a car means that I could run from him.

He seems to realize the moment the thought crosses my mind because his smile drops off into a look of deep hurt.

We stare at each other in tense silence for a moment, aware that we've acknowledged that I can't leave and he'd stop me if I tried, which is something we don't acknowledge. The sharp reality that this isn't just a weird relationship where Theo has unmitigated access to my life cuts through our illusion for a minute.

He grabs my hand and smiles at me weakly.

"Hey, why don't we go out there this weekend? I haven't been in forever. It'll be nice." He's trying to push us back into what we're doing here, the way we're purposefully ignoring the situation he's created, so I force a smile and nod. The rest of the night is a little awkward, but by the time we go to bed, we're both lying to ourselves again, and it's kind of working.

It's working for him, anyway.

***

From the moment I get into the car after work the next day, Theo doesn't stop touching me. We drive east for a few hours and check into a nice hotel, and I roll my eyes at the sheepish smile he gives me when there's champagne and flowers in our room. We have a light dinner at the hotel bar, get a little drunk and listen to the piano player, then go back to our room and have the kind of rough sex I love, the kind that makes me so physically overwhelmed that my brain shuts off and I don't have to feel any of my feelings.

The less of my feelings I have to face when I'm around Theo, the better.

We get up early, and Theo seems excited and slightly high-strung as he grabs us coffee. It's cold and raining, and I accept the brand-new ankle-length puffer jacket he swears he had to pick up because he forgot my rain jacket. I shoot him an exasperated look, but I take the jacket all the same.

We drive west to a gorgeous overlook point, and Theo wraps his arms around me as I take in the Columbia River Gorge. I've never seen anything like the steep, tree-covered rock walls that seem to shoot out from the broad, grey river, and Theo talks softly about the geology of the place as I appreciate the beauty. We start driving back east on an old scenic highway, and he stops at every waterfall along the way.

The one I like most is a sheet of water that drops down a mossy wall of columnar basalt formations. When I almost slip and fall trying to get close enough to examine the clusters of slim, hexagonal strips of rock, Theo catches me and frowns at my shoes, telling me I need hiking boots and that it's too wet to do any of the hikes he wanted, so we'll have to come back again in the spring. I ignore him making future plans for us, pretending not to have heard him over the roar of the water.

I just focus on the feeling of the coarse, wet rock under my fingertips.

We drive to the next waterfall, a towering thing that cascades into a small pool before pouring into another fall. It's swarming with people, and we sip hot cider and climb the slick path to view the upper part of the falls from an old stone bridge, hand in hand like all the other couples around us.

As we drive back on the interstate, I watch the fog drift through the trees and the tiny waterfalls that run down the craggy, mossy walls of volcanic rock, and I look up to notice the barest dusting of snow at the highest peaks on either side of the river.

Theo drives us into Hood River, where we drift in and out of art galleries and shops and a small, cramped bookstore with ridiculous art on the walls before we have lunch at a brewery. Theo seems slightly anxious, constantly checking to see if I'm having a good time. I can tell he's trying to make things okay and show me we're a normal couple having a normal, romantic weekend.

We're not, but I let him try because it's easier not to fight it.

I ignore the fact that I don't even feel like fighting it anymore.

As we drive back to the hotel, Theo sheepishly tells me I have a massage at four-thirty, but that it's not a *gift*, that I deserve to relax and he'd do it himself, but he'd just end up fucking me. I realize he's apologizing in his own way, so I allow it.

The moment I'm alone with the massage therapist, I start crying. I apologize profusely, and she tells me it's more common than I think, so I just let myself cry.

I don't cry in front of Theo anymore unless we're having sex. I only let myself cry where I think he can't see me, like the bathroom at the rec center or the trivia bar, and only for a few minutes at a time, because I'm worried he has cameras there, too.

When I get to the hotel restaurant after my massage, Theo ignores that I've obviously been crying, and we both pretend everything is fine.

We go back to our room and have the kind of slow, emotional sex we've been having more often, the type of sex where I can't help letting my guard down with him. I keep my eyes closed so I don't have to see how he looks at me, but he begs me to look at him and be present with him, so I am. Whenever I see the way he looks at me, I realize how completely trapped I am.

How I feel when I see him looking at me like that is an even bigger problem.

***

The line between Theo's fantasy and my reality gets blurrier as the days slip by. We're so comfortable with each other now that we have fun together even when we're not doing anything. When I pretend he's my boyfriend, I get these glimpses of something good that could have existed between us, and I see that he's kind of perfect for me. I find myself wanting to share things with him, wanting to be open, wanting to make him laugh, wanting to be affectionate for no other reason than to see him happy.

The most fucked up thing about this situation Theo's created is that even when I remind myself he's stalking me and that none of this is *real*, I can't help feeling like it should be real between us.

I want it to be real between us, but it can't be.

That's the biggest fucking problem.

34

THEO

"How's everything going?"

"It's going *really* well, actually." Dr. Mills smiles a little at the dumb fucking grin I can't keep off my face.

"That's great to hear. What's going well?"

"Things with Alex are amazing." Dr. Mills nods, smiling a little.

"Do you want to talk about it?"

"We're just connecting so much lately. I feel like she's really starting to let me in."

"I'm happy to hear that. What else is going well? Besides Alex?"

I blink at her, confused for a moment. "What do you mean?" Her eyebrows raise slightly in surprise.

"Theodore, are you telling me that your relationship is the only thing in your life?" I scoff and shake my head but say nothing. "Okay, so what else do you do with your time?"

"Normal stuff. I read, I cook, I clean, I jerk off, I watch TV, I work out, I do projects around the house, I occasionally have to talk to someone about the company, things like that."

From the look on her face, I might have listed all of those out a little too quickly.

313

"Well, you sound busy, but are you passionate about any of those things?"

"Um, I love to cook. Food is...important to me." The way her brows quirk slightly makes me think I revealed something by accident, but I don't know what.

"What about other people in your life? Have you made any friends or gotten established in any sort of community?"

"I've definitely been more social since Alex and I have gotten together. She's good for me like that."

"That's progress, but that centers Alex again. I think we should focus on building up your life *outside* of Alex." Is she stupid? Alex is my entire life.

I give her a tight smile. "*Fine.*" This is such fucking bullshit.

"So, what's something outside of Alex that interests you?"

"Um, I was kind of into coding in high school and college, I guess." Hacking, technically. "Lately I've been working on some coding projects for fun." I've been making better phishing emails to trick Danny into letting me into his computer, which finally *worked.*

Dr. Mills smiles. "That's great. Let's start there."

***

"I want you to be good for me, okay?" Alex glances at the things on the bed and looks at me with barely concealed excitement.

"What does *that* mean?" I laugh a little and pull her dress off, kissing her skin as I go.

"It means you're going to get on the bed and stop asking questions." She shoots me a heated look as I unhook her bra and pull her thong off.

"Theo -"

"Get on the fucking bed," I growl at her, and she does immediately, looking eager. I'm pretty sure she's learned that when I talk to her like that, she gets into that headspace she likes so much, the one I've figured out how to get her into fairly quickly now. All I have to do is overwhelm her, which is relatively easy anyway.

She lets me tie her wrists tightly to the headboard, watching me with pure desire on her face, her lips pink and parted and ready for the ball gag I slip into her mouth. I climb onto the bed, bending her legs and binding them, tying her ankles tightly to her thighs, praising her with every knot. She's flexible, so I know it won't hurt her if I leave her bent up like this for a while, which is good.

I have no idea how long this will take.

I look at her lying on the bed, her legs bent and her cunt exposed to me, her perfect tits on display, her expression nervous and excited and needy, and I'm so hard for her it hurts.

"You're so fucking pretty tied up like this for me," I coo, and her eyes flare wide and her cheeks flush. I slip a thumb into my mouth to wet it, rubbing her clit for a moment until her eyes roll back in her head and she makes a low, sultry sound through the gag.

I do *not* want to leave her here unfucked, but I have things to do.

I slip an eye mask over her eyes, and she makes a high-pitched sound, trying to question what's happening.

"Sweetheart, I have to run some errands. I'll be back later, okay?" Alex whines in protest. "If you're good for me and come while I'm gone, I'll reward you when I get home." I slip a pair of headphones over her ears and pull up the audio porn she likes, putting on a playlist of things I know she's gotten off to before. She freezes the second she hears it and laughs a little. I pull a few more things out of the nightstand for good measure. I bend down and suck one of her nipples into a tight peak, biting gently, then slip a clamp around it and tighten until she makes a little squeaking sound.

"You like that?" She doesn't respond, which means the noise-canceling headphones are working, but her breathing is harder. I tease her other nipple the same way and slip the clamp on, eliciting another little squeak from her. I could leave her like this, and I'm sure it would be enough to drive her wild, but I want her to feel good while I'm gone. I run a finger against her cunt to find that she's already dripping, and I palm myself through my jeans for a moment as I touch her.

Fuck, this is torture for me.

I pull out a rabbit vibrator from the nightstand, coating it in lube before I push it slowly inside of her, and she lets out a series of short, surprised moans. I lift up one headphone, and she mumbles something around the gag that sounds suspiciously like *fuck me*.

"Be a good girl for me," I whisper in her ear before I turn the vibrator to its lowest setting, and the sound she makes goes straight to my dick. I don't know how long I'm going to be able to hold out listening to her from the other room, so I lower the headphones and launch myself off the bed and away from her. I can't help standing in the doorway and watching her writhe on the bed, tied up and perfect and ready for me to use when I'm done.

She's so fucking gorgeous, and she's all mine.

I just need to figure out how to keep it that way.

I listen to the sounds she makes around the gag, and I can feel my cock straining hard against my jeans as I head to my office. I pour myself a drink and focus on my breathing, because I know this will be unpleasant. Danny might be a stupid fuck, but he's paid attention to whatever training on phishing they give cops, because it took me weeks before the dipshit finally clicked on something I sent.

Now that I'm in his computer, the first thing I look for is information on Alex, and he has quite a bit. He tracked her for a while using a sophisticated image-tracking software I'm sure he got from work, but she's been so fucking smart about hiding that he lost her in Seattle. That's too close for comfort, but it's far enough away that it won't cause problems.

No matter what, he's never going to fucking touch her again.

On second look, Danny's slightly less stupid than I'd like to think he is. He's fairly organized and keeps good records, but nothing's secured or encrypted, so he's still kind of stupid. His tax returns indicate that he makes a good living, but not enough to explain how he owns two very expensive cars and a motorcycle outright, how he and Alex took long, expensive international vacations every year, and how he affords a lifestyle that shouldn't be available to him on his salary alone.

He keeps bank account statements for Alex's accounts in a separate folder, and that fuck has spent close to *half* of Alex's inheritance. She inherited *so much* money, and he's spent almost everything that wasn't tied up in investments. I drain my glass and look up at the ceiling, furious.

He's *really* fucking stupid, because mismanaging that amount of money is criminal.

Alex makes pretty little whining sounds in the other room, which calms me down.

Danny keeps everything in his calendar. He works long hours, but he's consistent about what he does in his time off. Gym, golf, bar, strip club, most of it with his friends and his brother. He gets a lot of massages, randomly scheduled and sometimes up to six times a month, so I'm going to guess he frequents sex workers. If I go back through his calendar, it looks like he took Alex to a nice dinner once a month.

Is this how she got through it for so long? Because he was out of the house most of the time, fucking other women? What did she even do all day besides work out and cook and clean? Read, probably, and she mentioned she took online classes. I'm sure she shopped, and she *definitely* drank a lot.

Now that I know where he goes and what he does, I can start planning to kill him. He's a cop, so I need to make sure I'm very fucking careful. I can't risk getting caught, and it can't get connected back to Alex. I should probably shoot him from a distance, as unsatisfying as that would be. It's been over a decade since I've been hunting, so I need to get Boss' guns from Yachats and start practicing again. Luckily, I have time. I can't go to Boston until I'm off parole unless I get permission.

I wonder if Officer Dent would approve it if I told him I'd be meeting my girlfriend's family.

Either way, I need to wait until I'm absolutely positive Alex won't run away once she gets access to her old life. Not that she could, but things are finally getting where I want them with her. Since I beat the shit out of Ben, it seems like she's almost entirely adjusted. She calls me her boyfriend. She's more relaxed. She's sharing more. She's playful. She initiates sex just as much as I do. She's starting to do things for me, little things I'm not sure she notices, but little acts of service all the same. She smiles at me, *really* smiles at me, all the time.

We have fun together.

Her trust issues are still a big problem, though. She's still not *entirely* open with me and hides her feelings from both of us. It'll still take time to get her fully adjusted, and I don't feel like losing any of the progress we've made.

From the long, low moans coming from the bedroom, I know Alex is close, but she hasn't come yet, so I still have to wait. I keep poking around in Danny's computer, but I'm not finding much else of interest. His taste in porn skews exclusively towards teen girls, he's got a bit of a gambling issue, and he's been sleeping with a coworker's wife for a few months – all shit that I don't care about.

I navigate to his photos, which are mostly photos of him with his family and Alex. There are so many photos of him and Alex on vacation, always stretched out somewhere on a sunny beach. I wonder where she'd like us to vacation together once I'm off parole. Knowing Alex, somewhere with lots of wine and huge art museums, but I don't know where I can even go after being incarcerated. I'm thinking about that as I absently open up the videos folder, but I stop dead when I see a folder labeled BUNNY. I click it open to see dozens of thumbnails of him and Alex fucking, and one subfolder labeled FF.

I get up, pour myself another drink, and leave the room, making a beeline for Alex.

I'm not doing it. I can't watch those videos. I can't watch him fuck her. I already know Danny was abusive, and I don't want to see Alex be miserable. I'm just going to stand in the doorway and drink and watch Alex come for me. I watch her chest flush as her body shakes and listen to her gorgeous, stifled moans as she does exactly what I told her to do.

Then I finish my drink and go watch the videos, because I can't help myself.

Thankfully, most of the videos are boring. Alex's orgasms are so fake it's kind of funny. They're studied, like she watched a lot of porn and mimicked it, which is possibly exactly what she did. She does the right things, makes the right sounds, but she's fucking *lying*. Either she can lie to other people much better than she can lie to me, or Danny didn't care enough to notice.

I notice with a level of juvenile satisfaction that there's an apparent size difference between Danny and me, not that it matters. The thing that actually matters is how different Alex is with him. She's so unenthusiastic, and it seems like she'd rather be doing anything else.

A long, sweet, keening sound echoes down the hallway, and I force myself to stay at my desk, eyeing the subfolder with unease before I open it. It has a few dozen videos, and I can tell from the thumbnails that these are *apologies*. I click on one, then another, getting progressively angrier as I watch them.

He makes her beg forgiveness for the dumbest shit before he brutally fucks her face. It's not rough the way Alex likes, it's meant as a punishment. How he talks to her makes me sick – he's degrading her in a way that's obviously not supposed to be enjoyable, and I can tell he's actively trying to hurt her feelings. His favorite thing to call her is a stupid, worthless, pathetic fuckup, and it makes me sick to my stomach to hear it over and over and over. Alex cries in the earlier videos, but her face is relatively blank in the later videos, her eyes glazed over, and I can't tell if she's drunk or zoned out or both.

Either way, she looks like she's just not there.

I'm fucking nauseous. Nine years of *this*?

I think about her reaction to being asked to apologize back in October, and I stare down at my feet, my head in my hands. I have been *such* a shitty boyfriend by accident.

I close out of Danny's computer and take deep, shaking breaths as I leave the office because I'm so fucking furious. I go to the basement and sprint on the treadmill for a few minutes, thinking about killing Danny the entire time, which helps calm me down.

Once I'm calmer, I go back upstairs to Alex.

I lean in the bedroom doorway and watch her writhe on the bed, listen to her whine and take harsh breaths through her nose, watch her shake as she starts to come again. Suddenly, being tied up and used isn't what I want for her right now. She likes it, I like it, but I can't get that blank fucking look of hers out of my head. I can't stop hearing Danny tell her what a stupid, worthless bitch she is.

I want to be tender with her right now, treat her with the kindness she didn't have before, wrap her up in my arms and make her feel safe and warm and secure.

I need her to know she's loved.

I get undressed slowly, watching her. She's so different than I thought she was, and I don't know how to handle that. I don't know how to help her with all the hurt she's been through, but I can do this, I can make her feel good.

I kneel on the bed, and she makes an excited sound, tilting her hips up a little as I pull the vibrator out of her slowly and untie her, massaging the stiffness out of her legs and hips, which makes her purr behind the gag. I unfasten the nipple clamps and slip the headphones and eye mask off, and her eyes are heavily lidded and adoring when they meet mine. I unbind the gag and slip it out of her mouth, massaging her jaw gently, and she hums in pleasure.

"Welcome home," she murmurs, her eyes closed and her face dreamy. A thrill goes through me, and I know I'll do anything to hear her say that to me every day for the rest of my life.

The thought makes me slightly uncomfortable, for some reason.

"Hi, sweetheart. You were *so* good for me while I was gone. What do you want as a reward?" She smiles and laughs a little, keeping her eyes closed and leaning into my touch.

"*You*," she whispers.

I'm grateful her eyes are closed, because I'm so fucking in love with her and I can't hide it anymore. I bite my tongue and unfasten her wrists, and her hands go immediately to me, loosely holding my shoulders. I make love to her slowly, saying anything I can think of to tell her how wonderful she is. Her orgasms are long and languid, almost like they're going half-speed, and once she can't handle any more, she pulls me tight and begs me to come for her.

I hold her in my arms after, loving the way she drapes herself across me and falls asleep instantly. I stroke her hair gently and stare at the ceiling, anger flooding back into my body.

The second I get off parole, I'm going to fucking kill him.

***

"What happened with Danny?" I focus on caramelizing the onions, not looking at Alex when I ask. I've found it's easiest for her to talk to me about hard things if I don't look at her, but I watch her out of the corner of my eye as she sips her wine.

"I told you. He pulled a gun, and I ran."

"No, I mean, how did you end up with him?"

"*Oh*. Um, I don't know." I frown over at her, and she looks up at me and shrugs. "I don't, kind of. One day, he showed up and blew up my life, and then he was always sort of there, texting me, calling me, telling me he'd take care of me, shit like that." I feel a twinge of discomfort that I shove down. What a fucking prick.

"Then he, um...we...he...*anyway*, then we were together." I don't push it, but I'm nauseous thinking about what she's not saying. She shrugs, draining the glass of wine and pouring herself another glass.

I look back at the onions, and I wait.

"I...I think Danny was able to get me to do things and make choices for me because I was so lost after my parents died. I was trapped inside the feeling that I should have been in the car with them. I was *supposed* to be, and I wished I had been most of the time."

I wince. "What do you mean?"

"Um, my parents and I got into a fight right before they died. I got a D on a calculus test, and I thought it was going to fuck my life up." Alex laughs bitterly. "It did, kind of. I ditched track practice to get drunk, and I forgot we were supposed to go to this gallery opening of my mom's that night because I didn't put it in my fucking planner. My parents came home to get me, and I was shitfaced, and they were *furious*, telling me I was ruining my future with my irresponsible behavior. I got so mad at them because they expected so much out of me, and I was so fucking tired of it. We got into this huge screaming match, and they left me at home, and they got hit on the way to the gallery." Alex's face is bunched up, her hand covering her mouth, and I can tell she's trying not to cry. "The last thing I did before they died was disappoint them," she says, her voice watery, "and I thought it was *my* fault they died."

"It wasn't," I say softly, and she lets out a bitter laugh.

"I know that now, but when I told Danny I felt that way, he made me feel like I had to be perfect to make up for it."

"*Motherfucker*." She nods and takes a few deep breaths, rubbing her arms in a soothing motion. I want to hold her, but I genuinely don't know if it's the right thing to do right now. She's never been *this* open before, and she seems reluctant to keep going. She pours herself another glass of wine, and I eye the nearly empty bottle as I wait for her to keep speaking.

"It started slow, you know? He made everything so easy for me at the beginning, and then once I kind of realized what had happened, I had no idea what to do. I got mad at him once, and then I found out I didn't get to *be* mad at him. He told me I was spoiled and immature, that I didn't know how to be a good wife, that he needed to show me my place, that he took care of me and I needed to take care of him." I grit my teeth and move the onions around, focusing on my breathing.

"His family was awful, too. His parents died when he was young, which is kind of how he got me to talk to him, but his aunts were really involved in our lives and *extremely* critical of me. They bossed me around constantly, and it took me fucking *years* to realize that I was being pushed around and manipulated by everyone. I was just trying to get through it and figure out how to not make Danny angry. He got so angry about *everything*, and it took me a long time to figure out how to handle him."

"Why didn't anyone fucking help you?" She snorts.

"People tried, but I didn't want to acknowledge what was going on, so I lied to everyone and pretended it wasn't happening."

"Why didn't you-"

"No more, Theo." Her voice is sharp. "It's your turn to share. Tell me about your grandparents." I shoot her a frustrated look, but she's being open, and I know she wants that from me, so I indulge her.

"Um, yeah, okay. They were great, I guess. I spent every summer with them as a kid, basically. I always wanted to be here instead of with Jason and Melissa."

"Why didn't you live with them?" I shrug, taking a deep breath.

"They tried to adopt me when I was born because Melissa was only seventeen, but she wanted to keep me, so she and Jason moved out to Yakima when she was pregnant. The two of them ended up using me to get money out of Nana and Boss." Alex makes a sharp, disapproving sound.

"What did they need the money for?" I blink down at the onions for a second.

"Jason's drug habit, probably. It worked, because Nana and Boss loved me, but things were shitty for years, and then I killed Jason, and then Melissa fucked off, and then I came here, and then things were *fine*."

"Uh-*huh*," she says, her voice dripping with disbelief. I take a deep breath and look over at her skeptical face, forcing a smile.

"Seriously, things were fine. Nana and Boss were great, and they loved me even though I was a fucking handful." Alex folds her arms over her chest and raises her eyebrows at me expectantly, and something tightens in my throat.

She shared, I can share.

"Um, I mean, I think they viewed me as a chance to fix whatever they thought they'd fucked up with Melissa, so they were super strict and expected a lot out of me. I felt like they wanted me to be someone I wasn't. Nana tried really hard to fix my behavior, which made things between us difficult because I wanted to make her happy, but I couldn't control my impulses or my emotions or *anything*.

"Boss expected me to take over the company, so he was on my ass to shadow him and learn the business, which I had *no* interest in. He pushed me to do well in school, which was hard because school was fucking boring, and then he pushed me to study business in college and work for the company during the summers, which I *hated*. I wanted to make him happy, so I did all of it. I hated every fucking second of it, but I did it."

"What did your grandma want for you?" I laugh and force myself not to look directly at Alex.

"She wanted me to find a nice girl, settle down, have a shit ton of kids, and be as normal as fucking possible." Alex sips her wine slowly, not looking at me.

"What were you like in college?"

I shrug. "I dunno, I was mostly normal. I did well in school because there would be hell to pay if I didn't, and I was better at socializing. Managing my impulses was easier, too. Not easy, necessarily, but easier. I also fucked around a lot." Alex laughs a little too loudly, and I eye the almost empty wine bottle beside her. "Can you bring me that? I need to deglaze the pan." She does, leaning against the counter next to me and sipping her wine quietly as I upend the bottle into the pan before pouring in the stock and seasoning the soup.

"Then what?" I laugh bitterly, shaking my head at her.

"*Then* I met Ashley, and everything in my life was great for the first time ever, and *then* she left me, and *then* I found out she was in love with my roommate, and *then* I tried to kill him, and *then* I went to prison. My grandparents hired great lawyers, but there's still a mandatory minimum for what I did.

"I disappointed the ever-loving fuck out of Boss, who *never* forgave me for being the reason he had to sell his majority in the company instead of passing it down, and then he died. Nana forgave me, mostly because she thought I couldn't help being such a fuck up, but then she got breast cancer, and I couldn't be there for her or do anything to help her because I was in fucking prison."

"I'm so sorry."

"Yeah, she died three months before I got out. Oh, and *then* I had to deal with *Melissa*, who hates me even more than she used to. I had to pay off my own fucking mother to get her to leave me alone, which was awesome. Can I *please* stop fucking sharing now?" I exhale hard, looking away from her. "I'm so sorry, sweetheart. I didn't mean to snap at you."

"I know, baby," she says, and she runs her hand run up and down my back. I stare at the simmering soup, breathing deeply and pushing everything back down. Alex picks up the wedge of cheese and inspects it for a long time before her arm snakes around my waist.

"My dad always used Gruyere when he made French onion soup. I've never had it with Comte, but they're not really different, right?" I catch her eye and try to smile at her.

"They're a little different, but they're mostly the same." She hums and sets the cheese back down. I wrap my arm around her shoulders, and we stand there quietly, embracing.

35

ALEX

FRIDAY, DECEMBER 22

Theo's been cagey all week about our Christmas plans, and I don't want to deal with it. He wasn't even home last night, which was the first night I've spent without him in over a month. He seems excited when he picks me up from work, and the backseat of his car is full of a cooler, grocery bags, a small duffle bag, and a nice, brand new weekender bag.

I don't even ask, I just raise my eyebrows.

He looks sheepish. "I thought we could do Christmas away."

"Theo, I *hate* Christmas. I didn't even get you anything." He sighs as he opens the passenger door.

"Just get in the car, Alex." I roll my eyes and get in.

At this point, I know there's no fighting him on things.

He starts driving south down the coast, soft Christmas music filling the car, and he glances over at me as we pass through Seaside.

"Why *do* you hate Christmas?" he asks, and I groan, looking up at the roof of the car. I don't want to talk about this, but we've been sharing so much more, and I like talking to him. It blurs the lines too much, but they're already so blurry that I don't think it matters anymore.

"I loved it as a kid. My parents and I had all these weird traditions." I smile, thinking about my dad in his stupid running outfit. "And then there was Danny, and he and his family had all these insane expectations around Christmas. It was a huge production every year, with parties, and caroling, and gingerbread houses, and lights, and midnight Mass, and Christmas dinner, and there was this unspoken *right* way to do everything. I hated it, but I had to fall in line and host and look the part and act the part, and everything had to be *perfect* every fucking year. His aunt Mary was a controlling little tyrant about it, and the fucking bitch always said *something* that made Danny mad at me," I say bitterly.

Talking about this stuff with Theo is easier now, but it's still not easy to talk about. He gives me a minute to calm down, rubbing my leg soothingly.

"Tell me about what you did with your parents." He's looking at the road, and his voice is soft, and I cross my arms and look out the window at the dark ocean. I don't think I've talked about this with anyone in years.

It might be nice to talk about it.

"Well, my dad always did a charity run on Christmas morning in this *stupid* elf outfit. It was so dorky, with big fake ears and a ridiculous hat my mom made, so we'd go stand in the snow and drink cocoa and wait for him to finish after we opened presents. Once I was in high school, my mom would put peppermint schnapps in my cocoa, *fah wahmth*," I say, mimicking my mother's thick Boston accent. Theo looks at me, his eyebrows raised, but I ignore him.

"Also, my mom had this dumb story she told every year about her entire extended family meeting in Milan for Christmas when she was eighteen, and *everyone* brought a panettone, so there were twenty of them or something. They ate them until they got sick, but it was so funny that my mom always wanted a panettone at Christmas. I *loathed* them until I was, like, nine. Have you ever had one?" Theo shakes his head. "They're pretty great, honestly."

"What else?"

"As a little kid, I was *very* nervous about Santa coming down the fireplace, so my mom had an artist friend of hers weld this insane-looking grate that turned our fireplace into a spike pit so that I felt safe that no one could come down the chimney." Theo laughs, squeezing my knee. "I'd find all the presents from Santa skewered on these spikes on Christmas morning, but somehow the presents were never damaged. How she got a fucking bike on there, I'll never know." I laugh again, thinking about it sticking out of the fireplace at a weird angle. "Once I found out Santa wasn't real, my mom told me arranging gifts on that thing was her favorite part of Christmas, so we kept doing it until -" My voice catches in my throat as I sob.

When did I even start crying?

I wipe the tears from my face, exhaling harshly. "Anyway, Christmas is hard. Don't make me do it." Theo reaches for my hand and pulls it towards him, kissing it softly.

"You got it. We can skip everything except the ham, okay? I fucking *love* Christmas ham and it's my first one in nine years, so please indulge me." I laugh and shake my head at him. He's so weird about food.

"Okay. Just ham."

"Ham and gifts?"

"*Just ham.*"

"Fine," he sighs. "But I booked you a spa day tomorrow, which isn't a gift, technically." I close my eyes and lean back against the headrest, sighing loudly in exasperation.

"I wish they'd never let you out of prison."

He laughs, but I can't tell if I'm joking or not.

***

A few hours later, we pull into a quaint coastal town and turn off the highway, heading up a small, steep road into the wooded cliffs. The houses here are few and far between, and all set far back from the road. We finally pull down a long driveway through a small copse of trees, revealing a large, low, mid-century house with a view of the coast.

I help Theo take the bags in, and I'm floored when we step inside. It's a spacious, open-concept room with the living room and dining room flowing into each other. The kitchen is tucked away off the dining room, barely visible. The walls along the back of the house have floor-to-ceiling windows, showing an expansive view of the town, the coast, and the cliffs. An insane-looking suspended fireplace hangs down into the corner of the living room with split logs piled beneath it, and the house looks like a spread from a mid-century catalog. Unlike the furniture at Theo's place, everything here looks well-kept but actually vintage.

"Shoes off, suitcases downstairs. I'll deal with the *tree*." It's only then I notice a hilarious, ancient silver aluminum tree in the corner of the living room, decorated with large blue ornaments and pink tinsel.

He must have come down here yesterday to set this up.

"Leave the tree. It's kind of amazing." He grins at me as I slip off my sneakers and take the suitcases down a staircase off the entrance, walking down into a lower level not visible from the driveway. The house is built into a hillside, so it's colder downstairs. It's got a wood stove in the central seating area, with doors on either side and a huge window looking out into the trees. I peer into the four doorways, finding two small guest rooms, a bathroom, and a master bedroom with a large ensuite bathroom.

I put our bags in there and start snooping.

Everything is neat and tidy, and there aren't any personal effects – it might be a rental, but something about this place seems too familiar for that.

There's nothing in the main room or the larger guest room, but in the smaller guest room, I find a box tucked up in the corner of the closet. I pull it down onto the bed, finding it full of framed photos featuring the same couple, spanning decades. The man is tall, with curly brown hair, blue eyes, and a square jaw, and the woman is medium height, with tan skin, straight black hair, and a warm smile.

There are photos of them taken in this house, horseback riding on the beach, hiking in the Gorge, smiling at the Coliseum, and they always look completely wrapped up in each other. Further down in the box are photos of them with a girl with curly dark hair and hazel eyes, and she's all sorts of ages in the photos, but never older than a young teenager. She's beautiful, with a long face, startlingly bright hazel eyes, and a warm, slightly crooked smile bracketed by dimples.

Theo looks *so much* like his mom.

Further down, there are a few photos of Theo with his grandparents, and he ranges from a cute little kid to a sad, awkward-looking preteen to a handsome, put-together-looking teenager.

There are no photos of him with his mom.

I leave the pictures scattered on the bed and keep snooping. In the nightstand drawer, hidden underneath some papers and a flashlight, I find two more photos, both taken in front of the silver tree upstairs. One photo is of Theo, his mom, and a man who has to be his dad. Theo has his sharp jawline, nose, and general build, but his dad is thinner, his muscles are ropier, and his skin is pale and a little sallow. Theo's mom is still young, certainly younger than his dad, but she looks wildly different from the photos of her as a teenager. She's thinner, with dark circles under her eyes and pockmarked skin, and her teeth are all sort of yellow.

In her arms is Theo, maybe three or four, smiling and happy and clutching a big teddy bear. God, he was *such* a cute kid, all dimples and wavy curls.

I don't know why the photo is making me so sad.

The other photo shows Theo, maybe eighteen or nineteen, thinner than he is now and with short hair, smiling broadly next to a handsome kid his age with ginger hair and blue eyes, their arms around each other's shoulders. Theo's wearing the college sweater languishing under my bed, and the kid is wearing a crewneck sweater with a cartoon duck. I flip the photo over, seeing "Theo & Kevin, Christmas 2011" written in a looping cursive on the back. I stare at the words for a second, processing them.

Oh, my *god*.

"Sweetheart, do you wa-" My head whips up as Theo walks in on me and sees all the photos spread over the bed. His eyes widen, and he tenses up immediately, and we stare at each other for a long moment.

"Put. Those. Away," he says, his voice low and clipped.

"Theo, what -"

"Don't," he snaps.

"I have questions." He closes his eyes and breathes deeply.

"*Alex, please,*" he begs quietly.

"Baby," I say, keeping my voice soothing. "I've never told anyone about the fire grate. Danny didn't even know about it. I shared, and now it's your turn." He looks at me like I'm fighting dirty, which I am, before he takes a shaking breath and nods.

"Were you and Kevin friends?" He pushes out a small, bitter laugh and looks away from me, shaking his head.

"He was my best friend, actually. Kind of my only real friend ever. We were roommates freshman year and we just clicked, I guess. We were inseparable after that. His parents sucked the same way my parents sucked, so he spent holidays and summers with me in Astoria, and Nana and Boss *loved* him. It was like having a brother, I think," he says, grimacing up at the ceiling. "When Ashley came along, we all spent a ton of time together, and I was fucking *ecstatic* that they got along so well. I was just too stupid to see what was happening." He lets out a low, angry laugh. "They were careful enough that I didn't catch them, and I'm sure that piece of shit would have kept fucking her behind my back if I hadn't told him that I was going to propose. She broke up with me right after that, and I *still* didn't see it." Theo crosses his arms and shakes his head at his feet. "I would have beaten the shit out of anyone I'd found Ashley with, but I wouldn't have gotten angry enough to kill anyone else. I don't feel bad about it, honestly, because he fucking deserved it," he says in a small, hurt voice.

I stare at him, my mind whirring.

"Is that why you don't have any friends?" He gives me a look I don't entirely understand.

"I have you," he says quietly, and a strong wash of pity rolls through me. I have to look away from him so he doesn't see my expression, so I look down at the photos in my hands. After a moment, I hold up the one of him and his parents, but he doesn't look at it.

"Can I have two questions?" He groans but gives me a jerking nod. "Why do your parents look sick?" Theo snorts and rolls his eyes.

"Because they're fucking meth addicts, Alex." I blink hard, looking back down at the photo. His mom looks so much sicker than his dad. I look back up at him, tense and upset in the doorway.

"You said it was just your dad." I see a muscle in his jaw twitch, and he shakes his head slowly.

"I never said that." I stare at him for a second, thinking about everything he's told me about his parents, and things start clicking into place.

"Is *that* why you didn't give your mom the money?" He narrows his eyes and looks up at the ceiling.

"I gave her enough to get her to fuck off, but yeah. She's got three other kids now, and I knew from experience she wasn't going to spend anything on them. I set up trusts for them anyway, structured so the money can only be used for college or a down payment or something like that, so Melissa can't get to it. I'm hoping maybe it'll fix their lives, but I don't know. I have a couple of years before the oldest one turns eighteen, and then Melissa will be a fucking headache again, I'm sure." I stare at him, shocked. I knew he was closed off, but I had no idea how much he was hiding from me. I have so many questions now.

"Wait, so -"

"You said *two fucking questions*," he snaps. He closes his eyes, rubbing his hand over his face. "*Sorry,* sweetie. I'm not mad at you, I just don't think about this stuff, *ever.*" I nod, no longer surprised by that.

"It's okay. Last question, and it's easy, I *swear*," I say in a soft voice. I look down at the photo of him as a little kid and smile a little, holding up the picture again, pointing at him and the bear.

"Was your childhood nickname Teddy?" His face goes blank instantly as he looks at the photo, and he shakes his head slowly.

"No, I didn't have one. Pretty much everyone except my grandparents called me Ted."

"What did they call you?" Theo glances at me, and I see his jaw clenching.

"Nana always called me Theo, and Boss just called me son," he says through his teeth. He closes his eyes and sighs as he turns away from me, his body rigid and his voice tense. "I'm going to be in the kitchen. Please leave me alone for a little bit," he says as he walks back upstairs. I stare after him, still stunned.

I pack the photos away and put them back in the closet and curl up the guest bed, looking out the window, thinking. It's dark outside, so I mostly see myself reflected back in the window.

I can see on my mirrored face that things have just gotten a lot more complicated for me.

I unpack our bags, noticing Theo packed his college sweater in my bag even though I never wear it anymore. I'm in so deep that I don't know which way is up, so I change into soft leggings and put on the goddamn sweater and head upstairs. It's been almost two hours, which is probably long enough. The fireplace is going, and the dining room table is set, including a wine glass for me, and Theo is in the kitchen, leaning against the counter and staring at the oven, drinking whiskey straight from a half-empty bottle.

I go into the kitchen, watching him warily. Aside from being a little red around the eyes, he doesn't seem drunk at all. He lets me gently slip the bottle out of his hands but just keeps staring at the oven, his face blank.

I look over and see that he's watching a chicken roast, the timer on the oven showing another fifteen minutes. I pour him a glass of water, and he sips it slowly, still not looking at me. I stare at him, but I have no idea what to do, so I put my arms around his waist and hold him tightly.

If he can share, I can share.

"If you think I've got a problem with my drinking, you should have met my mother," I say, resting my head on his chest. "She was the worst when she was drunk, super mean and critical, and she drank a *lot*. My dad was controlling and *really* passive-aggressive, so between the two of them, I couldn't do anything right, no matter how hard I tried." Theo doesn't respond, but he wraps his arms around my shoulders and holds me tightly, his thumbs tracing slow circles on my skin. "I tried so hard," I whisper, and he pulls me closer and kisses my forehead before he rests his cheek on the top of my head.

We stay like that until the chicken is done.

Theo says nothing, makes me a plate, cups my face in his hands and kisses me softly, and goes to bed.

I drink a large glass of wine, put the untouched plate in the refrigerator, and go downstairs shortly after. When I crawl into bed, Theo's already asleep, so I wrap my arm around his waist and tuck my other arm underneath his pillow, curling around his back.

I try to ignore how I feel when he relaxes back into me, how I feel as my hand finds his under the pillow, how I feel as I twine my fingers through his and press a kiss to his shoulder, but I can't.

There are no lines between us anymore. Everything's blurred together into a huge mess.

36

THEO

The day after Alex finds the photos, I have such a bad hangover that I can't even make her breakfast, so I give her the car keys and the details for the spa and go back to bed. She'll be irritated when she realizes I've booked her for every service they offer, but she won't say no.

She acts like she hates gifts and hates being pampered, but she doesn't.

I was supposed to need her to be out of the house for hours to set up decorations and put gifts under the tree and make gingerbread for us to build a house and all the other shit I thought might make for a perfect first Christmas together, but now that's pointless.

I scrap all my plans for the day, and I drink instead.

I don't think about the photos, or about Kevin and Ashley, or about Melissa and Jason, or about Boss and Nana. I just drink and think about the fact that after Thanksgiving, I didn't bother to ask Alex how she felt about *other* holidays because I'm a selfish fucking asshole who wanted to have something nice with her.

I lie on the couch and stare into the fireplace, somewhat drunk and exceptionally angry that this isn't going how I wanted.

Fuck it, I'm going to do *one* of the things I had planned for this weekend. I already have everything I need to make a panettone because there was always some in the photos of her and her parents at Christmas, and she should have one thing that feels familiar to her, that lets her know her traditions matter in this relationship.

As I make the dough, I think about what I need to do to kill Danny. I've never planned to kill someone before, and figuring out what I need to do to not get caught is annoying. He's a cop, so I have to factor in that the cops will give a shit that he's dead and actually investigate it. Still, it shouldn't be that hard. I cover the dough and slip it into the fridge to rest overnight, trying to figure out if Alex would be likely to run away back to Boston if she got her old identity back.

I don't think she would anymore. I think we're in a good enough place that she'd stay with me, where she fucking belongs.

I cut myself off from drinking after the dough is made so that I'll be relatively sober when Alex gets home. I don't want to be drunk around her again, because I almost told her I loved her last night when she came upstairs to comfort me.

She's not quite there yet, but she's close.

Alex comes home pampered and glowing and exasperated. I smile and try to act normal, but she's not buying any of it. She wraps her arms around me and tells me I'm a shitty liar and tries to get me to open up to her, but I don't. We talk about virtually nothing over dinner, but it's comfortable.

When we're sitting on the couch afterward, Alex crawls into my lap and kisses me, undoing my belt and telling me she wants to make my day better. For the first time ever, it takes me a while to get hard for her, but she doesn't say anything. She keeps kissing me and touching me, and I lose myself in her affection until she kneels between my knees. I can't tell exactly why she's sucking me off, but the idea that she might be apologizing makes me uneasy. I watch her closely, but she's so engaged, her face flushed and not blank at all, and she looks up at me adoringly as her cheeks hollow out around me.

I think she's trying to take care of me, which makes me come immediately.

Alex curls up in my arms after, shyly asking me if that made me feel better. It did, but I don't know how to feel about the fact that she's using sex like this, so I make her come instead of answering her.

This isn't going how I wanted.

This was all supposed to go so fucking differently.

When we go to bed, Alex gently turns me away from her and curls up around my back with her arm around my waist, pressing soft kisses into my shoulders.

I think she's trying to take care of me again, and it's the best I've slept in a long time.

The next morning, I wake up early to find a naked, mostly asleep Alex halfway on top of me with my thigh between hers, her hips moving the tiniest bit. I roll her carefully onto her back, touching her until she's wet enough that I can push into her. She wakes up to me fucking her, humming with delight as she wraps herself around me. Once she's fully awake, I fuck her hard the way she likes, loving her screams and the way she begs me for more. I leave her lying on the bed with that dreamy smile she gets after sex and go upstairs to make breakfast, relieved that things feel back on track.

She comes into the kitchen in my sweater and nothing else, her hair fucked up and her thighs still messy with me, and I'm finally calm as she smiles up at me before pulling me down into a long, sweet kiss.

This is what I wanted.

I tell her we have plans all day, starting right after breakfast, and she says she needs two hours for her own plans, which she won't tell me anything about.

In return for not asking any questions, she lets me give her *one* gift.

***

"What is this place?"

"You'll see." I help Alex down the slick rocks, grateful she's wearing the nice hiking boots I bought her for this exact purpose and not the canvas sneakers she brought with her.

We finally get onto the flat part of the rocks and start ambling across them, Alex taking her time peering into tide pools and pointing out starfish. I watch her, feeling more relaxed. This is how I wanted this trip to go. She smiles up at me from the edge of a tide pool, and she looks so picture-perfect that I wish I could fill my phone with photos of her.

I can't, not while she's still worried about Danny, but I'll fix that problem for her soon enough.

"Honey, we need to time this right. Can you follow me?" I reach my hand down to her, and we pick our way across the rocks, headed for Thor's Well. I know the best time to see it is at high tide, but that's a more dangerous time to navigate the rocks, so I get her there just before the tide starts coming in so she can watch it change.

There's a burst of water ahead, and she looks at it, confused and excited. It's fun to see this from her eyes, and I pull her closer to the collapsed sea cave as a wave crests over the rocks. She watches with wide eyes as a bigger wave rolls in, the water covering the rocks before it pours down into the cave mouth, making it briefly look like there's a sinkhole in the ocean. A minute later, a large wave hits the inside of the cave exactly right, and the water bursts up through the hole like a geyser.

Alex is *delighted*, taking photos with her phone and watching with an amazed smile, seeming to enjoy it most when the water creates the illusion of a hole in the ocean. I lead her closer, but she gets nervous about getting too close. I keep going, stopping a few feet from the cave opening and looking down at the churning water, waiting. I see the right wave come in and step back quickly, watching the water surge into the air, and I laugh as the water sprays my face.

When I grin over at Alex, she's putting her phone away with a shy smile.

We walk around the perimeter, and I keep my eyes on the waves and the water level gathering on the rocks so Alex can enjoy it. We stay until the water on the rocks starts getting too high, then I lead her away, watching her feet for her so she can peruse the tide pools. Alex is nearly giddy, chatting animatedly about rock formations and tidepools, googling Thor's Well and reading up on it as we return to the car.

We navigate down the coast, and Alex slips her hand into mine almost absently as she changes the radio dial from news to Christmas music, and something in me unwinds a bit.

She makes me pull off into a large store down the coast and tells me to wait in the car and to give her as long as she needs, and she seems excited as she hurries into the store. She left her phone in the car, so I open it, looking through her photos. There are mostly scenic photos of the coast or Portland, a few of Miles and Bailey, some of Anna and Jessica, and now a handful of *me*.

She's never taken a photo of me before, and my chest loosens entirely.

There's a few of me looking at tide pools, a photo where I'm looking down into the cave, another where I'm laughing at the water shooting upwards, and yet another where I'm looking over at Alex with a stupid smile.

I put her phone down and sigh in relief. She's been more adjusted lately, but *this* is different. She wants these reminders of me, of the time we're spending together, and they're proof of me as an established part of her life. I have worked so fucking hard to make this relationship work because I knew we were connected, and I fucked it up over and over again, but I finally fixed it.

We're *finally* on the same page now.

When I see Alex coming out of the store with a cart full of bags, I get out to help her put them in the trunk, but she points her finger at me, her expression stern.

"No! Stay in the car. You can't see anything!" I grin and do what she says.

I keep asking her teasing questions about the bags, trying to guess what's inside, and she keeps deflecting, trailing off in the middle of sentences as she looks out at the water. I forget she's never been this far down the coast, so I drive slowly and stay quiet, letting her enjoy the fog drifting off the grey, frothy ocean and into the evergreens that jut up out of the cliffs. She slips her hand into mine again, and we drive like that, quiet, with slightly staticky Christmas music playing softly in the car.

I glance over at her any time I can, and she mostly looks happy, but occasionally she looks contemplative, and once she seems downright sad. She's probably thinking about her parents, or about her asshole ex who ruined every possible holiday for her in some way or another. We're going to have to spend years building up new traditions and getting her to like holidays again.

Years. I smile at the thought.

We stop for lunch at a crab shack in Bandon, and Alex is thrilled. She cracks open the legs with efficient, practiced movements. She eschews the melted butter completely, just pops the tender crab in her mouth, her lips closing around her fingers and sucking quickly before she cracks open more of the leg. I have to remind myself to eat, remind myself that I love this place, that I haven't been here in ten years, but everything is obscured by the fact that Alex is here with me, happy and enjoying herself, stealing one of my crab legs since she doesn't seem to like the body meat as much.

"You're lucky I like you," I tease as she pulls another one of my legs to her plate.

"More like the other way around," she mutters, smiling up at me. I stare down at my food for a second, overwhelmed by the impulse to tell her I love her.

I have other plans for the day, a hike, more tidepools, maybe taking her to that ridiculous dinosaur garden down the coast, but I scrap them all. Instead, I drive us back to Yachats, lead her downstairs, and make love to her slowly. I bite my fucking tongue, and I try hard to keep how much I love her off my face, but I fail. She starts tearing up, pulling me closer and kissing me so that I don't see the look on her face, but I see it.

We're on the same page.

I leave her asleep in bed afterward and go upstairs to finish making the panettone. I'm letting the dough rest again and making a fire when she comes upstairs in leggings and my sweater, some of my socks on her feet.

"Teddy?" Her voice is sweet and endearing, and the nickname stops me cold. Why is she calling me that? I stand up and back away from the fire, looking down at how she's smiling sweetly up at me. She's being different right now, but I can't tell how. "Can you do me a favor?"

"Anything." She smiles wider at the supplicating tone of my voice.

"Can you go away?" A pit opens in my stomach, and all the joy vanishes.

"*What*?" My voice is sharp, and her smile falters, her eyes going wide for a second before she exhales exasperatedly and rolls her eyes at me. She steps closer, her arms winding around my neck and her fingers combing through my hair, and I relax instantly.

"Like, to the *kitchen*, baby," she says, pressing up on her toes and kissing me softly. "I need you to stay in the kitchen and not leave until I say you can. I have to deal with the stuff in the trunk, and I'd love it if you could just be good for me and do what I tell you." Her voice is low and sultry, and I'm putty in her hands as she kisses up my neck and jaw, pushing me back slowly until she's walking me backward toward the kitchen, undoing my pants as she goes.

I'm already hard from how her voice sounded when she asked me to be good for her, which is *new*. She slips her hand into my pants and grips me tightly as she kisses me, and when I gasp a little, she sweeps her tongue into my mouth, moaning softly, stroking my cock in long, slow movements as she guides me into the kitchen. She shoves me back against the counter roughly and pours a little olive oil into her hand before she goes back to stroking me, twisting her hand as it glides along my shaft. I close my eyes for a second, overwhelmed by the feeling.

Why is she being like this?

"Are you going to stay here?" she asks sweetly, and I nod, looking down at her with wide eyes. She gets this sly little smile on her face before she kisses me hard, biting my bottom lip and making me moan. She pulls back, looking into my eyes as she grips me harder and starts stroking me faster, her thumb rubbing over my head with every stroke.

Her other hand moves up my chest and neck, cupping my face, her thumb grazing over my bottom lip and pushing into my mouth. My breath starts coming harder as her thumb glides against my tongue, and a wave of heat courses through me.

What is *happening*?

"Do you want to prove you'll be good for me?" I'll do whatever she wants right now, so I nod again, unable to speak. She watches my mouth as she pushes her thumb further in, her face satisfied when I curl my tongue around it and suck.

Why the fuck is this so sexy?

She pulls her thumb out of my mouth and drags it across my bottom lip, laughing a little, and then her other hand wraps around me like a vice, and a small, needy whimper I had no idea I could make escapes me as she starts jerking me off, her hands twisting in opposite directions.

"*Oh, fuck*...Alex...shit..."

"Yeah?" She looks me directly in the eyes and makes soft, encouraging little whines when my breath starts coming harder. I lean my head back against the cabinets as I try to hold out longer, but that's not what she wants.

"Come for me, Theo." Her voice is a low, breathy, insistent thing, and her telling me what to do is so surprisingly hot that I come immediately, my orgasm so intense that my vision swims and my hips jerk harshly.

Everything seems sort of hazy when I look down at Alex, who slowly holds her hand up to me. Olive oil and cum cover her palm and fingers, and a wicked smile spreads across her face as she presses one of her fingers against my lips.

"Clean it up," she says softly, and I nod and start sucking her fingers clean and dragging my tongue across her palm. "Look at me, baby." I meet her eyes as I slip her pinky finger into my mouth and suck. Her pupils are dilated, and she keeps glancing between my eyes and mouth, and she smiles at me as I suck the last of my cum off her fingers. "Such a good boy." My eyes go wide, and I stop breathing, my head emptying out entirely and my chest filling with warmth as I stare down at her.

I like being good for her.

She steps into me and pushes onto her toes to kiss me, sliding her tongue against mine with a satisfied moan, and being touched by her feels good in a new way. I whine in protest and grip her tightly as she tries to pull away, and her face is smug in a way I haven't seen before as she looks up at me, cupping my jaw in her hand.

"Stay in the kitchen for me."

"Uh-huh," I breathe out. She laughs a little and kisses me sweetly before turning away from me.

"I fucking thought so," she mutters under her breath as she walks back into the living room. I hear her turn on the radio and tune it until it's playing Christmas music, and I stand there staring after her, confused and kind of dazed.

What just happened? Why is she acting like that? I pull my pants back up and wash my hands, reeling. Seriously, what just happened? Alex doesn't act like *that*. I preheat the oven absently, pouring the rested dough into the panettone collar. That's not how she is with me usually, but I *definitely* liked that. I put the panettone in the oven, turning on the oven light to watch it bake. Did I only like that because she liked that? Probably not, because I'm not into her rape thing, so I liked that regardless of her.

That's interesting.

I make coffee, leaning against the counter and watching the panettone start to rise, and I struggle to think. God, I fucking loved that. She *thought* so? How did she know I would like that if I didn't? I want to ask, and I desperately want to be close to her, but she told me to stay in the kitchen. She's turned up the music so loud in the other room that I can barely hear what she's doing. What *is* she doing?

A pit opens in my stomach as the haze in my mind slowly clears.

She's fucking manipulating me.

She's using sex and my affection for her to *manipulate* me. She's being so obvious about it, too, and I'm just letting her get away with it. I shake my head up at the ceiling, hurt and frustration building the longer I think about it. All I do is try to take care of her and make her happy, and she's treating me like a pathetic fucking doormat. I didn't think she was like that.

This is *bullshit*, and I'm not putting up with it.

"Alexandria, what the *fu-*" I storm out into the living room and freeze when I see her crouched by the tree, slipping a few perfectly wrapped presents underneath. All the anger dissipates from my body as I look around the living room. There are empty shopping bags, a roll of wrapping paper, and some scissors and tape discarded near her.

Alex seems exasperated when she looks up at me.

"I didn't say you could leave the kitchen yet, Theodore." Her voice is chastising and sexy at the same time, and I want to melt. "I was going to reward you for being good, too," she pouts.

I blink at her, my mind emptying.

"*Reward?*" She smirks and I shake my head quickly, trying to focus. "Uh, we *need* to come back to that later. What are you doing?" Alex suddenly goes from sexy to shy, taking a deep breath as she stands up and crosses her arms, looking out the windows behind me.

"Um, I, uh...I already ruined your Thanksgiving, and since it's your first Christmas out of prison and my first since Danny, I thought we could do...something?" She looks embarrassed but still won't look at me. "Nothing big. Not whatever crazy, over-the-top bullshit you had planned, but something. A few presents. Holiday movies. Your precious ham, obviously," she says, rolling her eyes and smiling, finally making eye contact with me, her face nervous and hopeful.

She's maybe the most vulnerable I've ever seen her, and my heart skips a beat.

Oh. She was manipulating me so she could *surprise* me. That was my cute, sweet, exceptionally sexy girlfriend manipulating me with sex because she knew it would work, and she apparently knows what works better than I do, because she *knows* me. She was manipulating me because she knows she can, because she knows I'm wrapped around her finger, because she knows I'll do anything for her.

This is all so *new.*

She's taking photos of me, calling me by a nickname, buying me gifts, trying to surprise me, trying to take care of me. I don't think there are any more barriers or trust issues between us anymore. I think she can feel our connection now, because she's *finally* doing this with me.

I need to tell her I love her.

"There's a panettone in the oven." She closes her eyes and laughs, and I can tell she's trying not to cry as she walks towards me and wraps her arms around me.

"You're kind of the best, you know that?"

37

ALEX

MONDAY, DECEMBER 25

I wake up on Christmas morning wrapped around Theo's back, my arm tight around his waist. I press a series of soft, open-mouth kisses to his broad shoulders as I slip my arm out from under his pillow and prop myself on my elbow, looking down at him. I take in his straight brows, the sweep of his eyelashes and the long lines of his cheekbones, the stubble on his jaw, his slightly aquiline nose, and his soft lips, affection and attraction welling up in my chest.

He's so handsome, but he looks different right now. He's usually so intense and so frenetic, wound so tightly that he never fully relaxes, even when he's asleep, but he seems so calm right now. I like Theo normally, but I *really* like him calm and vulnerable like this, even though that's a big fucking problem.

He's only like this when he's happy.

I'm *so* fucked, but I'm not thinking about that. I'm choosing to be happy today. I reach my hand down to grip his half-hard cock, stroking him slowly. He makes a slight noise and shifts in my arms, turning his hips slightly toward me, but he doesn't wake up. I stroke him a little harder, and his lips part, his brows twitching together. I roll him gently to his back and slip him into my mouth, sucking him slowly until he's fully hard, enjoying the deep, breathy sounds he makes. I wonder if I can get him to come before he wakes up – he's definitely gotten me to do it before. I take him deeper into my mouth and he moans a little, his hips thrusting up slightly and his chest starting to flush. I can tell he's close, so I add in both hands, watching his face closely.

He starts to wake up, his hands coming to my head and his eyes snapping open and rolling back as he starts to come, his hips jerking up slightly as my mouth floods with his cum. He swears softly and looks down at me with wide eyes, his face flushed and surprised. I smile up at him, watching him process waking up in the middle of an orgasm.

"That's your first present," I say, and he stares at me for a long moment before he sits up, reaching for me and pulling me close.

"You're the fucking gift," he says before he pushes me to my back and takes a long time giving me my first several presents.

***

Theo makes us coffee while I stare at the tree, frowning. I got him three gifts, and I told him he could choose three gifts out of the pile of bags he brought, but there are five gifts for me under the tree. I look up at him as he brings us slices of panettone and coffee, his hair sticking up weirdly in the back, his face soft and relaxed.

Fuck it, if I get to be happy, he gets to be happy.

"Teddy?"

"Hmmmm?" He sets down the coffee and panettone in front of me.

"I'm accepting any and all gifts for today *only*." His face lights up, and he kisses me hard and fast before heading downstairs. I sit on the couch and eat some of the panettone, warm nostalgia running through me at the taste. I haven't had one in years. Danny wouldn't have cared, but it was a small way I kept things separate, a defined before and after. It feels weird to have it now, here, in this situation, but I'm not thinking about that. Theo comes back up and puts a pile of bags under the tree, and I squint at them.

"Why are there so *many*?"

He looks up sheepishly. "Uh, there are a bunch of gifts that I gave you that first weekend that you've *never* used, so I thought I'd give them to you again."

I shake my head at him, sipping my coffee. He's insane. Sweet and thoughtful, but kind of insane.

I open his gifts first, finally putting on the cashmere cardigan and perfume he got me months ago, some small part of me thrilled to have things I wanted but felt like I couldn't have or shouldn't accept. I let myself react honestly, telling him how much I love everything, and he seems thrilled to have pleased me. He's especially happy about me wearing the perfume and tells me he loves how it smells on my skin. The house is warm enough from the fire that I put on some of the lingerie he bought me, slipping the cardigan back on but leaving it open, and he's *delighted*, constantly running his fingers over my skin.

I look at the few gifts I got him with increasing anxiety. Me deciding to get him something was so last minute that the gifts aren't perfect, maybe aren't exactly what he wants or likes, but I think he'll appreciate the thought more than anything. I give him the sweater first, explaining it's to replace the one I ruined when I threw a wineglass at him, which he seems to find funny. Next is the large enamel-coated Dutch oven, which I tell him I'm sure he already has a better version of, but it was the nicest cooking thing I could find at the store. He seems touched, and when I teasingly tell him I'd love it if he could make me coq a vin with it sometime, he tells me he'll do whatever I want, although he seems less than enthused at the idea. I turn over the last present in my hands for a moment, hesitant. I know he'll love this, but it feels like a point of no return.

I swallow the feeling. If I get to be happy, he gets to be happy.

He smiles when he opens the small Polaroid camera and film, but he seems a little confused until I take it out of his hands and load it. I lean against him and angle the camera back at us, kissing his cheek and snapping a photo. He looks at me in surprise, his bright eyes wide and focused intently on my face, and I feel a little embarrassed as I hand him the developing photo.

"Um, I thought you'd want a photo of us, and these ones can't be seen online." He looks at the photo of us and back up at me with a tender, overwhelmed look on his face. He kisses me gently, telling me over and over again that he loves it, kissing me harder and pushing me back on the couch, his hips fitting between my legs easily, like they're meant to be there.

I'm glad I bought him more than one pack of film, because he's a menace with the camera for the rest of the day. He takes a photo of my face right after he kisses me, of me in lingerie with my legs on his shoulders as he fucks me, of me laid out on the couch, blissfully zoned out after, of me drinking coffee, of me putting panettone in my mouth, of me pulling out his laptop to put on a movie, of us curled up together. I take the camera occasionally, snapping photos of Theo smiling and relaxed in a way he's usually not.

There are small piles of polaroids on the coffee table and dining room table that I sort through as he starts to make lunch. Many of the photos are washed out or out of focus, giving them a hazy, dreamlike quality, but there's one of us that I can't stop looking at. It's us in front of the tree, the tree dark and barely visible in the background, and we're smiling. Our smiles are so different, but they seem like a matched set. Theo's is crooked and his dimples are showing, and mine is broad and toothy and reaches my eyes. As I look at the photo, I realize both our smiles are completely real. We look like we fit together, like we're a real couple.

In the moment, we were.

For one second, it breaks the fantasy, and the feeling I've been pushing down hits me hard, and I choke down a sob. Theo sticks his head out of the kitchen and asks if I want champagne, and he looks so genuinely calm and happy that I'm able to swallow the feeling again. I put the photo down and join him, sipping champagne while he snaps the ends off green beans, taking a picture of him lovingly preparing his goddamn ham. I bring the laptop into the kitchen and make him watch *A Muppet Christmas Carol* with me while he cooks. He says he never watched it as a kid, and he doesn't seem to like it, but eventually admits that it's shockingly faithful to the book.

"You're *so* pretentious," I tease, and he laughs.

"You're worse than I am!" he protests. "*Look at the perspective in this painting. You can tell Monet was strongly inspired by his collection of ukiyo-e prints,"* he parrots back at me in a high, snobbish voice with an exaggerated Boston accent. *"If you'll notice the color choices -"*

"I do *not* sound like that," I interrupt, shoving him gently.

"You do, a little." He winks at me and kisses me quickly before refocusing on the green beans.

It feels normal to tease each other and have fun with him like this. I want to be happy like this all the time, but I'm not going to have any of this for much longer, so I just focus on being present in the moment.

I snap a photo of Theo pulling the ham out of the oven, laughing at his excitement. We sit down to lunch and Theo eats a *lot* of ham, the look on his face pure bliss. He explains, without prompting, that he got out of juvie and moved in with his grandparents right around Christmas, and that's why he loves it so much, especially the food. While we eat, we watch a storm roll in off the ocean, the wind whipping through the trees and the rain pattering against the large windows.

We curl up on the couch afterward and watch *It's A Wonderful Life*, which is Theo's favorite. We fall asleep on the couch facing each other, our legs tangled together under the blanket, breathing each other's breath as we drift to sleep. It's dark when we wake up, and we spend a long time holding each other, kissing lazily, enjoying just being together. Theo opens another bottle of champagne, and we drink by the fire, completely comfortable with each other.

I'm fully immersed in the fantasy of a perfect Christmas with my perfect boyfriend in my new, perfect life, and I want it to be real so badly.

This is so far beyond fucking and playing house. We *know* each other now. I've told him things I've never told anyone else about, and I know he's done the same.

I wish, not for the first time, that I was as delusional as he is.

I know how I feel about the situation, about *him*, but I don't let myself think about it. I don't let myself feel it because I don't want *my* feelings, I want *his* feelings. If I can't have those, I want the warm and hazy way he makes me feel after sex.

Adored. Cherished. Cared for.

I climb into his lap, and his hands span my back and grip my waist, pulling me into him. He slips my cardigan down my arms, trailing kisses along my collarbones and up my neck. We kiss slowly, feeling the warmth of the fire, feeling the warmth of each other as we take our time, being present in the moment together.

I let myself be happy in his arms, because I get to be happy sometimes.

I close my eyes, just trying to feel the pleasure and his adoration and ignore the feeling in my gut. I'm not feeling *that*, I'm feeling him inside of me, his fingers moving against me, his lips on my chest. He's doing what I need him to do – he's making the feeling disappear. I moan, my hands gripping his shoulders tighter as tension builds in my spine. He exhales hard and grips my hips, thrusting up into me, and there's no reality right now, just the fantasy of us.

"I want you so badly." It slips out of my mouth, and my voice is so achingly affectionate that it hurts to hear myself. The feeling swells and starts creeping into my chest, tightening around my lungs.

"I'm yours," Theo says, his voice tender and adoring. I tuck my face against his neck because I can't look at him. I know what I'll see on his face, but I can't see it.

I can't let him see how I feel, either.

I pull off him and lie down on the couch, pulling him on top of me and begging him to fuck me. He'll fuck me hard, and it'll just be sex, and then I'll get that hazy, warm feeling he gives me, and I'll have the fantasy back.

Theo starts to make love to me instead, cupping my face in his hand as he kisses me sweetly. I know I need to keep my eyes closed, otherwise I'm beyond fucked.

"Sweetheart, please look at me," he begs, and I do because I'm stupid. He's got that look on his face, the one he's been giving me all weekend, for much longer, and I see how he feels, and I want to cry.

We're telling ourselves two different versions of the same lie right now. Both of us want the fantasy, both of us want what we can't have, but the only difference is that I don't get to believe it's real.

I try to focus on the sex, focus on separating my body from my feelings, but it's not working. Instead, I'm feeling everything all at once, and I can't get rid of the feeling, can't ignore it anymore. It's suffocating me.

The sex was supposed to make it better and let me sink deeper into the fantasy, but it only made the reality worse.

It's been so good with Theo lately, especially today. It's been a perfect day, the kind of day I want to build my life around. A wave of longing chokes me as the reality of the situation comes rushing in hard on its heels, overwhelming me.

For the first time in a long time, I'm *loved*, but I don't get to have it or return it because I don't have the option to. Theo ruined it, just like he's ruined everything else. He's taken everything away from me, leaving only him, and I can't even have him now that I want him.

Something in his face changes, and he's less and more and different and the same, entirely vulnerable with me for maybe the first time ever. Something raw and electric courses through me as I look at him, and I know what's coming, and I know I can't handle it.

I can't handle any of this anymore.

I'd rather die.

"*Alex?*"

38

THEO

TUESDAY, DECEMBER 26

This is the happiest I've ever been in my life.

The storm howling outside sounds so soothing from the couch, and the dim firelight illuminates Alex, warm and soft and perfect beneath me. We're so fucking connected right now. I know she's still scared, but I can see how she feels when she looks up at me.

She loves me, too.

"Alex?" My voice is barely audible, and I can see on her face that she knows what I'm going to say. Her eyes go wide and tear up, and she starts sobbing. For a split second, I'm thrilled she's so overwhelmed with happiness, but I go cold when I realize she's not crying tears of joy. I pull out of her and hold her close, shushing her, touching her, trying to soothe her and ignore the panic I'm feeling.

This can't be her reaction. She's a fucking *wreck*.

"Sweetheart, what's wrong?" She buries her face in her hands and sobs, her body heaving in my arms. She hasn't cried like this in a while, maybe ever.

She *loves* me, I know she does, so there has to be something else going on.

It takes her a long time, but eventually she calms down enough to take a few deep breaths, pulling out of my arms and facing me. I reach for her immediately, but she backs away.

"Honey, what's going on?" She looks at me with a devastated expression and shakes her head, wiping her cheeks. "*Please* talk to me. What happened? Everything was going so perfectly." I wince at how desperate I sound, but Alex doesn't seem to notice. She just stares at me, her bottom lip trembling.

"That's the problem, Theo," she whispers. "Everything going perfectly is making me fucking miserable." Ice courses through my blood. That can't be true. She finally adjusted to our relationship, and she's been so happy since then.

She's *not* miserable, she's just not.

"I don't understand." She sighs and looks into the fire, chewing on her bottom lip and crying softly. She seems torn about what she wants to say, opening her mouth and closing it several times, but eventually, she closes her eyes, nods to herself, and takes a deep breath.

She seems like she's steeling herself for something, which makes me nervous.

"Theo, I didn't stay married to Danny for nine years because things were always bad. You know that, right?" She looks at me and must see on my face that I didn't know that, and she sighs. "I know it's probably easier for you to think he's just some horrible bastard, which he *is*, but he's also the only reason I didn't kill myself after my parents died.

"I was so fucking lost, and he came into my life and made everything worse, but I let him make choices for me and take care of me and he let me completely withdraw into myself. It took me years to realize that it wasn't good for me, that he'd let me isolate myself in a way that made controlling me easier, but at the time, it was all I wanted."

My knee starts bouncing quickly, and I can feel my shoulders tense. I don't understand why she's telling me all of this, but it's making me really fucking uncomfortable.

She looks over at my leg and smiles sadly.

"Danny, at his best, was a provider. He grew up working class, and his dad died when he was eighteen, so he felt like it was his job to take care of everything. He got a decent job and took care of his mom and his little brother, and after his mom died, he made it his job to take care of his aunts and his cousins however he could. When he met me, he wanted to take care of me, too. He was really controlling, and it only got worse over time, but if I toed the line, he made my life easier. He could also be sweet when he wanted to be, and I was happy sometimes."

It feels like she's just hit me over the head with a bat. That can't be true. She can't possibly have been happy with Danny. He was fucking *abusive*, so there's no way. She takes in the shocked look on my face and raises her eyebrows, looking down at her hands and exhaling hard.

"Look, anytime Danny lost his shit and hurt me and made me apologize the way he liked, he'd feel *so* guilty afterward, and my life would become extremely easy. He'd apologize and dote on me and feel so ashamed that he'd take on extra shifts at work so he didn't have to see me. Danny likes to stay really busy, so I had a lot of time to myself anyway, but if he felt guilty for hurting me, it was basically like I lived alone. I got to do whatever I wanted, within reason. I took online classes, I read, I helped organize precinct fundraisers, I worked out, I had a book club with his coworkers' wives, and I spent pretty much every Saturday shopping and going to movies and restaurants by myself. It was fucking great, honestly." She laughs humorlessly, pressing her forehead against her knees for a moment before she curls in on herself tighter, resting her chin on her knees and staring into the fire.

"That would go on for weeks or months before he'd be around more, and then he'd start getting angry about everything again. I tried to do everything to keep him from getting mad at me. I looked the way he liked, I played nice with his friends' wives, I endured his family with a smile, I let him fuck me whenever he wanted, everything. I was on my best behavior all the fucking time, and it was never enough. Any time he'd get mad at me, I'd get angry with myself for being this absolute fuckup, and it always kind of felt like I deserved what happened to me. I know that's not true, but I felt that way for a long time." She takes a deep breath and wipes her cheeks with her palms quickly.

I want to touch her, to comfort her, but I feel frozen. She's sharing so much with me, but something about how she's acting has me extremely on edge.

"Theo, the point I'm trying to make is that things going well *sometimes* made it easy for me to pretend things were normal. I was able to ignore what was wrong and occasionally buy into the fantasy that my marriage was good. I was still trapped in it, still fucking miserable, but I got to lie to myself most of the time." She looks at me and shakes her head, sighing. "Now I'm trapped here with you, but I can't lie to myself about it." Shock and indignation flood my body.

I can't believe she's comparing me to her fucking husband.

"I'm *not* like that, Alex. This relationship isn't like that." She levels me with a pitying look that sets my teeth on edge.

"I know you care about me, Theo, and I don't think you mean to be the way you are, but you're more delusional than I thought if you can't see how hard you worked to trap me here." What she's saying doesn't make sense, but a chill runs down my spine at her words anyway.

"You know, Danny was the wrong person at the right time. I was young, and I had just lost my parents. I needed somebody, and he took advantage of that to create a situation that worked for him. That's not how he sees it, but that's what happened. He had some level of access to me, though. *You* came out of fucking *nowhere*. You stalked me, you figured out that I was vulnerable, you inserted yourself into my life, and you've used the fact that I'm hiding to keep me under your thumb." My temper flares, hot and sharp in my core. Why does she keep lying to herself like this? That's *not* what's happened between us, not at *all*.

"I didn't fucking do that," I snap.

"Yeah, you did, and you did a great job," she snaps back. "You knew I would run and found a way to stop me. You knew if I went to the cops, I'd have to use my real identity and Danny would find me. I know you know who he is, Theo. I know you know about my life in Boston, my real name, my parents, all of it. I'm sure you've known everything since before you broke into my house, and you used all of it to trap me here with you." Something inside me cracks slightly, and anxiety buzzes under my skin. Is that what she thinks happened? She's so wrong about this.

I mean, she's not wrong about *some* of it, but I didn't do *all* of that.

I shake my head at her, too anxious to talk, and she looks over at the fireplace and lets out a long sigh.

"My only options now are to go home to my husband, who'll kill me because I ran away, or stay here with you, and you'll kill me when you don't get what you want. It's him or you, but it ends the same for me." I look at her incredulously, my heart sinking.

Is she seriously fucking afraid of me?

"I...Alex, I wouldn't...*no*," I force out, and she gives me a tight, sad little smile.

"I believe you *think* you won't hurt me, but I can't trust you. You're violent and delusional and wound so fucking tightly that you'll snap the second you realize you can't ever have what you want from me, which will happen soon." Tears prick behind my eyes, and I try to hold them back. I can't believe she's saying these things.

I'm not like that at all.

"Sweetie, what the *fuck*?" Alex reaches out for my hand, squeezing hard. I'm so confused and hurt and angry right now, but I twine my fingers through hers and hold on tightly, focusing on the feel of her skin against mine. She gives our joined hands a conflicted look as she runs her thumb against mine soothingly.

"I never really *liked* Danny, you know? We didn't have anything in common, and I think he sucks as a person." She laughs bitterly and shakes her head, looking over at the fire. "I like *you*, though. After what you did and how everything played out, it was *such* a shock for me, but we sort of fit together." A brief wave of relief calms me down enough to kiss the back of her hand. She closes her eyes, wiping her face quickly with her other hand before turning and looking up at me. "Theo, I like you *so* much. I have fun with you, and I like talking to you and getting to know you and spending time with you – all of it. Oh, and the *sex*," she laughs and rolls her eyes, her thighs clenching together a little bit. "The sex is fucking incredible. Everything feels so good with you."

This is exactly how I want her to feel, so why is hearing her say this so upsetting? It feels like she's trying to break up with me somehow. She takes a deep breath and pulls her knees tighter, shaking her head as she looks at me with pity.

"You're a sad, lonely mess of a person, you know that? You have no friends, no family, no life, no *boundaries*, and you're kind of fucking scary." I recoil in pain like she's just hit me, and she gives me this soft, sad smile and lifts my hand to her lips. "You're also smart, and funny, and sweet, and you're *so* fucking thoughtful. You're amazing most of the time, even if you're so fucking intense about *everything*, but I like that. I like you, *all* of you, so much. You're my best friend," she says quietly, looking up at me and squeezing my hand, tears streaming down her face.

Everything's so confusing right now, but I feel that familiar hum of connection between us, and I cling on to it. She's my best friend, too, even if she's hurting my feelings in every possible way. I take a shuddering breath and squeeze her hand, struggling to push down my anger.

Goddammit, this was just getting good, and now we're right back here.

"Sweetie, I think you're *really* confused right now, okay?"

"Can you please just listen to what I'm saying?" she asks, her voice pleading.

"I *am* listening, and you're lying to yourself again," I say, failing to keep the edge out of my voice. She shakes her head slowly, maintaining eye contact with me.

"I'm not lying to myself, Theo. You are." My temper breaks.

"No, Alexandria, you're fucking *wrong*," I snap, pulling my hand out of hers and running my hands back through my hair. "*Fuck*, Alex! I thought we worked past this! I thought we finally got you over these bullshit trust issues of yours and got you to stop fucking lying to yourself. I don't know why you're so insistent about pretending this is something other than what it is, but you need to *stop*. We're fucking *connected*, and we're *supposed* to be together. I *know* you can feel it, so you need to stop fucking fighting it." She stares at me, her wide eyes pitying.

"Oh, *Theo*," she says sadly, "That's the basis of your delusion, isn't it? You think that we're *connected*? That's not real."

"You need to stop with your fucking *bullshit*!"

She flushes angrily and points back at me. "No, *you* need to stop," she snaps back. "Listen to me, Theodore. *You're* the one who's lying to yourself, okay? You're *delusional*. You trapped me here and forced me into this fucked up situation where you get to be in something *like* a relationship with me, and you want it to be real so badly that you've been lying to yourself the whole time, but this is a *delusion*."

What is she talking about? Why is it making me so angry to hear this?

"What the fuck are you saying to me?"

Alex makes a loud, aggravated sound. "You hijacked my fucking life, Theo! I deserve to have my own life, and I worked so fucking hard to build something for myself after I left Danny, and you took it all away overnight! I struggled so hard to get to make choices for myself, and then you fucking took away *all* of my choices. Don't you get that?"

That sounds horrible. I would never do something like that to her. Her words start sinking in deeper, and something clicks a little bit.

What she's saying seems almost possible.

No, she's lying to me and manipulating me. That's what she's doing. I didn't do that to her.

"*Stop fucking lying to me, Alexandria.*" Why does my voice sound like that? That's not what I sound like. Why does she look scared?

"You know what's so frustrating, Theo? I really liked you when I met you, and I was *so* attracted to you, and I would have said yes if you'd just *asked me out.* You could have gotten to know me like a normal person, and then this would have been a real relationship for both of us, but whatever this is, it *isn't* a relationship. It *never* has been." Nothing about what she's saying makes sense, except that it seems like it *could* make sense, like it *should* make sense, and that scares the shit out of me. My skin is crawling, and I start to shake involuntarily.

I grab her face in my hands and pull her towards me a little too roughly, and her breath catches. I can tell that she's afraid of me right now, and I hate it so fucking much, but I need her to stop.

"I'm begging you to stop lying to me, sweetheart," I say, my voice soft and shaky, and her face contorts in pain.

"I'm *not*, and you know that. I know you can tell when I'm lying, so look at me, okay? You did all of that to me. You stalked me, you deluded yourself into thinking this was a relationship, and you trapped me in this situation. This isn't real, Theo. You took away the option for this to be real." I stare at her mouth in horror as her teeth don't touch her bottom lip.

Did she learn her tell?

She has to be lying.

"Please don't do this to me, honey. This is real, okay? You *love* me, I *know* you love me, so stop fucking lying to me, *please*," I say, my voice cracking on the last word. Alex starts crying and reaches out for me, her hands gripping my wrists hard, her face devastated and angry and resigned. I don't know why she looks like that, but it scares me. I want to fix it, but I don't even know what's going on. I'm so confused.

"I *don't* love you, Theo."

Time stops.

"I *can't* love you," Alex says quietly, and something deep inside me breaks apart. "It's not that I don't want to, because I *do*, but you're so fucking damaged that you needed to take away the option for me to leave you. If I can't choose to leave, then I can't choose to be here. You chose *me*, but you won't let me choose *you*."

She doesn't love me.

No, that's a lie. It has to be a lie.

"Teddy, I need you to know I would have chosen you, okay? If you'd given me the option, I would have loved you. I *promise*." She's speaking quickly, like she's trying to get it all out as fast as she can, and the resigned tone of her voice makes me instantly panicky. "I need you to know that," she says, her words cracking with tears. She looks so sad and terrified, and everything she's been saying is bouncing around in my head, crashing into things and knocking them loose. I don't understand anything she's saying, but it starts to seem more and more solid, making everything feel less and less real.

She doesn't love me.

I try to make eye contact with her and ground myself in her presence, but she's crying too hard to look at me. I don't want to make her feel like this. I want to make her happy. My understanding of things starts fracturing, and I try desperately to make sense of everything as a black hole opens up in my stomach, pulling in everything good that exists between us. The only thing anchoring me is Alex, but she's starting to slip from my fingers, so I hold on as hard as I can.

She doesn't love me.

I can't feel my body, and there's a loud buzzing sound in the back of my head, and my hands are shaking so hard that Alex's head is moving a little. I think I'm hurting her, and I don't want to hurt her, but I'm so fucking angry and confused right now that I'm not in control of my body anymore.

"What's happening?" My voice sounds wrong to me, too quiet and so scared, and Alex finally looks me in the eyes. Her face is still shaking in my hands, and the miserable, exhausted, relieved look on her face terrifies the shit out of me. She's so quiet that her words are barely audible, but I hear them perfectly.

"You're going to kill me, Theo." My vision starts to go red, and I panic as my mind spins.

I would never fucking hurt her. I would never intentionally hurt her. *I didn't hurt her.* I did hurt her, though. *She has to be lying.* She hasn't been lying. *I wouldn't do any of that to her.* I did all of that to her. *I didn't ruin her life.* I ruined her life. *What we have is real.* None of this is real.

I hurt Alex.

Oh my god, I hurt Alex.

She thinks I'm going to kill her.

Something inside of me snaps, and everything goes red.

39

ALEX

TUESDAY, DECEMBER 26

Terror floods through me as Theo's eyes go wide and he makes a horrible choking noise, his body tensing up and his hands gripping my head shaking so hard that I feel like my teeth are rattling.

I fucking *knew* it, I knew that he'd kill me once he figured out he couldn't have what he wanted from me, and I pushed him anyway.

I need to get out. I'm not going to spend the rest of my life trapped in a situation where I want to love someone but can't, or where I want to leave but can't, or where I don't get to make any real choices for myself. I'm so tired of not being able to live my life on my terms, so I'm choosing to let it go.

It was going to be him or Danny, and I'd rather have it be him.

I sob, rubbing my thumbs over the soft skin on the inside of his wrists and slamming my eyes shut. I don't want to see his face when he snaps. That's not how I want to remember him. I want to remember his stupid fucking crooked smile, or his dumb, smug smirk, or the soft, awestruck way he looked at me right as he was about to tell me he loves me.

I just hope he loves me enough to make it quick.

He makes a guttural groaning sound and shoves my head back roughly, yanking his wrists out of my hands. I fall back on the couch and curl into a tight ball, tensing up and waiting for the first blow.

It doesn't come.

I hear his breath, gasping and rough, and I keep my eyes closed for a few seconds longer, but when I open them, I see he's far away from me on the couch, his body curled in on itself. He's rocking back and forth, his head buried in his hands, his chest heaving rapidly as he hyperventilates.

Oh, my fucking god, I'm *alive*.

I launch myself off the couch and run downstairs, grabbing his wallet, phone, and car keys off the dresser. I can finally get the fuck away from him. I don't know how he's tracking me, but I've got all his shit, and that means I can leave him here and get away long enough to beg someone for help. Maybe I can seek sanctuary somewhere from him and Danny? I don't know, I'll figure it out. I run back upstairs and throw the front door open, but I freeze when I hear Theo crying.

I pushed him until he fucking snapped. This was the thing that would have made him kill me, *should* have made him kill me. I'm sure he was *about* to kill me, but he didn't.

That doesn't matter, I need to leave. I need to step through this door and fucking *run*. I go to take a step out of the house, but I can't.

Instead, I turn around and watch him as he freaks out, watch his breath saw in and out of him, watch tears stream down his face as he has a massive panic attack.

Why didn't he kill me?

I stare at him, considering him for a long time, stunned.

I look out the door towards his car and then look back at him. I should walk out this door right fucking now, I know I should. I have everything I need to run. I watch Theo for another minute longer before I turn away, closing the front door behind me.

I sigh, shaking my head as I walk towards him.

I'm more insane than he is.

I think of what he does when I have a panic attack, so I wrap him in a blanket and talk to him. I attempt to help him regulate his breathing the way he does for me, but he won't look at me or listen to me or react to me at all. He stops rocking at some point, and I keep my hands on his chest and stomach to help him breathe. Eventually, his breathing slows down and gets very shallow. I help him uncurl his body and sit back on the couch, and he just lets me move him because he's completely dissociated. I make him tea, but he doesn't drink it.

He just stares into the fire, catatonic.

I don't know what to do, so I slip on his flannel, wrap him in another blanket, and stoke the fire. I drink a very full glass of wine, sitting at the dining room table, staring at him and trying to figure out why I'm still here. I pick his t-shirt and sweats up off the floor and fold them, putting near him. He's still just sitting there, staring at the fire. I pour myself another full glass of wine and sit on the couch, trying to read the thick tome about Sylvia Plath he got me for Christmas, but I can't make any sense of the words, so I finish the bottle of wine as I lean against him and listen to the storm.

I'm probably stupid for being here, but I don't care. He didn't kill me and I'm alive, so I'm going to do whatever I want, whether or not I think I should.

I definitely don't think I *should* be here taking care of him.

I want to be here, though.

After three hours, it's either very late or very early and I'm exhausted, but I don't want to leave Theo alone. I know he wouldn't leave me alone, and I'm worried about him.

I don't think he's going to kill me anymore, but I think there's a pretty big chance he might kill himself.

I bend down, getting directly in his line of vision. His eyes are dull and unfocused, and he doesn't seem to register me at all. He's still so pale, but his breathing has finally evened out.

He's done scaring me now.

"Theo?" No reaction.

"*Theodore*," I say, my voice stern. Nothing.

I hold his face in my hands, stroking his cheeks. "Baby?" He doesn't respond. I stare at him for a second, thinking, then pitch my voice low and sultry, the way I did when I told him to stay in the kitchen.

"*Teddy*?" He blinks, his eyes focusing on me slightly, and I almost roll my eyes. Of course *that* worked. I softly stroke his temples with my thumbs and smile at him. "Teddy, can you come back to me?" His eyebrows twitch together, and he finally seems to register me somewhat, his eyes going wide when he does. "Can you talk to me?" He closes his eyes and shakes his head in small movements. "Can I get you anything?" He shakes his head again. "Are you okay?"

"*Fuck*, no." His voice is hoarse and unbelievably soft. I push my fingers through his hair, but he pulls away. "Don't." I stop touching him as he leans his head back against the couch and covers his face with his hands, exhaling hard. "Oh, my fucking god," he whispers.

He repeats it over and over and starts crying.

I stand there watching him, concern and pity and something warm and soft flooding through me. I want to take care of him, but I don't know what to do, so I follow a vague impulse and go into the kitchen. I start rifling through the fridge and pantry, looking at what we have, pulling out ingredients and piling them on the counter. I put on quiet jazz music, the kind my dad always listened to when he cooked, and start putting things together slowly.

I used to *love* watching my dad cook. He wasn't methodical in the kitchen like Theo, he was messy and unorganized. It was the one area of his life where he wasn't controlling. He would improvise and try things out, put things together that shouldn't have worked and made them work anyway.

That's how I thought you were supposed to cook before I married Danny. I thought it was supposed to be fun, that it was something you did for people you loved, and that things didn't have to be perfect to be good. Danny disagreed, and freaked out if I didn't cook something flawlessly the way his mom used to, but he's not here. I'm done letting him or my memories of him dictate any part of my life.

It's my fucking life, and neither he nor Theo are in control of it, not really.

I wish I'd figured that out a little sooner.

I haven't actually cooked anything in almost a year, and I'm so much worse than I used to be, but it doesn't matter – it doesn't need to be perfect. I remind myself of that as I feel nervous when I slice the bread a little too thick, or tense up when I have to fish a bit of eggshell out of the bowl, or almost cry when I dump a little too much cinnamon into the egg mixture by accident.

I focus on my breathing, reminding myself why I'm cooking in the first place.

Theo drifts into the kitchen eventually, his t-shirt on inside out, his tear-stained face somewhere between devastated and confused. When he sees me cooking, his head cocks to the side a little and his face goes entirely blank. He leans against the counter and watches me with wide, confused eyes, and that same warm, soft feeling spreads through my body as I smile at him a little.

"I'm making French toast. Do you want coffee?"

40

THEO

TUESDAY, DECEMBER 26

I'm dreaming.

Alex is in one of my flannels, the hem halfway down her bare thighs, puttering around the kitchen and humming along to French jazz. Her hair is pulled up into a bun and she looks calm when her eyes flit over to me as she whisks milk into the eggs, and her smile is soft when she hands me a cup of coffee.

I know it's a dream because Alex doesn't cook.

I know it's a dream because Alex fucking hates me, which she *should*.

My world is falling apart, and I might not know what's real anymore, but I know this *can't* be real.

I thought I was better. I thought I'd done enough work on myself in prison, and that Dr. Mills was full of shit. I honestly didn't see how out of control I got with Alex.

I look at Alex's back and close my eyes to block it out. Okay, maybe I knew I was a *little* out of control, but everything I did made so much sense when I did it.

Now, nothing makes sense.

I think Dr. Mills has been trying to talk to me about this for months, and I've been doing my best not to listen to her. She's been trying to protect Alex from me, and for good reason. She was right that this situation has been a nightmare for Alex. God, I'm such a piece of shit.

Alex is absolutely right, too. Did I work hard to trap her? Fuck yeah, I did. I took every opportunity I saw, I made opportunities where I could, and I did everything in my fucking power to trap her. To make matters worse, it *worked*, and now she's here the way I wanted.

I'm living inside a dream, but it feels empty now. Alex was always supposed to want to be here, was always supposed to love me back.

For the first time, the tight rush of obsession dwindles as I stare at her. I don't know that I've ever really seen Alex as a whole person before, but I'm starting to now, and it's painful. I've been ignoring so much about her, like the fact that I've been making her fucking *miserable*. Instead of the unmitigated happiness I felt a few hours ago, I feel a thick, oily slide of guilt in my stomach.

God, I think I barely even know her.

The first pieces of French toast come out dark, and Alex fiddles with the gas range to get the right level of flame, slipping more butter into the pan. Why would she be cooking? There are so many leftovers in the fridge. This is a dream, so it's probably just wish fulfillment.

My brain seems to be exceptionally good at that.

I stare at her, my mind skipping over everything she said on repeat, always landing back on the fact that she *could* want me, *could* love me, but that I've fucked it up. That's a new level of fucking up I wasn't even aware I was capable of.

I can't believe I did this to her. I'm no better than her husband.

Actually, I'm still much better than her husband. Unlike him, *I* would never fucking hurt her. I'm unsure about pretty much everything else in my life, but I know *that* for a fact – she does too, now.

I can't *believe* she thought I was going to fucking kill her. It's almost like she tried to get me to do it, but that's ridiculous.

Alex isn't like that.

I watch Alex grab some more butter, staring at her back. Jesus, I can't believe I did that. Where the fuck did that impulse even come from? My impulses have never made me want to do anything like that. That's objectively insane.

Fuck, I wish I was the version of me she wants, someone who just asked her on a date and slowly built something with her. Then we'd be here for real, and this would actually be perfect, or at least good. All I want is to go back and start over, to give her *that,* but I don't think I can.

I think this is maybe the last time I'll ever see her.

I watch her glance back at me, and I want to keep her. I still feel like we're connected, even though I probably shouldn't. I still feel like she's mine, even though that's probably wrong. She likes me and *wishes* she could love me, even though I'm ruining her life, so maybe I can fix this. Maybe I can undo everything I did that's ruining her life, and we can start over.

That's the dumbest fucking idea I've ever had.

I don't think I can fix it, and I don't think I deserve a chance, but all I want is to beg her to let me try. I shouldn't, I *know* I shouldn't. I should leave her the fuck alone, but I can't help it. Everything is fucked, and I have one desire in my life right now, and it's to try fix this and make it real so I can keep her.

God, I'm a selfish prick.

I take a deep breath, pushing down the impulse. If I *did* ask her, she'd say no. She fucking hates me, I know she does. Even if she doesn't hate me, it probably wouldn't fix anything.

"Alex?" I'm so fucking stupid for even attempting this.

"Hmmm?" Alex plops the next pieces of toast into the pan before she looks over at me, concerned. I think I'm going to vomit or pass out, so I take another deep breath.

"Is there any way I could fix this?" She looks confused, and I rush to explain. "If I stopped stalking you, could I fix this? I'll stop following you, I'll take the cameras out, I'll remove the trackers, I'll give back my keys to your place – if I do all of that and I ask you out like you wanted in the first place, would that fix anything between us, even a little bit?" Her eyes go wide but she doesn't say anything, and I'm absolutely going to vomit. "You can say no, and if you do, you can stay in Astoria or you can leave, but I swear I'll leave you alone no matter what. I just want to fix this." Her expression becomes incredulous, and she tilts her head a little, staring at me with wide eyes. She seems to be considering what I'm asking, which quells some of my nausea. She turns away from me, staying quiet for an agonizingly long minute.

"Theo, are you seriously, after *everything*, trying to ask me on a fucking *date*?" I grip the cold tile of the counter, trying to stay present in my body and not vomit. When she puts it like that, it sounds really fucking stupid.

"Uh, yeah, pretty much." A sharp laugh escapes her, and she shakes her head slowly.

"Are you fucking joking?"

"No. I want this to be real, and I'll do fucking anything to make that happen. I *know* you're going to say no, but I need to try. I can't help it, I really can't. I just need to try." She looks at me over her shoulder and gives me a strange, conflicted look before sighing heavily and turning back to the food.

"Why try if you know I'm going to say no?"

"Because I love you, Alex." She makes a sharp little inhale as she flips the next two pieces of French toast out of the pan. She takes her time soaking more pieces of bread before putting them into the pan, turning away from the stove to start slicing a banana at a glacial pace.

It feels like the oxygen is being slowly sucked out of the room as I wait for her to respond.

"I kind of figured that out when you didn't snap my fucking neck," she says quietly. Dread lances through me, and I repeatedly run my hands through my hair, trying not to panic. She's going to say no, and she absolutely should say no if that's what she thinks happened.

I watch her chop walnuts into fine pieces, my gaze landing in the space between her shoulder blades. I need to take that tracker out of her no matter what she says to my asinine, delusional fucking request.

She'll say no, and I know I won't be able to deal with her saying no. There's no fucking way I'll ever leave her alone if left to my own devices. The only way I'll be able to stay away from her is to go back to prison.

Either that, or I'll kill myself, which seems like the more appealing option.

I'll go to Boston and kill Danny either way as an apology, so she can get her life back, so I can make him fucking pay for how badly he hurt her, so I can make sure he won't ever hurt her again. If I kill him and then myself, I can fix two problems for her, but if I kill him and go back to prison, she could always choose to come see me, which she probably wouldn't.

When she finally speaks again, she's turned away from me so I can't see her face, but I can hear the wariness and frustration in her voice.

"You're seriously asking me for a chance to fix this fucked up situation *you* made?"

"I'm *begging* you."

"Do you honestly think that giving me a choice now will fix everything?"

"Uh, probably not."

"It *won't*," she snaps.

"I want to try anyway. Please."

She shakes her head, flipping the toast. "Theo, you're asking for something impossible here."

"I know that."

"You don't even *deserve* a chance after what you did." It feels like she's lodged a knife in my gut.

"Believe me, I know."

"If I say no, you'll leave me alone?"

"Yes," I choke out.

"You think you could *actually* leave me alone?" My heart plummets. She's going to say no.

"I'll make sure of it, I promise." One way or another.

She slides the last pieces of toast out of the pan and turns off the stovetop before walking over to me, crossing her arms and frowning up at me.

"You know you're delusional to even *ask* for this, right? I think you might *actually* be insane." I shrug. She's probably right. She gives me a hard stare, searching my face for something, but I don't know what.

She's slipping further out of my grasp, so I focus on memorizing her face. She's so angry and sad, and I know that's partially my fault, and I want to undo that.

She should get a choice, and she should be able to say no, but I'm such a selfish fuck that I want her to say yes. I want to give her life back, but I want her to share that life with me. I want to give her a choice, but

I want her to choose me. I want to give her what she wants, but I want to be what she wants. I love her, and I am so desperate for her to love me back that I would do anything she asks. I know she *could* want me. She doesn't, but she *could*. She'll say no, and then I'll kill Danny and then figure out what to do with myself.

I want to fix the mess I've made of her life, give her something back, make her happy however I can.

I have no idea what she sees on my face, but eventually her expression becomes exasperated, and she rolls her eyes, sighing and shaking her head.

"*I'm* fucking insane," she mutters. What does that mean? She steps into me, grabbing my jaw hard in one hand and yanking my face down towards hers, and I stop breathing. She's so close that I could kiss her, but I'm frozen as her eyes focus on mine for a long moment.

"*Maybe*," she says slowly. "I'll *think* about it."

I can't believe it. This can't be happening. This *has* to be a dream, or another delusion, or something. She backs away from me and walks back to the stove, plating the French toast and speaking quickly, her voice shaking with anger.

"Regardless of whether or not I choose to give you a shot, everything goes. I mean it, Theodore, *all of it*. No stalking me, no following me, no watching me, *nothing*. Don't even *think* about texting me. I will be looking for you *everywhere*, and if I so much as see you at the grocery store while I'm there, I will fucking kill you. I'm pretty sure you'd just let me at this point." That's probably true.

She pushes a plate of French toast towards me, pointing at me with a fork angrily.

"You're *very* lucky you're good in bed. That is the *only* reason I'm even thinking about it." I watch as she skates her teeth over her bottom lip because she's *lying*, and hope blossoms in my chest. She's absolutely going to give me a chance.

"Sweetheart," I reach out for her, but she shakes her head hard and flinches away from me.

"Don't even fucking think about it. You need to earn *everything*, if I even feel like letting you." She looks down at the plate of French toast and shrugs a little, her shoulders dropping. "Except this, I guess," she says, her voice soft. "I already made it for you." I blink at her, confused. She made it *for* me?

Alex, who staunchly refuses to do anything close to cooking, made me food.

I'm frozen to the spot as I watch her take her plate to the dining room and start to eat, frowning down at the plate angrily.

"I swear I used to be really good at this," she says, almost to herself. I stare down at the plate of food she's shoved towards me, taking a slow bite. The toast is a little too dark, she went heavy on the cinnamon, she drowned it in maple syrup, and she didn't even sauté the bananas, but it's fucking perfect.

It could be burnt to a crisp and still be the best thing I've ever eaten.

I stay in the kitchen, eating slowly while I watch her stare out the window at the paling sky, her frustrated face becoming more illuminated as dawn creeps on.

She's going to let me try, I'm fucking positive. She'll let me try to give her what she needs, try to be what she needs, try to salvage the colossal fucking mess I've made. I don't deserve her, but I'm going to try – right after I figure out whether or not this is happening.

I'm not entirely sure this *is* happening.

I might need to talk to Dr. Mills.

That is going to suck.

***

We pack up and leave after eating. We don't talk at all, and Alex barely looks at me. During the drive, we listen to a program on public radio about therapy programs for inmates, and Alex keeps shooting me an irritated and slightly amused look.

The closer we get to Astoria, the more nervous I get. When I follow her up to her apartment, my anxiety is so bad I'm on the verge of a panic attack.

I want this. I want her. I'm so lucky she's even *considering* giving me a chance, but I don't want to lose this access to her. Alex gives me a hard look, and I sigh and start to pull the small cameras down.

She's looked for them before and never found them, so she follows me around, looking to see where I hid them, constantly asking me if there are any more. She only stops when I pull up the camera feeds on my phone, showing her there are only the ones in her office and the rec center left, which I tell her I'll grab tomorrow.

I uninstall the hidden tracking apps on her phone, slip the microtracker out of the back, and go through her laptop and remove the programs I installed. She makes us some tea and sits down next to me, peering down at her laptop with mild curiosity as it reboots. I look at the tracking chip on the table and smash it with the edge of my empty mug.

"The little tracking chips? How many?" Her voice is suspicious, and my jaw clenches as I look at her.

"*That's* going to take a while." I get tweezers from her bathroom and grab my phone, starting to pull them out of hems and linings and shoes, breaking them as I go, leaving a growing pile on her dresser.

She leans against the door, watching me with raised eyebrows.

"You are *terrifying*, you know that? You *should* still be in prison," she says, but there's no heat to her voice. If anything, she's teasing me. I rub the back of my neck, shame thick in my stomach.

"Yeah, I'm realizing that."

She eyes the pile of trackers on the dresser thoughtfully. "Is that all of them?"

I look away from her and think about the last one. I should tell her, but she'll freak out and leave for good if I do, and I'm not jeopardizing any possible chance with her.

It's also the only way I have left to make sure she's safe.

I *am* going to take it out, I just need to figure out when. It's okay if it takes me a while to figure it out, right?

I nod to myself, but she takes it as an answer to her question. She walks over to me and leans her head on my arm, trailing her fingers down my spine as she looks at all the broken trackers.

"Teddy?" She sounds so sweet right now, and hope races through my body. I think she still wants this. Maybe she's already decided to give me a chance. Maybe she'll ask me to stay. Maybe we can talk, and I can try to fix this right now.

"Yeah, sweetheart?"

"Can you leave me alone now?" My heart sinks as she holds her hands out for my copy of her keys.

***

I get to see Alex the next day when I take the cameras out of her office, and she doesn't speak to me at all, but she accepts the coffee and pastry I bring her with a small smile.

I leave to take the cameras out of the rec center, and when I text her to show her that all the feeds are dark, she doesn't respond.

Days pass, and she doesn't talk to me at all.

I try extremely hard not to check on the tracker.

I don't really sleep, I don't really eat, I just stay in my house and do anything I can think of to deal with my anxiety, but it doesn't work. Every day that passes convinces me more and more that she's not going to give me a chance.

I start to lose my mind a little bit.

***

"Can you stop asking me stupid questions already? Just do your fucking job and help me *fix this*." Dr. Mills raises her eyebrows at me in reproach for snapping at her, but I don't apologize.

"Theodore, *that's* not my job. My job is to help you build a healthier relationship with yourself and help you manage the stresses of reintegration, and there's more to both of those things than your relationship with Alex." I force myself to take a breath and try a different approach.

"*Fine*. Will you *please* tell me how to fix this?" I hear how frustrated and desperate I sound, but I don't care.

I am desperate.

"I think the way to fix the situation is to work on yourself, do some healing, get a broader life, and come back to this when you have your feet more firmly on the ground." I look up at the ceiling and cross my arms over my chest, shaking my head at her.

"I don't even know why I thought you would help me," I mutter, and Dr. Mills sighs.

"Theodore, I'm *trying* to help you. Right now, it sounds to me like neither you nor Alex have had enough time and healing from your individual traumas to be in a healthy relationship. It's not my place to give my opinion, but if you'll allow me to say so, I think it would be wise for both of you to take some time away from the relationship." Panic grips my heart at the idea.

"That is *not* a fucking option," I snap.

"Do you see that it *could* be an option, at least?" I drop my head into my hands, pushing my hair back and groaning in exasperation.

"Yeah, I do, I *really* do, but I'm a selfish fuck and I can't do it." I roll my eyes and sit back in my chair, staring at the clock. She looks at me for a long moment before glancing down at her notes.

"Can we talk about some of the more concerning elements you've brought up?" I shrug. "From what you've just told me, you felt the impulse to stalk Alex. Can we speak about that?" I look up at the ceiling and shrug again.

I'm such an idiot for letting that slip.

"It was just an impulse. Nothing happened." I avoid looking at her face to see if she thinks I'm lying.

"Be that as it may, I think we need to better understand why you feel the impulse to interact with Alex in a way that doesn't respect her safety or privacy. You've felt these impulses before, right?" I nod, still not looking at her. "Was it just with Ashley?" I keep my eyes fixed on the ceiling and nod once, hoping it reads as sincere. No one else actually counts, anyway. "I know you said you did some work on this topic while in prison, but I'd like to explore it further with you."

"No." Dr. Mills clears her throat and waits, but I don't say anything.

"It may be uncomfortable to talk about, but ideally we'll want you to have a much better understanding of these impulses before getting into anything romantic, especially with Alex."

"I said *no*," I snap.

"I'd like you to spend some time thinking about *why* you don't want to talk about this." I glare at her but say nothing, and the silence between us becomes uncomfortable. "You also told me that you're questioning your grasp on reality because you and Alex viewed your relationship so differently. What does that mean, exactly?" It was such a mistake to speak to her about any of this. I should have just tried to figure this out on my own.

"We weren't on the same page, and now nothing seems real," I say, doing my best to sound nonchalant. "That's all." I don't even need to watch her to know she's blinking and pursing her lips.

"I need to be honest, I don't think that's all. I feel like you're leaving a *lot* out."

She has *no* idea.

"No, that's pretty much it." She makes a small noise of assent.

"Ideally, one misunderstanding shouldn't be enough to destabilize your grip on reality. I know you may not want to hear this, but the medication you refuse to take might have helped you from getting to this point. I think you should speak to a psychiatrist."

"*No.*"

"I think you might benefit from the medication."

"I think *you* might benefit from fucking *dropping it*," I snap. I push my hands back through my hair and exhale hard, glancing at her. "*Sorry*," I force out, "I'm having a bad day." Every day has been a bad day lately.

Dr. Mills looks genuinely concerned. "Thank you for apologizing, Theodore. I'd like to see you more often for the time being, if that's alright. I think you need more support, because it seems that you're in a fragile state of mind right now." I laugh bitterly.

"No fucking shit."

***

Therapy becomes twice weekly, and there's fucking homework.

Reading the books Dr. Mills assigns is hard. I can understand what the books are saying, but even the things that seem to apply to me don't feel real to me. I have to start trying to untangle what is and isn't real, and I can't talk to anyone about it.

I'm supposed to talk to Dr. Mills about it, but keeping my lies straight with her becomes harder. I start letting things slip by accident, and while I'm not stupid enough to admit to anything outright, I'm positive that she's beginning to suspect what's actually been going on between Alex and me.

I have to keep a journal, which I hate, and I use it to second-guess everything I think is real. I spend days going back through my entire relationship with Alex, trying to see it from her point of view, listing out what might have been happening from her perspective.

I get *very* drunk and freak the fuck out when I think about the first time we had sex.

I'm constantly being faced with the realization that there's no way Alex will ever speak to me again.

She shouldn't, honestly.

I put almost all of the polaroids of us away in the attic because it's fucking torture to see Alex look happy with me when I know she was miserable. She's either not that shitty of a liar, or I was so desperate to buy into her lies that I ignored them, but I don't know which it is. I keep one polaroid in my office, one of us in front of the tree, because I can tell for certain that Alex was happy.

I see Alex once in person downtown. She's at a wine bar with Bailey, and as they chat and laugh, Alex looks happier and more relaxed than I've ever seen her. Her smile is so wide and honest, and my heart breaks to see it. I leave the area immediately, even though she doesn't notice me, and I go to the soggy, freezing beach and sit out on the dunes and cry.

I've been crying so much lately. I didn't cry for almost ten years, and now it's happening constantly. This must be how Alex feels, and it's fucking *awful*. I know I'm part of the reason she cries so much, and I know she'd be better off without me.

Everyone else always has been.

I decide then and there that I'm going to kill myself after I kill Danny.

I don't want to live without Alex, and she doesn't want me. I'll wait until she tells me as much, but at this point, it's a foregone conclusion. I leave the beach, going home to make a list of things I need to do before I kill myself.

I need to get a will drawn up and leave Alex everything, but I need to make sure Catherine doesn't talk to her about it. I need to figure out what to do with my shares in the business, whether I can transfer them to Alex or if I should just sell them.

I need to get the trusts for Melissa's kids taken care of in advance, find a fiduciary and make some things explicitly fucking clear about safeguarding the money from Melissa.

I need to start preparing to kill Danny.

I need to write Alex a letter, explaining how sorry I am and how much I love her.

I'll do all of that while I wait for her to break my heart, which she will.

41

ALEX

Waking up the next day feels like a dream. I walk to work, still unsure of my new reality, but it feels real once I see Theo waiting at my office to take the cameras out.

He looks *miserable,* which he should, and he brought me breakfast, which I only accept because he seems so miserable. He takes the cameras out, shows me the camera feeds are off on his phone, and leaves. Once he texts me with proof that the cameras are out of the rec center, I go to yoga and relax fully for the first time in months.

After work, I walk home, but he's *nowhere.*

My life is just for me again.

It's fucking *awesome.*

Everyone can tell I'm in a good mood, and I try not to let it bother me when Bailey asks about Theo. I answer vaguely and turn the conversation away from him.

When I get home, I take all the presents he's ever given me and put them in bags under my bed and ignore them. I've run out of the food he bought, so I go grocery shopping for myself. I don't cook dinner, and I enjoy eating canned tuna directly from the tin without being questioned.

I spend the night painting a big, abstract canvas in warm colors, and when I prop it up to dry, I notice the small painting of Theo reading, which also goes under the bed.

The next day, I chat with some of the regulars at my dance fitness class, just because I'm in a good mood and I can. I get dinner at a brewery I haven't tried and walk home slightly drunk. I pull up the stupid Purple Ribbon Yoga video and recite the long-abandoned affirmations to myself. I masturbate successfully for the first time in months, and I don't think of Theo once.

I spend the rest of the night masturbating, thrilled to have control over my body back.

On Friday, I babysit Miles, and we play dinosaurs, hang out on the couch together with Biscuit, and watch cartoons. Bailey drives me home, and I stay up late, drink a bottle of wine, put on a face mask, and watch a dumb movie just because my time is my own.

I take the bus to Portland on Saturday, and since Theo's not hovering over me, trying to see what I like or don't like, I go shopping and buy myself whatever I want as a treat for being free again. I see whatever movie I want, since I'm the only person I have to consider when I choose the movie. There's no leg bouncing out of boredom next to me, and no one reminds me it's not real butter that they pour on my popcorn.

Anna, Jessica, and I get brunch on Sunday, and I finally feel like I can start being more open about myself and my feelings because Theo's not hanging around, trying to listen. I deflect when they ask about him, being as vague as possible without seeming suspicious. After brunch, I swing by a stationary store downtown and buy a planner for the new year, almost crying when there's no blocky handwriting in red ink anywhere in my new planner.

I go to Bailey's for New Year's Eve and tell everyone that Theo is sick when they ask about him, and then I don't mention him again. I get drunk on champagne and walk home drunk, open another bottle of champagne, play loud music, and dance around my apartment. No one freaks out about my safety, or criticizes my music, or asks why I'm getting shitfaced, or makes a stupid little concerned face when I fall on my ass.

I show up to work the next day *very* hungover, and no one texts me to ask me if I'm feeling okay or shows up with lunch, ibuprofen, and a disapproving look.

My life is back in my hands, and I focus on how amazing it feels to be in control again.

I work hard to ignore any of the other feelings I'm having.

I go to trivia on Tuesday, and I run into Ben for the first time since Theo beat the shit out of him. Anna and I ignore him, mostly talking to each other and Zach. Ben seems nervous, looking around occasionally, but Theo's nowhere to be seen. He doesn't text me or show up at the bar or at my house after. I'm almost disappointed, but I become elated when I realize that it means he actually isn't following me or watching me.

I go out to a wine bar with Bailey on Wednesday, thrilled I have so much time to socialize. After work on Thursday, I go to the small bookstore downtown and pick up a used copy of a self-help book about shame and vulnerability that Bailey recommended.

I reread the section on numbing yourself to keep from being vulnerable twice.

On Saturday, I go to the beach and paint, and I allow myself to think about Theo. When I get home, I spend hours writing out color-coded pros and cons lists of reasons why I should or shouldn't give him a chance, and every list has more red ink than green. All the evidence points to Theo being a bad fucking idea, and I try to convince myself that should be enough for me to make the right choice about him.

The next morning, I go on a long run along the waterfront, not used to running alone anymore. I walk back to my place slowly, and I finally stop ignoring the feeling I've been shoving down since I got back from Yachats. I look at the pros and cons lists, but they don't cover everything, so I throw them all out and start over, using a third column to list how I feel about him.

I know how I feel about him and the fucked-up mess he made of my life, but I don't know what to do about it. I want to give myself the time to fully consider every option, so I let myself think about it for another week. I go through my routine, go to work, see my friends, but in the back of my head is a constant churn of what to do about Theo.

The next Sunday, I think I'm finally ready to see him, but I know I need to make up my mind before I talk to him. I spend my entire run trying to decide what to do, but by the time I get to his house, I'm still unsure.

I know what I *should* do, and I know what I *want* to do, but I don't know what I'm going to do until I take the first step down the dead-end road that leads to him.

I twist the knob on his weird, vintage doorbell, but he doesn't answer the door. His cars are all here, so I doubt he's in Yachats. Maybe he's out, but he knows what time I run on Sundays, and I don't think he'd risk it.

I turn the handle and find the door is unlocked, which is unusual because he *always* locks his doors. I slip off my running shoes and look around, seeing that his house is spotless. Theo's a neat freak anyway, but it had begun to look like someone might live here. Right now, it's basically a showpiece. I head upstairs to his bedroom, and it's spotless except for a bag of my things set neatly in the corner with a thick envelope on top.

I stare at the bag and letter with apprehension, but I don't touch either.

His office has a large, organized pile of brand-new therapy and self-help books on his desk, as well as a notebook and some highlighters. There are some unmarked sealed manila envelopes and a few stacks of paper on his desk, and everything is tidy. I resist the strong urge to go through his things, but I don't like the look of the envelopes, which look exactly like the ones we put documents in at work. I notice he's got the Polaroid of us in front of the tree taped to one of his monitors, and I pick it up and look at it for a long time.

We look so happy.

I check the guest rooms he never uses, and they're all perfectly tidy and recently cleaned, but he's not there. I open a small door that leads to a narrow staircase, which must be the entrance to the attic, and I get a little nervous as I climb the stairs slowly. I keep my eyes on the rafters, but it's just a cramped attic full of boxes and no Theo, and I breathe a sigh of relief.

I'm probably being ridiculous.

I check the rooms downstairs that he never uses, but he's not in any of them. When I head into the kitchen and see that his fridge is empty, I start to panic.

I hurry towards the detached garage, but when I pass the basement door, I hear something, so I open it and head down the stairs.

His basement is a huge home gym, and Theo's facing away from me with headphones on, shirtless and in workout shorts, jumping rope rapidly. I know that he works out when he's wound up, which is why he's in such great shape despite the absurd amount of food he eats, but I just thought he ran a lot and had some dumbbells. I'm pretty sure he's got a nicer gym down here than the rec center. He's got a weird, curved treadmill, a weight rack, a cable machine, and a wide variety of other equipment, including a Pilates machine that looks untouched.

This is *so* excessive for one person, but I shouldn't be surprised.

He's not usually one for restraint.

He still hasn't noticed me, so I sit on the steps and watch him over the low wooden railing. On further inspection, the gym looks like the most used room in the house right now. It's almost messy, which is probably a bad sign. I wait, watching the clock, and he only starts to slow down after about ten minutes.

God, he must be really stressed.

It's a few more minutes before he finally stops, hanging the rope on a hook on the wall and breathing hard. He puts his face in his hands and tilts his head back, his chest heaving, and I can see rivulets of sweat rolling down the lean, defined muscles of his body. As I look at him, I become extremely aware of an ache between my legs that wasn't there when I walked into the basement.

We need to get out of this house.

Theo turns around and startles when he sees me, swearing loudly as he whips off his headphones. The music filtering out is so loud and aggressive that it's no wonder he didn't hear me. He hasn't shaved in a few days and he's very pale with dark circles under his eyes, and he looks a little leaner than the last time I saw him. His face morphs from shock to elation and he jolts forward as if to get closer to me, but seems to stop himself.

"*Sorry*, honey, you scared the shit out of me. I've been leaving the door open for you, but I did *not* think you'd be here. Holy shit, I've missed you. How long have you been here? *Fuck*, you look *gorgeous*." He takes a deep breath, running his hands back through his hair. "You didn't tell me you were coming, or I wouldn't have been down here. I would have made you something to eat after your run. Do you want something to eat? Actually, I don't even have any food, I'm so sorry. How was your run? How have you been? Are you okay? *Why are you here?*"

He doesn't let me answer any questions before he asks the next one, and I stare at him, concern and affection warring for my attention. He seems wound so much tighter than normal, but he looks as if he hasn't slept in days. His eyes are wide and searching my face rapidly, and I can tell it's bothering him that I haven't said anything yet.

"Theo, come here." He walks towards me quickly and leans against the stair railing, close enough to touch me, but he doesn't.

"Hi, sweetheart," he whispers. He's looking at me in the intense way he did in Yachats, like he's trying to memorize my face, and it makes me more nervous. I take a deep breath and let it out slowly, trying to keep my expression neutral.

"I think it's time we talked." His face goes blank instantly, and he looks away from me, nodding to himself.

"I'll leave you alone, I promise," he says quietly, and his resigned, hollow tone makes me feel like I was right to be nervous. I reach over the railing and stroke his cheek softly, and he looks back at me, shock and a slight flush creeping across his face as he leans into my touch.

"I don't want that." His eyes go wide, and he stares at me, confused. I smile at him, trying to hide how deeply concerned I am about him. "Let's go get lunch, okay? It'll be our first date."

***

Theo doesn't seem to know how to act around me. He's nervous, his leg bouncing constantly, and he's so distracted that he lets me pay for lunch, which I know he doesn't like. He doesn't order anything but coffee, but he drinks a *lot* of coffee.

He looks at me in that weird, intense way, and starts asking me a litany of inane questions about the last three weeks – what did I eat, where did I go, did I read anything, etc. I indulge him, but I don't know if I trust that he doesn't know the answers.

When I ask him how he's been, he gets cagey and doesn't make eye contact.

"I'm fine," he says quickly, and I force myself not to roll my eyes.

"You don't seem fine," I say gently, and he shakes his head down at his coffee.

"I'm good, I promise."

"When was the last time you slept?"

He shrugs, not meeting my eyes. "Last night."

"When was the last time you *ate*?"

"This morning."

"Theo, you're a shitty liar, okay? *Please* talk to me." He still won't look at me, and I get irritated. "You want this chance? Stop fucking lying to me, *now*." Theo finally meets my eyes, looking at me for a long second, his mouth a thin line and his jaw tense.

"*Fine*. I'm *not* good, I haven't slept in days, and I can't remember the last time I ate. I've been trying to exhaust myself to get some sleep, but it's *not working*. Also, Dr. Mills has me doing therapy twice a week until parole ends, which sucks." He rolls his eyes. "I have *homework* now, like a fucking kid."

"I noticed the books." He shakes his head and looks out the window.

"Yeah. It's...hard." I can see that he's trying, but I don't know if I can trust him yet.

"What did you do Tuesday night?"

He frowns at me. "What I've been doing for the past three weeks: locking myself out of my phone and in my house. I mostly clean and work out and read the stupid books, why?" I don't think that's all he's been doing, but I'm not going to push it right now because he's so on edge. He obviously doesn't know that Ben showed up to trivia again, so I keep it to myself.

He's so wound up that he might kill Ben on principle if I tell him.

"No reason. Do you want to get dinner with me on Wednesday?"

His eyes go wide. "Fuck, yes. I'll make you whatever you want, you name it." *Coq a vin*, a desperate voice in my head whispers, but I shake my head at him.

"Um, I think we should go out. I don't think we should be alone together right now," I say slowly, and I know he understands. For just a second, he's himself again, and he flashes me a wolfish grin.

"I miss you, too, sweetheart," he says quietly before his face falls back into a tense, nervous expression, and he's back to being this version of himself that's worrying the shit out of me.

"Um, do you want to go grocery shopping after lunch?" I can't keep the concern out of my voice, and he shoots me a knowing look.

"Alex, stop *asking*. My answer is always going to be yes. Just tell me when I get to see you and what we're doing."

"I'm always going to give you a choice, Theo." His expression becomes pained, and he nods slowly as he looks away from me.

***

On Wednesday, Theo's calmer and seems like he's slept, but he still seems more wound up than usual. He's so subdued and self-conscious, and he won't even touch me. It's weird to see him like this. I'm used to him being high-strung, but he's usually confident, bordering on arrogant, and overbearingly affectionate.

It's what I've come to like from him, and adjusting to something else is uncomfortable.

We go for dinner at a restaurant on the waterfront, and it's empty enough that I ask for a table near the window, away from other people. Theo orders a double whiskey, and I know immediately that he's pretty stressed out if he's drinking. I order my drink and watch him fidget and try not to look at me.

"How are you?" He glances out the window, and I watch his jaw tense.

"Better than Sunday," he says quickly, looking back at me and trying to smile. "So fucking happy to see you again." I stare at him, knowing I should reassure him, but I want to know how he'll react when I don't. He anxiously searches my face for any reaction and starts to ask me a question when our drinks arrive.

I order enough food for both of us because I'm almost positive Theo won't eat without prompting, and the moment the waiter leaves, Theo downs his whiskey.

"Why are we here?" He says it so quickly that all the words blur together, and I almost laugh, but he's so serious that I stop myself.

"We're on a date," I say slowly. I get a glimpse of the Theo I know as he smirks and rolls his eyes before his face drops back into uncertainty.

"*Why*, Alex?"

I look at him, confused. "Um, I took my time to think about it and decided I want to give you a chance." He cocks his head to the side and looks at me with disbelief. "I thought that was obvious. Why didn't you ask me this on Sunday?" He looks over my head, and the table shakes as his knee bounces.

"Uh, I hadn't slept in a few days, and everything seemed so surreal that I wasn't *totally* sure it was happening. The only reason I know it happened is because there's food in my house now. I had to talk to Dr. Mills about that yesterday," he mutters unhappily, and I desperately want to reach out and take his hand, but I hold myself back.

"What did she say?" His eyes widen, and his mouth becomes a thin line.

"*Please*, no. I'm not trying to keep it from you, but it fucking sucked and I'd rather talk about anything else tonight."

"We don't have to talk about it." He looks at me gratefully, and I give him a soft smile, which makes him relax a little. "If we're going to do this, I have some conditions, but -"

"I'll do fucking *anything*, Alex. I want to fix this," he says, his voice pleading. I try to keep the pity off my face, but I'm not sure I'm successful.

"Theo, you *can't* fix this." He instantly looks devastated. "That's not what's happening here. I'm giving you a chance because I want to, not because I think it will fix anything you did." He stares at me intently as though I've spoken in a different language and he's trying hard to translate it.

"Wait, *what?*" I smile shyly at him and nod. He opens his mouth to say something, but our food arrives, cutting him off. I smile at the waiter and thank him, catching Theo's displeased glare at how the waiter smiles back at me.

I have a hard time not rolling my eyes.

"Theo, stop it," I hiss as the waiter walks away. "I'm not on a date with him, am I?" His face relaxes a little. "Listen, we can't start over, but we can make something new, right?" He nods, looking very nervous and very hopeful. "*Please* eat something, and then we'll talk about my conditions."

We eat in silence, and Theo seems to relax a little more every time he looks at me. I gently tap my foot against his under the table, and he smiles at me, but it doesn't reach his eyes.

It takes him all of three minutes before he finally can't help himself.

"What do you want me to do? I'll do *whatever* you want." I take a sip of my wine, watching him closely.

"The biggest thing for me is that you have to be completely honest with me about *everything*. I want to get to know you, so I don't want any more lies or half-truths. I'll be honest with you, too, I promise." He seems extremely uncomfortable but nods slowly. "Good. I'm also making all the choices for the time being. I'm making our plans, I'm choosing when to contact you, I dictate how physical we are, everything. I need to be the one in control of things this time." He winces a little, but nods enthusiastically.

"Yeah, of course. Whatever you need. What else?" I take a long sip of my wine, trying to brace myself for his reaction to the next condition.

"We can't spend time at either of our places because we're *not having sex*." He pouts immediately, and I can't help but laugh.

"Can I at least ask why not?"

I frown at him. "Theo, I don't think we have a real shot at seeing if this works if sex is involved, at least in the beginning. The sex is so distracting for both of us, but it's maybe a little more distracting for you?" He cringes, looking down at his food. "At least we already know the sex is fucking *amazing*," I mutter, and he's himself again, smirking up at me and chuckling.

"That's an understatement, honey," he mutters back. "Okay, what else?" I grimace a little.

He's going to *hate* this one.

"I want you to work harder in therapy," I say slowly, and his face falls. "Like, *actually* be open with your therapist." He pales and groans in protest.

"Please, no," he begs.

"I know it's hard on you, but I think you need it. You've got a lot of problems, and I'd like you to at least know whether or not something is real." He takes a deep breath, and his knee starts bouncing again.

"Sweetie, I can't tell my therapist everything, and I kind of hate her."

I shrug. "That doesn't mean you can't work on yourself, and you can always talk to me if you want." Theo's jaw sets as he leans back in his chair and crosses his arms, and I know he's going to push back. "Whatever I want, right, Teddy? It's important that you do this for me," I say in a soft voice, and he sighs.

"*Fine*. Anything else?" I shake my head. "Do I get to ask anything of you?"

My eyebrows shoot up in surprise. "What do you want, besides the chance you *begged* me for?" He looks at me for a long moment, his expression somewhere between confused and desperate.

"Why are you giving me a chance?" he asks, and I laugh a little.

"Because I like you." It's not a lie, but there's no way I'm telling him the real reason until he proves himself to me. He stares at me for a second before he nods slowly, and we go back to having our slightly awkward dinner.

He barely relaxes, and he tries hard not to look displeased when I interact with the waiter. We both drink more, and I can tell we're both trying to figure out how to be with each other now.

I let him drive me home, and he's thrilled when I ask him if he wants to get brunch and see a movie on Sunday. I'm delighted when I watch him restrain himself from kissing me when he drops me off.

He's trying.

42

THEO

THURSDAY, JANUARY 18

"How did your conversation with Alex go?"

I suck in a quick breath and push my hands back through my hair. "Really good. She's open to dating again, so that's fucking amazing." Dr. Mills' eyebrows shoot up.

"You sound excited, and it's nice to hear you happy, but based on what we've talked about before, is there anything you're worried about?" I shrug, avoiding her gaze and her question and the roiling anxiety in my gut.

"Alex had a list of conditions."

"Like what?"

"No sex, for starters," I scoff, shaking my head. "Um, being totally honest, working harder in therapy, letting her take the lead, stuff like that," I say, speaking quickly enough that I hope Dr. Mills will ignore the one that pertains to her.

She doesn't.

"Therapy is work that you have to do for yourself, not someone else," she says in a patient voice.

"I *am* doing it for myself." Dr. Mills blinks at me, pursing her lips just a little.

"Do you think it's fair that Alex has made participating in therapy a condition of getting back together?" I sit back, crossing my arms over my chest.

"I want to give her anything she wants, so it's fine."

Dr. Mills scrutinizes my face for a long moment. "Theodore, how familiar are you with codependency?"

I groan and roll my eyes. "I read the stupid book you gave me."

"Then I think we should talk about attachment styles. What do you think?"

"Just ask your fucking questions already."

"Can we talk about your relationship with your parents?" I drop my head back against the chair and start laughing bitterly.

***

After the appointment, I lean my head against my steering wheel, my body tense with anxiety as I desperately try to breathe and compartmentalize. I'm fighting off a panic attack when my phone chimes.

Alex, 1:03 PM:

still good for sunday?

I exhale, relief flooding through me and easing some of the sharp pain in my chest.

Three more days before I can see her again.

Three more days of not sleeping and trying hard not to do anything wrong, like looking at the tracker or jogging past her apartment at four in the morning or *accidentally* catching a glimpse of her in public when I know she won't see me.

Theo, 1:04 PM:

I can't wait.

43

ALEX

FRIDAY, JANUARY 19

Anytime I'm not with Theo, I focus on myself.

I try to, anyway.

I make dinner plans with Anna and Jessica, I go to drinks with Bailey, I get lunch with Suzie, and I don't talk about him at all. I run, I paint, I watch movies, I wander through Astoria, and I don't wish he was with me. I lay in bed at night, not missing his arms around me and definitely not thinking about him when I'm masturbating.

The next time I see him, he still seems nervous. I try to get him to engage with me, and he tries, but he keeps giving me this look like he thinks I'll disappear at any moment. He doesn't relax at all throughout the movie, constantly keeping himself from touching me.

It's jarring. I don't know how I feel about stressed out, unsure Theo.

***

Alex, 11:25 AM:

hey

Theo, 11:53 AM:

What's wrong?

Are you okay?

Why are you texting me?

> i hope therapy goes well today :)

Thanks, Alex.

That means a lot.

> see you tomorrow?

I can't fucking wait.

***

On Wednesday, we go to the sports bar where I first met him, which makes him extremely uncomfortable, but I flirt with him until he finally relaxes a little.

I choose a secluded booth and let him order the drinks so he doesn't have to watch me interact with the bartender, and I sit close to him and make him watch the Blazers game. Neither of us cares about basketball, but it's a neutral subject that we can make stupid jokes about, and the easy conversation seems to make him feel better.

By the end of the night, he's almost the Theo I'm used to.

Almost.

***

Alex, 11:57 AM:

how was therapy?

Theo, 1:00 PM:

I will do anything to not answer that question right now.

anything?

Whatever you want.

oysters from the place on the pier?

Fuck yes.

Pick you up after work.

It feels normal. Not normal for us, but what normal dating is supposed to feel like.

***

On Saturday, we drive out to the beach and walk up the shore, not talking, but our silence is comfortable again. We sit up on a dune and watch the waves come in, the wreck of the *Iredale* visible down the beach. It's cold and rainy, so I sit close and lean into Theo, and I can feel his arm jerk against mine as he keeps himself from wrapping it around me.

"How are you feeling?"

He snorts and shakes his head. "I have no idea. Not great." I slip my hand into his, interlocking our fingers and squeezing his hand.

"How are you feeling about *this*?" He grips my hand tightly, not looking at me.

"I don't know. I'm so grateful and excited, but I'm stressed and confused, and I feel so fucking guilty all the time. Mostly I'm just terrified that I'm going to fuck it up or hurt you again. I'm really worried that you don't want to be here, or that it's unhealthy for you to be with me, which is probably what Dr. Mills thinks." He runs his hand through his hair quickly and huffs out an angry breath.

I pull his face towards me, and I can tell he's searching for any indication of how I'm feeling, so I smile softly at him, rubbing my thumb over his cheekbone.

"Well, *I* feel good about this so far," I say as I lean in to kiss him. He makes a soft noise and kisses me back but doesn't move, letting me set the pace of the kiss. I can tell he wants more, and I can feel him holding himself back, and I grin against his lips.

He's trying so hard.

"I feel really good about it, honestly," I say, kissing him again. "I feel really good about *you*." Theo's smile is small and fragile, but it reaches his eyes, and I don't think he can help how he melts into me, wrapping his other arm around my waist and pulling me closer. He looks down at me, and I can tell he's unsure, but I'm starting to see that means he's thinking about me, and warmth spreads through me.

I like that I'm the one in control now, and I like making him feel good.

I like *him*, even like this.

***

Outside of our dates, we start running together again on Sundays, even though it's usually pouring. We always end our runs at the coffee shop by my work, which I find out Theo started frequenting when he was following me. When I make a joke about him stalking me, he gets so upset that he leaves immediately, and I bring him his coffee and a pastry, and we end up sitting on his porch and talking for hours about everything that happened between us.

We're both completely honest, and Theo has a panic attack when we talk about the first few times we had sex. He swears he's *never* making coq a vin again, and I have to hide my disappointment, mostly because I want to reinforce him having boundaries, even if they're boundaries I don't like.

The more we talk, the more I get to see what his perspective was from inside the delusion. I had a decent understanding of what his delusion was from pushing to find the limits, but it was *so* real to him. His justifications for his behavior are almost well-intentioned, and his understanding and interpretation of my behavior was so off base, but not entirely. I feel so much softer towards him after hearing his side, knowing that he always genuinely cared about me in his own insane way.

Knowing that makes me less nervous about us making this work.

When we talk about his behavior, there are things Theo can accept and take accountability for, and things he can't. He feels terrible about scaring me, about triggering me, about making me feel like I'd lost control of my life, about anything that made me feel bad, and he takes accountability and apologizes profusely.

He knows he shouldn't have stalked me or broken into my apartment, and he does apologize, but his apologies seem so pale in comparison to how he apologized for hurting me that I don't think he feels bad about any of it.

He gets *exceptionally* cagey and evasive when I try to address his stalking impulses, and he won't give me a straight answer on how many people he's stalked besides Ashley and I, so I drop it.

He'll have to tell me eventually, though.

The only thing he can't seem to accept as part of the delusion is the connection he thinks we have. He tells me he logically recognizes it's most likely delusional, but he explicitly avoids answering whether he thinks we're connected. I drop that, too.

It's delusional, but it wouldn't be the worst thing in the world if it were true.

***

After that conversation, it gets easier to talk about things. Both of us struggle to be open, but we work hard to answer questions honestly and to volunteer information, and being vulnerable with each other starts to feel good. On top of that, we get back to just enjoying each other's company, and things start to feel real between us.

We agree not to go out more than three times a week, besides running on Sundays, and the more comfortable we get together, the more Theo starts asking me about my days in minute detail. He acts casual when he asks, trying not to make it obvious how much he misses stalking me.

It's *very* obvious.

I start to feel calmer, more in control of myself and my life as time goes on. Being in control is good for me, and I'm able to emotionally invest so much more because of it. It's my choice to go slowly with him, to make sure he's proving himself to me, but I miss what we had.

I miss spending days on end with him. I miss his constant, overwhelming amounts of affection. I miss him showing up randomly when I'm not expecting him. I miss the fridge full of homemade food and coming home to him when he shouldn't be there. I miss the weird, unexpected texts about what I'm doing in the moments we're not together.

I'm horrified once I realize I kind of miss the stalking, too.

I don't tell Theo.

Over the weeks, Theo's mood seems to pick up and even out. He seems less anxious and more sure of himself, and I see more and more flashes of the Theo I know. He second-guesses himself more and seems unsure if things are what they are occasionally, but he starts to feel more secure in what's happening between us.

I think the therapy is helping, even though I know he's only trying because I've asked him to.

He really doesn't like his therapist.

He also doesn't seem to like himself.

That makes one of us.

Because my biggest demand of him is honesty, and we're talking so much, I'm getting to know Theo on a deeper level. He's not great at being vulnerable, but he tries hard to let me all the way in. He's got so many fucking issues, but he's genuinely a sweet, caring person at his core. The more I learn about him, the more sense he makes to me, and every time I look at him, I see a depth that I didn't see before.

I let Theo get to know me, too. He made a *lot* of assumptions about my life based on stalking me and what information he could find online. While he wasn't entirely off base, he never really knew everything, either. I get to tell him whole, messy truths about my life and let him see the parts of myself I tried to hide from him. The more he gets to know me, the more it feels like he sees me as less of an idea and more as a person, and he loves me all the more for it.

For the first time in my life, I don't feel like I have to do anything to earn the love I'm receiving. It gets harder for me to ignore and push down and manage my feelings about him, so I stop trying.

After that, it's hard to go slowly.

***

Alex, 10:03 AM:

no gifts! no valentines day!

Theo, 10:05 AM:

Flowers aren't technically gifts.

And they have nothing to do with Valentine's Day.

i love them

thank you

I hope you have a good day, sweetheart.

After a lonely day and a lonelier night with a bottle of wine and my vibrator, I take a photo of myself for the first time, making sure not to get my face.

Theo, 11:50 PM:

When I get my fucking hands on you, you won't walk for a week.

Alex, 11:51 PM:

sexting counts as sex

But nudes don't?

i'm not nude

Close enough.

i'm close enough

How close?

almost there

Get there for me, sweetheart.

Right now.

i miss you

I just missed you, too.

> This doesn't count as sexting, right?

> shut up

***

Theo takes me to a nice restaurant on Saturday, and I sit on the same side of the booth as him, pressing myself against him and flirting with him as I drink too much champagne and we eat oysters. He slips his fingers through mine and kisses me just under my jaw when no one is looking, and I'm giddy.

I love having a nice, normal date with my nice, normal boyfriend who doesn't stalk me anymore.

When Theo drops me off at my apartment and kisses me good night, I grab his jaw and slip my tongue into his mouth, unable to stop myself from crawling into the driver's seat and straddling him. He freezes, his body tense beneath me, his hands shaking against my waist.

"Alex, is this-" I cut him off with a long, deep kiss, grinding down into him.

"*Theo*," I beg quietly against his lips, "*please*." He lets out a low, aggressive sound and drags me against him, my every nerve lighting up at the feel of his fingers digging into me as he kisses me desperately. He's entirely himself again, and it feels so good to touch him, to feel his hands grip my ass hard, to hear him moan when I reach my hand between us and rub my palm against his length. He starts pushing my dress up, his fingers grazing against me through my thin lace panties, and I gasp when he circles them against my clit. I reach for his belt, undoing it frantically as he slips one long finger inside of me, and I cry out in pleasure.

"Oh, *fuck*, I missed you," he mutters as he slips a second finger inside of me, and I drop my forehead against his shoulder, panting hard as I undo his pants. He swears loudly when I take him in my hand and start to stroke his cock, and I start begging incoherently for *more* as he fucks me with his fingers.

"More," he agrees in a guttural whisper, pushing me back against the steering wheel and crooking his fingers hard inside me. I accidentally lean back into the horn, and the loud sound startles us enough to break the moment.

We both freeze, breathing hard and staring at each other, his fingers inside of me and my hand tight around him. Theo's shaking underneath me, his fingers inside of me but unmoving, his pupils wide and his expression starving.

He's holding himself back, *barely*, and I adore him for it.

Still, I have to get away from him immediately, or my restraint will completely break.

"I need to get out of the car," I say, forcing the words out.

He shakes his head furiously. "Please don't."

"I'm going," I choke out.

"You could come first," he pleads.

"We're not having sex." Theo raises his eyebrows and glances down between us.

"Sweetie, what do *you* think we're doing right now?" His voice is condescending and desperate, and I exhale a laugh that's more of a groan than anything else.

"*No*, Theo." He nods, his face pained as he slips his fingers out of me, and he makes a slight noise of protest when I release him. I barely stop myself from reaching back down and guiding him inside of me, grabbing my bag and opening the driver's side door instead.

Theo grabs my hand, pressing a soft kiss to the inside of my wrist.

"We can hold off as long as you want, sweetheart, I mean it. Whatever you need. I'm not fucking this up again." My chest fills with warmth and my body aches for him, but I force myself to get out of the car and walk to my door alone.

I send another photo that night and get one in return, and I have to stop myself from begging him to come over. Going slowly with Theo is getting impossible, but I have to keep trying.

I'm not ready to tell him yet.

***

I see him the following Monday, and I force myself not to drink anything because I'm barely holding on to my inhibitions as is.

"Not thirsty?" He teases, staring at me hungrily.

"Very thirsty," I mutter into my water, and he laughs.

He walks me home, our interlaced fingers somehow becoming the warm, comforting presence of his arm around my shoulders. When we get to my apartment, he pulls me tightly against him and kisses my neck in a way that makes me moan.

"You're so fucking needy, honey," he whispers just below my ear before nipping at my neck. I whine and reach for him, and he pulls back and laughs at the look on my face.

I freeze. For a split second, it's October and he's my stalker making me beg for sex, and I hate how much I want him. I involuntarily step away from him and blink hard, staring at him, trying to figure out how I feel. He immediately looks concerned and frustrated.

"Fuck, Alex, I'm sorry." I shake my head, smiling at him, figuring out what to say.

"No, I just...you...it felt like *before*." His face falls instantly, and I realize he doesn't understand that I liked being back there with him, that it's so much fun to have him act like this again.

I've realized that I like all versions of Theo, even this fragile, moody version who thinks I hate him.

"*Great*. Sorry," he says tightly, looking away from me with a clenched jaw.

"I liked it," I say quietly, and he looks back at me like I'm insane. I shrug, smiling a little. "I like *you*. Come here." He steps towards me tentatively, and I pull him down into a searing kiss, burying my hands in his hair and pressing up into him. He makes a harsh, wanting sound in the back of his throat as his hands grip my hips and he hauls me closer. I lean back and look up at him, smirking as I feel him hard against me.

"I'm not the only one who's needy, huh?" Theo laughs weakly and lets me go as I back away from him, staring at me with a bemused expression. I have to force myself to step backward towards my apartment, both of us staring at each other hungrily as I open the door.

I don't think I can hold out much longer, mostly because I don't want to.

***

By the time I get off work on Thursday, I've decided to end the no sex rule. I sprint towards Theo's place, ready to throw myself at him. The second I see him I can tell something's wrong, and all thoughts of sex fly out of my head instantly.

He's worked up, pacing on the porch, not looking at me or answering anything directly, his body vibrating with tension. I sit down on one of the porch chairs and gesture to the other, but he shakes his head and keeps pacing.

"What's wrong?" He huffs out a frustrated breath and rolls his eyes at me.

"I'm *fine*, Alex." I cross my arms and raise my eyebrows at him, trying to be patient with him.

"Please talk to me, Teddy." He freezes and gives me a look that tells me he thinks that me using the nickname is playing dirty, which it is.

"I said I'm *fine*," he snaps, and my patience breaks.

"Your *one* chance hinges on you being honest with me, remember? Sit down and talk to me, right *now*." Theo shoots me a desperate look and nods tersely, perching on the edge of the seat and bouncing his knee quickly as he looks down at his feet and runs his hands through his hair.

"Therapy is *very* fucking difficult," he grits out. "Tuesday was bad, but today was worse. Dr. Mills fucking sucks," he spits.

"Can't you get a new therapist?"

He rolls his eyes. "I'd have to petition the court, and '*I don't want to talk to her*' isn't a good enough reason. I'm on parole for another year and a half, but I only have six months of therapy left, so the less I interact with the system until I'm done, the better."

"Do you want to talk about what happened?" I usually don't ask about his sessions, but this is such a massive reaction that I think I should. Theo's face is drawn, and he won't look at me.

"You asked me to try, so I'm trying," he says miserably, "and I fucking *hate* it. Now that I'm being even *slightly* more open with Dr. Mills, she's been asking all these invasive fucking questions about my impulses, and my family, and my relationship with Ashley, and my friendship with Kevin, which is all shit I *don't* think about. She's so goddamn nosy and she's digging deeper than I want her to, and it's fucking *awful*." He shakes his head, exhaling harshly.

"What's worse than that is she keeps getting in my fucking head about this. The better things go between us, the harder dealing with her gets. I can tell she's always thought us dating was a bad idea, but she seems very against us being together now, especially because I'm almost positive she knows I was stalking you." I look at him in surprise, and he shrugs. "I was so fucked up after Christmas that I tried to actually talk to her, and it was a huge mistake."

"How much does she know?"

He snorts. "Nothing concrete. I'm delusional, honey, not *stupid*, but everything was so hard to deal with that I accidentally let some things slip. I can tell from her questions that she's put it together, she just has no evidence to give to the parole board."

"Well, I'm not surprised she's figured it out. You're a pretty bad liar, except to yourself." This earns me a pained look, and I shoot him a small smile and tap his foot with mine. "So, she doesn't even know everything and still thinks we shouldn't be together?" Theo runs his hands through his hair and lets out a derisive laugh.

"Yeah, pretty much. Dr. Mills thinks that this relationship is keeping me from addressing any of my issues, which is *wrong*, and that you haven't dealt with how deeply traumatized you are from Danny, which I'm *positive* she's right about, and she keeps insinuating that you probably feel coerced into giving me a chance, which I'm *terrified* of, or that I'm taking advantage of you and pushing you into some fucking codependent situation, which I have *no idea* about, but she's probably right about that, too."

No wonder he doesn't like his therapist.

He leans back in his chair and drags his hands down his face, sighing heavily. "I'm just having a hard time acknowledging that she might be right about some of it. It's all so fucking different from how I feel, but that's the big problem, right? I'm painfully aware that I'm not the most in touch with reality when it comes to you or this relationship. I'm really worried that it *is* bad for you, but I have no fucking idea. She seems to think it's not good for me, but that's because she's a fucking idiot." He laughs bitterly.

I look out at the river, considering what he's saying. I've been trying to focus on myself – what I want, what I need, how I feel, and if this is right for *me* – but I've never even considered that us dating might be bad for Theo.

My heart catches in my throat and I swallow it down, trying not to panic.

"Well, what do you think about what she's saying? Would it be better for you if we didn't keep doing this? Is that what you want?"

Theo goes very still, staring at me intensely.

"I want to prioritize what's right for *you*," he says slowly, his voice apprehensive but warm. Something loosens inside of me, and a rush of affection for him passes through me.

"I appreciate that, but I care about you, and I want to know what *you* want." Everything about Theo's demeanor sharpens and his gaze becomes deadly serious as he leans forward towards me.

"Alex, I want *you*." My stomach flips and my breath catches at the intensity behind his words. "I want *everything* from you, and I want it right fucking now. I hate this dating bullshit we're doing. I can't stand being away from you for a second and I miss you all the fucking time. I try not to think about you, but it's all I do. I can't even go an hour without thinking about you, and that's on a good day. Dr. Mills says I'm supposed to do things for myself, but I'd rather do everything for you. Fuck, I'm only even working on myself in therapy because you want me to. I want to give you everything you want, but I want you to want *this*. I want you to wa-" He clears his throat and looks away from me, staring at his feet, and I can feel tears pricking behind my eyes.

"Listen, I think Dr. Mills might have a point that it's a bad idea for you to be with me, but I'm too fucking selfish to walk away from you. I can't do it. I don't deserve you, but you're all I want, so I'll take whatever you're offering me."

I look away from him, blinking quickly to keep my tears from falling. I sit back in my chair, pulling my hair up into a ponytail and taking it out repeatedly just to have something to do with my hands as I watch the cargo ships drift slowly up and down the river, working through my feelings and trying to keep from crying.

I wasn't ready to have *this* conversation with him, but it's already happening, so I take a deep breath and exhale slowly, bracing myself.

"Theo, I think your therapist is right that I shouldn't be seeing you." I hear him stop breathing, but I can't look at him. "I can see that you're trying hard to be better, and whether you're doing it for me or not doesn't matter, because it's good for you either way. No matter how much work you do, though, you still fucking *stalked* me and forced me into a relationship. You took over my whole life, a life I had just started to build after escaping Danny, and that *sucked*. I mean, it sucked so badly that I pushed you to get you to kill me, just so I could get away from you."

Out of the corner of my eye, I see him place his head in his hands, his knees jumping so hard that his whole body shakes.

"Oh, my fucking god," he mutters under his breath over and over, his voice panicky, and I feel a slight pang of guilt. He apparently hadn't put that together, and this was the wrong time to tell him. I give him a minute to calm down before I take a deep breath and continue.

"It's my choice what to do here, Theo, and I'm trying to make sure that if I choose this for myself, it's something I do completely outside of how you're feeling. Part of why I'm going slow with you is to give myself every opportunity to walk away from you, which I know I *should*." I can see him watching me closely out of the corner of my eye, but I can't look at him or I'll start sobbing. I look upwards at the porch roof instead, trying to keep it together.

"I'm not stupid enough to think dating my former stalker is a good idea. I *know* that I shouldn't be with you. I've weighed out all the pros and cons and you lose every time, by a *huge* fucking margin. I know the right move, the *smart* move, is to walk away from you, and I'm trying so hard to be smart about this." I take a shaking breath and finally look over at his shocked and devastated face. "It's not working, Theo, it's just not." His face goes blank and his whole body starts to shake, and I can't help laughing a little.

"Teddy, I've thought about this so much, and I'm done giving a shit about what I should do." His eyes widen as his face shifts from devastation to confusion. "I should have left you in Yachats, but I didn't. I shouldn't have given you a chance, but I did. I should get up and walk away from you right now, but I'm not going to. I only care about what I want to do, and I want *you*." Theo looks like he's going to cry, and I can feel my eyes start to water too. "I have all the choices in my life back, and now I get to choose you."

Theo stares at me for a long minute, and I can see he's trying to figure out whether this is real.

"Alex, are you fucking serious?" His voice is soft and disbelieving. I laugh a little and shrug, wiping away the tears forming on my lash line.

"Of course. I meant it when I told you I'd choose you if I had the option." His expression softens into something completely vulnerable and hopeful, and his eyes roam over me, landing on my lips, and he starts leaning towards me, slowly crossing from his space to mine.

Fear lances through me as he leans forward, and I jerk away from him, standing up and stumbling back a few steps. He looks confused and hurt, and I shake my head, wrapping my arms around myself to attempt to contain how I'm feeling.

This is exactly what I want, but I know everything is going to change the second he touches me. We're about to be together, *really* together, and I don't know if I'm ready.

I've never been in love before.

It's fucking *terrifying*.

I stare at him, trying to explain. "Theo, I *want* this, but it's...it's *so* much, all at once, and things...I don't...I wasn't ready...I want *you*, I'm just...I need..." I drag in a harsh breath and trail off, unsure I can explain my feelings.

Theo's frozen, leaning forward in his chair, scrutinizing my face, and I'm glued to the spot under the weight of his gaze. He finally gives me a knowing smile and gets to his feet, walking towards me slowly and stopping in front of me, so close we're almost touching. His eyes are fixed on mine and he's so focused, so intense, so *overwhelming*.

I missed this.

"You don't have to be scared, sweetheart," he says quietly. I stare up at him, my arms tightening around my waist to keep from grabbing him.

"We're taking this slowly," I breathe out unconvincingly. Theo raises one eyebrow at me in amusement as he bends toward me, bringing his face close to mine.

"Oh, I can take you slowly," he teases, grinning when I laugh a little. I look down at my feet and shake my head.

"I *should* leave," I say, my voice shaky. Theo places two fingers under my chin and tips it back until I'm looking at him again, and he searches my face intently. I can feel myself blushing under the intensity of his gaze, and a small, crooked smile appears on his face.

"You don't *want* to leave, do you?" I shake my head a little, and his face becomes satisfied and smug. He's entirely himself again in this moment, and I love him like this. "That's my fucking girl," he whispers, and my heart skips a beat. "Tell me what you want, and I'll give it to you."

I can't keep myself from reaching for him, and his body tenses as my hands drift up his chest and wind in the hair at the nape of his neck. It's even longer now, which I like, and I focus on the feeling of his hair in my fingers as I figure out how to tell him what I want. He looks down at me, barely blinking as we stare at each other, and any defenses I had left crumble as I look up at him.

"Theo, I want to go *home*," I whisper. He looks at me intently for a moment before his eyes widen, and his smile softens from smug to something surprised and tender. He winds his arms around my waist and drags me against him as he hovers his lips over mine, his words almost inaudible.

"Welcome home." I melt into him, tilting my face up a fraction of an inch and grazing my lips against his. My entire body is a live wire the second I kiss him, and the kiss immediately deepens to something frantic and hungry. His hands come to my ass as he bends down to pick me up, groaning as he pulls my body flush against his. My legs lock around his hips, and my arms wind around my neck as I kiss him. I grip his hair and the back of his shirt and his neck as I pull him closer.

He keeps one arm locked around my waist as he stumbles towards the front door, his hand frantically, blindly reaching for the door handle. Somehow, he finds his way into the house and into the living room, never breaking our kiss. We topple down onto the couch, laughing a little before his lips find their way to my throat, and I whimper, dragging him closer. He pulls away instead, yanking his sweater off, and I'm pulling mine off in the next moment. He leans down to kiss my chest, but I push him off and start undoing his jeans.

He makes a rough, frustrated sound and grabs my wrists with shaking hands, stopping me. I look up at him, confused, finding his face lined with tension and hope and desperation.

"Is this real?" he begs. "I'm supposed to fucking *ask* you, and this seems too good to be true, so please tell me I'm not delusional." I can't help but laugh a little, shaking his hands off and undoing his belt.

"*Baby*, I promise this is real," I say, looking up at him as I pull his belt off. His eyes go wide, and he makes a low groan and starts unbuttoning my jeans frantically, trying to yank them off. He starts swearing when they don't slide off immediately, and I laugh and lift my hips, and he rips them and my thong off in one smooth motion.

I reach for him once I'm bare, but he's already out of his clothes and on top of me again, kissing me deeply, his hands roaming over my touch-starved skin, his muscles tense beneath my fingers. He's hard between my thighs, and I can already feel how wet I am for him when his head nudges against my slick entrance. I whimper, and he looks at me with wanton need, his body vibrating with tension.

"I need you," I beg quietly, and he nods, his pupils blown wide. We both moan as he pushes inside of me slowly, gripping each other tightly. My head kicks back and my nails dig into his back as I stretch around him, feeling the familiar pressure and friction and fullness that I've missed so much. It's been almost two months without him, and I can barely handle him anymore.

He takes his time working his way inside of me, kissing my throat and jaw and cheek as he goes, my breath coming in soft pants with every inch that he gives me. He pushes in the final bit, moaning loudly in my ear before he stills, his eyes shut tight for a long moment before he looks down at me, his expression vulnerable and tender as he moves in me slowly.

"I'm so fucking sorry," he whispers, and I shake my head as I tilt my hips up to take him deeper.

"It's okay." He exhales hard, nodding faintly and pulling himself back out again, slow enough for me to feel every delicious inch of friction before he rolls his hips, filling me again.

"I'm going to make you happy," he says into my neck, and my eyes flutter closed, a soft moan escaping me as he presses a soft, open-mouth kiss right below my ear. I arch into him, running my hands over his back, clinging tightly to him.

"You already do." He sighs and kisses me deeply, and I whimper and drag my nails along his back as he starts to thrust faster.

We move in tandem, finally back together where we belong, where everything makes sense.

I pull him tight, my legs wrapping around his hips and my arms around his shoulders as he lifts me into him, and I whine softly as he fills me with long, deep strokes. Every nerve crackles with electricity and I can feel heat slipping down my spine and building in my core. My leg tenses and twitches against his waist, and he grins, picking up his pace.

"*Already*? That's my girl."

"I'm yours," I whisper, and his breathing picks up, his expression turning reverential. I know that look, know what's coming, and my heart skips a beat in anticipation as he opens his mouth.

"I love you so fucking much, Alex," he says, his voice thick with emotion, and my entire body hums as something electric passes through me. Tears heat the corner of my eyes, and I open my mouth to tell him, but an unfamiliar emotion courses through my body and overwhelms me, choking me, and nothing comes out. I gasp, trying hard to say something, *anything*, feeling desperate as I look up at him, dying to tell him how I feel.

"*Teddy*," I force out, but nothing but breath comes out after that.

Why can't I say it? I know I love him. I knew the second we got into the conversation today that I would finally tell him, but there's so much emotion in my throat that I can't speak. I take his face in my hands, nodding quickly, trying to make him understand. He looks surprised, his breathing picking up, his eyes darting between my eyes and my lips, his face hopeful and unsure. I nod harder, my breathing getting quicker. His bright hazel eyes flare wide, soft and hopeful when they meet mine, and a dam inside me breaks.

My body floods with warmth as I come around him, too overwhelmed by everything to do anything other than cling to him and bury my face in his neck as my body shakes. I fall apart in his arms, my vision blacking out around the edges as the most intense pleasure I've ever felt courses through me. I keep my hands fisted in his hair, and I hear him whisper *I love you* again and again before he comes with me, his body tensing and his hips jerking, driving him deeper into me before we both go slack.

We stay there, panting hard and clinging to each other. I can feel his heart pounding through my chest, matching mine beat for beat. When we lock eyes, he looks as overwhelmed and scared as I feel.

Theo kisses me softly before he pulls out of me, holding me so closely he's almost on top of me, his hand roaming up and down my body, his touch reverent and possessive. I tuck my face into his neck, my eyes tearing up as something I didn't remember I'd lost slips back into place.

It takes me a minute to realize what I'm feeling, and when I do, I close my eyes and laugh a little, a few tears running down the side of my face.

"Honey, are you okay?" Theo's quiet voice borders on panicked, and I grin up at him broadly, grazing my fingers over his cheek. He relaxes instantly, and his eyes crinkle at the corners as he beams down at me.

"I'm *happy*, Theo," I whisper, crying harder. "I'm so fucking *happy*."

"Me, too," he whispers, leaning down to kiss me. He wraps me in his arms and holds me as I cry, making soft shushing sounds. I cling to him, humming softly as I stroke his face, running my fingers through his hair and down his neck, dragging my fingers slowly down his arm until I can twine our fingers together.

We get to have this now. I wanted the option to choose him, and he gave it to me.

He's mine now, and I'm his.

Everything is perfect.

44

THEO

I might have already fucked this up.

Alex sits on the counter in my flannel with a dreamy smile as she drinks a glass of wine and watches me cut vegetables. I shouldn't be using a knife right now because I'm so distracted, but I try to focus on the process and not on the growing ball of anxiety in my chest.

I pause what I'm doing and look over at the angel sitting on my counter, her dark hair in a messy high ponytail, her freckled cheeks flushed, her light brown eyes soft and adoring as she looks at me, her kiss-swollen lips curved in a happy, satisfied smile. I've *never* seen Alex happy like this, and it's hard to believe it's because of me.

I only make her this happy because she has no idea I'm lying to her.

I've been doing *almost* everything she asked of me, and it's all been making me fucking miserable. I have mostly kept myself from stalking her since we came back from Yachats, which has been excruciating. I have begrudgingly been trying to internalize what I'm learning in therapy, which makes me fucking hate myself. I've been dating her in a way that makes me want to tear my hair out because I'm only getting a fraction of what I want from her at any given time.

The only thing I haven't done is be totally honest with her.

I keep thinking about the tracker, and how she only wants to be here because she doesn't know about it. We're *actually* together now, and I think she just tried to tell me she loves me, but only because she doesn't know I put a tracker in her and I'm still *technically* stalking her a little bit, even though I'm trying hard not to.

"*Fuck!*" I pull my hand back, my finger gushing blood from where I've accidentally sliced it open. Alex makes a small yelp and hops off the counter, running into the bathroom for the first aid kit. I run my finger under the faucet, washing the blood off and examining it while I get my thoughts back under control. Alex hurries back into the room, flipping through the first aid kit for ointment and bandages before she starts tending to the cut.

"This seems familiar, right?" she asks with a sly smirk as she carefully dries my hand and dabs ointment on the cut. I laugh, resting my other hand on the small of her back and pulling her into me.

"Somehow, *I'm* still the one getting threatened with knives." She giggles, wrapping the bandage tight and kissing my finger softly. She looks up at me, her eyes brimming with adoration, and it feels like I'm in a dream.

Why am I so worried? Now that we're together, I can remove the tracker, which will fix everything.

Everything is fine.

Alex loves me.

At least, I'm *almost* positive she loves me. I'm not entirely sure, and I need to know. I'm supposed to be asking, checking in, making sure, seeing if what I think is real *is* real, especially with her.

"Um, I need to ask you something, like earlier. I suck at reality with you, supposedly." She laughs as she hops up on the counter, sipping her wine again. "You want to be here, right? That's real?" I look at her, and she nods. "Words, please, honey." She smiles, slightly amused.

"I want to be here. That's real." She's not lying.

"You really want to do this? You want to be in a relationship with me, even though you think you shouldn't be? Is that seriously real?" She smiles, nodding again, sipping her wine.

"I *really* want to be in this relationship with you." She smirks at me. "You just want to hear me say you're my boyfriend again, right?" I shrug, smiling sheepishly, and she laughs at me. "You're my fucking boyfriend, Theo." I laugh weakly, sucking in a breath as she sips her wine.

Okay, here goes.

"When we were having sex, were you trying to tell me that you love me?" She spits her wine out in surprise, covering her mouth in horror. I laugh, handing her a towel, watching her face flush a bright red as she dabs at the stains on my shirt.

She takes a deep breath, exhaling quickly, looking distressed. "Um, I tried, but I couldn't say it." Panic grips me and my brain starts running sideways and in reverse, second-guessing everything about what happened. I try to breathe, but my chest feels too tight.

"I didn't expect you to say it back," I say quickly. "I couldn't help it, but you already know how I feel about you. Please don't say it if you don't mean it. I don't want you to lie to me, especially not about that." She cocks her head to the side, giving me a fond, slightly sad smile.

"Oh, baby, that's not what's happening. I think I just got overwhelmed because I felt so happy and connected to you." My brain speeds up to the point that it shuts down entirely, leaving me standing there staring at Alex like a fucking idiot. She frowns and slips off the counter, standing before me, her hands gripping my shoulders and pulling me towards her.

"Theo, this isn't a delusion, okay? This is real. I have the option to be here, and I want to be here. I have the option to love you now, and I do." A sharp thrill runs down my spine at her words, and she kisses me quickly, pulling back to look at me with a vulnerable and tender expression. "I love you so fucking much, Teddy." She smiles up at me, and it's the first time I've seen her so happy and unguarded, so genuinely joyful. Her smile looks like it did in the photos of her before her parents died, but broader, sweeter, and infinitely warmer.

I take her face in my hands and kiss her, and a slick slide of guilt in my stomach ruins the best moment of my life.

I don't want to keep lying to her.

I should tell her about the tracker, but I can't because I'm a weak, selfish asshole who just got everything I ever fucking wanted. She's here, she loves me, and she's so fucking happy right now, so there's no way I'm ruining this for myself. Instead of telling her about the tracker, I tell her I love her over and over while I make love to her on the kitchen counter. She wraps herself around me and looks at me with an open, adoring expression as she talks constantly between kisses, telling me that she's mine, that she loves me, that she's so happy this is happening, and every whispered *I love you* that pours out of her fills a space inside of me that's always been empty.

Being loved by Alex makes me feel completely whole for the first time in my life.

There's no fucking way I'm giving this up.

I shut everything else out and stay in the feeling with her all night. Food tastes better, her laugh sounds like music, every smile is a gift, her kisses make me feel like I'm burning from the inside out, the slow, passionate sex is the closest thing I've ever had to a spiritual experience, and beneath everything is the constant hum of our connection resonating between us.

It's the best night of my fucking life.

I'm able to stay in the feeling as we lie there, talking softly until she falls asleep in my arms, and then it slowly fades away, the familiar emptiness returning. I wait until I'm sure she's asleep before I slip out of bed and head down to the basement, where I sprint on the treadmill to keep from freaking the fuck out.

It's fine. As long as she doesn't find out I'm lying, I can fix this and keep her forever. All I need to do is remove the tracker, which will make this whole problem disappear. I just need to focus on the fact that she's here, even though I'm a massive fucking asshole, and that she wants to be with me, despite the warnings of my concerned therapist, and that she *loves* me, even though I don't deserve it.

It'll all be fine.

I'll take out the tracker and tell her about it when our relationship isn't so new, like in a few years when we're married and have kids. She'll be mad at me, but she won't want to leave at that point. She'll know how happy I can make her, and she'll let me spend the rest of our lives making it up to her.

I'm not going to fuck this up again.

I *can't* fuck this up again, because I won't get another chance with her.

I don't even deserve the chance she gave me, but Alex gave it to me anyway because she's a kind, wonderful, forgiving person who I don't remotely deserve.

That's real. That's not a delusion. I know that for a fact.

45

ALEX

FRIDAY, FEBRUARY 23

Alex, 9:45 AM:
baby you need to stop

Theo, 9:46 AM:
Indulge me.

we've talked about the gifts thing

Flowers don't count.

i love you but you're crazy

I love you, too.

Last one, I swear.

The next bouquet arrives around the same time Catherine does, giant pink peonies spilling out of a rectangular glass vase. Every table in the office is covered in different bouquets of various sizes, so the florist puts the vase on my desk next to two others. Catherine comes in after the florist, looking shocked.

"The Anderson boy?" I nod. Her eyebrows raise in question, and I blush.

"He's insane. Things are going...*well*, and he's a gift-giving person." She laughs and lowers her voice in a conspiratorial tone.

"He takes after his grandfather, then. When we reviewed the estate, Dottie had an extensive list of all the gifts Robert had given her over the years, and *why* he had given her the gifts, which she was very...open about." She laughs slightly. "You probably shouldn't ask Theo if he knows the story behind the house in Yachats." She gives me an arch smile as she heads into the kitchen for coffee, exiting with one of the large homemade almond croissants I was sent to work with this morning.

"You're taking Monday off for your birthday, right?" I nod, and she gives me a sly look. "You should prepare yourself for more of this." I groan and drop my head into my hands, and Catherine laughs as she walks up to her office, passing Bailey on the stairs. Bailey looks around at all the bouquets, counting, and raises her eyebrows.

"*Another* one?" Bailey asks. I blush, pointing at my desk, and she cackles as she dips her head down to smell the peonies.

"Please take some home," I beg. "Suzie already promised to take three."

"I can take some to the nursing home after work. They'll love them."

"*Thank you.* I'd take them myself if I had a car."

Bailey barks out a laugh. "Babe, he's probably spent the money it would take to *buy* you a car."

"Yeah, well, he's being ridiculous."

"Ridiculous isn't always bad," she says, heading into the kitchen for another croissant. I look at the card sticking out of the huge bouquet of peonies on my desk and add it to the pile of cards on my desk, all of them reading the same thing:

I LOVE YOU SO FUCKING MUCH, ALEX

I smile, looking at the polaroid of Theo I've kept all this time and finally put out on my desk. It's him laughing, pulling his stupid Christmas ham out of the oven.

He's certainly ridiculous, but it's not bad at all.

***

It's raining when I get off work, and Theo is waiting for me outside my office with an umbrella. The second I lock the door, he grabs me and kisses me until I'm dizzy.

"Are we back to you showing up places like a fucking stalker?" He grins and opens the umbrella for me, pulling me down the stairs towards his car.

"Not if you don't want, but I think I get special dispensation to be a *little* over the top right now." He kisses the top of my head as he opens the car door, and I notice a few bags in the back. I look at him as he starts the car, a tiny thread of concern breaking through my good mood.

"How did you pack me a bag?" He gives me a serious look before shifting into reverse.

"It's all your stuff that was still at my house." I'm instantly relieved, and I love that I get to trust him now. I run my hand down the back of his neck, and he hums contentedly as he starts driving us out of town.

"Where are we going?"

"Yachats, for the weekend. I'm pretty much set on not letting you out of my sight until your birthday is over. We can go back to *dating* then, if you want," he says, his voice disdainful as he says the word dating.

I stare at him and consider it for a minute. It's been nice having time to myself, and I think we should still take our time, but I want *this* back.

"Maybe a middle ground?" He interlocks our fingers, pulling my hand up to kiss it, his lips warm against my skin.

"I'll give you whatever you want for as long as you want, no exceptions."

"I'm going to take you up on that tonight."

He flashes me a crooked grin. "Yeah, you fucking are."

***

"Theodore, absolutely *not*." He ignores me as he brings another bundle of gift bags in from the trunk, placing them with the rest of the pile on the dining room table. "Seriously, return *everything*." He laughs.

"I can't. I bought most of these months ago. There are only two new things."

"This is insane. You're insane."

"Sweetheart, I need you to be a little forgiving here, okay?" he says, pulling me closely, his lips grazing against my neck. "I love you, and this is how I show love." He kisses me just above my collarbone. "I'm going to make you a nice dinner while you go through these, because that's also how I show love." His lips trail up my neck as his hands grip my waist. "Then I'm going to tie you down and make you cry before I fuck your brains out, which is your *favorite* way I show love." I moan a little as he bites the soft skin just below my ear.

"I can't believe I gave you a chance," I tease.

He pulls back, his face instantly serious. "Me, either."

I lean up to kiss him, smiling at him as I pull away. "Will you be telling Dr. Mills about this development?" Theo shoots me a dirty look as he steps away and walks into the kitchen to open a bottle of wine.

"Don't mention that horrible woman to me right now. Let me be fucking happy this weekend, *please*. I'll go back to being a better, more miserable person on Tuesday, I promise." I laugh as he hands me a glass of wine before pouring one for himself. "Now go open gifts. And maybe put some of them on? Especially the lingerie." I groan and start in on the pile of gifts.

I want to say I didn't miss this, but I did, because Theo's *very* good at gifts. The bags contain an assortment of nice things I looked at in shops months ago, along with some books I want to read, some *very* nice paints and brushes, a *lot* of lingerie, some of which I change into, a pair of spiky black heels, and two small black velvet boxes.

I stare at them, freezing up.

"What the fuck are these?" Theo pops his head out of the kitchen and smiles shyly.

"Um, I bought those for your birthday, but I can't wait to give them to you. You don't wear much jewelry, and you've never really looked at it, so I had to guess. If you hate them, I'll return them, and you can pick out whatever you like." I stare at the smaller box, picking it up delicately and holding it out to him.

"Theo, is there a ring in here?" He levels me with a serious look.

"*No*. You want to go slowly, so we're going slowly. Minus this weekend, which I'm going to spend spoiling the shit out of you because it's your birthday on Monday, and you're going to fucking take it because we're *together* and *you love me*." He grins at me before glancing at the box in my hands. "That's not how I'm going to propose, by the way." I nearly choke on my wine. "Also, you're still *technically* married," he says, rolling his eyes and making a face. "For now," I hear him mutter as he ducks back into the kitchen. I shake my head at him, amused, before I turn back to the table, eyeing the velvet boxes with apprehension.

I close my eyes and take a deep breath before I pry them open to reveal a matched set of earrings and a necklace. They're minimal and elegant, large rectangular emeralds set in thin gold bezels, and I relax as I look at them. They're beautiful, and exactly my taste. With Danny, jewelry was usually an apology for hitting me, but it was always diamonds, always platinum, always something that looked gaudy to me. This is different. This is Theo being fucking insane, but not like that.

I look down at them, considering his choice.

"Emeralds?"

"Uh, yeah," he says, dragging out the vowels. "So, the first time I saw you, you were wearing this green dress, and it's always been my favorite color on you. Also, my birthday is in May, so I couldn't help it." I laugh and clasp the necklace on. He's so ridiculous. I'm getting more used to his gifts being a show of love. He was apparently raised this way, which reminds me of what Catherine said this morning.

"Baby, why did your grandparents buy this house? Catherine said not to ask you." I hear a disgusted sound coming out of the kitchen.

"Do *not* make me think about that."

"Come on, *indulge me*," I say, mimicking his low voice as I enter the kitchen. He looks at me in the jewelry and his eyes soften, his smile small and crooked.

"Do you like them?" I lean up and kiss him gently.

"I *love* them, but no more jewelry, please. There's a reason I don't wear it."

"Will you please tell me why?" I shrug, sipping my wine. I can talk to him about this stuff now. I *want* to talk to him about it now.

"In my marriage, gifts were apologies, and jewelry was the big apology. I had a *lot* of jewelry." Theo chokes and gives me a horrified look.

"*What?*"

"Yeah." He looks furious.

"*Fuck*, I wish I'd known that," he says, looking up at the ceiling. "I honestly just thought you were being stubborn or something about the gifts. Fuck, I'm so sorry, honey." I wrap my arms around his waist, lying my head against his arm.

"It's okay. I didn't tell you before because I didn't want you to know me. Now I do." He kisses the top of my head.

"I'm going to fucking kill him." Theo's voice is cold and venomous, like nothing I've heard from him before, and it sends a chill down my spine. I frown down at the chicken he's preparing.

"Please don't go back to prison. I just started thinking you should be out." He laughs.

"Oh, I'm *never* going to go back to prison. I'd starve myself to death, I hate the food so fucking much." He slips butter under the skin of the chicken he's preparing, rubbing gently.

Oh.

"Is *that* why you're weird about food?"

"I don't think liking to eat well counts as being weird about food, but not really. My parents were bad about keeping food in the house when I was a kid, so I had to just eat whatever I could find, and it usually sucked." I hold him tightly. "Whenever I visited my grandparents, there was *always* food, and it was always *good*. When they adopted me, Nana taught me how to cook, and I got super into it. Maybe I went a little overboard about it after I got out of prison, but again, I don't think I'm weird about food." I hum, pulling him closer and kissing his shoulder.

"Well, either way, you're a good cook, and I *hate* cooking." He looks down at me, curious.

"Why *do* you hate cooking so much?" I take a large sip of wine before looking at my feet.

"My dad taught me how to cook when I was a kid, and I was fine at it, but I wasn't great. After the first year of being married, Danny stopped being as nice to me and started listing out his expectations of a wife. He expected me to be his personal fucking chef and learning how to cook the way he liked came with a lot of yelling and some *gifts*. Remember Thanksgiving?" Theo stills, taking a long, deep breath.

"The first Thanksgiving we hosted was the first one I ever cooked. I'd never even had turkey for Thanksgiving, and the one I made was both raw *and* burned, somehow. We had to throw it out, and his family gave him so much shit for it, *especially* his aunt Tricia. He got drunk and told me I humiliated him, and he shoved me so hard that I broke my arm when I fell. I got a brand-new wedding ring a week later with a *big* fucking diamond, and he was super nice to me for six months." I can tell Theo's trying hard not to react, but he's so livid that he's shaking a little as he leans over and kisses my forehead softly.

"Okay," he says slowly, his voice strained. "We're *never* doing Thanksgiving again, and I'm going to break every bone in his fucking body." I pull his face down and kiss him before I lean against the counter, refilling my wine glass to the brim. I shoot him a forced, flirty smile.

"*So*, the Yachats house?" Theo eyes my glass of wine and takes a deep breath before rolling his eyes.

"*Fine*. Nana once drunkenly told me that Boss bought it for her after she 'put out' for the first time. She was very drunk, and there were *details*," he says, shuddering. "He was married at the time, so this was where they came every weekend until his divorce was finalized. That part of the story also came with details, unfortunately." He raises his eyebrows at the chicken. "They got married here the weekend after his divorce went through," he says softly, smiling a little and shooting me a quick look.

"That's sweet, but you're telling me this has always been a weekend sex house?" He grimaces and nods. "So, who else have *you* brought here?" He shrugs as he puts the chicken in the oven.

"Besides Ashley, I don't remember." I raise my eyebrows.

"You don't *remember*?" He gives me an amused look as he washes his hands.

"Honey, I came here a *lot* in college. High school, too, a little bit." I stare at him for a second, thinking.

"Theo, how many people have you slept with?" He laughs, shaking his head.

"I don't know. You're the only one that counts, though, since you're the only person I plan on fucking ever again." I blush, my whole body feeling warm as I look down into my wine and set it on the counter.

"I like the sound of that." I keep my voice almost inaudible, but I know he hears me because he freezes for a moment before he grabs me around the waist and hauls me into the living room. He's inside of me immediately, fucking me hard, but his eyes are soft every time they meet mine.

***

Theo's in the kitchen finishing dinner, and I'm stretched out on the couch, blissful and hazy, when one of the floodlights goes off. Theo walks through the living room quickly, his face and body tense, and he shakes his head at me as I sit up.

"Stay there, sweetheart." He peers out of the window next to the door before he opens the hall closet and grabs a shotgun and two rounds. I sit up, frowning at him.

"Have you always had a gun?" Theo shrugs.

"I have a few, but I keep them here since I'm on parole. Pass me the laptop?" I grab it from under the couch and hand it to him as he sits beside me. He pulls up the camera feed and watches it, frowning.

"I don't fucking like *that*," he mutters, cracking open the shotgun and loading it.

"What is it?" Theo turns the laptop towards me and replays the video. There's some quick movement in the trees, but the cameras are old, and the image is too dark and grainy to make out precisely what it is. The floodlights flare on, and the screen is white for a second as the camera adjusts. Then, it shows the front of the house and the edge of the woods lit up, but there's nothing there. I pass the laptop back and run my hand down the back of his neck.

"Baby, it's nothing. Animals always set those lights off, so it was probably just a deer who got spooked by the lights." Theo makes a displeased noise and watches the video again.

"I'm going to go check it out," he says, standing up.

"No, you're not." I grab his hand and pull him back down towards the couch, but he doesn't move. He looks towards the door, his body rigid.

"Alex, it's a security issue." I roll my eyes at him.

"Teddy, it's a fucking *deer*. Dr. Mills is going to have a field day when she finds out that you're paranoid as well as delusional." His head snaps towards me and he shoots me a dirty look. I smile at him sweetly, and he sighs, cracking open the shotgun again and pulling the rounds out. He puts the gun away in the hall closet, shooting me a wry look over his shoulder.

"You're kind of an asshole, you know that?" I grin at him and watch his face soften.

"You *just* figured that out?" He laughs as I lie back down on the couch, stretching my legs out as he walks towards me and bends down to kiss me.

"I actually figured that out when you threw a glass of wine at my head," he says, kissing me again quickly when I laugh at him.

"To be fair, you deserved it."

He shrugs. "Debatable."

I jerk my head away from him as he tries to kiss me again. "*Is* it, though?"

He flashes me a quick, sheepish grin. "Depends on who you're asking. Come on, dinner's ready."

***

"Fuck, baby," I moan, stretching my arms out in front of me as I press my hips back. "This feels so fucking good." Theo hums softly.

"Nice try. You're still not getting me to join you. I fucking *hate* yoga." I look up from my yoga mat to where he's lying on the couch reading a book.

"You're viewing this all wrong," I say, pressing onto my hands and knees. "You could be over here *helping* me stretch." Theo smirks at me.

"Sweetheart, I helped you *stretch* so much this morning that you could barely walk upstairs. You want more already?" I shake my head as he stands up quickly and I press up into a down dog, pushing my heels to the floor.

"No, you've been *helping* so much that I'm going to be in pain if we don't restrain ourselves a little bit." He snorts and sits back down, and I hear a page turn.

"Considering how fucking happy I am, I *have* been restraining myself." I laugh as I start walking my feet towards my hands.

"You're insatiable. How did Ashley deal with you being this insanely horny?" I hear his book snap shut quickly, and by the time I'm standing, he's got his arms crossed and he's obviously irritated.

"Alex, can you not ask shit like that right now? I'm having a perfect fucking weekend." I cross my arms and narrow my eyes at him, trying to decide if I want to push.

"If you answer three questions, I'll reward you for sharing."

He rolls his eyes. "You can't use sex to manipulate me."

I laugh at him as I walk towards the couch. "Yeah, I can, because it fucking *works*. Three questions and everything is on the table." His eyebrows raise slightly. "I'll be your perfect little fucktoy all night long," I whisper, leaning down and biting his lip gently, and I feel smug as I watch his pupils dilate, his gaze trained on my lips.

"*Everything* is on the table? Like, weird shit you don't know I'm into?"

"Please don't pee on me." His head kicks back as he laughs.

"*Not* my thing. Can we go get lunch before you force me to share? There's a place here with the best fish and chips on the coast." I look at him, surprised.

"You *hate* fried food." He shrugs.

"Exceptions can be made for quality. Let's go."

Theo seems to get less and less relaxed as we drive down to the restaurant and order. I grab a table in the outdoor seating area while Theo brings us beers and our number. He sits down and takes a deep breath, crossing his arms, obviously defensive.

"You want three questions? You have three holes, and I'm going to tie you up so tightly that you can't move, and then I'll take my time with each one. If I don't *like* your questions, *you* won't be coming. Those are my conditions." I raise my eyebrows at him and smirk.

"If that's what you want, I should force you to answer questions more often." He laughs a little, relaxing a bit. "What were you like with Ashley?" I lower my voice slightly. "I want to know about the stalking, too, so it all counts as one question." He groans and sips his beer.

"You're *definitely* not coming." I roll my eyes, knowing that's unlikely. "Uh, from *my* perspective, things were easy, and I was really good to her. We met at a party, I pursued the shit out of her, and then we started dating. We had a great sex life, we went on nice dates and weekend trips, I spoiled her, I was nice to her friends, I helped her study, I tried to take care of her and be who she needed. You know, boyfriend stuff." He exhales hard, looking at the table.

"From *her* perspective, I was intense and closed off. She said everything started out normal, but after I told her I loved her, I started scaring her with how I was acting. She thought I was obsessed with her, and she said I turned into an overbearing sex addict who wouldn't leave her the fuck alone for two minutes at a time." I look away from him, biting the insides of my cheeks to keep from laughing and working hard to school my face back into neutrality.

"I guess she and Kevin started fucking around that time. She said they both thought I was losing it, but neither of them knew what to do about me. The brain damage fucked up his memories, so I have no idea how Kevin felt, but he acted like nothing was different at the time. They both did, honestly. When Kevin told her I bought a ring, she said she knew she needed to *escape* me," he says, his voice hurt. He pauses as someone brings out our food, and I sip my beer, waiting until he leans closer and lowers his voice.

"Uh, I'd been mostly good about keeping my impulses in check until she broke up with me, but after that..." I raise my eyebrows, and he looks away from me, shrugging. "I just gave in. I followed her around, attended her classes, showed up at her internship, hacked her Facebook and her email, stuff like that. She blocked me, so I kept calling and texting her from different burner phones. I wanted her back, and I wanted...access to her." He shrugs again, finishing his beer quickly. "Then I learned how to pick locks so I could get into her place whenever I wanted, and *that's* when I found out about her and Kevin." I nod, thinking about my next question as I squeeze lemon juice on everything.

I should ask more about the stalking, or about Kevin, or about literally anything *other* than what I want to ask. I'm getting very hung up on one part of it, but I know it's the wrong thing to focus on. It doesn't even *matter*.

"You bought a ring?" I flush, slightly embarrassed that I asked.

He looks at me incredulously. "Yeah, Alex, of course I fucking did. I loved her, and my grandparents loved her, and all I wanted was to be with her. I would have proposed a few months into dating, but she was really practical, so I was waiting until she got accepted to med school." I nod, looking at my food and thinking for a minute while I eat.

I'm not sure how to say what I'm feeling, so I throw caution to the wind and just start talking.

"I'm glad she left you." Theo looks at me, shocked and hurt, and I raise my hands placatingly. "To be clear, I think it's super shitty that she and Kevin fucked around behind your back. You didn't deserve that. I mean, you shouldn't have stalked her or tried to kill him because of it, but still, I'm sorry it happened. And I'm sorry prison sucked, but it kind of feels like if you hadn't gone, maybe we wouldn't have...it's just, I feel like everything awful that happened to us in the past made sure that we ended up here right now, you know?" Theo freezes, huffing out a short breath.

"I'm happy we're here. Together. For real," I say quietly, smiling at him a little. My smile fades when I see his jaw is clenched and his knee is bouncing quickly, and I'm instantly worried that I've fucked up and expressed it wrong. "I'm so sorry, I didn't mean to upset you. I was just trying to...I don't know, I'm sorry." He shakes his head, and his legs tangle with mine under the table as he looks away from me, blinking quickly and running a hand over his mouth.

I reach over and squeeze his other hand, relaxing as his fingers immediately intertwine with mine and squeeze back. I wait for him to look at me again, and when he does, I lean forward across the table and kiss him, running my free hand up the side of his neck and cupping his jaw.

"I love you," I whisper against his lips before kissing him again. "You're the best person I know and you're *mine*, and you make me so happy." I kiss him again, and he makes a soft, content sound. "I mean, you're absolutely fucking *insane*, but I love it. Thank you for letting me choose you." He ducks his head down, rubbing a hand over his face.

"*Jesus*, Alex. Don't make me cry in public," he says, shooting me a tender look. I sit back down and rub my leg against his under the table.

"You can punish me when we get home, if you want?" He laughs, shaking his head down at his food before taking a bite.

"Depends on your last question." I run a fry through the tartar sauce slowly, debating.

I should ask him things he still avoids talking about, like the stalking, or his friendship with Kevin, or his mom and why she left. None of that is what I want to ask about, but I shouldn't open that door with him. It's way too soon, and he'll be a fucking nightmare about it.

I look up at him, at his adoring expression, and I let myself lean into my feelings and do what I want. Fuck it – we're in love, everything is amazing, we're having a perfect weekend, and I want him to know how I feel about him. We cracked open that door last night anyway, and I know I can ask about everything else later. I take a sip of my beer to hide my smile.

"You know I don't like diamonds, right?" I finger the necklace around my neck, zipping the pendant up and down the chain with my left hand, trying not to smile. Theo's eyes go wide, and his head cocks slightly to the side as he stares at me.

"Are we talking about this?" His voice is a low whisper, and I shake my head.

"*No*. We're being smart and going *slow*, but I just wanted to make sure we're on the same page." He laughs weakly, his smile growing wider.

"We're on the same page," he says quietly, and I can tell from the look on his face that I've ruined us going slow in any real capacity.

That's fine. I hate going slow with him, anyway. I still need him to prove he can do it if I ask him to, but I won't make him prove it forever.

"So, do I get to come when we get home?"

He gives me a wicked grin. "Oh, sweetheart, that's *all* you'll be doing today."

"You promise?"

"Fuck, yeah. Also, for future reference, I keep my promises." He and I stare at each other, our ankles interlocked under the table, and a swell of happiness fills my body.

This is perfect.

***

"You've been *such* a good girl for me," Theo coos against my neck as he finishes inside of me again, running his hands down my body, kissing me as he starts to undo the knots in the rope. I whimper in protest as he pulls out of me and helps me straighten my legs.

I don't know how long we've been in the bedroom or how many times I've come, but *everything* is sore and I'm so exhausted that I'm on the brink of passing out. The room is so soft around the edges that it's all blurring together, so I close my eyes and relax into the feeling until I'm blurring at the edges, too.

"I could do this forever," I whisper, and Theo laughs softly.

"Honey, could you even *handle* more right now? You are *so* fucked out." I grin up at him lazily as I shake my head, and he's quiet for long enough that I start to drift off. "Sweetheart, were you talking about the sex?" I shake my head again, and he sweeps me up into his arms and holds me tightly, stroking my oversensitive skin and pressing gentle kisses along my face and neck.

He doesn't say anything, but I can feel his heart pounding in his chest, and it lulls me to sleep.

***

"This is *such* bullshit. Nadya should have chosen James, because this guy fucking *sucks*. God, all these people are fucking *idiots*."

"Mmhmmm," I murmur, kissing Theo's shoulder softly. Even hours later, my body feels like jello, my mind is hazy and blissful, and everything still has a washed-out, glowy quality. I lean further into Theo's arms, delighting at getting to be so happy just sitting here and watching dumb reality TV with my perfect boyfriend after being fucked stupid.

This is what I want for the rest of my life, and I probably should have kept that to myself, but I'm not great at doing what I should with Theo. I look up to see him staring down at me, his expression adoring and almost confused.

"I can't even explain how happy you make me," he whispers.

"Makes two of us," I say quietly, and he grins, both of his faint dimples visible. I see the moment the thought crosses his mind, and he rolls his lips and works his jaw as he tries not to bring it up.

I watch with amusement as he fails.

"Can we talk about it a little bit? *Please?*" I laugh as I look back over at the laptop.

"*No,* Teddy. We're taking things slow, remember?"

"Yeah, right," he mutters.

"We *are,*" I protest. When I glance up at him, he's got a gooey, affectionate expression on his face as he sweeps my hair behind my ear, and I can't help but melt into him a little more. "We'll be dating for a while."

"Forever, ideally," he says softly.

"*Theodore,*" I warn, and he smiles at me sheepishly. I shake my head at him, turning back to the show again. "Ideally, yeah," I add very quietly.

He shuts the laptop, shoving it towards the foot of the bed before kissing me deeply. I sigh contentedly and wrap my arms around his neck as he whispers promise after promise against my skin. I let myself get swept away in the moment, in my own joy, and I start whispering soft, affectionate things I shouldn't be saying yet in between slow, deep kisses.

Fuck it, I don't care about going slow anymore.

We're on the same page, and we'll probably get to the next one much sooner than we should, but it'll all work out anyway. Things seem to work out for us, even though they shouldn't.

This kind of happiness feels impossible, but it's not. It's *real*. It's all finally real.

46

THEO

SUNDAY, FEBRUARY 25

It's three in the morning, and I should be asleep with Alex in my arms, peaceful and calm and dreaming about our future, the future we're finally on the *same fucking page* about. If I'm awake, I should be emailing the jeweler to see how long the ring I ordered on Friday will take to make, and then figuring out where and when and how I'm going to propose.

I should *not* be fighting off a panic attack and drinking whiskey like it's my fucking job.

All I wanted was one perfect weekend to ignore everything and live blissfully in the bubble of time between Alex telling me she loves me and Dr. Mills telling me something that will make me hate myself more than I already do.

I didn't think it was too much to ask to have one weekend where I get to pretend everything is perfect, to not think about what a fuckup I am, to just be happy with the woman I love.

It was all going exactly how I wanted until Alex told me how grateful she was that I did everything she asked me for.

She told me that her *trusting* me made it possible for her to choose me, and she wanted to spend the rest of her life choosing me. The second she said that, the thoughts and feelings started creeping back in.

I can't let them in, otherwise I'm going to lose my shit.

I would never resent Alex for anything, but I *really* miss my delusion right now.

I take another long swig of whiskey from the bottle, trying hard to compartmentalize. I'm already drunk, but I need to dull myself down enough that I stop thinking or feeling *anything*.

Alex's drinking problem is understandable, because it's fucking effective. Hers seems to be going away, though, and I think mine is just starting.

Once my mind is muddled enough that I can slip back into the bubble I've created around this weekend, I head back downstairs and brush my teeth as I stare at Alex's sleeping form, illuminated by the moonlight coming through the large bedroom windows. Her arm is stretched across my side of the bed, like she reached out for me after I left.

I'm still astounded by the fact that she's here, in love with me, committed to me in a way I'm almost positive I'm making up, and genuinely happy in a way she hasn't gotten to be in a long time, if ever.

If she gets to be happy, I get to be happy, at least for another two days.

***

I wake up late in an empty bed, slightly hungover. I lie there and listen to the quiet sounds of Alex doing something in the kitchen, so I slip on sweatpants and walk upstairs to make her breakfast. I stop dead when I find her waiting for me in lingerie and tall black heels, sipping her coffee and eating some toast. She smiles at me sweetly, pouring me a cup of coffee.

"Good morning." Her voice is soft and sultry, sending a wave of heat down my spine. She hands me the coffee as she pushes me back against the counter, and I stare down at her, thrilled but unsure of what's happening.

Then she gets down on her knees in front of me, looking up at me with a sly smile.

How have I never had this specific fantasy about her?

"I have a feeling it's about to be a *very* good morning," I say as I sip my coffee. Alex grins as she starts slipping my sweats down, kissing my hips as she goes, looking up at me as she drags her pretty pink tongue up the underside of my cock before she sucks me into her warm, wet, gorgeous mouth. I moan at how good she feels, and she moans back, running her hands up my body. I have to set down the cup of coffee she made me because I'm afraid I'm going to drop it.

This is the best morning of my life.

This kind of happiness feels impossible, because it *is* impossible. It's not real, but Alex doesn't need to know that, and I'm going to keep it from her as long as I can. I'll kill her husband, marry her immediately, come in her three times a day until she's pregnant, and then spend the rest of my life trying to make up for something that she doesn't even know I've done.

Nope, I'm *not* thinking about that right now.

"That's it, sweetheart, *just* like that." Alex looks up at me and moans as her fist works in concert with her mouth, and I lean my head back against the cabinets, enjoying her. She's so perfect, and she's all mine.

I know that's not how I'm supposed to think about her, but no amount of working on myself in therapy can convince me that she's not mine, especially not right now. I don't deserve this, and I don't deserve *her*, but I'm in the bubble again, so I look down at her as I run my fingers through her silky hair and grip the back of her head.

"Be a good girl and relax for me." Her eyes stay locked on mine, and she nods quickly, whimpering as I push myself deep into her throat. She gags a little, and I pull her head back, giving her a break before I push in again.

"Can you take more of me?" She makes a small sound of acquiescence, and I push in deep, keeping her there until she starts to gag harder and drool a little. When I pull her head back, she's staring up at me adoringly and swirling her tongue around the head of my cock, and I have a hard time not coming right then.

I could spend the rest of my life having mornings like this, and I'm going to do everything in my power to do that. I'll make her dinner on Tuesday, *slightly* drug her wine, and remove the tracker while she's asleep.

It's small and inserted shallowly, so I won't have to make a big incision. I've been practicing on various cuts of meat for weeks, and I've gotten the technique down well enough that it won't hurt her, she won't notice, and it won't leave a scar.

She'll never even know it was there.

I can't think about *any* of that right now. I can only think about how perfect Alex is, how in love we are, and how this is all real now. That, and how good it feels to have the woman I'm going to spend the rest of my life with sucking my cock like this first thing in the morning, moaning like it's getting her off, too.

I look down and see that she's touching herself, and heat builds at the base of my spine quickly.

"Oh, *fuck*," I say, my voice low and harsh. Alex pulls off me, smiling as she jerks me off against her lips.

"Please give it to me," she begs, and she keeps jerking me off quickly as she slips me back in her mouth, hollowing her cheeks around me. I try to hold out, but I can't, not when she's looking up at me like this, flushed and wide-eyed and begging. I swear loudly as I come, and she moans excitedly, closing her eyes as she swallows. I reach down to cup her face, pulling her off me and running my thumb over her swollen, wet lips.

"That's my perfect fucking girl," I whisper, and she blushes a deep pink.

"All yours," she says, her voice sweet and a little raspy. I look down at her, overwhelmed. She *is* mine, and she wants to keep it that way. We both do.

I'm never going to tell her about the tracker.

No, I'm *not* thinking about it.

She stands up, taller in her heels and covered in thin green lace, and leans into me, kissing me slowly. I hold her tight, gripping her ass and tasting myself on her tongue as I deepen the kiss. I pick her up, setting her on the edge of the counter and slipping her thong off before I step in between her legs.

"I'm going to take such good care of you," I whisper, and Alex looks up at me lovingly, taking my face in her hands and stroking my cheekbones.

"You do take care of me. You're so good to me, Teddy."

No, I'm not, but she doesn't need to know that, and I'm *not* thinking about it.

I loop an arm around her waist and hold her tightly, kissing her hard as I start to touch her soft, slick cunt. She loosely wraps her arms around my shoulders as I slip two fingers inside her, pulling away from the kiss and dropping her head against my shoulder. She pants into my skin as I slowly fuck her with my fingers, placing soft, open-mouthed kisses on my neck and chest.

I hold her close and take my time, loving the small, whining gasps she makes as I bring her to the edge. Once her leg starts to tense up, I back off, stilling my fingers and biting her neck gently. She whines, and I laugh when I feel her start pushing down on my shoulders.

I keep my fingers inside her as I get down on my knees for her, looking up at her for a moment. She smirks at me, her hands carding through my hair and pressing my face between her legs. I drag my tongue against her clit, sucking gently as I crook my fingers towards me, pulling out until I find the right spot and massaging her there while I alternate between sucking and flicking her clit with my tongue.

I listen to the soft whimpers she makes for me, working her until her leg tenses up next to me, and then I press a little harder, suck a little harder, bringing her closer and closer until I feel her clenching around me, her release coating my mouth and fingers as she moans out my name. When I look up at her, she's flushed, looking down at me with a smug little smile.

"Good boy," she whispers, grinning down at me. My head empties out, leaving nothing but a need to make her happy, so I bury my face between her legs again.

Making her happy is all I can think about.

I can't think about the fact that I'm still lying to her, which is the principal thing she asked me not to do. I can't think about the fact that I'm still *kind of* stalking her, which is also something she asked me not to do. I can't think about the fact that she'll leave me if I tell her the truth, or the fact that I'm so desperate to tell her the truth because I love her.

I'd lose my fucking mind if I thought about any of that, and there's plenty of time to do that when we get back to Astoria.

I get one fucking weekend to be happy, so I work hard to lock all of it away and have a perfect weekend with my perfect girlfriend who loves the version of me she thinks she's getting. We're back to sharing a fantasy, except this time it's real for *her*, and I do my best to lose myself in it, too.

I push down the thoughts, and I fantasize about her letting me put all the cameras back up and follow her around again, about getting full access to her at all times the way I want. I fantasize about moving her out of her shitty apartment and into my huge, depressing house and making it a *home* with her. I fantasize about killing her husband and giving her every part of her life back, and her turning around and sharing it all with me. I fantasize about marrying her, about building a life with her, about having a family with her, about getting to spoil the shit out of a kid with my eyes and her freckles and then getting to spoil the shit out of her for making me so fucking happy. I fantasize about spending the rest of my life making her happy in any way I can.

I ignore that I'm fantasizing about everything I want but can't have, just like I'm ignoring everything else this weekend. I ignore that I've been trying to memorize the open looks of adoration she's giving me because I know I'll never see them again if she finds out what I've done. I ignore that Dr. Mills is probably right when she implies that I'm a manipulative fuck who's abusing Alex. It isn't what she says, but I can tell it's what she thinks.

I especially ignore the fact that I know, deep down, taking the tracker out of Alex isn't going to fix *anything*.

I force myself to stay in the bubble and have another perfect day with her. I take her hiking, and we go tide pooling afterward. We make love and lie in bed, talking and joking and holding each other for hours, and I drink myself to sleep in the middle of the night again. I'm on the brink of losing my shit, so I resolve to keep her in a hazy, slightly dissociated state with sex on her birthday.

She'll love it, and she'll be too zoned out to notice that I'm stressed.

The next morning, I spend a long time with my head between her legs until she wakes up in the middle of an orgasm, and then I pin her down and fuck her mercilessly. She's blissed out and dreamy when I make her French toast and give her more gifts, and then I tie her up on the couch and shove a vibrator between her legs as I touch and kiss every inch of her body, forcing her to come until she's a tired, crying mess.

She's barely coherent when I take her to the spa, and she practically floats out two hours later because she's so relaxed and happy and, most importantly, *thoughtless*.

I drive us home that afternoon, reveling in her dreamy, giddy happiness and pushing down the feelings that get harder to ignore the closer we get to home.

We go to her place, and I put away all the gifts I have finally badgered her into accepting before I give her soft, slow head. I make her come over and over to keep her distracted, because I'm barely holding it together.

Afterward, I draw her a bath, pour her a glass of wine, and leave her to relax while I make her dinner and a cake, trying not to hyperventilate. I dote on her and cling to the happiness I can when she tells me she loves dinner, she loves the cake, and she loves me. I open a bottle of champagne, get her a little drunk, and give her a small, wrapped box with a set of my house keys in it.

She's so ecstatic she fucking *cries*, and I fight off a panic attack.

She goes to bed happy and spoiled and relaxed, having noticed nothing wrong with me, and I lay in bed with her in my arms, all the thoughts and feelings I've been fighting off for days worming their way back into my brain and body. I pull Alex closer as a black hole opens inside of me, sucking away all the happiness from this weekend.

None of it was real in the first place.

I've fucking ruined everything, *again*, except this time I've ruined my life instead of hers.

All the therapy has ruined any chance of me being happy. Alex wanted me to try hard in therapy, and I wanted her to love me, so I tried really fucking hard for her, and I wish I hadn't. Enough of the shit I've begrudgingly learned has gotten through to me to know that, by her own definition, Alex *can't* love me back.

I wouldn't have known or cared when I was in my delusion, but now I fucking care. Now I don't want her to love me back unless it's real, unless I've actually earned it.

She believes she loves me because she thought she had the *option* to, but she didn't. I've worked so fucking hard to give her back control of her life, but I didn't give up *everything,* and I lied to her about it. I've had so many opportunities to tell her, but I kept lying to her because I wanted her to give me a chance, and then because I didn't want to ruin my chance, and now because I want to keep her.

She told me she wanted to choose me, and I didn't believe she would, but I was wrong. Based on how absolutely in love with me she thinks she is, I'm starting to suspect that she still would have given me a shot if I'd told her about the tracker right after Christmas.

I wish I could tell her about it now, beg for forgiveness, tell her that I never checked her location, never *kind of, sort of, technically* stalked her after she asked me not to, but that would be another lie.

I'm so fucking tired of lying to her.

I stupidly thought I could just fix it by taking the tracker out, but that won't fix it. I can take it out and pretend that everything is fine, but no matter what, I'll always know that she can't truly love me back. I told her at one point that I'd take whatever she was offering, but that feels wrong to me now.

I know I can make her happy, I know she can love me, I know this can work for real, I know that she can want me the way I want her, and I want *that* so badly it hurts.

I wouldn't be in this situation if I'd just killed myself when I had the motivation, which I probably should have done. It would have saved us both a lot of pain, because she'll be fucking devastated if she finds out.

I look down at Alex's relaxed, sleeping face, and I think about how incandescently happy she was this weekend. For a second, I wonder if I could deal with hating myself forever just to keep making her that happy, but I know I'm too fucking selfish for that.

I want to be that happy, too.

I slip out of bed, making sure she doesn't wake up as I change into running clothes, and I lean in the doorway for a moment to watch her sleep, feeling a deep ache of longing as I stare at her. She's such a wonderful person, and I'm a miserable, selfish fucking bastard.

I need to make an impossible choice, and I have to do it tonight. I can either lie and keep her forever, or I can tell her the truth and lose her forever.

I can't stand the idea of spending a life with her knowing she can't love me back, but I can't lose her.

I have no idea what to do.

I'm fucking trapped.

47

DANNY

The alert hits my phone just as I get home from work with a 96% match, but I'm not getting my hopes up. It wouldn't be the first time the facial recognition software has given me a false match, and the alerts have been coming in less frequently for almost a year.

The first few times it found matches, it *was* her, mostly on security cameras. I flew out to look for her anywhere she popped up, and I contacted the local police to help me. She was careful, even changing her clothes a few times to try and hide, but there are so many goddamn cameras everywhere now that it was easy to track her as far as Seattle before she completely disappeared.

I don't want to give up on her, but I'm almost positive my poor Bunny's dead.

I shower before I pour myself a drink and head to my office, exhausted from work and expecting disappointment. When the software gives me a photo from a website in Oregon, and the girl in the picture is in a Pilates class at a recreation center, I pay attention. I set my drink down and lean in closer, unsure if it's her. Her hair and body are different from Bunny's, but I try not to get hopeful when I look closely at her face.

That honestly might be her. She's got the same nose, the same big eyes, and the same shaped lips. I look up at the painting of her as a little girl holding the white bunny, and I realize the expression on the woman's face is eerily similar.

Oh my god, I think I found her.

How the *fuck* did she disappear like that?

I call Captain Rodriguez to let him know that I found a promising lead on my wife, and I put in an immediate time off request. He approves it because he's a good guy, even though he probably thinks it's another dead end.

People don't want to say it to my face, but everyone thinks she's dead.

At first, when I thought something bad happened to her, I was a fucking wreck, but I didn't tell anyone once I finally noticed the money was gone and realized she'd run away.

I still don't understand *why* she ran from me.

Sure, we got into a fight the night before, but couples fight. She was being so disrespectful, drunk and screaming at me about ruining her life, calling me all sorts of horrible things, and I couldn't help but lose my temper with her.

I was a jackass, maybe, but she needed to be put in her place.

Bunny has always been so understanding when I lose my temper, but not this time. I don't know what changed, but it's time for her to come home. I need to show her that I can change for her, that I can be better.

I stare up at the painting of her as a little girl, sweet and lost the way she was when I found her. She needed me to take care of her then, and she needs me to take care of her now, *better* care of her.

Once I find her, Bunny's never going to run away from me again.

***

I grab my gun and my surveillance camera, pack a bag, and spend the entire redeye to Portland trying to keep my emotions in check. I'm fucking furious that she ran away from me, but I'm so relieved she's alive.

I was such a piece of shit that night, but I still don't know why she hasn't come home.

Maybe she's afraid that I won't take her back or something.

Bunny's always been so fragile and irrational, but she deserves me to be better, so I'm going to try to be understanding and figure out how to fix things with her. We can try that bullshit couples counseling my partner Marquez's wife forced him into.

Maybe Bunny would appreciate that.

It's early, so I get through the airport and get my rental car quickly, navigating to the small coastal town's recreation center. Bunny likes routine, so she'll be there for the Pilates class today. I'll find her, tail her for a while, see what she's been doing, and then I'll figure out the right way to make her come home with me.

At twelve-eleven, I see her walk up to the building quickly, her gym bag slung over her shoulder and a large vase of flowers in her arms. After all this time, seeing her is like getting hit with a freight train.

God, I didn't realize how much I missed her.

She looks *terrible*. She's obviously been depressed, the way she was that first year we were married, because she's completely let herself go. She looks like a completely different person now, and I don't like it. It's going to take her a lot of time and effort to get her back to herself, but she can do that when we get home.

Fuck, what are we going to tell people when we get home?

I chain smoke while I wait for the class to be over, trying to calm myself down. I'm still shocked that she's not dead. Once I see her leave, I get back in my car, following her at a distance. She's walking quickly, texting occasionally before finally reaching a small house and climbing the stairs with a bounce in her step.

She doesn't seem depressed.

I park two houses down and get out of the car, keeping a ball cap pulled down over my eyes and walking past the house quickly, seeing a sign that shows the house is a law office.

Does Bunny have a fucking *job*?

She's never had to work a day in her life because I'm a good husband, and I've always provided a comfortable and easy life for her, but I guess she'd have to work without me. She'll be suspicious if the office gets a call with a Boston area code, so I hide my number when I call the firm, and she picks up immediately.

"Cairn and Reed, Alex speaking," she chirps over the phone. "Hello?" I hang up quickly, grabbing my pack of cigarettes with shaking hands and lighting up.

She's using a fake name, she looks different enough that cameras haven't caught her before this, and she found a job where she got hired without using her legal name or social security number.

Alice didn't just run, she's been *hiding* from me.

How would she even know *how* to do all of this? I checked her phone, her tablet, and her laptop, but there was nothing in her search history that would have helped her disappear like this. Why would she do this to me over one stupid fight? I know it was bad, but she's making me feel like a fucking monster. My temper starts to rise the more I think about it.

I want to know just what the fuck she's been up to out here.

I light another cigarette and walk around the block, grabbing a cup of coffee once I'm done smoking and walking past her office again, keeping my face turned away. The house is raised off the street, so I can't see inside, but that doesn't mean she can't see out. It starts raining hard, so I get back in the car and wait, only occasionally leaving to smoke under the shade of a tree.

Around four-fifty, I see her leaving her office with a few massive bouquets in her arms, a plump woman with a mass of black curls following her, also carrying bouquets.

What's with all the flowers? Did someone die?

She helps the woman load them into her car that's parked right across the street from mine, but Alice doesn't notice me. I look closely at her hands and almost bolt out of the car.

She's not wearing her fucking wedding ring.

Has Alice lost her goddamn fucking *mind*? She's still my wife. I watch as she hugs the other woman and hurries back inside to get out of the rain, and I barely notice as a car turns down the street and parks in a spot the woman just vacated.

ARIANA RIVERS

I only clock it because the tall guy who gets out of the old silver hatchback walks up the stairs to the door and leans against the wall, checking his phone. My hands tense on the steering wheel.

This better not be what I think it is.

Alice comes out a few minutes later in a long, puffy coat, and he grabs her aggressively and bends down to kiss her. My blood starts to boil as she leans into him, wrapping her arms around his neck and pulling him down towards her to deepen the kiss, her hands running through his hair.

Alice isn't that affectionate.

I start my car and tail them, noting down his license plate. I assume they're going back to one of their places, but I end up following them down the coast for hours. I don't know what's going on here, but I'm starting to get really fucking angry. Her running was one thing, but the fact that she hasn't come back home to me because she's too busy whoring herself out is fucking unacceptable.

I wait for them as they stop at a small grocery store, sickened by how casually possessive of my wife this asshole seems, draping his arm around her shoulders as they cross the small parking lot.

I follow them as they head up a hill into a neighborhood with nice houses, passing the driveway they turn down and parking my car out of sight up the road. I whip out my work laptop and link it to my phone's hotspot to search for the guy's license plate, and my blood runs cold when the search comes back.

The fucker is a violent offender who went to prison for stalking and assault.

I can't believe Alice is this fucking stupid, but it's why she's always needed me to protect her. She has no idea what she's gotten herself into, and she needs me to save her.

She probably doesn't even know what sick fucks like this do to women.

I grab my gun before I sneak down the long driveway, keeping to the shadows. I notice floodlight cameras on every corner of the house, so I stay in the tree line, navigating slowly until I can get a good view of the main room through the enormous windows that make up the side and back of the house.

There's a pile of gift bags on the dining room table, expensive gifts strewn all over the table, and I can see the two of them talking in the kitchen. When I get closer, I see the stupid bitch is in nothing but strappy, lacy lingerie.

She's a literal whore.

I watch him look at her, his face focused and predatory, before he aggressively picks her up around the waist. She screams as he hauls her into the living room, throwing her down on the chaise of the couch and undoing his pants quickly. He wraps one of his hands around her throat and shoves into her hard, and she screams again.

I reach for the gun concealed under my shirt, flipping the safety off. He's going to kill her, and no one treats my dumb whore of a wife like that.

I've got my gun cocked and aimed at him when I hear her moaning loudly, and I freeze, focusing on Alice. There must be a window open somewhere, because I can kind of make out what they're saying if I listen hard enough.

"Yeah? Is this what you want?" I can hear her moan something out that sounds like *more,* and he laughs. "That's my fucking girl."

What the *fuck*?

I still have my gun aimed at him, but I don't pull the trigger as I watch her run her hands up and down his arms before he grabs her legs and hauls them over his shoulders, slamming into her and making her scream again. I can hear a low, constant stream of words from her, but her voice is quiet enough that I can only make out a few here and there between the sounds he's making.

"...*baby, please*...more...I need...*there*...harder..."

He pushes her knees down towards her face, bending over her and fucking her brutally, and she starts losing her mind, moaning out his name and clawing at his chest.

I feel myself get hard as I watch her arch off the couch, watch her body starting to shake as she comes, and it takes me a second to realize I've *never* seen her like this.

Why haven't I ever seen her like this?

She pushes him off, and he barks out a sharp laugh, kissing her quickly as he pulls out of her and stands up.

"Fuck, you're perfect. Come here." She sits up, and he grips a fist of her hair and shoves his cock so far down her throat that she starts gagging. She *hates* that, I know that for a fact, so I'm shocked when I hear her moan. My hands tense around my gun as I watch her blow him enthusiastically, watch her whine and drool and look up at him as he comes down her throat, watch as she smiles up at him sweetly afterward.

My gun starts shaking in my hands as I watch my wife give this asshole something I've always wanted from her.

Alice is sweet, but she's a frigid fucking bitch. She's *always* hated sex. The first time I fucked her, she cried like a baby the whole time and didn't even appreciate how good I was to her. I knew she was a virgin, so I spent months trying to show her what she should do for me, but she's never done it the way I want her to. She learned quickly to let me fuck her whenever I want, but she's never been enthusiastic, she's never wanted to try anything new, and she wants it over with as fast as possible.

I fuck her mouth whenever she owes me an apology, mostly because she hates it so much that she tries everything to get out of it.

I've assumed for years that I'd just married someone who needed to be babied, that she couldn't ever give me what I wanted in bed, and I'd have to pay to get what I wanted occasionally. I don't want to cheat on her, but she's forced me into it. It's always sucked having a wife who can't please me, no matter how rich or pretty she is.

Apparently, she *can* please me, she just doesn't fucking *want* to.

I'm her goddamn husband, and she owes me everything I want from her. Instead, she abandoned me after I spent almost a decade taking care of her, and now she's whoring herself out to a violent criminal.

She even seems to think it's better than what she has at home.

"I love you so fucking much, sweetheart." I freeze, and scorching heat rises in my chest and the back of my neck.

It's one thing that he's fucking my stupid whore of a wife, but this is beyond unacceptable. She's *my* wife, which she seems to have forgotten, because she looks up at him with a sweet smile and blushes. Her mouth moves, and I can't hear her voice, but based on the dumb, smug look he gets on his face as he walks away, she says it back.

I'm going to kill that worthless fucking cunt.

By the time I can finally stop my hands from shaking, he's in the kitchen and she's laid out on the couch, and I don't have a good aim on either of them. I head for the front door, ready to kill both of them.

Just as I step out of the tree line, the floodlight cameras go off.

I jump back into the trees, crouching and aiming for the front door. He doesn't come out, but as I make my way back slowly to the windows, I can see he's got a shotgun in his hands.

I lean against a tree and holster my gun as I watch the two of them. The floodlights shocked me out of being angry for long enough that I can start to think about this rationally. If I kill Alice, I can't take her home to Boston and make her spend the rest of her life apologizing to me for running away.

After watching her, that's what I fucking want.

I know I can get it, too, because she's sensitive and she's always been so easy to tell what to do. I just need to be sweet to her, to save her from herself and show her why she needs me, why she should come back home to Boston and let me take care of her again, and she will.

Then, I'll spend the rest of my life getting the love and respect I deserve from her.

I wait until they're busy eating dinner to head back to my car, heading down into the tiny town they're staying in and renting a hotel room. I start looking into the guy, who's a rich trust fund fuck. Alice is such a spoiled little princess that it makes sense she'd go for someone with money, and guys like that always get away with murder.

When I get access to the crime scene photos, I realize just how right I am.

It'll be so easy to show her why she should run away from this guy and back into my arms. I'm going to be her fucking hero, and she'll realize what a mistake she's made and want to come home and make it up to me.

***

I trail them all weekend, watch her and take photos of her, watch all the things I'm going to make her do for me when we get home, getting

447

progressively angrier every time I hear the dumb fucking whore tell him she loves him.

They spend the weekend mostly fucking, hiking, and eating, and I follow them at a distance when they leave the house wearing a ball cap and a hoodie, but neither of them seem to notice me.

I see him packing their bags the day before her birthday, so I use the hotel's printer to print out the crime scene photos and the photos of them.

Alice and I are going to have a long fucking talk before she even gets on a plane back home.

I trail them back to some old shithole house in Astoria, and once I realize he's not leaving for the night, I rent a secluded cabin close by, unpacking and setting up to show her what a fucking idiot she is.

I head back to her place early enough to catch her as she goes to work, but he drives her to work like a fucking chauffeur, so I park near her office and wait.

He's finally gone, for now, and she'll come out eventually.

Around noon, I watch her running down the street, the skirt of her dress flapping around her legs underneath her long jacket. I start to follow her, but I can't be seen chasing her down the street, so I turn back halfway and smoke while I wait.

She'll come back to the office at some point.

I only have to wait impatiently for about ten minutes before I see her sprinting back in my direction. She's going to pass right by me, but she doesn't see me at all. She's never been that aware of her surroundings, which is just another reason why she needs me to take care of her.

From now on, she'll be taking good care of me, too.

48

ALEX

TUESDAY, FEBRUARY 27

I wake up to an empty bed and quiet sounds coming from the kitchen, but when I check the time on my phone, it's too early for either of us to be awake. I walk into the kitchen, half asleep and confused to find Theo in running clothes, sweaty and pacing quickly in the small space while he waits for coffee to brew.

"Teddy?" His head snaps up towards me, and he looks pained to see me.

"Go back to bed, sweetheart," he says, his voice soft. I rub my eyes, trying to wake up.

"Why are you up? It's three in the morning." He runs his hands through his hair.

"Um, I'm just stressed about today." He gives me a tight frown and pours himself a cup of coffee. "I don't want to deal with any of it."

"Deal with what?" He shakes his head, not looking at me.

"I'm going to tell Dr. Mills that we're together and that you love me, and she's probably going to tell me I'm a piece of shit, and she's going to be right," he says quietly.

I step closer to him, but he shrinks away from me a little, and I'm instantly more awake and concerned. I know therapy is hard for him, but

I don't know how he went from ecstatically happy back to this version of himself overnight.

"Teddy, *please* don't think like that. You're a wonderful person, okay? That's real." He chokes out a harsh laugh and shoots me a disparaging look.

"*You're* fucking delusional if you think that." I sigh, knowing I need to be gentle with him when he's like this. I step into him, crowding him against the wall and running my hands over his shoulders, keeping my voice low.

"Baby, I love you, but you've got horrible self-esteem. I don't think you see yourself as clearly as I do." He makes a pained face and looks up at the ceiling.

"No, I see myself pretty clearly now because of all the goddamn therapy," he says, his voice bitter. "Dr. Mills is probably right that we shouldn't be together," he mutters.

"You can't let her opinion about our relationship matter more than mine, okay?" He scoffs and shakes his head, shooting me an irritated look.

"Last time I checked, *you* don't think we should be together, either," he snaps, and I step back from him and cross my arms.

"I thought I made it obvious this weekend how much I want to be with you," I say quietly, trying not to sound as hurt as I feel. Theo crosses his arms and sighs harshly, looking at his feet and nodding faintly.

"Yeah, you did." I step close to him again, running my hands up and down his arms.

"Is this seriously all because you don't like your therapist? This came out of nowhere." He laughs humorlessly.

"Honey, you have no fucking idea." Maybe I don't. This is the first time I've seen him before a therapy appointment, and maybe he always gets this worked up.

"You don't have to tell her about us." He looks down at me, shocked.

"Are you telling me to lie to her?"

I shrug. "You do already, so what's one more lie? You only need to be honest with me." He winces slightly and looks away from me.

"I know," he says quietly. I lean up to kiss him, but he turns away and runs his hands through his hair. I pull back from him, shocked.

I don't think Theo's *ever* rejected affection before.

"I'm going to go on a run," he says and tries to walk away, but I grab him around the waist and hold him closely.

"I need you to come back to bed."

He shakes his head. "I'm not tired."

"You don't need to be tired to come back to bed," I say softly, rubbing his back. "I don't like seeing you upset. Let me take care of you." He sighs hard and nods but starts giving me that look like he's trying to memorize me, which makes me concerned.

His mood switched overnight for some reason, and I want to switch it back. I try to make him feel better, and sex always works with Theo, but not this time. He gets *very* intense and presses me down into the mattress, fucking me slowly, his expression serious.

"I'm so sorry," he says quietly, "I'm so sorry about everything." I stare up at him, unsure how to react.

"Baby -" He shakes his head, and I stop speaking.

"I love you, Alex. You're the best thing in my life, and I don't deserve you."

"Theo, what -" He cuts me off with a bruising kiss.

"I'm going to fix it," he mutters quickly against my lips, his thrusts picking up. "I'll spend the rest of my fucking life making it up to you if you let me, I *promise*," he whispers.

I have no idea how to respond to anything he's saying, so I nod and try not to let him see how anxious he's making me. He pulls me impossibly tighter as I start to come, and he just keeps saying *please* again and again until he's coming with me.

Afterward, he rolls off me and doesn't hold me at all, he just lies there and covers his face with his hands, his whole body so tense he's shaking. I watch him for a moment, horrified and concerned when I realize he's either crying or trying hard not to cry.

"Teddy?" He doesn't respond and I have *no* idea what to do, so I just wrap him in my arms and kiss his hands and wrists and face and hair. "Everything's okay. I love you," I whisper into his ear. "I'm so lucky to have you." He laughs bitterly.

"You have no fucking idea what you're talking about," he snaps at me, and I unwind from him immediately, lying next to him and staring up at the ceiling, confused and extremely hurt.

After a minute, he pulls me close and apologizes profusely, holding me so tightly it's almost uncomfortable.

I look into his conflicted, upset face, and for just a second, I wonder if he's hiding something from me, but I know that's unlikely. The only reason we're together now is because we're honest with each other, and I trust him not to hide anything from me.

At this point, I doubt he could tell me anything that would push me away.

***

Alex, 10:01 AM:

let me know when you get there

Theo, 11:51 AM:

Here.

feeling any better?

Fuck no.

I start zipping the emerald pendant along the chain as I stare down at my phone, worried about him. We barely slept after the weird, upsetting sex, and he was stressed and clingy all morning.

There's got to be something I can do to make him feel better.

let me make you dinner tonight

> **You don't have to do that.**

> please let me take care of you

> **I don't deserve you.**

> teddy stop it

> you're mine and you're the best and i love you

> **I love you, too.**

There we go. I knew that would work. He'll come home from therapy stressed out, I'll go over after work and make him dinner, he'll bitch and moan about how much he hates his therapist, and I'll spend the rest of the night doing my best to reassure him that I love him in every way I can think of.

We need to talk about his self-esteem at some point, but right now I'll just focus on taking care of him.

I'll even see if I can take a late lunch and call him after he gets out of therapy so I can spend the hour calming him down. I'm sure that will make him feel a little better.

I forgot to sign up for my workout class today anyway, so I can do that.

I open my web browser and navigate to the rec center website. I got an email that they recently redid it, and now I can sign up for classes for an entire week ahead of time instead of the day of, which is much more convenient. I navigate to the reservations page and stop dead.

There's a photo of a Pilates class on the website, and I'm clearly visible in the photo.

I start to panic. Who took this? When did they take it? How did I not notice? I won't even let Theo take pictures of me with his phone, which was the whole point of the polaroids he has hung up all over the fridge. How long has it been up? When did they redo the website?

Fuck, this is bad.

I take a few deep breaths and email the rec center, asking them to take it down immediately. It's fine. I'll go down there right now and talk to the administrator, and it'll be fine. You can't even see all my face, just *most* of it, but my hair is different, and I've gained weight since I left Boston, so I don't look like Alice Murphy at all.

Everything is going to be fine.

I change out of my boots into the pair of running shoes I keep under my desk and run down to the rec center. It's only a fifteen-minute walk, but I need to deal with this *right now*. I wonder if Theo could take the photo down if they won't. He's good enough with computers that he might be able to hack their website.

I reach for my phone and realize I left everything at the office in my hurry to get out the door.

I get to the rec center two minutes later and ask to speak to the office administrator, but she's out sick for the day. I ask to speak to anyone who can edit the website, but most of the employees are retirees and they contracted it out. I ask them how long ago they updated the website, and my blood runs cold when they tell me it's been up for a week.

Oh, fuck.

That's long enough that Danny's probably seen it, which means he's either here or he will be soon. We were out of town this weekend, so if he's already here, he hasn't found me yet. That's good, because if he finds out about Theo, he'll go off the deep end. He's always been so fucking jealous, even worse than Theo. I open my mouth to ask to use the rec center phone before realizing I don't know Theo's phone number, so I turn and jog back toward my office.

I'm trying to think if I've noticed anything off in the last week when I stop dead in the middle of the sidewalk.

The floodlight camera.

What if that wasn't a deer?

No, no, no.

I take off for my office in a dead sprint. I don't notice the people as I shove past them, I don't notice the car that stops short and honks at me as I run in front of it, I don't notice that it starts raining, I don't notice anything around me – the only important thing right now is me getting back to the office.

I need to get to my phone and tell Theo what's happening. He's going to freak the fuck out, but he'll get home in a few hours, and then I'll be safe. Everyone is at the office today, so I'll let them know what's happening, and they'll keep me safe until Theo gets back from Salem.

They won't let anything bad happen to me, and Theo sure as hell won't let anything bad happen to me. He loves me, he's protective, he has enough money that I'm sure he can do *something* to keep Danny the fuck away from me, and if worse comes to worst, he can be pretty fucking violent.

Danny won't be able to get to me if Theo's around.

I'm two blocks away from the office when someone steps right out in front of me, and I'm sprinting so fast that I can't stop myself from slamming right into him. He stumbles back from the impact, and I lose my balance and start to fall, my feet slipping on the wet concrete, but he wraps his arms around me tightly and sets me back on my feet.

"Sorry, sorry, sorry!" I don't look at him as I start to push away from him, but I freeze when his arms tighten around me, and I go cold when I smell cigarette smoke and Old Spice.

Oh, no.

"Where are you running to, Alice?" Panic rushes through me as I look up into Danny's concerned, angry face. I start shaking my head quickly. There's no fucking way this is happening to me.

I was so close.

"You've gotten yourself into a bad situation, but I'm here now, babe. It's time for you to come home." I can tell he's trying to be calm and sweet, using that patronizing voice he uses when he thinks he can talk me into doing something without yelling first.

Usually, that voice makes me acquiesce immediately, but not this time.

"*No.*" He looks surprised as I start struggling against him, trying to kick and hit him. "Get the fuck off me!" I'm screaming loudly, hoping someone can hear me. Danny claps a hand over my mouth and starts pulling me up a driveway towards a car, growling into my ear furiously.

"Jesus Christ, Alice, what the fuck is wrong with you?" I start screaming behind his hand, shaking my head and trying to bite him. He swears and releases my body for just a second before he pushes a gun against the back of my head, and I freeze.

"Hands behind your back. Don't make a sound." I don't know what to do, but I hear him cock the gun, so I put my arms back. He releases my mouth and ratchets handcuffs around my wrists so tightly they bite into my skin.

"I hate that you're making me do this. We both know I'm not this guy," he says as he grabs a fistful of my hair roughly and yanks me towards the car. He opens the back door and shoves me in like I'm being arrested, hitting my head against the car on the way down.

Fucking bastard.

He gets in and starts driving, heading out of town on a road I'm not familiar with. I look out the car window, trying to figure out where we're going, but I have no idea where he's taking me. We're quiet for a while, and I can tell he's working himself up.

Fuck, I shouldn't have fought back. Fighting back is only going to make this worse for me.

"I don't understand why you did this to me," Danny says, his voice hurt.

Great – he's kidnapped me *and* he's playing the victim.

"I was scared, Daniel," I say slowly, using his full name the way I do when I'm trying to make him listen to me. "You pointed a gun at me and threatened to kill me."

"It's your fault I even got that angry," he says petulantly, and I roll my eyes because I know he can't see me. I keep my voice low and soothing when I talk to him.

"I was telling you how I felt. I'm allowed to have feelings."

"Bullshit," he spits. "You were drunk, and you were saying insane things to me." I grimace. I said *a lot* of things to him that I shouldn't have. "I'm a good guy, Alice. I didn't ruin your life, and I didn't fucking take advantage of you, I took *care* of you."

He's more delusional than Theo ever was.

"You took care of yourself," I mutter before I can stop myself.

"What the fuck did you just say?" Shit, I can't talk back like this with Danny.

"Nothing." Danny's quiet for a few minutes, and I can tell he's trying to calm down, but the air in the car is tense, and I start curling in on myself, making myself smaller.

I remember this. I *hate* this.

"You know, I'm surprised you could disappear like this. You're not that smart." *Because I play dumb to placate you, you fucking prick*, I think bitterly.

"I saw something like it in a movie." He shakes his head, exhaling hard.

"Yeah, well, you shouldn't have done it," he says, and I can hear how furious he is. "You should have just let me apologize to you, and everything could have gone back to normal." That's exactly what I was running from, but I can't tell him that.

"You're right," I say quietly, trying to appease him.

We're quiet for the rest of the drive, but I can feel him getting angrier and angrier in the front seat. I breathe and tell myself it'll all be okay. I can handle Danny. I did it for nine years, I can do it again until Theo shows up, or until I can run again.

We pull down a long dirt road and park in front of a tiny little red cabin along a small river, and I get a bad feeling. I need to be really fucking careful with him if we're going to be so far away from other people.

"What is this place?" He parks the car and turns around to glare at me. I force myself to smile at him and I watch him relax a little. Good, okay, I can still handle him.

"I thought we should have some time together before going home, so I picked something nice for you." I can hear how tight his voice is, but I know he likes to provide, so I lean in towards him to de-escalate.

"That sounds nice, Danny. Thank you," I say, trying to sound sincere and smile at him more. It works, because he seems less angry when he gets out of the car.

He doesn't uncuff me, but he pulls me out of the car more gently and leads me inside, sitting me down on a couch. He looks down at me, his thick arms folded across his chest, and it's obvious he's barely restraining his anger.

"We need to talk about something, Alice."

Shit, he hasn't called me Bunny once.

This is really fucking bad.

Danny sits down next to me, his hand gripping my knee hard. When I look up at him, his face is that same sort of anger tempered with concern from earlier. "You've been gone for a year. Why haven't you come home?" I take a deep breath and nod, knowing I need to placate him.

"I wanted to come home, but I was scared you'd be mad. It's been so hard without you." It should be the right thing to say, but it's not. I watch rage flash over his face, and I know it's coming a second before he slaps the back of my head hard, causing me to pitch forward and my vision to swim for a second. He launches off the couch and disappears for a second, placing a thick folder on the coffee table when he comes back, like he's about to interrogate me.

When he flips open the folder to a photo of Theo and I tangled up together, I know I'm fucked. Theo's face isn't visible, but the overwhelming love is evident in my expression as I look at him.

My body goes ice cold.

"I know how *hard* it's been for you," Danny hisses, and I close my eyes and try not to panic. "Don't you fucking lie to me and say you wanted to come home. You've been out here whoring around for a *year*."

"Dan-"

"Shut up. You're so fucking stupid, you know that? You don't know anything about the world, and you've put yourself in so much danger without me to protect you. The guy you've been spreading your legs for is a dangerous fucking creep, and you couldn't even tell." His face shifts into more concern than anger, and I know I've got a way out.

He figured out who Theo is, and I just need to play dumb and act grateful.

I stay quiet, trying to look confused, and Danny removes the photo of us to show a mugshot of a college-aged Theo with short hair, a black eye, and a cut lip. I gasp on purpose, but all I feel is a pang of pity as I look at how young and miserable Theo looks in the photo.

"He's a fucking *criminal*, Alice. He almost killed his college roommate just because he wanted to fuck the guy's girlfriend. He stalked her and everything." Danny pulls the mugshot away to reveal a close-up photo of someone from the shoulders up, their battered face peeking out between a neck brace and the slightly bloody bandages wrapped around their head.

It has to be Kevin, but you'd never be able to tell.

My eyes widen as I lean forward to look at the photo. Seeing what Theo did is so different from just knowing about it. Kevin's face is covered in deep cuts and purple and black bruising, his eyes are swollen completely shut, his nose is obviously broken beneath a cast, and his lips are split so badly they need stitches.

Looking at this, I'm positive I saved Ben's life.

"The poor kid has permanent brain damage, and that's not even the worst part. This fucking guy killed his dad when he was a *kid!* Look at this shit," Danny spits, pulling the photo of Kevin away to reveal a crime scene photo of Theo's dad dead on a living room floor, blood pooling on the carpet beneath his head. There's a handgun next to his dad's head, the handle coated in blood.

My gasp is involuntary this time.

I lean farther forward and stare at the photo for a minute, feeling nauseous. Theo *severely* downplayed what happened. He might have shot his dad in the head, but I can't even tell if it's true. His dad's face is collapsed in on itself, brain matter splattered in the pool of blood and along the handle of the gun.

Theo said he lost it, but he was just a kid. I didn't realize he could have done something like *this*.

Realization washes over me as I look at the photo, followed by an enormous amount of pity and anger. Watching him do that is probably why his mom abandoned him. I wonder if his grandparents saw these photos, if this is why they pushed him so hard to be normal.

I'm so absorbed in the photo that I almost forget Danny is there until he starts talking again.

"It's horrifying, right? You had no idea you were whoring yourself out to a fucking psychopath, did you?" Danny's voice has gone from frustrated to furious, and he pulls away the photo of Theo's dad to reveal more pictures of us in Yachats. Danny flips through them slowly, laying them out on the coffee table so I can look at all of them.

There are so many photos of us, but they're only of us having sex. Most of them are in the living room or dining room, but Danny even climbed down the hill and got photos of us in the bedroom.

Did he seriously watch us all weekend?

I get why Danny's so angry now.

He has to be aware that I've never enjoyed sex like this with him, never looked at him like this. My eye catches a photo of Theo and I in the kitchen, me on my knees and his hand in my hair. I'm sure Danny was pissed watching that – I've never once blown him without him asking for it. When I see how Theo's looking down at me, possessive and adoring and so obviously in love with me, I lose focus for a second and smile a little.

It's a fucking mistake.

Danny grabs my shoulders and I'm suddenly looking at him, his pale blue eyes wide and his face turning red.

"What the *fuck* is wrong with you, Alice? Have you lost your fucking mind? He's a goddamn *murderer*." I swallow hard and nod, remembering that I need to pretend that I didn't know that Theo had done those things.

"I'm just...shocked. I'm so stupid. Thank you for saving me from him, Danny." The words are bitter in my mouth as I force them out, but they have the intended effect. Danny relaxes a little and sighs angrily, shaking his head at me as he looks down at the photos.

"I don't know what the fuck is wrong with you, I really don't. You ran away from me, you hid from me, you cheated on me, and you're acting like it's fucking *nothing*, like I'm fucking nothing to you. You don't even seem sorry that you did this to me."

Oh, *of course*. That's why we're here. He's going to make me apologize.

"I'm *so* sorry, Daniel," I say slowly, trying to seem sincere. "I want to make it up to you." I'm grateful he doesn't have Theo's preternatural ability to know when I'm lying.

He huffs out a breath and nods. "You've really fucked up here, but I'm going to try to forgive you. You'll have to work hard to make it up to me, Bunny, but I'll let you." I'm Bunny again, which means I'm calming him down. I just need to keep him calm.

"Thank you. I'm so sorry, pumpkin. I'll do anything to earn your forgiveness." When he looks at me, I can tell he believes me, and I struggle not to flinch when he pets my hair.

"God, you're lucky I love you so much, babe. You're coming home with me, and we'll get back to normal." I nod eagerly, knowing I'm not going to Boston. Theo's going to show up, just like he always does. He's not just my boyfriend, he's my fucking *stalker*, and he's going to find me. All I need to do is run out the clock until he can get home from Salem.

"You're right, Danny. I'm so lucky to have you. When are we going home?"

"We'll go tomorrow morning. You're not leaving anything you want here, anyway. It's not like you love this guy or anything," he says slowly, and he looks at me sharply, his jaw set. "*Right?*"

My mouth goes dry. Danny's not stupid, and he's exceptionally observant when he wants to be, so there's no way he missed how Theo and I are with each other. He might have even heard us. I just need to lie to him and tell him that I don't love Theo. I open my mouth, trying to make myself say it, but nothing comes out except a soft rasp of air.

My eyes widen in surprise and fear.

I can't say it.

Danny goes very still, his face turning redder and redder.

"Tell me you're not fucking serious." I shake my head hard, but he knows I'm lying now. His eyes go wide, and his lip curls in anger as he punches me in the face. My nose snaps, and I scream as searing pain radiates out from the center of my face. I taste my own blood as it runs into my mouth, and I start crying as my nose throbs and stings.

"You stupid, worthless fucking *bitch*!"

Anger boils in my veins. I know getting angry with Danny is dangerous, but I can't help it. It doesn't matter, anyway, because Theo's going to be *furious* when he gets here and sees that I'm hurt.

That's not going to end well for Danny.

"My boyfriend's going to fucking kill you," I spit out at him, and he laughs harshly, getting in my face.

"Your *boyfriend* doesn't know where you are, dipshit," he spits back. It takes me a second to realize that he's right, and freezing numbness starts creeping up the back of my neck.

Theo *doesn't* know where I am.

He wanted our relationship to be real, which meant no more stalking, so he can't find me anymore. I still think of him as my stalker, but he's just my normal boyfriend who *doesn't* stalk me now.

How could I forget that?

Oh, shit.

I'll be back in Boston for a while before Theo can get to me, so I need to be much more careful with Danny than I have been. I just have to get through this the way I used to.

Minute by minute, hour by hour, day by day.

49

THEO

"What I'm hearing you say is that you started this new version of your relationship with a serious breach of Alex's trust. Is that correct?" I nod once, running my hands through my hair and looking at the clock instead of at Dr. Mills. I don't know why I'm telling her about this situation. Maybe I'm just trying to punish myself.

I certainly fucking deserve it.

"Are you being the partner you want to be for Alex?" I shake my head slowly. "Do you think Alex deserves to be lied to and manipulated like this?" I drop my head into my hands and stare down at my boots, shame coursing through me.

I'm *definitely* trying to punish myself.

"No, but I can fix it," I grit out.

"How do you propose doing that?" My knee starts bouncing quickly as I think about how I have to take the tracker out tonight and how I know it won't fix *anything*.

I still don't know what to fucking do.

"I'll figure it out. I can fix it, I *know* I can fix it. It's all going to work out." I don't bother looking at her.

We both know I'm lying for my benefit, not hers.

"Theodore," she asks hesitantly, "can I ask you if you think you're capable of loving Alex?" I snap my head up and glare at her.

"How fucking *dare* you?" Dr. Mills frowns and holds up her hands in a placating gesture.

"I'm not questioning your *feelings* for Alex, I'm asking if you think you have a genuine understanding of what love is," she says, her voice calm and gentle.

"What the fuck kind of question is that? Of course I do." She blinks and purses her lips, and anger courses through me.

"Are you familiar with bell hooks at all?" I shake my head, and Dr. Mills's eyebrows raise slightly, as if to indicate she's not surprised. "She proposed a definition of love that goes beyond sex and desire – one that's based in care, respect, trust, and honesty. Importantly, she makes the point that love and abuse can't coexist. She said that most people will cling to a false notion of love that makes abuse acceptable, because embracing a definition of love without abuse would mean people may need to accept that love wasn't present in their families." My knee bounces faster as I stare at Dr. Mills, her words ricocheting around in my brain. "What do you think about that?" She watches me patiently as I process what she's saying.

I get angrier the longer I think about it.

"What the fuck are you trying to say to me?" Dr. Mills sighs a little and leans forward in her chair, speaking gently.

"From what you've told me, I'm not sure you had real love modeled to you, so I'm not sure you know what it feels like." I'm instantly nauseous and much angrier. "I know you care very deeply for Alex, but do you think you can love her by the definition I've provided?"

"I *do* love Alex," I snap.

"You said earlier that, by her own definition, Alex *can't* love you because you're lying to her and manipulating her, right? How is the inverse not true?" Panic tightens every muscle in my body.

"You're fucking wrong." Actually, she *might* have a point, and I hate her for it.

"Do you think Alex wants to be in another relationship where she isn't treated well?"

"Don't you dare compare me to her piece of shit husband," I spit at her. "I'm not a pedophile, or a cop, or a wifebeater. All I did was *lie* to her."

Among *lots* of other things.

"I think you're missing my point, Theodore. Don't you think Alex's husband believed he loved her? I'm sure he tried to fix things with her at one point or another." I shoot her a warning look, and she gives me a piteous frown. "People don't always want to acknowledge the way they abuse others, especially if they believe they love them." My eyes widen, and Dr. Mills raises her eyebrows at me and says nothing.

I stare at her for a long moment, a low, angry buzzing starting in the back of my brain, the edges of my vision getting red.

Oh, *shit*. I need to get out of here, *right now.*

I shoot up out of my chair and grab my coat.

"Theodore, please sit down." I take a step towards her, bending down quickly and getting in her face. Dr. Mills leans back in her chair, her eyes widening in fear.

"*Fuck. You.*" I storm out of the room before I lose my shit. I won't do that, no matter how much I hate her.

I'm only this angry because she has a point.

I throw myself into the car and try hard to keep myself from having a panic attack, try to regulate my breathing, try to figure out what the fuck I'm supposed to do now.

Goddammit, I know what I have to do.

Dr. Mills might have a point, but she's fucking wrong about me. She has no idea how much I love Alex. All I want is to make her happy, and to do that, I have to give her back all her options, which is what I should have done in the first place.

I'm going to go home, pull her out of work, tell her about the tracker, take it out, relentlessly apologize, and fucking beg her to stay. She'll probably never forgive me, but I love her enough to tell her the truth, and I'm miserable enough about lying to her that killing myself will be a fucking relief if she leaves me.

Still, she might forgive me. She might even understand why I lied in the first place and give me another chance. I don't deserve it, and I don't deserve *her*, but maybe she sees it differently. She spent all morning telling me how much she loves me and how wonderful she thinks I am.

She's the fucking delusional one now, but that might work in my favor here.

I call Alex the second I'm on the road, but she's not answering because she's at her stupid fucking Pilates class.

I know she'll be done soon, but I keep calling her anyway, texting her between unanswered calls, getting progressively more upset the longer she doesn't respond.

I need to talk to her, need to hear her voice, need to tell her I love her and hear her say it back one more time before I ruin everything.

Theo, 12:35 PM:

Sweetheart, please answer the phone.

Theo, 12:39 PM:

I need to talk to you, Alex.

Theo, 12:42 PM:

I love you so fucking much.

Theo, 12:45 PM:

Honey, please pick up.

Theo, 12:48 PM:

Call me back as soon as you can.

Theo, 12:51 PM:

Sweetie, I know Pilates is over.

Theo, 12:57 PM:

Alexandria Marie Shearer, answer your god-damn phone.

Theo, 1:02 PM:

Sorry, I'm upset. Please pick up.

Theo, 1:06 PM:

Are you okay?

Theo, 1:09 PM:

Alex?

By one-fifteen, Alex still hasn't called me back or answered any of my texts, and I'm getting increasingly nervous. I call her five more times, but I keep getting her voicemail. I call the office several times and get the office voicemail, and I start to lose it.

I wish I still had those fucking cameras, because I just need to see that she's alright. I think about checking the tracker, but Dr. Mills' words are still bouncing around in my brain.

I'm not going to check it.

I need to control myself for once in my fucking life.

I can prove to Alex that I can love her however she needs, no matter how wrong it feels to me. I have to give her the option to *actually* love me, and if I'm extremely fucking lucky, she might still want to.

I struggle to focus on my breathing, but all that goes to shit when I get a call from Catherine fifteen minutes later. I answer the phone, and she starts talking before I can.

"Theo, have you seen Alex?"

"I've been in Salem. What the fuck is going on?" I hear her swear softly.

"She's been gone since noon, and all her things are here. Normally, she's back around one, and we're getting worried." Panic races through me.

"I'm coming back right now. I'll be there as soon as I can, okay?"

I know Alex's phone is at the office, but I call her anyway before I look back at our texts. There's nothing to indicate something's wrong. I call the hospital, but no one matches her description. I call the police station, but I get nothing from them. I call the rec center, but no one even answers.

My thumb hovers over the tracking app, but I stop myself. I don't need to check it. I won't have it after today, and I can handle this situation without it.

I drive as fast as I can, but it still takes me an hour, and I'm panicking when I run into Alex's office and see Catherine, Suzie, and Bailey all in the front room, their faces nervous.

"*Where the fuck is she?*" Suzie startles at my tone, but I can't help it.

"She never came back," she says somberly. My mind starts spinning, and for one very brief second, I wonder if she ran from me.

My hand twitches towards my phone.

"Can I look at her desk?" Suzie nods, and I rush over and look closely. There's a cold cup of coffee, a small stack of cards from the flowers I sent her on Friday, a polaroid of me and the Christmas ham, half a muffin, and her phone with fifty-seven missed calls from me. The heeled boots she wore this morning are under her desk, and her running shoes are gone, but she left her gym bag and purse.

This doesn't make any goddamn sense. *Did* she run from me?

I open her desktop, and fear hits me like a freight train.

There's a photo of her online.

Danny.

"*MOTHERFUCKER!*" I scream, hurling the coffee cup across the room. It shatters against the wall, and Suzie flinches, making a terrified whimper. "Sorry! Fuck, I'm so sorry," I say as I frantically look through Alex's inbox. I see an outgoing email to the rec center begging them to take down the photo at 11:57 AM.

Alex *just* found out about this, so she probably went down there to ask them to take it down. I look through the website quickly and see it was updated a week ago, and my blood starts boiling. I exhale hard, running my hands through my hair, pacing rapidly as I think.

"Theo?" I ignore Catherine.

How long has he been here? It can't have been more than a few days, and we were out of town this weekend, so maybe he doesn't know anything about her life here yet. Nothing weird has happened in the last week, so that means he's probably just –

Wait.

"Theo, what's going on?" I barely hear Bailey because I'm thinking about the floodlight camera that went off in Yachats this weekend.

Oh, shit.

I drag my hands over my face and try not to throw something else. Danny knowing Alex is here is one thing, but him knowing about us is another.

"It's her husband," I choke out. "He found her." Catherine wraps her arms around Suzie, and Bailey lets out a strangled gasp. I rush for the door, but Bailey gets in my way, standing right in front of me and looking like she's going to cry.

"*Wait!* Shouldn't we call the cops?" I can feel my temper flaring.

"Fuck, no, the cops won't help her. *He's* a cop, and they stick together." I reach for the door, but Bailey is still there, blocking me from leaving. "Bailey, I need to go," I grit out.

"Where are you going?"

"I'm going to go get her, so I need you to move." She doesn't, and my hands are shaking from the effort it takes to restrain myself from shoving her out of the way.

She's getting in between me and Alex.

"How are you even going to find her? I think we should -" Fuck this, I'm done being nice. I lean down quickly, getting in Bailey's face as I reach around her and grab the door handle.

"*Get out of my fucking way,*" I snarl at her, but my voice sounds wrong to me, too venomous and cold. Bailey's eyes widen with fear, and she scrambles away from me as I throw the door open and sprint out of the office.

I pull out my phone and open the tracking software as I get in my car.

Alex is close, twenty minutes away down the Youngs River, but I know I can make that drive in half the time. I start speeding, constantly checking my phone, but Alex's location isn't moving. She went missing between twelve and one, which means she's been there for at least an hour, maybe closer to two.

Danny's dead either way, but he better not have fucking hurt her.

This is all my fault. I can't believe I fucked up this badly. I didn't want to let Alex out of my sight this morning, and I should have paid attention to that. I should have taken more precautions to protect her, namely killing Danny the second I wanted to. I should have checked the tracker the second she didn't answer the phone.

The fucking tracker.

Lying about it was the right thing to do.

Fuck everything Dr. Mills said to me today. Honestly, fuck everything Dr. Mills has *ever* said to me. She's a fucking idiot, and I *never* should listened to any of her bullshit in the first place. I never should have let her get in my head or make me doubt myself, especially not when it comes to Alex.

I did everything for a reason, even if I didn't understand it at the time. I listened to my fucking impulses, and they were right, *again*, because Alex and I are connected. I *never* should have tried to convince myself that we weren't connected.

Not that I tried that hard.

I'm not sorry about anything I did anymore. I was right to do *all* of it. Every impulse I've ever had about Alex feels completely rational and entirely justified now. Even my delusion feels justified, because I was absolutely right about us. Honestly, the delusion is kind of *how* we got together, so it served a purpose.

Tight knots of guilt inside of me start to loosen and unwind as I realize that I'm not the awful person I thought I was.

Me stalking Alex isn't wrong, or crazy, or abusive.

It's how I show love.

Fuck trying to be a different, better person to convince Alex to love me. She loves me anyway and she needs me exactly how I am, which she's about to realize. I know she'll understand everything when I explain it to her, which I'll do right after I kill Danny.

I'm going to find her, I'm going to save her, I'm going to keep that tracker in her, and I'm never letting her out of my fucking sight again. Everything is going back to the way it was. I'm putting back all the cameras, all the trackers, everything. Fuck it, I'm adding more. She can be angry with me if she wants, but it's not like she's going anywhere. We'll get back to where we are right now, even if it takes us years. I'll spend the rest of my life begging her to forgive me if I have to.

I'll be able to, because she'll be alive.

Unlike Danny, who will be *very* fucking dead.

I'm two minutes away from her when I realize I don't have anything with me that I can use to kill him. Not a knife, not a gun, not a screwdriver, absolutely nothing.

Whatever, fuck it. I'll kill him with my bare hands if I have to.

50

ALEX

The force of the blow to the side of my head sends white dots swirling across my vision, and one of my ears feels like it's going to explode.

"You're *my* fucking wife, you stupid cunt! You love *me*. You need to remember how good I am to you, even though you don't fucking deserve it." I keep my head down and nod, forcing myself to play along instead of screaming at him.

"You're right. I'm sorry."

"You're *sorry*? Then it's time for you to apologize." Oh, my god, is he fucking serious? He is, apparently, because he stands in front of me and starts undoing his pants, and I can see he's already hard.

I wish Theo were here to beat the shit out of him.

"None of the half-ass bullshit I normally get from you. You're going to make it good." I look up at him and see how angry he is, how resentful, how excited he is to make me do this for him.

He's so fucking pathetic.

I roll my eyes at him before I can stop myself, and he slaps me again. My head snaps to the side, my broken nose stinging and starting to bleed again.

"Don't you fucking disrespect me," he spits at me. I nod my head and steel myself for what I know is coming. Danny grabs a fistful of my hair, but he doesn't do it correctly and it hurts. I gasp in pain, and he shoves his cock into my open mouth. I can taste the blood from my broken nose start to mix in with the saliva as he starts to use me.

I close my eyes and focus on breathing. I just need to get through this for a few days. We'll go back to Boston tomorrow, and then Theo will show up. Knowing him, he's already freaking out that I'm not answering my phone. I'm sure the girls at the office will call him when I don't come back, and he'll figure out what happened and start driving to Boston immediately. He might even get there before us.

Danny starts screaming at me, berating me for what a stupid fuck up I am. That was the worst part in the past because I believed what he was saying. Now, I don't listen to him – I just breathe and zone out and try to get through it, but it's hard because he's being so much rougher than usual. He keeps pulling my head back and slapping me, and I can't help but start crying from how bad my nose hurts, and he hits me for that, too.

He grips my throat so hard that I can barely breathe, fisting my hair with his other hand and pushing in as far as he can, holding me there so long that I start gagging too hard. He pulls me off him and I lean forward to vomit, blood and saliva and bile pooling on the floor beneath me.

When I'm done, he keeps going.

Danny's always been an absolute bastard when he makes me do this, and it's always been a punishment, but this time is different. He's not using it to get off at all. He's *only* using it to punish me, and he's making a point to hurt me. I breathe and focus on how much I hate him, and when he finally comes, all I can think about is how fucking stupid he sounds and how disgusting his cum tastes.

Danny yanks hard on my hair and starts criticizing me for not doing a good enough job, but I don't look at him and I bite my tongue to not snap back.

If Theo wants to kill Danny, I'm not going to stop him.

Fuck it, maybe I'll kill him myself. He has to sleep sometime.

Danny's still yelling at me, working himself up and telling me what a piece of shit I am in every possible way he can think of. I try hard to ignore what he's saying, but he knows me well enough that he's starting to hit on some of my insecurities. When my constant stream of apologies starts feeling less like lies, I get furious.

I like myself now, and I refuse to let him manipulate me like this. I deserve so much fucking better than that. He's the terrible fucking person here, not me, and I'm not listening to a word coming out of his mouth anymore. He keeps yelling and berating me, but I stop responding.

Fuck him.

"...isn't that right, *Bunny*?" I wasn't listening to what he was saying, so I don't know the correct answer. I default to what I usually do and just nod, but that's the wrong choice.

He grabs me by the throat and throws me onto the floor, and I scream as I feel my shoulder pull out of the socket and the handcuffs cut into my wrists. Everything seems too sharply in focus from all the pain, and I can't pull away from my body, no matter how hard I try. He kicks me in the stomach hard enough to knock the wind out of me, and I struggle to take a breath, curling into a ball.

"Stupid fucking worthless *cunt*." I'm gasping, trying to breathe, and I hear a small metallic sound before he shoves me on my back. I look up and see his face is red with anger, his blue eyes are cold and flat, and he's got his pocketknife in his hands. I scream, and he backhands me hard enough that my vision swims.

"Shut the fuck up." He takes the knife and starts slicing off my jacket and dress, cutting me with the knife as he goes. I try not to scream or cry, clenching my sore jaw as hard as I can to let out as little sound as possible, but I can't help whimpering in pain.

Danny keeps dragging the knife over my skin, nicking me and slicing into me as he cuts my clothes off. Once he's got my clothes cut to pieces and pulled off me, he tears the necklace off and rips the earrings out of my ears, calling me a whore as he does.

He's too angry right now, and I need to calm him down.

"Pumpkin, listen to me, okay?" My voice is shaky and weak, but I start talking quickly. "I'm *so* sorry. I *love* you so much, and I never should have run away. I'm so stupid, and I don't know what's wrong with me, but I was wrong to cheat on you and *I'm sorry*. You don't need to do any of this, okay? We can go back home, and everything can go back to normal, and I'll do my best to make it up to you. Let's just go home, okay? We can go to the airport right now. I want to go home and make it up to you. I'll do whatever you want. *Please.*"

Danny looks down at me, his face disgusted, and I panic because I can tell he's not buying a fucking thing I'm saying. I've never seen him this angry in my life, not even when he pointed that gun at me.

"You're goddamn right you're never running away from me again. I'm going to put you in your fucking place." I eye the knife in Danny's hand with terror and start to push away from him, my feet scrabbling on the floor, but he pins me down by the throat. "I don't want to do this, Alice, but you've given me no choice."

"Danny, *no,*" I choke out. "Please don't do this, Danny, I won't leave, I sw-" I get cut off by my own scream as he plunges the knife deep into my outer thigh, dragging it down a little. He pulls it out and stabs me again and again, and the edges of my vision start to go black as fire radiates from my thigh. The pain is so bad that I can't even cry, I can only scream. Danny yanks the knife out and walks away, and the shock finally numbs me a little bit, so I struggle to breathe through the pain and nausea as I force myself to look down at my thigh.

There's so much blood.

Danny comes back in with a first aid kit, and I watch him press a large gauze pad to my thigh and loosely bandage it. By the time he's done, the wrap is already turning red.

I think that's too much blood.

"Danny, I need to go to the hospital," I beg, and I look up at him. His eyes are narrowed at me, and his cruel, satisfied expression sends a chill down my spine.

"You're not going anywhere, Alice."

"*Please,*" I choke out, crying harder. "Let me go. Don't do this. I won't say anything."

"You're goddamn right you won't." Danny grabs a rag from his back pocket and jams it into my mouth, and I scream as he pulls some tape from the coffee table and winds it around my head. I'm still crying, and breathing is harder with the blood clogging up my nose, and I feel like I'm starting to suffocate. I turn my head to the side and try hard to stop sobbing and slow my breathing.

"I'm tired of hearing you cry like a fucking baby," Danny spits before kicking me in the side. Something snaps, and then I'm screaming through the gag and crying and trying not to vomit or pass out from the pain. He stands up and pulls his belt off, and I flinch as he doubles it up in his hand.

"I tried to be good to you and take care of you, but you fucking ruined that. This is what you fucking deserve." He grips the belt tight in his hand and brings it down across the side of my head, and I scream. He pulls his arm back and brings the belt down hard across the stab wound on my thigh, and I go limp as my vision goes black for a minute. He pushes me onto my back with his foot and brings the belt down over my chest, and everything is so overwhelming and painful that I start to feel dizzy.

I forgot how much the belt hurts, and Danny keeps reminding me. I start to lose feeling as the shock sets in, leaving me clearheaded enough to realize I'm not making it back to Boston.

I can't believe loving Theo is what's going to get me killed. I think I could have survived if I'd lied. They're just words, and I should have been able to say them, but I couldn't fucking do it. The one time in my life I truly *needed* to lie, and I couldn't.

Not about that.

I know there's no way for Theo to find me, but in the back of my mind, I still thought he'd appear out of nowhere. I know he didn't mean to break his promise to always show up, and I know he would have if he'd had a way.

I wish he still had a way.

Danny grabs me by my dislocated arm and yanks hard, dragging me backward. I'm too dizzy and in too much pain to even scream, and I watch with confusion as I leave a trail of blood behind me. I look down at my leg in horror and realize I've already bled through the bandage.

That *is* too much blood.

Danny picks me up and throws me on a bed, and I moan in agony as I land hard on my wrists, feeling something in my other shoulder tear. I'm in so much pain that it's all blending together, and the shock is blurring out and dulling everything into one constant thrum of pain through my body.

Danny rips my underwear down my legs and grabs my knees, shoving my legs open. I try to pull them together, but he's already kneeling between them and undoing his pants. He babbles as he jerks himself off, using that harsh, rapid tone of voice he uses when he's about to do something I know I'll hate.

"You're such a stupid fucking cunt. You're so fucking pathetic, you're not fit to be my fucking wife anymore. You humiliated me, you stole my fucking money, and you whored yourself out to that piece of shit. You wanna be a goddamn dirty fucking *whore*, Alice? I'll treat you like one, don't you fucking worry. I saw how he treated you. You like it rough? You have no idea how rough I can be. I'm finally gonna give you what you fucking deserve." Danny's hand grips my throat, and I start to choke as he pushes down on my windpipe, and then he's on top of me.

No.

I fucking *refuse* to have this be the last thing I experience before I die.

My mind finally pulls away from my body as he forces his way inside of me, and I go somewhere *else*.

It's not the numb, grey state I remember living in after my parents died. It's not the cold, staticky zoning out I felt anytime Danny got angry and started yelling. It's not the buzzy, confused way I feel when I'm too upset to handle something. It's not the hazy, pleasurable floating outside of my body feeling that Theo gives me.

This is different.

This is *terrifying*.

It's a painful shrinking, an excruciating feeling of smallness, and it feels like I'm falling down, down, down into a deeper part of myself than I knew existed. I'm lucid, but nothing makes sense. I can see something above me, and I know it's Danny's face, but it's just a vague jumble of colors and shapes. I can hear something, and I know it's Danny yelling at me, but I can't distinguish what he's saying. My body can feel pain, but I'm not connected to my body, which is getting number by the second anyway.

I know what's happening to me, but I can't process it.

The only thing I can process right now is that I'm going to die, and I'm pushed farther inside of myself as a wave of hopelessness hits me.

I don't want to die.

Maybe Danny was always going to kill me, but I really thought I'd gotten away from him.

I really thought everything was going to be okay.

I ran to the other end of the country and rebuilt myself, built a life out of *nothing*. I built something imperfect, maybe, but it's mine and I love it.

I *loved* it, I guess.

I loved this small, beautiful town. I loved my tiny, shitty, freezing apartment that I covered in my art. I loved my friends, who I was finally feeling closer to. I loved the women I worked with and how they sort of became my family. I loved my job, my routine, my structure, and my color-coded planner covered in red ink. I loved my sweet, damaged, slightly delusional ex-stalker of a boyfriend who almost ruined my life.

Fucking *Theo*.

I hope he knows he was the best choice I made, besides leaving Boston.

I'm going to miss making choices.

Before, I'd always let other people tell me how to be, what to do, and how to live. Here, *everything* was a choice I got to make. There were confines to the choices, maybe, but I got to make them all the same.

I didn't realize that's what life was supposed to be – a series of choices you made for yourself until you built something that fit you.

I wish I would have known that earlier.

I don't know what it would have changed, but it might have changed something. Maybe I never would have let Danny in. Maybe I would have accepted help earlier. Maybe I would have run sooner. Maybe nothing would have changed, but I still would have known I could have lived differently.

God, I wish I'd known I could have been as happy as I was this weekend. That's what my life was going to be moving forward, and if that little bit is all I got, it was fucking worth it.

I just wanted so much more.

I don't know what happens next, or even what I *think* happens next, but I hope I get to see my parents again. I hope they're not disappointed that I never made anything of myself the way they wanted. Maybe they'll be able to appreciate that I made something *for* myself instead. Something small, nothing impressive, but something all mine nonetheless.

I hope they'll appreciate that I was happy and in love before I died.

Somewhere far above me, I can feel my body getting weaker, and I know I'm going to be gone soon. I let that knowledge push me to drift farther down inside of myself, allowing myself to shrink smaller and smaller as I go.

I let go of the fear, the anger, the helplessness, the pain, the resentment, all of it. I don't have space for anything but the love, and I hold on to that as long as I can.

That's the only thing I want to take with me.

That's the only thing that's still mine.

51

THEO

I drive past the small turnoff twice before I see it. Danny will hear me if I drive up to the house, so I slam my car into park and sprint up the long dirt road.

I've never run a faster mile in my fucking life.

I slow down to catch my breath when I see the small, well-kept cabin sitting along the river, a shiny rental car parked out front. I need to be smart about this. I need to make sure Alex is safe and get her out of here before I fucking kill him.

I stay low as I approach the cabin and slowly try the handle, but the front door is locked. I peer through the living room window and panic races through me. There's a bunch of scattered photos, a discarded first aid kit, some duct tape, and a small pool of fresh blood on the floor with a trail leading away from it.

Oh, *fuck*.

I need to get her out of here, *now*.

I notice a door in the kitchen visible from the living room, so I keep low and walk around the side of the small cabin quickly. I slowly turn the handle of the back door, closing my eyes briefly and sighing in relief because it's unlocked.

Alex and I *have* to be connected, because there's no other way I'd be this fucking lucky.

I leave the door open a fraction of an inch and go scope out the other rooms first. I need to know where they are before I go in, and I need to see if he's got a gun.

I duck low, keeping under the windows except to peek in the rooms. The small back bedroom has an open suitcase, a camera, a laptop, and an empty holster. Shit, of course he has his gun *on* him. I round the corner, peering into the empty bathroom as I sneak toward the other bedroom window. I can hear muffled sounds through the wall and raise my head just enough to look inside.

I freeze, and my head empties out, everything replaced by a deafening, furious buzzing as I see Alex's pale, naked body on the bed.

Her arms are tied beneath her, and her shoulder looks pulled out of the socket. There's tape around her mouth, and it's covered with blood from her nose, which looks broken. She's got finger-shaped bruises starting to appear on her arms and throat, and huge bruises starting to blossom over her stomach and ribs. Thick red welts and long, irregular cuts are strewn all over her body, and she's got a soaked, bloody bandage wrapped around her mid-thigh. The bed beneath her leg is dark with blood, and Danny's on top of her, her limp body moving with the impact of him. Her eyes are open, staring blankly at the ceiling, but she's not reacting. She's *so* pale, and her skin has a sickly grey pallor.

My heart stops beating, the world stops turning, and time freezes.

I'm too fucking late.

He killed her.

She's dead.

The panic in my body transforms into something icy and horrible as I turn around and head for the back door. This is so different from anything I've felt before. All I see is red, all I can feel is fury, but I'm entirely present and completely in control.

I know that I need to be quiet, and I know I have time, so I do everything carefully.

I enter the cabin quietly and slip a kitchen knife from the block before I head towards the front bedroom. My control wavers when I see them again through the open door, but I'm clear headed enough to notice his gun is on the bedside table. I can't let him get close to it, so I go slowly, but my control starts slipping as I hear how much he's enjoying himself.

He's taken so much from her. He ruined her life, then he took it, and he's still fucking taking from her.

I'm going to enjoy taking everything from him.

I tighten my grip on the knife and hang on to the last threads of my fading control as I approach him from behind. I just need to get a little closer, and then I'm going to rip this motherfucker's guts out.

"Stupid - fucking - dead - bitch," he says, punctuating each word with a thrust. He hauls off and slaps her, and her head falls to the side with no resistance.

There's no control after that.

By the time hears me, I'm already shoving the knife deep into his side, twisting it as much as I can. He starts to scream, and I rip the knife out and pull him off her, throwing him back into the wall and stabbing whatever I can reach. He yells in pain, blocking me and hitting me hard as he tries to fight me off. I register the impact of his fists and feel something snap in my side, but I can't feel any pain, so I keep stabbing him.

He's slightly taller than I am, larger and definitely stronger, but none of that matters.

He has something to lose. I don't.

He's trying to grab me, but he's getting weaker, and his hands are slick with blood, so he can't get a good grip. His blood is getting on my hands, and the knife almost slips from my grasp at one point as he blocks my stab. The momentary distraction of me regripping the knife gives him an opening to punch me in the face, and my nose breaks as my head snaps back. Danny bodychecks me into the bed, scrambling away from me, and I fall onto Alex's injured leg.

For a fraction of a second, I'm grateful she can't feel any pain.

I launch off the bed and rush after him as he grabs his gun, but I've got the knife lodged in his throat before he can take aim. His eyes go wide, and he starts gasping out these horrible, wet sounds as he falls to the floor. I follow him down and rip the knife out of his throat right before I feel the impact of something tearing through my left shoulder and my left side.

Oh, *right*.

The gun.

I drop the knife and wrench the gun out of his hand and shoot him until it's empty, then I bring the butt of the gun down on his ugly fucking face. I smash the gun into his face twice more, then throw it to the ground and grab his head with both hands, picking it up and bashing it into the floor, throwing my whole weight into it. My left arm isn't working that well, so I'm mostly using my right, but he's not fighting me anymore.

I don't know when he stops moving, but I can't stop moving.

I pick up his head and slam it into the floor again and again until it cracks open, and then I keep fucking going. What's in my hands starts to get less solid and harder to hold, and the pool of blood beneath us keeps getting bigger, but it's only when a jagged piece of bone slices my palm open that I'm able to stop, and only because it cuts so deeply that my hand becomes hard to use.

I drop what's left of his head onto the floor, vaguely aware that I'm exhausted and in pain, but it doesn't matter.

Nothing matters.

As I stare down at what used to be Danny, the buzzing inside my skull starts to fade as the reality of the situation sets in.

Alex is gone. She's just...*dead*. I can't fucking fix that.

A black hole opens in my stomach and my fury is replaced with despair. It's my fault she's dead. I fucked up and got here too late. I didn't do enough to care of her, to *protect* her, and she got fucking tortured to death because of it. This is all my fault. I failed her.

I struggle to my feet, looking down at Danny's annihilated face.

At least I did *that* right.

I close my eyes and take a shaking breath. I don't want to look at Alex and see how badly I let her get hurt, but I can't leave her on the bed like this, tied up and fucking abused. She's mine and I still need to take care of her, even if she's not there anymore.

I force myself to look at her, and my body involuntarily convulses in horror. Alex's body is limp on the bed, her head turned towards me, her wide eyes looking towards Danny's corpse.

I'm feeling some of the pain now, and it's excruciating, but it's nothing compared to this.

I don't want this to be the way I remember her. I want to remember the way she looked at me this weekend, how she looked when she felt happy and loved and cared for. That's what she deserved, not *this*. I reach for her slowly, hating that Danny's blood is even touching her as I gently turn her face up towards me and brush the hair away from her eyes.

I can feel the faintest hum of connection between us, but I know it's just my brain playing tricks on me because I don't want to accept that she's gone.

"Sweetheart, please wake up," I beg softly. I shake her shoulder gently, but there's no response at all. This can't be fucking happening. Alex has always been *such* a liar, so maybe this is just another lie she's telling. I press my fingers to her neck gently, and I sob when I don't feel anything.

Why can't *this* be a fucking delusion?

"Come on, honey, wake up." I want her to be alive more than I've ever wanted anything, so I press harder against the delicate column of her throat. I know I'm being stupid, but I just want her back.

Deep beneath my fingers, I feel a faint, sluggish pulse.

Everything instantly snaps into sharp focus.

Her chest is barely moving, and my ears are ringing from the gunshots, so I can't hear if she's breathing, but that doesn't mean she *isn't*. Even with my fucked-up hand, I manage to rip enough tape off her face to pull the gag out of her mouth, but she doesn't even react.

"I've got you, sweetheart, just hang on for me," I beg rapidly. I try to be gentle as I roll her to the side, and she's completely unresisting. At least one shoulder is dislocated, and her wrists are handcuffed, raw and bloody beneath the metal, and I lay her down gently before I tear through Danny's clothes looking for the keys.

"Everything's going to be okay, sweetheart." I unlock her wrists and move her arms to her side gently before I rip my bloody flannel off, ignoring the pain in my left side as I jerk my arm free. I wrap her in the shirt to try and get any amount of warmth into her before I pull her from the bed and into my arms as best as I can.

"Please fucking stay with me, Alex. Don't leave me, okay?" She's like a rag doll, absolutely limp in my arms, and I take care of getting her out of the cabin, snatching the keys to Danny's rental car off the coffee table as I go.

Now that some of the adrenaline has worn off, I'm starting to move slower, starting to feel the pain from the gunshot wounds and the snapped ribs and the deep cut on my right hand, but none of that matters. Getting Alex to the fucking hospital matters. The hospital is twenty minutes away, but she doesn't have twenty minutes.

I don't know if she even has ten.

"Stay with me, honey. Everything is going to be okay if you stay with me, Alex, I fucking *promise*. I *promise*, okay?" Alex doesn't even register me as I get us in the car and start speeding as fast as possible.

Her eyes are unfocused, her head is lolled to one side, and her pulse is getting slower and weaker. I keep checking it as I drive, having to push my fingers deeper into her throat to feel it. I keep talking to her, telling her it's going to be okay, that I love her, that I've got her, that I can fix this, that everything will be okay if she can just fucking hang on, and I beg her over and over to stay with me.

We're halfway to the hospital when her eyes start to drift closed.

"*Alexandria, don't you fucking dare!*" I start screaming at her, begging her to wake up, but she doesn't.

I almost hit someone as I bring the car to a screeching halt right in front of the emergency room doors. People are yelling at me and I'm yelling for help, almost falling in my rush to get Alex out of the car. Nurses move me aside and do it for me, getting her on a gurney and rushing her into the ER.

The second Alex is taken away from me, blinding pain hits me all at once. I slump against the side of the car and stare after her as two large nurses rush over and haul me onto another gurney.

I close my eyes for a second, and when I open them, I'm being wheeled quickly down a brightly lit hallway. I'm in so much pain that I can barely understand anything, but I can hear people talking to each other over my head.

When I ask them if Alex is alive, no one answers me.

I keep asking until I lose consciousness.

52

THEO

FRIDAY, MARCH 1

I'm vaguely aware of sound and light for a long time before I can open my eyes. Everything seems blurry, out of focus and wrong, and it takes me a minute to process that I'm in a hospital bed on an IV drip and surrounded by machines.

I'm barely awake, and half formed thoughts pass through my mind like water through a sieve, with one glaring exception.

Alex.

I'm in so much pain that I can't get up, and I try to yell but my voice is too weak. I look around to find the button to call the nurse, pushing it repeatedly with the edge of my hand because my fingers are stiff and in pain under all the bandages. After what feels like an eternity, a tall nurse hurries into the room and starts checking my vitals.

"Is she alive?" My voice is rough and quiet, and I start to panic when he doesn't respond immediately. "Tell me she's alive, *please*," I rasp out. The nurse gives me a terse look and nods once, and I pass out again.

***

Danny shot me just below my left collarbone, grazed my left side deeply with the other bullet, broke my nose and three of my ribs, and the bone from his face sliced into my hand deep enough to tear through most of the tendons. On top of all that, he did a great job at beating the absolute shit out of me.

I didn't feel any of it at the time, but I can feel it all now.

It fucking *sucks*.

I've been asking to see Alex for days, but the nurses keep telling me I have to rest. I don't listen to them. Sitting up alone is a struggle, and I'm so dizzy and tired from the effort that I fall over, and I get chastised by the nurses that rush in. They tell me that I have to stay in bed, and I tell them I have to see Alex.

When I try again a few hours later, I make it to the hallway before one of the nurses sees me. She takes pity on me, or on herself, and puts me in a wheelchair and takes me to the critical care ward to see Alex.

She's *covered* in bruises and bandages, hooked up to IVs and heart monitors, lying in bed and staring at the ceiling, her eyes unfocused and glassy. She doesn't look at me, and I start to panic.

"Sweetheart?" She doesn't respond, and she doesn't react at all when I reach out to take her hand.

Her heart rate doesn't even change.

I try not to panic, keeping my finger pressed against the pulse point in her wrist and watching her vitals as I interrogate the nurse. She tells me Alex is like this with everyone, that she mostly sleeps or stares at the ceiling. They did an MRI that showed her brain function is completely normal, but she's not there.

I know how Alex gets when she's stressed, and it's just a matter of time and her feeling safe. I explain that, but the nurse doesn't seem to listen to me and wheels me out of her room shortly after.

The hospital won't let me stay in her room and they won't give us a room together, no matter how much I beg, or offer to pay, or threaten to sue.

I wasn't even supposed to be allowed to see her, apparently.

***

Two police officers show up to ask questions, an older balding man and a younger blonde woman who looks at me sharply. I'm so miserable from being separated from Alex and so loopy from the painkillers that I stupidly start to answer their questions.

"Your girlfriend's in a bad way. Did you do that to her?" I level the blonde with a look of pure disgust.

"Her piece of shit *pig* husband did that to her," I say slowly, and her face hardens.

"Detective Daniel Murphy was found brutally murdered yesterday by the property manager of the rental he was staying in. Did you do that to *him*?"

I look up at the ceiling for a minute, realizing just how much shit I'm in. I'm probably going back to prison, and I don't think I'm ever going to see Alex again, because I think she might have seen what I did to Danny.

Still, I want a chance.

"I need to call my lawyer." The balding detective frowns.

"Mr. Anderson, we're just wondering -"

"Nice try. Fuck off."

***

Catherine comes to the hospital, showing up after she visits Alex. She tells me Alex is the same as when I saw her yesterday, and I quietly tell Catherine that I need an excellent criminal defense attorney as soon as possible.

A few hours later, Elise Hughes arrives from Portland, tall and well dressed and extremely displeased that I spoke to the police. I give her as much information about Alex's past with Danny as I can quickly, I tell her how Danny found Alex, I tell her the truth about how I found Alex, and I tell her what happened in the cabin. I do *not* talk about Alex and my relationship, aside from the fact that we've been together for the last six months.

The police and the hospital decide to keep Alex and I separated, so on top of not seeing her, no one at the hospital is even allowed to tell me how she is.

My nurses get *very* tired of me asking, very quickly.

I'm losing my mind being separated from her and not being able to take care of her, and the doctors have to put me on sedatives just to manage me.

Officer Dent comes down and lets me know that I'm going to be detained on murder charges once the doctors clear me for release. He tells me *if* I'm acquitted, there will be a parole revocation hearing. Either way, the chances I go back to prison are incredibly high.

Dr. Mills comes down, and I'm so upset and on so much medication that I openly talk to her about my feelings for the first time. I don't tell her how I found Alex or what happened to Danny, but I tell her about my feelings when I saw Alex on the bed. I talk about thinking she was dead, about what happened to her, about how badly I failed her, and I'm a fucking mess by the end of it.

To her credit, Dr. Mills mostly just listens.

She tells me I did something remarkable in saving Alex, and that I didn't fail her at all, so she's still a fucking idiot.

She's also an asshole, because at her request, the hospital sends in a psychiatrist.

I do my best to lie to them, and I get out of taking everything but anxiety meds and antidepressants, but those still fucking suck.

***

After a few days in the hospital, Bailey walks into my room, looking me over with wide eyes. I sit up as quickly as I can, wincing in pain, and Bailey and I speak at the same time, our voices overlapping.

"Theo, what *happened*?"

"How is she?"

"Why is there a police officer outside your door?"

"*How's Alex?*" Bailey's face falls as she pulls up a chair near my bed.

"She's not talking, but the nurses told me to expect that," Bailey says, her voice heavy. "She looked at me, though, and nodded and shook her head when I spoke to her." A wash of relief rolls through me, followed by the sharp, overwhelming longing to see her. "Haven't you seen her?" I shake my head in frustration.

"They won't let me," I mutter, and Bailey's eyes narrow.

"Why not?" Her voice is hard and flinty, and we stare at each other for a long minute. "Theo, what did you *do*?" I eye the open door and the officer standing at the doorway in a silent question, and Bailey scrunches her nose and shakes her head.

"When I found them," I whisper, "I thought she was dead." Bailey looks pained for a second before her eyes widen in understanding and her expression slowly drops into horror. "I need you to take care of Alex," I say quietly. "I'll give you whatever you want. I'll pay for Miles to go to college, I'll buy you another house, whatever. Alex is going to try to ignore it, she won't eat and she's going to drink, and I need you to keep an eye on her and make sure she gets better." Bailey nods slowly.

"You don't need to worry. Catherine, Suzie, and I are already figuring out what we need to do to help her, and Dylan and I cleaned out the guest bedroom in case she needs to stay with us." I close my eyes and lay back against the pillows, exhaling sharply.

"Thank you." Bailey stands to leave, pausing and looking at me with a conflicted expression before resting her hand on my uninjured shoulder, squeezing tightly.

"Thank *you*," she says, and she gives me a small smile before she leaves.

***

Catherine and Suzie visit and tell me Alex still isn't talking, but that she's engaging slightly more, humming in response instead of just nodding and shaking her head. Bailey visits again with some containers of food, and I notice with relief that one of them is half-eaten. Anna and Jessica

490

drop in quickly to tell me that Alex *still* isn't talking, but they got her to eat an entire plate of food for the first time in a month.

Elise comes the day before I'm released, but before I can even open my mouth, she smiles at me.

"She finally spoke to someone yesterday," she says cheerfully, and my heart soars.

Once Elise leaves, I frantically ask the nurse if I can please see Alex, please speak to Alex, if I can call her or pass on a note to her or *anything*, but the answer is always no.

***

I'm released into the jail's custody and the arraignment is set a month out. I call the hospital every day, which is the only thing I can do besides take pain medication and rest. I still haven't spoken to Alex, and I'm getting desperate.

In the hospital, we were forcibly separated, and she wasn't even speaking. Now, I'm almost positive that Alex isn't speaking to me on purpose.

She *must* have seen me kill Danny.

I did it because I love her, and I don't want her to be afraid of me and leave me because of it.

Every conversation with Elise starts with me asking how Alex is and what the nurses and doctors have said. Alex is getting better, sort of, but she's not doing well. She's engaging with the hospital staff more, but she still barely speaks, and she doesn't say much when she does. One of the nurses caught Alex crying in the middle of the night, but she shut down entirely when she realized the nurse was in the room.

After I've been in jail for two weeks, Elise comes in for a meeting more tense than I've ever seen her, and I'm immediately concerned.

"What's wrong? How's Alex?" She raises her eyebrows at her bag as she pulls out her laptop.

"She was having a tough day. Listen, Theo, you need to stop calling the hospital." I straighten up quickly, studying Elise's face.

"You talked to her? Did she say anything to you? Why was she having a bad day? Is she okay? Is she going home soon? Did she ask about me?" Elise levels me with a hard look, and I go cold.

"I went to talk to her, I told her who I was, and she gave me this to give to you." Elise pulls a small slip of paper out of her pants pocket and hands it over. There, in a shaky, faint version of Alex's bubbly handwriting, is my fucking death sentence:

they found the tracker

"The doctors found it during an MRI after they stabilized her. She's known about it since she woke up," Elise says quietly. Something inside of me breaks completely as I stare at the note.

Alex isn't *afraid* of me.

She fucking *hates* me.

"Leave," I choke out as a black hole forms inside of me, every ounce of energy sucked out of my body. I return to my cell in a daze. I don't eat or sleep, and time starts speeding up and slowing down at random until I lose track of the days.

I've felt like this before, when Melissa left or when I lost Ashley, and even a little bit when I killed Jason. Still, in comparison, none of those things even bothered me. Nothing has ever felt this bad.

If I had the energy to kill myself right now, I would.

I'll do it later. I have nothing but time now.

Dr. Mills visits twice a week for therapy, but I don't see the point. She reminds me that seeing her is part of my parole, and since I'm still *technically* on parole, I'm required to sit in a room with her for an hour twice a week. She tries to speak to me, but I stare at the clock, not really seeing or hearing her.

She has me put on suicide watch, which is fair.

***

Time without Alex blurs and stretches oddly. The arraignment happens, but I barely notice. I show up at the courthouse, Elise enters a plea of not guilty by reason of self-defense, bail is denied, and I go back to jail.

I know that Alex will be fine eventually, but without her, I don't care what happens to me anymore.

Elise visits to talk about next steps, to discuss offers for plea deals and talk about the vague possibility of trial, but I don't care. My only request is to get out as soon as possible so that I can kill myself in Yachats, where I got to make Alex happy for one weekend.

A week after the arraignment, Elise tells me we have a potential plea deal, but it would mean ten more years in prison. Ten years is a long fucking time, but Alex should have the option to talk to me before I kill myself. I know I'll probably never see her again, but she'd know where to find me if she wanted to talk to me.

Ten years is long enough that she might even want to.

I tell Elise I'll think about it.

53

ALEX

TWO MONTHS EARLIER

FRIDAY, MARCH 1

I don't know what being dead is supposed to feel like, but I'm pretty sure it's not supposed to be this painful.

I can hear a soft beeping somewhere, and as I open my eyes, a dimly lit ceiling slowly comes into focus. I close my eyes again, muddled thoughts drifting across my mind.

Everything blurs and I fall asleep again, or maybe I don't. I can't tell.

Once I'm fully awake, an older woman with greying blonde hair appears in the room and introduces herself as Dr. Goodman. I'm too tired to respond as she tells me I've been out for a few days, that I got to the hospital just in time, and that I'm lucky to be alive. She tells me something nicked a small branch of my femoral artery and I lost a lot of blood, and that's excluding the rest of the injuries.

Injuries?

Danny.

What happened to Danny?

A vague, blurry memory of screaming and gunshots and so much blood flits across my mind.

Theo happened to Danny.

He showed up.

As I open my mouth to ask the doctor where Theo is and if he's okay, she pulls out a small biohazard bag from her pocket and holds it up to me. There's a tiny, slightly bloody item in the bag, and I blink slowly, trying to figure out what I'm seeing.

"This was found in your body during your MRI. We didn't know what it was at first, but one of the nurses did some digging. It's a subcutaneous tracker. Did you know about this, Mrs. Murphy?" I don't answer her, I just stare at the bag.

If Danny had put it there, it wouldn't have taken him a year to find me.

My eyes slide past the doctor and land on the ceiling as a different kind of excruciating pain shoots through my body. I shut down to try and escape it, but I'm too overwhelmed to be numb. The pain triggers more pain, and soon I'm staring at the ceiling, frozen as I feel every emotion I've been pushing down and outrunning for ten years.

It's so agonizing that I can't do anything but lie there and *feel*.

I'm hiding too far inside myself to do anything other than stare at the ceiling, and I'm put through another MRI because I can't acknowledge any of my doctors or nurses. I think Theo visits at some point a few hours later, but I'm not sure. The police must come at some point, but I can't remember.

I can't crawl out of the black pit I've slipped into.

At some point, on some day, when the room is dark and everything is quiet, I start to cry silently, and I don't stop for hours, not until a nurse makes her rounds. I shut down and wait until she's gone before I start sobbing again.

Catherine and Suzie visit, Anna and Jessica visit, and Bailey visits almost every day. They all tell me that Theo's a wreck and asking about me constantly, but they can't see how much pain hearing about Theo causes me.

Theo, who microchipped me like a dog and fucking *lied* to me about it.

When I know I'm alone, I cry about *everything*. I barely sleep for days on end, followed by days where all I do is sleep. I have flashbacks and nightmares of Danny that span a decade, and nightmares of Theo killing Danny, and dreams of Theo standing over me, broken and defeated and covered in blood.

I start engaging with the hospital staff, but I can't speak to anyone. I'm too overwhelmed to open my mouth.

I'm afraid that if I do, I'll never stop screaming.

After a few weeks, Bailey brings Miles' favorite stuffed cat and rests it by my hand.

"Miles wants me to tell you he hopes you feel better," Bailey says quietly, and I grip the little orange cat tightly. "He's been asking about you every day. Can I bring him?" I nod, trying not to cry.

The first time I speak to anyone is to thank Miles and tell him that his cat made me feel better. It's not a lie, and it makes him smile.

The next time I speak to anyone, I tell the nurses to keep Theo the fuck away from me and that I'm not taking any of his calls.

I'm not talking to that absolute fucking *asshole*.

Once I start talking, the police show up again. I tell them I don't remember anything about what happened, aside from Danny kidnapping me and nearly killing me.

My memories and my feelings are my fucking business, and I haven't made up my mind about what to do with them yet. Mostly, I haven't made up my mind about what to do with *him* yet.

On top of crying and sleeping and feeling, I start to think.

***

I'm talking to a newer doctor on rotation about when I'll be able to go home when a tall woman in a fashionable suit knocks on my door as she walks in. I've seen her in the hallways before, and I know my nurses have turned her away, but I don't know who she is.

"Sorry to interrupt. Should I come back?" I look at her with trepidation and shake my head, beckoning her in before turning back to the doctor.

"Anyway, Mrs. Murphy, like I was saying -" I flinch hard. Definitely a new doctor.

"*Shearer*," the woman interrupts smoothly but sharply. "It's Ms. Shearer, doctor. That should be explicitly listed on her charts." I'm not sure how she would know that, but I shoot her a look of appreciation anyway.

"Right. Sorry about that, Ms. Shearer. I was saying we'd like to keep you for a few more days, but you can check out at any time." I nod and look at the woman pointedly. The doctor clears his throat and flips my chart closed. "I'll let you two talk, then." I ignore him as he walks out, still looking at the woman.

"Thanks," I say, my voice soft and hoarse from disuse. "How'd you know?"

"I'm the one who made sure that was listed." She smiles at me, offering me a soft, well-manicured hand. "I'm Elise Hughes." I shake her hand quickly and stare at her, waiting. "I'm Theodore Anderson's attorney." I groan and drop my head to my knees.

"He's resorted to *this*?" If he can't stalk me himself, he'll pay someone else to do it.

"He doesn't know I'm here. He won't know I saw you unless you want him to." I look over at her, and her face is serious. "May I sit?" I nod, and she pulls a chair to my bedside, tossing her long, sleek ponytail over her shoulder. "I have his side of the story, but I assume you wouldn't be dodging his calls if he were telling me the truth." I laugh humorlessly, pulling my knees to my chest.

"Theo's not great with the truth," I say bitterly.

"Good to know. Would you consider talking to me?" I look over at her, scrutinizing her.

"Why?"

Her face softens. "You're the only other person who knows what happened, and from what I understand, you've told the police almost nothing. To be completely frank, I think you remember more than you're saying, and if anyone could tell me the truth about what happened, it would be you." I stare down at my hands, thinking.

"You're not my lawyer, so why should I tell you anything?" She hums, crossing her legs.

"I'm *not* your lawyer, but my client starts every conversation by asking me how you are and ends every conversation by begging me to see if you need anything. He's the one that made sure I had the hospital get your name right." I press my hands over my face to hide that I'm tearing up.

Fucking *Theo*.

"Plus," she says quietly, "he told me *how* he found you, so he's telling the truth about some things." I freeze, my breath catching in my throat and betrayal dripping down my spine like ice water, washing away the warmth that had been gathering in my chest.

He told his fucking *lawyer*?

I look over at her, unable to stop my tears. "I'm glad he told *one* of us," I spit, "he just chose the wrong one." Elise raises her eyebrows and looks out the window as I start to cry, covering my face and trying to keep myself from completely breaking down in front of her.

"Okay, well, that's…" Elise sighs heavily. "Look, Alex, on the record, I'm going to ask you to consider speaking to me and testifying or submitting a statement on his behalf." She stands, slipping her bag back over her shoulder. "Off the record? He's pretty fucking stupid," she says quietly. I look over at her in surprise and she pulls out a card and places it on the table near my bedside. "Please let me know if you need anything, and I mean *anything*. I won't tell him what you asked for, and he'll pay for it either way."

"I don't want anything from him."

She nods once. "Of course. Can *I* get you anything before I go?" I nod slowly, anger and resentment coursing through me.

"Yeah. Hang on," I say, tearing a piece of paper off a notepad near my bed and writing out a quick note, handing it to her. "Can you give him this?" She takes the note, glancing at it quickly before folding it and slipping it into her pocket. "He's going to lose his shit when he sees that," I warn her quietly, and she exhales slowly.

"*Got it.* Do you want me to tell him anything, or just give him the note? Our conversation is entirely confidential, by the way." I shrug.

"You can tell him I've known about it since I woke up. They found it in an MRI." I look down at my hands. "Please don't tell him this, but I haven't told anyone what I remember because I haven't decided how I feel about him yet." I look up at Elise, but her face stays neutral. "Your job will be *very* hard if I decide that I hate him as much as I do right now."

***

A few days later, Bailey picks me up from the hospital, bringing clothes and a bag of my things that I left at the office, as well as some food. We don't really talk on the short drive, and she frowns up at the attic of the dilapidated house when she pulls up.

"Alex, why don't you stay with us for a while? We'd love to have you."

"I want to be in my own space," I say quietly, and she looks back at me with concern.

"I get that. Do you need help up the stairs?" I shake my head. "I'll come over tomorrow, yeah?" I nod, trying not to cry as I lean across the center console and pull her into as tight of a hug as I can handle.

"I love you, Bailey." She squeezes me back lightly.

"I love you too, babe. Let me know if you need anything, okay?" I nod again, getting out of the car and walking slowly towards the house. It's so surreal to be home that I don't even think about how much has changed until I grab my keys from my bag and see the extra keychain with the shiny new keys to Theo's place dangling there.

My heart gets ripped out of my body all over again, and I start to feel numb as I make the slow trek up to the third floor. I haven't moved this much in over a month, and the healing scars on my thigh twinge deeply as I pass through the second-floor landing.

I'm so tired by the time I get to my apartment that I put the food Bailey got me in the fridge and strip out of my clothes, pulling on sweats and Theo's college sweater and crawling into bed. It takes me a second to realize that I can still smell Theo faintly on my pillow and in my sheets. I grip the pillow tightly, pull the duvet over my head, and sob until I fall asleep.

I was so fucking stupid to fall in love with him.

When I wake up a few hours later, I stand in the center of my small apartment, remembering how happy I was the last time I was here. So much of that happiness had to do with Theo, who was fucking *lying* to me the whole time.

I drift into the kitchen and pull a polaroid I took on my birthday off my fridge, staring at it closely. I look stupidly happy because I was both stupid and happy, but I stare at the way Theo's not looking at the camera but at me. I can see the longing in his eyes, the slight tension in his jaw, and how fragile his smile looks.

I can't believe I didn't see how miserable he was.

He wasn't delusional this time, either. He knew he was doing something wrong, *knew* he was betraying my trust, and he did it anyway. I think about how he acted that morning, how stressed he was, the way he held me tight and told me he was sorry, how he promised that he'd make it up to me while he fucked me.

I thought he was talking about things that had *happened*, not things that were *happening*.

My heart breaks a little more, and I set the polaroid face down on the counter. I should have known better than to let him in. I *did* know better, but I chose him anyway because I'm a fucking idiot.

I grab a bottle of wine and head into the bathroom to draw myself a bath.

I've felt enough pain today.

I've felt enough pain for the rest of my life.

***

I'm terrified to walk *anywhere*, so I mostly stay in my apartment. I have a hard time eating, but I'm mostly able to keep from drinking like I used to because of the Xanax and the antidepressants they prescribed me in the hospital. I want to avoid my feelings, but it's hard to do, so I lie in bed and reckon with them the way I did in the hospital.

After a week at home, I cook for myself for the first time in a year. It's just pasta, and I barely eat it, but it feels good.

It feels like a *fuck you* to Danny.

Bailey comes by every day for the first two weeks, spending time with me and bringing food and taking me anywhere I need to go. She brings me over to her place for dinner as often as I'll let her, and Dylan pulls me aside and lets me know that he and Bailey have an extra room, and I can stay with them for as long as I need. Miles, who doesn't understand what happened, occasionally asks me if I'm still sick.

Catherine and Suzie frequently stop by my apartment after work, and Suzie's the first to realize that I haven't left the house on my own since I got home. Two weeks after I get home, she offers to go on a walk with me, and I refuse until she pulls a small gun out of her purse and tells me nothing bad will happen to me. I look at her, surprised, and she pulls me into a brief hug before she shepherds me out of the house. We start going on walks to Shively Park every time she comes over, and after another two weeks, I make the walk by myself.

I cry the whole time, but I still do it.

Anna and Jessica come over on Tuesdays instead of going to trivia, and we order takeout and watch dumb TV together, keeping our conversations light and easy. Jessica ragging on a dating show as though nothing happened to me lets me feel almost normal for a little while, but I don't miss the concerned looks she and Anna occasionally shoot at me.

No one asks me about Theo, but I can tell they all want to.

***

I know I have to talk to Theo before I can make a decision about him, so I call Elise and ask her to help me register to visit the jail without him knowing. I tell her I have no idea how our conversation will go, but since she'll have to deal with the fallout, I tell her she should be prepared for the worst.

I certainly am.

54

THEO

MAY 17

I don't know what day it is when I'm called to the visitation room, but I saw Dr. Mills two days ago, so it's probably Elise coming to ask about the plea deal. When I'm led to the public visitation room instead of the private one, I assume it's Catherine or Bailey, who both visited when I first arrived.

I freeze the second I enter the room, and everything else disappears instantly.

It's Alex.

It's been two and a half months since I've seen her, and she's so fucking beautiful, but she looks *terrible*. She's in a dark green dress with long sleeves, but it's too loose on her. She's noticeably thinner and worryingly pale with dark circles under her eyes. Her nose is slightly crooked now, and the scar across the bridge is still a swollen dark pink. Her roots have grown out and her nails are all bitten to the quick, and she looks beyond exhausted.

I don't know why she's here, but she's *here*.

She tenses up the second she sees me, but I can't understand her expression at all. Her face is blank, but her gaze is sharp and exacting as I walk towards her slowly. We sit there, staring at each other for a long time, and hopeless longing churns in my stomach.

I know what I want to say to her if she gives me the chance, but she probably won't. I have no idea what she wants to say to me, but I know it won't be good. I don't think either of us know how to start, so I wait for her to talk first, mostly so I can enjoy the last few minutes I get in her presence before she destroys me.

"You're not a shitty liar after all," she says finally, her voice as flat and indecipherable as her expression.

I wince. "I didn't know how to tell you about the tracker." She looks at me blankly, cocking her head to the side slightly.

"You lied in the *car*," she says slowly, and I go cold. "You said if I stayed with you, everything would be okay." Her voice breaks on the last word and her mask cracks, leaving her looking miserable. She swallows hard, her eyes tearing up as she looks away from me. "*Nothing's* okay," she whispers. She's trying hard not to cry, and I sit there speechless, what's left of my heart breaking as I watch her try to hide her feelings from me.

I'm dying to comfort her, but I know I can't.

It's painful to see her like this, to know I let this happen to her, but at least I get to see her one last time. She's miserable now, but she won't be forever. I might have fucked up her life, but I killed Danny, and I'll leave her everything after I kill myself, so now she'll have a real chance to start over. She'll build something new for herself and be happy again someday, and she'll find someone who loves her.

Whoever she chooses will be so fucking lucky to be loved by her.

It just won't be me.

"Your lawyer wants me to testify on your behalf," Alex says in a hard voice, and I shake my head quickly.

"I don't expect you to do that." She stares at me, raising one eyebrow slightly. "I mean it. You don't owe me anything, Alex. I'm just so fucking glad you're alive, and I'm *so* grateful that you're even here. Thank you for coming." She frowns at me.

"Theo, I-" The guard cuts her off by telling the visitors they have thirty minutes, and she sighs and shakes her head before taking a deep breath.

I know what's coming, and I can't handle it.

I think it might kill me.

"*Theo*, I'm -"

"Don't." She closes her mouth, her brows knitting together as she frowns at me. "Will you just listen to me first, *please*?" She narrows her eyes and stares at me for a long moment before she nods, and relief washes through me. She's giving me one last chance to be honest with her, so I start talking quickly.

"There's no way you would have given me a chance if I told you about the tracker, but I was way too fucking selfish to give up a chance with you, so I lied. I didn't know what the fuck else to do. I felt bad that I was lying to you, but you would have left me if you knew I'd lied to you, and I didn't want you to leave me. I promise that I was going to take it out and tell you about it, I fucking *swear* I was, but I'm glad I lied about it. You would have made me take it out, and then you wouldn't be sitting here." Alex's face slides back into that blank mask, but her eyes are sharp and focused on mine, so I drag in a breath and keep going.

"I'm sorry that this happened to you. I'm sorry that I failed you and didn't protect you from Danny, and I'm sorry that you're in pain, and I'm so fucking sorry that I hurt you, but I'm not sorry about anything else I've done, not a single fucking thing. We're connected, and I knew that, and I was right to do what I did. I was right to stalk you, I was right to start our relationship when I did, *how* I did, I was right to put that fucking tracker in you, and I was right to lie about it. You're alive because I did all of that, so I'm not sorry about any of it." She scoffs and raises her eyebrows a little bit, and I lean forward slightly and lower my voice to a whisper, looking into her eyes.

"I'm especially not sorry about killing Danny. You should know I was going to do it anyway, after I got off parole. He deserved to die for what he did to you as a kid, much less every other fucking thing he ever did to you, and I'm so fucking happy I got to make him suffer." Her eyes widen in surprise, and I drag in a ragged breath, terrified she's about to walk away after hearing that.

"Sweetheart, I thought you were fucking *dead*. I saw you lying there, and my entire world ended. I have nightmares about you dying every night." I can feel the tears starting, and I try to fight them off. "I thought us being connected meant we were supposed to be together, but if the *only* reason we're connected is because I was supposed to get rid of Danny for you and get you to that fucking hospital, I'm okay with that.

It's honestly the only thing I've ever done right in my life, besides loving you. I'm glad I got to do *something* good for you, at least." I can't stop the tears at this point, and I wipe them away quickly before I keep talking.

"I *know* you hate me, but I'm grateful you're here anyway, and I'm *so* grateful you're even listening to me right now. I know you're going to walk out that door and I'm never going to see you again, so I need you to know how much I fucking love you." Her lips purse slightly, and I wince.

She definitely hates me.

"I know I fucked everything up from the start, but loving you is the best thing that's ever happened to me. I tried to give you the option to love me the way you wanted, I really did. I know you never got to love me back, not *really*, but for that brief moment you thought you did, it was so fucking amazing. You're so good at loving people, Alex, and you're going to be the best part of someone's life. You were the best part of mine." I look away from her quickly, wiping my eyes again before looking back at her blank, unfeeling face.

"I'm so fucking glad you're alive, Alex, and all I want is for you to be happy. You deserve all the love and happiness in the fucking world, and I hope you get it." Her eyes widen and I watch as she cocks her head to the side a little, frowning at me, saying nothing. I wipe my face and try to breathe, grateful that she let me say all that to her face instead of the uncertainty of knowing whether she'd read the letter I wrote to her.

I memorize her as she contemplates me intently, and we sit there for a few long, uncomfortably silent minutes before she closes her eyes and sighs, shaking her head slightly and letting out a huff of air that might be a laugh in a different situation.

"You're a fucking *asshole*, you know that?" Her voice is quiet and shaky, and for just a second, she sounds almost exasperated. I can't help but smile at her a little bit.

"You just figured that out?" It slips out of my mouth before I can stop myself, and her face flushes as she looks at me, blinking once before her eyes narrow. She takes a deep breath, exhaling hard as she leans across the table towards me, and my faint smile slides off my face as she gets ready to fucking obliterate me.

"No, *Theodore*, I figured it out when the doctors pulled a fucking tracker out of me," she snaps. "You're not sorry for that, right? Well, I'm not sorry for shutting you out. I'm sure you've been a fucking wreck, but I don't give a shit. I needed space to figure out how I felt about everything that happened, how I felt about *you*, and you know what? I'm so fucking *furious* with you and all your bullshit. Against my better judgment, I chose to trust you, to *love* you, and what did you do? You lied to me constantly and broke my fucking *heart*." Her voice cracks on the last word, and I stop breathing.

The black hole inside of me starts pulling in everything that's left of me, leaving only cold, bitter numbness.

I'm going to kill myself the second I leave this room.

"Please just try to remember that I loved you, okay?" I beg quietly. She looks, for one second, almost concerned before she rolls her eyes at me and passes her hands over her face, letting out an irritated sigh.

God, she *really* fucking hates me.

"What do you think is real right now?" I stare at her, numb but slightly confused.

"Alex, I'm not delusional anymore. I know what's real. I know I fucked everything up, I know you hate me, and I know this is the last time I'll ever see you." I don't think there's a point in me telling her that I love her again, so I don't.

She stares at me for a long moment before her face softens a little.

"You're still delusional," she mutters quietly, and I watch her closely, trying to figure out what she's saying. "I'm so fucking angry with you, but that doesn't mean I hate you. I mean, I *do* hate you a little bit right now, but not really. The only reason I even get to be mad at you is because of you and your stupid stalker bullshit, and I'm so grateful for that." She glances down at her hands quickly, drawing in a sharp breath before looking up at me with wide, teary eyes.

"I don't think I can ever thank you enough for saving my life," she says, her voice quiet and warm, and the numbness is suddenly replaced by sharp, painful longing. Her breath hitches and she wraps her arms around herself, and I wish I could touch her one last time. "Theo, I...I *knew* I was dying, and all I could think about was how much I wanted to live. I was...I think I was almost gone before you showed up." She lets out a sharp exhale and shakes her head. "I didn't think you were going to find me, but you *did*. I hate to admit it, but your stupid lie saved my life." A small, dangerous amount of hope starts to blossom in the center of my chest, and I raise my eyebrows in surprise. She shrugs, turning away from me.

"I still can't believe you didn't tell me you put that fucking thing in me. You had *so many* chances." I cringe and she takes a deep breath, still not looking at me. "Nothing would have changed for me if you'd told me about the tracker, Theo. *Nothing*. I still would have given you a chance. You should have believed me when I told you I wanted to love you."

The hope withers away as she looks back at me, quickly brushing tears from her cheeks. "I hate that you lied to me, but what broke my heart was that you didn't love me enough to *trust* me. I wanted you so badly, and I spent weeks and weeks trying to talk myself out of it, but you were *all* I wanted the whole time. Why couldn't you have just trusted me?" I look down at my hands as I start to feel numb again.

"I don't...I just..." I trail off, trying to swallow down the guilt lodged in my throat. "I'm so sorry for hurting you," I whisper. I can't think of anything else to say. She's quiet for a minute before she lets out a long, loose exhale. In my periphery, I see her lean further across the table towards me, but I can't look at her anymore.

I'm tired of seeing how much I've hurt her.

"I forgive you."

What the fuck did she just say?

My eyes snap up to hers, and I'm deeply confused when I see her soft, adoring expression. "I'm going to yell at you the next time we talk, though. I think I've earned that," she says, the corner of her mouth quirking up.

I stare at her, my mind skipping. "*What?*"

She smiles at me a little. "You know I can be angry at you and still want you, right?" I stare at her mouth in confusion. I *know* that's a lie, so I must have missed her teeth on her lip. She studies my face as I struggle to smother the hope I'm starting to feel again, and she gives me a small, warm smile. "I don't *hate* you, Teddy. I love you." Her teeth don't touch her lip as she speaks, and my brain shuts down entirely.

Alex looks almost amused as I stare at her.

There's no way this is happening.

This is fucking *impossible*.

"This is real," she whispers, and I shake my head slowly. I don't think it's real. I think it's a dream, or another delusion, but I'll take it no matter what it is. I lean over the table and reach for her, gently cupping her face in my hands as I kiss her. It's fragile and tentative, barely even a kiss, but my entire body feels like it's on fire when our lips meet. It's like the feeling I had the first time I kissed her, but infinitely stronger, resonating in every nerve.

The only thing that permeates the feeling of our connection is the overwhelming certainty that it's *real*.

Alex's hands come up to mine, her thumbs brushing softly over the skin on the inside of my wrists, and there's no black hole inside of me anymore, there's only *this*, there's only *her*. She makes a soft, content noise and I lean farther into her, deepening the kiss as I chase after that small sign of her happiness.

Someone whistles and a guard yells at me, telling me to let her go, but I can't.

I'm not letting go of her ever again.

Alex gently pulls my hands away and breaks the kiss, pouting just a little as she looks at the guard. I'm so shocked that I can't say anything, so I just stare at her as I sit back down. She stares back, her light brown eyes brimming with tears, and I can feel our connection humming between us, deeper and more complete than it's ever been.

She smiles at me again, tapping my foot with hers, and I trap one of her ankles between mine, desperate to hold her in any way that I can. She huffs out a soft laugh and I have no idea how to react besides grinning at her like a fucking idiot, which is precisely what I do.

She reaches up to wipe tears from her face and I can see scars from the handcuffs peeking out from her sleeve, which instantly grounds me. This might be real, but I still fucked everything up. I'm in jail, I'm probably headed back to prison, Alex has been through something unimaginable, and it's all my fault.

Wait, why the fuck does she still love me?

"Visitors, time to go!" I stand up quickly to help Alex up. I don't know how much pain she's in, so I keep my touch light as I pull her close as gently as I can, every point of contact between us burning. Alex leans into me, her hands coming up to the sides of my face and her thumbs grazing over my temples as she pulls me down towards her.

"I love you," she whispers against my lips. "You're *mine*." I feel dizzy when she kisses me. The guard snaps at us and I reluctantly let her go, holding on to any part of her as long as I can before she leaves.

***

I call Elise the second I'm allowed to use the phone and start talking rapidly, letting her know that I refuse to take the ten year plea deal she's been negotiating, that under no circumstances can I go back to prison, that she needs to do whatever she can to get me the fuck out of here immediately, and that they can take me off suicide watch now.

Elise is quiet for a second, then laughs softly. "Would you be surprised if I told you I had a similar conversation with Alex about an hour and a half ago?" I can't help the manic laughter that spills out of me.

"*Surprised* is a fucking understatement. I don't care what you have to do, who you have to hire, or what hoops I have to jump through, but I need to go home. *Now*."

Elise hums. "I'll be there Monday to discuss our options, but you *cannot* make a snap decision. Trial is the only way you get out of serving time, but if you're found guilty, your *best* case scenario is ten years. Judge Ramstead isn't known for lenient sentencing." I groan. "And no matter what we do, Alex *needs* to submit a statement or testify." I shake my head even though Elise can't see me.

"Absolutely not. I'm not making her talk about what happened."

"You realize she's your entire case, right?"

"You have no idea what happened to her."

"I've read the hospital reports and I've spoken to you, so I know that I'll need to hire a trauma therapist to help me prepare her for whatever we need from her."

"No."

"Take it up with her. She told me she'll do it, whether you like it or not." I laugh a little, shaking my head. She's so fucking stubborn. Elise is quiet for a long moment, then sighs again. "Theo, you know that if we go to trial, you won't be able to speak to her until the trial is over, right?" I stop smiling instantly.

"Why the fuck not?"

"It could be seen as witness tampering."

"For how long?"

"It could take months," she says slowly, "maybe even a year."

"*Are you fucking kidding me?*" The guard snaps at me for yelling so loudly.

***

"You seem different today." I shrug, not saying anything, and Dr. Mills waits patiently for a minute before trying again. "Your lawyer's put in a request to have you taken off suicide watch. What's changed?" I raise my eyebrows at her.

"I don't want to die anymore," I say slowly, enunciating every syllable and giving her a tight, condescending smile. Dr. Mills closes her eyes briefly, exhaling what sounds like a laugh.

"Thank you, Theodore, I'd gathered that," she says, sounding slightly amused. "Would you care to tell me why not?"

"Are you seriously this stupid?" Her eyebrows shoot up in reproach.

"Excuse me?" Her tone is sharp and no longer amused, and I smile a little.

"I asked you if you're fucking stupid," I say slowly, and the corners of her mouth tighten.

"May I ask why?"

"Because you're a shitty fucking therapist," I snap, and she looks at me curiously. "I've been saddled with you for almost a year, and you've spent every minute trying to make me feel like some insane, damaged fuck up. The only reason I've ever participated is because of Alex, and you used that to get in my fucking head. I even *believed* you for a minute, honestly, and it made me miserable." Dr. Mills considers me for a long moment, nodding faintly. "You're fucking wrong about me, by the way." She sighs, looking down at the notepad in her lap, and I look over her head at the clock behind her.

Time seems to pass so slowly whenever I'm around her.

"I think there's a *lot* to unpack there," she says gently. "I'd like to come back to it in a minute, but I'm going to hazard a guess and say you've spoken to Alex recently?"

"No shit."

"How do you think it went?" My eyes snap back to hers, and I can't help but smile.

"I *know* it went well." The phone calls have gone well too, even though Alex kept her promise and spent the first one yelling at me for everything I did to hurt her.

I thought I couldn't possibly hate myself any more than I already do, but I was wrong. I know she's already forgiven me, but I'm going to spend the rest of our lives trying to make all of it up to her.

"So, am I right to assume you two are together again?" I roll my eyes and sigh impatiently.

"*Obviously*, otherwise I would have killed myself. You ask the dumbest questions sometimes, you know that?" Dr. Mills looks shocked.

"Theodore, do you realize how concerning that is?"

"See, *these* are the kinds of dumb fucking questions that make it apparent to me that the state has no interest in hiring someone even *remotely* competent to work with parolees." Her eyes flash with irritation. "Of course I see why *you* think it's concerning, but you're a fucking idiot if you think there's any point to me living without her." She nods down at her notes and clears her throat before looking at me sharply.

"Do you think the codependent dynamic present in your relationship is healthy for either of you?" I raise my eyebrows at her.

"*You* obviously think it's unhealthy, but I think Alex and I can decide what works for us." She looks down at her notes again, and I can tell she's getting upset under that neutral facade of hers.

"Let me ask you this: considering what she's been through, do you think Alex is in a stable enough emotional space right now to make the right choice for herself regarding your relationship?" I raise my eyebrows at her in amusement.

"You do *not* know Alex. Believe me when I tell you she knew all her options and took her time deciding what to do. I know her well enough to trust that she chose what's right for her, so I'm not questioning her decision."

Technically, I've *already* questioned her decision. Not because I didn't trust her, but because I needed to understand.

I wish I hadn't asked.

Dr. Mills gives me a sharp look. "Do you think one of your motivations for not questioning Alex's decision is because it ultimately benefits you?" I cross my arms.

"No." Her eyebrows raise quickly.

"I'll speak very plainly, Theodore. I know you care about Alex, and I think it's wonderful that you saved her life, but I don't think you're prioritizing her needs in this situation."

I narrow my eyes at her. "You have no idea what you're talking about."

"Well, I'd love to hear your perspective, because it seems to me that Alex is in an extremely vulnerable emotional state and you've found a way to reel her back into a relationship that is, by your own previous account, unhealthy for her." Dr. Mills' voice is sharper than I've ever heard, and I laugh and shake my head.

"You've got a fundamental misunderstanding about how our relationship works if you think *that's* what happened."

"What am I misunderstanding? Please enlighten me."

"No." Dr. Mills raises her eyebrows.

"Why not?"

"Because Alex no longer gives a shit about me participating in therapy, so your misconceptions about me or my relationship aren't my fucking problem anymore."

Dr. Mills clears her throat and gives me a terse smile. "Did Alex say why she no longer cares about you trying to work on yourself?" I grit my teeth for a moment.

"*She* feels like all the work I've done in therapy has made me a better person and a better partner." I hate that Alex thinks the woman in front of me had even the slightest hand in it, and I really hate that she might be right. "She thinks I should be thanking you for helping me *reel her back in*," I say, putting as much disdain as I can manage in the words. Dr. Mills looks like she's tasted something extremely bitter, and she stares at me for a moment, her mouth tightening.

"You're completely aware that you're taking advantage of her, aren't you?" Her voice is quiet and tense, and I bristle immediately.

"Oh, for fuck's sake," I snap, rolling my eyes, "I'm using *your* words, not mine, and I'm done listening to you about my goddamn relationship anyway."

"Why is that? Is it because I've pointed out that you consistently take advantage of Alex's inability to make healthy choices for herself at this point in her life?" I lean across the table instantly, and Dr. Mills jerks back, looking uncomfortable with how close I am.

"Do *not* disrespect Alex by underestimating her ability to make decisions for herself, do you fucking understand me?" I see Dr. Mills look towards the door and shake her head quickly at the guard I'm sure is watching, so I sit back slowly, crossing my arms over my chest again.

"Let me be very fucking honest with you, for *once*. You don't understand our relationship because you've never had all the details, so you've based your bullshit opinions on whatever it is *I've* decided to tell you. I don't tell you a lot of things, and I usually lie about whatever I do tell you." She looks astonished that I've admitted that. "I don't lie to Alex anymore. I've been honest with her about fucking *everything*, and she's still chosen to love me for who I am. I don't deserve her, but I *respect* her choice, and so should you." I look away from Dr. Mills, focusing on the clock, my knee bouncing quickly.

There's only one reason I'm even talking to her, and I need to stop dicking around and say it.

"Alex gets to make whatever fucking choices she wants to because she's *alive*." I close my eyes for a minute, trying to breathe and fight off the memory of her on that bed. "She's only alive because I found her in time, and I only found her in time because you pissed me off so fucking badly that I left Salem half an hour early, so *thank you*," I grit out, keeping my voice quiet.

Dr. Mills looks mildly shocked, and I look back at the clock as tears prick at the corner of my eyes. I technically have twenty-five minutes left, but I need to leave immediately.

When I look back at Dr. Mills, she has a scrutinizing look on her face that sets me on edge.

"Theodore," she asks quietly, "how exactly *did* you find her?"

I respond by standing up and walking away.

55

ALEX

MAY 17

I'm home for over a month before I'm ready to talk to Theo, and I can't sleep at all the night before I see him. I lie in bed, trying to imagine what might happen, but every scenario seems wrong.

When Bailey picks me up, she glances at me as I get into the car, concern clear on her face.

"Can I ask?" Bailey's voice is quiet as she pulls away from the curb, and I sigh.

"I saw him do it," I say quietly. "I don't know how I feel about him now." Bailey doesn't say anything, but she grips my hand in hers and squeezes hard, and I barely talk to her for the rest of the short drive there. I sit there and bite my nails, which I haven't done since I was a kid, steeling myself for dealing with him.

I want to take a Xanax because I'm so nervous, but I can't be off guard with Theo. I don't know how he's going to act, but I'm expecting that he'll lie to me and try to manipulate me to get what he wants.

That's all he does, apparently.

I'm a ball of nerves as I sit there, waiting. I'm so grateful that he saved me, but I'm also furious and heartbroken, and I can't even begin to explain how I felt watching him kill Danny. I'll thank him for saving my life, but after that, I don't know what I'll do.

I could leave him here to rot, which is probably what I should do.

The second I see him enter the room, I go numb. Theo looks *terrible*. He's thinner, his hair is longer, he hasn't shaved in days, and he has such defined purple circles under his eyes that it seems like he hasn't slept in a long time. He moves slowly, his eyes cast downward, and I don't think I've ever seen him so subdued.

The second he sees me, he jerks in surprise and his face transforms from a drawn, blank look to something almost feral, terrified and upset and *wanting*. Familiar tension returns to his body instantly, and he freezes in place for a moment before walking towards me slowly.

Everything about him seems sharper to me now, like there's an edge to him I'd missed.

I don't move as he sits across from me, and we watch each other warily. I know this is probably the last time I'll see him, but I don't know how I feel about that yet. All I can feel is pain as I look at him, and it takes me a long time to pull myself together enough to speak to him without screaming at him.

"You're not a shitty liar after all." Theo flinches as if I've slapped him.

"I didn't know how to tell you about the tracker," he says, his voice hoarse and quiet like he hasn't spoken much lately.

"You lied in the *car*," I say, forcing down my tears. "You said if I stayed with you, everything would be okay." Theo freezes, his eyes widening. "Nothing's okay," I choke out, and he looks so horrified that I have to turn away from him.

Not for the first time, I wonder if it shouldn't have listened to his bullshit lies, shouldn't have clung to his every word and fought to stay with him. I didn't want to die, but if I'd kept shrinking into nothingness, I wouldn't have to live with all this pain.

I wouldn't have to sit here and wait for him to break my heart again.

I force down all my feelings and I watch him closely for any signs that he's lying or manipulating. I watch the way he looks at me, his hopeless face full of love and concern and longing, and I listen closely to the desperate, resigned tone of his voice as he tells me I owe him nothing.

When he begs to speak, I let him, trying hard to keep my face neutral as I brace myself for his bullshit. He starts speaking rapidly, like he's expecting me to get up at any moment.

"...I'm *glad* I lied about it," he rushes out. "You would have made me take it out, and then you wouldn't be sitting here." For just a moment, I want to kill him because he's such a fucking asshole.

He's also *right*.

He keeps talking, and his rationalization for why he refuses to take accountability for his bullshit is somewhat understandable. I can begrudgingly see where he's coming from, and that he wasn't being malicious, just extremely fucking selfish. None of it makes me less angry, but the more he talks, the more I can tell something about him is different, but I can't tell what.

He leans towards me, and something about his expression changes from desperate and pleading to smug.

"I'm *especially* not sorry about killing Danny," he says, and I freeze, watching him carefully as he tells me he was *always* planning on killing Danny.

Oh, my god.

"...*so* fucking happy I got to make him *suffer*," he says in a harsh whisper, smiling for a fraction of a second. My eyes go wide at how predatory and unhinged he looks, at how delighted he is with himself, and I realize what's different about him.

He's exactly the same person, but he's finally being honest with me.

None of this is what I expected from him, and I sit there trying hard to hide my shock as he apologizes for hurting me and flatly refuses to apologize for anything else. He seems so devastated, so fucking resigned to the fact that he's lost me, but he doesn't beg, or plead, or manipulate – he just accepts it. When he tells me he just wants me to be happy, I know it's the truth.

My heart breaks for a fraction of a second as he lets me go, but when I realize what it means, my breath catches as my heart lodges itself in my throat. All the hope I've been shoving down and pushing away leading up to stepping into this room breaks free and floods back into me.

I've spent the last two months thinking Theo couldn't put what I need above what he wants, and maybe he wasn't able to before, but he can now. I thought he'd saved my life for himself, so he could *keep* me, but now I'm realizing he might have done it purely for my sake.

Something fundamental has changed between us, because something's changed with *him*.

I didn't know he could love me like this.

I try to keep a grasp on my anger, on the betrayal and the heartbreak, but a deep pang of longing cuts through all of it.

Theo looks so completely devastated and hopeless, and for a second, I'm back on that bed with him standing over me, covered in blood and begging me to wake up. Something warm and soft and aching flows through me, and I let myself truly feel it for the first time in months as I watch him sit there and give me that look like he's memorizing me.

Fucking *Theo*.

I remind myself that it's entirely my choice what happens. I've got all the control now, and I could walk out and leave him for good. I could scream at him and insult him and force him to feel all the pain I'm feeling, and then I could testify against him, just to spite him.

Or I could forgive him.

I could have him back.

He stares at me with his teary, bright hazel eyes, leaning slightly forward across the table as if drawn to me, and I hear my dad's voice run through my head for what feels like the millionth time.

"*Alice, there's no such thing as a second or third chance when you truly love somebody – there's only another chance.*"

I could give Theo another chance. I think he *deserves* another chance. I don't have to give him one, and I probably shouldn't, but I want to so fucking badly.

I have spent months trying to talk myself out of loving him, but nothing has worked. No matter how hard I've tried to convince myself that I hate him, all the anger and heartbreak haven't made the slightest dent in my feelings for him. I curl up in bed alone every night, afraid to go to sleep and desperately missing Theo's arms around me, and whenever I wake up from a nightmare, I reach for him.

I walked in here assuming that he'd lie and try to manipulate me and break my heart all over again, that I'd have to walk away from him for good, but that's not what's happening. Instead, he's finally giving me the option to love him, and he's not even *trying* to.

I think some of that therapy got through to him, even if he'd never admit it.

I want to make the right choice, but I don't know if there is one. I think I just have to choose if I want Theo exactly as he is. He's so sweet, and thoughtful, and gentle, and insecure, and wonderful. He's so desperately, pathetically in love with me that he'll do anything for me, even if it means growing as a person. He's also kind of insane, and *terrifying*, and manipulative, and deeply damaged, and my fucking *stalker*, but choosing him means choosing all of him.

I know he's *mine*, whether I want him or not.

Fuck it, I want him.

I was always going to choose him if he gave me the option, and he just did. I have no reason to trust him, but I'm going to anyway.

I can't tell if I'm insane or if I'm making the best choice of my life, but I think it's possible that both are true. I almost laugh at how ridiculous it all is.

"You're a fucking *asshole,* you know that?" The corner of Theo's mouth rises slightly in a small, crooked smile, and my stomach flips.

"You just figured that out?"

God, I missed him so much.

For one brief moment, everything feels impossibly good between us, and then all the pain and rage floods back into me, and I remember precisely how fucking angry I am with him.

"No, *Theodore,*" I snap, "I figured it out when the doctors pulled a fucking tracker out of me." Theo flinches slightly, and I let my anger get the better of me and start tearing into him, watching him grow paler and wider-eyed the more I speak. When I tell him he broke my heart, he seems to implode, leaving him looking completely hopeless and empty.

I've seen him look at me like that before, and the rest of the words die on my tongue.

"Please just try to remember that I loved you, okay?" Panic and concern race through me at the quiet, hollow sound of his voice. I think about the thick letter perched on the bag of my things, the envelopes on his desk, the fridge with no food. I'm almost positive he was planning on killing himself if I didn't give him a second chance, and he's probably much more suicidal right now than he was then.

Oh, *Theo.*

"What do you think is real right now?" I ask gently. He blinks once, slowly, looking a little lost.

"Alex, I'm not delusional anymore. I know what's real. I know I fucked everything up, I know you hate me, and I know this is the last time I'll ever see you." I can hear the unspoken *I love you* hanging in the air between us, and it breaks my heart that he doesn't say it.

He's still in deep shit with me, but I think he needs a lot of reassurance before he can handle my anger.

God, he's so fucking fragile.

I don't know why that's so endearing, but it is.

"You're still delusional," I tease softly, but he just blinks at me in confusion. Theo can't hide any of the emotions flashing across his face as I thank him, and I watch his face transform from despair to confusion to despair again the longer I speak. He seems baffled when I forgive him, and I can almost see the moment he starts wondering if what's happening is real.

"I don't *hate* you, Teddy," I say softly, my heart pounding in my chest. "I *love* you." Theo stares at my mouth with a look of intense confusion, and I know for a fact he doesn't believe me.

I'm going to spend the rest of my life making sure he never doubts that again.

"This is *real*," I whisper, and he looks desperate and unsure as he reaches for me.

Our lips barely meet, but something intangible starts passing between us over and over on an endless loop, solidifying more and more each time, linking us tighter and tighter together until all I can feel is the unbreakable, invisible thread connecting us to each other.

Time seems to stretch and distort, and I spend a lifetime in that moment with him, back where we belong, where everything makes sense, where we're two halves of one inextricable whole.

***

I hardly make it out of the visitation room before I break down, trying and failing to keep myself from sobbing as I check out and hurry back to Bailey's car in the parking lot.

She looks deeply concerned the second I open the car door. "Babe, are you okay? What happened? Do I need to kill him?" I wipe my face and choke out a laugh as I shake my head, catching my breath.

"Please don't," I say, my voice watery and faint as I start crying again. "It's...we're good. Everything's okay." Bailey smiles at me and squeezes my knee.

"He really loves you, you know that?" I nod, wiping away my tears.

"Yeah, he does," I say quietly as we pull out of the parking lot. "More than I realized."

***

Elise's firm is located on the seventeenth floor of a large glass and steel building in downtown Portland, and she greets me warmly and ushers me back to her large corner office. It's stylishly decorated in cream and rose colors, full of large, lush houseplants, and has an expansive view looking east over the river.

I sit in a plush chair as Elise makes coffee with a small espresso maker in the corner, and I slip a bottle of Xanax out of my bag and take one quickly while her back is turned. She hands me my coffee and sits in the chair across from me, crossing her legs and looking at me, obviously intrigued.

"So," she says slowly, "do I get to ask why you're sitting here instead of in the district attorney's office? Your phone call Saturday afternoon was a surprise." I look down at my coffee, smiling a little.

"Yeah, well, Theo surprised me. Um, how much has he told you about our relationship?"

"Essentially nothing." I laugh nervously and look out the window, taking in the view of Mount Hood as I take a deep breath, trying to push down my anxiety.

"How much do you need to know to get Theo out of prison?"

"You're his entire case, so pretty much everything." I turn back to Elise and stare at her apprehensively for a moment.

"Is this all confidential?" She nods once. "Well, you're either going to think I'm a fucking idiot, or you're going to understand why I'm sitting here. Maybe both." Elise leans forward, resting her elbow on the arm of her chair and cupping her chin in her hand in a way that reminds me of Jessica when she listens to gossip. I laugh and look back out the window, taking a shaky breath.

"Um, so Theo's not just my boyfriend, he's my *stalker*. He, um, he kind of forced me into a relationship because he was delusional and thought we were together, or that we belonged together, anyway." I flick my eyes back to her, and she's seemingly unfazed. "And then I fell in love with him." Elise doesn't even blink. "Please don't judge me." She shakes her head.

"I'm not judging you, Alex," she says softly, smiling at me, "but now I have a *lot* more questions for you." I laugh and shake my head before I take a long sip of my coffee and answer every question she asks.

***

Elise tells us she can give us three weeks to talk before she initiates trial preparations, so the first thing I do is spend an entire phone call yelling at Theo for everything he's done wrong, keeping my language vague enough that no one listening in would know what I'm talking about.

I don't give a shit if we're connected, or if he saved me, or if he's the love of my life – he's still a fucking asshole who betrayed me and broke my heart. He apologizes for hurting me and for not protecting me, but refuses to apologize for anything else. I can tell from his voice that he's smiling every time he speaks, so I yell at him for that, too.

I let him talk the entire next phone call, and he instantly starts in on a rapid litany of questions about how I'm doing, and I get increasingly irritated with how often he asks if I've spoken to a therapist yet. When I tell him to drop it, he's quiet for a long moment and then lets out a long sigh.

"Sweetheart, can you please tell me why you still love me?" he asks in a soft, desperate voice.

"Because you put me first and *finally* gave me the option to choose you," I say, my chest filling with warmth. "As much as you hate her, I think your therapist probably helped you get to a place where you could do that." Theo lets out an aggravated sigh.

"You seriously think the therapy you emotionally blackmailed me into worked?"

"Yeah, I do, actually."

"Well, if you think therapy works, you should see a therapist."

I snort. "I walked right into that one, didn't I?"

"You *need* to talk to someone about it, Alexandria," he snaps, his tone commanding.

"No," I snap back at him, "I *need* it to go away."

"Honey, it won't go away, and you *know* that," he says, his voice softening, and a wave of dread washes over me. I know he's right, but I can't talk about it. I can barely think about it.

"How's Dr. Mills? Don't you see her today?" He groans, and I hear the phone ping, letting us know we only have one minute left.

"Don't think I'm dropping this," he warns, talking quickly. "I think I have to thank her for something, but I don't want to."

"You definitely have to thank her for making you a better person," I tease, and he makes a choked, disgusted sound.

"Oh, fuck *off*, she had nothing to do with that."

I let out a soft laugh. "Whatever you say, baby. What do you have to thank her for?"

"I'll tell you in person. Listen, I need you to do me a favor before I see you again."

"The people at the jail said I can't bring you food."

"That's not – wait, you *asked*? God, I fucking love you. No, I want you to move into our house." My heart skips a beat. "If you want to, I guess. Your choice," he says almost shyly.

"Theo, I –" I hear the line go dead as the call disconnects automatically. I stare at my phone, still stunned by how casually he called it *our* house. I look around my shitty, tiny little apartment, the first place I've ever had that was *mine*.

Now I want something to call *ours*.

I have a moving company pack up my few belongings and move them to Theo's, texting Roger that I've moved out and slipping my keys and my last month's rent underneath his door.

It takes me a few days to move all my clothes into *our* closet, to put my things away in *our* room and *our* bathroom, to make it *our* house instead of his house.

I want to make it our *home*, but he's not there.

***

Theo looks better the next time I see him, like he's slept and eaten something. I ask him why he had to thank Dr. Mills, and he gets quiet for a minute, his jaw tensing up. His legs reach for mine under the table, and he explains what she said to him, why he left early, why he didn't check the tracker, and everything that happened up to him getting to the cabin.

I start to hyperventilate when he talks about it, and Theo's leg rubs against mine soothingly as he talks me through breathing, helping me calm down.

"Honey, do you...do you remember me...being there?" I wrap my arms tightly around my waist and look up at him warily. He seems extremely nervous, his eyes darting from my eyes to my mouth quickly. "You don't have to talk about it, but I just...you were barely conscious, so I don't know if..." He trails off, his voice tight with anxiety.

I'll have to tell him eventually, so I might as well do it now.

"Um, kind of," I say, holding myself tighter. "I don't...it's sort of fuzzy, and I don't remember all of it, but I, um, I heard you screaming and I...I wasn't *there,* but then I...was? Um, I, uh...I saw it. I watched you do it," I say, whispering the last part. I feel the table start to shake as his knee starts bouncing, and when I look up at him, he looks genuinely terrified.

"Why are you here?" I let out a long sigh, caressing his ankle with mine.

"I'm not your mom, Theo." His eyes widen, his body stills, and I think he stops breathing. "Danny figured out who you were and showed me photos of your dad. That's why she left, right? Because she saw you do that?" We sit there quietly for a minute before his knee starts bouncing again, and I know I'm right. "She didn't actually leave without saying anything to you, did she?"

"*Don't,*" he snaps, his tone venomous.

"You're going to have to tell me eventually," I say quietly, and his jaw clenches as he looks over my shoulder at the clock. A guard calls out that we have ten minutes left, but Theo keeps staring at the clock. "Teddy, can you look at me?" He shakes his head quickly, and I press my ankle against his, but he pulls away. "*Baby,* I remember what happened, and I'm still here, okay? I love you and I'm not afraid of you." His eyes finally dart towards me, and he stares at my mouth.

"Can you say that again?" His voice is quiet and stressed, and I trap one of his ankles with mine and lean forward.

"I love you, and I know you'll never hurt me." He looks extremely skeptical, even though he knows I'm not lying. "I wouldn't have just moved into *our* house if I was afraid of you, right?" His eyebrows rise slowly, and a small smile spreads across his face before it starts to slip, and he begins to look extremely concerned.

"Honey, if you remember anything about what happened in that room, you *need* to talk to a therapist."

"*I'm not fucking talking about it,*" I snap at him, and he looks taken aback for a moment before his face becomes almost pitying.

I can tell he's thinking about what Danny did, and I fucking hate it.

***

Theo spends the next two weeks trying to talk me into seeing a therapist at every opportunity. He begs, he pleads, he tries to manipulate me. I give him every excuse I can think of, but he counters everything.

I tell him I barely want to leave the house, and he tells me most therapists do it over video now. I tell him I don't want to find someone, and he says he'll have Elise do it. I tell him I can't afford it without health insurance, and he just laughs at me. I tell him I want to just bury it and pretend like it never happened, and he looks at me with concern and begs me to please just fucking *try*, if not for me, then for him, *please*.

I think about it, and I talk to Suzie. She's very encouraging, but much gentler about it than Theo is. She shares some of how therapy helped her, and I realize that I not only need the help, I *want* the help.

I tell Theo during our last in-person visit, and he's thrilled. We spend the rest of the hour talking quietly and frantically, trying to get everything straight before the trial, including what to say about the tracker, because we know it will come up. The closer we get to the end of the visit, the more he starts getting that look like he's memorizing me again, and the guards snap at us for being too affectionate when it's time to go.

Our last phone call is a few days later, and it's mostly Theo telling me how much he loves me and that everything will be okay, and me telling him that I love him and he needs to come home.

The following week, Suzie introduces me to an EMDR therapist, and I start seeing her once a week.

It sucks, but it helps.

My therapist encourages me to go to domestic violence support group meetings, so I do, but I don't talk for weeks. I listen to other people talk about their lives and experiences, and so many of the things they say resonate with me, and I just sit in the back and cry quietly during most of the meetings.

Eventually, I work up the courage to start sharing, and it's terrifying to be honest about it.

Well, mostly honest.

I tell the whole truth about Danny, and I tell some truths about Theo, as well as a *lot* of lies.

Things start to get better slowly.

I build a new routine, which grounds me, and I pull out my planner and start filling it out. Anna and Jessica come over on Tuesdays, I have therapy on Wednesdays, and on Fridays, Catherine, Suzie, and Bailey take me to lunch or dinner or come over and let me cook for them. I use Theo's extra car to drive into Portland on Saturdays to go to my support group, and I start using the gym in the basement instead of returning to the rec center.

I start to feel a little more normal, but there's still no red ink in my planner.

After a few weeks, I tell Suzie I'd like to come back to work, and she lets me come back part-time, which goes a long way towards making me feel more in control of my life again.

Theo's house – *our* house – is close to the office, and I force myself to walk. I'm more aware of my surroundings than I've ever been, and I have to take a Xanax when I get to the office the first few times. I'm eventually able to make the short walk to work without panicking, and it's one more thing that Danny tried to take from me that I can take back.

Over the weeks, my therapist and I start getting deeper about things other than what happened with Danny, which is highly uncomfortable for me. We talk about my drinking, my self-esteem, my marriage, my relationship with my parents, and I tell the truth about all of it.

When she explains codependency, I get anxious and try to change the subject, which doesn't work. I get to a place where I can talk about it in the context of my parents and Danny, but I lie through my teeth about my relationship with Theo.

I don't know if she buys it.

Elise keeps me apprised of what's happening with the trial, and we have trial preparation every few weeks. She reassures me that we're moving quickly, even though it takes months.

The last month leading up to the trial is tough. Elise and I have to go over everything in excruciating detail, including what she'll ask and what the prosecutor might ask. I'll have to talk in detail about my relationship with Theo, my marriage, and what happened with Danny.

I've only had to speak to my therapist about *everything* that happened, and since part of trauma therapy is processing things I buried and I have *no* interest in talking to strangers about it, I tell one crucial lie while we're preparing for trial.

It won't jeopardize Theo's chances of getting out, so it's fine.

He'll know, but he won't push me about it.

Between the trauma therapy and preparing for the trial, I stop sleeping well. I'm back to lying in bed alone, desperately missing Theo and afraid to go to sleep. Every time I wake up from a nightmare, I grab a shirt or a sweater of Theo's and put it on a pillow, curling up with it and burying my face in it, inhaling his scent to try and comfort myself until I'm able to fall back asleep.

By the time the trial rolls around, I've run out of shirts that still smell like him.

56

THEO

The psychologist Elise hired, who I lied to carefully and relentlessly, testifies that I'm a reasonable, mostly stable person with complex trauma, and while I was afraid for my own life, I was genuinely terrified for Alex's.

The doctors testify that while I was severely injured when we got to the hospital, they almost lost Alex, which I did *not* know.

The rental owner testifies that the body was horrifying to see, which is a little fair, because I completely lost my mind.

The cops testify that no one who could do what I did to Danny should be allowed to walk free, but they're fucking cops and they're being melodramatic because *he* was a cop.

After two days of sitting in this courtroom impatiently listening to people I don't fucking care about, we get to the most important testimony. When Alex walks into the courtroom, everything else fades away, and I have to work hard to seem somber.

She still looks too thin and tired, but she seems a lot more like herself. She's obviously nervous, but her shoulders drop slightly the second she sees me, and she seems calmer immediately. I'm not supposed to interact with her, but I can't help smiling at her a little bit and giving her a quick wink. She blushes, trying not to look at me, and Elise clears her throat sharply, so I look down at the table until I can control myself.

Once the prosecutor starts asking questions, I have to work hard to keep my shit together. I didn't want Alex to testify because I thought it would be too hard on her, but I didn't even consider that listening to her would be hard on me, mostly because I'm a fucking idiot.

The prosecutor asks her tough questions about what happened, and it's a series of stops and starts because she keeps crying. I'm stuck at this fucking table, and it's making me miserable to have to watch her cry with no way to comfort her. I want to do anything I can to take care of her, so every time she looks over at me, I take a deep breath, and she follows suit.

It calms both of us down.

Alex gets into the details of what happened to her, some of which I knew and most of which I did *not*. My knee bounces quickly as she talks about getting kidnapped, and I shut down entirely when she starts talking about what Danny put her through in the cabin. When the prosecutor asks Alex if she remembers being raped by Danny and she says no, I go cold and work hard not to freak out in front of all these people.

She's fucking *lying*.

"Mrs. Murphy, will you please review Exhibits 1 through 20?" The prosecutor gestures to the photos in front of Alex, but she stares at him for a second, not looking at the pictures in front of her or at the large crime scene photos printed and displayed for the jury to her left. I can tell she's tired, and when her eyes finally dart to me, I help her breathe. Alex finally looks down and shuffles through the photos slowly, and I watch her face anxiously, my knee bouncing quickly.

"Now, you were the only witness to the altercation between Mr. Murphy and Mr. Anderson, correct?"

"Yes, I was," she says, still looking down at the photos and cautiously not reacting to them.

"Do you believe Mr. Anderson acted out of self-defense when he did this?" he asks, waving a hand at the large, blown-up photos of Danny's body.

"Yes, I do." No, she doesn't. She knows I did it for her. Everyone in this fucking courtroom knows I did it for her.

"You said earlier that you were experiencing some level of psychological dissociation as you witnessed the altercation, correct?" Alex raises her head and stares at the prosecutor, and I can tell she's irritated.

"That's *correct*," she says, her tone sharper.

"Do you feel as though you were able to accurately assess the situation, given your psychological state at the time?" I grit my teeth as Alex's face flushes and her eyes narrow.

"Being brutally beaten and raped isn't fun, so *excuse me* for coping," she snaps. I draw in a sharp breath and hear Elise exhale slowly beside me. "Seeing as Danny was raping me *while I was dying*, and Theo got shot and beaten half to death trying to *save my life*, I think I have an exceptionally accurate assessment of the situation, thank you very fucking much," she says slowly, her voice acidic and condescending.

There's a flurry of whispering in the courtroom, and the prosecutor looks irritated. Alex looks at me, her face tense and anxious and furious, and I mime breathing in and out for what feels like the hundredth time in the last two hours, giving her a small, encouraging smile. She closes her eyes and takes a deep breath, and I see an older woman on the jury catch the exchange.

The judge looks down at Alex, who has started to quietly cry again.

"Mrs. Murphy, I understand this is upsetting, but you need to calm down," she says gently. Alex quickly wipes her eyes with a crumpled tissue and nods down at her hands.

"Yes, Your Honor. I'm sorry." She looks up at the prosecutor. "I'm sorry, Mr. Franco." He nods at her, and Elise hums in approval from beside me.

"That's alright. I understand that you've been through a lot, but I thought you testified that you don't remember being raped?" Alex pales and looks at her hands.

"I remember it starting," she says quietly, "and I had to deal with all of the injuries, so I know it *happened*." Those aren't lies, but they also aren't the truth. I have to look down at the table because I don't need anyone on the jury to see how furious I am.

"Understood. Do you believe that this level of violence was justified as an act of self-defense?" I look back up at Alex as she nods down at her hands.

"Yes, I do."

"Can you explain why?" She straightens up and looks at the prosecutor, her jaw set.

"Danny was *terrifying*. He was a big guy, he was really strong, he knew how to fight, he was trained with firearms, he had horrible anger issues, and he was extremely jealous. He would have used the same amount of violence to kill Theo, if not more. Danny seriously injured Theo, and that was *while* he was defending himself. I think the level of self-defense was entirely justified." Alex's voice is soft and insistent, and Elise surreptitiously draws a small smiley face on the notepad in front of her.

"I'm still having a hard time seeing how the level of *extreme* violence in these photos makes sense as an act of self-defense." Elise makes a slight noise of irritation but doesn't object.

It *was* an extreme level of violence, and the photos are jarring.

Danny's head barely looks like anything anymore from how it's collapsed in on itself, his face bashed in and the entire back of his head cracked open, his brains spilling out on the floor beneath him. His arms, chest, and torso are covered in stab wounds and a few bullet holes, and he's bloody everywhere.

All I see when I look at the photos is how much I love Alex, but I don't know what she sees. I watch her closely as she looks at the pictures again, and my heart skips a beat as her face softens almost imperceptibly.

No one else would catch it, but I do.

Months ago, she and I briefly spoke about the fact that she remembers me killing Danny, but she never told me how she felt about it.

Now I know that she saw the love in it.

That's my fucking girl.

"The photos make sense to me," Alex says softly before looking back at the prosecutor. "Knowing Theo, he was *terrified*, and I'm sure he wanted to be absolutely positive that Danny couldn't keep hurting me." She shoots me a tender look, and I mouth *I love you* as subtly as possible.

"How did you feel about watching Mr. Anderson do that to your husband?" I focus on Alex's mouth very carefully as she looks back at the prosecutor and takes a deep breath.

"It was horrible, but he only did it to protect me," she says quietly, and I bite my cheek to keep from smiling at her when she looks at me with soft, adoring eyes. "I know Theo *never* would have done anything like that if it wasn't a life-or-death situation," she lies, and the prosecutor gears up to ask her another question.

"She's doing well," Elise whispers quietly after the judge calls for a break. I watch the bailiff escort Alex out, catching her eye and giving her a small smile. "Now we just need her to make you look sympathetic." I give Elise a brief, amused look.

"Tough ask," I say quietly. Elise makes a big deal of putting her papers away in her bag, making a lot of noise as she does.

"Not as tough as you might think," she whispers.

***

"Your Honor, I'd like to move to refer to the witness by her preferred name of Alexandria Shearer during my questioning." Alex shoots Elise a look of deep gratitude, and the judge thinks for a moment before nodding.

"I think that's fine," the judge says, glancing at the court reporter and asking her to add it to the record.

"Thank you, Your Honor." Elise, sharp and imposing in her tailored suit and high heels, softens as she approaches Alex. "Ms. Shearer, how did you meet Daniel Murphy?" Alex swallows hard.

"Um, he was one of the cops who came to tell me my parents had died in a car accident." I hear some faint murmuring in the room.

"What were your respective ages at the time?"

"I was seventeen and he was twenty-eight." More murmuring, and Elise hums in concern.

"How did you two enter into a romantic relationship?"

Alex laughs bitterly. "Uh, I wouldn't say we entered into a relationship so much as he forced a relationship on me." I'm slightly uneasy about the way she's phrasing that, and my knee starts bouncing.

"How so?"

"Danny knew my foster parents, so he was around constantly, and he just inserted himself into my life. He wouldn't stop texting me, and he started showing up everywhere and he wouldn't leave me alone. He kept telling me he wanted to take care of me." My stomach knots up, and I look down at my hands to keep the jury from seeing my face.

She's never told me *this*.

"Then he...he offered me a ride home from school, and he...um, he..." I glance up and watch as Alex looks up at the ceiling and wraps her arms around her waist. This *also* isn't something we've ever talked about. "Um, he drove me out to a secluded area and raped me and told me that I had wanted it and that it meant we were together." A pit opens in my stomach as I watch her, but she still won't look at me.

I wish I wasn't finding this out in front of a room full of people.

Some of her behavior early in our relationship makes a lot more sense.

"What was that like for you?" Alex's eyes well up with tears, and she shakes her head, looking back at Elise.

"It was awful and overwhelming. I had no idea what to do." I feel a slick churn of guilt in my stomach. "I was a kid who just lost my whole family, and he took advantage of me. I didn't feel like I could ask anyone for help because he was older and a cop, and I thought no one would believe me, so I just let it happen. He took over my whole life." Elise nods sympathetically, and Alex still won't look at me.

Of *course* she never told me any of this.

Elise gets Alex to recount years of manipulation and abuse, more details she's never told me. She talks about finally having enough, about Danny pulling a gun on her, about running away and building a life in Astoria. She doesn't talk about the fact that I did almost the same thing to her that Danny did, but it hangs unsaid between us.

I am *never* going to stop making that up to her.

I sit there, staring at her, really listening to what she's been through, aware of everything she's not saying about our first few months together, and I think about my conversation with Catherine on Thanksgiving.

Alex is the furthest thing from fragile I can possibly imagine.

"Ms. Shearer, how did you and Mr. Anderson meet?" Alex finally looks at me, and her lips twitch into a small smile.

"He approached me at a bar back in September." I keep my face as neutral as possible. I'm probably supposed to look like I enjoy hearing this part, but it's just making me nauseous.

"When did you start dating?"

Alex huffs out a quick laugh. "We had our first date a few weeks later, and then we were just sort of together after that," she says, shooting me a quick, amused look.

Is this *funny* to her? She's got a very dark sense of humor if it is.

"How early into dating did you reveal to Mr. Anderson that you were living under an assumed identity?"

"Almost immediately. I've always felt safe with Theo." I hate that it's a fucking lie.

"What's your relationship like?" Alex's face softens almost entirely. A small, warm smile plays across her lips, and I watch her mouth very closely.

"It's amazing." Not a lie, thank god. "After being with Danny, I didn't know what a good relationship was even supposed to be like, but I have that with Theo. He's my best friend. He's kind, and he's sweet, and he's very gentle with me. He understands my past, and he does his best to accommodate the PTSD I have from it. My therapist says our relationship provides me with a lot of reparative experiences. He makes me feel safe and loved, and like I'm good enough without ever trying."

I can't help smiling at her. I love that I make her feel this way, and I especially love that she's not lying about any of it. Hearing this is slightly tempering the overwhelming, painful knowledge that I do *not* deserve her.

"I was married to Danny for almost ten years, but I'd never been in love before I met Theo. I didn't realize loving someone was supposed to be easy." I have no idea what my face does when I hear that, but my expression makes Alex tear up a little when she glances at me.

The questioning moves on to other aspects of our relationship, and Elise and Alex have carefully crafted a narrative of selective truths that make me look like an even-tempered, reasonable person, a perfect boyfriend, and a fucking saint compared to Danny.

When Elise asks Alex about the tracker, Alex tells a somewhat convincing lie about how we found the tracker to be an imperfect solution to making Alex feel safe.

"How did you decide on that as a solution?" Alex looks up at Elise shyly.

"I know it seems unconventional, but I was so afraid that Danny might show up and hurt me, and I couldn't trust the police to protect me. I was vulnerable, and it made me feel safer knowing that Theo always knew where I was, just in case." She seems so earnest when she talks about it, and she's making it sound almost believable. Judging from the face of at least one person on the jury, I think she's fairly decent when it comes to lying to other people.

"Can you tell me why, after only a few months of dating, you'd entrust Mr. Anderson with something like that?" Alex smiles softly and tucks her hair behind her ear.

"Well, I was *certain* he wasn't going anywhere." She shoots me another amused look, and I struggle not to smile at her.

She's fucking flirting with me.

"You'd only been dating for a few months. How could you be sure?"

Alex shrugs. "It took me a while to open up emotionally, but that was *not* the case for Theo." She looks down at her hands, laughing weakly. "He was very open about how he felt about me from the beginning, and we only put the tracker in after we started talking about a real future together."

I sneak another swift glance at the jury, who are all focused on her sweet, vulnerable face as she lies through her teeth. Some of them look skeptical, but most of them don't.

Elise transitions to asking Alex about the kidnapping and the cabin again, but she gets a *lot* of details out of Alex that the prosecution didn't, which makes Alex cry so much that she has to be granted a five-minute break.

Someone on this fucking jury *has* to understand that Danny forfeited the right to his life the second he touched her.

Alex's testimony takes all day, and the prosecutor is a dick during cross-examination, calling her Mrs. Murphy again. I can tell Alex is wrung out and exhausted by the end of it, and then Elise has to go again.

Alex is completely withdrawn as she gets escorted off the stand, and I lock eyes with her as long as possible. She tries to smile and mouths *I love you*, and it takes everything in me not to rush after her.

I'm slightly calmer as I watch Bailey get up from her seat in the gallery. She locks wide eyes with me and nods at me quickly before she wraps a protective arm around Alex and leads her out of the courtroom.

I need to find a way to thank Bailey, even though I'm not sure anything will ever be enough.

Once the jury is dismissed for the day, Elise leans close, keeping her voice almost inaudible as she slowly packs up her bag.

"She made you look like a knight in shining armor," she whispers, barely moving her lips.

"I believe the word is *perjury*," I mutter through my teeth, catching Elise's sharp look out of the corner of my eye. "*Sorry*. Bad joke," I say, glancing at my feet.

"Do *not* throw away the gift she just gave you," she hisses at me.

I shake my head slightly. "Story of my fucking life."

***

"Mr. Anderson, can you please explain what happened in that room?" I grit my teeth and take a deep breath, blowing it out quickly.

I *need* to keep my shit together.

"Yes. I looked through the window and saw Danny raping Alex on that bed, and I was positive she was going to die." I have to pretend I didn't think Alex was *actually* dead, otherwise it doesn't legally count as self-defense. "I entered the house, took a knife from the kitchen to defend myself, and went in to save her. Danny and I fought, I defended myself to the best of my ability, and then I got Alex to the hospital."

"Alex being Mrs. Murphy?" I scowl at him. The whole fucking room knows she goes by Alex.

"I've only known her as Alexandria Shearer, which she *prefers*." Prick.

"Can you explain why you thought Mrs. Murphy was going to die?" I nod, taking another deep breath.

Despite the sedatives, the breathing exercises, and the fact that I know I need to keep my emotions under control, I have a tough time staying calm. My knee starts bouncing instantly, and I push my hands back through my hair as I describe in graphic detail what I saw through that window and what I saw in the bedroom. I watch the prosecutor pale a little when I tell him what I heard Danny saying to her, and I need a minute after sharing it to keep my shit together.

I still have nightmares about it every single fucking night. In the future, this will be one of the things I *never* think about, but right now I need everyone in the courtroom to know what that bastard put her through.

I think it makes the crime scene photos look like an underreaction.

"Mr. Anderson, can you please review Exhibits 1 through 20?" I pointedly ignore the large printouts to my left and look down at the crime scene photos in front of me, focusing just to the left of the photo, then just to the right before I slowly flip to the next one.

Elise had to coach me not to look at the pictures. Apparently, I can't hide the look of satisfaction on my face when I see them, no matter how hard I try, and the jury can't know that I'm thrilled that I killed Danny.

"Would you consider this to be an extreme level of violence?" I take a deep breath, working hard to keep my face neutral, but I accidentally glance at one of the photos.

"Given the situation, I view it as the appropriate level of violence." Elise's face is neutral, but her gaze becomes very sharp, reminding me I need to be wildly fucking careful with how I answer these questions. "I used the force I thought was required to defend myself and Alex. She had told me how violent Danny was, and I was terrified of him." I work hard to deliver the lie effectively because I hate having to say it. "When I found Alex, she had been kidnapped, beaten, stabbed, and was being brutally raped while she bled to death. I was terrified for her, to say the least, and I was shot and severely injured trying to rescue her. I did my best to make sure we were both safe." The prosecutor looks skeptical.

"Don't you think you could have just incapacitated Mr. Murphy to defend yourself?"

"No, I *needed* to kill him," I say slowly, and I see Elise purse her lips at me from the defense table. "During the fight, it was obvious that he wouldn't stop until he killed me, and I needed to defend both myself and Alex." The prosecutor gestures at the crime scene photos.

"*That* level of violence was required to defend yourself?"

"Yes," I say a little too quickly, and Elise looks *pissed*. Fuck, I need to reign it in and get myself back under control.

"Do you regret killing Mr. Murphy?" I nod, trying to look pained. From the look on Elise's face, I need to try harder.

"Of course I regret killing him," I say, taking a deep breath and looking down at my hands. "I wish it hadn't come to that, but the only way to get Alex out of that room was to kill Danny, and I would have done fucking *anything* to keep her alive." My eyes prick with tears as I think about her on that bed, and I look back up at the prosecutor. "I would have let him kill *me* if that's what it took to get her to the hospital, without hesitation. I truly regret what happened, but I don't regret doing what I needed to do to save her. I *never* would have killed him if her life hadn't been at risk. It's horrifying to live with the guilt." My eyes dart to Elise, who looks much less irritated with me now.

Several rows behind her in the gallery, I see Dr. Mills. I haven't spoken to her since I thanked her, and I didn't realize she'd been here, watching the trial.

I don't miss how she blinks and purses her lips.

Shit.

***

After several days of deliberation, I'm decided not guilty by three votes.

Once the decision is read and the jury files out, Elise leans in and very quietly tells me she thinks I would have been put away for life if Alex hadn't testified. I snort, looking down at Elise and trying not to smile.

"Oh, I'm *aware*. I'm going to spend the rest of my life showing her just how grateful I am." I look over my shoulder at where Alex is waiting in the first row of the gallery, and from the blush creeping across her face, I said that loud enough that she heard me.

I need to go pick up that ring I ordered back in February.

"Can I *please* go home now?" She's right there, and it's been fucking *months*. Elise raises her eyebrows at the impatient, adolescent whine in my voice.

"Do *not* leave this courtroom with a smile on your face. I'll see you in a week." I nod and walk away from her quickly, keeping my head down as I embrace Alex, kissing her forehead before I lead her out of the courtroom, my arm wrapped tight around her shoulders.

On our way out, I pointedly avoid looking at my very concerned-looking therapist loitering in the back of the small courtroom.

I don't like how she's looking at Alex.

***

The day before the parole revocation hearing, Elise visits, spreading out all the paperwork I need to review across the dining room table and explaining the proceedings to Alex, who stands close to me, my arm around her waist.

"Um, how likely is it that Theo's parole *will* get revoked?" Elise smiles at Alex, but her smile seems insincere to me.

"We can't know for certain, but his parole officer is advising against it, so I think it should be fine." Alex nods and walks out of the room, saying something about making coffee, and Elise levels me with a wary expression once she's gone.

"Things have changed," she says under her breath as she hands me a sheaf of paper from her bag. "This was submitted to the board yesterday." I stare down at the papers, and all the panic I've been pushing down comes to the surface.

Dr. Mills filed a last-minute recommendation to revoke my parole.

"Can she *do* this?" I hiss, and Elise shrugs.

"Yes, but some of her reasoning seems unethical. We'll have you two testify against it – I've included a list of questions I'll be asking – but you both *need* to keep it together, especially *you*."

The edges of my vision swim red and my hands shake the more I read.

I can't go back to fucking prison. I spent the entire last week making preparations just in case, but I wasn't planning on *needing* them. The week home was way more complicated than I expected, and I can't be away from Alex again.

I need to take care of her.

"Should I let you tell Alex?" Elise asks quietly as we hear Alex's footsteps in the hallway. I tuck the papers away, nodding once and forcing a smile as Alex walks into the room.

I have no idea how I'm supposed to tell her.

***

I keep it from Alex until the next morning. She starts crying angrily as she reads it, and she barely calms down enough to read the questions she's going to have to answer.

I don't stop touching her until we reach the hearing room.

The board hears Officer Dent's report first, which claims that I've met every term of parole and recommends strongly against revocation.

Dr. Mills disagrees.

She tells the board it's her professional opinion that I'm an extreme recidivism risk. According to her, I'm a dangerous, dishonest, unstable person who has spent the better part of a year stalking Alex. It's her opinion that, although I was acquitted of his murder, I either enjoyed killing Daniel Murphy or genuinely believed it was the right thing to do, and most likely perjured myself to get acquitted.

She's not wrong.

Dr. Mills finishes by telling the board that she recommends that my parole should be revoked, mostly to protect Alex's safety.

When I hear that, I shoot a quick glance at Alex, who looks fucking mutinous.

Elise calls Alex and I to testify in my defense, but Alex can't keep her cool. She starts to cry as she vehemently tells the board that Dr. Mills is full of shit, that I've *never* stalked her or abused her, and that we have an extremely healthy relationship.

From the look on Dr. Mills' face, I might not be the only one who can tell she's lying.

When Elise questions me, I try to stay calm as I explain that I believe Dr. Mills is unprofessionally biased against me based on her own misunderstandings and professional insufficiencies, which are not reflective of myself or my actions.

It's a mistake to look over at Alex, because she's on the verge of tears and biting her nails. I know she did that as a kid, but I've *never* seen her do it, and I lose my temper.

My voice is caustic as I tell the board that Dr. Mills is unethically abusing her power to punish me for not respecting her, and that she's willfully conflating a traumatic case of self-defense with recidivism because she's an incompetent fucking idiot who should be fired at once.

Only Alex and Dr. Mills look unsurprised by how angry I am.

When the board revokes my parole, Alex becomes furious and calls Dr. Mills a fucking cunt in front of the whole room, which is shocking even to me. Alex is so upset she has to be removed from the room, and as I watch her get escorted out, I catch her eye and mouth *I love you* right before I start losing my mind.

I'm unwilling to let her out of my sight for a *minute*, much less a fucking *year*.

I can't keep her safe if I'm in prison.

I turn to stare at Dr. Mills, and I let her see on my face what I think about her and her bullshit interpretation of my relationship, how I feel about going back to prison, and just how much I agree with Alex.

57

ALEX

WEDNESDAY, AUGUST 28

Bailey sits with me outside the courtroom as I wait to be called to testify, rubbing soothing circles against my back as I focus on grounding techniques my therapist has taught me.

"Do you want me to come in with you? I can stay here," she offers quietly.

"Um, if...if I say yes, can...will you pretend you never heard any of it?" Bailey slips her hand into mine and squeezes.

"Of course, babe. I'll be there for you however you need." I grip her hand, unable to look her in the eye, and we sit there until the bailiff comes to collect me.

***

I'm nervous as I'm sworn in, catching the eyes of Bailey, Elise, and Theo to ground myself as I stutter through the oath. When the prosecutor starts asking me questions, I have to work hard to focus on staying present and not dissociate. Elise and I prepared extensively for the testimony, but talking to the prosecutor is still harder than I thought it would be.

I don't want to talk about any of these things, but I need Theo to come home, so I sit on the stand and I cry and I answer all of the questions the way Elise and I practiced and I let everyone on the jury pity me, even though I fucking hate it. I pretend the crime scene photos aren't as horrifically brutal as they are, and I pretend like watching Theo kill Danny wasn't terrifying, and I do my best to carefully playact around the truth of what happened, the truth that everyone in the room knows but that no one can acknowledge.

What Theo did wasn't self-defense.

It was an act of love.

***

Elise instructed us to act dignified and somber if Theo got acquitted, so I bite my cheeks not to smile, and we keep our heads down as we hurry to our car. We're barely out of the courthouse parking lot when Theo leans in towards me, his dimples bracketing his wide smile as he slips his fingers through mine.

"Hi, sweetheart," he whispers, and I grin at him, squeezing his hand and trying not to cry.

"*Hey*, baby."

"You're a fucking angel," he says softly, "a lying, manipulative little *angel* who just saved me from a lifetime of prison food." I laugh, crying because it's the first time I've laughed in six months and because I've missed him so badly.

When I pull up to a red light, he's immediately in my space, halfway in the driver's seat as he cups my face in his hands, whispering that he loves me in between soft, deep kisses. I'm lost in the kiss until someone behind us honks, and Theo swears, flipping off the driver behind us as I push him back to his seat and start driving again.

"I didn't even lie that much," I say, and Theo rolls his eyes at me. "Okay, well, your legal argument couldn't be 'he fucking deserved it,' which he *did*," I say a little more bitterly than I intend. Theo doesn't respond, and when I look at him, his face has gone entirely blank, his knee bouncing quickly.

"Teddy?" He shakes his head, running his hand through his hair.

"What? Sorry, I was just...yeah. Anyway, it's over. We don't ever have to think about it again." His hand grips mine hard, and I grip his back.

"No, we don't. I'd rather think about what you'll do to me when we get home," I say, trying hard to keep my voice light. He looks over at me and smirks, but the corners of his mouth are tight and he's much more tense than he was a minute ago.

I swallow my creeping anxiety and focus on the fact that everything can finally go back to normal now.

***

I start sobbing the second we're through the front door, all the stress of the last six months overtaking me in a heartbeat, and Theo pulls me into his arms immediately, kissing every part of me he can reach.

"It's okay, sweetheart, I've got you. Come here," he whispers as he bends down to pick me up, and I wrap my legs around him and bury my face into his neck. He grips the back of my thighs as he walks us into the living room, holding me closely on the couch, one hand cupping the back of my head and his other arm locking around my waist.

He talks to me as I cry, telling me how much he missed me, how much he loves me, how he's going to make up for everything, how he's going to make sure I'm happy from now on, and his breath catches as he starts to cry, too.

We stay like that for a long time until he takes a deep breath and I follow, and we calm each other down. I pull back and smile at him, taking his face in my hands and looking at his teary, vulnerable expression.

"Welcome home." His face lights up with an ecstatic smile, and he pulls me into a slow, deep kiss.

It takes me a minute to realize that we're home, completely alone, and that I'm straddling him on our couch. Every nerve comes alive as I feel his body responding to mine, and for the first time since everything happened, desire rushes into my blood. I push the kiss from something sweet to something far hungrier, pressing my body into Theo's and grinding my hips down into his. He makes a soft, deep sound as his hands grip me, and I break the kiss to trail my lips along his jaw.

"I need you," I whisper into his ear as I reach between us and graze my fingers against his hard cock. His hips jerk and he makes a harsh sound in the back of his throat, but he tenses up and stops me as I start to undo his belt. I look at him in surprise, and he seems anxious as he gives me a forced smile.

"Can we take this slowly?" I laugh and shake my head, continuing to undo his pants and swallowing the anxiety flooding the back of my throat. It's fine, everything is fine. Theo very gently moves my hands away, and panic slices through me. "Sweetheart, I think we should talk about this, okay?" I can't look at him, so I stare down at my hands as the happiness drains out of me.

I was worried about this, but I didn't think it would actually *happen*. I thought it was so unlikely that I didn't even bring it up to my therapist. Dread starts to numb me as I climb off him, curling up into a ball and burying my face in my hands.

"Alex? What's going on?" I focus on breathing, trying not to cry. This isn't *fair*. "Honey, can you *please* talk to me?" Theo's voice is panicky.

"I can't fucking believe you," I spit, finally looking over at him to see that he's gone pale. "I didn't think you were a piece of shit, but I guess I was *wrong*." Theo looks confused as he reaches a hand out for me, and his face becomes devastated as I flinch away from him. "Don't you fucking touch me. I can't believe you don't *want* me because of what happened." Once it's out of my mouth, I can't keep myself from sobbing.

Theo looks at me, stricken, then leans over quickly and grabs me around the waist, hauling me into his arms and holding me tightly as I try to push away from him.

"*Fuck, no*," he says harshly. "That's not...I wouldn't...no fucking way, Alex, not a fucking chance." I collapse into him, and he holds me closely as I cry, rubbing my back and whispering reassurances I can barely make out. Once I've calmed down slightly, he cups my face, gently wiping my tears away with his thumb and looking at me with concern. "I will always want you more than anything, I fucking *promise.* Nothing will ever change that, do you understand me?" I nod, the anxiety draining out of me, and I rearrange myself in his arms until I'm straddling him again, running my hands along his chest.

"I'm just worried that sex isn't a good idea," he says quietly. I close my eyes, trying to keep my face neutral to hide my anger. This is bullshit, and he and my therapist are both wrong. It's fine, *I'm* fine, and I want to feel normal again. I *need* to feel normal again. I force myself to smile at him, trying to be reassuring as I run a hand through his hair.

"I think it's a good idea," I say, leaning down and tracing his neck with soft, open-mouthed kisses. He groans as I drag my teeth against his neck, and I feel him getting hard again as his hands slide up my waist, gripping my ribcage and pulling me closer.

There we go.

"I still think we should go slowly," he says softly. I scoff and push back from him, frustrated.

"*Why?*" He looks surprised at how harsh my tone is.

"Sweetheart, we don't have to rush this. I want to make sure you're okay," he says quietly, tucking my hair behind my ear, and I bite back a sharp response. I can tell he's thinking about what happened, I can see it in the concern on his face, and I fucking *hate* it.

I want him to be the way he was with me before.

I want that warm, hazy feeling he gives me, not *this.*

"I'm *fine*, Teddy," I say sweetly, running my hands down his body. "I just *need* you." I kiss my way along his jaw, biting his earlobe gently, and his hands flex against me. I pull back to look at him as I press my hips into his, grinding against him, and I can tell he's not going to hold out much longer. "*Please* fuck me, Theo," I whisper in a low voice, and I smile as I watch his pupils dilate and hear him swear under his breath.

He's always been so fucking easy.

"Only if we take this slowly, okay?" I nod as I kiss him and start undoing his shirt, knowing we're not going to go slowly. "God, I fucking missed you," he whispers against my lips before kissing me again, taking his time, as though we've never kissed before. My entire body feels electric, and I start to feel good as I run my tongue against his. His hands roam over my body frantically, and everything starts to feel like it should between us.

I work hard not to tense up when his fingers pass over the scars on my leg as he moves his hands up my thighs.

His hands roam over my hips and grip my ass, and he groans as he digs his fingers into me, seeming to forget that we're going slow as he pushes up against me. I know he can't help himself when it comes to me, so I grind down against him and he moans, pulling off my dress and trailing his hands down my body appreciatively.

I ignore how his mouth tightens when his eyes land on the scars on my skin. I push his shirt down his arms, throwing it to the ground and lean back to pull his t-shirt off. I run my hands over his taught, tense muscles, ignoring the scars on the left side of his body.

I pull him back into a kiss, and he finally gets lost in me the way I want. He slips my bra off, sucking one of my nipples into his mouth, and I whine as he spends a long time focusing on one breast and then the other, kissing and biting and licking until I'm finally lost in him. I moan, reaching down between us, but he grabs my hand gently and moves it away.

"Theo, *come on*," I whine, and he pulls back, looking at my face intently.

"Let me take care of you first," he says sweetly.

"*No*," I snap. I'm done waiting. "Just fuck me," I beg, standing up and slipping my thong off and undoing his pants. He stares at me apprehensively as I straddle him again, but he slips a hand in between us, barely grazing his fingers over me. I flinch, startled by the touch. My skin crawls, and I fight to keep from pulling away from him.

No. This is *not* happening.

His hand stills instantly, his eyes searching my face nervously. "Alex, are you okay?" I don't say anything, I just nod tightly and try to keep my body loose, but it's not fooling him. He stops touching me, his hand going back to my hip, and I get pissed.

This is bullshit.

He makes a soft, raspy sound as I reach between us with one hand and grip him hard, and he thrusts into my hand involuntarily. He tenses up and jerks back, looking at me anxiously as his hands grip my hips and push them back slightly.

"*Goddammit,* sweetie, can you fucking *slow down?*" My temper flares, fury rushing through me.

This is *not* getting taken from me. No fucking way am I letting Danny ruin sex for me. I just need to push myself through this, and then I'll be back to normal.

"Shut *up*," I snap. I grip him and line myself up, tensing up the second I feel him against me, and I fight off tears as I notch him into my entrance. Theo's eyes widen and he goes rigid beneath me, grabbing my hips and pushing me away harder.

"*Alexandria, don-*" I force myself down onto him and cry out immediately at the pain. Every muscle in my body locks up as panic floods through me, numbing everything.

For one brief moment, I can see Danny's furious face overlaid on Theo's horrified one, and I start to hyperventilate as I pull away from my body.

"Oh, *fuck*. Fuck, fuck, *fuck*." I hear Theo freaking out, but I'm already so deep inside of myself that it sounds like it's coming through water. I can feel my body being moved and I can hear vague sounds, but I let everything fade.

I can't believe this is happening.

I thought my therapist was full of shit when she said sex might be hard. She said Theo and I should go slow, but I thought if we could just get there, it would mean that everything was finally over, that everything was back to how it should be, that everything was back to normal.

It would mean that *I* was back to normal.

I guess not.

I know I'm safe because I'm with Theo and we're at home, so I close my eyes and drift down into myself. The only thing that permeates is Theo's warm scent, which calms me down.

I don't know how long it takes, but I slowly become aware that I'm wrapped up in a large blanket on our bed, Theo's arms around me and his soothing, low voice speaking softly. I can feel his lips moving in my hair and one of his hands stroking my back gently as his words finally come into focus.

"...be okay, honey. It's not going to last forever, I fucking promise. We'll figure it out, okay? Everything will go back to -" I lean into him slightly, and he stops talking as one of his hands raises to cup my cheek and turn my face up towards him. His brows are knit together in concern, and his eyes search my face.

"What do you need? Can I draw you a bath? Would that help?" I nod, and he leans down to kiss my forehead. "I'll be right back." I watch him slide off the bed, his posture rigid as he walks down the hall to the bathroom. I blink, looking around the room for the clock, realizing it's roughly two hours after we got home.

I curl up into a ball on the bed, holding my knees close to me, letting waves of despair crash over me. Theo comes back into the room and gently pulls me into his arms, carrying me into the bathroom and setting me in the bathtub as the warm water pours into it.

"Do you want tea?" I nod, and he tries to smile at me.

I lay in the large bathtub, turning the cold tap down until the water is scalding, staring out the window, thinking. Theo comes back up a few minutes later with two mugs of tea, placing one on the bathtub tray before he sits down next to the tub, staring at me intently.

"You want to talk about it?" I turn the water off and shrug, curling into a small ball and resting my arms on my knees. "Are you okay?" I look up at the ceiling, shaking my head a little.

"It's not fair," I say quietly. "He's still taking things from me." I look over at Theo, his jaw clenched and his face blank as he tries not to freak out. "I'm sorry I pushed it, but I just wanted everything to be normal again. I didn't think it would be...I mean, it's *you*. I feel so fucking safe with you." He smiles at me a little. "Everything is hard, but *this* wasn't supposed to be hard. I don't even know if you'll be here after next week, and I can't connect with you the way I want, and I just...*fuck*," I sob, and Theo rubs my back.

"Everything's going to be okay."

"You can't lie to me," I choke out, and he pulls my face into his hands, kissing my forehead.

"Sweetheart, I'm not," he whispers, his voice pained. "I fucking *promise*."

***

Theo spends the rest of the day trying hard to take care of me. He doesn't let me out of sight and barely lets me out of his arms. I pretend I'm fine, but it's impossible to hide how devastated I am, and I can tell it's making him more and more stressed. He can't figure out how to take care of me, and I can't figure out how to get him to calm down.

Once it's time for bed, he holds me tightly and curls around me protectively, and I feel so safe that I fall asleep easily for the first time since my birthday. I wake up in the middle of the night from a nightmare and reach out for Theo, only to find that the bed is empty, and I panic. I flip on the lamp on the nightstand and see a quickly scrawled note that just says *basement*, and the panic ebbs.

I find him running with his headphones on, and I sit on the stairs and watch him for a while, noticing that he lost more weight in jail than I realized. When he finally gets off the treadmill, he lays on the ground, breathing hard. He covers his face with his left arm and starts flexing and gripping his right hand, which doesn't have a full range of motion anymore.

I watch him for a minute before I go down and sit next to him, gently taking his right hand in mine. He startles a little and pulls his headphones off, and I can tell from his eyes that he's been crying. I start massaging his hand, being mindful not to pull too hard on the skin of the large, deep pink scar that spans his palm. He sighs, closing his eyes for a second.

"Why are you up, sweetheart?" I dig my fingers against the base of his thumb, and he groans appreciatively.

"I had a nightmare." He shoots me a pained look. "What about you?"

"Me, too." I lace my fingers through his and stretch his hand gently. We stay there for a minute, Theo looking up at me with concern as I focus on easing the tension in his hand.

"What happens in yours?" I ask, and he closes his eyes, squeezing our interlaced fingers.

"You die," he whispers. "If it's a good dream, I get you to the hospital first." I ignore the tears pricking in the corners of my eyes as I push his damp hair back from his forehead, staring at the puckered, deep pink scar beneath his left collarbone before I graze my fingers over it gently.

"Can you come back to bed?" He nods and stands up, keeping his hand in mine as he follows me upstairs. He takes a quick shower before curling up in bed with me. He winds his fingers through mine, placing our hands on my chest and stomach, and we lay there for a long time, synching our breath and helping each other relax.

"I promise we're going to get through this," he whispers into my hair as I drift off.

Lying there, half asleep and at home in his arms, I almost believe him.

***

After that first day, we try to act normal, but nothing is normal. We don't talk about what happened, and we don't talk about what might happen, we just try to be present with each other.

I'm able to get real sleep, but Theo can't. The second day we're home, I wake up at three in the morning to him shaking me awake, begging me to wake up as he shoves his fingers into my neck. After that, he barely sleeps at all, and he spends most of the time I'm asleep preparing for if he has to go back to prison.

He won't talk with me about it because that makes going back feel like a real possibility, but he makes me sign a lot of paperwork, tells me I should get my bank cards to his accounts within a week, and has the most expensive, aggressive security system he can buy installed.

He won't acknowledge that any of it is a precaution, and I don't push it.

When I talk to my therapist about what happened when we tried to have sex, Theo's in the same room on his computer. He has headphones on, but I know he's listening because when my therapist recommends trying again, he gives my laptop a dirty look and shakes his head. Later that day, I walk into the office wearing nothing but his college sweater and sit on the edge of his desk while he's on a call with someone at Anderson Timber. His pupils dilate as he sees the hem of the sweater riding high up my thighs, but he looks away quickly, his knee bouncing rapidly.

I want to push, but I don't.

As the week goes on, we get moments together where everything feels right. For an hour here or there, we feel normal, wrapped up in each other and smiling and joking like nothing happened. We spend most of the week in the kitchen, on the couch watching TV, on the porch watching the ships, or in bed holding each other tightly.

When I make dinner for him one night, he leans against the counter next to the stove, watching me with wide eyes and smiling the whole time. We run together on Sunday, and it feels like any other week as we finish our run, chatting and walking to the coffee shop hand in hand.

Being in the coffee shop is a different story, however. It's packed, and Theo's tense immediately. When a man steps too closely into my space, Theo's arm is hard around my waist as he hauls me against him. His entire body is rigid and slightly shaking, and when I look up at him, his face is blank. On the walk home, he keeps his arm tight around my shoulders and makes us cross the street twice to avoid walking near other people.

When I ask him about it, I find out that his anxiety about my safety has gotten *much* worse than I realized.

The day before the parole hearing, Elise visits to talk us through what will happen and tells us it should be fine, but after she leaves, Theo's a wreck and won't let me leave his side for a second. I lay in his arms that night and he promises me that everything will be okay, that no matter what happens he's going to take care of me, that if worse comes to worst there's only a year left on his sentence anyway, and I start to get more and more nervous.

I don't want to be away from him ever again.

I don't feel safe without him.

***

I pace in the hallway once I'm removed from the hearing room for screaming at Theo's therapist, furious and heartbroken and fighting to ground myself before I have a panic attack. Elise finally exits the room and sighs when she sees me.

"I'm sorry this was the outcome," she says, gripping my shoulder briefly. "Theo's already asked me to pursue every avenue to have that woman's license revoked."

I sigh angrily. "Good. When can I see him?"

"Alex," Elise says gently, "you won't be able to see him for at least three weeks while he's processed back into prison." I gape at her in horror. "I'll swing by tomorrow to help you get registered, okay?" I go numb and nod absently, wandering away from Elise in a daze.

I don't remember a minute of the drive home.

When I walk into the house, I realize I don't like being alone in it anymore. It feels empty without Theo now, too big without his intense, frenetic energy taking up so much space, and it makes me feel like I'm shrinking away again. I text Suzie that I won't be at work for a few days before I grab two bottles of wine and head for the bathroom, sitting in the hot bath and drinking.

For the first time since I got out of the hospital, I remember exactly why I had such a bad drinking problem for so long.

***

The first time I visit Theo in prison, he's a nervous wreck. He holds me so tightly it's hard to breathe as he kisses me desperately before asking me question after question about how I'm feeling, what I've been doing, how therapy is going, if I'm eating, how much I'm drinking, *everything*.

We've talked about all this over the phone, but I think he wants to see if I'm lying.

I try to calm him down, but his anxiety is worse than I've ever seen it. The table is shaking because his knee is bouncing so hard, and his hands are so tight around mine that it hurts. I ask him how he is, but he doesn't want to discuss it. I beg, and he tells me prison is worse than he remembers. He hates the people, hates the food, hates the lack of agency, but all of it pales in comparison to how much he hates being away from me.

"Fucking Dr. Mills," he spits. His jaw clenches, and he exhales hard. "I swear to god I'm going to kill her the second I get out of here," he mutters under his breath, shaking his head slightly. I snort and roll my eyes at him.

"Yeah, *right*. We've already filed a complaint against her with the state board, and Elise says she's looking into every avenue to get back at her."

"I want her to lose everything," Theo says quietly. When I look at him closely, he seems like he's staring right through me, and a wave of dread rolls through me.

"Oh, you better be fucking joking," I hiss at him. He nods absently, and I lean forward, yanking my hands out of his and fighting off tears.

"Look at me, Theodore." His eyes focus on mine, his gaze sharp. "Danny was one thing, but I *will* leave you if you even *think* about killing her," I whisper harshly. He frowns, his jaw tensing.

"It was just a joke, Alex." I lift my thumb to my mouth and start biting my nail, and Theo begins to look nervous. "Honey, I'm just upset, okay? You *know* I'd never do that." I stare at him, scrutinizing his face, my stomach churning.

"You're not allowed to lie to me anymore," I say quietly. His eyes go wide, and he opens his mouth to say something, but the guards cut him off by calling out that we have five minutes, and I wince. "I'm not going to be here next week," I say quickly, and Theo's face drains of all color as he leans forward, reaching for me.

"Alex, *listen to me*, okay? It was a bad joke, I promise, so *please* don't fucking do this." His voice is panicked, so I slip my hands back into his and rub my foot up his calf slowly to calm him down.

"I have to go to Boston," I say. "Suzie helped me with Danny's estate, but I've been putting off dealing with the house for months." Theo's mouth becomes a thin line, and he shakes his head slightly as his grip on my hands becomes almost bruising.

"*Don't*. Wait until I'm out, or hire someone to do it, but *please* don't go back to Boston," he begs.

"Teddy, you know I'm coming back, right?" He looks away from me quickly, shrugging. "*Baby,*" I chide, and he exhales harshly.

"How long will you be gone?"

"I don't know. A few weeks, maybe?" Theo swallows hard, looking nauseous.

"Fuck, Alex. When do you leave?"

I glance up at the clock, sucking in a sharp breath. "Um, in about six hours." Theo makes an aggravated noise and yanks his hands away from me, running them through his hair and shooting me a dirty look.

"You *seriously* didn't mention this to me at *any* fucking point this week?" I wince, feeling a surge of guilt. I don't think it's a good idea to tell him that I was putting off this trip so he could come with me.

"I only bought the tickets last night. I need to get it over with." He nods tersely, running his hands through his hair again.

"Fine. Where are you staying?"

I look at him incredulously. "The *house*, Theo."

"Absolutely the fuck not," he snaps. I open my mouth to argue, and he shoots me a sharp look. "This is non-negotiable, Alexandria. I'm not letting you stay in that fucking house. I want you to be comfortable and I need to know you're safe, so you'll stay at a nice fucking hotel." He clears his throat, his jaw tightens, and he leans across the table, taking my hands in his again. "*Please* don't be stubborn about this." I take in the dark circles under his eyes and how on edge he seems, and I squeeze his hands.

"Whatever you want." He nods, looking down at the table for a minute, trying and failing to compose himself.

"Could you *not* drop these things on me out of nowhere? I'm freaking the fuck out about being away from you as it is," he snaps.

"Yeah, of course. I'm so sorry." He sighs and looks up at the ceiling. "*I'm* sorry. I didn't mean to snap at you."

My heart breaks a little at how panicked he looks when the guard tells us it's time for the visitors to leave a minute later. Theo kisses me urgently before we have to separate, holding my face in his hands.

"I love you. Be safe. Answer when I call," he begs.

"I love you, too. I'll be back soon, okay?"

He doesn't look like he believes me.

58

ALEX

SATURDAY, OCTOBER 5

Boston feels strange to me – the familiar sights and well-traveled roads feel foreign. I check into my hotel and order room service, spending the rest of the night in the bathtub with a bottle of wine.

The next morning, I take a rideshare to the house, and when I pull Danny's keys out of my bag, I'm shaking so hard that I can barely open the door. The door swings open and walking into the house feels like stepping back into a different version of my life, and it's so overwhelming that I sprint upstairs for the big guest room, my old childhood bedroom with the Alice in Wonderland murals long since painted over, and I hide in the closet and cry the way I used to when I was a kid.

When Theo calls, I talk to him as I walk through the house, and he helps me keep a handle on my anxiety until I step into the bedroom I shared with Danny. I run to the bathroom and vomit immediately, and when Theo begs me to go back to the hotel, I do.

The next morning, I go to the cemetery near my old house and visit my parents' graves for the first time since I buried them. They were two miles away for nine years, but I never visited them because I thought they would have hated who I'd let myself become.

I sit on the grass with my coffee and tell them everything that happened after they died, about Danny, about running away, about my life in Astoria, about Theo, about wanting to see them when I was dying, all of it. I cry on and off for hours as I talk to them, feeling lighter with everything I tell them.

By the time I leave the cemetery, I feel unburdened.

Theo calls as I walk to a nearby restaurant that my mom used to love, and Theo starts to lose his cool when he hears the sounds of cars and people in the background. He begs me not to walk anywhere alone again, sounding close to a panic attack. I don't want to lie to him, but I know he needs to look at me to tell if I'm lying, so I agree.

What he doesn't know won't hurt him, in this instance.

***

Going through the house is overwhelming. I never realized how many *things* Danny and I had, and I have to decide what to do with *all* of them.

I've been in Boston for a few days when Danny's family realizes I'm there, and his brother David shows up and tells me that if I were a decent person, I would give *Danny's* family *Danny's* house and *Danny's* money.

When I laugh at him and tell him he's insane, he turns an ugly shade of red and tells me it's my fault that Danny's dead, that I'm an ungrateful whore, and that I never deserved him. I stand in the doorway and watch him try to push me around and manipulate me the way Danny used to, and a savage joy spreads through my body when I tell him to fuck off and slam the door in his face.

David, his aunts, and several of his cousins show up the next day, so I answer the door with one of Danny's guns, which scares all of them enough that they don't try to push their way into the house. The gun is unloaded, which is for the best, because all the rage I suppressed for a decade wells up and I start screaming at them.

I tell them about what Danny did to me in the cabin, what he did to me when I was a kid, everything he'd *ever* done to me, and I tell them to get away from *my* house, my *parent's* house, that they'll get fucking *nothing*, that they can all rot in hell with Danny, and I'll send them there myself if they show up again.

They're all so shocked that they don't say anything before I slam the door in their faces.

I'm so furious when they leave that I destroy anything personal of Danny's that I can find in the house, anything he loved, anything I can get my hands on.

The house is a fucking wreck by the time I'm done, and so am I.

When Theo calls an hour later, I sob through telling him what happened. He says he's proud of me, that he loves me, and then he offers to send Danny's family copies of the crime scene photos so they can see that Danny got exactly what he deserved. I laugh and tell him he's insane, but that I love him and I'll think about it.

I take myself to a nice dinner afterward and walk around Beacon Hill, soothed by the familiar old, red brick buildings, happy to be a different person than I was the last time I was here.

The next day, I hire cleaners to deal with the absolute mess I made. While they clean, I spend the day selling all the jewelry and watches at a pawn shop, selling the cars for much less than they're worth to a used car dealership, and sticking Danny's motorcycle and all the paperwork out on the street with a FREE sign, mainly because all of it would have pissed Danny off to no end.

I take a break from dealing with everything and go to Cape Cod for a few days, staying in Hyannis, as close to my grandmother's old house as possible. I walk along the beach, taking photos of everything to show Theo the beaches I grew up on. He calls when I'm tide pooling, and I spend the time describing it to him, telling him how much I wish he was with me and that I'd like to bring him out here someday.

It's the first phone call we have where Theo sounds even remotely calm, and I know it's because it's the first call we've had where I'm not a nervous wreck.

By the time I head back to Boston, I'm ready to leave, so I hire movers to donate everything in the house that didn't belong to me before I met Danny. The only things left in the house after that are my books, a few boxes of my keepsakes, some of my parents' things, and my mother's paintings.

I stand in the mostly empty house, waiting for the movers to come pack and ship all my things back to Astoria, and I stare at the painting of me and the rabbit. I refused to look at it before now, but it seems different from the painting I looked at before I left Boston.

For the first time in my life, it feels good to look at, because I can finally see all the pain and the joy and the love that my mother put into it.

As the movers take the boxes of my parents' things downstairs from the attic, they find the fireplace grate with the long spikes tucked away in a corner under a tarp, and I start to cry. When Theo calls, I tell him we can have a real Christmas when he's out, with the ham and the grate and the aluminum tree and French toast and whatever other insane bullshit he wants. He asks if we can skip the life-altering panic attack, and I tell him maybe, but only if he's good.

He's quiet for a long moment before he tells me that he likes being good for me, and a small wave of heat courses down my spine for the first time since the day he got acquitted.

I want *that* back.

I have almost everything else back.

I finally have access to my identity, my past, and my *life*, but with a few exceptions, like my bank accounts and my keepsakes, I don't want it.

It's not mine anymore.

On my last day in Boston, I donate Danny's entire life insurance policy to a local domestic violence organization, find a realtor to sell the house for me, and go to the cemetery to say goodbye to my parents.

I schedule my flight so I can drive directly from the airport to Salem to see Theo, but I don't tell him I'm coming.

The second he walks into the visitation room, his face relaxes into relief, and he holds me so tightly I can't breathe.

"Is this why you didn't answer the phone this morning? I wish you would have told me, I was freaking out. How was the flight? How are you?" I lean forward over the table and smile, trapping one of his ankles between mine and lacing our fingers together.

"I'm just happy to be home." He blinks, his face blank for a moment before a broad, crooked smile spreads over his face, filling my chest with warmth.

***

Once my childhood home sells and nothing legally ties me to my old life anymore, I change my name to Alexandria Marie Shearer.

I chose it, and it's mine.

"It's so annoying," I complain to Theo, sipping the piss-poor excuse for coffee the visitation room vending machine serves. "It's so much effort to change a *name*. I have to get a new driver's license, a new passport, a new social security card, my bank accounts changed over, *all* of it, and it's a fuck ton of paperwork." He shrugs with one shoulder, his other arm tight around my waist because the guard on duty is less strict and we can sit next to each other.

"That sucks, honey. I don't remember the process of my last name getting changed, but I was a kid," he says, sipping his own coffee.

"Yeah, well, I should have changed *my* last name to Anderson. It would have saved me the trouble of doing it later," I say, sipping my coffee to hide my smile as Theo's body goes rigid next to me. I glance up at him, and his head tilts slightly to the side as he pulls me closer. He smiles at me slowly, one side of his mouth picking up more than the other, and he's unable to speak for a minute.

"Um, you don't have to change your name again," he says finally, and I raise my eyebrows in surprise.

"Really? I thought you'd be thrilled about that." He shrugs, trying and failing to seem nonchalant, and I feel his thumb tracing circles on my hip.

"I mean, *yeah*, but I'm thrilled either way. I want you to be happy, so it's your choice." I'm the one who can't speak for a minute after he says that, and then we get yelled at by the guards because excessive displays of affection are *not* allowed.

"I fucking hate it here," he mutters as he lets go of me, shooting the guard a dirty look as I begrudgingly move to the other side of the table.

***

The year passes quickly. I rebuild my life in Astoria in a more permanent way. I'm not hiding here anymore, and everything truly is my choice, so for the first time in my life, I feel like I'm standing on solid ground.

I slip back into my old routine and expand it. I go back to work full time, mostly because I love the women I work with, who are more family than anything else at this point. Catherine, Suzie, and Bailey come over for dinner once a month, and I have Sunday dinners with Bailey and her family. I babysit Miles whenever I can, and he even comes to my house occasionally.

Anna and Jessica and I go out for brunch every other week, and I start going back to trivia with them. The first time I go, I see Ben, and he pales when he sees me and sits as far away from me as possible.

I ignore him, but the girls don't.

Anna smiles a little too wide when she asks me how Theo's doing and tells me how much she hopes he'll start coming with us when he's out. Jessica joins in, sweetly asking Ben if he's ever met my boyfriend, and I have a hard time not laughing at the terrified look on his face.

He never shows up at trivia again.

Theo gets slightly calmer and less panicked as the months go by, but he *hates* prison. He gets thin because he hates the food and exercises as much as possible to help with his separation anxiety, which has gotten extremely bad.

The prison psychiatrist puts him on medication, and he seems different, calmer and more solid somehow, but less like himself. He doesn't like it, although it *does* help with the anxiety, much to his chagrin. He's also forced to see a therapist in prison, who he either refuses to speak to or lies to constantly.

I don't care, because I buy two copies of every book my therapist recommends, books about trauma and self-esteem and domestic violence, and I make Theo read them with me.

We both struggle with it.

We read things that apply to us individually, but have difficulty addressing them whenever they interact with our relationship. We read things that apply to our relationship and feel like they're right for other people, but wrong when it comes to us. There's a level of intense codependency and trauma bonding that we can both acknowledge and recognize is *technically* unhealthy, but it doesn't feel wrong to either of us.

I get comfortable enough in therapy and my support group that I start to let little things about Theo slip by accident. When my support group leader pulls me aside and starts trying to address my relationship with Theo, I stop going to the group. When my therapist starts trying to address my relationship with Theo, I stop going to therapy.

Without ever explicitly discussing it, Theo and I decide to do nothing to change how our relationship works, because it works for us.

We start fitting together in a much deeper way. We get to know each other better, *really* know each other, because neither of us lies anymore. We write each other long letters about the things that are too hard for us to talk about, and we talk on the phone every day, and I visit every week. Because there are no conjugal visits in Oregon, it feels like a weird, continued version of us dating.

I miss him constantly, but I make a point to enjoy my time without him. I have the distinct feeling that once he gets out, it'll be a while before I'll be alone again.

I don't mind.

He doesn't want to let me out of his sight, and I always want him to know where I am.

I get the desire to start painting again a few months after Theo goes back to prison, and then I start painting a *lot*. It becomes a fixation, and it's all I do with my time outside of working and seeing my friends. I paint abstract canvases in varied colors, but they always have the same general shapes. Every time I finish a painting, I feel slightly lighter, but I don't know why. I keep painting the same thing in different forms for weeks until I finally feel like painting something else.

After a month, I look at one of the canvases and realize I've been painting various abstracted versions of Danny's face hovering over me in the cabin, and then I tuck all the paintings away in the attic.

I *almost* have everything back that he took from me.

It takes me six months after my failed attempt to have sex with Theo to start masturbating again, and I don't push myself, but I do everything I can to feel in control of my body again. I talk to Theo about it, and he begs me to take it slowly.

It doesn't work at first, but I eventually get there, and I cry from sheer happiness the first time I have an orgasm. I work to get used to the feeling of having something inside me again, which takes a *lot* longer to adjust to, but I finally get to the point where I can feel pleasure with no undercurrent of fear.

Once I have back the final thing Danny tried to take from me, I bring all the paintings down from the attic and burn them. Once they're burnt, I write Theo a long, detailed, explicit letter about what I want him to do to me when he's home, complete with a small pile of polaroids.

The next time I see him, he looks at me like he's starving.

***

When his release is a few weeks away, we talk about what we're going to do when he gets out.

Theo tells me that besides marrying me immediately and getting me pregnant as soon as I let him, *if* I let him, he'd like to take me somewhere, anywhere I want to go, because we both deserve a fucking vacation. I ask him if he wants to help plan it, but he says he doesn't care where we go, what we do, or how long we're there, as long as it's somewhere he won't lose sight of me easily.

He tells me he wants one week at home before we leave, to decompress and cook and fuck and relax, and I flash him a big, shit-eating grin.

"So, what you're saying is that you want to fuck and play house?" He shakes his head at me, smirking.

"That's pretty much all I've ever wanted, Alex."

"I fucking *knew* it."

59

THEO

SUNDAY, AUGUST 3

The meds made time pass faster and made my separation anxiety easier to manage, but I stop taking them a week before I get out. Alex notices the difference immediately, but she doesn't say anything.

I can tell I'm not the only one who prefers it when I'm not on them.

Once they wear off, I've got so much energy that I feel like I'm crawling out of my skin. I can't sleep much, and I have no appetite anyway because the food, even the stuff from the commissary, is all fucking *disgusting*. I notice that my anxiety and nightmares are much worse without the meds, but I know it'll all go away once I finally get my fucking hands on Alex again.

The day before I'm released, she visits wearing the exact green dress she wore the first time I saw her in Catherine's office two years ago, and I freeze when I see her.

She's still stunning, but she looks so different now. She stopped dying her hair, changing it back to her natural honey-colored blonde, and she cropped it halfway up her long, delicate neck. The stress of dealing with everything killed her appetite for a long time, but she's been eating regularly and looks healthy again.

She's healthy for the first time since I've known her. She's calmer and confident, more stable and grounded in herself. She drinks a lot less than she used to, and she won't drink at all if she's upset. She's better at regulating and dealing with her emotions. She doesn't shut down as often, and she doesn't lie to me at all anymore.

She's so fucking perfect.

I pull her tight and give her the short kiss I'm allowed to before we sit down. I look at the guards on duty and know I'm not going to get away with sitting next to her, so I reach my hand across the table and touch any fucking part of her I can. I have less than twenty-four hours, and then I can touch her as much as I want.

A sly smile spreads across her face as she slowly massages my right hand.

"Change of plans for tomorrow. We're not going home right away." I'm too worked up to handle this right now, and I close my eyes and exhale hard, trying to stay calm, but my knee starts bouncing instantly.

"Sweetie, what the *fuck*? Why not?" She grins at me and drags her fingernails across the inside of my wrist, and being turned on by her calms me down slightly.

"Um, I told Bailey that a three-hour car ride after a year without you would be torture, and she surprised us with a nice hotel room ten minutes away." She blushes as she speaks, and I relax at once. "I'm checking in after I leave here. We'll go straight there tomorrow, and then we'll go home the next morning." I make a mental note to add more money to the trust I had Catherine set up for Miles. "She also tried to give me a box of pregnancy tests," Alex mutters under her breath, and I grin.

"Have I ever told you that I *really* like Bailey?" She laughs.

"Constantly, and the feeling is mutual. *Anyway*, the hotel is nice and the reviews on the restaurant are good. I called ahead and asked about room service, so we don't have to leave the room."

"You're so fucking wonderful."

She smirks at me. "I also brought some things I thought you might want."

"I love you."

"I haven't come in a week," she whispers, blushing hard.

"Can't say the same." Especially not now that I'm off the meds and I have a stack of those fucking polaroids she sent me.

"Oh, I'm sure." She looks at me, her eyes full of desire, and I lean forward, keeping my voice low.

"You look *so* fucking needy, sweetheart." She blushes a deep pink as she stares at my lips, nodding slowly.

"You have no idea." I have to reach down and adjust myself so I'm tucked into my waistband, and she looks at me with her beautiful, wide brown eyes, licks her plush pink lips, and starts whispering to me all the things she wants me to do to her tomorrow.

She's driving me fucking crazy, but I know I need to be careful. It's been a year, but I remember the panic attack she had when we tried to have sex last time, and she only just started masturbating again a few months ago. I don't want it to be anyone but us in that room tomorrow, which means I *need* to keep my shit together for once in my life and take my time with her.

By the time the visit is over, Alex has spent an hour working me up so much that when I kiss her goodbye, she drags her fingers down my back and pushes her hips against mine as she slips her tongue into my mouth, and I come from that alone.

I have to bite my tongue until I bleed to not openly react in the room full of people, and she laughs so hard that she starts to cry when she realizes what's happened. I shoot her a dirty look.

"You're an *asshole*, you know that?" She smiles beatifically up at me as she steps away.

"You just figured that out?" I laugh as she turns away. "I'll see you tomorrow, baby," she calls over her shoulder, glancing back and winking at me.

***

I give my cellmate everything I've bought from the commissary and pack all the letters and drawings and photos Alex sent me over the last year, and then I almost lose my mind when I realize I have another eighteen hours before I get out.

Time slows to a crawl, and I live ten years in the time between Alex leaving and when I get called up to the office the next morning. I only start to feel somewhat calm once the checkout process begins, but I'm so wound up that it feels like it takes another ten years. One of the guards looks amused at how I'm bouncing on my toes and checking the clock every thirty seconds.

Once I'm finally out in the parking lot, I barely have to look for Alex before I spot her. She's parked right in front, leaning against my car and grinning at me, looking like a fucking wet dream. She's done her hair and makeup, and she's wearing a pair of tall black heels and a very short, very low-cut, silky black dress that might *actually* be lingerie, and I can tell from here she's wearing nothing underneath.

I hate that other people can see her like this, but I don't care about anything except getting my fucking hands on her.

I run over to her, throwing my bag down and bending down to pick her up as she pulls me in and kisses me. My whole body feels like it's on fire the second I touch her, and I moan as she wraps her legs around my hips and her arms lock around my neck. I grip her ass, pushing her back against the car, and she makes a soft whine in the back of her throat as she buries her hands in my hair.

I'm seconds away from undoing my jeans and fucking her right there until a few whistles and jeers from other people leaving snaps me out of the moment.

I don't want anyone else to have access to this side of her, *and* I'm supposed to be taking this slowly. I pull away from her, looking into her gorgeous, flushed face, her pupils wide with want and her lips already swollen, and I work hard to tamp down my desire.

"Hotel. *Now*," I choke out, and she laughs as I put her down, wobbling on her heels for a second when I press her against the car and kiss her again before I shove my bag in the back and get into the passenger seat.

Alex is a *terrible* driver, but that may have something to do with the fact that she's trying to pay attention to the road and her GPS and my lips on her neck and my fingers circling against her clit all at the same time. I'm almost positive that someone in the car next to us at a red light

PERFECT

watches us, but I'm too preoccupied with making Alex come for me to notice.

She pulls up to a nice hotel along the river, and the idea of sleeping in a comfortable bed makes me think that Bailey, Dylan, and Miles would *love* a vacation.

We leave the car with the valet, who smirks at me as he turns away, but I don't know why until I catch our reflection in the door. I start laughing when I realize that I'm in prison release clothes and Alex is basically wearing lingerie, her lipstick is already gone, her hair is messed up, and she's flushed.

She pulls me quickly through the mostly empty lobby and towards the elevators, repeatedly jamming her finger into the button. She looks back at me with a sly smile as I grab her by the hips and pull her back into me.

"The elevators are mirrored."

"*Fuck*, yeah."

The elevator takes *forever*, but that doesn't matter because I've got Alex in my arms, kissing her neck and pressing my hard-on against her lower back, just breathing her in and reveling in being able to touch her as much as I want again. She pushes back into me, making tiny whimpering sounds, and my plans to go slowly with her disintegrate.

I'm going to fuck her against the mirrored wall of this elevator so I can watch her come on my cock from every angle.

Just as the elevator doors open and I push her inside, slipping my hands up her skirt, someone calls for us to hold the elevator. I hear Alex swear, and I jam my finger on the door close button, but the door is slow enough that the man catches it and slips in with us.

I genuinely consider beating the shit out of him for a second until I see Alex's face in the mirror. She looks equally pissed, but she's so fucking cute when she's angry at anyone *other* than me that it calms me down enough to be able to focus on her again.

I grip her waist and lean down, dragging my tongue up the shell of her ear and laughing quietly as she shivers against me.

"I'm going to make you fucking *cry*," I whisper into her ear, and I watch in the mirror as she bites her lip hard to keep from moaning. God, this elevator is slow. I splay one hand across her lower stomach, pulling

569

her flush against my body. "I'm going to fill your pretty little cunt with so much cum you'll be a mess for days." I keep my eyes on hers in the mirror, and she blushes and looks at me adoringly. "You won't be able to walk for a fucking week once I'm done with you, sweetheart."

I'm not actually whispering anymore, and the man who insisted on joining us is highly uncomfortable. He's trying to ignore us, but he looks up and catches sight of gorgeous, frustrated, needy Alex, and his eyes land on her hard nipples poking through the thin, almost see-through silk of the dress.

He stares at her a little too long, a little too appreciatively, and my temper flares immediately. I catch his eye and give him a tight smile as I protectively wrap an arm around her waist.

"I killed the last man who touched her," I say, my voice quiet and cold, and the man looks at me with a horrified expression before quickly looking away. I feel nails digging into my forearm and look down to see Alex frowning up at me.

"That's *not* funny," she chides. I shrug as the elevator finally fucking stops, looking back at the man, who has moved closer to the door and is pointedly not looking at us.

"Neither were the crime scene photos."

He blanches and keeps his head down as Alex gasps at me.

"*Theodore!*" The doors open, and she laughs in delight as I haul her out of the elevator and drag her down the hall.

I'm so determined to get her alone that I don't even realize I have no idea where our room is until Alex laughs and pulls me back, leading me down the other hallway. I look around quickly, and once I'm sure we're alone, I press her up against the door to our room and slip a hand between her legs. I moan into her ear when I feel the smooth, velvety skin of her cunt dripping wet for me, and she fumbles with the key card, finally opening the door. I pick her up and slam the door behind us, throwing her onto the bed and dragging her to the edge, dropping to my knees and slipping her legs over my shoulders.

"Finally, something I want to fucking *eat*." Her giggle turns into a moan as I drag my tongue against her slowly, coating it in the taste of her arousal. Has she always tasted this sweet? I reach up and pinch her nipples through the silk of her dress, rolling them in the way she likes as

I devour her cunt, making her gasp and whimper. I'm delirious as she moans out my name loudly and rakes her hands through my hair.

I don't need to go slowly, I need her to come in my mouth right fucking *now*.

I suck on her clit, flicking my tongue against it, pulling one of my hands away from her perfect tits so I can push two fingers inside her and crook my fingers against her g-spot, pulsing hard in a way that makes her arch off the bed. Her leg starts to tense up, and I drag my other hand down her body and press my hand against her lower stomach, pinning her hips down as she writhes on the bed, pulsing my fingers and sucking her clit until her whole body starts to shake. She shrieks, gripping the duvet as she gushes into my mouth, liquid dripping down my chin.

That's new.

We both freeze, and when I look up at her, she looks as surprised as I am. A slow, smug smile spreads across my face.

"You *really* missed me, didn't you?" She flushes a deep pink and laughs.

"God, yes. Come here." I'm on my feet and undoing my pants when I pause for a second.

I *think* I'm getting carried away here.

Wait, did I seriously mention killing Danny to the guy in the elevator just to get him to stop looking at her? Oh, *goddammit*, I'm absolutely getting carried away. I need to keep my shit together, so I drop back to my knees quickly.

"Sweetheart, I want you to come for me again. You taste so fucking good." Alex sighs and sits up, reaching for me.

"Theo, I need you to *fuck me* right now." Her voice is low and demanding, and my cock throbs in response. I take a deep breath, trying to calm down. I'm not fucking this up, not letting the sex trigger her, no matter how much I'm dying to be inside her.

"Honey, we can take this slow, okay?" She gives me a sweet, impatient smile.

"You can take *me* slow, okay?" I laugh and start to go very slowly, pulling our clothes off as I kiss my way up her body, pinning her hands down when she tries to grab me, drawing long lines up her body with my tongue, every moan and whine and gasping breath she makes going straight to my cock. I slide her wrists above her head and hold them down while I kiss her slowly, taking my time with every nip and suck and glide of my tongue against hers.

It's fucking torture for both of us.

She starts squirming underneath me, pleading with me to just fuck her already, begging frantically in half-formed sentences that devolve into the word *please* repeated over and over until I can't hold out any longer. I kneel between her legs and drag the head of my cock over her warm, dripping cunt, but I have to stop almost instantly because I can feel heat building in my spine.

"*Theo*," she whines, and I work my way inside of her slowly, inch by inch, trying hard to ignore how perfect she feels around me and focusing on watching her for any signs of a problem instead. She doesn't seem anxious, she doesn't freeze up, her face doesn't go blank, she just whimpers and runs her hands over my body frantically as she pulls me closer and looks up at me with so much love I feel like I'm drowning in it.

She tilts her hips up to take me deeper as I push inside of her fully, and I have to stop again so I don't come right then. I bury my face in her hair and breathe her in for a minute, smelling her perfume and the warmth of her skin, and something deep inside of me falls back into place. I start to feel overwhelmed as her legs wrap around my hips, and I pull out and thrust back into her slowly.

Why does this feel so different?

I'm confused as tears prick at my eyes, and I don't understand what I'm feeling. We're finally back together, we're on the same page, we're completely connected, we got everything back, and *everything* is okay now.

Why the fuck am I starting to cry?

She whimpers and arches up into me, her hands running over my neck and chest, her expression becoming concerned.

"Teddy, are you okay?" I nod, staring down at her as I roll my hips and push deeply inside of her. "Theo, stop." I freeze, looking for any signs that she's upset. "What's wrong?"

"Nothing." Nothing *is* wrong. "I'm okay, sweetheart." I *am* okay. "I'm just really fucking happy."

Oh.

That's what I'm feeling.

Alex starts tearing up, pushing my hair back from my face.

"Me, too." When I kiss her again, it's like I'm kissing her for the first time. Being with her now feels so different, like we're truly connecting for the first time. I give her everything I have, and she gives me everything of herself in return, and there's no place where I end or she begins – there's only us as a whole. I lock eyes with her as she starts to come undone underneath me and takes me down with her, and my vision goes black for a second from how intense it is.

Everything seems soft and slightly out of focus as we lay together afterward, our foreheads pressed together and our breath mingling as our hands wander over each other. We stay there for a long time, staring at each other, touching each other, feeling our connection resonating between us, just being together again. I pull her into my arms as I roll to my back, and every ounce of worry and anxiety and tension washes out of me.

Lying there with Alex, I feel fucking *peaceful* for the first time in my life.

"Okay, sweetheart," I say, kissing her forehead, "I need to eat some actual fucking food, and then I'm going to spend the rest of my life buried inside of you."

***

I don't care that the hollandaise isn't lemony enough, that the eggs aren't perfectly poached, or that the potatoes aren't seasoned the way I would prefer. The food is much better than anything I've eaten in a year, excluding Alex, and I'm too distracted to enjoy it anyway.

Alex looks happy as I stare at her sitting across from me, and that's all that matters. Her ankle rubs against my calf, and I trap it between my legs, making her laugh. We sit there for a long time, not speaking, enjoying the moment.

She gets up and pulls me to the bed, kissing me and stroking me until I'm hard before dropping to her knees. I try not to let her see how nervous it makes me, but she doesn't seem to notice. I watch her for any signs of distress, but she's so relaxed and engaged that it becomes almost impossible to do anything other than enjoy what she's doing.

She does it differently now, and I already know what I can and can't do. I cup her face gently, keeping my touch light as I press my thumbs into the hollows of her cheeks and feel my cock sliding in and out of her mouth. All it takes after that is looking down at how her lips are wrapped around me and the soft blush spreading across her cheeks as her wide, pretty eyes meet mine. She moans in delight as I come in her mouth, and she sighs contentedly as she swallows, like she's missed this as much as I have.

I pull her into my arms and spend a long time showering her with affection and praise afterward, because I know she needs it.

There's one letter Alex wrote me that detailed things she needs me to know but *never* wants to talk about, things that are off limits, things I can't do or say anymore and why not. She didn't visit for two weeks after I read it, not because I didn't want to see her, but because she didn't want to see my reaction, which was fair. I couldn't calm down for a long fucking time. When she did visit after that, it was the first time we'd lied to each other since everything happened, because we both said we were fine.

I make her lie on the bed and masturbate for me afterward because she does that differently now, too, and I want to see what's changed. I watch her closely, and when she's a panting, needy little mess, I start tying her up because she begs me to. I don't use handcuffs, I don't tie her hands behind her back, I don't use the ball gag she brought, and I take my time and watch her like a fucking hawk, but she's relaxed and excited.

I spend a long time making her come any way I can, watching her closely, noticing what she does and doesn't react to in the same way anymore. It takes longer than it used to, but for the first time in a year and a half, when Alex cries, it's because she's overwhelmed the way she wants to be.

When she slips into a slightly dissociative state, the look on her face isn't the blank, tired look I'm afraid to see, and I breathe out a sigh of relief. She looks soft and dreamy and a little smug, the way she always looks when she's been fucked right.

I ignore how hard I am, how much I want to be inside her, and how much I *love* fucking her when she's like this as I untie her, and I pull her into my arms and hold her. I kiss her and trail my fingers up and down her soft skin, telling her how perfect she is, how gorgeous she looks, how much I fucking missed her, how much I love her, and how happy she makes me. She lays in my arms for half an hour before she comes back to herself, and then she starts sobbing because she wasn't sure she'd get *this* back.

I wasn't sure she would, either, but she fucking does.

***

We're not used to constantly fucking anymore, and we're both exhausted before noon. Alex lays in my arms, holding me tightly, her head tucked against my neck and her leg slung across my waist. I run my hand up and down her thigh, my fingers passing over the scars there, and sharp anxiety creeps back into my body.

Now that I've got her back, I'm never letting her out of my sight. I can't let anything bad happen to her ever again.

"Baby?" Her question is soft and quiet, and her lips move against my neck in a way that makes me shiver.

"Hmmm?"

"If you ever go back to prison, I'll kill you," she murmurs. I laugh and run my hand up her back, kissing her temple.

"The only way I'm leaving your side from now on is if I'm dead, I promise."

"Does that promise come with a ring?" I try not to react until I realize that there are no prison guards and no stupid fucking rules, and I can be as excessively affectionate as I want when she says something like that.

I'm not *that* exhausted, apparently, but she is when I'm done with her.

***

"Sweetie, what the *fuck*?" I cross my arms over my chest as I stare down at the array of sex toys on the bed. She gives me a coy little smile and pulls me close, kissing me softly as she pushes me back onto the bed.

"Do you trust me?" I nod, eyeing her warily. "Good. Now come here," she says, snatching up the ball gag and bondage tape with a wicked smile.

Apparently, Alex didn't tell me what *she* wanted to do to *me* when I got out, and I have a lot of fucking questions.

I forget them all the second one of her small, well-lubed fingers slips inside of me.

"Oh, *Theo*," she coos, drawing out the vowels as she looks down at me, absolutely delighted. "Do you like that?" I nod slowly, keeping my eyes on hers. "I thought so. Now be good for me, okay?"

According to Alex, I'm *exceptionally* good for her.

I gasp as she gently pulls out of me, leaving me feeling empty in a foreign way that I love and hate. I lay there, dazed, lost in the feeling of her soft tongue dragging slowly against my skin as she licks my cum off my stomach and chest. I moan softly when she unfastens the ball gag and pulls it out of my mouth, gripping my jaw to keep it open so she can spit my cum into my mouth. She smiles down at me, running her hand through my hair.

"Swallow for me." I do what she wants. Everything seems out of focus and nothing really makes sense, but I start to feel anxious when she moves away from me to unfasten the strap-on harness and let it slip to the ground before she unwinds the bondage tape from my arms and legs. The longer she's not close to me, the worse I feel, and then she climbs back into bed and pulls the duvet over us, holding me tightly, whispering sweet things into my skin and touching me everywhere, and everything feels right again.

Her hands on my body feel so good, and I reach out for her and pull her closer, resting my head on her chest and listening to her heartbeat.

I have *no* idea what I'm feeling right now, but she's the only thing grounding me from floating away.

"Baby? Are you good?" I look up to see her, flushed and happy and a little concerned, and I don't think I can speak right now, so I nod faintly. She smiles at me as she takes in my expression.

"Yeah, you are," she says, laughing slightly. "You're *such* a good boy." A warm wave of contentment rolls through me as she holds me, and I feel so cared for in her arms. Everything feels so fucking perfect when I'm wrapped up with her like this.

Only once the hazy feeling starts to fade a little bit do I realize that *this* is what Alex must feel like after we have sex.

Adored. Cherished. Loved.

Safe.

***

Alex lies naked on the bed, and I lean over her, pushing her hair back from her face.

"Sweetheart, wake up." She doesn't respond, and I start to get desperate. She's so pale, *too* pale, staring at me with dull, unfocused eyes. Her body is limp beneath me and the tape across her mouth is coated in blood from her broken nose. I press my fingers to her throat, the blood on my fingers smearing across her skin, but her pulse isn't there. I grab her shoulders and gently shake her, but her head falls to the side.

No, no, no.

"Alex, *please*. Don't leave me, okay? I'm here now." I frantically shove my fingers deeper into her neck, searching for a pulse that isn't there. It should be there. She's fine, she's just a fucking liar. I start to panic, shaking her harder, her head jerking back and forth.

"Alexandria, wake the *fuck* up." I think I hear something faintly through the ringing in my ears, but I can't make it out, so I just keep shaking her. She's not dead. I wouldn't let this happen to her. She *can't* be dead. I *can't* have failed her like this.

"You can't fucking do this, honey, you can't-"

"*Theo, wake up!*" My head jerks to the side and heat blooms across my cheek, and then everything looks *different*.

I blink rapidly, confused as Alex comes into clearer focus with every second. It's darker and we're on a different bed. There's no blood or tape on her face, and her hair is different. Her eyes are wide and teary, but bright and focused on me. I don't know what's happening. I can feel the breath dragging in and out of me, and I'm aware of her hands on my face, of my hands gripping her shoulders hard enough to bruise. I let go of her at once, cupping her face in my hands and kissing her quickly.

It was just a fucking *nightmare*.

"Sorry," she says, stroking my cheek. "You wouldn't wake up." I shake my head quickly.

"You okay?" I can't help but move one hand down and shove my fingers into her throat so I can feel her pulse beating rapidly underneath my fingers. I let out a harsh sigh of relief the second I feel it, and she circles my wrist with her hand as she blinks back tears.

"I'm okay, baby. I didn't know they were still this bad." I shake my head, still focused on the feeling of her heartbeat beneath my fingers. The nightmares are constant, but they're not *this* bad anymore. I'm usually aware I'm dreaming, but this one felt real again. She pushes her other hand through my hair, making soft shushing sounds as she strokes the back of my neck, and I can tell she's trying not to cry.

"Theo, I'm right here. I'm okay. This is real." I stare down at her, and I can't say anything, can barely feel anything but the adrenaline and panic still coursing through me, but I need her. I kneel between her legs and spit on my hand, leaning down to kiss her again as I start touching her desperately.

She makes a soft whimper and pulls me into her tightly, kissing me back hard. I do the bare fucking minimum to push inside her, and she gasps harshly when I do. I grab one of her wrists and pin it to the bed, keeping my fingers on her pulse as I fuck her frantically, focused solely on the feeling of her rapid heartbeat. Her other arm winds around my neck and I hear her soft gasps turn ragged as she starts crying beneath me.

It's the wrong kind of crying, I know that, but I'm already too far gone.

I barely feel the orgasm before I start crying, too, pulling her against my chest so hard I can hear her struggling to take in breaths. I let go of her a little, keeping my arm locked securely around her waist and cupping the back of her head with my other hand. She tangles her legs into mine, her fingers digging into my skin as she tries to get closer.

We lay there crying for a long time before one of us takes a deep breath and the other follows, and we start to calm each other down slowly, anchoring each other. We lay like that, syncing our breath to each other, feeling our hearts beat out the same rhythm at different times, a call and response of connection.

***

Later that morning, Alex drives us home so I can look at the scenery. I look at her instead, but I don't bother trying to memorize her anymore.

I know her as well as I know myself, if not better.

She takes the long way, driving along the coast, one of her hands in mine the whole way home. We don't talk about anything. There are no more scheduled visits, no more timed phone calls, no more rush to get everything out as quickly as possible.

We have nothing but time now.

When we drive through Warrenton and I finally see the low hill of Astoria rising out of the river, I grip Alex's hand tightly and let out a long breath, relaxing a little more. She drives us along the highway, turning off and heading up the hill towards our house.

I hated living in the big, empty house I grew up in when I got out of prison the first time. It was a reminder of exactly how badly I'd fucked my life up, of what a disappointment I was, of who I should have been but wasn't. When Alex pulls up the driveway, the house looks different to me, almost the way it did when I was a little kid.

It seems inviting again, like a sanctuary, like a *home*.

"Welcome home," Alex says as she parks the car and flashes me a wide smile. I look over at her and feel myself melt. I don't know what I did right or how the fuck I got this lucky, but I know this is real. I kiss the back of her hand, flashing her a quick smile.

"I got home yesterday." She rolls her eyes at me, failing miserably to hide that she's tearing up.

"Me, too."

60

ALEX

The second Theo walks in the door, his hand grips mine tightly as he kicks off his shoes. He drops his bag and drifts slowly down the hall, dragging me along with him, looking around with wide eyes.

"Holy shit, Alex," he whispers. "This place feels like a *home*."

"It's *our* home," I say quietly, and he looks down at me with something close to confusion. A moment later his expression clears, and his shoulders lower and the tension in his body unspools until he's completely relaxed, vulnerable and happy and calm in a way I've *never* seen. Warmth floods my chest as I watch him, and he pulls me up into his arms and spins me around, which he's *never* done before, and he seems giddy as he kisses me over and over.

This is the happiest I've ever seen Theo, and I love that I get to make him feel like this.

I follow him from room to room, trying to see the house through his eyes. I'm used to it now, but I did so much redecorating over the last year that the house is barely recognizable. I kept some of the furniture Theo bought, but replaced a lot of it with pieces that fit better with the house.

I also went through everything in the attic and brought down things I liked – photographs, some mid-century wall art, and a collection of large, intricate handwoven baskets. The house is warm and eclectic now, with lots of my and my mom's art on the walls, and framed photos of Theo and I and our families scattered around the house.

I only chose pictures of us where I could tell we were happy, and the polaroid of us in front of the tree at Christmas is in the living room, pride of place on the mantle.

Theo's thrilled about every change I've made, and as I trail him around the house, I start to feel comfortable in the house in a way I haven't been before. I've made the house entirely suited to my tastes, but it's always just been a big, empty house that I lived in. Theo's ecstatic energy fills up the space so much that the house feels warm and welcoming.

It's *finally* a home now.

Theo bounces in between rooms, and when he enters the living room, he freezes, staring at the huge, slightly abstract version of the wreck of the *Iredale* hung over the mantle.

Theo looks over at me, surprised and excited. "Alex, this is *insane*. You're super talented, you know that?"

I blush in embarrassment, crossing my arms. "Do you like it?"

"I fucking *love* it." I smirk at him. I knew he would love it, especially once I found the pen and ink drawing he'd stolen from my apartment in his desk drawer, along with a minuscule painting and one of my thongs.

Fucking stalker.

I framed all of them for his office, he just hasn't noticed them yet.

He pulls me tight and stares at the canvas mounted on the wall for a moment longer before he finally drags me into the kitchen, where he starts laughing deliriously at the small painting of a Christmas ham hanging up on the wall.

I painted lots of small canvases with different dishes and food items and hung them up all over the kitchen, and Theo likes all of them except the one of coq a vin. He shoots me a look that's equally irritated and amused when he sees it, and I grin at him.

Then he's desperate to cook something.

We have food at home, but he insists on spending almost two hours at the little co-op anyway. He won't let me leave his side, his arm around me as he spends a long time examining every available option and piece of produce. I have to remind him that we're leaving in a week and that he can't buy too much food. When I tell him I'm cooking him dinner later, I'm pretty sure he almost has an aneurysm.

He makes us salmon and a nice salad for lunch, and even pours himself a glass of wine from a bottle I have chilling in the fridge. We sit out on the porch, eating and watching the ships drift up and down the river, enjoying the nice weather, and then I climb into his lap and take my time enjoying him.

We nap on the small couch on the porch, although Theo startles awake at one point when a car alarm goes off several blocks away, and it takes him a few minutes to calm down, his arm tight around my waist the whole time.

When it's time for dinner, he sits in the kitchen and watches me with a soft look as I make him a porcini risotto, and it's not lost on him that it's the first dinner he ever cooked me. We curl up on the couch to watch a movie afterward, but neither of us pays attention to the movie because he's inside of me almost immediately. We sleep face to face, wrapped around each other tightly, and Theo sleeps for the whole night.

He has nightmares, but it's nothing as intense as that first night together, which was apparently the worst one he's had in over a year. We have frantic sex after his nightmares, but when he wakes me up from one of my nightmares, he's barely touching me.

We don't have sex after my nightmares.

He cooks elaborate meals three times a day and eats constantly. He sleeps for long hours, holding me tightly in bed or falling asleep on the couch with his head in my lap. He doesn't let me out of his sight to the extent that he follows me into the bathroom, which I don't even complain about the first time.

He won't stop touching me, and we can't stop fucking, even when it starts to hurt. He gets out on Sunday morning, and I'm so sore by Wednesday that I can barely walk. I lie on the couch in pain, my cunt throbbing and core aching, and look at him in horror when he kneels between my legs, undoing his belt.

"How are you not in pain right now?"

"Oh, I *am*," he says, wincing a little, "but I can't help myself." He winks at me as he leans down to kiss me, but I shove him away.

"Can you help *me* and get me an ice pack and stop touching me? You have the rest of your life to fuck me, so please calm down." He laughs and retreats to the kitchen, returning with an ice pack wrapped in a thin dish towel.

"I'm holding you to that 'rest of my life' thing," he says as he hands me the ice pack, and I groan as I press it between my legs.

"Baby, I will let you buy whatever insane goddamn ring you want if you just stop fucking me for a minute. Whatever you want, I swear, just *stop* touching me." He grins.

"I'm *definitely* holding you that 'buying you whatever I want, whenever I want' thing." I shoot him a dirty look.

"That's *not* what I said." He leans down and kisses me, grinning.

"Indulge me?" I roll my eyes and nod.

I like how he shows love.

***

The packages start to arrive the next morning. It's two new phones, hundreds of miniature chip trackers, a variety of larger trackers, a shit ton of cameras, and a package Theo doesn't open.

I lean against the kitchen island and sip coffee as I watch him unpack everything, preparing for a conversation I knew was coming. He seems tense, constantly glancing over at me as he neatly lays all the items on the counter. I just stare at him and wait, sipping my coffee and steeling myself.

"*So...*" he trails off, running his hands through his hair and shrugging as he flashes me a sheepish smile.

"You know I don't have a crazy husband looking for me anymore, right?" He relaxes a little and smirks as he pulls me into his arms.

"Not yet, you don't," he says, kissing my forehead. I laugh at him and shake my head, looking at everything on the counter.

I was expecting this, just not to this extent.

"Teddy, we talked about this," I say slowly. His face gets very somber, and he tilts my chin up, forcing me to look at his determined expression.

"I told you I wanted everything back, and you said you wanted options, right?" I nod, and his expression turns steely. "Your options are *this*, or you're never leaving the house again unless I've got my fucking hands on you. Preferably both." I give him an incredulous look and laugh at him.

"You *can't* be serious." Theo raises his eyebrows. "Baby, we live together, and I don't plan on being away from you that often, so you've got all the access to me you could possibly want. This is...a *lot*."

He shrugs. "It's basically everything I had before." I look pointedly at the enormous piles on the counter, easily double or triple what he pulled out of my apartment, and he sighs heavily. "Sweetheart, it's different now, okay? It's not just about...*access*, it's..." he trails off, shrugging and looking vaguely uncomfortable. He hates talking about the stalking impulses, so I don't push.

"Theo..."

"Alex, listen to me," he says softly, pushing my hair behind my ear, "I have nightmares about how I found you every single night, and then I was kept away from you, worried sick about you every single day for a fucking year. When I told you that I was never letting you out of my sight again, I fucking *meant* it." I raise my eyebrows at how harsh his tone gets, and he shoots me a tense look before kissing my forehead and sighing heavily into my hair.

"With *that* said, I don't want to stop you from having a life outside of me, so I'll settle for slightly less than what I want. It's a compromise." I snort as I look over the items on the counter again, shaking my head slightly.

I know to pick my battles with Theo, and this isn't one I'm interested in fighting, partly because I'd lose, but mostly because I see this for what it is.

It's love.

I pick up the unopened package, turning it over in my hands. I know exactly what's inside, and I knew this one was coming no matter what. I hold it out to him, and his expression closes off and becomes wary, and I can tell he's getting ready to fight me on it.

"Non-negotiable," he snaps, and I lean into him.

"My feelings exactly." Theo's eyes go wide. "I was hoping we could start with this one?" He's on me immediately, kissing me violently and tearing off my clothes, and the package with the tracker falls out of my hands as he slams me back against the counter.

"That's my fucking girl," he whispers harshly as he shoves his hands between my thighs and starts touching me desperately. He's almost feral, biting my lip and making low, aggressive moans deep in his throat as he starts fucking his fingers into my sore, swollen cunt, kissing and biting his way down my throat as he rubs my clit with his thumb, and I whimper, unable to speak.

He's being *so* rough.

He pulls his fingers out of me and spins me around, bending me over the counter and undoing his pants quickly. I hear him spit right before he pushes my head down onto the counter, and I scream as he shoves himself inside of me in one long, smooth thrust. I'm so tight that it hurts, but he doesn't give me a moment to adjust to him before he starts fucking me hard, swearing constantly under his breath as he slams into me over and over.

I forgot what *this* felt like, being completely overwhelmed by him like this.

I can barely hear him over the sharp gasps I'm making. My cunt is still swollen enough that I'm tighter than usual, but the pain is heightening the pleasure. I feel my leg tense up, and I whine. Theo's hand lifts off my head, and he grabs my hips, lifting them slightly so he can get deeper, and the counter bites against my hip bones on every thrust.

I scream as I start to come, and Theo loses his pace and becomes frantic, moaning loudly as he comes. He drops my hips and his hands land beside my head as he bends over me, his breath hot on my back as he kisses me softly between my shoulders, scraping his teeth over my skin gently.

I lay on the counter, shaking slightly as he pulls out of me, completely stunned as everything gets hazy the way I like. Theo's been thoughtful about how we've been having sex, but he's been holding back. He didn't think about anything this time, didn't hold back at all, just took me hard the way he used to, the way I like.

I missed this.

"Oh, *fuck*." I look up at him, and he seems anxious. "Sorry, I just...shit, honey, are you okay?" Affection floods through me, and I smile up at him lazily.

"I am now," I whisper. Theo stares at me for a moment, seeming to understand what I'm saying, and his face drops into a wolfish smile, his gaze possessive and adoring, and I have the urge to cry.

I *love* having this back.

"Not if you can still talk." He takes me upstairs, ties me down to the bed, and spends an hour making me come until I'm a sobbing, thoughtless mess.

I'm so blissfully zoned out that I barely notice when he starts talking to me, untying me and rolling me onto my stomach. He's gone for a minute, and then he's talking to me again, and I laugh softly when I realize what's happening. I feel him swab my back and then feel a soft pinch, and he kisses my neck slowly while he waits to make sure I'm numb between my shoulders. There's a tug and slight pressure for a second, and then I don't feel anything other than *safe*.

He turns me back over and kisses me for a long time before he fucks me very gently, telling me what a good girl I am, that I took it so well, that I'm so perfect for him, that he's got me now. I revel in the security of knowing that he's always going to know where I am, and I come apart underneath him knowing that he'll never let anything bad happen to me again.

I lay in his arms afterwards and feel truly and completely relaxed for the first time in a long time.

Everything feels like it's supposed to again.

***

Theo spends the next few hours putting trackers in my clothes and bags and shoes and all the cars. I put on his college sweater and trail around after him, feeling increasingly relaxed as he goes.

He puts cameras up all over the house, which doesn't make any sense to me until he says he wants to watch me if he's not at home for some reason, or if he needs to be in another room for a long time, and that he's putting some in my office again, and the trivia bar, and any other place I spend time regularly.

"You are *such* a stalker," I say, handing him another camera.

He winks at me. "You seem to like it."

I shrug, fighting a smile. "I like how you love me." He looks up from adjusting a camera aimed directly at our bed, his eyes wide and his smile soft, and I start to laugh as I realize what he's doing.

"Baby, how long do you have access to the camera feeds?" His expression turns sheepish instantly.

"Uh, about 72 hours, unless I download something."

"How many videos do you have of me?"

He shoots me a wicked grin. "Just you, or us together? Either way, the answer is *a lot*. I have a locked terabyte drive that I keep all the videos on, and I missed that fucking thing in prison," he says, shaking his head.

"I bet you did. So, can I stalk you, too?" He laughs, stepping towards me and wrapping me in his arms.

"You don't need to. I'm never going to be away from you again."

"I know, Teddy," I say quietly, "I just want to know how long it'll take you to get to me." Theo shoots me a pained look and kisses me slowly before he pulls out his phone and shares his location with me.

"I'll do whatever else you want, too," he says earnestly, and I eye the camera on the dresser.

"Then be a good boy and get on the bed." He follows my gaze towards the camera, and he grins before he does exactly what I want him to.

61

THEO

MONDAY, AUGUST 11

There's no way around getting the ring without Alex knowing, but I try anyway. I tell her I want to replace the necklace and earrings I'd gotten her before we leave for vacation, and she gives me a knowing look but doesn't say anything.

I let her choose what she wants this time, and it takes her less than a minute to pick out a set identical to the ones I got her for her birthday, the ones lost at the cabin.

I feel a rush of excitement as Alex tries on the necklace, and I lock eyes with the woman behind the register, surreptitiously pointing to my ring finger. She gives me a conspiratorial smile and nods before complimenting Alex's taste.

"Sweetheart, it's going to take a minute to check out. I'll meet you in the coffee shop?" Alex's eyebrows shoot up in surprise before her gaze darts to the woman behind the counter and back to me, her face settling into a smug smile. She presses up on her toes to kiss me, and I watch her cross the street nervously, trying not to run after her. Once she's in the cafe, I turn to see a small velvet box laid next to the necklace and earrings.

I open it to see the ring I ordered a year and a half ago, a large, flawless emerald set in a gold bezel that matches the necklace and earrings I got her for her birthday.

When I made this appointment the day I got out of prison, I specially ordered the same set so she could choose them for herself this time. She could have chosen something else, but I knew she wouldn't.

I just wanted to give her options.

***

It only takes two minutes in the airport to realize I made a mistake agreeing to go on vacation with Alex. There are so many people and so many bad things that could happen to her. I don't let her out of my direct line of sight, even pushing in front of two people to ensure I'm behind her in the body scan line. I keep my hands on her at all times as we walk through the airport, trying to breathe deeply when people get too close to her.

Alex, on the other hand, seems relaxed and comfortable navigating the airport, and she keeps trying to get me to calm down. When I get up to follow her to the bathroom, she rolls her eyes and hands me her bottle of Xanax, telling me to be good and take one for her.

I do, but it doesn't help that much, and I still wait outside the bathroom and watch the tracking app.

I don't like small spaces and I've never flown before, and I instantly hate how cramped the airplane is. We're flying in the front of the plane in a row with just the two of us, and when I complain to Alex about how small the seats are, she just laughs and tells me I have no idea what I'm talking about.

She tries to sit in the aisle seat, but I make her take the one next to the window so I can have control over who gets near her. She sees how tense I am and puts her hand on my bouncing knee, promising everything will be fine. She's patient with me, indulgent and even a little amused, but she makes me take another Xanax when I freak out as the plane starts moving. It finally calms me down enough to focus on holding her hand and listening to her go over the detailed itinerary she's already told me twice.

She's *so* excited, and that calms me down more than anything else.

The flight is eight hours long and I get tired from the Xanax, but Alex is exhausted, so I keep asking for coffee so that I can stay awake and let her sleep. I start one of the books she's got on her e-reader and watch a Norwegian crime drama on the small TV, but I glance over at her constantly, taking the blanket they gave me and putting it on top of the one she already has wrapped around her to make her even slightly more comfortable.

She makes a slight whimpering noise and her body jerks at one point, so I shake her hand gently until she wakes up. Her eyes snap open, and she seems nervous and tense for a moment until she sees me. Then, her face relaxes into relief, and she threads her fingers through mine and smiles at me before going back to sleep.

I spend the rest of the flight watching her.

***

At the car rental place, I learn that Alex can drive a manual. She proudly tells me that she's been practicing in Boss' truck, and I make a mental note to replace the transmission when she stalls the rental the second we get into it and grinds her way into each gear.

She's excited and chatty as we drive the hour to Reykjavik, pointing out volcanic rock formations and tuning the radio to Icelandic pop music. I have no idea why she chose Iceland, and she's been vague about it. When I ask her again, she shrugs and said she thought it sounded nice.

We stay in Reykjavik for two days, and Alex has a long itinerary with things for us to do and restaurants for us to try. The city is small and busy, but between never letting go of Alex and her being excited about absolutely everything, I start to relax enough to enjoy what we're doing.

I follow her into museums and an insane-looking church, down shopping streets and through a flea market, where Alex looks at everything with delight. I buy the thick wool sweaters she chooses for us, and anything else she seems even remotely interested in, including a very stupid looking stuffed puffin.

She takes me to restaurants she chose specifically because she thought I'd like them and makes me try local foods like fermented shark and reindeer, although she looks at me reproachfully when I order whale and refuses to try it. The food is fantastic, but Alex having put so much thought into what I'd like is what I enjoy most.

Once we're out of the city and drifting through the countryside, I realize Alex put *much* more thought into what I'd like than I realized.

Iceland is beautiful and spacious, and taking a road trip around the island makes it so we're always together and usually alone. We stay as far away from other people as possible and mostly in small cabins, including one made almost entirely of glass. Alex packed our itinerary with hikes, waterfalls, restaurants, hot baths, and anything else that seems halfway interesting. She's planned for us to always be doing or seeing something new, and after a year of horrible monotony, the constant stimulation relaxes me.

Our days are spent mostly fucking, hiking, and eating, which is exactly what I want to be doing anyway.

Alex carries around a sketchbook and spends time painting, and as she tries to capture the shocking blue of glacial ice or the sweep of green hills or the deep charcoals and blacks of the beaches, I sit with her just enjoying the scenery, or listening to the crackling sound of the ice splitting apart, or eyeing other tourists who get too close to us, or taking photos of Alex with the polaroid camera we brought.

I spend as much time inside of her as I can, in the rentals and the car and anywhere outside that I think we'll be alone for a few minutes, constantly claiming her and making her moan and cry and whine and come for me. She's needier in bed now, constantly wanting to be held tighter and fucked harder, always begging for more. She also wants to be in control more often, wants me to be good for her, and wants to fuck me as hard as I fuck her.

I didn't think our sex life could get better, but I was wrong.

She's more relaxed than I've ever seen her, peaceful in a way that feels contagious, and I can feel something unknotting inside of me slowly throughout the trip. At one point we're relaxing in a large hot bath set into a lake, Alex floating on her back in front of me, the soft swells of her breasts and stomach and the tops of her thighs protruding from the water, and I realize that I haven't felt anything but pure happiness for days.

There's been no anxiety, no nightmares, no concern about Alex's safety, no panic in the back of my mind that something's about to go wrong, no nagging suspicion it's all going to fall apart. There's only a content, peaceful joy I've never experienced before, and I know it's all because of her.

Sulfurous steam curls up around Alex's face, and she opens her eyes and looks up at the bright, open sky before looking over at me, smiling with that hazy, relaxed look on her face she usually only gets after sex.

"I love you," she whispers before closing her eyes again.

I have no idea how I ended up here, how any of this is real, but I want to stay with her in this feeling forever.

My mind drifts to the ring for the hundredth time, but it's still not the right time.

She knows it's coming. I carry the ring around with me everywhere, and even though she's spent the last year telling me she'll say yes, I still want to do it right. Whenever I think it might be the right time, it never is. There are always too many other people around, or Alex is too distracted sightseeing, or I get too overwhelmed and fuck her instead.

Even after everything, it still feels like the easiest way to connect with her.

***

About two weeks into our trip, we wake up early to go whale watching in a small town in the north of the island. I lean against the boat's railing as it sails out of the harbor, staring down at a sleepy, excited Alex, the early morning sun illuminating the hair whipping around her head in a halo.

I barely listen to the tour guide, barely look out at the water, barely even notice the birds and seals and whales that Alex loses her mind over. Instead, I watch her looking out at the water and think about the last time we did this, which was the first time it felt easy with her, the first time she actually smiled at me.

A familiar hum resonates inside me, followed by a powerful impulse, and I grin as I lean down towards her, pressing my lips against her ear.

"Alex?" I have to speak loudly over the sounds of the wind and waves and the seabirds, but even I can hear how soft my voice sounds. She pulls down the binoculars, takes one look at my face, and she starts to cry immediately, dropping her binoculars against her chest and nodding quickly.

"Yes," she says, kissing me hard, and I laugh against her mouth.

"Do you want me to ask?" She nods, leaning into my chest and looking up at me, her face open and adoring and her smile radiant.

"Alexandria Marie She-"

"*Fuck yes,*" she cuts me off, and I laugh, grinning at her like an idiot and trying to figure out, just for a second, if I'm dreaming. I kiss her softly, and she makes a sweet, content sound before pulling away and laughing a little. "It took you long enough," she teases, and I kiss her again quickly.

"I wanted it to be right," I say quietly as I pull the box from my jacket pocket. Alex makes a little cooing sound when she sees the ring and beams up at me.

"Good choice," she says as I slip the ring on. She kisses me and leans her back against my chest as she puts the binoculars back up to her face, trying to point something out to me. I hold her close and stare at her left hand wrapped around the binoculars, watching the emerald ring glint in the sunlight, satisfied in a way I didn't know I could feel.

She's right. It was a good choice.

I'm just not sure it was ever mine to make.

***

Alex slips back into the hot spring, a silicone cup of beer in hand, and she grins as she positions herself in my lap.

"We're getting married next month," she proclaims, and I laugh.

"You're *so* impatient. Can you even plan a wedding in a month?"

She rolls her eyes. "Theo, we barely know enough people to *have* a wedding. Bailey's ordained, you'll cook, and Miles will be the ringbearer. We'll do it at the house in Yachats, and I'll rent a small block of rooms at one of the hotels so everyone can stay the night." I raise my eyebrows at her, a little surprised.

"Wow, you've thought about this a *lot* in the last two hours."

"No, I've thought about it a lot in the last *year*," she says softly, kissing my shoulder. "I already invited everyone and made hotel reservations."

"When did you have time to do all that?" I ask, trying to figure out when she's been out of my sight long enough to make that many calls.

"Oh, I did it before you got out of prison," she says sheepishly, and I laugh, pulling her close and kissing her in a way that makes the people around us avoid looking at us.

"So," I ask, kissing her temple, "when are we getting married?"

A wicked smile spreads across her face. "September 21st." I think for a second and then start laughing so hard she slips out of my lap.

"You're fucking *kidding* me, right?"

"Baby, it's our *anniversary*," she says sweetly, wrapping her arms around my neck and kissing my cheek.

"*That's* our anniversary?"

"It's our *real* anniversary, anyway," she mutters, and I groan, sinking further down into the steaming water and looking out over the cliffs at the ocean stretching out behind her. "I promise I won't throw a wine glass at your head this time," she says sweetly.

I look back at her, shooting her a heated look. "I promise I'll make you cry," I say quietly, and she gives me a smug smile.

"That's the *only* reason I said yes." I watch her teeth skate over her bottom lip, and I grin at her, not calling her out on the lie.

***

The wedding is small – just us, Bailey and her family, Catherine and Suzie, as well as Anna and Jessica and their plus ones. Alex spends the night before we get married at the hotel with her friends, and the only reason I don't freak out is because I'm ten minutes away and I trust Bailey, but I still barely sleep.

Instead, I spend all night replacing the floodlight cameras with state-of-the-art ones and keeping an eye on Alex's location, which doesn't move. I spend all morning making way too much food, mostly because I'm on the verge of a panic attack.

I have the distinct fear that Alex is going to walk in and tell me that none of this is real, or that I'll wake up in that tiny, uncomfortable bed in that tiny, uncomfortable cell and find that I'm still counting the hours until I can see her again.

When Alex and the guests walk in, I freeze. She's stunning in a loose, lacy white dress, her hair is curled in soft, golden waves, and her cheeks and lips are a gorgeous pink that matches the bouquet of flowers in her hand, but everything about her pales in comparison to the look she gives me.

It's pure, unfettered, unconditional love, contentment and joy and excitement all wrapped into one smile. For one fleeting moment, I'm confused as to how someone so perfect exists.

I have no idea what she sees on my face, but it makes her tear up.

The ceremony is casual, and Miles ties our rings to a stuffed cat, which makes Alex cry. A moment later, she has to reassure Miles that she's crying because she's happy.

The words *I do* are barely out of Alex's mouth before I cup her face in my hands and pull her into a deep kiss. Her hands wrap around my wrists, and I only remember that we're not the only ones in the room when I hear Jessica whistle. I shoot Alex a quick, guilty smile and brush the tears off her face before letting a very amused Bailey walk me through my own vows.

We put on music and drink and eat, and Alex gets drunk with her girlfriends while Miles eats far too much cake and passes out on the couch. The longer the festivities go, the more I start glancing at the clock on the wall. I want to celebrate, but everything feels too surreal.

I got everything I ever fucking wanted, and it's so much better than I thought it would be.

I pull Alex tightly against me as we finally shepherd everyone out of the house. The second the door is closed and locked, I spin Alex around and press her up against the door, dropping to my knees and telling her I love her over and over again between slow, soft kisses that make her moan before I drag her downstairs and spend the rest of the night showing her exactly how her husband *should* treat her.

***

"Honey, *no.*" I grab Alex's left hand in mine, momentarily distracted at the sight of the rings on our fingers, and she yanks her hand out of mine, shooting me a dirty look. I groan as she grabs the boxed mac and cheese and drops it into the basket.

"I'm not going to make *you* eat it. It's for Miles."

"I don't understand why Bailey and Dylan allow him to eat that garbage, and I don't understand how he prefers it to what *I* make him."

Alex laughs at me, rolling her eyes. "You tried to feed him duck a l'orange last time."

"So?" She snorts and grabs more mac and cheese.

"He's *six*, Theo. He wants kid food. Our kids are going to eat this, too," she says, shaking the box at me. I cross my arms and glare at her.

"Over my dead fucking body, Alexandria. It's not even real *chee-*" I stop talking when I see Ben round the aisle.

Ben, who has *never* apologized to Alex. Ben, who still lives in the area, surprisingly. Ben, who freezes when he sees me and looks scared when I smile at him.

Before Danny, I'd have beaten the shit out of him purely on principle, but seeing him doesn't bother me at all now. Alex follows my gaze and notices him, and I feel her hand press into my thigh, her nails digging in.

"Hi, Ben." He turns around and walks away quickly without so much as looking at her. "Okay, rude," she mutters before she looks up at me suspiciously. "Why are you so chill? You've never been chill about *anything*, especially not Ben."

I shrug. "I know for a fact he's not stupid enough to bother you."
She narrows her eyes at me, her face becoming apprehensive.

"Why? What did you *do*?"

"Depends on your definition of *doing* something." I lean down to kiss her, but she pulls away, leveling me with a stern stare that I'm sure will terrify our kids someday.

"What the fuck does *that* mean?" I pull her close and tuck her hair behind her ears, smiling softly at her. She's going to hate this, but I'm not going to apologize for it.

"Ben *might* have received a copy of the crime scene photos." Her jaw drops.

"Theodore Robert Anderson, you *didn't*," she hisses.

"Technically, *no*, because I had someone else mail them." I flash her a guilty smile. "I told him once that I'd kill him if he ever touched you again, and I wanted to make that point explicitly clear while I was away." I study her face carefully as she frowns at me briefly before snorting out an exasperated laugh and shaking her head.

"No wonder he never showed back up to trivia," she says quietly before she levels me with another stern look. "Don't threaten people like that again. Ben could file a restraining order because of those photos, and I *never* want to talk to another cop again in my life." I nod, running my hands up and down her arms.

"Whatever you want, sweetheart."

"I mean it, Theodore," she says sternly.

"So do I."

She melts against me slightly. "Promise?"

"I promise." Alex seems satisfied, giving me a small smile and winding an arm around my waist as I wrap my arm around her shoulders and hurry her away from the aisle of processed foods before she reaches for more mac and cheese or thinks too hard about our conversation.

I promised to give her whatever she wants, and I know what Alex wants more than anything is to be safe and happy. I don't think it's unreasonable to threaten or hurt anyone who jeopardizes her safety or happiness, but I don't need to send those photos to anyone else.

I already sent them to Danny's family.

62

EPILOGUE

DR. MELISSA MILLS

ONE YEAR LATER

SATURDAY, JULY 25

"Okay, buddy, that's enough out of *you*," Kayla chastises gently as she picks a crying Henry up off the ground and carries him out of the small grocery store as he starts wailing louder. June looks on the verge of tears as she watches them.

"Mom, I'm so fucking tired," she says, rubbing her hand over her protruding baby bump. "I don't know how Kayla did this last time."

"Kayla didn't have a teething toddler to contend with," I say gently, rubbing her back. "She also had a much easier pregnancy. You've got this, Junie." She sighs, pressing one hand over her eyes and blowing out a thin stream of air.

"Can you please finish shopping? We'll be outside." She hands me her basket and follows her wife and son. I bend down and grab the chocolate bar Henry wanted before wandering the aisles, looking for what we'll need for the week.

It's a small store, and it doesn't take long to turn down the last aisle. I reach for the oat milk without looking up from the grocery list, and my hand knocks against someone else's.

I glance up to see a short young woman in an oversized University of Oregon sweater.

"Sorry," she says in a bright, bubbly voice, "I was looking at my phone." She waves the phone in her hand before she slips it in her back pocket, giving me a small, friendly smile as she gestures at the oat milk. "You can take it." I look at the lone carton and back at her, sighing in relief.

"Would you mind? My daughter is vegan, and *pregnant*, and she hates every other type of alternative milk."

"It's all hers," the woman says warmly, and I smile at her as I slip the carton into my basket.

"Thank you so much. I know she'll appreciate it." She nods, grabbing a carton of almond milk instead.

She looks familiar, somehow, but I'm not sure where I'd know her from. I glance at her sweater. Maybe I've seen her around campus?

"I hope you don't mind me asking, but do you go to U of O? You look familiar – maybe you work there? I lecture in the psychology department occasionally." The woman glances down at the sweater and shrugs.

"No, I just love this sweater." Her smile broadens, then softens as she looks at me closely. "You look familiar, too, actually. I'm Alex," she says, offering her hand. I reach out to take her hand, and it hits me exactly where I know her from.

She looks so different that it's no wonder I didn't recognize her at first. Her stylishly cut hair is a warm blonde now, her oval face is fuller and rosy, no longer gaunt and pale, and her posture is straighter, her shoulders lower and no longer curved in on themselves. She's relaxed and happy, and an entirely different person than the woman I watched testify.

I wonder how Theodore is doing.

I've thought about them on and off over the last two years. I should have known better than to get so emotionally involved, but I've always been hopeful that having Theodore's parole revoked allowed Alex to escape him.

It wasn't the right choice to make, and with how hard he worked to have my license revoked, it almost cost me everything, but now I feel that I might have been right to do it.

"Hi, Alex. It's so nice to see you again." She looks at my face for a long moment before the wave of recognition crashes over her, and she looks stunned. She recovers quickly, arranging her face into a tight smile as she glances away from me briefly.

"Hi, Dr. Mills. Um, how are you?"

"I'm doing well, thank you. How have things been going? If you don't mind me saying this, you seem different. You seem *happy*." She blinks, taken aback, but her face relaxes back into a warm, friendly smile after a moment.

"Things are good, and I'm really happy now," she says softly, a sweet smile on her face. I breathe a sigh of relief.

"That's so wonderful to hear. Do you live here now?"

"No, I'm just here for the weekend. What about you?"

"My family and I are on vacation," I say, gesturing to the oat milk and basket of food. She nods and reaches up to tuck her hair behind her ear, and I notice the obscenely large emerald ring and slim gold wedding band on her left hand. Anxiety pulses through me, but two years is plenty of time for her to have fallen in love and gotten married to someone new.

I hope.

I gesture to her hand. "That's a beautiful ring."

She looks down at her hand and smiles wider. "Thank you. He did a good job, didn't he?"

"Did you get married recently?"

Her expression tightens slightly as she glances back up at me. "We got married about a month and a half after he got out." My stomach drops and any trace of a smile slides off my face.

Oh, *no.*

"You and Theodore are married?" Her mouth tightens as she tilts her head slightly to the side.

"Of course we are. Why wouldn't we be?" she asks in a challenging tone.

"I just...I thought...well, how's married life treating you?" Alex narrows her eyes slightly, scrutinizing my face momentarily before sighing.

"Look, I understand and appreciate the idea of what you're trying to do here, but your concern is misplaced. It's *always* been misplaced." I feel a rush of frustration.

"I don't think that's true, frankly. I think Theodore is a dangerous man and an abusive partner, and I think being with him puts you in danger." She laughs and rolls her eyes, shaking her head at me.

"I'm not in any danger, *trust* me." I notice she doesn't address the other points I've made. "Theo's the only reason I feel safe, and I know he'd never hurt me."

Oh, this poor woman.

"Stalking *is* a form of harm, Alex." Her eyes widen and she flushes angrily, and it's all the confirmation I need. He absolutely *was* stalking her, and most likely still is.

"Oh, *shut up*," she says harshly. "Theo loving me the way he does is the only reason I'm alive, and I'm *very* fucking happy to be alive." She looks away from me briefly as tears start welling up in her eyes. "God, Theo's right – you *are* a shitty therapist. You seem incapable of believing that I *want* him the way he is, and you took a *year* away from us because of it. Do you have any idea how hard that was?" I feel a mix of guilt and pity as I look at her, and I keep my tone gentle when I speak to her.

"Alex, do you truly believe this is what's best for you?"

"Do you think I'm a fucking idiot?" she snaps. "You realize that I know *exactly* who Theo is and what our relationship is like, right? I chose him because he makes me happy."

I'm not sure if I believe that's true, but it's heartbreaking if it is. I did my best to give her an opportunity to escape him, but there's nothing I can do for her if that's how she wants her life to be.

I should have known better than to get involved.

"My family is waiting for me, so I should be going," I say softly. "I wish you all the best, Alex, I really do."

"Whatever," she mutters as she glances away from me, wiping her eyes quickly. I turn around and startle as I almost bump into a man standing close behind me, and I take a quick step back, grabbing for my purse as it slips down my shoulder.

"Excuse me, I'm so sor-" I stop speaking as I look up and see Theodore standing before me, his arms crossed over his chest and his face locked in that cold, blank look that he used to give me during sessions, the one that means he's deeply upset about something.

Exactly how long has he been standing there?

He looks almost as different as Alex does now. His hair is longer than I've ever seen it, down to his collarbones, and he's filled out significantly since the last time I saw him. He looked thin during his trial, but now he looks more like he did before he killed Alex's husband, except healthier and broader in the shoulders.

Not for the first time, I'm viscerally aware of what a large man he is.

"Hello, *Melissa*," he says in an icy, condescending voice as he steps into my space, looking down at me with barely restrained hatred. "Why the fuck are you making my wife cry?"

Oh my god, he's *furious.*

"We were catching up," I say, trying to keep my voice from wavering. He barks out a laugh, not breaking the direct, unsettling eye contact he's making with me.

"That's *not* what you were fucking doing," he says quietly, and the hair on the back of my neck stands up. I work to keep my face from revealing how absolutely terrified I am of him, but from the way his eyes narrow appraisingly and the small, predatorial smile that creeps across his face, he can tell.

"Theo, it's *fine*," Alex says from behind me, her voice exasperated, but he's so focused on me that he doesn't seem to hear her. I pull back involuntarily as he leans down slowly, bringing his face closer to mine.

"Do you *really* think it's in your best interest to get in between us again?" His voice is low and lethal in a way I've never heard before. I try hard to stay calm, but my heart pounds in my chest and my breathing becomes shallow as he stares at me, fury radiating from his gaze.

If he didn't view me as a threat to his relationship before, he certainly does now. From what I remember, he draws a clear boundary around physically hurting women, but I'm almost positive I've made myself the exception to that rule.

I've worked with a lot of dangerous, angry men over the years, but this is the first time my life has ever been in danger because of it.

"*Teddy.*" His eyes widen slightly at the close sound of Alex's soft, disappointed voice, and his gaze darts in her direction. She's moved to my side, zipping a pendant along a necklace chain as she glances between us, her mouth tight. His demeanor shifts instantly to something less angry but still tightly wound, and he stands back up to his full height as he looks over at her.

"Yeah, sweetheart?" His voice is still sharp, but infinitely more gentle when he speaks to her. I keep my eyes on him, unwilling to get distracted from the threat in front of me, but I can see Alex step close to him and off to the side, making him turn away from me to face her. She seems on the verge of more tears as she lifts her anxious face towards him, and I watch Theodore soften further as he looks down at her.

It's although I've ceased to exist to him entirely, and I want to keep it that way.

"I'm going to leave," she says quietly, but he winces like she's yelling at him. "Do you want to go home, or do you want to stay here? It's your choice." His eyes flare open, and his arms unfold, his hands flying to her face with terrifying speed, and he pulls her close as he brings his face down towards hers.

I realize at that moment that he's got his wife's small, fragile head gripped in his hands the same way he must have held her ex-husband's head when he cracked his skull open, and it's terrifying to see.

I watch them, unsure of what's happening but deeply unsettled by the intensity and tension radiating from them.

"I want to go home," he says quickly, and there's a panicked undercurrent to his voice that I don't understand. She nods, a few more tears running down her face.

"Good," she says with a small smile as her hand comes up to his wrist. The moment she touches him, the tension melts off his face and out of his body entirely, and the pure hatred rolling off him a moment ago completely evaporates. Watching him become a completely different person right in front of my eyes is jarring. I honestly can't tell if it's his ability to lie so adeptly or his extreme emotional volatility, but he's exceptionally blatant about it. The man was on the edge of losing it a moment ago, and now he's acting calm and smiling at Alex lovingly, seeming warm and almost soft as he gently brushes the tears off her cheeks.

This must be how he's so effectively manipulated her.

He leans down and kisses her forehead before he drops his hands from her face, threading his fingers through hers and taking the full handbasket from her with his other hand. Alex tilts her head toward the exit, and he nods, starting towards the front of the store without looking back at me.

Alex, on the other hand, looks over her shoulder and flashes me a wide-eyed look of warning, mouthing the word "*go*" before she turns away. I stand there, frozen to the spot, reeling.

I think she just saved my life.

I think she *knows* she just saved my life.

I take a few deep, shaky breaths, trying to calm myself down as I drop my handbasket on the ground and walk quickly towards the exit, keeping my eyes averted from where the two of them stand at the checkout counter, his hand on her upper back.

I head for where June and Kayla and a sleeping Henry are parked in front of the small grocery store and start sobbing the second I get into the car. I feel June's hands on me instantly, rubbing my back.

"Mom, are you okay?" I shake my head at her as I catch my breath.

"Mel, what *happened*?" I wipe my face, trying to calm down.

"I, um, I...," I trail off as I look up and watch Theodore and Alex leave the store and head for the car right next to ours. He has the grocery bag in one arm and his other around her shoulders, smiling down at her as she says something. They seem relaxed, chatting animatedly and laughing as though nothing happened.

She notices me as he holds open the passenger door for her, her eyes widening slightly as she takes the groceries from him. He doesn't see me until he opens the driver's side door, and the moment we make eye contact, his face transforms into that same cold, furious sneer he gave me at the parole hearing. A chill rolls down my spine at the sight, and I keep my eyes on him as I turn on our car and shift into reverse.

The moment he's in the car, Alex leans over to pull him into a passionate kiss, and he seems entirely distracted by her again.

I watch them, morbid curiosity piercing through my fear.

I'm beginning to believe that I *have* misunderstood their relationship. I always thought Theodore was lying through his teeth about Alex mindfully choosing to be with him, but he seems to have been telling the truth. She *does* seem to know exactly who he is, and she certainly knows how to manipulate him.

Their dynamic is *horrifying*.

"Mom?" June's anxious voice snaps me out of watching them, and I reverse quickly, navigating us towards our rental house.

"Girls," I say in a shaky voice as I speed up the narrow road toward our rental, "we need to see if there's anywhere else you'd like to spend the week. We're leaving. *Immediately*." I ignore June and Kayla's questions as I help grab Henry and hurry them into the house to pack.

I'm not taking any chances with our safety. I don't know why Alex saved my life, but I don't want to stick around for her to change her mind.

I never want to see either of them again, but knowing that terrifying, vindictive bastard, I'll need to take some precautions to make sure of it.

ACKNOWLEDGMENTS

I owe endless gratitude to the following people:

To my husband, Joshua. He believed in me when I didn't, he pushed me to try when I didn't want to, and then he did every possible thing he could do to support me along the way. Sometimes our relationship feels like my own personal delusion, and I seriously don't know how I got so lucky. I love you so much and I'm grateful to get to wake up and choose you every day.

To Athena, who alpha read, beta read, sent memes, made suggestions, copy edited, helped proof the physical copies, and overall showed up for me and *Perfect* in such an insane, ride-or-die way that feels unreal.

To Katie, who alpha read, beta read, and is also one of the best people I know. I'm aggressively lucky to have you in my life.

To my sisters Jackie and Emma, and my friends Gabby, Kat, Dahlia, Kirsten, and Bethany, I am eternally grateful for your love, your friendship, your guidance, and your support.

To Tuesday, the walking book encyclopedia who gave me the confidence that *Perfect* is, actually, the book I thought it was.

To all my beta readers and their amazing comments that helped make *Perfect* what it is.

To the members of Portland Romance Writers, thank you for welcoming me with open arms and offering endless advice. Everyone should go check out all of these wonderful authors and all of their books.

To Carson Wright, for your artistic vision and for hearing what I wanted and making my cover better than I could have imagined.

To Oregon. Many years ago, I pulled a geographic in the midst of a crisis and wound up here, and I can't imagine a better home.

To me. Impostor syndrome comes for all of us, but if no one ever reads this book, or if the people who read it absolutely *hate* it, I'll still have I made a lifelong dream come true by writing a novel that I'm proud of and putting it out into the world. It doesn't need to be perfect to be good, but I think *Perfect* is pretty good.

Lastly, to you, the reader. Words can't express my gratitude that you picked up this book and spent your valuable time reading it. Thank you.

ABOUT THE AUTHOR

Ariana Rivers studied Literature at San Francisco State University, and lives in Oregon with her husband and their very demanding cat.

Perfect is her debut novel.

When she's not writing, Ariana enjoys pole dancing, rainy beaches, a chilled glass of white wine, and gossiping relentlessly with her friends.

Learn more about upcoming projects at arianarivers.com

TRIGGER WARNINGS

Abusive Relationship(s)
Alcoholism
Anxiety / Panic Attacks
Assault
Attempted Murder
Attempted Rape
Blood & Gore
Bondage
Bones
Breath Play
Child Abuse (referenced, not explicit)
Cops
Cumplay
Death
Delusions
Depression
Drug Addiction (referenced, not explicit)
Domestic Violence
Dubious Consent
Dubiously Consensual Non-Consent
Eating Disorders
Edging
Emotional Abuse
Exhibitionism
Explicit Violence

Grooming
Gun Violence
Hospitalization
Kidnapping
Manipulation
Mental Health Issues
Miscommunication
Murder
Orgasm Control
Pedophilia (referenced, not explicit)
Pegging
Physical Abuse
Rape
Rough Sex
Serious Injuries
Sexual Abuse
Sexually Explicit Scenes (I promise!)
Somnophilia
Stalking
Substance Abuse
Suicidal Ideation
Torture
Toxic Relationship
Voyeurism